Wordsworth Dictionary of Homonyms

The Wordsworth Dictionary of

HOMONYMS

David Rothwell

Wordsworth Reference

In loving memory of
MICHAEL TRAYLER
the founder of Wordsworth Editions

1

Readers who are interested in other titles from
Wordsworth Editions are invited to visit our website at
www.wordsworth-editions.com

For our latest list and a full mail-order service, contact
Bibliophile Books, 5 Thomas Road, London E14 7BN
TEL: +44 (0)20 7515 9222 FAX: +44 (0)20 7538 4115
E-MAIL: orders@bibliophilebooks.com

First published in 2007 by
Wordsworth Editions Limited
8B East Street, Ware, Hertfordshire SG12 9HJ

ISBN 978 1 84022 542 6

Typeset in Great Britain by Antony Gray
Printed and bound by Clays Ltd, St Ives plc

To my two children,
who give me a reason for living.

INTRODUCTION

Since this book is entitled *A Dictionary of Homonyms*, it is perhaps reasonable to assume, as you've just bought it or borrowed it, that you already know what the word 'homonym' actually means. If you do, then you are among a small minority. Hence I am going to spend some time explaining exactly what homonyms are.

Doubtless to your disappointment, my definition of the word *homonym* will have a distinct tinge of Humpty Dumpty about it. If you recall, in *Alice in Wonderland*, Humpty Dumpty declared that a word meant what he decided it meant. I am going to be equally autocratic. There is not really very much alternative. The definition provided by the *Shorter Oxford English Dictionary* is so terse as to be inadequate, and that is true of the full *OED* as well. The *Oxford Dictionary of English* – 'each of two or more words having the same [homo comes from the Greek for same] spelling or pronunciation but different meanings and origins' – is fine, but it is almost alone in being so. Trailing through the Internet files will produce semantic indigestion but no clarity. Bill Bryson in *Troublesome Words* tries hard, but is misleading, while Thomas Parrish in *The Grouchy Grammarian* is amusing but imprecise. And so I could go on. In many ways, this confusion is not terribly surprising. Words come into being by chance. Apart from scientific nomenclature where words are devised to assist in classificatory clarity, most words arrive on the scene because someone needs such a word and promptly invents it. The inventor is not concerned that his or her word fits neatly into current usage, that it is grammatically congruent with other words and that its spelling reveals its kinship to Mesopotamian precursors. When, sixty-five million years ago, Cedric shot an arrow at a dinosaur and shouted 'Blast!' because he missed, he did so because the sound of the word 'blast' was ideally suited to relieving his frustration. When someone else, a few million years later, saw a man eating ham pressed between two slices of bread, he called the edible object a 'sandwich' because it was, at the time, being eaten by the Earl of Sandwich. This is how words happen. I do not know how and why 'homonym' and its related words first came into existence – nor does anyone else – but you can be fairly sure that some innocent bibliophile in the sixteenth or seventeenth century thought, 'There needs to be a word for this,' and promptly invented it.

The reason that there is confusion and a lack of clarity over *homonym* is that it is closely related to two other words, *homograph* and *homophone*. I shall, therefore, define these words first.

1. A *homograph* is a word that is spelt identically to another word but none the less has a different meaning and probably a different origin. You will doubtless be annoyed if you tear your trousers while climbing over a fence. Indeed, you may be so upset that you shed a tear. As you can see, 'tear' and 'tear' are spelt identically, but they are pronounced differently and have entirely different meanings. They are good examples of a homograph. Many homographs are not even pronounced differently. Thus the word 'hide' sounds exactly the same whether you are talking about the skin of an animal, a measure of land or the verb meaning to conceal or keep out of sight.

2. A *homophone* is a word that sounds exactly like another word, but has a different meaning and a different spelling. If you stand on the stair and stare at the picture, you have a good example of a couple of homophones. As you know, *stair* and *stare* sound identical, but they have very different meanings. They also have different spellings.

It is possible for a word to be a homograph or a homophone. However, whatever the word may be, it is also, by definition, a homonym. In other words, *homonym* is a conceptual word that embraces both homographs and homophones. Hence 'homonym' can refer to a word that is spelt the same way as another word but sounds differently, to a word that is spelt the same way and sounds identical too, and to a word that sounds the same as another word but is spelt differently. Hence 'homonym' is just the collective noun for 'homograph' and 'homophone'.

If these terms are relatively new to you, it will take a little while before they become second nature to you. There is nothing complicated about them, but it takes all of us some time to adjust to strange vocabulary. Just have a look at the list below. They are all homonyms, but it will be useful if you just go through them and identify which ones are homographs, which ones are homophones, and which ones are both homographs and homophones.

race	race
bow	bow
sight	site
read	reed
left	left
wound	wound

You may have found this tiny little exercise mind-numbingly easy, but just in case, let me go through them one by one.

a) The word *race* can mean a running competition or someone's ethnic background, so it clearly has at least two very different meanings. Therefore *race* is a homograph, but since the words sound the same whichever meaning is being intended, they are also homophones.

b) If you *bow* to the Queen and are wearing a *bow* in your hair, the word 'bow', though it has the same spelling in both cases, has none the less got two different meanings and two different pronunciations. It is therefore a homograph but not a homophone.

c) 'Site' and 'sight' cannot be homographs because they are not spelt the same, but they are homophones because they sound the same.

d) 'Reed' and 'read' are homophones, but not homographs.

e) 'Left' is a homograph and homophone.

f) 'Wound' is a homograph, but if you wound up some wool, it would sound differently from the wound in your leg, so the word is not a homophone.

I hope that those six examples provided a little consolation into the homonymic world with which this book is concerned.

Homonyms can be confusing for both foreigners and native English speakers. Indeed, such difficulties have even attracted academic attention. The article by Michael H. Kelly and Anjani Ragade from the University of Pennsylvania, entitled *Grammatical Relationships Between Homonyms: Effects on Language Comprehension and the Structure of the English Vocabulary*, is a good example. Hence it is convenient to have a reference book that will serve as a banisher of any confusion. If you don't know the difference in usage between 'there' and 'their' or between 'where' and 'wear', then this book will tell you. Consequently this book will be useful to people who are trying to learn the English language, and equally useful to native English speakers who want to avoid possibly embarrassing mistakes in their usage of their language. It will also be useful to that enormous tribe of crossword solvers. Most of all, perhaps, this book will be fun for that remarkably large section of the population who are wordaholics, i.e. people who just enjoy playing around with words. Indeed, there is a distinct possibility about which you need to be forewarned, that someone who begins using this book as a reference tool may, as a result, also turn into a wordaholic. This may well make you shunned and despised by many – but it will increase your enjoyment in life enormously!

One or two warnings need to be made. First of all, the selection of homonyms is not an exact science. Do you, for instance, class *which* and *witch* as homophones? Strictly speaking, you shouldn't. There is a slight aural difference in the sound of the two words. The same is true of *while* and *wile*, *were* and *where*, and scores of other words. The trouble is, in most cases we never actually hear the slight difference anyway. Few of us speak as correctly as Professor Higgins in Shaw's *Pygmalion* or its off-shoot *My Fair Lady*. Hence words that are not homophones in theory, turn out to be so in practice.

Secondly, and much more importantly, it is by no means easy to decide whether a word really does have a series of different meanings or whether the variations are merely nuances of the same basic meaning. For instance, everybody's favourite four-letter word 'love' can mean a surprising variety of things. 'I love Susan', 'I love custard tarts', 'I love the music of Byrd' and 'I love playing chess' are all sentences with the same main verb, but does anyone seriously think that loving Susan is the same sort of emotion as loving custard tarts? Yet, in all cases, the word 'love' means a strong liking, an affection for, a devotion to. Is 'love' therefore a homonym or not? It is a question of judgement, and there will doubtless be many instances in this volume where you disagree with my judgement. Nor can I even claim any consistency in the selection of words. I look at a word like 'detail' and decide that it is or is not a homonym on what is basically just a gut feeling. With, for instance, a word like *porridge*, there are no problems. That word clearly and distinctly has two entirely separate meanings. With a word like *ledge*, it is nothing like so clear cut. All three meanings given by the dictionary are so conceptually linked that I personally don't think that it can be counted as a homonym, but who is to say? Hence this volume cannot claim to be complete if only because the idea of completeness will vary from person to person. In addition, of course, I'm bound to have missed some perfectly valid homonyms through carelessness, stupidity or sheer verbal exhaustion. All I can do is apologise.

There are two other forms of incompleteness also. I have excluded most obsolete words, so you won't find *eke* or *frere* within these pages. Nor have I made any attempt to deal with dialect. For instance, in Bristol the two words *idea* and *ideal*, words with very different meanings, are both pronounced identically. In Manchester *book* and *buck* are homophones. They are not so in this book. Standard Received English is merely an accent like all the others, but it is the accent that is taken as the norm in this book. To have coped with other dialectal variations would have been impossible.

In addition, a vast number of nouns in English can be easily transferred into being a verb. Clearly their function within a sentence changes markedly, but the basic meaning remains unaltered: 'I live in a house'; 'I need to house my son.' By and large, such instances will be ignored.

There is no real difference in meaning, and hence the basic homonymic criterion is missing. Furthermore, there are many words that are internal homonyms, that is, the word concerned has two or more different meanings. It therefore follows, if the word is a verb, that its associated noun will also have different meanings, but that the meanings will be identical, apart from grammatical function, to the verbal instances. Where this is the case, I have tended to opt for just the one instance. Thus you will find the verb 'to succeed' in this dictionary, but you will not find the word 'success'. I am sorry if this irritates any of you, but it would have expanded the length of this book enormously, and I did not think that the matter was worth the death of so many trees.

As you will probably already have realised, homonyms are the source of that quaint British disease known as the pun. The poet Thomas Hood was fond of using them:

> And even the stable boy will find
> This life no stable thing . . .

Shakespeare has Hamlet toying with the words 'son' and 'sun' in an embittered fashion. Many of us have friends who are incorrigible punsters. So, if this book serves no other purpose, it will help to make you the linguistic scourge of your neighbourhood.

And that brings me to a final point. Words are fun. I have made every effort to make this book as full and accurate as I can, but I have made no effort whatsoever to make this book solemn. Most of the examples herein that illustrate the usage of words are examples invented by me. Many of those examples are silly, and some of them display rank bias. This is irrelevant. The definitions that I provide are accurate ones, and the usages cited are perfectly valid. In other words, the facts are as clear and accurate as I could make them, but the opinions sometimes expressed in my illustrative examples are not facts, and, strictly speaking, are not germane to the argument. Therefore, don't let your disapproval or distaste for my opinions (should that ever happen) get in the way of the genuine utility of this book.

Clearly such a book as this could not have been compiled without massive help from a number of sources. The books that were used are listed in a brief Bibliography at the end. Those books were invaluable, and the vast majority of the definitions that I have provided have been lifted without acknowledgement from one or other of those books. The *Shorter Oxford English Dictionary* was my staple diet, though I was surprised to find many omissions in its 2,515 pages, omissions not always remedied by the full *Oxford English Dictionary*. Ironically, many of those omissions were corrected by a newer Oxford publication, *The Oxford*

Dictionary of English, a volume that it was a delight to use. The Internet, as ever, was invaluable, and shortened my labours immensely. I have pinched unashamedly the quizzes at the end of this book from the Internet, just modifying them slightly for my purposes. The friends who provided aid included (in alphabetical order) Anna Dearden, Patrick and Wendy Keane, Christopher Rothwell, Megan Rothwell, Sue Rothwell, Jocelyn Ryder-Smith and Michael Stewart. Needless to say, any deficiencies that this completed volume may possess are all their fault, and I am in no way to blame.

Finally, let me end with some examples of what you are letting yourself in for. The daughter of a friend of mine sent me the following examples of homonyms within a sentence:

1 The bandage was wound around the wound.
2 The farm was used to produce produce.
3 The dump was so full that it had to refuse more refuse.
4 We must polish the Polish furniture.
5 He could lead if he would get the lead out.
6 The soldier decided to desert his dessert in the desert.
7 Since there is no time like the present, he thought it was time to present the present.
8 A bass was painted on the head of the bass drum.
9 When shot at, the dove dove into the bushes.
10 I did not object to the object.
11 The insurance was invalid for the invalid.
12 There was a row among the oarsmen about how to row.
13 They were too close to the door to close it.
14 The buck does funny things when the does are present.
15 A seamstress and a sewer fell down into a sewer line.
16 To help with planting, the farmer taught his sow to sow.
17 The wind was too strong to wind the sail.
18 Upon seeing the tear in the painting I shed a tear.
19 I had to subject the subject to a series of tests.
20 How can I intimate this to my most intimate friend?

If you are English and literate, the twenty examples above will present you with no problems. If you are not English and/or not fully literate, the twenty examples above will be a nightmare. This book, among other things, will banish such nightmares.

A

A, a, Eh!

These two words could hardly be more different. **A**, as you doubtless know, is the first letter of the English alphabet, and it also is a word on its own, normally used as what is called the indefinite article. That means that **a** is placed before a noun in order to indicate that you are referring to a single object. Thus you would say 'I saw **a** bus', to indicate that you are referring to a single bus. It is, in fact, quite difficult to construct an English sentence without using the word **a**: 'I went to a party'; 'We saw a film'; 'He had a headache'; and so on. However, although use as the indefinite article is so overwhelmingly common in English, **A** does also have other uses. It is, for instance, the name of a key in music: 'He played a piece in A major.' In such instances, the letter is normally capitalised. It is also normally capitalised when A is used to denote the first in a set of items, as in: 'Suppose A was here when the explosion occurred . . . ' The best roads in Britain are called A roads. The population of Britain is divided into sundry socio-economic categories, the highest of which is labelled A. On a chessboard, the leftmost file viewed from White's side of the board is termed the A file. The letter 'a' tends to be used for the first constant used in an algebraic expression. There is a type of blood group called A. Geologist use A to denote the uppermost soil horizon. The letter also forms a part of a number of Latin expressions that have been incorporated into the English language, expressions like 'a priori' and 'a posteriori'. The letter is also often used as an abbreviation in common terms like a.m. (*ante meridiem*, before noon) or AD (*anno domini*, in the year of our Lord). **Eh**, however, is very difficult to pin down to any specific definition, while 'a', as we have seen, has many of them. 'Eh!' is always an exclamation, but it can be an exclamation of enquiry, of surprise, or even of sorrow: 'Eh, are you sure he meant that?'; 'Eh, I was never so surprised in my life'; 'Eh, it was sad to hear about Joe.' Indeed, **Eh** can be considered more a sound than a word, a sound whose intonation will indicate in what mood or feeling it is being expressed. We know that this exclamation has been used in England since the sixteenth century, though clearly it could go back even further.

aback

This word has three entirely different meanings. There is the nautical term to indicate that the wind is blowing in the wrong direction so as to prevent forward motion, there is the rare term to signify a square tablet or compartment, and, most commonly, the word means to be disconcerted or surprised: 'I was taken aback when she announced that Brian was now engaged to Wendy.'

abacus

Most of us know about the calculating frame which has sliding balls on wires and is used for arithmetical operations. Indeed there are reputed to have been people so skilled on the abacus that they rivalled the speed of a computer. However, like **aback**, abacus is an homonym that is both a homophone and a homograph, since the same word with the same pronunciation also refers to a board strewn with sand for drawing figures, and, architecturally, to the upper part of the capital of a column.

abandon

The verb 'abandon' means to desert, to give up to someone else's control, to cease to control something or someone. Hence you might say, 'I must abandon my child to the vagaries of fate.' Equally you would abandon ship if the ship itself was sinking. However, the word can also mean a freedom from constraint or convention, in which case it becomes a noun rather than a verb: 'He acted with total abandon at the party.'

abate

The most common use of this word is as a verb meaning 'to reduce or diminish'. Hence you could have a sentence like: 'The neighbours did nothing to abate their noise.' But it is also a legal term meaning, according to the *Shorter Oxford English Dictionary*, 'To thrust oneself tortiously into a tenement between the death of the owner and the accession of the legal heir.'

abba

This is the Greek word for 'father', and in the New Testament of the Bible it is applied to God. However, it is also a title accorded to bishops and patriarchs in the Syrian Orthodox and Coptic churches. Its meaning remains 'father' in both cases, and hence it could be quite reasonably argued that this is not a homonym. None the less, the gulf between a divine father and a pastoral one seemed to me to merit the word's inclusion.

abet

In its most common usage, this verb has rather shady connotations. The word means 'to assist or encourage', but it is invariably used within a criminal context. Hence you might abet someone in hiding some stolen goods or abet someone in breaking into a jewellers. As a noun, now very rare, it means a fraud: 'His attempt in claiming that the picture was by Cézanne was an abet.'

abide

This verb normally means to reside in, to stay with or to wait: 'I will continue to abide in my house.' It can also be a little stretched in meaning to mean obey or acquiesce: 'I will abide by your rules.' The word is also used in what Eric Partridge calls a low-class colloquialism: 'I can't abide him,' where it means 'tolerate'.

abode

There are a number of English words which double as a noun and a verb, though the meanings of both are similar. Thus 'abode' can mean a place of habitation ('It was good to return to my abode for a good night's sleep') and be the past tense of the verb 'abide': 'It was rarely I abode in so comfortable a hotel.' One can consequently argue over whether or not this is a true homonym. On most occasions, such examples will be omitted from this dictionary.

about

This is one of those not uncommon English words that is very useful but quite difficult to pin down. First of all, it is commonly used as a preposition relating to position. Thus one might say, 'She was wandering about the market,' or, 'He stood round about the middle of the field.' The word can also signify that something is shortly about to happen: 'I was just about to lock up.' The word can also be used as a synonym for 'approximately': 'It is about six o'clock.' In addition, there are connotations of motion attached to the word: 'He likes to get about,' or, more figuratively, 'She is always beating about the bush.'

abridge

If you were to **abridge** a book, you would shorten the book. If you were to 'abridge' a speech, you would make it less lengthy. However, in a legal context, if you abridge a right or privilege, then you curtail it.

abrupt

If you are **abrupt** in your speech, you tend to be brief and curt to the point of rudeness. If you are walking along and encounter a sudden steep hill, you might describe the terrain as being an abrupt climb. If you are listening to a lecture and the lecturer suddenly dies of a heart attack, you would say that the lecture came to an abrupt end. There are similarities in these three examples, but they seem to be sufficiently diverse for 'abrupt' to count as a homonym.

absence

This word would not have appeared in this dictionary had I not discovered from Brewer's *Dictionary of Phrase and Fable* that **absence** was the Etonian term for 'roll-call'. Until then I had assumed that the word only meant the state of being away, of not being present.

absolute

If something is **absolute**, then it is not qualified or modified in any way. Thus you can demand absolute secrecy, or live under an absolute ruler. However, the word can also be used in grammatical contexts. If you use a transitive verb but do not have an object to the verb, then the verb is said to be absolute: 'Guns kill.' In philosophy, if a value or principle is regarded as universally valid or may be viewed without reference to other elements, then the value or principle is termed an absolute. Clearly there is a conceptual kinship between these uses, so whether you count 'absolute' as a homonym or not is virtually a matter of taste. Yet, with uses like 'absolute zero' to signify a temperature of -273°C, 'absolute music' to describe music with no narration attached to it, and 'absolute pitch' as a synonym for 'perfect pitch', the contexts in which 'absolute' can be used do seem strikingly diverse.

abstract

The adjective **abstract** indicates that something is mental rather than physical. Thus to discuss whether *Bleak House* or *Great Expectations* is Dickens's greatest novel is an abstract discussion. The books themselves have a physical reality, but the evaluation of their merit does not. Words like 'love', 'hope' and 'despair' are abstract words because you cannot see, touch, hear or taste the objects those words describe. As a verb, however, 'abstract' means to remove something. Thus you can abstract all the blue-eyed men from a group and take them off to the lab. You can abstract all the soft centres from a box of chocolates, and leave only the nutty or hard ones. There is, though, another use of 'abstract' as a noun. If you prepare an abstract of someone's speech, then you are providing a summary of that speech.

access

If you have **access** to something, then you have the means and opportunity to visit it or use it. At the moment I have access to a computer, but I do not have access to the planet Mars. However, the word may also be used to indicate an outburst of emotion: 'I was overcome with an access of hope.'

accident

Most of us have been involved in an **accident**, a mishap of some kind from a trivial one like tipping too many black peppercorns into the stew to a more serious one like driving into the back of another car. However, in philosophical terms, an **accident** can also be some quality or property which a thing possesses, but which is not an essential element in defining the thing concerned. Thus the height of a person or the redness of a brick would both be counted as accidents.

acclamation, acclimation

It can certainly be argued that these two words are not homonyms: there is too great a distinction between the 'clam' sound of **acclamation** and the 'clim' sound of **acclimation** for them to be accounted as true homophones, and since they are spelt differently, they cannot be homographs. However, I note that both words are included in the homonym list provided in a somewhat odd and largely useless American publication called *Scholastic Dictionary of Synonyms, Antonyms, and Homonyms*. Hence, largely out of cowardice, both words have been listed in this book. The first, **acclamation**, is a noun signifying great support and applause for some person or cause: 'The pop group Knowle Knockouts was greeted with huge acclamation.' The second word, **acclimation**, must surely have virtually become obsolete by now, because the British certainly seem to prefer the much longer 'acclimatisation'. Both words indicate that someone or something is getting used to relatively new conditions: 'After three months in the Congo, I reached some form of acclimation.'

accommodation

Most of us live in some **accommodation** or other, whether it be our own house, a caravan or a room in a hotel. Thus the most usual use of the word is to signify some place of habitation. However, you can also make some **accommodation** for someone else's views or habits. Hence, when you go on holiday with your aunt, you accommodate yourself to her less rapid mode of walking. Furthermore, in commercial use, an **accommodation** can be a loan of money.

account

This is an elusive word. In some contexts it appears perfectly precise, so that an **account** can be a statement of the moneys (or monies) received and paid, with a calculation of the balance. You can also have something on account, which means that you do not pay for it there and then, but will settle up at the end of the transaction. Equally the word can refer to a narration, an **account** of the things that have occurred during the day. It can also act as an adjective, so that an account book is one used for the keeping of accounts. By extension, you can be called upon to give a good account of yourself, or possibly to call someone else to account. Here the word has a moral evaluation attached to it.

ace

Originally an ace was the side of a die with just a single dot upon it. Later the word came to be employed for the highest playing card in each of the four suits, one that carries only a single emblem of that suit. Since then, however, the word has been extended to mean anything that is supremely good. Thus you can be an ace at darts, at ballroom dancing or at learning languages. In 1989 the café attached to the Victoria and Albert Museum came up with the inspired slogan, 'An ace caff with quite a nice museum attached.' If you possess some secret advantage, you might claim to have an ace up your sleeve. If you serve at tennis and your opponent is unable even to touch the ball with his racket, then you have served an ace. There is, however, the expression, 'I came within an ace of death,' where the meaning of ace seems to have shifted to meaning 'very close'.

achate

This word is a rare verb meaning 'to purchase', a Middle English noun meaning an agate and a Middle English noun meaning a purchase or things purchased. You are likely to get through your life without ever using the word. I have.

ache

This can be a verb (I ache with pain) or a noun (I have an ache in my stomach), but as you can see, the meaning in both substantive and verbal form is virtually identical, and so ache could hardly be termed a homonym. However, ache is also the name for an umbelliferous plant, so that fact does place the word firmly into the homonym range (I had an ache in my back as I bent to pick up the ache).

acid

In its most common usage, this word has a precise meaning, since it is any substance that dissociates in water to yield a sour corrosive solution containing hydrogen ions, having a pH of less than 7, and turning litmus paper red. However, it is also a slang name for LSD, and, from its chemical nature, can often be used as an adjective to indicate that something or someone is sharp, cutting or hurtful. Hence, if you put the acid on, you are putting pressure on someone. You can also apply the acid test, that is, some way of determining the truth of the matter. The expression comes from the fact that if you place gold in nitric acid, there will be no reaction at all, but if the gold is contaminated in any way, then its colour will change. In geology the word acid is used to refer to rock (especially lava) which contains a relatively high proportion of silica. Children may be fond of having an acid drop, a boiled sweet with a sharp taste. Acid house is a kind of dance music with a fast, repetitive beat that was apparently popular in the 1980s. As an adjective, 'acid' is applied to many nouns: acid rain, acid salt, acid test, etc.

acknowledge

If you **acknowledge** that something is the case, then you admit that some fact or element in a situation has to be accepted as valid. Hence, when on trial in a murder case, you might have to acknowledge that you did possess a hatchet similar to the one that dealt the fatal blow. If you were walking down the High Street and met your acquaintance Helen Smith, you would acknowledge her by smiling or waving a hand. If you were compiling a dictionary of homonyms, you would acknowledge in the preface or somewhere all the help that you received in this enterprise from sundry people. Hence **acknowledge** always carries a sense of recognising someone or something, but the contexts in which the word can be used differ sufficiently for 'acknowledge' to be counted as a homonym.

acolyte

This word has a technical meaning in that it refers to a person assisting a priest in a religious ceremony, but the word has subsequently been extended to mean the follower or disciple of almost anything. Hence you could be an acolyte of chivalry, of the Acol system in bridge or of the latest pop group.

act

In its most usual sense as a verb, to **act** means to do something, to take action over something: 'We must act soon if we are to prevent Julian leaving for Africa.' If, however, you act a part in a play, then you take on the role of a character other than yourself. As a noun, an act is a deed, an action performed, something done. However, it can also be a division within a play, ballet or opera, or a written law passed by Parliament.

acts *and* axe

These two words are not precisely identical in pronunciation, but they are so close that, in everyday speech, few people are likely to detect a difference. The first word, **acts**, could be referring to deeds or actions, laws passed by Parliament, or divisions into which a play is divided. It could also be a verb referring to the mode of behaviour ('He acts strangely'; 'She acts joyously'; 'It acts like a chisel'). The word **axe** (or **ax**) refers to a chopping instrument, a tool used for cutting down trees or whatever. From thence, it is often used metaphorically: 'He has an axe to grind' (He has some selfish motive in the background); 'To hang up one's axe' (To retire).

acute

This word has a number of meanings, and although they are all similar to each other, there is enough difference for it certainly to count as a homonym. Thus some object can exist with a pointed end, in which case one could say that it had an acute end. A disease could reach a climax of dangerousness, in which case we would say that the disease had become acute. Someone might have extremely sensitive nerves, in which case we would say that their nerves were acute. Someone might be extremely shrewd, and hence might be called acute. A sound might be high and/or shrill, and hence might be described as acute. An acute angle is one of less than 90°.

ad, add

The word 'ad' is often used as an abbreviation for the word 'advertisement', but this usage is so common (I put an ad in the paper) that 'ad' can now be taken as a word on its own, just as 'bus' is now an accepted word and hardly anyone remembers that it started out as an abbreviation for 'omnibus'. In addition, **ad** is also a Latin preposition meaning 'to' and survives in English in such naturalised expressions as '*ad hoc*', '*ad infinitum*' and '*ad nauseam*'. The verb to **add**, of course, describes an arithmetical operation that one learns at primary school and, by extension, the action of increasing something: 'If we can add five acres to that field, we will be able to grow a third more strawberries.'

Adam

In the book of Genesis, **Adam** was the first human being created by God. This proper noun can consequently hardly be called homonymic in any way. However, in the eighteenth century, Robert Adam (1728–92) and his brother James created an elegant, neoclassical style of architecture, and their surname has subsequently become an adjective in phrases like 'Adam architecture' or 'in the Adam style'. Such usage, of course, is very different from saying that you don't know someone from Adam.

adamant

This was a somewhat mythical rock or mineral, sometimes identified as either diamond or lodestone, to which a number of contradictory properties were often attributed. The word stems from the Greek *adamas* meaning 'untameable, invincible'. Milton writes about: 'gates of burning adamant'. Since about the sixteenth century, however, the word has come to be used as an adjective signifying impregnable hardness ('He had an adamant heart') or that someone's mind was firmly made up ('He was adamant that he would not resign over this issue').

adda

This is a noun of Indian origin and signifies a place where people meet for conversation. However, it has since been extended to mean also a place for illicit drinking, or a junction point for public transport.

adder

An **adder** is someone who adds things up, or, in electronics, a unit that adds together two input variables. It is also a snake, the only poisonous British snake, with the alternative name of viper. The word has also been used figuratively as a synonym for the old serpent, i.e. the Devil.

addict

An **addict** is someone who is dependent upon something so that he or she cannot survive without it. Normally the word is used to indicate a dependence on drugs, but it can be extended to any compulsive addiction: 'He was an addict of *Coronation Street* / chocolate biscuits / Mozart,' etc. However, this noun can also be used as a verb, where it has a similar connotation but is perhaps sufficiently different to count as a homonym. Legally it can mean the action of delivering over someone to some form of judicial sentence: 'I addict you to seven years' hard labour.'

addition

As you would expect, this is the operation of adding numbers together, and most of us will remember having lots of practice in this at primary school: $3 + 7 = 10$. However, the word is not confined to arithmetic. You can have an **addition** to your name: 'Sir Henry Jones'; 'Sheila Davies, B.Sc.'. You can have an addition to a note of music by putting a dot just to its right and consequently lengthening the duration of the note by one half of its previous value.

addle

As a noun **addle** is the dry lees of a wine or another word for mire or liquidised filth. By extension an **addle egg** is one that has gone rotten. As a verb, you can addle someone, implying that you confuse or baffle them. More figuratively, you can call someone an 'addle-pate' or refer to them as being 'addle-headed'. In 1614 a Parliament called by James I became known as the addled parliament because it did not pass a single act.

address

This word has a whole variety of different meanings though they are all cognitively linked. As a noun, an address can be the place where someone lives: Jocelyn Smithers, The Cottage, Little Upston, Shropshire TF9 2PN. Also as a noun, an address can be a speech delivered on a formal occasion. In both these instances, the noun can be turned into a verb: 'I must address this letter'; 'I must address the House.' The word can also mean the action of preparing or researching something: 'I must address myself to the job of preparing this *Dictionary of Homonyms*.' You might also, if you are a man, address yourself to a lady, hoping thereby to gain her hand in marriage. Your address (i.e. your manner of speaking and presenting yourself) might also be described as commanding, abrupt, arrogant, oily or whatever. In this usage, the noun 'address' is never preceded by an article and has no plural.

adds, ads *and* adze

The first two, **adds** and **ads**, being merely the plurals of words that we have already encountered, would not appear in this dictionary if it were not for the fact that they are homophones with **adze**, an axe-like tool.

ade, aid *and* aide

I am somewhat dubious about **ade** because I have not found it as a complete word in any dictionary, but an Internet source lists it as being a fruit drink, and most of us are familiar with words like 'lemonade' and 'orangeade' which does add some credence to the idea. **Aid** is a verb meaning to help or assist. An **aide** is an assistant, normally taken to be a shortened version of **aide-de-camp**.

adherence, adherents

These two words are conceptually linked to the verb 'adhere' and have the same source in the French verb *adhérer*, which itself comes directly from a Latin verb of almost the same spelling. **Adherence** indicates the state of holding fast to some object, person or cause: 'My adherence to our noble leader is well known.' **Adherents** are supporters or followers of some leader or ideal: 'We are all adherents of the democratic principle.'

admiral

As most of us know, an **admiral** is the most senior commander of a navy, but it is also the name of a butterfly with bold red markings (red admiral) or white ones (white admiral).

admissible

This is an adjective which has two conceptually similar meanings, but distinct enough to raise the word to homonym status. The first meaning is concerned with one's right of entrance to some event or organisation: 'Women were admissible only on Saturdays.' The second meaning is often used in connection with the validity or otherwise of evidence: 'The Scotch bottle on the back seat was not admissible as evidence that Shawn had been drinking.'

admission

The same can be said for this noun as was said for its cognate adjective immediately above. An **admission** can be an acknowledgement of the truth of something: 'In an admission of his love, Christopher fell to his knees and poured out his heart.' Equally the word can mean the process or fact of entering or being allowed to enter some venue: 'Admission to the swimming baths now costs £2.'

admit

There are two common meanings for this verb. The first is to allow someone entry to some place or event: 'I am pleased to admit you into the General's study.' The other common meaning is when you own up to something or agree that something or other is the case: 'I admit I killed the canary'; 'I admit that the evidence is against her.'

adolescence, adolescents

Adolescence is the period during and immediately after puberty when a young person changes from being a child into being, physically at any rate, an adult. **Adolescents**, of course, are the young people experiencing this change.

adrift

If something is **adrift**, you picture it floating unattended upon the lake or sea, at the mercy of wind and tide. This concrete meaning has been extended to refer to mental or intellectual confusion: 'In understanding Kant, Christopher was all adrift.' In addition, in colloquial naval usage, the word can mean being late, overdue from leave, or absent from one's place of duty.

adulterate

This word is most commonly used as a verb, and as such means to debase something or to counterfeit something. Hence you could say, 'To adulterate a coin by incorporating base metal within it is a crime punishable by death.' The word can also be used as an adjective derived from the noun adultery: 'Her adulterate form was wracked with shame.' As you can see, both senses carry the connotation of debasement.

advance

The simplest form of this verb is when it signifies movement forward: 'The advance of the army was rapid.' The word can also mean the state of being in a forward position: 'We were in advance of the rest of the army.' More figuratively, the word can be used to signify promotion in rank or position or salary: 'His advance to stardom was remarkable.' It is also possible to advance an argument in the sense of putting forward reasons for supporting a particular view or course of action: 'I would like to advance the argument that being in debt is a desirable state while interest rates are so low.' As a noun, however, **advance** can signify a sum of money, normally one that is handed over before it was due: 'He made an advance to his son.' One can also make an advance to a lady, normally with romantic intentions: 'I made an advance to Sybil because I wanted to hold her in my arms.'

advert

As most of us know, the word **advert** is an abbreviated form of 'advertisement', but, as with a number of other words, the shortened form has now gained its own autonomy. An advert is a notice displayed publicly in some way that either seeks to persuade you to buy a particular product, to attend an event, to apply for a job or to use a particular service. But the word is also a not very commonly used verb. If you advert to something, you refer to it or draw people's attention to it: 'I would now like to advert to the recent work done on black holes.'

advice

In the most common usage of this word, **advice** means guidance that has been or could be provided: 'My advice would be to avoid Filwood Broadway on a Saturday night.' However, an advice can also be the formal notice of some financial transaction.

aeon

You can certainly be pardoned for thinking that **aeon** is simply a word that means an indefinite and very long period of time. In modern conversation, the word is often used flippantly: 'Doris is getting ready, so we should be able to leave in about an aeon or so.' However, certain academic subjects have adopted the word for more specific passages of time. For the astronomer and geologist, an aeon is equal to a thousand million years, still a long time but more definite than the everyday usage of the word. Philosophers of the past have also used the word. For the Platonists, Neo-platonists and Gnostics, an aeon was a power existing from eternity, an emanation or phase of the supreme deity.

aerie, airy

I am far from convinced that these two are homonyms, because I pronounce these two words differently. However, I understand that many people do not do so. The first word, **aerie**, is an eagle's nest, and the second word means breezy.

affair

Most of the time this word is used to signify business or the ordinary pursuits of life: 'Foreign policy is not normally an affair that need concern the Home Secretary'; 'John had his bicycle stolen, but that was no affair of mine.' The word can also refer to a sexual relationship between a man and a woman: 'Doris had an affair with Cyril, and regretted it ever afterwards.' The word is also often attached to any controversial issue. Thus in eighteenth-century France there was the affair of the diamond necklace when Marie Antoinette was wrongly accused of attempting to purchase an extremely valuable necklace.

affect

As a descendant of the Latin adjective *affectus*, the noun 'affect' is a term in psychology meaning a feeling, emotion or desire that affects behaviour. As a descendant of the Latin verb *affectare*, the English verb **affect** means to pretend or to assume a false position: 'She affected to be acquainted with the Duchess of Cornwall'; 'He had a very affected voice designed to make you think that he was an old Etonian.' Many people, of course, speak in so slovenly a manner that they make the two words, **affect** and **effect**, sound identical, but that does not make them homophones.

affinity

The trouble with a number of English words is that although they have different meanings, those meanings are so conceptually linked that it is difficult to decide whether or not they deserve the name of homonyms. Perhaps this is the case with **affinity**. In all its different meanings, it is concerned with relationships. Hence the word can be used to denote a kinship between parents and offspring, between cousins, nieces and nephews, and so on. Equally, on a more rarefied level, a pianist might be said to have an affinity with Chopin, if that is a composer that he or she plays particularly well. In philology, languages are said to have an affinity if they share some vocabulary and have structural resemblances. Hence Italian and Spanish have an affinity because they are both descended almost directly from Latin. In natural history, rocks, animals and plants that share a structural resemblance are said to have an affinity. Some chemicals have an affinity with each other in that they can relatively easily combine to form new compounds. As you can see, all these depend upon relationships, but the relationships seem to be sufficiently disparate for **affinity** to count as a homonym.

affix

This word has two meanings that are so conceptually allied that it could be argued that **affix** is not really a homonym. The first meaning relates to placing something firmly upon something else. Thus you might affix a stamp on to an envelope, affix a signature to a letter or affix a doorknob on to a door. The other meaning is a linguistic one. You might affix the suffix '-ing' on to a word: 'play', 'playing'. You might affix a prefix like 'un-' on to a word: 'comfortable', 'uncomfortable'.

affray

The noun **affray** denotes an attack or struggle: 'There was an affray outside the courtroom as supporters of the accused grappled with the police.' The adjective from the obsolete verb form of the word means startled, disturbed, or frightened: 'He was affrayed [afraid] of his own shadow.'

afield

Both meanings of this adverb are concerned with location, but they are certainly very different. If you say that the visitors came from as far afield as New Zealand, you are stating that visitors came from distant locations. If a fox hunter remarks to you that there is great satisfaction in having a day afield, then he or she is referring to the local location.

afloat

This word has a literal meaning and a figurative one. If you are lying in a swimming pool on your back being supported by the water, then you are afloat. If you are on board a ship crossing the Atlantic, you are also afloat. However, if your company is just about managing to make a profit, then your company can be said to be afloat. If a friend of yours is said to be having an affair with the headmistress of the local primary school, then there are nasty rumours afloat.

after

This small word can perform in a number of different guises. It can be an adverb qualifying a verb and meaning 'later in time' or 'behind': 'The speeches came after the meal.' It can be a preposition in expressions like 'time after time'. It can be a conjunction in a phrase like 'he came after I left'. In nautical language it can even be an adjective: 'He was in the after cabin.' There is also the slightly quaint expression 'after one's own heart' to describe exactly what one would have wished, and the even quainter one, 'be after doing something', which indicates that you are on the point of doing something or have just done it.

against

This word is often used as a preposition indicating that someone or something is close to or attached to something else: 'She leant against the fire.' It also indicates a state of opposition: 'They fought against the poll tax.' **Against** can also be used to signify a contrast: 'His body was a black outline against the pale sky.' The word can also signify protection: 'He drank a Lemsip against the danger of catching a cold.'

agape, Agape

These two words are pronounced quite differently. The first, **agape**, rhymes with 'rape' or 'crape' and is normally used as an adjective signifying a mouth wide open in amazement: 'His mouth was agape in wonderment.' The other, **Agape**, is often, though not invariably, spelt with a capital letter, and unlike **agape**, has a stressed 'A' and its final syllable, '-pe', rhymes with 'pay'. The word means 'a love feast' and is given its capital letter because it is often used to refer to the last supper of Jesus Christ. Such love feasts eventually became a scandal, and were condemned by the Council of Carthage in 397. The word and practice was revived in the Norfolk parish of Hilgay in 1949 in an attempt to bring Anglicans and Methodists together.

agate

The normal, everyday usage of this word is to denote an impure micro-crystalline form of quartz which is used as a gemstone or for making pestles and mortars, burnishers and polishers. However the name is sometimes used to denote a marble, and, even more rarely, is the North American term for printing type of about five and a half point. The *Shorter Oxford* also claims that **agate** is an adverb signifying 'on the way' or 'a-going', though I have never heard anyone, even in Oxford, say 'I am agate to the market'. Brewer's *Dictionary* also claims that a diminutive person has been called an **agate** from the custom of carving small figures on seals made from agate.

age

All uses of this word have to do with time, but they are such varied uses that **age** has to count as a homonym. Hence the word could denote a considerable stretch of time: 'In the age of the dinosaurs . . . '; 'In the age of Elizabeth I . . . ' Equally it can be used to indicate something much more specific and short-term: 'I have reached the age of twenty-one.' The word can also be a verb: 'I age a decade every time I hear a Tony Blair speech.' Shakespeare in *As You Like It* divides a man's life into seven ages: the infant, the schoolboy, the lover, the soldier, the justice, old age, and finally senility leading to death. The word is also used in numerous expressions like 'age before beauty', 'the age of consent' and 'the age of discretion'.

agglutinate

This verb has a few scientific uses, and although they all tend to mean something similar, their scientific disparity does mean that **agglutinate** counts as a homonym. Thus in chemistry, when a group of particles in suspension merge into a clump, they are said to **agglutinate**. In linguistics, when two or more words merge together to create another word, they are said to agglutinate. Thus 'sidewalk' is an agglutination. In building, when two or more articles are bound together by glue or cement, they have been agglutinated. In biology, you can agglutinate bacteria, red blood cells, etc. If you accept that these different technical usages are sufficient to make **agglutinate** a homonym, then the adjective **agglutinative** and the noun **agglutination** must also be homonyms.

aggravate

The common meaning of this verb is to irritate, to annoy. Thus I aggravate my wife when I play the French horn in the garden. However, the word also means 'to burden, to increase in difficulty'. Hence my son's English teacher aggravated his difficulties with metaphor when she tried to explain what a symbol was.

agonist

In biochemistry, an **agonist** is a substance which initiates a physiological response when combined with a receptor. In anatomy, though, it means a muscle whose contraction moves a part of the body directly. The word can also be used as a synonym for 'protagonist'.

aha

This is a noun meaning a sunken fence (sometimes spelt 'ha-ha') or an exclamation of surprise, satisfaction or irony. Its second meaning has led to a piece of psychiatric jargon, the aha reaction, used to signify the sudden achievement of insight or illumination.

aid *and* aide: *see* ade

ail *and* ale

Quite apart from sounding identical to ale, the word **ail** is a homonym of its own. Its normal usage is as a verb indicating that one is feeling ill: 'I ail from a sore throat.' By extension, one can have many ails, that is, a number of things that upset or trouble one: 'Among my ails, my son and daughter are the most troubling.' As you can see, the verb ail has here become a plural noun. In addition, the word used to have a connection with 'corn', but this usage is now obsolete. Its homonym **ale** refers to an alcoholic drink very similar to beer. Indeed, 'ale' and 'beer' were once synonymous, but 'ale' is now used to denote a slightly lighter liquid. Practices vary, however, and in many localities, ale and beer are interchangeable terms. Obviously, of course, drinking too much ale will make you ail.

aim

The meanings of **aim**, both as noun and verb, are all similar, but distinct enough to raise the word to homonymic status. If you aim a dart at the treble twenty on a dartboard, your intention is to hit the board in that small, circumscribed area. If you succeed in so doing, your aim has been perfect. David aimed his stone at Goliath, and his aim certainly was perfect. But the word can also be used for much less practical and concrete purposes. A television programme might be aimed at children aged under ten. A company might aim to increase exports by ten per cent. These sorts of aim do seem very different from aiming your gun at a target.

air, are, e'er, heir, err *and* ere

As you doubtless know, **air** is the compound gas that pervades Earth's atmosphere and which all animals breathe in order to maintain life. However the word can also refer to the general appearance of a person: 'He had the air of being very bored.' It is also a tune or melody: 'She sang the air like an angel.' As a verb, 'air' can also mean the activity of bringing something up for discussion: 'Could I air a long-standing grievance?' If you appear in a radio programme, you can be said to be on the air. Thus **air** is a homonym of its own. It also sounds exactly like **ere**, a preposition meaning 'before' (I was up ere dawn) and **e'er** which is a contraction of 'ever'. The word **are** does not normally sound at all like **air** ('We are tired tonight'), but it also means 1/100th of a hectare, and with this meaning its pronunciation alters. An **heir** is someone who is due to inherit something (Prince Charles is heir to the throne), and since the 'h' is silent, the word does sound like **air**. The word **err**, however, is not a true homophone of **air**, but is mispronounced by such a massive majority of the population that it would have been invidious to have omitted it. It is, of course, a verb and rather appropriately means to make a mistake ('I tend to err when in a hurry').

aisle, I'll *and* isle

An **aisle** is the passageway in between the church pews up which the bride walks for her wedding ceremony. So, of course, do other people on lots of other occasions, but this is the event with which the aisle is most commonly associated. **I'll** is the common contraction of 'I will', and **isle** is another word for 'island', though 'isle' perhaps implies a fairly small island. 'I'll take you to the isle of Lundy after you've walked up the aisle.'

ajar

A door can be slightly open, it which case it is often said to be ajar. Two people may not chime together very well, in which case their personalities could be described as being slightly ajar.

ale *see* ail

alert

If you are **alert**, then you are wide awake and capable of reacting to any unforeseen circumstance. Equally you can be alert to any danger. Hence the noun and verb have parallel meanings. But if you see or hear an alert, then you hear a siren or warning bell, or see a red flag or flashing light. Thus one noun is descriptive of a mental state, the other is pointing to a physical event, though both are conceptually akin.

alewife

If you want to keep your friends, you will only refer to an **alewife** when wanting to describe a NW Atlantic fish of the herring family. The colloquial use of the word tends to imply a slatternly and drunken housewife of extremely dubious reputation.

alien

As an adjective, **alien** means something that is foreign in nature, character or origin: 'Egyptian seers are alien to British culture.' As a noun, an **alien** is a person who is not naturalised to the country in which he is living and whose mode of living is strange to the majority of the population. The adjective and noun are clearly closely related, and do not merit being listed as a homonym. However, the word has more recently taken a slightly more bizarre meaning, and people are prone to talk (or see films) about strange creatures from outer space. Indeed, many people believe that such aliens have visited Earth and because their appearance and intelligence are so different from those of human beings the word **alien** has taken on a more specialised (and frightening) meaning. That this is almost certainly total nonsense is irrelevant.

alight

This word can be a verb meaning to dismount, to come down, to descend: 'She had some difficulty as she tried to alight from the bus.' Less commonly, it can be used as a verb meaning to light something up, from which the more common adjective comes: 'The fire was alight.' The word can also mean to accidentally find or discover something: 'He was lucky in that he soon alighted on his rarely used set of compasses.' The *Shorter Oxford* claims that this usage is now rare, but since I am frequently alighting on things which I had virtually forgotten, I would beg to differ.

align

If you are one of those meticulous people who like everything in its place, you are likely to **align** your pots of paint in the garden shed neatly along a shelf. You will find that in most classrooms, the desks are aligned neatly in rows. Yet at the same time, you can align yourself with some worthy cause. Here you are not putting yourself in a row, but instead signifying your support for Cancer Research or whatever.

all, awl

An **awl** is a small tool normally used for making small holes in leather or some similar substance. Hence, unless you are a shoemaker, this is not a word that will appear frequently in your conversation. **All**, however, is a word that most of us use every day. It can have varied appearances. As a noun, it means everything that we have or possess: 'I gave my all,' a phrase often used by actors who have just hammed the part of Macbeth mercilessly. As an adjective, it means the whole: 'All flesh is as grass,' as the apostle Peter comments in his New Testament letter. The word can even act as an adverb: 'The Government is all full of deceit.'

alley

The common use of this word is to signify some sort of passageway. Thus you can have a passage between houses, a walk along a passage in a wood, or, indeed, a free way between any other two objects. However the word has also been used as a variation of 'ally' (qv) which is a kind of marble, to refer to the area between the doubles tramlines on a tennis court, and to the area between the outfielders in left-centre or right-centre field in baseball.

allow

This verb means that something is permitted: 'I will allow you to kiss me under the mistletoe.' However, it can also mean that something is accepted as true or valid: 'I will allow that Henry is somewhat hard of hearing.'

allowance

This noun usually means the quantity of money payable in regular instalments that is available to someone: 'Brian was having difficulty living off his allowance.' However, it can also mean the granting of extenuating circumstances: 'I will make allowance for the fact that Sandra is tone deaf.'

allowed, aloud

The first word is the past participle of the verb 'to allow' and means 'permitted': 'Smoking is not allowed in the cinema.' The second word, **aloud**, means that something is audible: 'It is a pity that he made his criticisms aloud.'

ally

An **ally** is, in political terms, a country or state that collaborates with one's own country or state. Hence France could be an ally of Spain in dealing with the Basque problem, Britain could be an ally of the USA in coping with drug abuse, and so on. Equally one can have a personal ally: 'Rosemary is my ally in trying to ban gypsies from camping on Egdon Common.' An ally is also a toy marble made of alabaster, marble or glass. The two words are not homophones since the marble is pronounced with the 'y' having a short sound, while the partner or supporter 'ally' has a long 'y'. They have different derivations too. One is from the Latin *alligare* meaning 'to bind together', while the other is thought to be a diminutive of 'alabaster'.

alms, arms

Alms, an unusual word in that it is a singular noun despite ending in an 's', refers to gifts to the poor. It does, however, sound remarkably similar to **arms** (qv), the upper limbs of a primate.

alone

Few of us would think of **alone** as being a homonym. It simply means being on one's own, being without company: 'I went to the woods alone.' However, there are other ways in which this word is used. In a sentence like 'There were six bingo halls in the town centre alone', there is clearly no sense of loneliness. True, the sentence is pointing out that only one factor is being considered, but its adverbial usage here is clearly different from its previous adjectival use.

altar, alter

The first word is normally used to indicate the place in a Christian church where communion is celebrated, but it can also be used to indicate the raised platform upon which some sort of animal or human sacrifice is carried out. Metaphorically, the word can also be extended to give a spurious holiness to some perfectly secular thing or event: 'I worship at the altar of Manchester United.' The second word is a verb meaning to modify or change something: 'I must alter this dress.' **Alter** is also used in the Latin phrase *alter ego* which literally means 'other self' but is normally used to refer to a very trusted friend.

am

This entry is a fraud. The only real word, **am**, is the first person singular of the present tense of the verb 'to be': I am tired. There are no other words with the same spelling, and the only conceivable homophone is the word 'ham', so frequently spoken with its 'h' missing: 'Two slices of 'am, please.' However, the human capacity for getting things mixed up leads me to include 'am' in this dictionary because it is the chemical symbol for the element americium, and an abbreviation for amplitude modulation, ante meridiem, an American Master of Arts and *Hymns Ancient and Modern*.

amber

The noun **amber** refers to the hard, translucent fossilised resin that comes from extinct conifers. Typically yellowish in colour, it has been used in jewellery for centuries. However, the word is also often used to refer to the middle signal in a set of traffic lights, the one that commands caution, lying, as it does, between the red for 'stop' and the green for 'go'.

amount

The two meanings of **amount** are clearly linked, but sufficiently different to count as homonymic. In one sense the word means the conclusion reached when all the factors have been taken into account: 'Given the evidence, I do not think that it can be said to amount to a proof.' More narrowly, the word is commonly used to signify a total of money: 'The amount of money in my bank account would not permit a holiday this year.'

analogue

As a noun, **analogue** can refer to a person or thing that is seen as comparable to another, while in chemistry it refers to a compound with a molecular structure closely similar to that of another. As an adjective, however, 'analogue' signifies an activity that is using signals or information that is represented by a continuously variable physical quantity such as spatial position, voltage, etc. Thus a clock is normally analogue because it displays the time by means of hands rather than numerical digits. In the USA and increasingly in Britain, 'analogue' is spelt 'analog'.

analyst *see* annalist

anchor

This is another dubious homonym. As a noun the word means an appliance for keeping a ship stationary, but the word can be used figuratively and applied to anything that provides stability or security: 'The anchor to my life is my wife'; 'I anchor myself in the music of Bach.' It is also often used in connection with the presenter or coordinator of a television programme: 'Tonight our programme on players of the Jew's harp in Latvia will be anchored by Melanie Snodgrass.'

ancient

Normally this word refers to something or someone who is extremely old: 'These carvings are very ancient, probably dating back to the eleventh century'; 'I am so ancient that I can actually remember the days before television.' In Daniel 7:9, God is called 'the Ancient of Days'. However, though the usage must be almost obsolete by now, the word **ancient** can also refer to an ensign or flag, or even to the person carrying it. Hence Pistol in Shakespeare's *Henry V* is called 'ancient Pistol', not because he is old but because he is the standard-bearer.

angel

Normally seen as a messenger from Heaven, this word is extended to apply to normal human beings who have distinguished themselves by some act of great kindness. Furthermore, there used to be an old English golden coin that was called an **angel**, largely because it depicted the archangel Michael killing a dragon. In modern theatrical parlance, an **angel** denotes the financial backer of a play. The word can also be used as an adjective. Thus 'angel visits' refer to encounters that are delightful but rare. 'Angel water' is a Spanish cosmetic made originally from angelica.

angels

Apart from being the plural of the noun mentioned in the entry immediately above, **angels** is also RAF slang for an aircraft's altitude. Often linked with a number representing thousands of feet, a pilot might say, 'We are now flying at angels nine.' The plural word is also used in reference to an unexplained radar echo.

angle

An angle is formed when two lines meet. If those two lines meet at an angle of 90°, then the meeting point is called a right angle. This geometric term has, of course, been extended to other contexts. Thus you can agree to meet a friend at the angle of High Street and Poplar Avenue. More figuratively, you can approach a problem which is proving difficult to solve from a different angle, hoping that your new approach will be more productive. The word is also a synonym for the verb 'to fish', and can again be extended in a figurative fashion in expressions like 'I am angling for more money for this task.' Written with a capital letter, an Angle was a member of a German tribe that invaded England and eventually gave its name to the 'English' people. The Angles and angels are linked in the comment attributed to Gregory the Great. On seeing fair-haired English slaves in Rome, he is reputed to have said (in Latin), 'These are not Angles but angels.'

animism

This word can either mean the belief that plants, inanimate objects and natural phenomena possess a living soul, or the belief that a supernatural power organises and animates the material universe.

animus

This noun has three meanings. First of all, it can mean great dislike or ill feeling towards someone: 'Richard had great animus against John.'

Secondly, it can signify an urge to do something: 'The reforming animus sprang from the shop floor.' Finally, in Jungian psychology, it means the masculine part of a woman's personality.

annalist, analyst

An **annalist** is someone who looks after or researches into the annals of a person, town, area or country. He or she is thus a practising historian. An **analyst** is someone who makes an analysis. In other words, an analyst examines something (a chemical compound, a historical document, a poem, etc.) and tries to break it down so as to reveal its full nature. Closely linked, of course, are the two homonymic verbs, **annalise** (to record) and **analyse** (to break down, to separate).

anneal

This is a verb which relates to the process of heating metal or glass and then allowing it to cool slowly so that any internal stresses are removed. In biochemistry, however, the word refers to the recombination of DNA into its double-helix form.

annex

As a verb, **annex** means to unite or take over some other country, area, department or whatever: 'I am proposing to annex Poland as a further security against Russia.' As a noun, the word normally means something added to something else: 'We built a granny flat as an annex to the main house.'

annihilate

We normally use this verb to refer to the total destruction of a people or place: 'The hydrogen bomb could annihilate the population of the world.' In physics, however, the word means the conversion of a subatomic particle into radiant energy. Clearly the same distinction will apply to the noun **annihilation**.

anorak

This is an article of clothing, a lined jacket designed to keep out the cold. Reputedly, because anoraks were normally worn by people engaged in the entirely pointless activity of train spotting, the word was extended to refer to socially and intellectually inept people. Hence, in 1999, the *Sunday Times* referred to the Chancellor of the Exchequer as 'an anorak', and went on to observe that 'He has the social skills of a whelk.'

ant, aunt

An ant is a small insect typically having a sting and living in a complex social colony, and an aunt is your father or mother's sister. Strictly speaking, there is a difference in pronunciation between these two words, but in real life it is often not detectable.

ante, auntie, anti

Apparently an **ante** is the preliminary bet put up before the deal in a game of poker. Informally, the word can also refer to the sum of money representing a person's share in some joint financial operation. It is also the prefix for a number of words like 'antecedent' and 'antechapel'. An **auntie** is a child's term referring to his or her aunt. The word **anti** means opposed to: 'I am anti smoking in clubs and bars.'

anvil

We normally associate the word **anvil** with the village blacksmith, since an anvil is a heavy iron block on which metal can be hammered. However, the word also means the horizontally extended upper part of a cumulo-nimbus cloud, as well as, in anatomy, being another word for 'incus', the anvil-shaped bone within the ear.

Apache, apache

With a capital letter, the word **Apache** refers to an American Indian people living chiefly in New Mexico and Arizona. The same word is used for their language. However, the word has also been adopted by the French, and, with no capital letter, denotes a violent street ruffian.

ape

As a noun, this word refers to a member of the monkey family, one that lacks a tail. As a verb, the word means to mimic or to imitate. In colloquial usage, if you call someone an ape, you imply that he (very rarely 'she') is a primitive barbarian.

apex, Apex

If you reach the **apex** of your profession, you have reached its highest point. Thus the position of Director General of the BBC is the apex of the broadcasting industry. Equally the word can refer to the highest physical point of something, like the apex of the roof. With a capital letter, **Apex** is the system of reduced fares for scheduled airline flights and railway journeys which must be booked and paid for before a certain period in advance of departure.

apheresis

In linguistics, **apheresis** means the omission of the initial sound of a word when that word is merged with another. Instead of 'he is', we often say 'he's', thus omitting the 'i' sound. In medicine, the word refers to the removal of a particular component or substance from the blood.

aphrodite, Aphrodite

In mineralogy, an aphrodite is a soft opaque milk-white mineral consisting mostly of bisilicate of magnesium. In zoology, an Aphrodite refers to a genus of marine worms. In classical mythology, Aphrodite refers to the Greek goddess of love.

aplomb

If something is **aplomb**, it is perpendicular, the word deriving from the French *à plomb* meaning according to the plumb line (i.e. vertically). However, if you behave with **aplomb**, you conduct yourself with confidence and self-assurance.

apogee

You might want to call the Mona Lisa the **apogee** of Renaissance art. You might want to call Mozart the apogee of music. As you will have inferred, the word means 'culmination', 'highest point', 'climax'. In astronomy, however, the word refers to the point in the orbit of the moon or a satellite at which it is the furthest from the Earth.

apostrophe

The most common usage of this word is to indicate the little comma superscript that appears in words like 'can't', 'o'er' and 'boy's' to indicate that a letter or letters are missing. The British habitually misuse the apostrophe, giving rise to such idiocies as 'jean's not allowed' and indignant letters to the so-called quality press. Less commonly used, an **apostrophe** is an exclamatory address, normally directed to a specific person or thing. Thus the headmaster in his end of academic year address to the assembled school might suddenly call upon the muse of history: 'O Clio, remember, I pray, this year as one of the most glorious in our history.' That would be an apostrophe. Apparently in botany, the word is also used to refer to the aggregation of protoplasm and chlorophyll-grains on the cell walls adjacent to other cells.

apparatus

Many of us remember at school having to gather together the **apparatus** for a chemical experiment. In this sense, the word means the equipment needed for a particular purpose. Thus athletes need their apparatus (spiked running shoes, shorts, etc.), firemen need theirs (helmet, hoses, etc.), and so on. But the word can also be used to refer to the complex structure of some system.

Thus we might talk about the apparatus of government, the apparatus of the EEC, and so on. Equally we sometimes talk about the critical apparatus of a scholar, things like original documents, reference books, and so on. These meanings are all conceptually similar, but disparate enough for 'apparatus' to count as a homonym.

appendix

More properly called the vermiform appendix, this is a wormlike pouch extending from the lower end of the caecum in some mammals. In human beings, the **appendix** is vestigial, and can be removed with no ill effects. In books, however, an **appendix** can be placed at the end of a book, treating in more detail something that arose in the body of the book.

apply

If you **apply** for a job, you are making a formal request to be given the post concerned. If you apply paint to a fence, you are putting paint on to the fence in order to improve its appearance. If you apply the strict rules, then you are being meticulous in enforcing the formal details. If you apply yourself to the task given, you are giving your full attention and devotion to the job in hand. As you can see, 'apply' has a variety of kindred meanings.

appointment

If one has an **appointment** with someone, then there is an agreement to meet them at a particular time and place. If you have an appointment in the Foreign Office, then that is your job.

appreciate

If you **appreciate** the novels of Jane Austen, then you recognise their full worth, you enjoy their mastery and control. If you buy an antique, you will hope that its value will appreciate, i.e. rise in value and price.

apprehend

The two basic meanings of **apprehend**, the one physical and the other mental, are conceptually related. If you physically apprehend someone or something, then you lay hold upon them, seize them, arrest them. If you apprehend something mentally, then you understand it, conceptually grasp its significance.

apprehension

To be full of **apprehension** is to be full of fear and anxiety that something unpleasant is likely to happen. At the same time, if you have a full apprehension of something, you understand it completely. If, however, you are placed under lawful apprehension, then you have been arrested for some alleged crime.

apprise, apprize

To **apprise** someone of something is to inform them: 'I thought it right to apprise Harold of what had happened.' If you **apprize** something, you put a price upon it, you estimate its value.

approach

As a verb, **approach** can be used in three similar but distinct ways. You can approach a building or an area: 'We are now approaching Sheffield.' You can approach a person: 'I took the opportunity to approach the lord mayor and raise the issue of our Kurdish residents.' You can get close to a solution: 'In approaching genetics, Maslow and Grundy seemed to adopt a sort of biological Calvinism.' There are comparable uses for the noun. All use the word in the sense of getting closer to someone or something, but the senses of approaching Sheffield, the lord mayor and the study of genetics do seem so diverse that 'approach' has to be counted as a homonymic word.

appropriate

If something is **appropriate**, then it is suitable for the context or circumstances envisaged: 'I think that this prayer is appropriate for the occasion.' However, you can also **appropriate** something in the sense of taking it over or assigning it to some special purpose: 'I need to appropriate these keys because they may be relevant to our enquiry.' Although 'appropriate' is obviously a homograph, it is not a homophone, slight though the difference in pronunciation is between the two uses.

apron

In normal usage, an **apron** is an article of dress, normally worn in the kitchen or workshop in order to protect one's other clothes from dirt or injury. However, a theatre can also have an **apron** stage, one that juts out into the auditorium. In gunnery, an apron is a square piece of lead laid over the touch-hole. In plumbing, an apron is a strip of lead which conducts the drip of a wall into the gutter. The word 'apron' is also a technical term in ship building and in mechanics. You can also talk about the apron of a roast duck or goose, in which case you would be referring to the skin covering the belly. At an airfield, an apron is the hard-surfaced area used for manoeuvring or parking aircraft. In geology, an apron is an extensive outspread deposit of sediment. In all these cases, there is a conceptual similarity in that there is always the idea of something protecting something else, but the contexts are so diverse that it seems justified to call such usages homonymic.

apt

If you have a tendency to react in specific ways, then your friends may say that you are **apt** to lose your temper with lazy students or whatever. If something is particularly suited or appropriate to a particular occasion, then it might be described as apt for the time. If you are particularly adept at learning a new language, then you will be an apt pupil. The word 'apt' is derived from the Latin *aptus* which means 'fitted', but, as its subsequent usage shows, there are very different ways of being fitted.

aqua

This word is often used as an abbreviation for 'aquamarine' (qv), a light bluish-green colour. In pharmaceutical circles, the word is used as a synonym for 'water', and this is its usual meaning when the word is used as a prefix for other words like 'aqueduct' and 'aqualung'.

aquamarine

Normally thought of as a light bluish-green colour, this word can also signify a precious stone that is a light bluish-green variety of beryl.

arc, ark

An **arc** is part of a circle. Thus a rainbow forms an arc, the arch of a bridge can be an arc, a geometrical diagram can contain an arc, a comet in the sky can describe an arc, and so on. In mathematics, an arc indicates the inverse of a trigonometrical function. In physics, the word is used to describe the luminous electrical discharge between two electrodes. There is also a painful eye condition known as **arc eye**, a complaint caused by damage to the cornea from ultraviolet radiation during arc welding. An **ark**, however, can be a large, floating vessel or boat most popularly associated with Noah, or a chest or closed basket of some kind. In Jewish history also, the wooden coffer in which the tables of the law were kept was called the ark of the covenant.

arcana

This plural noun denotes the secrets or expertise of a particular profession or occupation. It also denotes either of the two groups of cards in a tarot pack, the 22 trumps being the major arcana, and the 56 suit cards being the minor arcana.

arch

An **arch** is the curved structure that normally connects two vertical structures, thereby creating an opening through which people or traffic may pass. Thus bridges or doors may be arched. The word **arch** may also be an adjective describing someone or something as the major or principal element in a situation. Thus someone may be your arch rival in the mathematics exam, or you may be the arch drug supplier in Taunton. The word can also be used to describe a remark or comment. If you are being arch to someone, your comments are normally semi-playful but with a distinct tone of superiority.

archetype

The meanings of **archetype** are all conceptually linked. First of all, it can be a superb example of a particular kind of person or thing. My friend David Hanson was the archetype of the traditional country doctor, caring, upright and conscientious. Equally, an archetype can be the progenitor of later developments. Hence someone might say that the hunting horn was the archetype of the trumpet, trombone and other brass instruments in the modern orchestra. More technically, in Jungian philosophy, an archetype is a primitive mental image inherited from the earliest human ancestors and supposed to be present in the collective unconscious. The word is also used to indicate a recurrent symbol in literature, art or mythology. Hence Ulysses is seen as the archetypal wanderer.

are *see* air

are, R, r

Are is the second person singular present, and first, second and third person plural of the verb 'to be': you are tired, we are tired, they are tired. The same word is used to denote a measurement equal to 100 square metres. In its normal pronunciation, 'are' sounds exactly like the letter R.

area

Most of the time, this word relates to a physical space. Hence you and I live in a particular area, south Bristol, north Glasgow, or wherever. Mathematicians amuse themselves by working out the **area** of a triangle, i.e. how much space it consumes. But we also use the word to denote a mental region of interest or concern: 'As far as history is concerned, I'm only really interested in the area of political conflict in Blackburn from 1832 to 1867.'

arid

If an area of land is particularly dry and barren, it can be described as **arid**, that is, incapable of supporting life. However, a topic or subject can also be described as arid if, for you, it lacks interest, excitement or meaning.

ark *see* arc

arm

This is a verb meaning to equip oneself with weapons, and derives from the Latin plural word *arma*: ('I will arm the squad with machine guns just in case we run into trouble'). An **arm** is also the upper limb of a biped, and derives from the Old English *arm*: ('The arms of a gibbon are surprisingly long'). Hence to be armless can mean that you possess no upper limbs or that you are carrying no weapons. Metaphorically, the upper limb has been transfigured in expressions like 'an arm of the sea', 'to chance your arm', 'at arm's length' and 'the secular arm'.

arms, alms

Obviously, given the entry immediately above, **arms** refers to more than one upper limb ('He raised his arms in the air'), but the word can also refer to the distinctive emblems or devices that make up the heraldic insignia of families, corporations or counties. The word can also refer to weaponry: 'He took up arms'; 'I must have the right to bear arms'; 'a nation in arms'. The homophone **alms** refers to money given to old and impoverished people. Indeed, in Britain there were alms houses erected for the housing of such indigent folk.

array

This word can be a verb meaning to set or place in readiness objects or people, either for an inspection or for battle. It can also be a reference to one's dress: 'I will array myself in my finery.' As a noun, an **array** can be an impressive display of something (an array of flowers), an arrangement of troops, or a list of jurors impanelled.

art

When one studies art at school or college, the word is confined to such visual activities as painting, sculpture, tapestry making, etc. However, the word is extended to any activity that requires skill. Hence you can demonstrate the art of a blacksmith or be proficient in the art of diplomacy. The word **art** is also an old-fashioned form of the word 'are', still sometimes used in jocular or mock-poetic contexts: 'Thou art a scurvy knave.'

artery

An **artery** is a tube that carries blood from the heart to all parts of the body. Because it is thus concerned with transporting blood, the word has been metaphorically used for man-made transport systems. Hence the A1 could be described as the main artery of Britain's road system, and so on.

article

Most commonly this is a piece of connected writing of moderate brevity on a particular subject, an item that might appear in a newspaper or magazine. Thus you might write an article about recent developments in genetics, your favourite football team or the problems of parking in Leicester. The words 'a' and 'the' are also articles, 'a' being referred to as the indefinite article and 'the' as the definite article. The terms of an agreement or a will or any similar legal document can also be referred to as an article: 'Please look at article 3, sub-section c.' However, the word can also operate as a verb, in which case it refers to a kind of apprenticeship as a solicitor, architect, surveyor or accountant: 'I was articled to a firm of solicitors in Newton Abbot.'

articulate

If you are **articulate**, you are able to speak fluently and coherently. However, the word also has anatomical meanings. If an animal is articulate, it possesses jointed segments. A brachiopod is also described as articulate because it has a hinge that joins the two halves of its shell. Hence, when you transform the adjective into a verb, it can mean either that you pronounce your words clearly or that two or more items come together to form a joint.

as, ass

An **as** was a Roman copper coin, but you are unlikely to encounter the word in this context much today. You will, however, encounter **as** as an adverb countless times. It can be used almost as a synonym for 'because': 'As John is not here, I will happily take his place in the team.' It can indicate the passage of time: 'We ate our sandwiches as the procession passed.' The word can be used as a comparative word: 'She is as good as me.' The word often introduces a dependant clause: 'As I have already mentioned, the ghost in *Hamlet* is something of a problem.' Certainly the uses of the word **as** are varied and manifold, and it is used in countless expressions: 'as good as gold', 'as green as grass', 'as pleased as Punch', 'as thin as a rake', etc. It also sounds very like the word **ass**, another word for a donkey. (See the separate entry on **ass**.)

ascent, assent

An **ascent** is a climb, a movement upwards: 'The ascent of Snowden exhausted us.' An **assent** is an agreement, and acknowledgement that something or other is in fact the case: 'I assent entirely to your claims.'

ash

This is a forest tree common to Europe, western Asia and north Africa, or the powdery substance left after something has been burnt. The first day of Lent is called Ash Wednesday because of the custom of applying the ashes of palms, made into a sort of paste, to the foreheads of penitent Christians.

aside

As an adverb, **aside** indicates that something or someone is being moved out of the way: 'He stood aside to allow other passengers to reach their luggage.' As a noun, 'aside' refers to a remark that is delivered to someone, but is not intended to be overheard by anyone else. For plays in the theatre, an aside is a convention by which the actor can say something for the benefit of the audience, but which no one on stage can hear.

ask

The verb to **ask** indicates the action of saying something in order to elicit an answer, normally an answer giving information that the enquirer lacks: 'May I ask which is the quickest way to the railway station?' As a noun, the ask is the minimum price at which an article is offered for sale. Colloquially, one can have a big ask, that is, one that is going to be difficult to answer: 'To expect Graham to increase sales by ten per cent is a very big ask.'

asp

A noun in all its meanings, an **asp** is either a poplar tree, a large predatory freshwater fish of the carp family, or a small, venomous, hooded serpent.

aspect

All the meanings of **aspect** are related. As a noun it means the appearance that something or someone presents to the naked eye: 'The aspect down the Avon Gorge is gorgeous, but I do not like the aspect of that evil-looking man leaning over the Clifton Bridge.' As a virtually obsolete word, 'aspect' can mean the action of looking at, and is so used from time to time by Shakespeare and Milton. However, in the spurious subject of astrology, the word means the relative positions of the planets at any given time.

aspirate

All animals need to **aspirate** because the verb means to breathe in. However, it can also mean to draw up fluid by suction from a vessel or cavity. In addition, the word is used to describe a common British disease, namely the failure to pronounce the letter 'h' at the beginnings of words: ' 'eather our 'ousekeeper gave me some 'addock and 'am for tea.' In that example, there has been a total failure to aspirate, that is, pronounce a sound with an exhalation of breath.

aspiration

This word is obviously the noun drawn from the verbs described in the entry immediately above, yet it also possesses a different and entirely unconnected meaning. If you have an **aspiration**, you have the hope or ambition of achieving something. In this case, the noun is linked, not to 'aspirate', but to the verb 'aspire'.

ass

This is a horselike quadruped often called a donkey. However, because donkeys have a simple, rather vacant expression, the word **ass** is also used to indicate that someone is a fool. In the United States the word is also used to refer to a person's bottom or buttocks.

assent *see* ascent

assistance, assistants

The first word refers to help provided: 'He was of great assistance in repairing the car.' **Assistants**, of course, are people who provide that help.

assume

This verb normally means that you accept something to be the case even though you haven't got actual proof: 'I assume that Hilda will want to go away this Christmas.' The word can also mean that you hold a position entailing some power or responsibility: 'When I assume the office of Lord High Executioner, all vegetarians will be executed.' The word can also mean that you or something begins to adopt a new quality: 'When Brenda became President of the Union, she began to assume a new arrogance in her behaviour.' You can also assume an entirely false demeanour: 'Knowing that he was about to be found out, Jack assumed an attitude of deep penitence.'

assumption

This is a noun, and most of the time refers to something that everybody accepts, to an element the validity of which is never doubted. Thus once upon a time, it was an assumption that the sun went round the earth. It is also possible for an assumption to refer to the taking up of an office or position: 'Jack's assumption of the role of Prime Minister was remarkably trouble free.' In addition, with a capital letter, the Assumption relates to the Roman Catholic belief that the Virgin Mary ascended to heaven in the same way as her son.

assurance

In the jargon of insurance brokers, **assurance** refers to life policies, but the word also denotes an almost arrogant self-confidence that a person may display. It can also mean a positive declaration designed to instil confidence: 'He gave an assurance that Patricia would pass her driving test.'

assure

This verb has three slightly different meanings. First of all, you can **assure** yourself of something, convince yourself that something is the case: 'Martin assured himself that she was asleep.' Secondly, you can be assured by someone else that something is really the case: 'Kevin was assured that the brakes of the car had been checked.' Finally, you can take out a financial policy that will assure you of a measure of security in the future.

astragal

This is the moulding round the top or bottom of a column, or a bar separating panes of glass in cabinet making.

astringent

This word can be an adjective describing the contraction of skin cells and other bodily tissue, or a word describing a sharp and severe verbal approach: 'She was astringent in her criticisms.' It can also be a noun depicting a lotion that is applied to the skin in order to reduce bleeding.

asylum

An asylum is an institution to which ill people, traditionally people with mental difficulties, are admitted. The word also refers to the protection granted by a country to people who have fled persecution.

at

This preposition can act in a variety of ways. First of all, it can express location: 'He was found at the railway station.' It can denote a particular point on a scale: 'The temperature remained at 24°C.' It can express a particular state of feeling: 'She felt at odds with him.' It can announce a purpose: 'My policy is aimed at reducing poverty.' It can indicate the way that something is or was done: 'He held the knife at my throat.' Hence you can sit 'at home, with the room at a comfortable temperature, your bottle of martini at hand, your husband at your side, and feel completely at ease'. To add to its versatility, the word at is also a noun signifying a monetary unit of Laos equal to one hundredth of a kip.

ate, eight, Ate

The verb ate is the past tense of the verb 'to eat': 'I ate all the mince pies.' The number eight is a homophone of 'ate', and is the numerical digit lying between seven and nine. The goddess Ate was taken by the Greeks to be in charge of mischief and random destruction.

atlas, Atlas

The common noun normally refers to a book of maps or charts. Thus you can have an atlas of Great Britain showing where the towns, rivers, hills, etc. of that country are located. Equally you can have an anatomical atlas showing where the different bones and muscles of a human being or animal are placed. In fact, one of those bones, the first cervical vertebra, is specifically called the atlas. The word also is used to indicate a specific size of drawing paper, 26 x 17 inches. In classical mythology, Atlas was a Titan compelled to hold the Earth on his shoulders, and the name has since been used to refer to any well-developed, muscular man. The name has also been given to an American intercontinental ballistic missile, and to one of the satellites of the planet Jupiter.

atmosphere

This is the word used to describe the spheroidal gaseous envelope surrounding a planet, though, so far as we know, only the atmosphere of Earth is capable of sustaining life. However, the word is also used to describe the tone or feel of a social gathering: 'I did not like the atmosphere at the party. Too many people were too bitchy.'

atrium

This noun denotes a hall, either an entrance hall or a central court. It also refers to each of the two upper cavities of the heart.

attend

This verb has two quite distinct meanings. First of all, it means to be present at some place and/or event: 'I will attend the concert next Friday.' Secondly, it means to pay attention to or to concentrate: 'I really did attend to my work.'

attendance, attendants

If you are in **attendance**, then you are present at some event: 'My attendance at his funeral was deeply upsetting.' **Attendants** are people who are present at some event, sometimes in an official capacity: 'The attendants made sure that the tents were firmly secured.'

Attic, attic

With the capital letter, the word refers to things pertaining to the area of Greece known as Attica or to the capital of that area, Athens. Hence the poet and dramatist Sophocles has been termed 'the Attic Bee', and Xenophon was called 'the Attic Muse'. In lower case, the word refers to a small room immediately under the beams of a roof. It is thus the highest room in a house, the garret, and is traditionally the low-rent habitation of a poet.

attrition

This is a noun signifying the gradual reduction in strength of something: 'Weeks of ease in Bermuda led to the serious attrition of James Bond's muscular tone.' However, in scholastic theology, the word also means a failure in expressing sufficient contrition for a sin.

auction

As verb or noun, **auction** relates to a public sale of something whereby the article in question is sold to the highest bidder. In the card game bridge, the auction is the process of bidding in order to decide the contract in which the hand will be played.

audience

Most of us have sat in an **audience**, a collection of people gathered together to see or hear something. Thus there is an audience at a flute recital, a cricket match, a public talk or a regatta. Television and radio programmes are also said to have an audience. More formally, however, one can have an audience with an important person, that is, a formal interview: 'Benedict demanded an audience with the Pope.'

auger, augur

The first word is a noun and refers to a small drill used by carpenters for boring holes in wood. The second word is a homophone and a verb that means to foretell or prophesy, though in ancient Rome there was an **augur**, an official who observed natural signs like the behaviour of birds, and proceeded to interpret such 'signs' as an indication of divine approval or disapproval.

aught, ought

In English writers up to the eighteenth century, **aught** and **ought** tended to be used as synonyms. Nowadays, they have quite distinct meanings. **Aught** means 'anything': 'For aught I know, Mars could be inhabited by purple dragons.' **Ought** today is a verb implying a moral imperative: 'I ought to post this letter.'

auntie

This is a child's affectionate name for an aunt, but since 1965, when Jack De Manio called his autobiography *To Auntie with Love*, the word has also been used as a nickname for the BBC.

aural, oral

Not only do these words sound almost identical, but they have allied meanings too. **Aural** is an adjective that relates to the sense or organs of hearing. Hence hearing a poet read out loud his own poetry could be described as an aural treat. **Oral** is also an adjective and refers to things connected with the mouth. Thus 'oral history' relates to reminiscences delivered by people who lived through sundry events. 'Oral hygiene' is concerned with effective tooth brushing, flossing, etc. However, just to be complete, the word **aural** could be an adjective referring to someone's 'aura': 'I felt the aural force of Nelson Mandela's personality.'

auricle, oracle

These two words are not exactly homophones, but once again you would be hard put to it to distinguish between them. The **auricle** refers either to the external part of the ear or to the two upper cavities of the heart. An **oracle** has a number of related meanings all referring to prophecy. Thus an oracle can be a seer who prophesies what is to come, or it can be the prophecy itself. Equally it can be the place or shrine where people go to hear some needed prophecy. In ancient Greece, that at Delphi was the most famous.

austerity

It is perfectly possible to speak with **austerity**. In such a case, one's voice would have a stern and severe manner. It is possible to have a room furnished with austerity, in which case it would be simple, plain and uncluttered. In addition, a country or a household could be experiencing austerity when they found themselves in difficult economic circumstances. Clearly all these instances share common factors, but they are diverse enough to count as homonymic.

auxiliary

In everyday life or in military operations, an **auxiliary** is a helper, ally, confederate or assistant. In mathematics, its meaning is similar, since an auxiliary is a quantity introduced to simplify an equation. In grammar, however, the term is applied to words that are short but helpful, words like prepositions or prefixes. Thus in 'submerge', the syllable 'sub' is an auxiliary. The term can also denote a verb (often the verb 'to be') that helps to form the tenses of other verbs. Thus in the sentence 'I am tired today', the word 'am' is an auxiliary.

average

This is another word that perhaps barely justifies inclusion as a homonym. In mathematical terms, an **average** is the sum you get by adding up a series of numbers and then dividing the result by the number of items you have added. Thus 11.6 would be the average of 5, 11 and 19. However, deriving from this precise usage, the word is now often used to indicate something or someone who is neither particularly good nor particularly bad: 'Jane's cooking skills are fairly average.'

avidity

If you have an **avidity** for something, you display a keenness and enthusiasm for it. In biochemistry, avidity is the binding strength between an antibody and an antigen.

away, aweigh

The first word is an extremely common English word and signifies either the action of moving more distantly from someone or something ('I moved away from the bonfire'), or the state of being so removed ('I was away from London during the summer'). In both cases, the word is an adverb. So too is **aweigh**, a word only used in connection with raising the anchor of a ship. It refers to the lifting of the anchor from its position on the seabed.

awe, oar, or, ore

To experience **awe** is to be in a state of almost terrified wonderment. Thus one could be in a state of awe in looking at Rheims cathedral, standing on the edge of the Grand Canyon, listening to the B minor Mass of J. S. Bach, or praying to God. An Internet source defines the next three words as a boat propulsion system, a Boolean deathtrap, and as mineral-laden dirt. This is amusing, but less than ideal for our purposes. An **oar** is a pole-like object flattened and widened at one end, and used as a lever to propel a boat, normally a rowing boat. **Or** is a word used to cite an alternative – 'We could stay in or go out' – or to link two words that mean much the same thing – 'We could revise or study this afternoon.' **Ore** is a native mineral that contains within it a metal in sufficient quantity as to make the metal worth extracting.

aweful, awful

If you are **aweful**, then you are full of awe (see above). If something is **awful**, then it is really bad. An Internet site that I encountered gave **offal** as a homonym for these words, but that strikes me as stretching things far too far.

awl *see* all

ax or axe *see* acts

axel, axil, axle

The noun **axel** denotes a jump in skating from the forward outside edge of one skate to the backward outside edge of the other. The noun **axil** refers to the upper angle between a leaf stalk or branch and the stem or trunk from which it is growing. The noun **axle** denotes the rod passing through the centre of a wheel or group of wheels.

aye, eye, I

The word **aye** is normally taken to be the nautical equivalent of 'yes'. The **eye** is the organ through which animals can see. **I** is the personal pronoun referring to oneself.

azure

This is the precious stone lapis lazuli, or the colour blue. The precious stone, of course, is normally the blue colour that the word denotes. Equally there is a small butterfly called 'azure' because it too is blue or purple in colour.

B

B, b, bee

As you know, **B** is the second letter of the English alphabet, and, like A, often used for grading someone's work: 'Doreen got an A, but Stephen could only manage a B.' **B** is also a key of music, and the bedbug has been comically referred to as B flat. The letter is also used in countless abbreviations: BBC, BA, BC, etc. A **bee** is an insect that makes honey, though apparently in nautical parlance, a bee can be a metal hoop. The insect, however, because it is a social animal, has been appropriated for communal contests like spelling bees. Furthermore, because the bee carries its pollen on its legs, the expression 'the bee's knees' has been invented to refer to something notable or outstanding.

baa, bah, ba

The bleating sound made by a sheep is a **baa**, while an exclamation of dismissal or disgust can be a **Bah!** Neither of these needs explication, but **ba** is more complex. It is a synonym for the word 'soul', and, according to the ancient Egyptians, it roamed burial places at night. Later teachings affirmed that the ba was a manifested appearance of a god. Thus the bull Apis was the ba of Osiris, and the star Sirius was the ba of Isis.

baby

While the most common usage of this word is to refer to the very young off-spring of an animal (including humans), the word is often extended to include new ventures in business: 'Our department of sociology is only a baby at the moment, but we expect it to grow rapidly.' The word can also be used as a verb: 'I shall baby him along.' Even so, in all uses of the word, the ideas of great youth and newness are present, and so one might reasonably challenge its status as a homonym.

bachelor

Normally taken as meaning an unmarried man, the word can also be used to refer to someone who has taken a first degree at a university. The word has also been used to describe a young knight who was a novice in arms. In Australia, the word **bachelor** has been shortened to **bach** or **batch** as a label for a holiday house or 'weekender' on the beach.

back

This word has a variety of meanings. With an object like a coin, a book, a car, etc., the back is the side of the object that is opposite to the front. In animals, the back is the part of the body that is closest to the spinal column. The word is also common in a wide variety of expressions: 'I shall come back'; 'I shall stand at the back'; 'I went back on my word'; 'The whole country went back to barbarity'; 'I'm just a back number'; and so on. The **back** can also refer to the surface of a river. It is also a verb meaning to place money on something in the hope of winning even more: 'I shall back David Rothwell to win the Booker Prize.' (That would be equivalent to throwing the money away.) If you use 'back slang', you pronounce words as if they were spelt backwards.

bacon, baken

Often accompanied by eggs, **bacon** is the back and sides of a pig, frequently fried for breakfast. However, it has also entered into colloquial use as a way of indicating that one has escaped from a perilous situation: 'Seizing that overhanging branch was the thing that saved my bacon.' As a past tense of the verb 'to bake', **baken** is a somewhat old-fashioned way of saying 'baked'.

bad, bade

If a person or object is **bad**, then they are the reverse of perfect. A bad person does criminal or selfish things, a bad apple tastes dreadful and might infect you with some disease, and a bad idea fails to lead to any very constructive outcome. Not surprisingly, the word 'bad' is attached to scores of nouns in a metaphorical or proverbial sense: bad blood, bad debt, bad egg, bad form, bad lot, bad news, bad patch, and so on. The word **bade** is the past tense of the verb 'to bid', and can be pronounced with a short 'a', in which case it is a homophone for 'bad', or with a long 'a', in which case, of course, it isn't.

badger

Most of us are likely to think of a **badger** as a nocturnal, hibernating animal that lives in a burrow called a sett. It does, however, have a number of other meanings. In the sixteenth century, a badger was someone who bought corn and other commodities to then sell elsewhere. Apparently anglers call a type of artificial fly a badger, and a shaving brush made of badger's hair is often referred to as a badger. Although it is unlikely to be useful to you, you might also like to know that an inhabitant of Wisconsin is often nicknamed a badger. All such usages are nouns, but **badger** is also a verb. It means to nag, to subject someone to continuous rebuking reminders: 'I had to badger Tony to get any spare electric bulbs.' There is also the so-called 'badger game' whereby a prostitute lures a client into a room, and then robs him.

baft

This is a coarse and cheap fabric, usually of cotton, and in nautical terms, another word for 'behind'.

bag

Most of us are used to carrying our shopping in a **bag**, a receptacle of flexible material open only at the top. Like most nouns, it can thus be turned into a verb – 'I bagged all the turnips' – but it also has a colloquial usage where it means that you reserve something for your own use: 'Let me bag the back seats.' The word is also used in a variety of colloquial expressions: bag of bones, bag of nerves, bag of tricks, old bag, and so on.

bagatelle

This word manages to refer to a game played on a table with a semi-circular end at which are nine numbered holes, to a piece of music or verse of a light nature, and to something of little consequence: 'Playing dominoes on Tuesdays is a mere bagatelle.' You could therefore, I suppose, say that playing bagatelle while listening to a bagatelle was a mere bagatelle, but I wouldn't recommend your doing so.

baggage

This word is customarily used to refer to a collection of luggage, but it can also be used to refer unflatteringly to a good-for-nothing woman.

bah *see* baa

bail, bale

Not only are 'bail' and 'bale' obvious homonyms, but each of them is a homonym on its own. A **bail** is one of the two small pieces of wood that lie across the top of the stumps in a cricket match. It is also the condition of being allowed to be out of prison while awaiting trial for some offence or other. It can also be the hoop or half-hoop that supports the cover of a wagon. As a verb, it can signify the deliverance of goods in accordance with the promise made or contract agreed to. Equally, it can be the action of allowing or enabling someone to have bail: 'I offer to bail Peter out of jail.' Furthermore, it can denote the action of pumping water out of a boat: 'I bailed sufficient water out of the rowing boat for us to be able to reach shore.' The other **bale** can signify an evil influence – 'Margaret was Roger's bale' – or a large bundle or package. The word is often used in agricultural contexts as in a bale of straw.

bailee, bailey, bailie

None of these is common, but they certainly exist. A **bailee** is a person to whom goods are committed for custody or repair. A **bailey** is the outer wall of a castle, and a **bailie** is a municipal officer in Scotland.

bailer, bailor, baler

These words are derived from the ones almost immediately above. A **bailer** is one who bails water. A **bailor** is a person who entrusts goods to a bailee, and a **baler** is one who bales hay or straw.

bailing, baling

Bailing is the action of pumping water out of a boat, and **baling** is an adjective to describe the wire used to tie bales.

bait, bate

If you **bait** someone, you torment them by withholding something that they need or by sneering at them in some way. However, you can also bait a fish hook by placing upon it something that will attract the fish. The resulting object is also called a bait. However, if you **bate** something, you lessen its force or reduce its strength. Hence you can be bated of energy by lying in the sun.

baize, bays, beys

Baize is a coarse, woollen cloth often used for the covering of snooker tables. The words **bays** and **beys** are clearly the plurals of 'bay' and 'bey' respectively, and there is an individual entry on each of those words.

balance

The word has a whole variety of meanings all concerned in some way or other with gaining an equality, achieving an equilibrium. Thus you can place an object on a pair of scales and by placing the appropriate weights on the other side of the scale, achieve a balance, thereby learning the weight of the object concerned. You can balance on a rope, thereby ensuring that you do not fall off the rope (or at least you can if you are a tightrope walker). You can balance accounts, thereby determining that money coming in is equivalent to money being spent. You can balance arguments, trying to determine which side of an argument has the more convincing power. In dancing, your movements act in balance with those of your partner. Hence it could be argued that **balance** is not really a homonym, but it seems to me that the contexts in which the word is used are so disparate as to effectively make it so.

bald, balled, bawled

If someone is **bald**, their head has virtually no hair. **Balled** is a slang word denoting sexual intercourse. **Bawled** is the past tense of the verb 'to bawl' and means 'cried aloud' or 'shouted'.

bale *see* bail

balk

This word, sometimes spelt as **baulk**, is the ridge in a field between two furrows, or a strip of ground left unploughed. It is also the part of a billiard or snooker table lying behind the transverse line. It can also be a verb meaning to refuse to do something: 'I balk at running five miles in the pouring rain.'

ball, bawl

A **ball** is a spherical object used in sundry sports (tennis, cricket, etc.) or for just playing with in catching games. Hence we get such metaphorical expressions as 'the ball is in your court' and 'the ball of fortune'. A ball is also a formal dancing event like the graduation ball at universities or the hunt ball in some of the rural English counties. To **bawl** is to cry, normally rather loudly.

ballast

Basically this refers to the heavy material (gravel, sand, etc.) that is placed in the hold of a ship so as to give the ship stability and prevent it capsizing. However, the meaning has been extended to morals or philosophical argument. Hence if one says that Kant's arguments have no ballast, one means that he has not given his opinions adequate weight or logical force.

balsam

In chemistry **balsam** refers to compounds insoluble in water and consisting of resins mixed with volatile oil. In botany, balsam is a particular flowering plant. Its most common usage, however, is as an oil for soothing or healing wounds.

ban

If you **ban** something, then you prohibit it taking place. Hence you ban people under the age of eighteen from seeing an X-rated film, or you ban smoking in pubs. The word though can also be a noun, in which case it refers to the governor or viceroy in certain military districts in Hungary, Slavonia and Croatia under the Austro-Hungarian Empire.

band, banned

A **band** is a group of people linked together by some common purpose. They could be playing musical instruments together, in which case they might be a brass band, a military band, a wind band, and so on. They might be a band of sightseers, tourists, criminals, schoolchildren, or virtually anything else. However, if something is **banned** then it is forbidden. Thus smoking might be banned in the ballroom, or riding bicycles might be banned in the park.

bandy

One might have **bandy** legs, in which case they are curved laterally. Something might conceivably be bandy in the sense that it is festooned with bands of elastic, plaster or cloth. One might bandy a ball in the sense of throwing or hitting it to and fro. One can bandy words in conversation in that one has an argumentative quibble about some matter of disagreement. Hence your superior at work might say, 'Don't bandy words with me about that.'

bank

Most of us keep some money in the **bank**, a financial institution that takes care of your money while making profits in using your deposits for its own purposes. The word can also be used to signify the accumulated total of something that you have been saving: 'I have a bank of logs in the shed.' Equally we could lie on the bank of the river or upon the sloping incline of a hill. In a casino, the dealer will hold the bank, that is the amount of money wagered by every participant in the game. In financial contexts, the word can also be used as a verb: 'I will bank my money in the bank.'

banker

A **banker** is someone who works in or manages a bank, but the word can also refer to a ship employed in cod-fishing on the Bank of Newfoundland, a labourer who makes banks of earth, a horse which can jump on and off banks that are too wide to be cleared or even a card gambling game.

bar

A **bar** can be the counter at which one is served a drink in a pub or club, a strip of wood or metal, a barrier of some sort, or the environment in which a barrister works. As a verb, you can **bar** or exclude someone from the premises, or bar them from pursuing a particular kind of activity. Equally you can bar a door by making it more difficult to break in. In the Jewish religion, a bar mitzvah is the initiation ceremony of a boy who has reached the age of thirteen and is regarded as ready to observe religious precepts.

barb

Apparently a **barb** is a piece of white plaited linen worn under the chin by nuns. The word is recorded from Middle English, and comes via Old French from the Latin word *barba* meaning a beard. From this developed in late Middle English the current sense of a sharp projection near the end of a arrow, fish-hook or similar object, which is angled away from the main point so as to make extraction difficult. Plants too can sometimes be described as having barbs. A barbary horse is also sometimes referred to as a barb. The word 'barb' can also be applied to a hurtful or derogatory comment.

bard, barred

A **bard** is a poet. Hence Shakespeare is often referred to as the Bard of Avon. If something is **barred**, it means that it is rendered physically stronger as in a barred gate, or is forbidden to be done or performed as in a barred film or play.

bare, bear

The first word means naked or unadorned: 'The bare [naked] woman gazed out at the bare [unadorned] moor.' A **bear** is a heavily built, furred quadruped, but also, in Stock Market parlance, a bear is a speculator who makes every effort to depress prices so that he can buy cheaply and then sell later at a profit. The word can also be a verb meaning to hold or carry. As such the verb is often used in a number of proverbial expressions like 'to bear one's cross', 'to bear arms', 'to grin and bear it', and 'to bear the brunt'.

barge

A **barge** is a freight-carrying boat normally used on canals or in rivers. It is also possible to barge through a crowd of people, meaning that you have no scruples about shouldering people aside as you progress.

bark, barque

A **bark** is the sharp cry made by some quadrupeds like dogs and foxes. By extension, the word can also be used for a human angry exclamation. You can also bark with a cough. It is also the outer rind of a tree trunk. A **barque** is a square-rigged sailing ship.

barker

Obviously a dog could be a heavy and loud barker, while a man could be employed as a barker, i.e. one who strips the bark off trees. The word is also used to describe someone who loudly extols the goods he is selling or the show that is about to be put on. In the USA, a barker is a baseball coach.

barman

A **barman** can be one who serves behind the bar of a pub or someone who prepares metal bars.

barnacle

This can be a metal twitch for the mouth of a horse or ass, useful in controlling the animal's restiveness. A **barnacle** is also a species of wild goose, or sundry types of marine crustaceans that firmly affix themselves to rocks or the bottoms of ships. By extension, the word can be employed to describe a man or woman who is difficult to shake off, but who persistently attaches him- or herself to you and bores you rigid.

baron, barren

The pronunciation of these two words is not quite identical, but, in most people's speech, close enough to be undetectable. A **baron** is someone in the lower ranks of the nobility, whereas if someone or something is **barren**, it means that they are unproductive, incapable of producing life, or uninteresting.

baroness, barrenness

The first word relates to a baron's wife, the second to the state of being barren.

barred *see* bard

barrow

In some parts of the British Isles, a **barrow** is the name for a hill. Artificial hills created as a grave-mound are also called barrows. Most common of all, a barrow is a one-wheeled vehicle in which goods are transported.

basal, basil

Basal is an adjective referring to something associated with the base of an object or building. **Basil** is a culinary herb.

base, bass

The word **base** can refer to a number of things. First of all, it can refer to the bottom of something: 'I will fasten this to the base of the cooker.' There are associated usages in gunnery, architecture, dyeing, fortification, botany, zoology, heraldry and doubtless other specialist fields. In English grammar, the term refers to the word to which a suffix is attached. Thus in a word like 'superimposed', 'super' is the prefix and 'imposed' is the base. However, the word also has a moral or evaluative meaning. If something is base, it is inferior to something else. A base action is one to be deplored. **Bass**, on the other hand, is a word of tonal significance. It refers to something that is very low pitched. Thus, in music, Willard White is a bass singer, and the tuba is a bass instrument. Apparently, however, a bass is the name for a member of the perch family as well as being the inner bark of the lime or linden tree.

based, baste

If something is **based** on something else, it is supported or buttressed by it. Thus your brilliant piano playing might be based on your practice of the scales, while success in Latin needs to be based on a mastery of the conjugations and declensions. If you are cooking, you might need to **baste** the meat with fat, or to baste the vegetables with gravy. The verb means to swab with liquid during cooking.

bases, basis, basses

Bases is the plural of **base**, though an Internet source informs me that bases are what baseball players like to steal. The **basis** of something is its principal constituent. Thus the basis of skill in chemistry is a proper understanding of the Periodic Table. **Basses** is obviously the plural of bass and could therefore refer to a collection of bass singers. Apparently the word can also stand for many four-stringed guitars.

bash

If you **bash** someone, you hit them in a decidedly unfriendly fashion. To be fair, though, a bash can be accidental, and hence carry few moral connotations. Hence you may bash your car into a lamp post or even bash your spouse as you dash into the lounge and collide in error. Somewhat mysteriously, 'bash' has at least a couple of other meanings. If you are compiling a dictionary of homonyms and reach the letter X, you might confidently say, 'I'll bash out X this afternoon, since I doubt if there'll be more than a couple of pages needed.' So, if you bash something out, you do it rapidly. Don't, however, make this sort of remark to your editor, because to bash something out implies not only rapidity, but also a certain lack of care. In addition, a bash could be an event of some nature, often a party. You might say, 'I'm going to Tony's birthday bash this afternoon.'

basil *see* **basal**

bask, basque

To **bask** in something is to luxuriate in it, to enjoy it to the full. Hence one can bask in the sun or bask in the music of Palestrina. A **basque** on the other hand is a tight-fitting bodice or tunic. With a capital letter, Basque can identify a language or the people of the Pyrenees who speak that language.

bass *see* **base**

basses *see* **bases**

bat, batt

In England and Wales, of course, the word **bat** is likely to conjure up that strange implement with a rounded handle and flattened blade known as a cricket bat. However, naturalists are more likely to think of a nocturnal, blind, flying rodent. The word can also refer to a felted mass of fur, often used in hat making, and frequently spelt **batt**.

bate *see* **bait**

bath, bathe

Some contemporary of Queen Elizabeth I once remarked that the lady used to have a bath once a month whether she needed one or not. Most of us today regard a daily bath or shower as an essential. The meaning, however, remains unaltered. A **bath** is a vessel large enough to contain a human being and into which hot or warm water is poured. The human being then lies in this bath and washes him- or herself. The verb refers to the activity of washing. However, the meaning of the word has been extended. Hence, when you are developing photographic prints or plates, you immerse them in a bath. More figuratively, it is possible to bath in the summer breeze, to bath in the perfume of flowers, or to bath in the music of Vivaldi. **Bathe** is more or less a synonym of **bath**, though 'bathe' has perhaps a more genteel connotation.

baton

A **baton** is the little stick that a conductor waves around when supposedly directing an orchestra. The word is also used to signify a staff of office, as in a marshal's baton. It may also be a short stick used as a weapon by the police.

In all these, the implement is short, but when used by a drum major, the baton is a long stick with a knob at one end. It is also a narrow, diagonal line used in heraldry.

batten

In carpentry and building, a **batten** is a piece of squared timber used in flooring. In sailing, a batten is a narrow strip nailed to the masts and spars to prevent them from chafing. It can also be a moveable bar in a silk-loom which closes the weft. As a verb, the word means to thrive or to improve in condition. It is often used in an exploitative sense: 'She used to batten on her boyfriend for all kinds of new clothes.'

batter

If you **batter** something or someone, you assault them or strike it. You can also make batter from flour and milk in order to make pancakes or Yorkshire pudding. You may also be a batter, as opposed to a bowler, in a cricket team.

battery

A **battery** is a source of electricity in a torch, lamp, car or other vehicle. A battery can also be a collection of objects. Thus you might have a battery of plates on hand to cope with a lunchtime rush in the café, or a battery of cleaners to tidy up after the Little Poddrington Fête. Legally, a battery can be an unlawful assault on someone.

bawd, baud

Once upon a time, these two words used to be synonyms, but they are very different now. A **bawd** is a brothel manager, or someone who lives off immoral earnings. A **baud**, on the other hand, is the rate at which bits per second are transmitted within a computing context.

bawl *see* ball

bay, bey

A **bay** is the name given to a particular tree or shrub, *Laurus nobilis*, which was used for flavouring in ancient times: 'I have seen the wicked in great power, spreading himself like a green bay tree' (Psalms 37:35). From the leaves of this tree, wreaths could be made to celebrate some achievement, though Andrew Marvell had scorn for the practice: 'How vainly men themselves amaze, To win the palm, the oak, or bays.' More commonly, a bay is a stretch of the ocean that is partially enclosed by spurs of land: the Bay of Cardigan, the Bay of Biscay. The word can then be applied to other recessed objects; there may be a bay under the gable of a house, or there may be a bay of land among some hills. A dog may bay when it howls or barks for a long time. An animal may also stand at bay when it is being chased. The word also means a reddish-brown colour. Hence **bay** is an homonym on its own. A **bey**, however, is a Turkish official.

be, bee

We all know that to be is, in the splendidly pompous words of *Collins Dictionary*, 'to have presence in the realm of perceived reality'. In other words, **be** is the infinitive form of a very irregular verb meaning 'to live, to exist'. **Be**, however, is the chemical symbol for beryllium. A **bee**, on the other hand, is an insect that makes honey, an insect delightfully defined in an Internet source as a 'pollinating buzzer'.

beach, beech

A **beach** is the area of sand and shingle at the coast that is visible when the tide is out. However, in the Merchant Navy, to be 'on the beach' is to be unemployed. A **beech** is a European forest tree.

beadle

Once upon a time, a **beadle** was a man who made proclamations in a court of law, or even wandered round the town making civic proclamations (a town crier). Today he can be a church official attending upon the minister, an attendant in a synagogue, or a university official. In all cases, the function is alike – a beadle is a minor official – but it seemed, given the disparity of contexts available, sensible to count the word as a homonym.

beak

As we all know, a **beak** is that hard, projecting jawlike appendage of a bird, but the fact that a bird's beak juts out from its head has led to the word being taken over into other contexts. Thus an architect might refer to a beak when he or she is mentioning the upper surface of a cornice. A chemist might call the part of a still or retort through which vapour passes to the condenser a beak. A person's nose might also be referred to as a beak, particularly if the person concerned has a large, projecting nose. The word is also used to denominate the chief official of an establishment. Hence, as a pupil, you might have to go and see the beak, i.e. the headmaster. Because you were caught speeding down High Street, you might have to appear before the beak, i.e. the magistrate.

beam

A **beam** is a large piece of squared timber often used for supporting the ceiling of a room, and therefore often producing imprecations from tall people who crack their heads on it. With similar meanings, a beam is also the wooden cylinder in a loom or the central shaft of a plough. The word is also used to indicate the main stem of a deer's antler, and the widest breadth of a ship. Totally differently, however, a beam can also be a ray of light, or a broad smile. Exactly which of these meanings lies behind the 1960s expression 'Beam me up, Scotty,' is perhaps arguable, but the television series *Star Trek* from which it originated should not be examined for linguistic exactitude.

bean, been

A **bean** is a plant, a legume, normally used as a food as in broad beans, kidney beans, and so on. **Been**, of course, is simply the past tense of 'be'.

bear *see* bare

beard

In its most common usage, a **beard** is the name given to the growth of hair on a man's chin and jaw-line. The word has since been applied to similar growths on the faces of other animals like the goat, and even in some cases to fishes. The tuft of long hair on some plants like barley and wheat is also called the beard, as are the gills of an oyster. The word is also applied to the barb of an arrow or fish hook, and is a technical term in printing to indicate the part of a piece of type that connects the face with the shoulder. However, **beard** can also be used as a verb to indicate that you are going to approach someone over some matter that is in dispute: 'I must beard the managing director about this parking problem.'

bearing

You can admire someone's **bearing** because they walk with a sense of purpose and behave with dignity. You can try to get your bearings when you are lost and want to discover where you are. A bearing is also anything that carries weight or acts as a support. It is also a device or emblem upon a heraldic shield.

beat, beet

The first of these words, **beat**, has a variety of meanings. If you beat someone with a cudgel, then you are hitting them with a view to causing pain and physical damage. If you beat someone in a race, then you complete the race before they do. If you tap your foot in time with some music, then you are making out the beat of the music. In a similar way, a doctor might check the beat of your heart. If you are exhausted to the point of collapse, you might say 'I'm completely beat now.' In Devon apparently, beat also means the rough sod of moorland that is sliced off and burned before ploughing begins. The other word, **beet**, is much simpler, it simply being an edible red root vegetable.

beating

As you would expect, **beating** is simply the action of thrashing someone or something, or, more pacifically, defeating them in a race. However, nautically the word also means sailing against the wind.

beau, bow

A **beau** can signify a man who is excessively concerned with dress and appearance, or, more neutrally, simply refer to the male companion of a lady. The word **bow** has two different pronunciations, but the one that rhymes with 'beau' refers to the medieval weapon with which you shot arrows at the enemy, or to a curve or bend or the double-slipped reef knot.

beaver

A **beaver** is an amphibious rodent remarkable for its skill in constructing huts for its habitation and dams for its supply of water. Consequently the noun has been transformed into a verb, and if you beaver away, you are being extremely industrious. However, a beaver is also the lower portion of the face-guard of a helmet. As Sir Richard Vernon says in *I Henry IV*, 'I saw young Harry with his beaver on.'

beck

A **beck** is another name for a brook or stream, but it can also be a mute signal like a wave, a nod, or what have you. Hence if you are at someone's beck and call (virtually the only usage of the word these days), you will respond to their gestures or their speech.

bed

Most of us sleep in a **bed** at night, but we are also capable of setting out a bed of flowers. The word can also be used to indicate the bottom of a river or sea, and is generally employed to denote almost any level surface upon which something rests, e.g. the bed of a printing press. In a somewhat slangy sense, if you bed someone you are indicating that you had sexual intercourse with them.

bee *see* B

beech *see* beach

beef

This is the food derived from the flesh of an ox, bull or cow. However, if you **beef** about something, you are complaining about it.

been *see* bean

beer, bier

The alcoholic drink **beer** is made from fermented malt flavoured with hops. A **bier** is the framework upon which a corpse can be carried.

beet *see* beat

beetle

Most of us know about insects distinguished by hard backs and biting jaws. Such creatures are known as a **beetle**, and they are unlikely to figure in most people's list of animals that they adore. Less well known but less disliked, a beetle is also a heavy hand tool used for ramming, pounding or beating. There is also a card game called beetle, and people go to beetle drives to play.

It is also possible for you and I to beetle about, in other words, to scurry and wander around in a not very organised fashion, rather like a beetle seems to be doing when it is discovered in the pantry. As a verb, the word can also mean to overhang, to threaten, to jut over. Shakespeare in *Hamlet* uses it thus: 'Or to the dreadful summit of the cliff / That beetles o'er his base into the sea.' It is in this sense that the word is often applied to eyebrows.

bel, Bel, bell, belle

There are some problems with **bel**. *Collins English Dictionary* cites it as a noun meaning a unit for comparing two power levels, equal to the logarithm to the base ten of the ratio of the two powers, but neither the full *OED* nor the *Shorter* gives this definition, though the *Oxford Dictionary of English* does. An Internet source tells us that a bel is an Indian thorn tree, but this is not listed by any of the Oxford editions cited in the Bibliography at the end of the book, nor the Collins. Most sources, however, agree that **Bel** was a god of the earth in Babylonian and Assyrian mythology. All agree that a **bell** is a hollow, usually metallic, cup-shaped instrument that emits a musical ringing sound when struck, often by a clanger hanging inside it, though one Internet source contents itself with simply saying 'ding ding'. The word 'bell' can also refer to the strobile of the hop plant, the cry of a stag or butt at rutting time, the end of a trumpet or similar brass instrument, or to a bubble. A **belle** is a beautiful woman, and the phrase 'the belle of the ball' is a common cliché, though the word can be used in other contexts too: 'belle époque', 'belle laide', 'belles-lettres', and so on.

belt

This can be a strap that encircles the waist, thereby helping to hold up a skirt or a pair of trousers, or be transformed into a verb meaning to thrash with a belt. In slang, you can belt along the road, meaning to travel at extreme speed. More technically, you can talk about a belt of earth, meaning that the area is much longer than it is wide. Furthermore, a belt is a series of thick iron plates running along the water-line in armoured vessels. The strap that encircles the waist, being the most common usage of the word, has given rise to a number of clichés: 'to hit below the belt,' 'to tighten one's belt,' 'to live in the Stockbroker Belt', and so on.

ben

In Scottish dialect, a **ben** can be an inner room in a house, a mountain peak as in Ben Nevis, or the winged seed of the horseradish tree.

bench

A **bench** is normally a fairly long low-placed seat of wood or stone. They are often found in parks and other open places so that local residents can rest when taking a walk or doing their shopping. The word is also used to refer to the seat upon which a judge sits in court. However, the bench is also a collective noun used to denote judges and magistrates collectively. One can also have a bench mark, a surveyor's mark cut in something like a rock or the wall of a building to act as a reference point when determining the elevation of an area.

bend

In the more normal usage of this word, a **bend** is a curve or inclination away from the straight. Thus you can go round a bend in the road, or you can bend your hosepipe round the tree. (As you have just seen, the noun 'bend' slips easily into being a verb.) However, in nautical parlance, a bend is a knot used to unite one rope to another. In heraldry, a bend is an ordinary formed between the two parallel lines drawn across the shield from the dexter chief to the sinister base. As you can see, heraldry has its own impenetrable jargon.

bent

Obviously, if you bend something, the object concerned will then be **bent**. However, the word also refers to a type of grass or to a place covered with grass. It is also a slang word to describe someone who is dishonest.

beret, berry, bury

A **beret** is a small flat cap traditionally worn by Basque peasants. In sound it is very similar to a **berry**, which is a small fruit. The word **bury** is a verb meaning to inter, to cover with soil and/or leaves. These three words are not identical in sound, but they are certainly close enough to give rise to possible confusion.

berth, birth

If a ship is at **berth**, then it is lying at anchorage. Equally one's living quarters on a boat are referred to as one's berth. A **birth** relates to the coming into being of an animal, person or organisation: 'I was present at the birth of my son'; 'The birth of the Leicester Operatic Society was a traumatic affair.'

better, bettor

If something is **better** than something else, it is more suited to its role, it performs more effectively. Thus you may be better than your friend at spelling, or your oven is better at producing a good stew than your microwave. The word also occurs in countless proverbs: ' 'Tis better to have loved and lost than never to have loved at all'; 'It is better to give than to receive.' A **bettor** is someone who bets.

bey see bay

bias

All the meanings of this word have similarities, but there seems to be a sufficient difference in context for the word to count as a homonym. Thus in a game of bowls, the bowls themselves have a **bias** so that they curve in their path instead of going straight on. Equally, one of your friends has a bias so that she tends to regard anything that she reads in *The Times* as gospel truth. More objectively, a bias can be a diagonal line cut across the weave of a fabric.

bier *see* **beer**

bight, bite, byte

These three really are complete homophones, with not a shade of difference in their pronunciations. The first word, **bight**, is a homonym of its own. A bight is the middle of a stretched-out rope, or the curve in the middle of such a rope. Geographically, a bight is an indentation in a coastline, or the space between two headlands. A **bite** is the snapping action of teeth into food or some other material. Thus you want to beware of the bite of a dog, but more metaphorically, the bark of your boss is worse than his bite. A **byte** is a group of eight bits that, together, can create a computerised letter or symbol. Thus a combination like 01100011 will be a byte and will represent a letter, a number or a punctuation mark.

bike

The word **bike** is an abbreviation of the word 'bicycle', but so widespread that it has attained full word status like PC or bus. As you doubtless know, a bike is a two-wheeled vehicle propelled by the legs of the rider. They can frequently be seen in bus lanes and going through traffic lights on red. In northern parts of England, however, a bike can be a nest of wasps, hornets or wild bees.

bilbo

This is a sword celebrated for the temper of its blade, or a long iron bar with sliding shackles to confine the ankles of its wearer.

bilge

Technically the **bilge** is the bottom of a ship's hull, but as a verb it is used to indicate that the ship's bottom has been staved in or sprung a leak. It is also a slang word meaning 'nonsense'.

bill

A **bill** is what you receive when you have bought something or when someone has performed some service for you. It lists the amount of money that you now owe for the goods purchased or the service performed. Normally the amount cited is too large. However, a bill is also the horny beak of some birds, the point of the fluke of an anchor, or the draft of a proposed Act of Parliament.

billed, build

If you are **billed** for something, you receive a bill for goods provided or services performed (see above). Some birds may also be described as 'billed'. If, however, you **build** something, then you construct it. Hence you can build a toy train set, a shed, a house or even a friendship.

billion

This is an extremely dubious homonym, but I include it because in Britain a billion amounts to a million million, whereas in the USA it only amounts to a thousand million (though the latter is becoming standard usage).

birch

This is the name of a northern hemisphere forest tree, or a bunch of twigs from that tree used for flogging some supposedly errant member of society.

birth *see* berth

biscuit

A **biscuit** is a kind of crisp, hard bread produced in small, handful sizes to be eaten on picnics or with your good night drink or any other time you fancy one. Yet this is the name also applied to pottery that has been fired once but not yet glazed. There is also the colloquial expression 'This takes the biscuit,' which indicates disapproval at someone's effrontery or amazement that something so unexpected should have happened. According to *Brewer's*, 'Biscuits and cakes containing special spices were formally regarded as representing certain desirable attributes and were given as rewards in a variety of competitions.'

bishop

This is a senior member of the Church of England, usually in charge of a diocese and empowered to confer holy orders. The word, however, can also be used as a verb, in which case it means the practice of filing and tampering with the teeth of a horse so as to disguise its real age.

bisque

In the game of tennis, **bisque** is the odds given to a player in the form of a point to be scored once during the set at any time he or she may select. The word is also the name sometimes given to unglazed white porcelain.

bit, bitt

Bit can be a variety of things. It can be the past tense of the verb 'to bite': 'The dog bit my leg.' As a noun it can be the cutting edge of a tool: 'Careful with this; it has a sharp bit.' It can also be the part of a key that engages with the levers of a lock, the mouthpiece of a horse's bridle or a small portion of something ('Have a bit of chocolate'). In the USA, a bit is $12\frac{1}{2}$ cents, i.e. half a quarter. In computer jargon, a bit is an electrical pulse represented by a o or a 1. A **bitt** is one of the posts, fastened in pairs on the deck of a ship, for fastening cables, ropes, etc.

bite, byte

A **bite** is the action of sinking your teeth into something, normally in the process of eating. A **byte** is the collection of eight bits that in IT represent a letter, number or other character.

bitter

Most of the time, the word **bitter** is an adjective used to indicate that something is unpleasantly acidic to taste. It can then be transferred to things other than taste, so that a person can be described as being bitter about Britain's current policy towards gypsies (or whatever). In nautical parlance, the word is used to indicate a turn of the cable round a bitt. In a British pub, the word is also transferred into a noun – 'A pint of bitter, please' – to describe a type of beer.

bittern

This is a heron-type bird or the lye which remains after the crystallisation of common salt from sea-water.

blad

This can be a firm, flat blow or a fragment of something.

blade

This can be the leaf of a herb or plant, most commonly used in connection with grass. Alternatively it can be the flattened part of any cutting instrument like a spade, bat, oar or dagger.

blank

Most of the time, the word **blank** means empty. Hence you can have blank paper, that is, white paper with nothing written upon it. You can have a blank mind, one with no thoughts passing through it. You can even have a blank domino, one with no spots upon it. A blank cartridge is one with no bullet within it, and a blank cheque is one with no sum of money specified. Hence, despite the differing contexts, 'blank' seems conceptually uniform. Yet I include it as a homonym because of 'blank verse'. Most of Shakespeare and Milton consists of blank verse, and their writing can hardly be termed empty. All that the term 'blank verse' indicates is that the poetry is un-rhymed, but that in no way prevents it from being full of meaning.

blaze

This word normally refers to the bright light produced by a powerful torch or a roaring fire. Hence the word is often transferred to anything that is striking and strident: 'The Oakham Dance Troupe produced a blaze of colour and movement in their display.' However, the word is also used to refer to the white spot that one can see on the faces of some horses or oxen. As a verb, the word is also used to refer to the practice of marking trees by stripping off a section of their bark.

blew, blue

The first word is the past tense of the verb 'to blow', and the second is the name of a colour, a colour associated literally with sunny skies and more metaphorically with pornographic films, a depressed state or women with literary tastes, i.e. blue-stockings.

blind

If one is **blind**, one is unfortunately deprived of one's eyesight. Equally you can pull down a blind over a window so as to prevent anyone outside from seeing into the room. The word can also be used somewhat metaphorically to describe someone who is ignorant of the situation in which he finds himself: 'Since everyone else in the meeting had read the proposed regulations, I found myself operating blind.'

blink

The most common usage of this word is to refer to a momentary closing and opening of the eye. This is normally an involuntary action, and can be irritating when one is watching some high-speed event, since a blink can cause one to miss some crucial moment. The word can also refer to a very brief glimpse of some light-bearing object: 'I just caught a blink of light over there.' **Blink** is also a slang word indicating that something is no longer operating properly: 'My television's on the blink.'

bloc, block

The word **bloc** is normally used to indicate a group of countries or organisations that are linked together by some common interests. Hence one might talk about the bloc of EU countries, or complain that reform of Sheffield City Council is hampered by a bloc of vested interests. As a noun, **block** normally refers to a lump of wood. Indeed, one used to be beheaded on the block. Yet the word can also refer to a group of buildings – 'I'll just walk round the block' – or to a defensive stroke in cricket. As a verb, to block something means to prevent its progress.

bloody

Literally, of course, this word refers to something or someone covered in blood: 'The Battle of Waterloo saw a bloody end to the French threat.' However, in Britain and elsewhere, the word **bloody** has become an all-purpose swearword indicating disapproval: 'If I had my way, I'd wring his bloody neck,' though the neck in question is not in any way besmeared with blood. As an adjective it has been attached to a wide variety of undesirable objects: the Bloody Assizes, Bloody Mary, the Bloody Tower and so on.

Although in the twenty-first century, 'bloody' is a swearword that is unlikely to shock even the most maiden of aunts, it was originally very shocking because it was wrongly assumed to have some reference to the blood of Christ.

bloom

Flowers **bloom** in that they display their petals and give an impression of freshness and beauty. In a similar way, a young lady can be said to bloom as she attends her first university dance or whatever. Entirely differently, a **bloom** is the name given to a mass of iron after it has been initially hammered.

bloomers

A bloomer is an error, a mistake, and so **bloomers** are a series of such errors. The word, though, is also used to refer to women's somewhat baggy knickers, such underwear first being advocated by Mrs Amelia Bloomer (1818–94) in the USA.

blot

In literal terms, a **blot** is something created when a drop of ink falls on to your paper. There can be few today who use fountain pens and ink, and so the original blots no longer occur. However, the word has been extended to refer to any blemish or disfigurement in almost any context. Thus the new Town Hall can be termed a blot on the landscape, so-called celebrity television shows are seen by some as a blot in the media, and the existence of Aids could be seen as a blot on the moral fabric of the world. Much less portentously, a **blot** is an exposed piece in the game of backgammon.

blow

A **blow** can be a violent striking of something or someone with a fist or some other implement. Metaphorically, a blow can also be some mishap or circumstance that impairs or prevents what you were planning to do: 'We were planning to go for a walk, so it was a real blow when it started to pour with rain.' A blow can also be the emission of air from the mouth or a gust of air from the wind. In this sense, you can also blow down a trumpet to produce a sound or blow away the dust on your book. More figuratively you can also blow a raspberry at someone of whom you disapprove, or blow away the cobwebs in order to clear your mind.

blue *see* blew

bluff

If you are a **bluff** person, you tend to be direct and blunt, though the word implies that you are good-naturedly so. As a noun, the word refers to either a cliff or headland with a broad precipitous face, or to the action of hoodwinking someone by pretending that x is the case when you know perfectly well that it is y.

boar, Boer, boor, bore, bor

Correctly enunciated, some of these are not true homophones, but once again, in casual speech, they are all going to sound identical. A **boar** is a male pig, a **Boer** is a South African of Dutch descent, a **boor** is a tasteless buffoon, and a **bore** is someone who is tedious. A **bor** is an East Anglian form of address to a boy or young man. According to *Brewer's*, this final instance is derived from the Old English word *gebur*, which meant neighbour.

board, bored

A **board** is a plank of wood, though as a verb it indicates the activity of getting on to a ship or plane, as you would expect from its Old Norse origin where *borth* meant the ship's side. The word has been adopted for a number of more figurative expressions. Hence if you go back to the drawing board, you attempt to redesign something. If something is 'across the board', then it applies to everything. If something is 'above board', then it is patently honest. Someone who is **bored** is just not interested in what is going on around him.

boarder, border

A **boarder** is someone who is getting on a ship or plane, or a lodger in some house who pays for a bedroom and possibly some meals. A **border** is a boundary or perimeter that separates one thing from another thing. Thus you can have a border between two different countries, or a border between a forest and the surrounding countryside. You can also have a behavioural border: 'John thought that he was being funny, but he stepped over the border into rudeness.'

bob

You can have a **bob** of hair (a knot or bunch), a horse's tail cut short, a weight on the tail of a kite, a bunch of coloured ribbons, a bunch of lob worms used to catch eels, the refrain of a song, a type of dance, an apparatus for polishing burnished metal surfaces, a slang term for a shilling, a term for certain changes in the pealing of bells, or the name for the action of rapping or bouncing one object against another. For many of these noun uses, you can also use the word as a verb. One idiosyncratic verbal use is to 'bob for apples', an English game where you try to catch with your mouth alone apples that are hanging up or floating in water. Since for most of us, **Bob** is simply a shortened form of Robert, its homonymic versatility will be a surprise.

bodkin

For many of us, our only acquaintanceship with this word will be from Act 3 of Shakespeare's *Hamlet*: 'When he himself might his quietus make With a bare bodkin'. Clearly here the word refers to a dagger, but is also used to refer to a long pin used by women to fasten up their hair, or, in printing, to refer to an awl-like tool used to pick out letters from set-up type.

Boer *see* **boar**

bogus

Most of us think of this word as describing something that is false, spurious or sham – 'It is totally bogus to argue that God created the world in six days' – but the word also refers to a drink made of rum and molasses.

boil

You can **boil** something like eggs or carrots by immersing them in water that is above the temperature of 100°C, but the word is also a noun when it indicates a hard tumour on the skin. The idea of boiling things in steaming water has also led to expressions like 'boiling with rage'.

bold, bowled

A person who is brave, daring or fearless can be described as **bold** (here printed in 'bold' type) as, of course, can the actions of such a person. Landscape can also be described as bold if it rises steeply from the sea or surrounding countryside. If you are **bowled** in the game of cricket, your innings has been ended by the bowler hitting your wickets. Equally you can use this past participle in reference to a game of bowls.

bolder, boulder

If you are **bolder** than someone else, you are braver or more self-assured. A **boulder** though is a lump of rock or stone, normally too large to be carried easily.

bole, boll, bowl

The little word **bole** that few of us ever use none the less has four different meanings. First of all, it can be the trunk of a tree, or anything with a similar shape, like a pillar. Secondly, it refers to sundry types of clay. Thirdly, it can be a recess in a wall, a small, square recess in which a small ornament can be placed or in which there can be a small window. Finally it can be a reference to a place where, in ancient times, lead ores were smelted. The equally small word **boll** is either a rounded seed-vessel or pod as of flax or cotton, or a measure of capacity for grain. A **bowl** is a rounded dish from which many of us eat our morning cereal, though it is also a round ball used in the game of bowls. As a verb, the word is not confined to bowls, but is also used in cricket.

bolster

This is a long, stuffed pillow used to support one's head in bed, though, as a noun, it also has a number of technical uses. Thus it can be a surgical pad, a block of wood fixed on a siege-gun carriage, on which the breech rests during transport, the transverse bar over the axle of a wagon, the spindle-bearing in the rail of a spinning-frame, and a number of others which are equally specialist and hence unlikely to be used by members of the general public. As a verb, however, **bolster** means to support or encourage.

bolt

There are two common uses of this word, one as a noun, the other as a verb. The noun normally refers to a means of locking a door by moving a cylindrical metal bar affixed to the door through a staple attached to the doorpost. In that way, you **bolt** the door by sliding the **bolt.** However, as a verb, bolt can also mean to run away rapidly: 'The horse bolted' or 'I need to bolt if I'm to get to school in time.' The word can, though, be used in other contexts. Sometimes a short arrow with a thickened head can be called a bolt. Indeed, this was its original meaning. You can bolt your food by swallowing it hastily and without chewing it. You can buy a bolt of woollen fabric in a roll of predetermined length. You can even bolt some material by passing it through a sieve.

book

A **book** is a collection of sheets of paper bound together and printed upon so as to be easily read. It is also a verb meaning to reserve attendance at some event. Thus one might book tickets for a play at the theatre, for a train or plane journey, or for attendance at some council meeting.

boom

If something booms, it emits a loud, deep and resonant sound: 'I heard the boom of the cannon.' On a ship, a **boom** is a long spar extended so as to increase the foot of the sail. The word can also be applied to a marked increase in commercial activity: 'Over Christmas there was a boom in the sales of chestnuts.'

boon

A **boon** is a request granted or a gift made. Hence one might pray to God for the boon of good health, or thank your secretary for the boon of coping with the e-mails. However, one can also have a boon companion, where 'boon' means 'favourite' or 'congenial'. In both cases the word seems to have derived from the Latin *bonus*, good.

boor *see* boar

boos, booze

The first of these words is simply the plural of 'boo', a lowing sound often emitted as a indication of displeasure: 'The Prime Minister spoke so badly that there were several boos from the audience.' **Booze** is a colloquial word referring to alcoholic drink: 'I went out on the booze last night', or, 'Have we got any booze in?'

boot

Confronted with the word **boot**, most of us would think of a heavy, strong piece of footwear more suited for rough conditions than a shoe. However, the word also refers to a form of torture that was practised in the past in Scotland, the area of a car where luggage may be stored, or even occasionally a verb meaning 'to profit' or 'to benefit': 'What does it boot you if the Liberal Democrats do well at the next election?'

bootless

Obviously if one is **bootless**, one does not possess any boots, but the word is also used to indicate that something is of no purpose or of no use: 'It is bootless to expect compassion from big business.'

border see boarder

bore see boar

born, borne, bourne

If you are **born**, you are brought into life. Although the verb is normally applied to the animal kingdom, it is also often extended to new ventures in a wide variety of fields: 'The Worksop Plainsong Society was born on Saturday 12 April 1967.' If something is **borne**, it is endured, sustained or carried: 'Mary's cancer was borne with great courage.' **Bourne** is the equivalent of the Scottish word 'burn', and means a small stream or brook. Occasionally the word is used as a synonym for 'boundary': 'The undiscovered country from whose bourne no traveller returns.'

borough, burgh, burrow

I am not happy at placing these as homophones – the final vowel sound is different in the two words – but once again, this is not the case for many speakers. Anyway, a **borough** is a town possessing a municipal corporation and special privileges conferred by royal charter. The Scottish word **burgh** is pronounced in exactly the same way. A **burrow** is a hole or tunnel dug by a small animal, especially a rabbit, as a dwelling. Hence the verb 'to burrow'.

boss

When at work, one is subject to the commands of one's **boss**, that is, the person in charge of operations. He or she may even turn the noun into a verb, and boss you around, i.e. issue a series of commands. Yet, though this is the most common usage of the word, there are at least five other meanings. A boss is a protuberance on the body of an animal or plant, a mass of rock protruding through strata of another kind, a plasterer's tray, an ornamental projection in a vault, or the projecting part of a stern-post of a screw steamer. Once upon a time 'boss' also meant 'to miss a target', and although this usage no longer survives, we still have the expression 'boss-eyed', meaning to have a squint.

bottle

A **bottle** is a vessel, normally of glass, with a narrow neck and used for holding liquid. It can also be used as a verb: 'I must bottle the wine.' It is also a slang word meaning 'courage' or 'bravery': 'Nathan didn't have the bottle to confront Stephen.'

bottom

Normally the word **bottom** refers to the lowest part of anything: 'My key-ring is now lying at the bottom of the sea'; 'He drank his way down to the bottom of the bottle.' More figuratively, one can try to get to the bottom of something by investigating it thoroughly. However, the buttocks of a human or animal are normally referred to as the bottom even though the feet of said creature are actually its lowest point.

bough, bow

From a normal tree, a number of branches grow outwards from the trunk, and each of these could be called a **bough**. A **bow**, however, is either the front part of a ship, a weapon with which one can shoot arrows, a respectful lowering of the head, an implement for scraping the strings of a violin or similar instrument or an arch shape as in a rainbow.

boulder *see* bolder

bourn *see* born

bow *see* beau, bough

bower

The word **bower** can still be used as a somewhat effete term for one's house, though it also means someone who bows, and is the name of two anchors, the best-bower and the small-bower, that reside at the bow of a boat. Apparently in the card game Euchre, the bower is the name given to the two highest cards.

bowled *see* bold

bowler

This can refer to a cricket player or to a hard felt hat, the latter being particularly associated with city businessmen, and named after William Bowler, the English hatter who designed it in 1850.

box

Although we all think of a **box** as a case or receptacle, often made of cardboard and usually possessing a lid, the word also signifies a genus of small evergreen trees or shrubs. As a verb, one can box the compass, lodge a document in a law court, attempt to hit another man within the confines of a boxing ring, or make a cavity in the trunk of a tree so as to collect some sap.

boy, buoy

Normally the word **boy** is used to refer to a male child, though it is also used, somewhat patronisingly, to refer to a male servant. The word can also be used in semi-jocular fashion among equals in conversation: 'My dear boy, have you heard?' A **buoy** is a floating object in the water positioned so as to identify the location of things under the water like rocks. As a verb, if you buoy something or someone up, you keep them afloat, either literally or metaphorically.

bra, braw

The word **bra** is an abbreviation for the word 'brassiere', an article of clothing used to support a woman's breasts. However, like 'bus', this is an abbreviation that has now achieved its own autonomy. **Braw** is a Scottish word that can mean well-groomed or brave.

brace

A **brace** is a carpenter's tool, having a crank handle and a pad to hold a bit for boring. It is also one half of a pair of braces used to hold up trousers when being worn. It is also one of the straps by which the body of a carriage is held up from the springs. It is a thong that helps to regulate the tension of a drum. A sign like this } is also called a brace, and is used to link together two or more lines of writing or music. A clasp or buckle can also be called a brace. Its most common usage as a noun is to signify a pair as in a brace of pheasants. As a verb, the word is used to signify the action of preparing oneself for some imminent ordeal: 'I must brace myself for this visit to the dentist.'

braid, brayed

The word **braid** is normally used as a verb, in which case it means to interweave something like thread, ribbons or hair. As a noun, the word can be used to signify a plait of human hair or a woven fabric of silken, woollen or cotton thread in the form of a band. **Brayed** is the past tense of the verb 'to bray' indicating the sound that a donkey makes. It can, of course, be insultingly applied to human beings.

braise, brays

If you **braise** something, you stew it in a tightly closed pan. As is clear from the entry immediately above, a donkey **brays**, thereby emitting a noise not renowned for its tonal purity and beauty.

brake, break

A **brake** is a tool attached to most vehicles which, when used, enables the vehicle concerned to slow down and stop. In the countryside, a brake can be a clump of bushes or briars. Apparently the word also refers to a baker's kneading machine and to a heavy harrow for crushing clods and to an instrument for peeling the bark from willows. The verb **break** is normally used to indicate that something is severed into separate parts, is destroyed or damaged: 'I must break his will'; 'Do not break your toy by throwing it at the wall.' It can, however, also be a noun indicating an intermission: 'I must have a break from my revision'; 'We always have a coffee break at eleven.' Allied to this is its sense of a gap or opening: 'There was a break in the clouds.'

brave

Although normally used as an adjective meaning courageous, fearless or intrepid, **brave** is also a noun referring to American Indian warriors.

braw *see* bra

bray

A **bray** is the somewhat unmelodious noise made by some animals, most commonly the donkey. It transfers automatically into also being a verb, and is sometimes applied unflatteringly to human beings: 'He brays like an ass.' As a verb, the word can also mean to bruise or to beat small.

brazen

If something is **brazen** it is coated with brass, but the verb is also used to refer to people who are impudent or totally lacking in the restraint and self-deprecation that is supposed to be the hallmark of the English.

breach, breech

The word **breach** has a range of associated meanings. It can be an unintended opening in something: 'There was a breach in the sea wall.' It can be lapse of courtesy: 'Tom's treatment of Matilda was a breach of good manners.' You can also have a 'breach of promise' and a 'breach of the peace'. The word **breech** normally refers to the lower part or bottom of something. Thus a person's breech is his or her bottom, the lower part of a pulley block is called the breech, and one can refer to the breech of a bridge.

bread, bred

Bread is a food made of flour and yeast, and customarily made into a loaf, though the word is often used to signify food in general. The word **bred** is the past tense of the verb 'breed'.

break *see* brake

bream

We normally think of the **bream** as a freshwater fish, but it also indicates the clearing of a ship's bottom of shells and seaweed by singeing it with burning reeds or faggots.

breech *see* breach

breeze

A **breeze** is a gentle, light wind that can cool you in summer or chill you in winter. Because of its gentleness, the word has passed into slang to indicate that something is easy: 'It was a breeze taking that exam in the use of counterpoint in sixteenth-century Flemish composers.' However, the word also refers to small cinders and cinder-dust used in burning bricks.

brewed, brood

The first word is the past tense of the verb 'to brew', the action of converting grain into beer, though the word is also used in connection with a pot of tea – 'Has the tea brewed yet?' – indicating that the tea needs to be immersed in boiling water for a little while before it is fit to be poured into a cup. The word **brood** can refer to a family (a brood of hens, for example), or to the action of somewhat dark reflection: 'I must learn not to brood about the way George Bush so tarnished the tenets of Christianity.'

brews, bruise

If one **brews** hops, one is engaged in the activity of making an alcoholic drink. If one has a **bruise**, one has discoloured skin caused by some blow to one's body. Equally bruise can be a verb, and most boxers expect to bruise each other in the ring.

brick

A **brick** is a hard clay object used for building houses and other structures. The word is also sometimes used in describing a person: 'Harold is a brick.' This means that he is good-hearted and reliable.

bridal, bridle

If something is **bridal**, it pertains to the bride in a wedding ceremony. A **bridle** though is headgear designed for a horse, though apparently it can also be the plate inside a gunlock, which holds the sear and tumbler in position. It is also possible to bridle at someone, that is, to show anger or indignation.

brief

If something like a letter, a speech or novel is **brief**, then it is short. However, a brief can also be the instructions delivered to a barrister regarding his or her objective in a legal case.

brim

A **brim** can be the edge of some object, like the brim of a hat, or filling a glass to the brim. It can also refer to the state of pigs when they are feeling amorous.

broach, brooch

If you **broach** something, you are suggesting that it is a valid topic for possible further discussion. If you wear a **brooch** on your dress, you hope that it will attract attention because of its beauty, and therefore, of course, attract attention to you who are wearing the brooch.

brook

A **brook** is a small stream, but you are also able to brook something in the sense of being able to tolerate it. Somewhat strangely the word in this context is normally preceded by a negative: 'I cannot brook the way John Prescott mangles the English language.'

broom

This is a plant often found on heathland. It has yellow flowers, and a long, thin stem. It is also an implement for sweeping. Normally provided with a long handle, it is similar to a brush, but the sweeping head itself is composed of twigs or stems, originally, of course, from the broom plant.

brows, browse

The first word is merely the plural of 'brow', a word meaning forehead, except that when used in the plural, the word tends to refer specifically to the area of the forehead just above the eyebrows. The word **browse** is a verb signifying the action of feeding on the leaves and shoots of trees and bushes, actions undertaken by cattle, goats and deer. However, the word is often used to indicate the human activity of dipping into a series of books in order to select one that particularly appeals to oneself. Thus one might be browsing in a library.

bruise *see* brews

buck

This word is normally used for the male of certain animals like deer, goats and rabbits. None the less, the *Shorter Oxford* lists twelve separate meanings in all, a number of which are now obsolete. However, the word is still heard sometimes to refer to a dashing fellow. As a verb, **buck** means to copulate, but it is also used in a colloquial fashion as a request to speed things up – 'Oh, do buck up!' – or as expressing a determination to operate outside the system: 'By refusing to carry my ID card, I shall buck the system.'

bucket

Most of us think of a **bucket** as a vessel in which water is carried, but it can also be a piston in a lift-pump, or the beam or yoke on which anything may be hung.

buckle

As a noun, **buckle** normally refers to the metal attachment at the end of a belt that enables one to fasten the belt by inserting the hinged tongue of the buckle at one end of the belt into an appropriate hole punched at the other end of the belt. However, the word is also a verb with at least three meanings. One can buckle on one's clothing and equipment in preparation for battle, one can grapple with another person, or one can bend an iron bar or some other metallic rod so that it is bent into a curve. It is also possible for one's mind to buckle under the strain of trying to grasp something.

budge

Normally this is a verb meaning to move or shift – 'He tried to budge me away from the fire' – but it is also a noun referring to a fur garment made out of lamb's skin with the wool on the outside.

buff

If you are in the **buff**, then you are naked, but the word can also be an adjective describing a dull light yellow colour, and that definition itself derives from an earlier meaning when 'buff' meant a soft, stout leather prepared from the skin of buffaloes. Apparently in some dialects, buff can be a verb meaning either to stutter or to burst out with sudden force.

buffer

You can see buffers on railway trains. A **buffer** is something which projects from the train at both ends, and is designed to take the full force of any impact should the train hit anything else. However, a buffer is also someone who buffs, that is, polishes metallic objects like cutlery or medals. It is also a slang word for a half-wit or foolish person. In Middle English the word was used for a stammerer.

buffet

Pronounced like the French word that it is, a **buffet** is an assortment of foods to which one helps oneself. Hence one may encounter a buffet at a wedding reception or at the AGM of some organisation. Pronounced with the 't' sounded, a buffet is a blow delivered normally by the hand or fist. Hence you might find that Hector was so anxious to get some smoked salmon at the buffet that he was forced to buffet one or two members out of his way. As you can see, it is useful that the word is not a homophone.

bug

This is a general word applied virtually indiscriminately to any insect or insect larvae, but over the last century or so it has also been used to describe a tiny apparatus hidden in a room with the purpose of picking up any conversation taking place in that room. It can also be used to describe an enthusiasm: 'He's bitten by the Sudoku bug.'

bugle

This is a musical instrument, similar to the trumpet but smaller and without valves. It is also the English name for plants of the genus *Ajuga*, and a tube-shaped glass bead, usually black, used to ornament clothing.

build, billed

If you **build** something, you construct and erect it. Hence you can build a house, a garden shed, a computer, a department of physics, or a good reputation. If you are **billed** for something, you are presented with a request for payment, a bill.

bull

A **bull** is the male of any bovine species like cattle, though the term is also used for the male of most large animals like elephants, whales, etc. It is also a constellation in the sky often known as Taurus. A bull is also someone who is active on the Stock Exchange in his or her attempt to raise prices. When the Pope or a bishop issues an edict, it is also often called a bull. According to the *Shorter Oxford*, it is also a contradictory expression, though my experience of the word used in a derogatory way suggests that to talk a lot of bull is merely to talk nonsense, and that it need not be self-contradictory. The word comes from the Old Norse *boli*.

bullfinch

Most British people will know that the **bullfinch** is an attractive bird with a short, hard, rounded beak. Fewer are likely to know that it is also a quickset hedge with a ditch on one side.

bullion

This word is commonly used to refer to a collection of gold and/or silver or to coins made of those metals. However, the word also refers to a type of hose where the upper part is puffed out, and to a fringe made of twists of gold or silver thread.

bully

Most of us know this word as pertaining to the unpleasant creature who at school or in the office takes pleasure in making life painful. A **bully** is someone who terrorises others. However, in order to start or restart a game of hockey, you need to bully off. In the States, however, the word is informally used to indicate excellence or approval: 'He's a bully fellow.'

bum

This is a synonym for a bottom or buttocks, but is also used to indicate that something is no good – 'It was a bum deal.' For Americans, the word tends to be applied to vagrants.

bun

A **bun** is a cake to be eaten, or a woman's hair gathered in a bun shape at the back of her head.

bunt

A **bunt** is a noun signifying a disease of wheat, the baggy centre of a fishing net or sail, the act of flying an aircraft in part of an outside loop, or a parasitic fungoid. It is also a verb indicating a gentle tap at a baseball ball. An Internet source also lists the homophone **bundt** as meaning a type of cake, but this word is not found in the *OED* or any other sources used in compiling this book, so I can only assume that it is an Internet error.

buoy *see* boy

burger, burgher

A **burger** is a shortened form of the word 'hamburger', a noxious food purchased in fast-food cafés and comprising some meat imprisoned between two fat rolls of a bread-like substance. A **burgher** was a member of the trading or mercantile class of a medieval town.

burn

As a verb, 'to burn' means to destroy by fire or to heat something to a degree that it causes damage or pain. However, the word is also a noun, normally used in Scotland, that is a synonym of 'stream' or 'brook'.

burr, bur

If you describe someone's voice as having a pleasant **burr**, you imply that they roll their 'r'-sounds much as they do in Northumberland. As for the other meanings of 'burr', it seems to be a matter of taste as to whether you spell it with one 'r' or two. The word can mean a siliceous rock suitable for millstones, a washer placed on the small end of a rivet before the end is swaged down, a circle of light round the moon or a star, or a rough ridge or edge left on metal or any other substance after it has been cut or punched.

bury *see* beret

bus, buss

A **bus** is a motor vehicle used for transporting passengers from place to place. Strictly speaking, it is an abbreviation of the word 'omnibus', but through usage, it has to be accepted as an independent word of its own by now. There can be single-decker buses holding about thirty passengers or double-decker buses holding about fifty-four. A **buss**, however, is a synonym for the word 'kiss'. Hence you can buss on a bus, though it is probably not advisable to attempt to do so with all the passengers.

bussed, bust

If you **bussed** Sophia, then you kissed her, but if you have a **bust** of Philip, then you have a head and shoulders sculpture of him. If you go bust, then you have no money left, but if you go on a bust, then you take part in a raid, search or arrest with your fellow policemen.

bustle

If you **bustle** around, then you hurry or scuffle around, often in a slightly disorganised way. If you wear a bustle, then you have a wire framework beneath the skirt of your dress.

but, butt

Since the word **but** can be a preposition, a conjunction or an adverb, it is clearly a versatile word. By and large though, it means 'except that' as in a sentence like 'I would go swimming tonight, but I have too much homework to do.' The word is also used in the Scottish expression **but and ben** which means a two-roomed cottage. Butt is largely speaking an American word for a person's bottom – 'He got kicked up the butt' – though one can also be the butt or victim of someone's humour. It is also a cask for wine, the thicker end of something like a whip, gun or fishing rod, a push or thrust with the head or horns of a person or animal, a short and rudely made cart, or the ridge between two furrows of a ploughed field.

button

A **button** is a small, rounded object attached to one side of a coat, shirt or dress so that it can be inserted into the button hole on the other side of the clothing, thereby affording the wearer some greater protection against the wind and cold. The word is often used in different contexts, but with the same under-lying sense. Thus a button mushroom looks a little like a button, and the knob at the end of a fencing foil looks a little like a button. It is also possible to use the word as a verb, and not just in doing up one's clothes. One can button or buttonhole a person in the sense that one engages his or her attention to the exclusion of anyone else wanting to approach him or her.

buy, by, bye

If you **buy** something, you purchase it. If you are **by** the church, you are close to it. If you say **bye** to someone, you are bidding them farewell, though it is also possible to have a bye in the game of cricket (score a run without actually hitting the ball) or to have a bye in a competition when you don't have to face an opponent.

buyer, byre

A **buyer** is someone who purchases something. A **byre** is a cow barn.

C

C, c, sea, see

C is the third letter of the English alphabet. Just on its own, it has a variety of functions. It can be, like A and B, a grading in an exam, or a list of items, sizes or categories. C also denotes a socio-economic category for marketing purposes, the third file from the left on a chessboard, the first note of the diatonic scale of C major, and the Roman numeral for 100. C is also a computer programming language, one that was developed for implementing the Unix operating system. C can also be an abbreviation for the element carbon, the speed of light in a vacuum ($e=mc^2$), 'caught' in the game of cricket, and so on. C is the traditional code name for the head of MI5 and the lowest category in the medical examination for service in the armed forces. The phrase 'the big C' is also a slang expression for cancer. There are even poems in which every word begins with C. It is also a homophone for **sea**, a noun denoting a large area of salt water, and **see**, a verb meaning to observe, to perceive, to witness. For fuller data about 'sea' and 'see', go to their individual entries.

cab

Originally a **cab** was a horse-drawn vehicle for public hire, a cabriolet, but when horses became replaced by cars, the name merely transferred itself as a taxi cab, a motorised version of the original. The word 'cab' is also often used to designate the driver's compartment in a lorry, bus or train. Apparently a cab is also the name of a cabinet containing a speaker or speakers for a guitar amplifier.

cabbage

Most of us have eaten **cabbage** at some time or another. It is a plain-leaved vegetable, a member of the *Brassica* family, which can be an ingredient of many meals. However, it is also a word used to describe shreds of cloth that are created when a tailor is cutting out clothes. It is also schoolboy slang for a crib, and, as an adjective for the noun 'head', can be used to indicate that someone is stupid. The word is also an adjective for a number of other less derogatory items: cabbage lettuce, cabbage moth, cabbage palm, cabbage roll and cabbage tree. There is even a butterfly called the cabbage white. 'The Cabbage Garden' is a nickname for the Australian state of Victoria.

cabinet

This word is normally used to indicate a small desk-like piece of furniture used for storing documents, letters, jewellery, etc. You can also have a cocktail cabinet in which drinks are stored. In politics, of course, the **Cabinet** is the committee of 15 to 25 ministers of the crown who are appointed by the Prime Minister to advise him or her on policy and legislation. In the USA, the cabinet is a body of advisers to the President comprising the heads of the executive departments of the government.

cable

This is a strong, thick rope of hemp or iron wire used for pulling a heavy object, connecting two or more objects together, or for being the means of transmission for electronic messages. Because of this last usage, the word has also been transferred to signify the message so sent. Hence you can have a cable sent by cable, that is, a message transmitted by telegraph. These days, of course, you can have cable television, a system in which television programmes are transmitted to the set of subscribers by cable rather than by broadcast signal. Originally the word was used to denote the rope or chain to which a ship's anchor was attached.

cache, cash

A **cache** is a hiding place, traditionally a hole in the ground or inside the trunk of a tree, where valuables or documents are hidden so as to escape detection. The word is also applied to the hidden store itself, so you can have a cache of diamonds hidden in the cache that is located under the abbey wall. **Cash**, on the other hand, is money. Colloquially it is generally used to refer to money that a person has available to them in their purse or wallet at the moment, but the word can also be used to refer to the amount in your bank account or to the billions that big business deal with daily. Apparently it is also a term for low-value coins in the East Indies and China. The noun can also be turned into a verb, so that you can cash a cheque, that is, convert the cheque either into an amount in your bank account, or into tangible money in your pocket.

cached, cashed

If something is **cached**, then it is hidden away in a secret place. If something is **cashed**, then it is converted into money.

cachet

This word, pronounced as its French origin would suggest without the 't' being sounded, normally indicates prestige or the condition of being respected. Thus you might say, 'No pianos have quite the same cachet as a Steinway.' However, a cachet can also be a flat capsule enclosing a dose of medicine. The *Oxford Dictionary of English* stipulates that it has to be unpleasant-tasting medicine, but this is not an integral part of the definition.

cachou, cashew

Cachou is a sweetmeat made of cashew nut, and used by smokers to sweeten their breath. As you will have gathered, a **cashew** is a tree that carries a cashew nut. It is a large tropical tree.

cack

As a noun, this word strictly means excrement or dung, but is frequently used informally to signify a load of nonsense: 'They talk such a lot of cack.' As a verb, if you cack yourself, you defecate in your clothes.

cade

This word, which most of us have never heard of, none the less has three different meanings. First of all, it can refer to young animals, often ones that have been rejected by their parents and are brought up by human hand. George Eliot apparently commented that 'It's ill bringing up a cade lamb.' Once upon a time, **cade** also meant a barrel of herrings, but, although this usage is now obsolete, the word is still used to refer to a cask or barrel. There is also a species of juniper which yields oil of cade, a substance used in veterinary surgery.

cadet

This word, with the 't' pronounced, refers to a young trainee in the armed forces or the police. In the French pronunciation, with the 't' not sounded, the word means a younger son or daughter, or, more normally, a junior branch of the family.

cadge

It is likely that most of us know this word as a colloquial synonym for 'borrow': 'Can I cadge some sugar off you, Marg?' Apparently in the early seventeenth century 'cadge' was a dialect word meaning 'carry about'. For those involved in falconry, however, **cadge** becomes a noun referring to a round frame of wood on which hawks are carried for sale. Here 'cadge' is probably an alteration of 'cage'.

cain, cane

A **cain** is a rent paid in kind, or, in Ireland, a penalty for an offence. **Cane** is stems of various reeds and grasses like bamboo and sugar cane which can be formed into rods or staffs for use as walking sticks. Said stick can also be used for beating another person with. Hence the verb '**to cane**', the practice of beating someone with a cane. Having been made illegal as a school or legal punishment, caning is probably today confined to slightly *outré* sexual practices.

cairn

As a noun, the word **cairn** normally refers to a mound of rough stones built as a memorial or landmark, typically on a hill or skyline. It could also be a prehistoric burial mound made of stones. The word is also an adjective to denote a small terrier with short legs, a longish body and a shaggy coat.

calculus

Most of us have heard of **calculus**, though few of us can do it. It is a branch of mathematics that deals with the finding and properties of derivatives and integrals of functions (whatever that might mean). A calculus is also a hard mass formed by minerals within the body, especially in the kidney or gall bladder.

calendar, calender

We are all familiar with the **calendar**, an object normally found hanging from the kitchen wall and which details the days of that particular year. The word can also mean a list. Hence, if you were told to calendar the documents relating to the case of *Dawson* v. *Pomfret*, you would be expected to make a lightly annotated list of those documents. In a sense, of course, both objects are lists. The calendar hanging from the wall is just a list of days, the calendar of Newgate Prison is just a list of prisoners on trial. A **calender**, however, is a machine which, by pressing cloth, paper, etc., makes the cloth or paper object smooth. Once upon a time though, a calender was a member of a mendicant order of dervishes in Persia.

calf

A **calf** is a young cow, bull or ox, though the term is sometimes applied to the young of animals other than bovine ones, animals like deer, elephants and whales. The word also applies to the fleshy hinder part of an animal's lower leg. The word can also be applied to an iceberg detached from a coastal glacier.

calibre, caliber

The first of these words, **calibre**, is British, the second, **caliber**, is American. Other than that, they are identical, and consequently both have exactly the same two meanings. The first refers to the type of bullet that a gun shoots (always a vital matter in television detective stories), while the second relates to the quality of the person or object that you are assessing: 'The calibre of the people getting MBAs these days has slumped alarmingly.'

calix, calyx

These two words are easy to confuse and often are. A **calix** is a cuplike cavity or organ. A **calyx** is the whorl of leaves forming the outer covering of a flower while in bud.

calk, caulk

A **calk** is an American word to describe a piece of iron projecting from the heel of a boot, a device that apparently prevents slipping. 'Calk' is also a verb meaning to copy a design by rubbing its back with colouring matter, and drawing a blunt point along the outlines so as to trace them in colour on a surface placed beneath. If you **caulk** a ship, you stop up its seams so as to prevent it sinking.

call, caul, cawl

Every native English speaker knows what a **call** is, yet the word does have a considerable range of application. You can call on someone at their home, you can call out to someone across the street, you can call someone a thieving bastard, or you can hear the call of the wolf. You personally may have a call, that is, an internal yearning, to become a nurse, a teacher, a priest, or whatever. On the Stock Exchange, a call is an option of claiming stock at a certain time at a fixed price. If you go hunting, it is the call of the hunting horn that will summon you. Hence 'call' is certainly a homonym in itself. But it is also a homophone with **caul** which is also an internal homonym. The word can mean a netted cap worn by women, or the inner membrane enclosing the foetus before birth. **Cawl**, another homophone, is now a dialect word for a basket.

calling

This participle can refer to someone **calling** across the street to you, or for you to have a calling to become a missionary or a postman. See **call**. There also exists a calling crab, so called because of its long claw which looks as if it is beckoning you, and a calling hare which itself has a peculiar call.

callous, callus

This word is applied to hardened skin. Thus, through constant pressure, the soles of one's feet can become **callous**. By extension, the word has been applied to people (or animals) who behave in an unfeeling and inconsiderate fashion. By definition, a professional torturer will be callous. So are most traffic wardens. A **callus** is the bony material thrown out around and between the two ends of a fractured bone in healing.

caltrop

This was the name given to an iron ball with four sharp prongs sticking out of it. This meant that, when thrown, one prong at least would always be pointing upwards. It was used to impede a cavalry charge. Since then sundry plants that entangle the feet have also been called **caltrop**.

cam

This word is normally used to indicate the projecting part of a wheel or other revolving piece of machinery. The **cam** then affects another piece of machinery, normally by pushing it. The word also means a ridge or mound of earth, though in some parts of Britain, 'cam' is a dialect word meaning perverse or awry. The Cam, of course, is also an English river which flows through the university town of Cambridge.

camel

This is a well-known beast of burden used in western Asia and northern Africa. It is a humped beast, one hump distinguishing the Arabian **camel**, two humps the Bactrian. However, a camel is also a machine for adding buoyancy to vessels.

camera, CAMRA

The **camera** is an optical device that takes pictures of whatever the camera is pointed at, York Minster, the Vale of Evesham or your mother-in-law. They, of course, are still pictures which you store in an album and periodically bore your friends with. Films and television programmes are shot by moving cameras, that is, ones that convert the moving scene into digital or electrical signals. However, a judge's private room is also called a camera, and hence, when a judge wants to hear a legal point in the absence of the public (or the accused), he retires and discusses the point *in camera*. The phrase has spread to denote all meetings of public concern from which the public is excluded. The word 'camera' also sounds very similar to **CAMRA**, the acronym for the Campaign for Real Ale.

camp

A **camp** is a temporary place of occupation. On holiday you may stay in a caravan camp or camp out in a tent. Troops on the move will camp out each night, normally in tents. More recently the word has become colloquial English for either implying that someone is a homosexual ('he's very camp'), or for describing rather *outré* behaviour.

can

This word is the present tense of the verb 'to be able'. Hence a sentence like 'I can tie my own shoelaces' indicates that you are able to perform this task. Yet 'can' has a variety of verbal uses. It is used to indicate that something is typically the case, as in sentences like: 'She can be very moody.' It also imparts permission to do something as in 'Of course you can go to sleep if you'd rather.' You even use the word as a request: 'Can you open the door for me, please?' As a noun, the word also refers to a metallic cylindrical container which can contain a variety of products from various kinds of food to paint or beer. It has also been used metaphorically in the expression 'a can of worms', where you refer to a complicated issue that is likely to lead to trouble and/or scandal. In addition, though the word 'cans' as a noun is obviously referring to more than one can, it can also be used as a verb signifying adverse judgement: 'He cans most of the books that he reviews.'

canary

The **canary** is a singing, finch-type bird often kept in cages for the delight of the insensitive household that owns it. The word is also the name of a dance, and a light sweet wine from the Canary Islands.

cancer

We all know that **cancer** is a feared disease caused by the uncontrolled division of abnormal cells in a part of the body, but the word can also be used figuratively as in: 'Racism is a cancer that is sweeping Europe.' With a capital letter, Cancer is a star constellation (the Crab) and, in astrology, the fourth sign of the Zodiac.

cane *see* cain

canker

To have a **canker** is always unpleasant, but its nature varies depending upon what sort of creature you yourself actually are. If, for instance, you were a tree, a canker would be a destructive fungal disease that results in damage to the bark. If you were a dog, cat or rabbit, a canker would be an inflammation of the ear caused by a mite infestation. If you are human, a canker is an ulcerous condition. Of course, just like 'cancer' immediately above, 'canker' can be used figuratively too: 'The Conservative Party is a canker that infects the entire body politic.' Shakespeare is better:

> To put down Richard, that sweet lovely rose,
> And plant this thorn, this canker, Bolingbroke.

canon, cannon

The first of these words, **canon**, is a homonym of its own. It comes originally from the Greek word *kanon* which means 'measuring rule', and you can detect that origin in many of its present usages. It is, perhaps, best known as a rule, law or decree of the Church, and one often hears of canon law. However, a canon can be a member of the church, in that a priest living with other priest, in the confines of a cathedral and observing canon law is also often referred to as a canon. A portion of the Mass service is also called the canon, and the accepted and received Scriptures for the Church (i.e. the Old and New Testaments) are also called the canon. In addition, in English literature, books which are universally accepted as great are often said to be in the canon. A canon is also a form of music, a form with resemblances to the fugue, and musical works whose authorship is uncertain are frequently labelled as not being in the canon. There is also a print size called canon, so as you can see, this five-letter word does sterling service. **Cannon**, on the other hand, is more modest. It is a large gun which, because of its size, needs to be mounted on firm ground or stone before being used. A cannon is also something that occurs in the games of snooker and billiards. When a ball hits one ball and then branches off to hit another ball or the cushion of the table, the event is known as a cannon.

cant, can't

One might argue that these two words are not homophones because **cant** is pronounced with a short 'a' and **can't** with a long one. As always, of course, pronunciations vary so much that generalisations are pointless. Cant is normally used to indicate spuriousness in speech. A statesman seeking to justify an illegal war could be said to be speaking cant. A religious leader trying to denigrate the theory of evolution might be speaking cant. Most politicians and priests speak cant most of the time. Rather differently, however, the word 'cant' is also used to refer to the specialist speech of sundry groups. Thus you can have thieves' cant, estate agents' cant, and so on. Notice, even in this usage, the word still has a disparaging tone, so you could refer to 'Stock Exchange cant' but would hardly mention 'Amnesty International cant'. But the word has other meanings also. It is the oblique line that cuts off the corner of a square or cube. In shipping, it is the piece of wood laid upon the deck of the vessel to support the bulkheads. **Can't** has only one meaning. It is a shortened form of the word 'cannot', and signifies that something or someone is unable to perform or do a particular action or activity.

canter, cantor

Given the entry immediately above, a **canter** could simply be someone who speaks cant. While this would be a perfectly valid use of the word, it must be extremely rarely used in this fashion. For most of us, a canter is an easy-going pace, normally on a horse, somewhat between a trot and a gallop. Apparently it derives from the expression 'Canterbury pace', the easy-going speed adopted by pilgrims to Canterbury Cathedral. A **cantor** is a singer, though the word is normally used for singers of liturgical music in church or synagogue.

canvas, canvass

With the single 's', **canvas** normally means a coarse unbleached cloth made of hemp or flax and used for making tents or sails. It is also, of course, the material upon which painters can produce masterpieces in oil. The double-'s' word **canvass** normally refers to the operation of going out and seeking support for some cause or person. Thus people knock on doors and canvass the virtues of the Tory Party, or seek your support for the High Street to be widened.

cap

Mostly we think of a **cap** as a flat shaped covering for the head, a kind of hat. However, almost any removable covering for the top of an object can be known as a cap. Thus you can take the cap off the toothpaste tube, a petrol tank or a fountain pen. Yet, purely as a verb, cap can also mean the action of outdoing someone else. Someone tells you a story about mis-diagnosis at a hospital, and you say, 'I can cap that,' and proceed to tell an even more alarming story of medical incompetence. In addition, when I was a boy a cap was a very small circular object that you put into your toy gun so that when you pulled the trigger of your gun, a satisfying bang was emitted. A cap is also an artificial protective covering for a tooth. It is also possible to cap prices, borrowing or expenditure, in that a limit or restriction will be placed upon them. Shakespeare uses the word as a synonym for 'top' or 'peak': 'A very riband in the cap of youth' (*Hamlet*) or 'Thou art the cap of all the fools alive' (*Timon of Athens*). There is also the quaint activity of capping verses. You are given a line of verse and then have to provide a second line that begins with the final letter of the first line. And so the group engaged in this game continue until they are thrown out of the pub.

cape

This is either a sleeveless cloak or a headland jutting out to sea.

caper

This is either a southern European shrub or the action of leaping, dancing or prancing in a light-hearted fashion. 'When I saw some caper on a cliff in Provence, I capered with joy.'

capital

This word has a surprising number of uses. You will have noticed that I always begin my sentences with a **capital** letter, that is, one in upper case. All countries have a capital city, the city which houses their seat of government. Most countries (I hope) have abolished capital punishment, that is the taking of life as a punishment for a crime. The head or top of a column or pillar is known as its capital. The amount of money that you have in your bank account or other funds is known as your capital. To indicate your approval of something, you might just exclaim, 'Capital!'

capitol

I nearly included this word with the preceding entry because **capital** and **capitol** are almost homophones. However, I decided that the 'a' / 'o' distinction between them just about ruled that out. A **capitol** is a citadel on the top of a hill, and for centuries that was its only meaning. However, the word has since been appropriated to refer to the building occupied by the USA congress, and even, in some American states, to the state house. Originally, of course, the Capitol was the temple of Jupiter in ancient Rome.

capon

This word is used to refer to a castrated cock, or to various kinds of fish.

capsule

Most of us think of a **capsule** as being a small case or container, normally one that contains a dose of medicine. However, it also has some precise scientific meanings. For the biologist, a capsule is the gelatinous layer forming the outer surface of some bacterial cells. For the botanist, a capsule is a dry fruit that releases its seeds by bursting open when ripe. A pea pod would be a typical example. However, the botanist could equally well be referring to the spore-producing structure of mosses and liverworts.

car, carr

While **car** is the universal shortening for 'motor car', with a double 'r', it can be a dialect word for an isolated rock or rocks off the Northumbrian or Scottish coast. With either a single 'r' or a double, it can refer to fenny ground.

carat, caret, carrot

The **carat** is a measure of weight used for diamonds and other precious stones that is equivalent to 200 milligrams, and a means of indicating the fineness of gold, 24 carats being pure gold. A **caret** is a mark like this ^ which you insert into your text when you want to indicate that the words or letter immediately above the caret need to be inserted. A **carrot** is an umbelliferous plant with a large red root which is edible. Eating carrots is traditionally said to improve your eyesight, though the word is also used to genially mock someone who has red hair. A carrot is also used as a symbol for something enticing, so you could say, 'The carrot that drew me to this tedious meeting was that Bernice was going to be there.'

caravan

For most of us, a **caravan** is a mobile home, normally towed along by a car to its destination, in the course of which, because cars and caravans are more difficult to pass, it delays one's own journey by half an hour. But the word is also used to signify a company of merchants, pilgrims or whatever travelling together. Equally you can have a caravan of ships sailing together.

carcass, carcase

Alternative spellings of the same word, though **carcass** is the more common. A carcass is a dead body of man or beast. The word is often used with a derogatory connotation, almost as if the body concerned was a piece of litter. The word can also be extended to refer to the damaged, derelict state of a building, car or ship. There is also a military usage, since a carcass (or carcase) can be an iron shell packed with combustibles and fired at a building so as to destroy it.

card

A **card** can be an item from a pack of cards, perhaps the queen of hearts or a two of clubs. Such objects tend to be called playing cards in order to distinguish them for other sorts of card. A card can also be a smaller rectangular piece of stiff paper on which your name, phone number and official status are inscribed. As salesman for Perfect Panties Ltd you will have a card to leave with all potential buyers. As secretary for the Lesser Wallop Tennis Club, you will have a card to demonstrate your importance. There are also cards to celebrate sundry events, like Christmas cards, birthday cards, or cards to mark your retirement. Such cards tend to have a jovial or pleasing front illustration and to have inside a piece of nauseous verse. In its basic meaning as a rectangular piece of thick, stiff paper, or in a playing-card context 'card' has become part of many common expressions: 'a card up one's sleeve' means that you have some secret plan; if you 'get your cards', it means that you have been sacked or made redundant; if you 'hold all the cards', you are in a strong position; and if you 'lay your cards on the table', you are being totally frank and open. A card is also the label given to a person who is prone to slightly eccentric behaviour. Although this usage is not cited at all by the *Shorter Oxford*, 'The Card' was the title of a short story by Arnold Bennett, and later made into a film. Although in real life, cards tend to be self-indulgent poseurs, they are viewed in Britain with amused tolerance. 'Card' can also be a verb, in which case it means the activity of raising the nap on cloth. Indeed, the invention of a carding machine was one of the significant developments of the Industrial Revolution.

cardinal

A **cardinal** is a high office in the Roman Catholic Church, and the cardinals form the Sacred College which elects succeeding Popes. More importantly, it can be a matter on which everything else hinges. Thus it can be of cardinal importance in the fight against global warming to abolish the motor car. In zoology, the cardinal is the hinge of a bivalve shell. There are also cardinal numbers (one, two, three, etc.) as opposed to ordinal numbers (first, second, third, etc.). There are cardinal points on a map: north, south, east and west. There are also cardinal sins, cardinal veins, and a cardinal grace. There is even a cardinal red, a deep scarlet colour, and a cardinal beetle that is so coloured.

career

Most of us hope that our children will have a satisfying **career**, namely a fulfilling occupation throughout their working life. However, the word can also be a verb meaning to gallop or rush: 'He careered through the town as if the police were after him.'

caries, carries

Caries is the decay of the bones or teeth, while **carries** is the third person singular form of the present tense of the verb 'to carry'.

carline

This is a thistle-like European plant or any of the pieces of squared timber fitted fore and aft between the deck beams of a wooden ship to support the deck planking. In Scotland it used to be a term for an old woman or even a witch.

carol, carrel

A **carol** is a song sung at Christmas, a song celebrating in some way the birth of Christ. A **carrel** is a small enclosed space in which one can sit and study. They are often to be found in university libraries.

carousel

There are three possible meanings for **carousel**. It can be a merry-go-round at a fair, a conveyor system at an airport from which arriving passengers collect their baggage, or, in the middle ages, a tournament in which groups of knights took part in demonstrations of equestrian skills.

carp

This is a freshwater fish, or a verb meaning to speak in a complaining and fault-finding fashion.

carpal, carpel

Carpal is an anatomical term referring to the carpus or wrist. **Carpel** is a botanical term referring to one of the cells of a pistil or fruit.

carpet

A **carpet** is a thick fabric used to cover floors. They can be of a plain colour or decorated in sundry ways. However, you can also be on the carpet, which means that you have been summoned for a rebuke. There is also a carpet moth, carpet snake, carpet shark and a carpet beetle.

carriage

This can be a mode of conveyance ('The Queen rode in her carriage'), normally a wheeled vehicle pulled by horses, or it can refer to the way in which a person stands and moves. If you stand erect with shoulders back and move with grace, you can be described as having a good carriage. The word can also be used as a synonym for luggage: 'I've got too much carriage to climb those steps.'

carrier

This word is a noun, and it always signifies a person or object that carries, holds or conveys something or someone. It cannot then be a homonym, you might, quite reasonably, argue. But **carrier** is used in such diverse contexts that there can, I think, be no objection to its homonymic status. You may go shopping with a carrier bag, you may ask for your jewels to be transported by a carrier (a professional person who provides this service), you may be looking at an aircraft carrier, you may be in charge of a carrier (a vessel or vehicle for transporting goods in bulk), you may have caught bovine tuberculosis off a badger because the badger is a carrier of that disease, and you yourself may be a carrier of the colour-blindness gene. The word 'carrier' certainly carries quite a lot.

carrot see **carat**

carry

Just as 'carriage' and 'carrier' squeezed in as homonyms, so the verb **carry** must do so as well. A train, bus, boat or aircraft service can carry you from A to B. The Clifton Bridge cannot carry very heavy transport. A woman normally has to carry her child in the womb for nine months. The Prime Minister has to carry the weight of massive responsibility. The television has to carry far more bilge than it ought to. I think the motion abolishing sword swallowing in schools will carry tonight. If you add 123 to 987, when you add the two digits to the right, you end up with nought and have to carry one. This gun has an excellent carry (i.e. its bullet travels a long way before dropping harmlessly to earth). Boycott was able to carry his bat throughout the entire day (i.e. this batsman was not dismissed). I always carry myself with confidence. Whatever the king of Solumbria has to say is bound to carry weight. I will not continue with any more examples, but if you look at each of the preceding sentences with some care, you can see that in each case the word 'carry' has a slightly different connotation. It increasingly baffles me how the English manage to learn English, let alone anyone else.

cartwheel

This is obviously a wheel of a cart, and less obviously a physical action whereby one leaps in the air, comes down on one's hands and then flips back on to one's feet. It is much favoured by children at primary school.

carve

The common-or-garden meaning for **carve** is to describe the action of cutting something. You can either carve a hard object, wood or stone, for example, into a design or figure. Hence you might go into a church to see the wooden carvings of Grinling Gibbons (1648–1721). More commonly, you may carve the Sunday joint each week. But a carve is also a turn in skiing whereby you tilt your skis on to their edges and use your weight to bend them so that they curve into an arc. In addition, you can carve someone up, either literally by slashing them with a razor, or more figuratively by ruining their reputation in some way. You can even carve up a geographical area as Africa was carved up by the Europeans in the nineteenth century.

cascade

A **cascade** can be a small waterfall, or a process whereby something, normally information, is passed on from person to person. You personally may also have hair that cascades over your shoulders.

case

This word has a surprisingly diverse range of meanings. A **case** can be an article for carrying or storing something. Thus you may go to work with your case containing documents, pens, paper or even your lunch. In such instances, you may dignify the case by calling it a briefcase. Equally you may be Sherlock Holmes working on a case, in which case the word refers to a criminal problem with which you are faced. By extension, a case can be any matter that demands attention: 'I need to work this morning on the case of parking provision in the Belmont area.' In grammar, a case denotes the role that a noun or adjective is playing in a particular sentence. In the sentence 'The boy kicked the ball', the noun 'boy' is in the nominative case (i.e. the subject of the sentence) while 'ball' is in the accusative case (i.e. the object). In printing, a case is the frame in which a compositor has his types. Letters can be in upper case (i.e. capitals) or lower case. The word can also be used to describe the state of something or someone: 'The town hall is a bad case after the floods'; 'Mary isn't a good case because of her eyesight.' If you are planning to burgle a house, it is a good idea to case the joint first, that is, inspect it carefully so as to learn its general layout and its possible exit points. The word is also linked with a number of others to act as an adjective: case history, case law, case work, etc.

cash *see* cache

cashed *see* cached

cashew *see* cachou

cast, caste

The verb 'to **cast**' means, normally, the action of throwing. You cast dice, you cast a fishing line, you cast nets, you cast a glance, you can cast your mind, and you cast someone into jail. A snake can cast off its skin. As you can see, if you cast something it is normally not the most violent of actions. Casting is a more restrained action than hurling or flinging. But a cast is also the characters in a play ('The cast for *Macbeth* were waiting for the director') or a mould into which metal is poured in order to make a medal or emblem of some sort. It can also be a slight squint in the eye. A **caste**, on the other hand, is one of the hereditary classes into which the population of India has long been divided. The word can also be applied to any group who keep themselves socially distinct, or who inherit exclusive privileges.

cat

caster, castor

A **caster** is simply someone who casts, whether it be clay on to the potter's wheel or aspersions at someone's reputation. If you are a fisherman, a caster can also be a fly pupa used as bait. A **castor** is the little wheel and swivel that you will find on the underside of some chairs and settees so that the article of furniture can be easily moved. A castor can also be a small vessel with a perforated top from which to sprinkle pepper or sugar on to your food. It is also what one Internet source simply describes as a beaver's smelly gland. This gland emits a reddish-brown unctuous substance having a strong smell and bitter taste which ironically is used in medicine and perfumery. With a capital C, Castor is also the first star in the constellation Gemini.

castle

A **castle** is a strong fortified building, normally built in the middle ages to be secure and to act as the locus for the subjugation of the surrounding area. It is also a move in chess whereby the king moves two squares laterally and the rook then jumps over the king. Unless you play chess, that explanation will have been meaningless, but if you don't play chess, you won't mind anyway.

castor *see* **caster**

casual

This is such a common word that it is not until one actually thinks about it that one realises that it has a number of differing meanings. The most common, I suppose, is where **casual** means without much thought, without much premeditated intention. 'I just made a casual remark about all Australians being descended from convicts, and he hit me.' Actions, as well as words, can also be casual: 'I went to the hospital with my broken arm, but they were so casual in their treatment of me that I might as well have been a parcel.' 'Casual' can also mean not regular or not permanent: 'He was only a casual worker', or, 'Martin only attends the bridge club on a casual basis.' Equally 'casual' can mean without formality: 'You can wear casual dress at the garden party.'

cat

This carnivorous quadruped is one of Britain's favourite domestic pets, though strictly speaking all members of the *Felis* genus, lions, tigers, etc., should be called cats. The word **cat** is also an abbreviation for the multi-lash whip known as the cat-o'-nine-tails, and an abusive term customarily applied to spiteful women. The word is also used to denote the tackle used to raise an anchor out of the water on to the deck of the ship. Normally capitalised, CAT can also be an abbreviation: clear air turbulence, computer-assisted testing, computerised axial tomography.

cataract

Most of the time, **cataract** is just a synonym for a waterfall, normally quite a large one falling over a precipice, but it is also the name for an eye disease and a governor for single-acting steam-engines.

catbird

Apparently there are two species of bird, one an American one from the mocking-bird family, and the other an Australian one of the bowerbird family that are both called a **catbird**. There is even a James Thurber short story called 'The Catbird Seat', and apparently if you are in the catbird seat, you are in a position of some advantage.

catch

If you **catch** something, you capture it or imprison it in some way. This can range from being as simple and innocent as catching a ball to as complex and dangerous as catching a criminal. However, you can also catch a train, and clearly no one then envisages a train flying through the air and your catching it with your upturned hands. You can also catch a cold, and in that instance it is the cold that does the imprisoning rather than you. Hence 'catch' has an active and a passive sense. If you catch a fish, then it is you doing the activity. If you catch the wind in your face or influenza off your neighbour, then it is the wind or the flu that is being the active agent. In addition, a catch can be a musical round in which one singer catches at the words of another, often producing comic effects. Furthermore, 'catch' is used in a wide range of common expressions, virtually all of them idiomatic and hence difficult to comprehend for anyone new to the English language. Here are a few of them with their literal meaning alongside:

Did it catch fire?	Did it become aflame?
Did you catch on?	Did you come to understand?
Did you catch his eye?	Were you seen by him?
Did you catch him out?	Did you fool him or get him to make a mistake?

caul *see* call

caudal, caudle

Caudal is an adjective relating to or belonging to the nature of a tail. Hence you can talk about caudal plumes on some bird's tail. **Caudle** is a warm drink, or thin gruel given to sick people.

cause, caws

At its simplest, a **cause** is merely something that produces an effect. Thus dropping a lighted cigarette on to dried twigs and grasses is quite likely to be the cause of a bush fire. Often, however, people undertake actions in order to accomplish a result, and they often describe this activity as working for the cause even if their activities produce no results. **Caws** is simply the plural of 'caw', the sound emitted by a crow.

caustic

This word is an adjective meaning burning or corrosive. It can be applied to substances like acid or bleach which can be destructive of organic tissue, or equally appropriately be applied to comment of a demeaning and derogatory nature. Apparently in mathematics, **caustic** is a word applied to a curved surface formed by the ultimate intersection of luminous rays proceeding from a single point and reflected or refracted from a curved surface.

caution

Most of the time, **caution** indicates a sense of hesitancy, an attitude of carefulness because one is uncertain about the outcome. Thus you and I cross the road with caution because we have no desire to be run over by a bus (or anything else). By a relatively simple extension, the word 'caution' can also mean 'a warning'. You see it in sentences like 'I must caution you against relying on tax cuts in the next budget.' But 'caution' also has a further meaning that is completely separate from these. If you describe someone as being a real caution, you are not warning against him or her, you are merely indicating that they are eccentric or wayward in some ways, normally in an amusing or surprising fashion.

cavalier

As most of us learnt at school, a **Cavalier** was a follower of Charles I in the English Civil War. You may also have learnt that Cavaliers were romantic but wrong, while their opponents, the Roundheads, were democratic but dreary. In fact, though, the word 'cavalier' can be applied to any horseman, particularly one serving in the cavalry. By a further extension, 'cavalier' can be a term used to describe any gentleman who is escorting a lady. Yet, as an adjective, the word has a very different meaning. If you are cavalier in your approach to studying Hebrew, you are likely to be slipshod, unfocused and far too casual. Hence, if you adopt a cavalier approach when you are talking to the Queen, she will regard you as offhand and lacking in respect.

cave

A **cave** is a hollow opening under the ground with the result that humans or animals can shelter or even live in the cave. It is also an exclamation meaning 'Beware!', though probably little used today now that Latin is so rarely taught. Note that the Latin exclamation is a two-syllable word.

caviar

This is the pickled roe of sturgeon or other large fish, regarded by some as a great delicacy. Because, it is argued, caviar (or caviare) can only be appreciated by a refined and developed taste (that is, not by peasants like you and me), the word has been made into a symbol of good things. Hence the expression 'caviar to the general' which is virtually the equivalent of saying 'pearls before swine'. In Tsarist Russia, certain matter in imported periodicals was censored by being blacked out with ink. Such matter came to be known as 'caviar' because its appearance was similar to black, salted caviar on a slice of bread.

caw, core, corps

The word **caw** is simply an onomatopoeic representation of the cry of a rook or crow. A **core** is the inner portion of an object. Hence, when eating an apple, you are forced to cease when reaching the apple's core. The word is often transferred from physical objects possessing a core to people or organisations possessing a core of belief or intention. Thus you might say that a desire to favour the rich lay at the core of a political party's objectives, or that a desire to play football for England lay at the core of young Martin's being. A **corps**, on the other hand, is a division of the army or, indeed, any body of people gathered together in a joint endeavour. Hence it could be a corps de ballet, a corps d'élite, the corps diplomatique, or even, one supposes, a corps de Red Lion every Thursday.

cay, key, quay

A **cay** is a low insular bank of sand, mud or rocks. The word **key** normally refers to an object for opening locks, but 'key' is an internal homonym and therefore has its own entry. A **quay** is a landing place for floating vessels.

cedar, seeder

The **cedar** tree is an evergreen conifer, sometimes called the cedar of Lebanon from its earliest location. A **seeder** is someone who plants seeds, or possibly, of course, a seed planting machine.

cede, seed

To **cede** is to yield, to give up, to succumb. Thus one can cede territory at the end of a war or cede a point at the end of an argument. A **seed** is the part of a plant from which a new plant grows.

ceil, seal, seel

The first of these homophones, **ceil,** is not a word that you are likely to encounter often today. It is a somewhat archaic verb to denote the lining or plastering of a roof. **Seal** has four or five meanings of its own, so you ought to see its individual entry. **Seel** is a verb that indicates the closing of a person's eyes when they die.

ceiling, sealing

A **ceiling** is the flat, top part of a room, normally the part from which the main electric light of the room hangs. More figuratively, however, the word can be used as the upper limit set on prices, wages or expenditure or to the maximum height to which an aircraft can rise. A glass ceiling, of course, is the purported bar that women experience in reaching top positions in business and industry. The activity of **sealing** is the activity of securing a document of some kind, either by sealing the envelope in which the document is placed, or by affixing a seal to the document itself. Hence King John sealed Magna Carta by affixing his seal to it and thereby accepting its terms. This is a smart-aleck remark to make when someone wrongly mentions King John signing Magna Carta.

cell, sell

The word **cell** is an internal homonym. It can mean a monastery or nunnery that is dependent on some larger religious house, it can mean a small and bare room in which a prisoner is confined, it can be a secret group of plotters, it can be the local area covered by one of the short-wave transmitters in a cellular telephone system, it can mean the smallest independent entity of which animals and vegetables are composed or, in electrical work, it can mean a vessel containing a pair of metallic elements. The verb to **sell** normally means the exchanging of goods or services in return for payment in money. It is, however, an internal homonym, so you need to see its own entry.

cellar, seller

A **cellar** is a room, normally below ground, in which objects are stored. Hence you can have coal cellar, a wine cellar or even presumably a Wellington boot cellar or a cough medicine cellar. A **seller** is someone who sells something in exchange for money or some service.

cellular

Something is **cellular** if it is composed of living cells. Hence you and I and our pet dog and our grass lawn are all cellular objects. The adjective can also denote a mobile telephone system that uses a number of short-range radio stations to cover the area that it serves. A fabric can also be cellular if it has been knitted so as to form holes or hollows that trap air and so provide extra insulation. A building too can be cellular if it consists of small rooms.

censer, censor, sensor

A **censer** is a vessel in which incense is burnt. A **censor** is either someone who helps to draw up a census, or else someone who checks that objects like books, films, television programmes, etc. are suitable for general consumption; such censors, as one Internet source delightfully puts it, are 'bad people who fear knowledge'. According to the psychoanalysts, we all have a censor in our brains. It is an aspect of the superego which is said to prevent certain ideas and memories from emerging into consciousness. A **sensor** is a device which detects that which it has been designed to detect. Thus a sensor will detect whether or not you have any metal objects on your person as you pass through passport control. Another sensor will detect if there is smoke in the room.

cent, scent, sent

All these are homophones, but very diverse in meaning. A **cent** in the currency of the USA is one-hundredth of a dollar. In music, a cent is one-hundredth of a semi-tone. A **scent** is a smell, though one that is normally felt to be a pleasant one. Thus the scent of flowers is generally regarded as pleasing. **Sent** is the past tense of the verb 'to send' and indicates that someone or something has been dispatched to its destination.

central

As an adjective, **central** normally depicts the point or area that is in the middle of something. Hence you can be in central London or in the Central African Republic. Something, however, can be central to your interests. 'The study of ornithology was central to Sheila's life, while drinking pints of beer was central to Brian's.' In phonetics, a vowel is described as central if it is articulated in the centre of the mouth.

centre

The word **centre** has only one basic meaning, but the applications of that meaning are so varied that one has to include the word in a dictionary of homonyms. If something is at the centre of something else, then it is in the middle. If you draw a circle, the centre of that circle will be equidistant from every point of the circle's circumference. The wedding cake is normally placed in the centre of the table. In politics, where people have a leaning to the left or right of the political spectrum, most political leaders try to appeal to the centre, which is why, when this entry was being written, it was virtually impossible in Britain to detect any difference between the Conservative Party and the Labour Party.

century

Most of us know that a **century** is a period of one hundred years. It can also be a score that you make as a batsman in the game of cricket or the amount you total in a game of darts. It was also a company in the ancient Roman army.

cere, sear, seer, sere

The word **cere** can be a noun or a verb. As a noun it relates to the naked, wax-like membrane at the base of the beak in certain birds. As a verb, it means to wrap in a cerecloth. The verb to **sear** means to burn or scorch something, or figuratively to have one's mind branded or wounded. A **seer** is someone who has second sight or who can prophesy. If something is **sere**, it is dry and withered. Shakespeare has King Lear saying that his life 'is fallen into the sere'. An Internet source has 'sere' meaning the 'natural succession of plant or animal communities', but neither the *Shorter Oxford* nor the full *OED* provides any confirmation for this.

cereal, serial

A **cereal** is either an edible grass cultivated for its edible seed like wheat, barley or maize, or a commercial product designed as a breakfast food and made in part from such grasses. Popular brands like Cornflakes, Shredded Wheat and Weetabix indicate their cereal origins by their names. A **serial**, on the other hand, is a narrative story that is delivered in instalments. Thus a magazine might have a serial so as to encourage its readers to buy the next issue. Many television programmes are serials, with some of them like *Coronation Street* apparently doomed to continue into eternity.

cerebral

If you suffer a **cerebral** haemorrhage, then blood has been released in the cerebrum of your brain. Hence it is not much of an extension to make 'cerebral' a synonym for intellectual pursuits: 'Simon preferred the cerebral activities of his maths course to the physical activities of the football field.' The word in phonetics is also a synonym for 'retroflex'.

certain

For most of the time, **certain** is an adjective. It can indicate that something is really going to happen, that something is valid: 'It is certain that Triple Arc will win the Derby tomorrow.' One can also use the word as a synonym for 'some': 'He had certain difficulties with the Sanskrit paper.' You can also use 'certain' when you are referring to someone whom you don't personally know: 'She brought a certain Mrs Sloams with her.' The word can also act as a pronoun, normally in conjunction with the word 'of': 'Certain of his habits are unappealing.'

cession, session

A **cession** is a giving up of something, normally an occupation or property. Hence, in a court of law, you might be commanded to a cession, a giving up of your property to someone to whom you owe money. A **session** is a period of time in which a person or group of people are devoted to accomplishing some task. Thus you might have a session on the piano trying to get your fingers round Bach's Goldberg Variations. A tutor might have a session with his students trying to understand Gladstone's policy towards Ireland.

chafe

As a verb, **chafe** normally refers to the activity of rubbing part of one's body against something and thereby making that part of the body somewhat sore: 'Be careful that you do not chafe your neck with that collar.' Yet you can deliberately chafe a part of the body in order to restore warmth: 'He chafed her frozen feet with his towel.' The word is extended to mean anything that you find irritating. Hence you could chafe that the council wanted to see your bank statements for the last two months, or you could chafe against the petty regulations of the British Legion. As a noun, 'chafe' refers to the wear or damage caused by rubbing: 'In order to prevent chafe, the beams have been raised.'

chaff

When you are threshing corn, you are bound to produce **chaff** because the husks of the corn are separated by the threshing process and become waste matter or chaff. In botany, chaff is the term used for the bracts of the flower of grasses. It is also possible to chaff with your friends, that is, indulge in light, frivolous conversation often involving wordplay or light-hearted insults that are as light and trivial as the husks of grain are. The word is also used to describe the thin strips of metallic foil that are released into the atmosphere by aircraft to deflect radar signals.

chair

As an article of furniture, a **chair** is a seat for one person, typically with a back and four legs. You may also be the chairperson at a meeting of Tweeton Labour Club, in which case you will take charge of proceedings at that meeting. You may also hold the Chair of Astrology at Ludlow University, in which case you will be the Professor of Astrology.

chalk

In the natural world, **chalk** is a white form of limestone. It can, of course, be transformed into small sticks of chalk which used to be omnipresent in schools for writing on blackboards. You can also chalk your cue in a game of billiards or snooker by rubbing the tip with chalk. The word can also be used figuratively in expressions like 'I'll chalk that one up against you, Dave,' even though no actual chalk is used to signify your grudge.

cham

This word is an obsolete form of the word 'Khan', but you still hear the word during discussions of Samuel Johnson because he was called the great Cham of literature. You also encounter the word in Shakespeare's *Much Ado About Nothing*: 'Fetch you a hair off the great Cham's beard' (Act 2, Sc. 1). However, the word is also a verb meaning to bite, chew or to mash. A Cham can also be a member of the indigenous people of Vietnam and Cambodia.

chamber

For most of us, a **chamber** is a room, often a somewhat private one. Thus a judge might transact relatively minor business in his chamber. The two Houses of Parliament are each called chambers. A chamber is also where you put the charge for a gun.

champ

If you chew vigorously at something, you are said to **champ** it. The word also indicates the state of fretting impatiently: 'He was champing for the flight to arrive from Paris.' It is also the timber of the Champac tree, and a common shortening of the word 'champion'.

chance, chants

Once again, these are not true homophones. If you pronounce **chants** correctly, its 't' sound distinguishes it from **chance**, but the real world is less precise. 'Chance', of course, is happenstance, the unpredictability of life: 'It was quite by chance that I discovered my birth certificate.' 'Chants' are not at all fortuitous. They are musical works, often of a religious nature, and frequently marked by very precise part writing.

change

Most of the time, the verb 'to **change**' entails the alteration of an object or person into something slightly different. The moon changes as it waxes and wanes. You and I frequently change our clothes. 'Eric used to be a keen Spurs fan, but now he's changed into supporting Chelsea.' 'The change in Sylvia following the death of her husband has been sad to see.' And so on. But if you change 'change' into a noun, it has two quite different meanings. If you buy a newspaper in the morning and hand over a five-pound note, you will get change, that is, money in the form of loose coins. Indeed, you often need some change if you are catching a bus, because many bus companies will no longer accept notes. In addition, you can have a change in the course of your bell-ringing stint. That simply means that ringing the bells in sequence A is now switched to a peal in sequence B or C or whatever. You may, quite rightly, feel that since 'change' always means a process or operation of becoming different, it is not a homonym. Even when you buy a paper, the change you get from your five-pound note only actualises the fact that your crinkly piece of paper, the five-pound note, has been transformed into some lesser-value coins. I do, of course, take your point, but surely the nature of such changes is so disparate as to justify being labelled homonymic. You can change address, change colour, change hands, change your mind, change the subject and change your tune. When driving a car or a bicycle, you can use the gears to change up or change down. This strikes me as being a homonymic galaxy.

channel

A **channel** can be a stretch of water separating two countries, wider perhaps than a strait, but much narrower than a sea or ocean. It can also be a band of frequencies used in radio and television transmission or an electric circuit which acts as a path for a signal. More loosely, a channel can also be the accepted norm for communications or distributions between countries or within an organisation. 'Jim failed to get his idea adopted because he didn't go through the proper channels.'

chaos

As a mass noun (that is, one that is not normally found in the plural and which does not use the indefinite article), **chaos** represents the normal state of things, namely, complete disorder and confusion. It is also a concept in physics used to describe the property of a complex system whose behaviour is so unpredictable as to appear random. In mythology, Chaos was the first created being.

chap

This word is merely a colloquialism for 'man', 'fellow': 'He's a nice sort of chap.' It originated as a shortening of 'chapman', a trader or merchant. But it can also mean a fissure or crack on the skin, either of the two bones that make up the jaw, or even a dialect word for buying and selling. It is also an abbreviation for 'chapter'.

chapel

A **chapel** may be a building designed to hold religious services, or, in a large church or cathedral, a section of the building designed for this purpose. In a religious sense, 'chapel' can also act as an adjective: 'Mrs Howard is staunch chapel.' Used in this way, it always means a Nonconformist body like the Methodists or Baptists, ones that use a chapel as opposed to a church. However, the word is also used for the members or branch of a print or newspaper trade union.

chapter

A lot of books are divided into **chapters**, thereby affording a convenient point for you to stop reading the book and going off to make a cup of tea. But if a chapter is a division or compartment within a book, it can also be a group of canons within a cathedral, a section of a treaty or Act of Parliament, a local branch of a society, or a distinctive period in history or a person's life.

char

If you **char** something, you slightly burn it so that it is scorched. As a noun a char can be a small fish of the trout family, a slang word for tea ('I'd love a cup of char') or a slang word for a female domestic help.

character

Each letter, punctuation mark or other symbol in this book is a **character**, since the word is used to signify any distinctive mark. Hence a crude cross daubed on a door is a character, as is a hieroglyph in an ancient Egyptian manuscript. But, as most of us know, a character is also a word used to delineate any person who is striking or distinctive in any way. Hence we might say: 'Gerald is a real character because of his habit of singing Polish folk songs in the pub.' At the same time, any person, distinctive or not, who appears in a novel, poem or play will be called a character in that work. Thus Falstaff is a character in *The Merry Wives of Windsor*, Pip is a character in Dickens's *Great Expectations* and so on. Equally we use phrases like 'Jason is a man of good character', using the word 'character' as a totality of a person's traits.

chard, charred

The word **chard** presents some problems. An Internet source defined it as a spinach-like vegetable, but the word did not appear in my edition of the *Shorter Oxford*. The full *Oxford* defined it as a thistle or as an intermediate between a chart and a card. My *Collins Dictionary* said that a chard was a variety of beet with large succulent leaves and thick stalks, and my *Oxford Dictionary of English* also defined it as a type of beet. Fortunately there are no problems with **charred**. The word simply means burnt, though a charred object has not been burnt to ash, merely burnt so that it bears the colouring left by the flames.

charge

A **charge** can be a massed attack on another group of people, a building or some other site. Hence in wartime one has charges of one group of troops against another. Of course, one does not need a group of people for something to be a charge. Someone might charge towards a telephone kiosk in order to make an emergency call. A child might charge towards the ice-cream van in his anxiety to buy a cornet. Whatever the context, a charge is a rapid advance by one or more people or animals towards something else. But a charge can also be an accusation by someone against someone else. Hence a policeman, before he can lock you up, has to charge you with some offence. Equally, of course, you may charge your husband with being a drunken halfwit, a teacher may charge a pupil with lack of attention, a newspaper may charge a city council with wasting money, and so on. A charge can also be the operation of storing electricity in a battery. If you are in charge of something or someone, you are responsible for looking after that thing or person. Equally, a charge might be a sum of money or the demand for a sum of money. Thus, when you want a garment altering so that it fits you, the tailor might say, 'I'm afraid that I'll have to charge you £50 for this work.' Finally, a charge can be the quantity of material needed to fill up or equip something else. Thus, if you charge your gun, you put into it the materials necessary for it to be able to fire. Equally you can charge the coal scuttle by filling it with coal.

charger

Clearly a **charger** is someone or something that charges, but it is also a descriptive term for a horse or an archaic term for a large flat dish.

charlie

This is the code word representing the letter C in radio communication, but it is also a slang word meaning cocaine, a member of the Vietcong, a silly or stupid person ('a proper charlie'), in black slang, a white man, or, in the plural, a woman's breasts.

charm

The quality of **charm** is difficult to define. Someone who has charm possesses an elusive attractiveness, seems capable of making you feel that he or she is entirely delightful. Because of this, the word is also used to describe a small trinket that may be worn by a person because of its attractiveness. Less pleasantly, a witch may evilly put you under a charm so as to force you to do her evil actions. It is also a word for a flock of finches or other birds.

charter

A **charter** may be the written document that formally establishes the power and existence of a country, a university, a borough or a company. As a verb, you can charter a ship, coach or aircraft to take you to an exhibition, a peace conference, a meeting or what have you.

chase

As a verb, **chase** describes the activity of pursuing someone or something. Thus you might chase a boy out of your garden, chase a fox across the countryside, or chase a jewel thief down the street. Yet chase can also be a noun depicting a tract of unenclosed land used for breeding and hunting wild animals, the sort of setting chosen for a jewel, the cavity of a gun barrel, a groove or furrow cut in the face of a wall or other surface to receive a pipe or wire, or a type of joint used in shipbuilding.

chased, chaste

If something or someone is **chased** they are pursued, normally with the intention of capturing them. If someone is **chaste**, they are not having sexual relations with anyone.

chat

As a noun, **chat** has a number of rarely used meanings. It is a term applied to several birds, it is a small, poor potato, a shortened form of 'catkin', or an ore with some rock attached to it. Its more usual meaning, however, is to describe an informal conversation, and that is also its usual verb usage. To chat to someone is to have a relaxed conversation with them.

cheap, cheep

If something is **cheap**, then it is low in price, inexpensive. Under the fallacious assumption that cheap goods are necessarily inferior ones, the word 'cheap' has also come to mean 'paltry', 'of little worth', or 'contemptible'. A parallel shift has also taken place in that 'cheap' can be applied, not only to goods on sale, but to virtually anything else. Hence if you describe Wendy Arbuthnot as 'cheap', you are not saying that she will only cost 75p but instead you are implying that she lacks taste, has low standards, or in some other way fails to measure up to your standards of acceptability. Equally an article in a magazine or newspaper might be cheap because it is underhand and fails to provide a balanced view. The original meaning of 'cheap' was 'market' or 'market place', and although this is now obsolete, it survives in place names like Cheapside, Chepstow and Chipping Camden. **Cheep** is much less complex. The word simply refers to the short, high squeaky cry made by a young bird.

check, cheque, Czech

The two final words are straightforward, but **check** has a variety of meanings. When the king in a game of chess is under attack and could be taken next move, then the king is in check. When a garment has a pattern of cross lines forming small squares, then it has a check pattern. If you want something not to happen, then you try to check it. If you want to make sure that something is in order, then you check it just to be sure. If, in poker, you decide not to make a bet when called upon, then you check. A **cheque**, however, is a written instruction to your banker to pay out a stated sum of money, while a **Czech** is a person who come from or lives in the Czech Republic.

cheek

Your **cheek** is the side of the face below the eye, but it can also be the side-posts of a door, a projection on each side of the mast of a sailing ship, either of the buttocks, or an instance of impertinent or insolent speech. The word is also part of some idiomatic phrases: 'cheek by jowl' (close together), 'cheek to cheek' (romantic embrace), 'turn the other cheek' (refrain from retaliation).

cheque *see* check

cherry

A **cherry** is the fruit of a cherry tree, a small, soft round-stoned fruit that is typically bright or dark red. The word is also a slang word for a woman's virginity.

chest

The front surface of a person's or animal's body between the neck and the stomach is called the **chest**. It is also a large, strong box in which, traditionally, your valuables are stored.

chesterfield

With a capital letter, Chesterfield is a town in Derbyshire, but for our purposes we need to note that it is a sofa with padded arms, and a man's plain straight overcoat.

chews, choose

If one **chews** one's food, one masticates it with one's teeth. This is the literal usage of 'chews', the third person singular present tense of the verb 'to chew', and all mammals, as far as I know, chew their food in order to obtain nourishment. However, the word can be figuratively extended so that it is possible to chew over a problem, that is, consider a problem at some length in an attempt to arrive at a solution. The verb 'to **choose**' means to select something from a range of options. Thus many of us choose to watch a particular television programme over all the other possibilities available.

chi

This is the twenty-second letter of the Greek alphabet, but also, in Chinese philosophy, the circulating life force.

chiasma

In anatomy this is the X-shaped structure formed just below the brain where the two optic nerves cross over each other. It is also a point at which paired chromosomes remain in contact during the first metaphase of meiosis.

chic, sheik

Something or someone is **chic** if they are elegantly and stylishly fashionable. A **sheik** is an Arab leader, and obviously there is nothing to prevent a sheik from being chic.

chicane

This is a sharp double bend in a road or racing track created so as to slow down the traffic. In a card game, a **chicane** is the name given to a hand devoid entirely of a particular suit, normally trumps. The word can also be used as a verb where it means to deceive someone.

chick

This is a young bird, especially one newly hatched. It is also a slang word to denote a young lady, and, since the 1990s, we have seen the emergence of 'chick lit', novels meant to appeal strongly to female readers mostly in their 20s and 30s. In the Indian subcontinent the word also means a folding bamboo screen for a doorway.

chicken

This is a domestic fowl kept for its eggs or meat, but also a word used to denote a coward or someone who fails to keep their nerve in a dangerous situation. Thus it is also possible to 'chicken out' when you withdraw from something through a lack of nerve.

chief

Most commonly the word **chief** denotes a leader or ruler of a people or clan, but it can also be employed more loosely for the head of an organisation (e.g. chief of police, chief technician, chief rabbi) or even as an informal mode of address to your boss, your husband, or whatever. In heraldry a chief is an ordinary consisting of a broad horizontal band across the top of the shield.

Chile, chilli, chilly

The first of these is a South American country, the second a dried pod of red pepper, and the last one an adjective indicating that something is uncomfortably cool. They are all virtually exact homophones.

chill

In its normal usage as a noun, a **chill** can either be a drop in temperature to produce a feeling of unpleasant cold ('There was a chill in the air'), or a feverish cold, a common complaint in Britain. The word can also be used metaphorically, often to suggest fear, in phrases like 'a chill ran down my spine'. A chill is also a metal mould designed to cool metal during the operation of casting. The word is also part of the expression 'to chill out', a phrase which means to relax after a period of strain or work.

chime

No one seems to know the exact origin of this word, though it can be traced back to Middle English. As both a noun and verb, it is associated with the sound of bells ringing. When you hit a bell with a suitable hammer-like object, the bell will **chime**. Indeed there are widespread customs associated with the chiming of bells; we are all used to bells chiming in the New Year, and, of course, the chime of church bells summons us to church each Sunday. A set of suitable bells is, indeed, sometimes called a chime, so it is possible to have a chime chiming. However, the word has at least two other meanings. A chime is the rim at the end of a cask, and, as a verb, denotes an almost indefinable connection between people. You have arranged, for the first time, to go out with Hazel. You say to her, 'I hope that this will be the first of many occasions.' She replies, 'Well, that depends on how well we chime together.' You can see this sort of chiming in action at a public meeting. Sometimes the speaker is able to establish a real rapport with his or her audience. In other words, they chime well together. Obviously, of course, this use of 'chime' is an extension of the idea of bells pealing harmoniously together, but it provides another interesting example of how words that have originated in one context can be transplanted into an entirely different one.

chimera, chimaera

In Greek mythology, a **chimera** was a fire-breathing female monster with a lion's head, a goat's body and a serpent's tail. These are not often encountered in Britain today, and so for most of us, a chimera either means an organism containing a mixture of genetically different tissues, or something that is hoped for but is extremely unlikely to occur – 'It is a complete chimera to expect intelligent television programmes during normal waking hours.' A **chimaera** is a cartilagineous marine fish with a long tail.

chimney

We all know what a **chimney** is. It is a vertical channel or pipe which conducts smoke and gases from a fire up through the roof and into the air. It is also the aperture down which Santa Claus descends on Christmas Eve to leave presents at the foot of the bed. Chimneys like this are becoming less common now that most people have central heating rather than coal fires. However, the word 'chimney' is also used for two other entities. It can be a glass tube protecting the flame of a lamp, or it can be a very steep narrow cleft by which a rock face may be climbed.

China, china

The capitalised word **China** refers to the most populous country in the world, and this dictionary has no direct interest or concern with the names of countries, though there is also a China aster, a Chinese plant of the daisy family. However, as we all know, the country name has been adopted to describe a type of porcelain or fine semi-transparent earthenware that was originally made in China until its adoption by European countries in the sixteenth century. Many of us drink our tea or coffee in china cups and eat our dinner off china plates. Much less well known though is the fact that 'china' is also the name for the thick fleshy root-stock of the plant *Smilax China*. In addition, 'china' is the name of a homoeopathic medicine made from the bark of the Cinchona tree. Finally, 'China' is a rhyming slang word for your closest friend. Starting with 'china plate', rhyming slang turned the 'plate' into 'mate' which eventually got dropped, leaving you simply with expressions like 'my old china'.

chine

This noun has at least four different meanings. It is the backbone of an animal as it appears in a joint of meat, it is a mountain ridge, in the Isle of Wight or Dorset it is a deep narrow ravine, and it is the angle where the strakes of the bottom of a boat or ship meet the side.

chink

The word **chink** is a not very respectful term for a man or woman from China, but there are other less opprobrious meanings. A chink can be a narrow slit. At night time you can often see that someone is at home because there is a chink of light visible through a chink in the curtains or the door. 'Chink' also denotes a sound. You might hear the chink of loose change in someone's pocket. You might hear your keys chink as you unlock a door. When having a glass of wine with a friend, you might chink your glasses together. In other words, a chink is the sharp, brief sound made by two or more metal or glass objects rubbing together.

chip

The **chip** is somewhat exaggeratedly often assumed to be the basic food of the British. You peel potatoes, cut the potatoes into longish thin rectangles, and then immerse these 'chips' into boiling fat until the potatoes go brown. You then drain the chips and eat them, either on their own and dowsed with salt and/or vinegar or with accompaniments like eggs and bacon. This greasy and fattening food is, it has been argued, the bulwark of British greatness. This, of course, is total nonsense, and is never proposed seriously, but fish and chips and other combinations are certainly a staple diet for many British people. Yet it seems likely that the name 'chip' for a wedge of potato stemmed from the earlier meaning of chip, namely a small, thin piece of wood. Indeed you could chip away with a knife in order to produce a chip of wood. Indeed, chips need not be of wood. If you are working with metal, and a small piece breaks off, that will be a chip of iron or whatever. In our technological age today, of course, many people associate the word 'chip' with computers. Here a chip is a tiny wafer of semiconductor material like silicon that has been processed to form a type of integrated circuit. These sorts of chips now store and manage so much of the world's data that they have become omnipresent and close on omnipotent.

A food, a sliver of wood or metal, and an integrated circuit are the primary uses for the word 'chip' today, but there are still a number of other specialised or colloquial usages. You can chip a ball with your cricket bat. You may chip a football over an opponent's head. You may be a chip off the old block. You may have a chip on your shoulder. When disaster strikes, you may admit that you have had your chips. The English language is so idiosyncratic that I marvel that anyone ever manages to learn it.

chipper

A **chipper** could, I suppose, be an article in which you fry your chips, and it is certainly used colloquially to refer to a fish and chip shop, yet probably its most common use is as an adjective to signify that you are feeling lively, cheerful or chirpy. As a verb, chipper can also be used as a synonym for 'to chatter', 'to twitter' or 'to babble'.

chippy

This is a colloquial term for a fish and chip shop, a slang term for a carpenter, and an American term for a prostitute.

chit

I personally have only ever heard this word used to denote a scrap of paper which acts as an authorisation for something: 'Take your chit to the counter and they will hand over the ordered goods.' Apparently, however, the word can mean a variety of things: a shoot from a plant, a small cleaving tool used by a cooper, a young child, and, as a verb, to sprout. You can also, of course, have a chit-chat with a neighbour, and in India give your savings to a chit fund so that they will gain interest.

chlorosis

For the botanist **chlorosis** is the loss of the normal green colour in the leaves of plants owing to iron deficiency in the soil. For the doctor, chlorosis is anaemia, again caused by a lack of iron in one's diet.

chock, choc

You can have a **chock** of wood or stone. A chock of wood can be used as a log for burning. A chock of stone or wood can be used to stop something else from rolling or moving out of place. **Choc** is a common abbreviation of 'chocolate', and has become a genuine word of its own in the phrase 'a choc ice'. Let me know if you ever hear anyone ask for a chocolate ice.

choice

The two meanings of **choice** are conceptually similar. You see an array of cheeses in the supermarket and you can have your choice as to which one you choose. Hence 'choice' represents the act of choosing. As an adjective, the word can signify the best available, something of real excellence: 'That is a choice turkey that you have there.'

choir, quire

A **choir** is a body of people gathered together to join in singing. There might therefore be a choir in church, a school choir, an amateur choir formed of local people who enjoy singing, or a professional choir who perform choral masterpieces like Bach's B-minor Mass. A **quire** on the other hand is a set number of sheets of paper, in fact the twentieth part of a ream, though it did originally mean the same as 'choir', as you can see from the *Book of Common Prayer* where it refers to 'quires and places where they sing'.

choke

You are likely to **choke** if something in your throat constricts the flow of air or someone tries to strangle you. Sometimes pure emotion can almost force you to choke: 'He was choked with anger.' Equally, if you break down in the middle of the High Street, your car may choke up the traffic. But 'choke' can also be a noun. A valve in the carburettor of a petrol engine is called the choke, as is the narrowed part of a shotgun bore near the muzzle. Apparently the inedible mass of silky fibres at the centre of a globe artichoke is also called a choke. The word is also part of other nouns like choke chain, choke cherry and choke point.

choler, collar

In the middle ages, human beings were supposed to consist of a mixture of four humours which, in combination, created or formed that person's character. One of those humours was **choler**. Equated with bile, it was supposed to cause an irascible temper, and even today the word is still used to depict irritability, short-temperedness or a general inability to tolerate the shortcomings of others. A **collar** on the other hand is normally used to depict the part of a blouse, shirt, coat or jacket that snuggles around the neck, and indeed the word is also often used to indicate that part of the neck itself. However, it is also possible to collar someone or something in the sense that you capture or entrap them. Thus in Harrods you might collar a pickpocket before he escapes with your wallet, or in a sale you might collar the last available leather armchair.

chop

You might walk into the butcher's and ask for a lamb **chop**, in which case you are asking for a slice of meat, generally one including a rib. You can have a mutton chop, a lamb chop or a pork chop, though my 1965 edition of the *Shorter Oxford* totally ignores this usage of the word completely, just another of the numerous instances where Oxford seems to be chronologically trapped in the eighteenth century. After all, most of us have eaten a chop for lunch quite often, far more of us, I imagine, than have ever chopped a tree down. This, of course, was the first usage of the word 'chop', a verb meaning to cut down, to hack or to hew. Hence you can chop a log into sticks, chop the branches off a tree, or presumably chop a lamb's carcass into chops. At a colloquial level, a chop can also refer to the jaw, or, in the phrase 'chop and change', indicate a change of mind. You may also get the chop from your work, that is, be dismissed, in which case you might like to console yourself by eating some chop suey. There is also the adverb and exclamation, chop-chop, meaning 'get a move on'.

chopper

A **chopper** is obviously something with which you chop, an axe or knife. It is also a colloquial term for a helicopter, a type of motorcycle with high handlebars, and yet another slang word for a penis.

choral, coral

You might object to these two words being linked together, because normally **choral** has a longer 'o' sound than **coral**. They are not, therefore, true homophones. But once again the vagaries of human pronunciation ensure their entry here. 'Choral' is an adjective. A choral work is a musical work sung by a choir, works like Bach's *St Matthew Passion*, Verdi's *Requiem* and so on. Most operas and musicals also have choral numbers in them. Coral on the other hand is a hard calcareous substance consisting of the continuous skeleton secreted by many tribes of marine coelenterate polyps for their support and habitation.

chorale, corral

A **chorale** is a musical religious work for choir, often no more than the orchestration of a simple hymn tune. A **corral** is an enclosure in which animals like horses can be kept, free to roam around but not free to escape.

chord, cord, cored

A **chord** can be at least five things. It can be a string or small rope, in which case it is almost identical to **cord**, or it can be a number of notes sounding together so as to produce a pleasant noise. It can also be a straight line joining the ends of an arc, the width of an aerofoil from leading to trailing edge, or each of the two principal members of a truss. Metaphorically also you can say that something strikes a chord when you simply mean that something has just reminded you of something else. If something is **cored**, its central part is removed. For instance, a cored apple is much easier to eat.

chorus

In virtually all of its manifestations, the word **chorus** carries the implication that there is a group of people (or animals) doing something together. Thus, in a musical work like an opera, many people singing together simultaneously is a chorus. When you arrive at work in the morning, all the office staff may simultaneously chorus, 'Good morning, your excellency.' A musical instrument may have a chorus pedal that gives the impression that more than one instrument is being played. In ancient Greek plays, several people, the Chorus, could comment simultaneously on the action. Yet, in contradiction to this group activity, in sixteenth-century English drama, the chorus was a single character who would speak the prologue and possibly other linking points of the play. Shakespeare's *Henry V* provides a good example.

chough, chuff

The word **chough** designates the black Eurasian and North African bird of the crow family, and a black and white Australian bird of the mud-nester family. A **chuff** is the sound that the old steam-driven railways used to make when they departed the station, a sort of puffing noise.

chow, chow chow, ciao

Chow is simply an informal word for food, but **chow chow** is a dog of a sturdy Chinese breed. **Ciao** is an Italian word, but it is frequently used by the British as a greeting, and is an almost perfect homophone with 'chow'.

chronic

The formal meaning of **chronic** is in relationship to an illness, in which case it signifies that the illness is persisting for a long time or constantly recurring. However, the word can be extended to other contexts. Hence a bus may suffer from chronic overcrowding or Thomas may be a chronic liar. Quite differently, though, 'chronic' can be a synonym for 'dreadful' or 'appalling': 'That was a chronic film.'

chub, Chubb

A **chub** is a river fish of the carp family. A **Chubb** is a patented name given to a type of lock for your door, one that is unpickable.

chuck

You can **chuck** someone under the chin, that is, lightly tap them on the underside of the chin. You can chuck something away, namely throw it into the bin. You can buy a chuck of beef from the butcher, normally a part of the animal taken from between the horns and the ribs. You can be addressed as 'Chuck', normally an affectionate endearment. You can chuck up your job, namely resign from it. You may stay in because it is chucking it down with rain. You may decide to chuck Felix as a boyfriend. You can listen to a hen chuck at her chickens as she calls them together. You can also use a chuck to fix the object to be turned on to a lathe or on to a drill.

chum

We normally think of a **chum** as being a friend. The word began as Oxford University slang, and arose as a shortened form of 'chamber fellow'. In America 'chum' can mean chopped fish and other material thrown overboard as bait.

church

Every British town or village has its local **church**, a building used for public Christian worship, but the word can also be a verb. If you church someone, you take her to church because she has recently given birth and needs to attend a service of thanksgiving.

churn

A **churn** is a machine for making butter, or a large metal container for holding milk. The word can also be a verb, either signifying the agitation of milk in a machine in order to produce butter or the action of producing something mechanically and in large quantities: 'We churned out 150 copies of the school magazine this afternoon.'

chute, shoot

A **chute** is a steep channel down which water descends, though man-made chutes can also be used to slide grain, coal, ore or whatever. It is also an abbreviation for parachute. The verb to **shoot** normally means the activity of firing a bow, bullet or other missile at something or someone. It also means to propel a ball towards the goal in an attempt to score in a game of hockey, football, *et al*. You yourself can also shoot forward in haste to do something, shoot a glance at something or someone, shoot a film with a camera, watch a plant shoot out buds, or, colloquially, shoot yourself with drugs by means of a needle.

ciao *see* chow

cinch

As a technical noun, a **cinch** is a Mexican saddle-girth normally made of separate strands of horse hair, but it is also a slang term meaning a certainty. 'It's a cinch that Battling Basil will beat Horrid Horace in the ring tonight,' some misguided punter will doubtless inform you. The word can also mean that something is very easy: 'The photocopier was a cinch to use.'

cinque, cinq

These two words are interchangeable, and they refer to the throw of a dice that turns up the number five, as you might expect because 'cinq' is the French word for 'five'. However, for reasons which a campanologist might be able to explain, the word is also used for the changes on eleven bells. There are also a group of five English ports (Hastings, Sandwich, Dover, Romney, Hythe) that are called the Cinque Ports.

cipher

A **cipher** is a message or communication that has been written in code so that no unauthorised person can understand it. The word can also be used to describe a person of no importance: 'As far as making Leftwich & Co. an efficient business is concerned, Donald Surcoast is a mere cipher.' The word can also be used to denote the continuous sound of an organ pipe caused by a mechanical defect.

circle

In geometrical terms, a **circle** is a round plane figure whose boundary (the circumference) is always the same distance from its centre. You can also have a circle of friends and acquaintances.

cirrus, serous

Most of us, I imagine, encounter **cirrus** as a type of cloud of high altitude, one with a wispy appearance looking rather like curls of hair. Indeed, the original word meant a curl-like tuft, and has consequently been appropriated, not just by weather forecasters, but by botanists who use the term for a tendril root, and by zoologists who call the wispy beard of some fishes a cirrus. **Serous** is an adjective to describe something that resembles or produces serum.

cist

In archaeology, a **cist** is a coffin or burial chamber made from stone or a hollowed tree. It is also the name for a box used in ancient Greece for storing sacred utensils.

cite, sight, site

If you **cite** something, you refer to it. Hence, in your major volume on the poetry of Milton, you doubtless often cite the writings of the critic F. R. Leavis. Even if you haven't written a book on Milton, you will cite many things during a day, even if it's only what Mrs Thompson told you about young Emily. The word **sight** is so commonly used that it barely requires explanation. 'Sight' is one of our major senses. It means the apprehension of something through our eyes: 'I caught sight of Kenneth in the market.' A **site** though is merely a location, a place: 'I was standing on the site of the old town hall.' The word tends to be used for a location where something that used to be there no longer is, or on the location where something new is going to be erected. All three words are perfect homophones, as are their past tenses (cited, sighted and sited).

civil

This is an odd word. Descended from the Latin word *civilis*, it ought to pertain only to citizenship, to the state of being a member of the community. Yet, over the centuries, other more peripheral meanings have become attached to the word **civil**. First of all, it means good-mannered. If you are civil, then you are polite and civilised, though the word does perhaps carry a connotation that you are formally polite but lacking in warmth. Secondly, the word is used as the opposite to military. 'Stanley did not join the armed forces, preferring to seek his fortune in civil occupations.' Thirdly, the word is used as a branch of law. You can appear in court on a criminal offence or a civil one, the latter being concerned with personal relations like divorce, misrepresentation, debt and so on.

clack, claque

The most usual meaning of **clack** is to describe a noise, mostly a sudden, rather dry noise, the sort that you get when a plank of wood falls on to another plank or an iron rod hits against a radiator. Yet the word can also be used to describe the chatter of human beings. The word **claque**, which sounds identical to **clack**, refers to a group of people who have been brought together for some social or political public relations purpose. For instance, your friend Alison Bridges is appearing in the lead at the Royal Opera House tonight. It is the opening night and she is singing the role of Tosca. You have bought tickets for yourself and eleven other friends, and during the opera you all will applaud wildly every aria that Alison sings. You have formed a claque. Equally when you and your eleven friends attend a public lecture given by Reginald Turncoat, your Conservative MP, you will act together to denigrate and disrupt that meeting as much as possible. Once again, you are a member of a claque, a group of dissatisfied voters.

claim

As a verb, you can **claim** that something is true, but you do not usually provide any evidence to support this assertion. You can also formally request something: 'I claim the £100,000 that Mrs Newbold left me in her will.' The nouns correspond to the verbs in the usual way.

clam

A **clam** is a marine bivalve mollusc, and an informal word for the American dollar. As a verb, you can clam up in the sense of abruptly ceasing to talk.

clamp

The most common usage for **clamp** is to describe a sort of brace or clasp that holds articles together. You might use a clamp to hold all your family photographs together. You might park your car in the wrong place and arrive to find a clamp making it immovable. But it is also a word to describe the large bivalve shell of the molluscs *Chama* and *Trudacna*. You can also clamp around the house, walking with a heavy, solid tread.

clap

When you are at a concert and the orchestra finish playing a piece, you tend to **clap**, that is, hit your hands together so as to make a percussive noise. It is a sign of appreciation for the music that you have just been hearing. But the word can also be used for almost any abrupt, explosive noise. Hence you might clap a friend on the back, or hear a clap of thunder. You may even, when you have said something that was ill-advised, clap your hand over your mouth. The word is also a term for the lower mandible of a hawk, and a colloquial term for the disease of gonorrhoea.

class

Basically the word **class** denotes a set or category of things having some property or attribute in common. Hence one might quibble about its homonymic status. After all, whether one is talking about socio-economic class or the class of university degree, one is still dealing conceptually with the same idea. Yet I have included 'class' for two reasons. First of all, 'class' in the biological sense is a precise demarcation and based entirely on scientific criteria. For the biologist, class is a principal taxonomic grouping, that above order and below phylum. Secondly, you were in a class at school, but that class was merely a random collection of boys and girls linked only by a rough equivalence in age. The gap between the biological classification and the school grouping seems to me to be massive. Furthermore, it is possible to use 'class' as an adjective, in which case it means 'outstanding' or 'excellent': 'Victoria Woods was a class act.'

clause, claws, Claus

In English grammar, a **clause** is part of a sentence that contains a verb. Thus, in the sentence 'Because it was a nice day, Wolfgang decided to go for a walk', there are two clauses. Official documents, however, also tend to be divided into clauses. This is not a grammatical distinction, but more a convenient reference point: 'If you could look at Clause 23 Sub-section b, you will see . . . ' As for **claws**, this is merely the plural of 'claw', a sharp horny nail arming the feet of some birds and animals. On the other hand, **Claus** is simply part of the name given to Father Christmas indicating that the origin of Father Christmas was St Nicholas (Santa Claus).

clay

Most of us know about the sticky earth-like substance that can be moulded when wet and is dried and baked to make bricks, pottery and ceramics. However, a **clay** is also a European moth with yellowish-brown wings.

clean

Whether as a noun or a verb, the word **clean** conveys the meaning of unspotted, free from dirt, and it is to produce that state that we wash our faces or polish our furniture. However, 'clean' also has at least a couple of less shampoo-like connotations. Thus your driving licence can be clean metaphorically when you have no offences listed upon it. The film that you go to see might be referred as a clean film if it had no sexual references contained within it, just as it would be termed a dirty film if it had. The Puritan revolution was in the seventeenth century, but its influence lingers on!

clear

As an adjective, **clear** has a number of functions. First of all it can denote something that is easy to perceive, understand or interpret: 'His instructions were very clear.' Secondly, it can mean that something is transparent or unclouded: 'There was clear water in the glass.' Thirdly it can denote the absence of obstacles or obstructions: 'The road ahead was clear.' Fourthly, the word can indicate that two objects are not in contact with each other: 'One wheel of his bicycle was clear of the ground.' The word can even mean 'complete': 'You must give me three clear days' notice.' Finally, as an adjective, 'clear' can denote a palatalised form of the sound of the letter 'l' as you get in the south-eastern pronunciation of 'leaf'. As an adverb 'clear' can signify the state of being removed from or not in contact with something else: 'He kept clear of Mrs Daniels.' In addition you can have the sense of 'completeness' again: 'He tried to get clear away.' As a verb, 'clear' is normally used in ways congruent with its noun meanings, though there are idiomatic variations. Thus clearing a ball at football, or clearing £15,000 in a business transaction both seem almost idiosyncratic. In addition, 'clear' is often associated with the prepositions 'off', 'out' and 'up', and there are a number of conventional phrases that use 'clear': 'clear the air', 'clear as mud', 'clear as a bell', 'clear one's throat', and so on.

cleat

This is a T-shaped piece of metal or wood on a boat or ship to which ropes are attached, or a number of projections on the sole of an athlete's shoe.

clew, clue

A **clew** is a ball of thread or yarn which when entering a maze you wisely release behind you so that you will be able to trace your way back. It is also the lower or after corner of a sail, or the cords by which a hammock is suspended. A **clue** is a guide towards the solving of a particular mystery. The fact that your wife has gone off for a month to stay with her sister might be a clue that she is finding you less than enchanting these days. Detectives look for clues to enable them to solve the crime. Crossword puzzles have clues so as to enable you to fill in the blank squares.

click

Most of the time a **click** is a short, sharp sound, the sort you get when you switch a light on or turn your key in the front door lock. However, it can also be a sudden illumination when the synapses in your brain suddenly reveal a connection that you had previously missed: 'I hadn't understood Sarah's death until I saw Geoffrey's bicycle, and then everything clicked.' People are also able to click (i.e. feel one-to-one with each other), and when this happens on a blind date, there is rejoicing all round.

climb, clime

If you **climb** something – a hill, some stairs, or whatever – you are ascending a steep place. More metaphorically, you can climb in your profession from office boy to managing director. Equally you can climb in some league sport like football or rugby, or you can climb in people's estimation because of your diligence or saintliness. Ironically, because the word 'climb' is almost invariably concerned with an ascent, you can also 'climb down' when you are forced to jettison a position that you have previously maintained. You can also climb into your suit, climb up the wall when you are feeling extremely frustrated, and you may have a mountain to climb when you are facing some difficult task. **Clime** though is just a synonym for 'climate', and a rarely used one too, though you occasionally hear the word in its plural, 'Shall we move to sunnier climes?'

clinch

When you **clinch** an argument, you settle it once and for all. When you are in a clinch with your opponent in the boxing ring, you are engaged in close-quarters grappling rather than boxing.

clink

The *Shorter Oxford* defines **clink** beautifully: 'A sharp abrupt ringing sound, clearer and thinner than a *clank*, as of glasses struck together.' The word is also a colloquialism for 'prison'. According to *Brewer's*, there was a jail in Southwark called The Clink, and it may have been so called because its gates clinked shut on the prisoner.

Clio

On the whole proper nouns are not included in this dictionary, but in the case of **Clio** there might some confusion. She is the Muse of epic poetry and history, but the same name describes a genus of pteropods found in the Arctic and, in astronomy, the 84th asteroid.

clip

To **clip** something is to cut it. Hence you might get the barber to clip your hair. The word suggests a relatively minor cutting operation. Thus, when you clip your hedge, you just remove a few projecting twigs rather than cutting down the whole thing. You can also clip someone around the ears. Here the word indicates a blow, a smack. You may also fasten a piece of jewellery with a clip, normally a spring-loaded device that grips the necessary portion of cloth. Finally you can clip along, indicating that you are proceeding at some speed. Your money will certainly disappear with some speed if you visit a clip joint, a night club where patrons are grossly overcharged.

clod

This word refers to a lump of earth or clay, a stupid person or a coarse cut of meat from the lower neck of an oxen.

clog

As a noun, a **clog** is a type of wooden shoe, typically associated with Holland or the north of England. Clearly, being wooden, they are noisy, and there is an entertainment called clog dancing where people dance together and beat out complex rhythms with their clogs. As a verb, to clog means to impede, to slow up, to obstruct. Thus your sink might be clogged with cabbage, the High Street is always clogged at 8.45 a.m., and the recent storm swept some branches into the stream which have clogged its progress.

close, clothes

This is a dubious homonym. The 'th' sound in **clothes** stops it from sounding too much like **close**, but the words would doubtless have sounded identical when spoken by Eliza Doolittle before Higgins got his hands on her. 'To close' is to end: 'The music came to a close.' It is also 'to shut': 'Please close the door.' Pronounced with a short 'o', it means proximity: 'He stood very close to her.' This closeness can also be a mental or spiritual one: 'Raymond was a very close friend.' The word 'close' is also often used to indicate that a particular street is a cul-de-sac. Indeed, like so many English words, 'close' has an alarming variety of idiomatic uses. You can have a close shave either literally or metaphorically, something can be close to the bone when it affects you emotionally, you can pay close attention to something, and maybe you were too close for comfort in catching the bus this morning. Clothes, of course, are the garments that you wear, and although they may present sartorial problems, at least they provide no linguistic ones.

clot

When you cut your leg, the blood will start to flow, but fairly quickly it will begin to **clot**, that is, to coagulate into a static lump. Indeed, as a noun, the word is often synonymous with a lump: 'There was a clot in the milk this morning.' It is also a slang word for a half-witted person.

cloud

A **cloud** is the visible mass of condensed watery vapour floating in the sky and threatening rain. However, you can also have a cloud in your life if something is troubling you or causing worry. It is also possible for something to cloud your judgement.

clout

You may well know that a **clout** is a heavy blow with the hand or some hard object, but, unless you are an archer, you are unlikely to know that a clout is also a target twelve times the usual size and used in long-distance shooting.

clove

One is surprised that one hears the word **clove** relatively rarely since it has a number of useful meanings. 'She clove unto her husband,' means that she was faithful to him, from the verb to cleave, to stick fast. 'He clove the log with one blow,' indicates that clove also means to split, to sever, to cleave. 'He handed her a clove of flowers,' makes 'clove' into a synonym for group or bunch. A clove is also the dried flower-bud of *Caroyphyllus aromaticus*, much used as a pungent aromatic spice.

club

One might belong to a stamp club, a bridge club or a football club. In all cases, a **club** is an association of people who meet together because they share the same interest. Equally, of course, a club is a staff or cudgel that you can use to help you over the rough terrain or to beat out the brains of your irritating next-door neighbour. Some games also employ clubs, golf being the best known. A club is also a suit in a pack of cards.

clue *see* clew

clutch

If you **clutch** at something, you grasp it firmly and hurriedly. Equally you might be clutched at by your baby, or you might clutch at the rail inside a bus as it suddenly moves off. In a car, of course, you will depress the clutch when you want to change gear. A clutch of eggs is a group of eggs fertilised at the same time, and the word can also be used for a group of almost anything.

coach

There are three types of coaches. First there is the **coach** in which you take a day trip to the seaside. Such vehicles are really buses, possibly slightly prettified, that are used to transport people to special events or to holiday resorts. Secondly, if you are the Queen, you will be transported to Parliament in a coach, a wheeled vehicle pulled by horses. Thirdly, if you travel by train, each separate compartment of the train is called a coach. So the first three meanings of this word are all close to being synonyms in that they refer to a means of transport. The final meaning is very different. You may decide that you need a coach to guide you towards your mathematics exam. You will be aware that all football teams have a coach to guide the training of the team. Thus a coach is a trainer or instructor in some specialised skill like Spanish or tennis or calculus.

coal, cole

Once upon a time, **coal** used to be a major fuel for household fires and factory furnaces. This is much less the case now, but this hard carbonised black vegetable matter is still mined in various parts of the world. **Cole** is a name for various sorts of *Brassica*, including cabbage, turnip and rape.

coaled, cold

If something is **coaled**, it is supplied with coal. If something is **cold**, one might argue that it is lacking in coal, but of course the word 'cold' means 'lacking in heat'. It is, though, an internal homonym, so see its individual entry.

coarse, course

If something is **coarse**, it is of inferior quality. In terms of material, the word implies a rather rough texture. In terms of speech, the word implies a degree of swearing and sexual content. If you are coarse (Heaven forbid!), you are lacking in refinement or delicacy. **Course**, however, is an internal homonym. There are race courses and motor cycle courses and so on where horses, bikes, cars, sledges, etc. race along striving for victory. In such cases, a course is a determined area of land along which or round which the competitors compete. Often though, the word is extended to relate to any journey. If you were travelling from Stoke-on-Trent to visit your uncle in Pontefract, you might be later than you had intended because you went off course. Here there is no race and no set route; it just so happened that, among the alternatives, you selected a lengthier one than was sensible. Equally one can use the word, not for a physical course, but for an intellectual one. I was studying the poetry of Cowper, but got sidetracked and went off course for a few weeks because I got captured by the poetry of Smart. In all of these uses, there is still the impression of a journey, physical or mental. On the other hand, you may be taking a course in mathematics or joinery. In this case, a course is a planned scheme of instruction in some skill. It is still a journey, but this time you are not doing the driving.

coast

Most of us have visited the **coast**, that area where the land meets the sea. Marked by sandy (or stony) beaches, the occasional seaside cliff, and invigorating breezes, the coast is a favourite holiday escape. Yet the word can also be a verb, normally indicating an easy and trouble-free progress from A to B. Thus you can say, 'I coasted down the hill,' 'I coasted through my exams,' or 'I had a relaxing holiday gently coasting through the Norfolk Broads.'

coat, cote

A **coat** is an outer covering. Thus, if it is cold or wet, you are likely to wear a coat. You may need to put a coat of paint over your fence. The coat of your terrier dog needs combing. You may also, of course, have a coat of arms, a badge or emblem indicating that you possess some form of title or position. A **cote**, on the other hand, is a shed or stall designed to shelter or store something. Thus you can have sheep-cote, a dove-cote or cote for the turnips.

coax, cokes

If you **coax** someone, you seek to persuade them to do something, and you will seek to do this by caressing them or by flattery. Thus you may try to coax your son to go to bed, coax your dog to go for a walk, or coax your husband to give up spending his weekends with Annabel. As for **cokes**, this is a reference to the omnipresence of a popular drink called Coca-Cola: 'We just went into town and had a few cokes.' Hence you might, I suppose, coax your son to mow the lawn by offering him some cokes.

cob

Few of us use the word **cob** these days, yet it has a wealth of meanings. It designates a big man, a great man. It is also the name for a male swan, a short-legged stout variety of horse, a type of clay mixed with gravel and straw and used for building walls, a blow, a species of gull, and the seeding head of wheat and clover. There are even some dialect and obsolete uses as well.

cobbler

A **cobbler** is someone who job is mending shoes, but it is also an iced drink made with wine or sherry, sugar and lemon, or a fruit pie with a rich, thick cake-like crust. In the plural you can exclaim **Cobblers** when you think something is total nonsense, or conceivably be referring to someone's testicles.

cock

The most common usage of this word is to indicate a male chicken, but it is also a spout with an appliance for controlling the flow of liquids through it, a conical heap of produce or material (especially hay), an upward turn of the brim of a hat, the ready-for-firing position of a gun, an informal term for nonsense, the notch of an arrow, and a slang term for the penis. As a verb, you can cock your leg, raise the cock of a gun, cock something up, or attempt something at full cock. Cock also appears in a number of colloquial phrases: cock-a-hoop, cock-and-bull, cock-horse, etc.

cocker

A **cocker** can be a casing for the leg, someone who puts hay into cocks, a follower of cock-fighting, a small spaniel with a silky coat, or a verb meaning to pamper.

cockle

As a noun, **cockle** is the name of an edible bivalve mollusc with a strong ribbed shell. As a verb, paper cockles when it forms wrinkles or puckers.

cockpit

This is a place where cock fights are held, or the compartment where the pilot sits in an aeroplane. The country of Belgium has also been called the cockpit of Europe because that country has witnessed many European wars.

cocks, cox, Cox

The first of these, **cocks**, is simply the plural of **cock** which you can read about in the entry immediately above. A **cox** is short for 'coxwain', the helmsman of a boat, and the capitalised **Cox** is simply a variety of apple, more fully known as Cox's Orange Pippin.

cocktail

The commonest use of this word is to describe an alcoholic drink consisting of a spirit or spirits mixed with other ingredients such as fruit juice or cream. However, the word can also mean a mixture of almost anything, though it is normally a mixture that is unpleasant or dangerous: 'He lives on a cocktail of beer and fags.' You can also have a mixture of small pieces of food, typically served cold as an hors d'oeuvre. A prawn cocktail is a common example. Ironically the word first came into use in order to describe a tail like that of a cock and more specifically referred to a horse with a docked tail.

cod

Most of us will think of **cod** being a species of sea-fish, one that we frequently eat with our chips, but the word can also mean a pod or husk, a pillow or cushion, a synonym for the scrotum ('not in polite use', says the *Shorter Oxford*) or one of the bearings of an axle. As a verb, 'to cod' means to trick or hoax. There is also the abbreviation COD which means cash on delivery.

code

Most of us think of a **code** as a system of letters, figures or symbols that is designed to hide their meaning from all but the recipient. However, computer programming languages are often referred to as computer code, and you also hear the word to describe a collection of laws or statutes, the code of law. You can also talk about a gene being the code for some quality or attribute.

codling, coddling

As you might expect, a **codling** is a young cod, but it also refers to a species of apple having a long tapering shape. Its homophone, **coddling**, refers to the action of comforting a small child, treating an invalid tenderly, being almost over-protective to someone.

cofactor

A **cofactor** can be the contributory cause of a disease, a substance other than the substrate whose presence is essential for the activity of an enzyme, or the quantity obtained from a determinant or a square matrix by removal of the row and column containing a specified element.

coffer, cougher

A **coffer** is a box or chest in which money or valuables are kept. A **cougher** is someone afflicted with a cough.

cog

We mostly think of a **cog** as one of a series of teeth on the circumference of a wheel, but the word also means an early form of ship, broadly built with a roundish prow and stern, a tenon on the end of a beam, and, as a verb, to practise certain tricks in throwing dice.

cohort

Originally a **cohort** was an ancient Roman military unit equal to one tenth of a legion, but since then it has been used to refer to any group of people engaged in a matter of mutual interest.

coin, quoin

A **coin** for most of us is a metal piece of money which we can use for buying things, but originally, until it transformed into **quoin**, a coin was the corner-stone of an arch. A quoin can also be a wedge or expanding mechanical device used for securing letterpress pages into a chase prior to printing, or a wedge for raising the level of a gun barrel or for keeping it from rolling.

coke

Coke is a solid fuel made by heating coal in the absence of air. It is also a slang word for cocaine, and a shortening of Coca-Cola, a popular drink.

cokes *see* coax

cold *see* coaled

collar *see* choler

collate

When you **collate** something, you collect and arrange the relevant items into a convenient order, but the word is also used for appointing a clergyman to a benefice.

collet

This noun can refer to three different articles. It can be a segmented band put round a shaft and tightened so as to grip it, it can be a small metal collar in a clock to which the inner end of a balance spring is attached, or it can be a flange or socket for setting a gem in jewellery.

collision

In everyday life a **collision** is when one moving object or person strikes violently against another. People collide against each other in a crowded market, and there are frequent vehicle collisions on our overcrowded roads. In computing, however, a collision occurs when two or more records are assigned to the same location.

colon

A **colon** is a punctuation mark that you were told at school is used to introduce a list like this: bat, stumps, gloves, bails, etc. In fact a colon is not quite as limited as that implies. It can also be used when you want to expand on something that you have just written. However, since punctuation seems to be taught but rarely these days, we can assume that the word is heading for redundancy. Not so, however, for the portion of the large intestine from the caecum to the rectum. That is unlikely to become redundant.

colonel, kernel

A **colonel** is a high-ranking officer in the army. A **kernel** is the seed contained within a fruit, and is often used figuratively as representing the heart of the matter: 'I think the kernel of truth lay in what Mrs Savage had to say.'

colony

In the days of imperialism, a **colony** was an area of land under the control of another country. Most colonies have since been given their independence, but a few still exist. The word is also used to describe a group of fungi or bacteria grown from a single spore or cell, or a community of animals or plants living closely together, and occasionally you hear the word applied to human groups like a nudist colony or a colony of painters on the West Bank of Paris.

colt

Although this word is of obscure origin, it appears in Old English as meaning a young horse, and this meaning it still retains. However, it has since been extended to refer to almost any young, inexperienced person or animal. Thus, when you first play for Lancashire Cricket Club, you are likely to be termed a **colt**. Ditto when you are in your first term as a barrister. However, as we know from many Western films, a colt is also a type of repeating pistol invented by Samuel Colt, and in nautical terms is also a piece of rope used for delivering a beating. As a verb, 'to colt' means to run around in a juvenile fashion.

column

This object can stand alone as a monument to something or someone (e.g. Nelson's **column**) or be part of a series of columns used as a support for some part of a building. It is a cylindrical body, often of considerable height, and normally tapering a little from base to top. However, the word also has a number of other technical meanings. It is a formation of troops long and narrow in shape. It is a body or division of ships. It is an article in a newspaper where, since the newspaper is divided into parallel columns, an article itself has come to be known as a column.

combine

If two or more things **combine**, they come together in some mutual enterprise. Hence you and I might combine in a joint attempt to raise the standards at Little Puddlington Junior School. Many people combined to protest against the Iraq War. Chemicals may combine to form a compound. However, in England, a combine harvester is often shortened, and farmers simply talk about the combine. It is a tractor-type machine for harvesting wheat and other grains.

come, cum

The verb 'to **come**' is a versatile word. It does not so much have a variety of different meanings as a variety of allied meanings. Thus it can mean 'to move towards something': 'All wine buffs will come to Harrogate next week.' It can mean 'to enter': 'Please come into the library.' It can indicate a position in a sequence: 'Doris hopes to come first in the competition.' Linked with a range of prepositions, 'come' can adopt a variety of stances: to come across, to come at, to come by, to come down, to come in, to come off, to come one, to come out, to come over, to come round, to come to, and so on. The word is also sometimes used to refer to ejaculated semen, though **cum** is more usual in that context. Of course 'cum' was originally the Latin for 'with', and the word can still be seen with that meaning in some place names like Chorlton-cum-Hardy. It also survives in some Latin expressions like *cum grano salis* (with a grain of salt).

comeback

After winning Olympic gold in the 100 metres, you decided to retire. However, a year later you decided to make a **comeback**, that is, a return to the activity in which you had previously excelled. A comeback can also be a witty response to your companion's remark, a return to fashion of a previous item, activity or style, the opportunity to seek a legal redress, or, very differently, a sheep bred from cross-bred and pure-bred parents.

comma

Most of us know the **comma** as a punctuation mark used normally to break up a sentence into its logical components. Thus it will be used to separate clauses or to demarcate items in a list. However, there is also a comma butterfly that has orange and brown wings.

commission

If you hold a **commission**, then you hold the authority to command others. Hence if you have a commission in the armed forces, you are an officer with command over other servicemen. However, a commission can also be a document setting out the task to be done. Indeed, if you were given a commission to close down the Tower of London, you might need to show your commission document at the Tower when you arrived to carry out your task. 'Commission' can also be a verb; you can commission someone to do something. You can also be paid commission, often for performing a task for which you have been commissioned.

commode

This used to be a tall headdress formally worn by women, but fashions have changed. It is still, however, a chest of drawers, though once upon a time, a **commode** was a piece of furniture containing a concealed chamber pot.

common

As a noun, a **common** is an area of land that is open to the public, and normally comprises merely land covered with shrubs and heather and the occasional tree. The term dates back to medieval times when some land was regarded as communal land and upon which the peasants could walk. This usage of the word still survives in terms like 'in common', that is, something shared by us all. But if you describe something as 'common', you could have two different meanings entirely in mind. Something is common if examples can be plentifully found. Thus the possession of a household dog is common, while the possession of a household anteater is uncommon. But 'common' can also carry a distinctly disapproving tone. Something is common if it is only done by the unsophisticated herd, by the unlettered lower classes. Hence you might regard spitting in the street as common, going to play Bingo as common or wearing a mini-skirt as common. Each of us has his or her own categorisation of 'common' things, and each of our lists is a reflection of our socio-economic and cultural position. As you can see, many things are common and common. For instance, spitting in the street is a very common sight (i.e. you can see it in most High Streets every day), but you may also regard it as very common (i.e. the action of an unhygienic lout). So, as you walk across the common, it is very common to see a lot of common people, some of whom doubtless regard you as common.

commune

As a noun, a **commune** is either a group of people living together and sharing possessions and responsibilities, or it is the smallest French territorial division for administrative purposes. As a verb, 'to commune' means to share one's intimate thoughts or feelings with someone else.

commute

If you **commute**, you have to travel some considerable distance from home to work each day, and consequently suffer the high fare costs and the intolerable overcrowding such an activity entails. If, however, you are in jail serving a sentence of twenty-five years for publicly insulting the Prime Minister, it is possible (though unlikely) that you might be able to persuade the authorities to commute your sentence to a less severe one.

comp

Words are often abbreviated, and sometimes those abbreviations become so standard that they effectively become genuine words on their own. In a number of different fields, this has happened or is happening to **comp**. If you attend a comp, you go to a comprehensive school. If you accept a comp from a friend, you have just received a complimentary ticket. If you are a comp, then you are a compositor.

compact

Few of us think about the words that we utter as a matter of course, yet **compact**, which is hardly an unusual word, has a variety of diverse meanings. As an adjective, it tends to mean closely and neatly packed together, and hence can apply to a car ('This compact car none the less has a large boot'), to a person ('James was a compact body as he weaved through the market'), to writing or speech ('She provided a compact account of the opera'), or to most other things. As a verb it indicates that force has been exerted so as to compress articles together: 'The rubbish was taken to the depot to be compacted.' As a noun it has at least three different meanings. It can refer to a small flat case in which a woman keeps her make-up, in metallurgy it means a mass of powered metal compacted together in preparation for sintering, and in international affairs it means a formal agreement between two or more parties.

companion

A **companion** is someone who keeps you company. Normally this is a friend whose company you enjoy, but elder people often have a companion living in the same house with them so as to assist the aged person feed properly and live in relative cleanliness. This companion may, of course, not be in any way a personal friend. However, this distinction between paid companion and friendly companion is hardly sufficient to include the word as a homonym. In nautical terms, however, a companion is a skylight or window frame installed so as to admit light to a lower deck or cabin, and that is ample reason for making 'companion' a homonym.

company

If you have **company**, you have companionship, you have other human beings with you. Strictly speaking, of course, it need not be human beings. You often hear people say, 'Oh, I have my cat/dog/bison to keep me company.' Perhaps they don't often say 'bison', but you get the idea. But the word is not confined to personal acquaintances and friends. Any gathering of people (or animals) can be described as a company, and from this came the use of the word to describe an enterprise or business that had been set up. 'What company did you use to get your drive coated with tarmac?' someone might ask, and your reply, 'DriveWay', will be the name of an organisation.

That organisation, of course, came into existence because a group of people combined together to carry out some commercial undertaking. They were a company of people, and so their business became known as a company. The word is also used to designate the full crew of a ship or that part of an army regiment that is under the command of a captain.

compare, compère

To **compare** one thing to another is to estimate or note the differences (and similarities) between them and possibly arrive at a evaluation between them. A **compère** is a person who introduces the performers or contestants in a variety show.

compass

A **compass** is a physical object that includes as its *raison d'être* a magnetised needle that always points in a northerly direction. Hence compasses are used by ships, aircraft or travellers so that they can determine accurately the direction in which they are progressing. Another physical object that is called a compass is that metal object that most of us used at school for drawing a circle. Comprising two arms linked at the top, and with a pencil secured in one of the arms, you use one arm as a fixed base, and can, depending on how far the two arms can stretch, then draw a series of circles of varying sizes. But the word is also used in a much less tangible way. You have just served a customer with a new shirt, and he might ask for a pair of grey flannels to go with it. You might say, 'I'm afraid trousers are not within my compass. You need to go to the first floor for those.' Here 'compass' is being used almost as a synonym for 'range' or 'ambit'. You are playing a piece of music on your flute when you stop and say, 'I can't play any more because the music goes too low, outside the compass of the flute.' In some uses of 'compass' there is also a distinct sense of describing a circular situation. 'I was compassed about by schoolchildren' is intended to give the impression that you were circled around by children. If you are thinking of moving house to the area known as Greymount, you might decide to compass the area to see what it is really like. Again the idea is that you will circle the region so as to assess its suitability.

compère *see* compare

complacence, complaisance

Watching someone exhibit **complacence** is often rather disagreeable. The word means 'self-satisfaction' and carries a hint of smugness with it. To show **complaisance**, however, is much better. It is the action or habit of making oneself agreeable, of being polite and even deferent. By and large, it is better to be **complaisant** than it is to be **complacent**.

complaint

If you express dissatisfaction or annoyance about something, you are normally uttering a **complaint**. Equally, if you suffer from some illness or medical condition, you might say 'I must receive treatment for my skin complaint.'

complement, compliment

These two words are often confused, which is not surprising since they sound almost identical and only have a single letter difference in their spelling. As a noun, **complement** refers to an object or quality that completes or fits in with some other object or quality. 'Roger's humility was the perfect complement to his scholarship.' A **compliment** as you probably know, is something said or done that expresses praise. 'You look more stunning than ever in that gorgeous dress,' is a compliment. There are, of course, what are known as 'back-handed' compliments. 'That gorgeous dress makes you look less frightful than usual,' would be a good example.

complex

If something is **complex**, it is complicated, multifaceted, difficult to disentangle. For many of us, the components that lie under the bonnet of a car are complex because we do not know our carburettor from our cam shaft. A group of associated buildings is sometimes called a complex, presumably because, if for instance it was a university, it is difficult to discover where the Modern Languages department actually is. In mathematics, a complex problem is one that involves numbers or quantities that are both real and imaginary. In chemistry a complex denotes an ion or molecule in which one or more groups are linked to a metal atom by coordinate bonds. Jung, however, used the word to describe a mental trait or a psychological obsession. Hence you may have an inferiority complex or a superiority complex. Thus, as you can see, 'complex' shifts from being a commonly used word with a generally accepted meaning to being also a technical word in a variety of disciplines.

complexion

The most common usage of the noun **complexion** is to denote someone's skin: 'She had a pale complexion', or, 'He had a ruddy complexion.' The word can also be used to refer to the general aspect or character of something. Thus a football commentator could say, 'The complexion of the game changed once they brought Twinkletoes O'Brien on to play,' or a literary critic could say, 'The complexion of Shakespeare's last plays is very different from that of his great tragedies.'

complexity

Clearly **complexity** is simply the state of being complex, and since complex has been defined above, there is no need to include the word in this dictionary. I was impelled to do so by a sentence in Philip Ball's wonderful book *Critical Mass* (2004): 'In this context, "complexity" has become a word that can mean whatever you want it to.' Alas, I quickly realised that this did not mean that I could say 'Look at my complexity' when I was pointing to the goldfish, or 'That complexity looks very crowded' when I was looking into Woolworths. The context that Ball was considering was the emergence of fractal patterns in bacteria and cellular automata. Indeed, this is closely linked to the theory of algorithms in computer science. For most of us, complexity means something that is complicated and often difficult to apprehend. For the scientist, it often means something that is much more localised on to matters like input parameters or wave-particle duality. Even were I capable, this would not be the place to explore such matters. Let us be content to say that 'complexity' simply means the state of being intricate. Hence for the average person, the word is not a homonym. For the research scientist, however, it is.

compliance

You exhibit **compliance** when you obey an order or request from someone else. In obeying the laws of the country, we all exhibit compliance. In physics, however, compliance is the property of a material undergoing elastic deformation. In other words, when you press on X, how much will it bend or sag inwards before it does something nasty like explode?

compose

When you **compose** something, you create it, you put it together. The word is most commonly used in connection with music – Beethoven composed the 'Moonlight Sonata' – but it can equally well be used for other forms of creation. Yet the word is also used for the action of soothing someone, for restoring tranquillity: 'Alice was deeply shocked by the actions of the police, but I managed to compose her.'

composition

This noun has at least four different definitions. First of all, one can talk about the **composition** of a substance or entity. The composition of the soil in your garden may be too claylike for your tulips to flourish. There is far too much salt in the composition of most fast foods. Secondly, a composition can be a created work, a novel, poem, symphony or painting. The C major piano sonata is one of Mozart's most enchanting compositions. Thirdly, the setting up the text of this dictionary, or the text of any other book, was an act of composition carried out by a compositor. If this book looks attractive and is easy to read, then the credit lies in its composition. Finally a composition can be a legal agreement to pay a sum of money that is less than you owe. If you owe Harrison & Co. £25,000 but only have £37 in your bank account, then Harrison & Co. may agree to a composition whereby you pay them £1,000 p.a. for ten years.

compound

If something is a chemical element, it cannot be broken down into anything simpler. A **compound**, however, can be. Thus sodium chloride is a compound because it can be broken down into the elements sodium and chlorine. From that scientific definition we have developed a usage by which 'compound' signifies a mixture of almost anything. But 'compound' also has at least two other meanings. Originating probably from the Malay word *kampong* which means an enclosure, 'compound' is often used to refer to a site on which there are a number of buildings relating to the same business or activity. Hence a health centre with its associated labs, offices, etc. might all be located in the health centre compound. The same term may also be used for military buildings, a school, even a shopping centre. As a verb, 'compound' is sometimes used to indicate that a legal matter, normally of a financial nature, has been settled. Thus Perkins might be persuaded to compound the debt that Wallace owes him at a rate of 85p in the pound. Equally the police might be willing to compound your attempted robbery into a mere caution if you are prepared to give them information about the whereabouts of Lightfingered Larry. These are the relatively normal uses of the word 'compound', but the word also crops up in one or two technical areas. Thus in physics you might use a compound engine as a condensing machine. In almost any science you might use a compound microscope, one that has more than one lens. In music, a compound interval is an interval of more than one octave. Finally, if you rent your house, you may pay a compound rent, that is, one in which your rates are also included.

comprehension

This is the state of understanding something. You may have full comprehension of the theory of relativity (in which cause you are a genius) or you may have a total lack of comprehension as to the causes of the First World War. When you were at school, you may have been set comprehension exercises. Here you would be given a passage to read and then asked questions about that passage just to make sure that you understood it. However, there is one other usage of 'comprehension' which has little to do with intellectual understanding. From the seventeenth to the nineteenth century, there was a religious current in favour of comprehension. What this meant in this context was that the members of the Nonconformist churches (Methodists, Baptists, etc.) should all join the Church of England and worship in Christian amity with each other. It was never achieved, of course, and Christianity continued in its schismatic fashion.

compromise

The most common usage of this word is to indicate an agreement in which the parties to the agreement all shift their positions a little so as to accommodate each other. So, if Raymond next door annoys you by playing rock music loudly at 11.30 p.m., you approach Raymond and ask him to be more considerate. 'That's a shame,' he says, 'I'm a night bird and like playing music into the small hours. Tell you what. Let's reach a compromise. If you could stop your dog barking at 6.30 a.m., I'll stop playing my CDs at night.' This was agreed, and so a happy compromise was achieved. Yet **compromise** as a verb has a very different meaning. If you compromise yourself, you place yourself in danger of physical or emotional or intellectual harm. Kirsty Malone was recently jailed for her part in the kidnapping of Sir Maverick Peascod. However, you were seen talking to Kirsty only two days before. Consequently your reputation has been compromised because you are a known associate of criminals.

con

You have a Latin exam next week, and so you anxiously **con** your Latin verbs: *amo*, *amas*, *amat* . . . Hence to con something is to study it, to learn it, to commit it to memory. But you can also con someone by deceiving them. 'I was conned out of £500 because I believed his promise that he could get it to snow in my garden on Christmas Day.' (You may feel that someone that stupid deserves to be conned, but that is another issue.) The word is also used as an abbreviation for convict. In Italian 'con' means 'with', and we encounter that in expressions like *con amore*, *con brio* and so on.

conceit

If you say that someone is full of **conceit**, you are saying that he or she is arrogant, full of their own importance. Yet that usage derives from the original and still current usage whereby a conceit is an idea, a witty notion, or a surprising connection. The term is frequently used in reference to poetry. Thus John Donne's idea of comparing two people in love with a pair of compasses is a conceit.

conceive

If you **conceive**, you are a woman, and your egg has been fertilised by a male sperm to create an embryo. But you can also conceive a plan, an idea or an artistic work. You have the same dual meanings with the noun 'conception'.

concentrate

If you **concentrate** on something, you give it your full attention. Equally you can concentrate something by increasing its strength or proportion. Hence you can concentrate your gin and tonic by putting in more gin. In such contexts, 'concentrate' is the opposite of 'dilute'.

conception *see* conceive

concern

I think that the most common use of **concern** is to denote a state of worry or anxiety. 'I have considerable concern about Doris's pet alligator, I am concerned about Michael's lack of progress in taxidermy, and my concern over the council's lack of interest in the playing of the mandolin is massive.' If concern in this sense is an emotional and possibly moral matter, the other meaning of 'concern' is more neutral. It merely signifies a connection. The council needs to concern itself with street parking, not because it is worried about it but because it relevant to the council's raison d'être. The frequency of mandolin playing, however, is not part of the council's concern. Equally it is no concern of mine as to what name is bestowed on the newly born baby of my neighbour. The word can also be extended to refer to a business: Sopes & Co. was a small engineering concern.

concert

A **concert** is a public performance of music, normally carried out by an orchestra and/or choir. If there are very few performers, the 'concert' tends to be called a recital. However, it is also possible to act in concert with a number of others without touching a musical instrument. My friends and I acted in concert when we sent that letter of protest to the National Union of Teachers. You can also describe your views as being in concert with someone else's when you completely agree with each other. The word can also be used as an adjective: concert grand, concert party, concert pitch.

conch

Given that this is a word that most of us never use at all, it has a surprising number of meanings. It can be the shell of a mollusc, a Roman vessel used for salt or oil, the domed roof of a semicircular apse, the external ear or a nickname for the lower-class inhabitants of the Bahamas.

conclude

When you **conclude** something, you finish it, bring it to an end. 'It is time to conclude this meeting,' said the chairman. When you conclude that something is the case, you arrive at a judgement, you decide that something is valid. 'I must conclude that the moon is not made of green cheese,' Neil Armstrong stated.

concord

If you and your friends are in **concord**, then you are in agreement about something. More formally, a concord can be an agreement reached in court. Even more pleasingly, a concord is two or more musical notes that, when sounded together, make a pleasing harmony.

concrete

Concrete is a building material made from a mixture of gravel, sand, cement and water. However, the word is then used to signify something that exists in a material form or even something that is definitely proven. 'I have concrete proof that dragons exist,' said ten-year-old Graham. Yet 'concrete' is also used in a number of idiomatic phrases. Thus the 'concrete jungle' is a city or town where the living quarters are unpleasantly cramped, a concrete number is one that refers to something actual like five boxes rather than the general concept of 'fiveness', and concrete poetry rests its appeal on its typographical shape rather than other more valid poetic techniques.

condensation

When warm air comes into contact with a cold window pane, you get **condensation** in that the air condenses into water droplets. Indeed the same word is used to describe the conversion of any vapour or gas into a liquid. But a condensation is also what you get when some literary work is shortened. *War and Peace* boiled down to 500 pages would be a condensation.

condense

When you **condense** something, you abbreviate it, make it more manageable in size. Hence you might condense Dickens's *Bleak House* and reduce it to a mere 300 pages. In the world of the chemist, however, if you condense something you make it more dense, more concentrated. The two meanings are clearly linked but sufficiently different in nature to be included in this dictionary.

condition

If you are in good **condition**, then you are feeling well and on top of your form. Hence the condition of someone or something – 'This chair is in poor condition' – concerns the overall fitness of someone or something for its purpose in life. However, you may also place a condition on something. Here you are stating that x can only be done if y also exists. 'I will only come to the fair if the weather stays fine.' This is a condition of your presence, a prerequisite. It is also possible to condition someone. For instance, if you are bringing up a child and are always telling it that walking improves one's health, then it is likely that the child will become conditioned to this and will automatically accept its validity and may even become an active walker because it wants to be healthy. It is also possible to condition one's hair. This is an activity more or less confined to women who anoint their hair with some substance in the belief that it will make their hair more attractive and healthy.

condominium

In political terms, a **condominium** is a situation where a state's affairs are jointly controlled by other states. It is also an American word denoting a building or complex of buildings containing a number of individually owned apartments or houses.

conduct

If you **conduct** Mrs Featherstone to the garden party, then you take her there, you lead her there, you escort her. If your conduct at this garden party then turned out to be reprehensible, then you behaved badly. Some schools have merit badges for good conduct, an award for pupils who have behaved excellently. If you heat an iron bar at one end, the heat at that end will slowly conduct itself along the bar until the whole bar is hot. Finally, if you conduct a meeting, an orchestra or a trip, then you are the one in charge, the one responsible for the successful outcome of that event.

conductor

If you are the conductor of an orchestra, then you are the one responsible for such matters as tempo, sound level and for keeping all the musicians in time with each other. If you are a conductor on a bus (an almost extinct species), then you collect the fares, and tell the driver when to stop in order to let a passenger disembark. If you are a conductor in a scientific sense, then you allow heat and electricity to pass easily through you. Most metals are good conductors in this sense.

conduit

This is a tube or trough for protecting electrical wiring or a channel for conveying water. Extending this second definition, a person can be a **conduit** if they act as a channel for the transmission of information.

cone

As a scientific term, a **cone**, according to the *Shorter Oxford*, is 'A solid figure or body, of which the base is a circle, and the summit a point, and every point in the intervening space is in a straight line between the vertex and the circumference of the base.' However, the word is also used to describe other things that are roughly shaped like a cone. Hence a sea shell can be a cone, an ice cream can be eaten from a cone, the fruit of some trees are cones, and cones make up part of the retina.

confirm

confirm

If you **confirm** that something is the case, then you are asserting that some previously held fact or assumption is definitely true. Hence you might wish to confirm that the pop concert is next Tuesday or that Paris really is the capital of France. But you can also confirm a young adult in the vows taken on his or her behalf at the religious ceremony of baptism. You can also confirm that someone has been appointed to a particular post.

conjugate

Basically this verb means 'to join together, to couple', but it is used in such a variety of contexts that it counts as a homonym. Leaves that grow in pairs are said to **conjugate**. Animals that have sexual intercourse are said to conjugate. You can conjugate a verb:

amo	I love
amas	you love
amat	he loves

In so doing, you are giving the different forms in a specific tense that an inflected verb can take. There are equally technical usages in optics, physics and mathematics. All carry the idea of coming together.

conjunction

In grammar a **conjunction** is a word used to connect clauses, phrases or nouns. The most common conjunction is 'and', though 'but' and 'if' are frequent ones too. But 'conjunction' also has a more technical meaning. In both astronomy and astrology, the heavenly and the hilarious, a conjunction refers to the alignment of two planets or other celestial objects so that they appear to be in the same place at the same time.

conjure

If you **conjure** your friends to all meet together for Derek's stag night, then you are earnestly beseeching them, almost conspiring with them. If you conjure a rabbit out of your hat, then you are producing something as if by magic. Furthermore, it is possible that a word or a sight will suddenly conjure up a memory of something else.

conk

Both the meanings of **conk** are much more colloquial English than formal and elegant English. It is possible that your car will conk out, that is, break down. It is also possible that your friend Ambrose has a large conk, that is, a large nose. I suppose that it is also possible that people refer to William I as William the Conk, but I think that we can safely ignore that.

conker, conquer

A **conker** is the hard shiny dark brown nut of a horse chestnut tree, whereas the verb to **conquer** means to defeat or subdue.

connexion, connection

This entry is not a homonym, it is simply that the same word with exactly the same meaning can be spelt in one of two different ways and be correct either way.

conscientious

If you are **conscientious** then you do a job of work as fully and carefully as you possibly can. However, you can also have a conscientious objection to something. Consequently you may refuse to allow your twelve-year-old daughter to have an abortion because you believe that abortion is equal to murder.

conserve

As a noun, a **conserve** is a medical or confectionary preparation of some part of a plant, preserved with sugar. As a verb, conserve means to keep in safety, to preserve in being, to keep alive. We are all these days being urged to conserve some animal or other that is nearing extinction.

consideration

If you act with **consideration**, then you are acting with thought for the feelings and attitudes of others. Giving up your seat to a pregnant lady on a bus or train is an example of consideration. But the word can also mean bestowing thought upon some problem. 'I gave the matter considerable consideration,' the chief inspector claimed. Equally a consideration can be something given in payment: 'Barry was good enough to mend my fence, so I gave him some of my apricot jam in consideration.' The word can also be a synonym for 'esteem': 'The Lord Mayor was held in great consideration.'

console

As a verb, **console** means to comfort or sympathise with. Hence I shall try to console you when you fail your driving test. As a noun, the word can mean three things. It is the keyboards and stops of an organ, a panel or unit accommodating a set of controls for electronic or mechanical equipment, or a type of bracket.

consonant

Two very different meanings here. A **consonant** is a letter that is not a vowel. Thus C, M and R are consonants, while A and E are not. However, if something is consonant, it sounds well with something else. Hence, while the violins playing alone made a consonant sound, it became even more so when the woodwind joined in.

consort

A **consort** is your companion or your spouse, a ship sailing in company with another, a small group of musicians playing together, or a verb meaning 'to habitually associate with someone'.

constitution

Unlike the USA and many other countries, Britain has no written **constitution**, that is a document laying down the fundamental principles to which the state is subject. However, unwritten though it may be, Britain does have a constitution made of laws and conventions. So does every country and the vast majority of large organisations. But 'constitution' is not limited to denoting organisational principles. It can be used to describe your general state of being: 'I'm afraid that my last pregnancy seems to have undermined my constitution.'

construction

A **construction** is an entity that is in the process of being built, whether this be a Lego model on the sitting room table or a grand hotel in the centre of town. But 'construction' need not be limited to physical, tangible things. We all construct beliefs and arguments out of abstract notions, and the construction of the English language, though it took centuries and is still being built, is a great deal less tangible than a Meccano set or a block of flats.

consul

Although today a **consul** is an official appointed by the state to live in a foreign city and protect the state's citizens and interests there, in ancient Rome a consul was an annually elected chief magistrate.

consummate

If you pronounce this word with the emphasis on the syllable 'sum', the word will mean 'perfect', 'sublime' or something equally praiseworthy. You might want to say that Maria Callas's performance as Gilda in Verdi's *Rigoletto* was **consummate**. On the other hand, on the day of your wedding, you might want to consummate your marriage by making love. Here the emphasis is on the 'con' – and the pun was accidental! Equally you might want to consummate (bring to an end) your period of being chairman of the Rotary Club by holding a grand dinner, or you might want to consummate your athletic career by winning the London marathon.

consumption

Your friend Horace may be an expert in the **consumption** of potato crisps. In other words, he eats them with astonishing avidity. The consumption of anything, be it potato crisps, bottles of Scotch or the coastline by the waves, means the disposal of or the disappearance of something. Hence the word has been transferred to describe a wasting disease of the human body: 'We were very sad when Vera died of consumption.'

content

If you are **content**, then you are perfectly satisfied with things as they are. The word indicates a state of being, not perhaps quite as satisfied as a happy state, but certainly a great deal better than a miserable state. The word can also refer to the items that work together to create a whole. You might say to a friend, 'You enjoyed Briggs's book, but what was its content?' 'Contents' is more common than 'content', but the latter is still current.

contest

If you witness a **contest**, you are watching a struggle, a battle for supremacy. This can range from a boxing match, an athletics meeting, a game of chess, a general election or a debate. However the word can also be used as a verb when you wish to challenge someone else's opinion: 'I contest your view that fox hunting is cruel.'

continent

Most of us learn at school that there are five continents: Africa, America, Asia, Australia and Europe. Hence a **continent** is a large land mass, and if you want to count ice as land, then you can include the Artic and Antarctic as being continents also. However, the word continent also signifies a mode of behaviour. Because you do not want to get fat, you can be very continent in your consumption of chocolate. Hence being continent means exercising great restraint over something or other, and the word is most generally used in connection with food or sex. Even more specifically, 'continent' is sometimes used to indicate your ability to control the movements of your bowels and bladder.

contrary

If you grew up knowing the nursery rhyme 'Mary, Mary, quite contrary', you will know that **contrary** means 'awkward, disobedient, contradictory' and similar perverse terms. But the word, much more neutrally, refers to an object, fact or quality that is the opposite of another. Thus to believe in democracy is contrary to also wishing to become dictator of the country.

control

As you know, if you **control** something, then you are in charge of it, able to dictate its movements. Hopefully you are always in control of your car; children and dogs are more difficult. 'Control' can also be a noun signifying the person or thing used as a standard of comparison. Thus, when designing a chemical experiment, you will have a control whose state can be measured against those elements being experimented upon. In addition, as many of us know from James Bond books or films, Control is a member of an intelligence service who personally directs the activities of a spy. Apparently a control in the game of bridge is a high card that prevents your opponents from establishing a particular suit.

convenience

This noun indicates the state of being able to proceed without difficulty: 'I was able to cross the market with convenience.' It is also an informal term for a public toilet.

convention

It has been decided to hold a large meeting for all those who are interested in making south Shropshire a National Park. It will be called the Ironbridge Convention. Hence a convention is a gathering of people to discuss some particular issue. But a convention can also be a written document. In our mythical Ironbridge Convention, the whole thing might result in the publication of the South Shropshire National Park Convention in which the rules for marking its new status are laid out. Equally a convention is the accepted way of doing things. In Britain and many other places it is a convention to shake hands with someone to whom you are introduced. In the game of bridge, a convention is a bid or system of bidding that tries to convey specific information to one's partner.

converse

If you **converse** with your friends, you talk to them. As you will have inferred, the word 'conversation' is closely related. Apart from conversation, it is possible to converse in an almost mystical sense. 'I went down to the lake to converse with God,' or 'When listening to Mozart I feel as if I was conversing with the eternal,' are both conceivable sentences. But if something is the converse of something else, then it is the opposite. Throwing bombs at your opponents seems the converse of negotiation.

conversion

This noun signifies the process of changing from one view to another. If you are a Christian and change to being a Buddhist, then that is a major **conversion**. On a much less metaphysical level, you might convert your loft into a bedroom. Equally, in the game of rugby, you might convert a try into a goal.

conviction

If you are apprehended after robbing a bank, you are likely to face a serious **conviction**, that is, a formal declaration by a judge or jury that you are guilty of a criminal offence. Very differently, you may have a strong conviction (i.e. belief) that the Sun moves round the Earth, and no physicist or astronomer can convince you otherwise.

convocation

In its general meaning, a **convocation** is an assembly of people. Hence you could hold a convocation in Leeds of all the people who wanted to support the city's bid to hold the Olympics in 2047. The word, however, certainly has two specific meanings. In the Church of England, a convocation is a provincial synod called together to deliberate on ecclesiastical matters, and Convocation is the legislative assembly of Oxford University.

convulsion

All three meanings of **convulsion** have things in common. Its medical meaning refers to a sudden, violent, irregular movement of the body, caused by the involuntary contraction of muscles. Geologically, a convulsion is an earthquake or other violent movement of the earth's crust. Politically, a convulsion is a violent social or political upheaval.

coo, coup

Doves and pigeons are said to **coo**, and human beings can make a similar softly murmuring noise, often when talking to a baby or in the arms of a loved one. A **coup** is an internal homonym of its own, and hence has its own entry.

cool

If something is **cool**, it is not very warm. Indeed, something cool is well on the way to becoming cold. Equally if you are cool to someone, you are not being very friendly. But the word is also used in a somewhat vague and ambiguous way as a term of approval. If you describe someone as 'cool', it implies that you admire them. If you play it cool, you adopt a somewhat arrogant and debonair approach to things. Or you can just utter 'Cool!' as an exclamation of approval and/or admiration. You can even use the word as a means of emphasis: 'He gave me a cool £10,000.'

coomb, comb, combe

These are all different spellings of the same word meaning a deep hollow or valley. However, **comb**, with a very different pronunciation, refers to a toothed implement with which one attempts to make one's hair tidy. Anything on a machine that also performs a similar function can also be referred to as a comb.

cop

In Britain **cop** can be a slang word for a policeman. It also means a conical mass of thread wound on to a spindle. As a verb, a cop is also what policemen attempt to do, namely, catch or arrest an offender: 'I shall cop you if you try to get into that orchard.' The word can also mean not very good at: 'He was not much cop at mathematics.'

cope

If you **cope** with running a home and bringing up three children, then you manage very well. 'To cope' is to succeed, to manage. But it is also an ecclesiastical vestment resembling a long cloak or the activity of paring the beak or talons of a hawk.

copper

For most of us, a **copper** is a colloquial term for a policeman, but it is also a metallic element, and an old pre-decimal term for a penny. Now rarely found, a copper also used to be a large copper or iron container for boiling clothes.

copse, cops

Both Collins *English Dictionary* and the *Shorter Oxford* tell me that **copse** is an alternative word for 'coppice', yet in my personal experience, I have often heard the word 'copse' used, but never 'coppice'. However, whatever their frequency of use, both words refer to a small wood. **Cops** as a verb means to capture or to be saddled with. Hence you can have sentences like 'I hope he cops the embezzler' meaning 'I hope he captures the embezzler', and 'I bet he cops all Andrew's work as well' meaning 'I bet he gets lumbered with all Andrew's work as well.' As a noun, 'cops' are policemen, an abbreviation of coppers.

copt, copped

A **copt** is (or was) a native Egyptian Christian belonging to the Jacobite sect of Monophysites, not an easy topic to bring into general conversation. If you are **copped** you are captured or apprehended, normally after committing some crime.

core *see* caw

corn

This word tends to be used as a generic term for cereal plants like wheat, maize and barley, though it is also a hardened spot that can develop on the hands or feet due to excessive pressure. **Corn** is also a slang term used to refer derisively to comic material that is old and well-used, and hence stale.

corner

When two objects meet at different angles, the space on the inside at the point of their meeting is called a **corner**. Hence, if you are in a room, the points at which the walls of that room meet are called corners. Normally the angle formed at the meeting point is a ninety-degree angle, though this is not always the case. When two roads meet at an angle, they too create a corner, and this is often convenient because it is easy to say to a friend, 'I'll meet you at the corner of Broad Street and Russell Avenue.' But a corner has at least four other meanings as well. You can take a corner in a game of football or hockey, so called because the ball is placed at one of the four corners of the pitch. You can create a corner in clarinets (or anything else) if you buy up all the existing clarinets in the country and hence then become the sole supplier. This is known as cornering the market. You can corner someone when you force him or her into a position from which there is no escape. You can even use a corner as a tool in book binding.

cornet

A **cornet** is a small, brass instrument that looks like a small trumpet and is played in exactly the same way. Trumpets you tend to find in orchestras, and cornets in brass bands. Cornet is also the name given to several organ stops, a kind of headdress formally worn by ladies, a piece of paper folded into a conical form and twisted at the apex, a conical wafer container for ice cream, and, in dress making, the cuff of a sleeve that opens like the large end of a trumpet or cornet.

coronet

This is a small or relatively simple crown, especially as worn by lesser royalty and peers or peeresses. It is also a ring of bone at the base of a deer's antler or the band of tissue on the lowest part of a horse's pastern.

corporal

Something is **corporal** if it is part of or pertains to the body. Thus corporal punishment is punishment on the body like a spanking or whipping, and our corporal needs (food, water, shelter, sex) are different from our spiritual needs (art, music, poetry or whatever). A corporal is also a non-commissioned military officer ranked just below a sergeant in the army, and a superior petty officer who attends to police matters in the navy. In a Christian service, a corporal is the white cloth upon which the consecrated elements are placed.

corporation

There are three possible meanings for **corporation**. It can be a large company or group of companies that are authorised to act as a single entity. It can also refer to the group of people who have been elected to govern a city, town or borough. It is also a semi-jocular reference to the stomach.

corps see caw

correspond

If you **correspond** with a friend, you write letters to him or her. But the word can also mean 'be similar to', 'be the equivalent' or 'match'. 'The President of the USA does not really correspond to the President of the YHA because their power and duties are so different.'

cosign, cosine

If you **cosign** something, you are merely signing a document that has already been signed by someone else. A **cosine** is simply the sine of the complement of a given angle.

cosy

As an adjective, **cosy** conveys a feeling of comfort and warmth: 'I settled into my cosy den.' As a noun, a cosy is a cover to keep a teapot or boiled egg warm.

cottage

Most of us think of a **cottage** as being a small dwelling place, often in the countryside. However, the word has more recently been used as a verb to signify the process of homosexuals procuring partners or, as a noun, the public toilet where such encounters often take place. There are also cottage hospitals, cottage flats, cottage loaves, cottage industries and cottage pies.

cotton

While **cotton** is a white fibrous material obtained from the cotton plant and used in the making of clothes, you can also cotton on to something in the sense that you come to understand it.

couch

As a noun, a **couch** is a long upholstered piece of furniture on which two or three people may sit. It is also a coarse grass with long creeping roots. As a verb, it can mean 'to bed down' or 'to lie down', and 'to express oneself': 'As I couched down on the grass, I then couched my belief that the country is a finer place to live than the town.' There is also the common expression 'couch potato' which denotes someone who takes little or no exercise and watches a lot of television.

council, counsel

A **council** is an assembly of people devoted to running an organisation. Thus you have county councils devoted to providing services for the inhabitants of that council, parish councils devoted to matters at a very local level, church councils discussing the appointment of a new vicar for St Mary's, and so on. The word **counsel** has two main meanings which are the obverse of each other. If you seek counsel (a noun) you are seeking advice and guidance. If you counsel (a verb) someone, you are providing advice and guidance.

count, Count

Most of us learn to **count** at school. It is the process of determining the number of objects or aspects: three chairs, six cups, seven thoughts. Proverbially, one also counts one's blessings, counts sheep when suffering from insomnia, and counts to ten in order to recover one's composure. Yet the word is also used to indicate significance: 'Tom doesn't really count for much in this affair.' Meanwhile count is a European title of nobility that is approximately equal to the English title of earl.

counter

Almost self-evidently, a **counter** is someone who counts, but it is also a small flat circular object used in many children's games like ludo or snakes and ladders. In addition, most shops have a counter, a flat-topped barrier between the customers and the shop assistants and to which the customer goes to be served. In addition, a counter can be the curved part of a ship's stern or that part of a horse's breast which lies between the shoulders and under the neck. Counter can also be an adverb signifying opposition: 'I am counter to this proposal, believing that it will wreck golf in Aberdeen for generations.' In this oppositional sense, counter also forms the prefix of many words (countermine, counteract, countermand), though there are even more words where 'counter' as a prefix has the sense more of balance than of opposition: counterpoise, counterpoint, countervail.

country

While a **country** is a political and administratively independent area of land like France, China or Bolivia, it is also an adjective that is the opposite of urban. People go into the country to enjoy the grass, trees, plants and birds, natural objects that are sparse in the cities and towns.

coup *see* coo

couple

This word is almost a synonym of 'two'. Thus we might talk about a **couple** of dogs, a couple of houses, or a married couple. We can even use the word as a verb, so if we couple a pair of dogs, we link or chain them together in some way. As a verb, the word can also be used to indicate sexual intercourse. In dynamics, the word is used to indicate a pair of equal and parallel forces acting in opposite directions.

course *see* coarse

court

A **court** is a clear space enclosed by walls or other buildings, a place where the sovereign of a country is residing, or a place in which justice is administered. As a verb, the word means the process of seeking to attract someone's attention ('I must court Perkins & Co. because they could lead to some useful contracts') or to indicate amorous intent ('I must court Rosie Lee because she has captured my heart'). The word also precedes a remarkable number of other words: court card, court circular, court dress, court hand, court martial, court of honour, court of love, court plaster and so on.

cove

This is a slang word for a man carrying with it a suggestion of a somewhat lower class and less than honest man. It is possibly derived from the Romany word *kova* which means 'thing' or 'person'. A **cove** is also a small bay or inlet at the seaside or even a hollow in a rock or hillside. In architecture a cove is a concave arch or vault.

cover

If you **cover** something, you place something over it so as to protect it from dirt, the weather or from being seen. But you might also decide to cover a particular subject, in which case you decide to study or expound upon a particular topic: 'Tonight at evening class we covered the Treaty of Versailles.' You can also cover a stretch of land in the sense that you travelled over it.

covert

If you are **covert** about something, you are secretive, possibly even underhand. 'The Foreign Secretary was very covert about his meetings with his French opposite number.' Yet a covert also signifies the feathers that cover the bases of the wing and tail feathers of a bird.

cow

As we all know, a **cow** is a bovine farm animal that in life provides milk and in death provides beef. The word is also used in mining to describe a kind of self-acting brake, and is a slang word to depict a disagreeable woman. As a verb, if you cow someone you intimidate them, you make them feel afraid and ashamed.

cowl, cowle

Monks often wear a garment that has a **cowl**, namely a hood. A chimney may also have a cowl placed over it in order to aid ventilation. A cowl may also be a tub, one normally used for carrying water. A **cowle** is an Anglo-Indian word meaning an engagement, lease or grant in writing.

cox, Cox *see* cocks

coy

A **coy** can be a shortening of the word 'decoy', a lobster trap, or an adjective meaning shy, reserved or retiring. In the final sense, the word has gained immortality through Marvell's wonderful poem 'To My Coy Mistress'.

crab

A **crab** is the general term for any decapod crustaceous animal. In Britain many of them are found at the seashore. In astrology the crab is the symbol for the star sign Cancer. It is also a type of wild apple, a louse that infests the human body, an anglicised name for a South American tree, or a small capstan. In music there is an entity called a crab canon, a musical work where the imitating voice repeats the notes of the theme in reverse order. The name stems from the mistaken belief that crabs walk backwards.

crack

If you hear a **crack**, you hear a sudden and sharp noise like the crack of a rifle, the crack of thunder or the crack of a whip. If you crack something you either break it or you solve the puzzle that it presented. Thus you can crack a cup by hitting it against the tap, or you can crack a criminal case by proving that it was Ethel Sprogget who committed the murder. (If there are any real Ethel Sproggets in the world, I apologise.) You can also crack a joke where 'crack' means 'tell', smoke crack where 'crack' means an illegal drug, crack up where 'crack' means to disintegrate either physically or mentally, or step on a crack where 'crack' means a tear or fissure in the floor or road. The word can even be a synonym for excellent. Hence you can be a crack shot or belong to a crack regiment.

crackling

You can hear the **crackling** of wood as the logs burn on the fire. You can hear the crackling of paper as you crumple the newspaper. In this sense, crackling is just the action of the verb 'to crackle'. But crackling is also the crisp skin or rind of roast pork, and some people love to eat the crackling.

craft, kraft

A **craft** is an occupation or hobby that requires skill or ability. The word is normally used in connection with physical skills like the craft of a potter or a wood carver. An aeroplane or ship can also be referred to as a craft, and Freemasonry is known as the Craft. **Kraft**, on the other hand, is strong wrapping paper made from a pulp processed with a sulphate solution.

crake

This word is a dialect word for the crow or raven, but is also a verb meaning to utter a harsh grating sound.

cram

If you **cram** a suitcase full of clothes, you have packed the case very tightly, leaving room for no additions. The word is a homonym because you can also cram for exams, in which case, you fill your mind with knowledge until it almost overflows. You can also, of course, cram food into your mouth.

cramp

A **cramp** is a portable tool that can be used for securing things together. If you park in an illegal place, you car may have a cramp affixed to it so as to secure it to the road. You may use a cramp to hold your holiday photographs together. But cramp is also a violent and painful contraction of the muscles, a condition that often occurs during running or other exercise. You can also cramp someone else by your very presence. For instance, your normal cheerful quick wit might turn into silent moroseness if you attend a dinner where the lady or man that you yearn for is also present. In other words, he or she has cramped your style.

crane

A **crane** is a large machine used for lifting, carrying and lowering objects that are too heavy for men to lift. It is also a bird noted for its long legs, neck and bill. It is also possible to crane your neck as you attempt to see something that is not quite in your range of vision. In this case, you bend and stretch your neck in an effort to see.

crank

In all its uses, **crank** carries the concept of something twisted or bent. Hence in motor mechanics, a crank is a portion of the axis bent at right angles. In bell hanging, a crank is an elbow-shaped device that changes the direction of a bell wire. Crank is also a slang term for an eccentric person. The term is also used for a poorly balanced boat, one that is likely to capsize.

crash

A **crash** always signifies the collapse or destruction of something, but there is a considerable difference between a car crash when the car concerned hits another car and is damaged beyond repair, and a financial crash when investors lose money because of a downturn in the Stock Market. Equally a computer can crash when it suddenly decides to stop working, Manchester United can crash out of the FA Cup when they are heavily defeated by Crewe Alexandra, and a business can crash when it becomes bankrupt.

cratch

This can be a disease in the feet of horses or sheep, or a rack or crib to hold the fodder for cattle. The word can also be applied to a wooden grating or hurdle.

crater, krater

Most of us tend to think of craters as the bowl-like openings of volcanoes, out of which pour the smoke and red-hot lava, but the word **crater** can be applied to almost any bowl-shaped hollow. Thus you have craters on the moon, and the explosion of a bomb or mine can create a crater. The word is also used for the cavity formed in the positive carbon of an arc light in the course of combustion. An Internet source also tells me that **krater** is an ancient Greek jar, but I am unable to find the word in the *OED* or anything else.

craze, Crays

Most of us know what it is to have a **craze** for something. One has an almost obsessive passion for something, be it the songs of the latest pop star, studying the Basque language, or taking part in cycle races. Crazes of this nature tend to be common among the young, and most of us become more controlled as we grow older. Entirely differently, one can craze a plate, cup or pot. You accidentally knock a plate against the tap when rinsing it, and a minute crack elongates itself across the plate. That is a craze, and you have crazed the plate. **Crays**, of course, shouldn't really appear in this book because it is a proper name, the name given to an extremely powerful supercomputer. I liked the Internet source that defined 'craze' as the sensation needed to buy more than one supercomputer.

creak, creek

If you hear a **creak**, you hear the sort of noise that is made by the unoiled hinges of a door, or the floorboards moving slightly as you cross the floor. A **creek** makes a very different noise because it is a small stream or a narrow inlet in the coastline.

cream

The more oily part of milk that gathers at the top of the vessel holding the milk is called the **cream**, and it is this portion of the milk that is converted into butter. Any paint that is the same colour as milk cream is called cream paint, and if you want to select the most outstanding people for some project, you are said to cream off the intake. Hence cream has come to signify the richest and worthiest of a group as in 'John Keats gives us the cream of romantic poetry.'

crease

If you **crease** a blouse or a shirt, you put a fold or wrinkle upon it. Indeed, it is in order to remove creases that we iron clothes after they have been washed. The crease is also a small area just in front of the stumps on a cricket field. Those who know the rules of cricket will also know exactly what I mean, and those who do not know the rules of cricket won't care anyway. The crease is also the area around the goal in a game of lacrosse or ice hockey. Apparently, as a verb, you can also crease a horse by stunning it through firing a shot in the crest or ridge of its neck. This does not sound like a friendly action.

credit

As a noun, **credit** can refer to the reputation or esteem in which someone is held: 'William Bishop is held in great credit in this town.' Equally the word can be synonymous with 'belief': 'It was beyond credit.' Financially, it is possible for you to be in credit, that is, have money in your bank account.

creep

You can also gain a credit by completing part of your university course, a credit that contributes to your final class of degree. As a verb, you can credit an amount to someone's account, or you can barely credit what you have just heard.

creep

If you **creep** around, you move in a slow stealthy fashion. Hence snakes and slugs are said to creep, and because snakes and slugs tend not to be our favourite animals, if we describe a human being as creeping, we tend to regard him as being nefarious or criminal. From that has come the slang word 'creep' to unflatteringly describe a human being, though it has nothing necessarily to do with his or her mode of movement.

crepitation

This is a cracking or rattling sound, often applied to the sound made when breathing with an inflamed lung. However, in entomology it refers to the explosive ejection of irritant fluid from the abdomen of a bombardier beetle.

crescent

This word refers to a shape, the curved shape of the waxing or waning moon, or the curved line of a street. It is also the name of a butterfly or moth that has crescent-shaped markings on its wings.

crest

You reach the **crest** of a hill when you reach the top. The top of a sea wave is also termed its crest. Your coat of arms, should you have one, can also be termed your crest, as can a tuft of feathers or fur on the head of a bird or animal.

crew

A **crew** is the complement of men in charge of a ship, but it is also an adjective to describe a haircut, the crew cut, adopted by men in the 1940s and 1950s. The hair is closely cropped and brushed upright.

crewed, crude

'The ship was **crewed** by men from Nigeria.' In other words, 'crewed' is the past tense of the verb 'to crew' and refers to the men and women staffing a ship. The word **crude** either means something not yet fully finished or thought out – 'My high-jumping technique is still fairly crude' – or refers to speech, writing or behaviour that is ill-mannered, rough, blasphemous and sexually explicit.

crewel, cruel

A **crewel** is a thin, worsted yarn used for tapestry and embroidery. If you are **cruel**, you enjoy inflicting pain and are merciless.

crews, cruise

The men and women who look after a ship while it is at sea are known as the crew of the ship. Obviously **crews** is the plural of 'crew'. A **cruise** refers to a trip by ship, normally for pleasure. Hence you can enjoy a cruise round the Greek islands or to the West Indies.

crib

A **crib** is a small bed for a child, normally with barred sides, a receptacle for animal food, a cabin, a framework of timber in a coal mine to prevent the coal shaft from caving in, the cards thrown out and given to the dealer in the game of cribbage, or the action of stealing someone's else work and passing it off as your own.

cricket

A **cricket** is an insect of the genus *Acheta*, or a game played between sides of eleven with rules that make calculus appear easy, and tactics that make philosophy appear simple. The game is popular in Britain, Australia, the West Indies, India, Pakistan and South Africa, and is totally ignored by the rest of the world. Devotees of cricket tend to confuse it with religion.

crimp

The most common current usage of the verb **crimp** is to signify a process of squeezing one's hair into plaits or folds. It also means the activity of causing the flesh of fish to become firm by gnashing it before rigor mortis sets in. It is also the name of an obsolete game of cards.

crisp

Like 'crimp', **crisp** can refer to the hair, in which case it signifies tight curls or a frizzy appearance. Some food too can be 'crisp', food like toast or bacon, in which a hard brittleness is indicated. There is even a food called 'crisps' comprising very thin and brittle potato segments. The weather too can be crisp when it is cool, fresh and invigorating, and you can speak in a crisp manner when you are being decisive and matter-of-fact.

critical

This adjective can certainly lead to misunderstanding. When you are being **critical** of a book, painting, person, *et al.*, you are not necessarily giving an adverse judgement on the entity in question. You are merely analysing it and trying to provide a balanced view. But in the real world, 'critical' now so often implies an adverse judgement that the original meaning is probably now beyond salvation. However, if someone is critical in hospital, it does not mean that they are complaining about the nursing staff, it means that they are close to death. Equally the word 'critical' is often used when a situation has reached crisis point and will shortly crash into disaster or possibly recover and move back to normality.

crocodile

This is large predatory semi-aquatic reptile. Its skin can be used to make crocodile shoes, purses, etc. The word is also used to describe a line of school children walking in pairs.

crook

Basically a **crook** is a staff or stick with a hook at one end. Crooks can be used for assistance in walking, and traditionally shepherds have them as they wander round the fields tending their sheep. A crook is also the pastoral staff of a bishop, the spiritual shepherd. However, a crook is also a dishonest person, someone who habitually breaks the law.

crop

This is another of many English words which have a surprising number of internal homonyms. First of all, a **crop** is the pouch-like enlargement of the gullet that you see in many birds. It is there that the food a bird swallows is digested. A crop is also a whip, and passes easily into the verb form so that if you know that you are about to be cropped, you are likely to be very apprehensive. The crop is also the total amount of vegetable produce that you can gather from a particular field or farm. Thus you might hear a farmer say, 'We had a good crop of wheat this year, but the sugar beet crop was disappointing.' As a verb, crop can also signify to reap a field, to cut one's hair, or to cut the heads off some plants.

cross

The **cross** is a major religious symbol because it was the object to which Jesus Christ was nailed to suffer his prolonged and painful death. A cross is also a symbol like this ✗, normally used in school exercise books to indicate that something is incorrect. One can cross, or alienate, a colleague, cross the road and also be cross in the sense of being annoyed or angry. The word is also a frequent prefix to indicate movement across: cross-breed, cross-channel, cross-index, crossroad, crosstalk, etc.

crotchet

A **crotchet** is a note of music which is half the length of a minim and twice the length of a quaver. On the page, it has a thin stem with a round black head at one end. You may also have a crotchet when you have some bizarre notion about something. Some people have a crotchet about unidentified flying objects, fairies at the bottom of the garden, whether politicians are genetically programmed to lie or whether the skill develops naturally, and so on.

crow

This is quite a large black bird of the genus *Corvus*, a bar of iron with one end slightly bent and shaped into a beak, or the action of exulting over some triumph or someone else's misfortune. It is not regarded as acceptable to crow over the latter, but many of us do.

crown

Most of us know that a **crown** is the bejewelled and ornamental headdress worn by kings and queens, but it is a number of other things as well. When you reach the crown of a hill, you have reached the top. Equally the crown of your head is the top of the head. The part of the tooth projecting from the gum is called the crown. There also used to be a British coin called a crown, and some are still minted for commemorative purposes.

crude *see* crewed

crunch

This verb is frequently used to signify the eating of something hard and brittle. Hence you crunch a biscuit or a crisp, but cannot crunch a jelly or soft cake. It is also used to indicate the prolonged processing of data by a computer: 'A 64-bit computer can crunch data at an incredible speed.' As a noun, **crunch** can denote the crucial point in a situation: 'When it comes to the crunch, we will have to make more toffee apples.'

crush

If you **crush** something, you deform it, you push it inwards with such force that it is pulverised: 'The man was crushed to death by the lorry.' The word can also be used to indicate emotional or intellectual collapse: 'Susan was crushed by Steven's rejection of her invitation'; 'I will crush Paul's invalid arguments in the debate.' As a noun, a crush can be a drink made from the juice of pressed fruit, a crowd of people pressed closely together, or an intense infatuation for someone.

crust

This is always the outer, hard surface of something, but it can be applied to so many objects that it becomes a homonym almost by default. Thus the crust of a loaf is very different from the crust of the Earth. It is also used metaphorically in the expression 'I've been earning my crust.'

cub

The **cub** is the name given to the young of many animals like the lion, bear and fox. It is also a stall or pen for cattle, and a junior member of the Boy Scouts.

cue, queue, Kew, Q

When you are acting in a play, and you are supposed to say, 'How fares your grace?' when the other character on the stage has said, 'And aroint thee, witch, aroint thee,' then 'aroint thee' is your **cue**. In other words, a cue is the signal for you then to do something. In the hundred metres, a bang of a gun is your cue for starting to run like mad. It may be that the end of the *Ten o'Clock News* is your cue for going to bed. But a cue is also a long, thin rod used for hitting balls in the games of billiards and snooker. A **queue** can also be long, because it is a line of people waiting for a bus to arrive or to be served in a shop. Queues have been described as a British disease because, it is claimed, we do far more queuing than any other nation. As for **Kew**, it is an area on the western outskirts of London and famous for its gardens which are accessible by the public. **Q** is the seventeenth letter of the English alphabet.

cuff

The end of the sleeve of a jacket, shirt or blouse is frequently referred as being the **cuff**. It is often decorated in some way with a button or decoration. A cuff can also be an inflatable bag wrapped round the arm when blood pressure is measured. If, however, you cuff someone, you strike them with your hand.

culm

This is anthracitic slack from the Welsh collieries, or the stem of a plant, especially the jointed stalk of grasses.

culture

This word comes from the Latin *colere* meaning 'to tend, to cultivate', and all the meanings of **culture** can be seen to stem from that origin. Thus if you have a culture of bacteria, you are deliberately tending these bacteria for scientific purposes. If you talk about the culture of the French (or any other nation) you are talking about the ideas, customs and social behaviour that have been cultivated over time. If you are interested in culture (i.e. art, literature, music), then you are interested in human activities that have developed over time and have resulted in works capable of providing immense pleasure. You may, as a result, be scornfully termed a culture vulture.

cum *see* come

currant, current

A **currant** is a small berry that can be eaten raw or else put into sponges and puddings to add taste. If something is **current**, then it is of the present, something that exists or is relevant now. But the word also refers to the passage of an electric charge – 'Is there any current going through this wire?' – and to a moving body of water – 'The current in the river is very strong.'

curry

As we all know, **curry** is a meat, vegetable or fish dish served with a sauce that makes it very assertive and hot to the mouth. As a verb, however, you can curry a horse by rubbing it down with a comb, you can curry tanned leather by soaking and beating it, and you can curry favour by behaving in a flattering and cajoling manner.

curser, cursor

A **curser** is someone who curses. A **cursor** is an on-screen positional indicator apparent mostly these days on the monitor of a computer.

cut

If you **cut** yourself, you make a thin opening in your skin with a knife, razor, thorn or rock, and normally release some blood. If you cut a scene from a film, you remove it. If you cut a sponge cake, you use a knife to divide the cake into smaller portions to be eaten. If you cut prices in your shop, you lower them. If you cut a pack of cards, you divide them into two roughly equal parts. If you cut a tooth, then you suffer the pain of the tooth slowly pushing its way through your gum in order to become a fully functioning tooth. If you cut a ball in cricket, you hit the ball with an almost lateral bat. If you cut someone short, you interrupt them. If you just cut someone, you refuse to acknowledge their presence. So, as you can see, 'cut' has a wide range of idiomatic uses, some of which are very disparate in meaning.

cutter

A **cutter** is someone who cuts, normally a dressmaker, a carver, a sculptor or one who castrates animals. A cutter is also a relatively small boat.

cygnet, signet

A **cygnet** is a young swan. A **signet** is an authenticating seal often contained in a ring.

cymbal, symbol

A **cymbal** is a member of the percussion family and comprises two brass circular plates that are banged together. A **symbol** is something that stands for or represents something else. Hence St George is said to be a symbol of England; in Dickens's novel *Bleak House*, the fog is often taken as a symbol of the confusing and prolonged court case with which the novel is concerned; and the stars-and-stripes flag is a symbol of the USA.

D

D, d

D is the fourth letter of the English alphabet, corresponding to the Greek delta and the Hebrew daleth. It represents a musical key, and is an abbreviation for 'doctor' in academic degrees like D. Phil. The letter also denotes the second lowest earning category for marketing purposes, as well a not very good academic grading. A D notice sent to newspapers and the media generally forbids their handling certain security information. A semi-circle marked on a snooker table is called the D, and d denotes the fourth file on a chessboard. Before Britain adopted decimal coinage, the *d.* was the symbol for pennies (£3 10s. 6d.), and d is an abbreviation in a number of different contexts.

dab

If you **dab** something, you give it a gentle blow or tap, normally with a soft substance. Hence you may dab your mouth with your napkin. But the dab is also a species of small flat-fish, and it is also possible for a person to be a dab hand at something or other. If you are a dab hand at finding information on the Internet, then you are skilled at that activity and can often find things more quickly than your peers. The word can also mean 'a small amount' as in 'She licked a dab of chocolate from her finger.'

dada

This is a young child's attempt to come to grips with the word 'daddy', and, through generations of hearing infants call '**Dada**', has become an accepted word on its own. In Indian English, however, in direct descent from the Hindi *dada*, 'dada' signifies an older brother or a male cousin. There is also, of course, the early twentieth-century movement in art, literature, music and film that was called the Dada movement.

dado

If you decorate a room and have the lower part of the walls decorated differently from the upper parts, then the lower section is called the **dado**. In North America, though, a dado is a groove cut in the face of a board, into which the edge of another board is fixed. In architecture, a dado is the part of a pedestal between the base and the cornice.

dag

The *Shorter Oxford* gives fourteen definitions of **dag**, and although some of these are now obsolete, it still seems an excessive number for a word that most of us have never used. A dag is one of the locks of wool clotted with dirt that you often find on the hinder parts of a sheep, and if you dag a sheep, you cut its dags away. A dag is also the simple straight pointed horn of a young stag, and a dialect word meaning 'to sprinkle' or 'to drizzle'. In Australia the word can denote either a conservative and unfashionable person or an entertainingly eccentric one.

dagger

A **dagger** is a short knife with a pointed end and sharp blade. You may recall that Macbeth was troubled with visions of the dagger that he had used to kill Duncan. There is also a dagger moth, so called because it has a dagger-shaped marking on its forewing. Since daggers were once common enough for people to carry one around as a matter of course, it is not surprising that they have entered into the world of common clichés. Thus you can be at daggers drawn with an opponent, or you can look daggers at someone who has offended you. The word probably derives from the Middle English verb *dag* which meant to pierce or stab.

dam, damn

A **dam** is most often thought of as being a structure designed to prevent the flow of a river or stream and consequently secure the creation of a reservoir. The word has also been borrowed in both mining and smelting when a partition has been needed to keep things separate from one another. A dam is also a female parent, though the word is more commonly applied to animals than to humans. **Damn** is a common swear word to indicate annoyance or condemnation. You might say, 'Well, I'll be damned,' in order to express surprise. You equally might say that something is not worth a damn when you mean that it is worthless. In theology, of course, to damn something is to ensure that the person or object in question goes on to suffer eternal punishment, a concept that religions of love seem quaintly attached to.

damage

To **damage** something or someone is to injure, spoil or harm the object in question. Thus a strong wind may damage some houses, a high tide might damage some sea chalets, and the fists of a drunken oaf might damage your face. In law, though, the damage is the value estimated in money of something lost or withheld, or the sum claimed or awarded in compensation for any loss or injury sustained.

dame

A **dame** is a woman, but there is a marked difference between someone who is a dame because she has been awarded the title of Knight Commander for services to the community, and a dame who is a comic character, usually played by a man, in a pantomime.

damp

If something is **damp**, then it is wet, though not excessively so. Thus the grass on your lawn may still be damp several hours after the last rainfall. But damp can also be a verb and a noun. Most pianos have a damp that serves to reduce or stop the vibrations of a piano string. You may also want to damp down the blazing fire in your hearth, that is, reduce the flow of air to the fire.

damper

Fairly obviously, **damper** can just be the comparative version of 'damp': 'This tea towel is damper than the other.' As a noun, however, 'damper' can mean any of six things. It can be a device for reducing mechanical vibrations in a car or lorry. It can be a pad for reducing the string vibrations in a piano. It can be a moveable metal plate in a flue or chimney used to regulate the draught of air. It can be a conductor used to reduce oscillation in an electric motor or generator. It can be a person, thing or comment that has the effect of casting a shadow over a meeting. Hence you might be at a tea party and discover that Mark's comment about Nichola's examination results cast a damper on the conversation. Finally, in Australia, it can refer to an unleavened loaf or cake.

dan

This is a small buoy supporting a pole which bears a flag by day and lamp by night. It is used as a mark in deep-sea fishing. A **dan** is also, in some localities, a small truck or sledge used to carry coal in coal mines. In judo you can mark your progress by successively gaining a higher dan; there are ten in all. The word 'dan' also used to be a title meaning 'sir' or 'master', and you can occasionally encounter it in sixteenth-century poetry.

dander

If you get in a **dander**, you lose your temper. But 'dander' can also be flakes of skin in an animal's fur or hair. Equally you can go for a dander, namely, a stroll.

dandy

Someone who dresses elegantly and fashionably can be called a **dandy**. There is a tendency for people who are so concerned with outward display to be vacuous in the extreme, but, perhaps surprisingly, this is far from being a universal rule. A dandy is also a relatively small boat, and a dialect word for a bantam cock. There are also some Anglo-Indian uses of the word to describe a boatman on the Ganges, or a hammock-type object in which you can be carried by two other men.

dane, deign

A **Dane** is someone who comes from Denmark, or a breed of dog. Presumably it is possible to be both at the same time. The verb 'to **deign**' indicates that you do something or speak to someone despite its being beneath your dignity to do so normally. Hence you may deign to do the washing up even though that is normally the housemaid's job.

dart

A **dart** is a small object with feathers at one end and a sharp protruding point at the other. This mini-missile is then thrown at a dartboard, which is divided into numbered sections, and the resulting score is then deducted from some mystic number like 301 or 501, and the first person to reach zero is the winner. This 'sport' is frequently shown on television, presumably as an aid to insomniacs. The word is also transferred to other objects that resemble a dart. The sting of a venomous insect or the dart-like organ in some gastropods may provide examples. A less bellicose example of the word occurs in dressmaking where a dart is the seam joining the two edges left by cutting a gore in the fabric. 'Dart' can also be a verb when it means to run or move somewhere suddenly and rapidly: 'She darted across the street.' In the late twentieth century, Dublin people used to speak contemptuously about 'the dart accent', the affectedly British accent adopted by some middle-class people in the area. In fact, 'dart' was an acronym for 'Dublin Area Rapid Transit'.

dash

If you **dash** to the post office, you get there as quickly as you can. If you dash a plate to the floor, you throw it there in anger or irritation, thereby smashing it. If you insert a dash in your writing like this – you break up the writing for the purposes of clarity or emphasis. If you dash something off, you do the task in a considerable hurry.

dassie

This is the name given to the hyrax, especially the rock hyrax of southern Africa. It is also the name of a silvery marine fish with dark fins.

date

This is the fruit of the date-palm, an oblong single-seeded berry, growing in clusters with a sweet pulp. The **date** is also the identification of a specific year or day. This dictionary entry was written on 22 February 2006. Equally you can arrange a date with someone, namely an arrangement to meet that person at a particular time on a particular day. Such meetings are often with someone with whom you have some romantic interest. Hence, on the date of 16 July, you may buy some dates to share with your date.

dawn

Early every morning you can witness the **dawn** as the sun slowly banishes the darkness of night and another working day begins. But because dawn is the first appearance of light in the sky just before sunrise, it not unnaturally has been used figuratively as well as literally. Hence the truth of something can suddenly dawn on you, and you are at the beginning of a new view of the world. A particular historical period can be called the Dawn of Something-or-other. Hence you might called the 1830s in Britain the dawn of the railway age, or claim, more dubiously, that the sealing of Magna Carta in 1215 marked the dawn of democracy.

day

Since a **day** is simply a period of time comprising 24 hours, there seems no point whatsoever in placing this word in a dictionary of homonyms. Yet, if one thinks for a moment, one realises that a day is not necessarily confined to those 24 hours. One can talk, for instance, of the day of Stone Age man, and here one is not talking about 24 hours but hundreds of years. Today we live in the day of the computer. Hence 'day' can become an emblematic word summing up an entire age in terms of its most striking feature.

days, daze

A day is a period of time that lasts 24 hours, and **days** is the simple plural of this word. Hence you may go on holiday for 14 days. If, however, you are in a **daze**, you are likely to be barely conscious, either because your next-door neighbour has just hit you on the head with his spade or because you have just woken up from a long sleep and are not yet fully conscious. Equally you can be dazed by a strong light or the sun, in which case you can barely see anything. However you can also be in a daze because you are suffering from an emotional or intellectual shock. Hence you can be dazed by the beauty of Muriel or dazed when you hear that the Prime Minister of Britain has just sold the British Isles to the USA.

dead

In a literal sense, plants, animals and humans are **dead** when they no longer have any sensations and no biological processes that previously sustained life. But one can also be figuratively dead. You might be dead to the magnificence of Mahler's music or to the mastery of Cézanne. In a ball game, when the ball is ejected from the field of play, it becomes dead. When you turn off the television, the screen becomes dead. If Saturn has no living matter upon it, then the planet is called a dead planet even though it continues to circle round the sun. The middle of the night is called the dead of night. So, as you can see, 'dead' is widely used in a variety of metaphorical contexts.

deal

When you are in the process of playing cards with someone, it may be your turn to **deal** the cards, that is, distribute the cards equally to all the participating players. Equally you may make a business transaction with someone, and this can be called a deal. You may buy something cheaply from a shop, and the shopkeeper may say, 'You have got a good deal there.' As a trade union official, you have to deal with both the members of your union and with management. The wood of fir or pine trees is often known as deal. Hence this four-letter word can mean distributing playing cards, making a mutually beneficial business arrangement, purchasing a bargain, interacting with people, or be a piece of wood. It is quite difficult to deal with such multifarious meanings.

dean, dene

A **dean** is an official position in some organisation. Thus you can be a dean in charge of some monks in a monastery, an officer in an Oxford or Cambridge university college, or, indeed, a senior member of almost any organisation. But a dean is also the deep, narrow and wooded vale of a rivulet, and as such is often spelt **dene**. However, a bare sandy tract or low sandhill by the sea is always spelt 'dene', and in that case the word has come from a Germanic origin and is related to 'dune'.

dear, deer

Most of us begin our letters '**Dear** Emily' or 'Dear Mr Snodgrass', in which case the word 'dear' is simply a polite and courteous convention. If someone really is dear to us, we like and esteem them considerably. Paradoxically, if something else is dear, that is because it is expensive. Hence, if you bought Brenda a bottle of perfume, you might say, 'The scent was very dear, but then Brenda is very dear to me.' 'Dear' can also be used as an exclamation of regret: 'Oh dear, I've forgotten my purse.' The word **deer** is simple in comparison, since a deer is simply a member of the family of ruminant quadrupeds distinguished by having antlers on their heads.

debug

One can literally **debug** oneself or one's clothing by removing all the insects that one can find. Inhabitants of Belfast or Birmingham or Bradford normally have no need to do this, but those working in the countryside or the Amazon jungle will find that it becomes a necessity. Equally one can debug a room by spraying pesticide within it. Interestingly though, the word 'debug' has also been taken over by the IT world, and if you debug a computer program, you remove all the coding errors that it contains.

decade

Most of us doubtless think of a **decade** as being a period of ten years, but the word also means each of the five divisions of each chapter of the rosary, and a range of electrical resistances, frequencies or other quantities spanning from one to ten times a base value.

deck

Many of us have walked on the **deck** of a ship, that platform or floor that extends across the width of a ship. However, you can also deck yourself in the sense of clothing yourself: 'I must deck myself out in my finest gear for this ball tonight.' People also talk about the deck of their audio equipment, and a DJ might even be handling several decks. A pack of playing cards is also often called a deck of cards: 'But, while he thought to steal the single ten,/ The king was slyly finger'd from the deck' (Shakespeare, *Henry VI, Part 3*).

declaration

A **declaration** is a formal statement or announcement. Two of the most famous are the Declaration of Rights of 1689 which established the joint monarchy of William and Mary, and the Declaration of Independence of 1776 which declared the breaking away from British rule of the thirteen American states. In addition, in the game of cricket, if the side that is batting decides that it has scored enough runs, then it will issue a declaration announcing that its innings is now at an end.

declension

If something is in a state of **declension**, then it is in the process of decay. You can also in Latin and other inflected languages have a declension for each noun in the language where the noun takes a different form depending upon whether it is the subject of the sentence, the object, a genitive part and so on.

decompose

We normally think of **decompose** as referring to the process of going rotten. We all decompose when we die in that the cells of our body break down until eventually our physical form has disappeared and we have dissolved into gases and earth. Clearly the same thing happens to all living things. For the chemist in the lab, something similar happens when he or she decomposes a substance, because the substance concerned is broken down into simpler constituents. Thus salt (sodium choride) could be broken down into sodium and chorine. In mathematics too a number or a function can be decomposed into simpler elements.

decompression

When there is a reduction in the air pressure, you experience a state of **decompression**. Thus a diver at the bottom of the sea will be experiencing high pressure while he is down there. As he slowly rises to the surface, he experiences decompression. In the computer world, data is often compressed so that it takes up less space on the hard disk. However, for humans to use this data, it has to be expanded to its original size. This process is known as decompression. As you can see, in all instances there is a similar process taking place, but the contexts and materials are so different that we have to include decompression as an internal homonym.

decorate

You may decide to **decorate** the house, that is paint the window frames, put on fresh wallpaper, pebble-dash the outside walls, and so on. To decorate something is to make it look more attractive. If, however, you decorate a serviceman, you present him with a medal for outstanding service in one of the armed forces.

decoration

In the home you might have a tapestry hanging from the wall as a **decoration**, that is, something which adorns the room. Equally your necklace may be a pleasing decoration to your body. However, the medals that a member of the armed forces wins are also called decorations, even if they have little aesthetic value.

deduction

There are two entirely different meanings to **deduction**. The first is when something is taken away from something else. Your weekly earnings are £200, but you actually receive only £110. This is because of sundry deductions like income tax, national insurance, pension fund, etc. The other form of deduction is an entirely intellectual operation. You are given a series of facts, and, by examining them, you are able to deduce that something else must also be true. This is known as a deduction. Sherlock Holmes was famous for it.

deed

If you perform some action, that action can be called a **deed**. If you write to Wordsworth and give them six homonyms that have been missed out from this dictionary, that will be your good deed for the day. But a deed can also be a legal paper or document setting out some agreement or confirming some right.

deem, deme

The verb 'to **deem**' means to regard something in a particular way. Thus you might deem the Eurovision Song Contest to be a public relations exercise for the tone deaf. You might deem autumn to be the loveliest season. You might deem Barbara Cartland to be a wonderful novelist. And so on. The word **deme** is much less subjective. It either means an administrative district in Greece or a subdivision of a population consisting of closely related plants, animals or people, typically breeding mainly within the group.

deep

If water is **deep**, it has considerable extension in a downwards direction. A deep mine is one that is a long way below the surface of the earth. More metaphorically, however, you can call a topic or subject deep if it demands considerable thought for its comprehension. The subject of human consciousness is a deep one because no one as yet fully understands it. Less portentously, your voice or a musical instrument can be deep if it emits tones that are low on the scale. You can also talk about a colour being deep when it is dark and intense.

deer *see* dear

default

You are said to **default** if you were meant to pay a debt and failed to do so, or were meant to appear in court on a particular day and failed to do so. Equally if you were due to play a tennis match with John McEnroe and he failed to turn up, you would win the match by default. In addition, computers do a large number of things by default. They select options for you unless specifically commanded not to do so. My computer selects the Times New Roman font by default unless I tell it not to, or select another default font in its place.

defer

If you **defer** to someone, you accept their judgement or acknowledge their superiority. If you defer doing something, you put it off to a more convenient time.

defile

If you **defile** something, you spoil it or treat it in a disrespectful manner. The verb is normally used when something esteemed or sacred has been abused or manhandled. As a noun, a defile is a narrow path along which troops can only march in file.

definition

When you explain the exact meaning of a word, you are providing a **definition**. However, visually, if something is blurred or indistinct, it lacks definition.

deflate

The three meanings of **deflate** all have conceptual connections. If you let the air out of something, then it will deflate. Thus you can deflate a balloon. It you deflate someone by your sarcastic comments, then they have lost confidence and feel deflated. If price levels in the shops begin to go down, then the economy is suffering from a deflation, and consequently prices deflate.

deflower

If you **deflower** a garden, you remove all the flowers or cut off their heads. If you deflower a woman, you remove her virginity.

degree

A **degree** can be a unit of measurement. Thus a thermometer marks the temperature in degrees. More loosely, the same action can vary in degree. If you kill someone, it is a crime, but it is less of a crime by several degrees if you kill someone because you are protecting yourself from death rather shooting someone because you want to pinch his walking stick. In addition you can gain a degree by completing a university course. The word can also be used as a near synonym for 'class' or 'status': 'He mingled only with people of his own degree.'

deign *see* dane

deliberate

An action that is performed as a result of thought is a **deliberate** action, one that you intended. If you deliberate about a problem or issue, you give pause in order to think about the matter.

delinquence, delinquents

If you have been guilty of **delinquence**, then you have been culpably remiss in some duty or other. Indeed, you may be so depraved as to belong to a gang of **delinquents**, a group of people who misbehave and break the law. Interestingly the word 'delinquents' was first applied to the royalists by their opponents during the English Civil War (1642–45).

delivery

The process of **delivery** is the handing over of items to someone else. The postman delivers letters, Parcel Force deliver parcels, the Chairman delivers a speech, and the Government delivers platitudes. The word is also used for the process of giving birth, and these days practically all deliveries take place in hospital.

delta

This is the fourth letter of the Greek alphabet, and still occasionally given as a not very pleasing mark in an examination. It is also a triangle-shaped area of alluvial land, enclosed and traversed by the diverging mouths of a river. The Nile and Ganges provide good examples. There is also a delta connection in electronics, again so called because the three wires involved form a triangular shape, which is itself the shape of the Greek letter. Delta is also a code word representing the letter D in communications.

deme *see* deem

demise

The **demise** of a person means their death, but the word is also used to signify the conveyance or transfer of property or a title by means of a will or lease.

demoiselle

This noun which few of us use can refer to four different objects. A **demoiselle** is a small crane with a black head and breast and white ear tufts. It breeds in SE Europe and central Asia. A demoiselle can also be a fly, a fish or a young woman.

demon

A **demon** is not your ideal dinner companion since it is an evil spirit or devil who takes possession of a person or who torments you in hell. Yet if someone calls you a demon cook, they are paying you a compliment. In such contexts, demon means skilled or expert. In Australia or New Zealand, the word demon is often used to refer to a policeman, which makes one wonder about law enforcement in the Antipodes.

demonstration

You might be asked to give a **demonstration** of a new computer program. In such a case you would explain the purpose of the program and show your audience how it worked. On the other hand, you might decide to go on a demonstration against the decision by Little Wallop Parish Council to allow cows to have grazing rights on the village green. In such an instance, your demonstration would be a protest. This difference between explanatory display and protest action can be seen in allied words like demonstrator and demonstrate.

den

This word is normally used to signify a wild animal's hidden home or lair. Thus you might see a badger emerge from his **den**. More informally, a den might be the room where you can go to relax or hide out. In the USA a den is a small subdivision of a Cub Scout pack.

dene *see* dean

denier

This is the unit of weight by which the fineness of silk, rayon or nylon yarn is measured, but a **denier** also used to be a French coin, withdrawn in the nineteenth century. With a different pronunciation, a denier is also someone who denies something.

denomination

A **denomination** is some independent branch of the Christian religion. Often the word is used to refer to small, sect-like bodies. Thus the Christadelphians are a Christian denomination. But denomination can be an adjective relating to bank notes, playing cards or postage stamps: 'He handed over several high-denomination notes.' The word can also mean the simple act of naming something: 'The denomination of this body will be the Praise Glory Institute.'

dense, dents

The word **dense** has at least three meanings. If something is closely compacted, it can be described as 'dense'. Hence you can have a dense fog or a dense mass of papers to get through. The word is often used to indicate that someone is being stupid: 'Oh don't be so dense, Clarice!' Finally, something that is complex, difficult to understand, or obscure can be described as dense. Thus, for most of us, Kant's *Critique of Pure Reason* will be extremely dense reading. **Dents**, of course, is simply the plural of 'dent', a slight hollow in a hard even surface normally created by a blow of some kind.

dental, dentil

Since you are highly likely to have received **dental** treatment in your life, you will not be surprised to learn that dental is an adjective relating to the teeth. Not, perhaps, surprisingly, **dentil** is a noun that also has a visual connection to teeth. A dentil is one of a number of small rectangular blocks resembling teeth, and used as a decoration under the moulding of a cornice.

dependence, dependents

Dependence is the state of being reliant on someone or something else. Britain's dependence on oil from Russia can lead to difficulties. Mary's dependence on her husband is total. **Dependents**, of course, are a group of people who rely on someone or something else. 'We are all dependents of the Earl of Knowle.' 'After a fortnight, we were all dependents on the opium from Afghanistan.' The word 'dependents' can also be used in English grammar. A clause, phrase or word can be dependent on another clause, phrase or word in the sense that it is subordinate to it.

deport

If you **deport** someone, they are expelled from the country in which they are currently living. Yet, though very rarely these days, one can still encounter 'deport' as a verb for mode of behaviour or general appearance in public: 'He deported himself with dignity at the AGM.'

depose

If you **depose** someone from office, they are suddenly and immediately relieved of their post. In the late 1990s and early 2000s, the Conservative

Party in Britain made a habit of deposing its leader and replacing him or her with someone even less effective. However, you can also depose by putting, under oath, what you believe to be the facts of the case in a legal proceeding.

deposit

If you have a **deposit** account at the bank, you have stored within it a sum of money which is gaining interest. If you go into a shop to buy a three-piece suite, they will ask for a deposit, namely a sum of money which you pay at once and then, perhaps, pay off the rest by means of monthly instalments. Hence, as you can see, a deposit is normally a sum of money handed over for some purpose or another. Indeed, in all of the uses of the word 'deposit', you have the idea of something being laid down. Hence you may find a deposit of dust on your desk if you haven't dusted it for the last fortnight. River deltas have deposits of alluvial soil laid down every year. So 'deposit' is barely a homonym since its basic meaning does not alter, but a deposit of money in a bank and a deposit of lava on a volcano seem such different types of operation that it was decided to include the word in this dictionary.

depravation, deprivation

If some people are living in a state of **depravation**, then they have virtually lost all moral sense and are content to live in a state that most of us would regard as immoral and wicked. If, however, someone was living in a state of **deprivation**, they would have a crippling lack of material resources. Most people in Great Britain whose only income is their old age pension live in a state of deprivation, though even that begins to look like luxury when one regards conditions in some other areas of the world.

depress

In all its meanings, the verb 'to **depress**' carries the sense of decline. Thus if you depress a person, you make them feel more miserable. If you depress a lever, you force it down. If you depress an economy, you make it less robust.

depression

Perhaps the most common use of this word is to describe a human feeling, a feeling of being saddened and uncomfortable in the world. Indeed, **depression** can be a crippling disease, and at its most extreme can lead to suicide. At the same time, the word has some technical meanings that are less distressing. When the column in your barometer goes down, that is because your area is suffering a meteorological depression. A concave area in the hills can also be called a depression.

deprivation *see* depravation

depth

To measure the **depth** of something, you start from the top and measure how far it is to the bottom. The depth of the well in your garden might be 75 feet. At the deep end, your town swimming pool has a depth of 6 feet. But depth is also used in a sense that is far from concrete. You might talk about the depth of your feeling for Stanley or Barry, or the depth of your research into the life of Einstein. Here a physical measurement has been transformed into an emotional or intellectual profundity.

derris

This is both an insecticide and a woody climbing plant of the pea family.

descant

If you have a melody and then place another melody on top of the first, then the second tune is called a **descant**. Alternatively, the word is occasionally used as a verb when it means 'to promulgate', 'to discourse upon'. The word tends to be used to describe portentous and self-important harangues: 'Once again we heard Derek descant on the evils of drink.' You can also have a descant recorder, the highest-pitched in the recorder range.

descent, dissent

The word **descent** has at least three separate meanings. It can signify a process of moving downwards: 'The rocks were a handicap as we made our descent.' It can apply to the origin or background of a person: 'By descent I have some Russian blood in me.' It can also be applied to a sudden attack: 'The Mercians were totally surprised by the Viking descent.' **Dissent** is simply the holding and expression of opinions that are contrary to others. The word is frequently used within a religious context, since all denominations other than the RC Church can be thought of as a collective dissent.

desert, dessert

As you doubtless know, a **desert** is an uninhabited and uncultivated tract of land. The Sahara Desert is one of the best known on Earth. But 'desert' can also be a verb meaning 'to abandon', 'to leave', 'to forsake'. Less commonly, a desert can be what you merit: 'That you won the Clarke Award was entirely your desert.' Finally, dinner might consist of a starter, a main course and a **dessert**. This last is normally a pudding of some kind. The two words are not quite homophones. The 'ért' in desert has a short sound, that in dessert a long one.

despite

Most of us use **despite** in only one way, as an equivalent to 'in spite of'. Hence you could say, 'Despite being bald, my head never gets cold.' But 'despite' can also mean 'contempt' or 'disdain'. 'I view the Prime Minister with despite,' is what a member of the Opposition might say.

dessert *see* **desert**

detail

A **detail** tends to mean a small part of a bigger whole. Parliamentary committees are meant to examine every detail of a Bill. When investigating a crime, the police must take note of every detail. But a detail can also be a small detachment of troops or police officers commanded to perform some specific duty.

determinant

When factor X inevitably produces outcome Y, then factor X is called a **determinant**. A particular gene, for instance, may be the determinant for your hooked nose. In mathematics, though, the word has a more technical meaning. A determinant is the quantity obtained by the addition of products of the elements of a square matrix according to a given rule.

determination

It is firmness of purpose that defines **determination**. For instance, when you ran the London Marathon last year, it was purely determination that got you over the finishing line. Equally it was Roger's determination that ensured that he was elected to the board of governors. But 'determination' has other meanings too. When a court case is completed, and the judge has handed out his decision, that decision can be termed a determination.

deuce

This word is a synonym for 'two' in games with cards or dice, a score in tennis when both players are equal on 40 points each needing two more consecutive points to win, or a mild oath.

development

The trouble with a verb like 'to develop' and all its kindred words like 'developable', 'developer' and **development** is that all its usages are conceptually akin, but the range of those usages forces one to include it as a homonym. The development of something is its movement from stage to stage until it reaches its current manifestation. Hence you could trace the development of Microsoft from its genesis in the brain of Bill Gates to its current position as the best-known computer company in the world. You could trace the development of the novel from its beginnings in the eighteenth century to its ubiquity today. But 'development' need not necessarily be a process. The word can also be applied to a single event. Your purchase of a dictionary of homonyms may be an important development in your linguistic career. The assassination of Franz Ferdinand in 1914 was an important development in international relations. 'Development' is also the process that a film endures before it becomes a photograph, and in a game of chess, the series of moves immediately after the opening is often called the development.

deviance, deviants

Deviance is the state or process of moving away from the norm and adopting a position that is not favoured by the majority. Normally applied in social or sexual matters, people who exhibit deviance are called **deviants**. Some deviants displayed their deviance by dancing naked outside Tescos.

device

The word **device** is often applied to relatively small mechanical or electrical equipment. Thus you may find your stapler a very handy device, or not be able to manage without your mobile phone. Yet 'device' can also mean a plan or tactic. You might find writing to the newspapers a useful device in your attempt to gain publicity for your abseiling exploits. 'Device' can even be used to refer to one's use of words: 'Using alliteration here was a clever device.' A drawing or design can be termed a device, particularly when it is relatively small and only forms a part of something bigger. Thus the frog that sits in the top left-hand corner of your writing paper might be seen as an amusing device. Indeed, one sometimes feels that 'device' is so versatile that one could use it in any context.

devil

The **Devil**, of course, is a major figure in the Jewish and Christian religions, being the supreme embodiment of evil. As such, he has naturally become a term of generalised abuse. If you call someone a devil, you will be expressing a strong distaste for their existence. Less personalised, the word can also be used merely as an exclamation of irritation: 'Where the devil did I put my pen?' However, there are two uses of the word that carry no moral tone whatsoever. A devil is a machine fitted with sharp teeth or spikes and used for tearing up something else. It is also the informal term for a barrister's (or printer's) junior assistant.

deviser, divisor

A **deviser** is someone who devises something, namely, he or she works out a new way of performing a task, or invents some facility to aid in such a task. A **divisor**, on the other hand, is someone who leaves something, normally real estate, to someone else in their will.

devour

This verb is normally used with reference to eating. If you **devour** your lunch, you consume it rapidly. In the same way, a fire can devour a building, and, more figuratively, you may devour a book because you are so enthralled by its subject matter.

dew, due

Dew is tiny drops of water that form on cool surfaces at night. Dew on the grass of the lawn is a common example. If something is **due**, it is expected.

Some money may be due to you from the bank, a lady may be due to give birth, or you may feel that you are due to receive the Nobel Prize.

dewed, dude

Dewed is the past tense of the verb 'to dew': 'Her face was dewed with tears.' A **dude** is a slang term for a man.

dey

A **dey** is a woman having charge of a dairy, or the titular appellation of the commanding officer of the Janissaries of Algiers who in 1720 deposed the pasha.

diaeresis

A **diaeresis** is a mark placed over a vowel to indicate that it is sounded separately. Examples are *naïve* and *Brontë*. The word is also used to indicate that there is a natural rhythmic break in a line of verse where the end of a metrical foot coincides with the end of a phrase.

dial

When we use the word **dial** as a noun, we are normally referring to the face of a clock or watch. As a verb, dial refers to the operation of calling a telephone number either by moving a dial (rare these days) or using a keypad.

dice

Most of us first encounter **dice** in playing games like ludo or snakes and ladders. They are small cubes, each face of which is marked with a different number of dots ranging from one to six. But dice can also be a verb. You might decide to dice the onions, namely cut them up into small cubes. In the colloquial phrase 'dice with death', dice is being used as a synonym for 'take a chance with'.

dick

This word does sterling service as a slang word. It can mean a penis, a stupid person or a detective.

die, dye

If you **die**, you cease to live. But 'die' is also a noun meaning a small cube, the singular of dice, that has the numbers from one to six marked by dots on its respective sides. A **dye** is a substance that will change the colour of some other object, be it hair or fabric. Both words have similarly homonymic parts of speech: dies, dyes, died, dyed.

diet

A **diet** is what half the people of Britain are supposedly following, namely a system of food intake that will lead to health and a pleasing slimness. Yet the Diet of Worms in 1521 was not an unpleasant meal but an important meeting, and the word 'diet' can be applied to sessions of any governmental or ecclesiastical body.

diffuse

This verb means to spread over a wide area. A strong wind will **diffuse** seeds over many acres. As an adjective, however, 'diffuse' means lacking clarity or too vague.

digest

You **digest** your food when it is broken down in the stomach and intestines. But you can also digest a book or an idea when you come to understand its concepts and meaning. Yet a digest of a book means a summary of the book.

digger, Digger

A **digger** is someone who digs, normally literally in the garden, but also more figuratively one can be a digger for information. In Australia, a digger can be a term for a soldier. During the English Civil War, a group of radical dissenters came to be known as 'Diggers'.

dike, dyke

In most cases, these two words are merely alternative spellings for the same object, namely an embankment of some kind, often an embankment to prevent the ingress of water. The dikes (or dykes) of Holland are a good example. However, a **dyke** is also a synonym for a lesbian, and although the *Oxford Dictionary of English* states that this usage can also be spelt 'dike', this is, I think, unusual.

dine, dyne

To **dine** is to eat: 'We dined at an Indian restaurant.' A **dyne** is a unit of force that, acting on one gram, increases its velocity by one centimetre per second every second.

dingo

A **dingo** is a wild or half-domesticated dog found in Australia, or Australian slang for a cowardly or treacherous person.

dinosaur

These large fossil reptiles of the Mesozoic period seemed to have entered public consciousness massively in Britain, so much so that the word **dinosaur** is now used figuratively to denote a person or thing that is outdated or has become obsolete.

dipper

Some birds that immerse themselves in water are called a **dipper**. The stars in Ursa Major and Ursa Minor are called respectively the Great Dipper and the Little Dipper. The word has also been applied to someone who practises total immersion in water as a mode of religious baptism. The apparatus for immersing negatives in a chemical solution is also called a dipper. No doubt someone who dips into a whole series of books could also be called a dipper. Indeed you may at this very moment be dipping into this dictionary. The word can also mean a scoop or ladle, and be a slang term for a pickpocket.

dire, dyer

If something is **dire**, it can either be extremely serious or urgent, or be of very poor quality. A **dyer** is someone whose trade is dyeing.

direct

This is an extremely common English word, yet we rarely consider in how many different ways we use it. First of all, if you **direct** something, then you are in charge. If you direct a play, you are responsible for guiding the cast through their lines and movements. If you direct a company, you are responsible for setting targets, introducing new developments, refining efficiency, and so on. Equally, 'direct' can have a more specialised meaning in that when you someone asks you where the Post Office is, you direct them along the correct route. But 'direct' also has a functionally purposeful meaning to it. When you say, 'We went the direct route to the station,' you mean that you took the shortest, most efficient route. Your air route from London to Copenhagen will be a direct one if you do not have to change at any point *en route*. You yourself can be direct in that you tend to go straight to the point, and have no time for euphemisms or digressions. Finally, if you are in a position of command, you can direct someone to do something. Thus a teacher may direct his or her pupils to do a particular exercise. Like so many English words, 'direct' has a multiplicity of connotations, as you can see from the phrases of which 'direct' is an integral part: direct access, direct action, direct mail, direct method, direct proportion, direct speech, and so on.

dirt

A substance, such as mud or dust, that soils someone or something is called **dirt**, but the word has developed metaphorical uses too. If you dish the dirt on one of your colleagues, you reveal something discreditable about him. You might treat someone like dirt, meaning that you barely bother to observe the normal standards of courtesy when dealing with that person. Films and books that have a pornographic content are often called dirty films or dirty books.

disarm

The two meanings of **disarm** have conceptual similarities. The most obvious meaning is when a person or body of people decide to relinquish their armaments or are forced to do so. Hence you may disarm a robber at the bank by seizing his revolver, or the Macclesfield Military Mafia might decide to disarm and rely entirely on charm to gain their ends in the future. However, you can also disarm someone literally by using charm. You go to meet your bank manager who is displeased that you seem to be using the bank's money on which to live rather than your own. You disarm him by pointing out that your business will shortly begin making a profit, and that over the next five years all your debts will be paid off.

disburse, disperse

Normally it is money that is disbursed. Your company has made a larger than expected profit during the year. As a result, they have decided to **disburse** some of that profit by giving an extra bonus to all their workers. If, however, you **disperse** something, you distribute it over a wide area. A storm will disperse seeds over a wide area.

disc, disk

More often than not, these are variant spellings of the same thing. A gramophone record or a compact **disc** can equally well be called a **disk**. In the computing world, a floppy or hard disk tends be spelt with the 'k', but there would be no problem or ambiguity if you spelt it with the 'c'. The k is also more common if you are referring to a thin circular plate of any material or any of the biological usages of the word, but I do not think that any international incident of any kind would be caused if you used the 'c' in such instances.

discharge

This word has a whole variety of related meanings with removal, unburdening or completing a task as its underlying concepts. Thus if you **discharge** an electrical circuit, you get rid of the electrical charge. If you discharge someone from their post, you sack them. If you discharge a gun, you fire it, thus ridding it of power. If you discharge a bankrupt, you relieve him or her of the stigma of bankruptcy. If you discharge someone from hospital, you restore them to the loving embrace of their friends.

discord

If you play two or more notes that are not in harmony with each other, you have a **discord**, which is why many people find the music of Schönberg one continuous discord. From dissonant music it is easy to stretch the idea to personal relations. You may experience perfect harmony with your mother-in-law, but many people experience discord with their partner's parents. You can also have discord in colours. It is possible, for instance, that although your brown trousers, pink shirt, green jacket and yellow tie look fine to you, others find them discordant. It is interesting that 'discord' literally means 'severance of hearts', from the Latin *discordia*.

discount

As Inspector of Police, you may **discount** the evidence of Amelia Constance because you know that she is a congenital liar. Here the meaning of 'discount' is equivalent to 'disregard'. When you bought a digital radio this morning, you got a discount because the shop was having a sale. Here 'discount' means 'reduction'.

discreet, discrete

If you are **discreet**, you display wisdom and reticence in your speech and actions. You are cautious in your approach, judicious in your behaviour and circumspect in telling others anything about your affairs. **Discrete** is quite different. Something is discrete when it is separate from other items, detached from the whole. Hence the case of the pickpocket at Fakenham Races is quite discrete from the case of the battered housewife.

discrimination

Most of us, alas, think of **discrimination** these days as meaning the unjust or prejudicial treatment of different categories of people, especially on the grounds of race, age or sex. Of course, 'discrimination' does mean that, but it also has two less distasteful meanings. If you have discrimination, then you are able to distinguish between the genuine and the shoddy, between the real and the apparent. Indeed, someone with discrimination would never be guilty of discrimination. In addition, discrimination in electronics refers to the selection of a signal having the required characteristic such as frequency and amplitude.

discussed, disgust

Perhaps this pair are not true homonyms. The difference in sound between the 'c' of **discussed** and the 'g' of **disgust** ought to be apparent. However, most of the time it isn't, and so these words sound like perfect homophones. 'Discussed', of course, is simply the past tense of the verb 'to discuss', and 'disgust' is the feeling you have when the President of the USA and the Prime Minister of the UK unite to demonstrate that keeping people who have been charged with no crime in jail and torturing them is perfectly congruent with the ideals of Christian charity.

dish

In everyday life, a **dish** is a shallow, flat-bottomed container for cooking or serving food. Many of us eat our breakfast out of a dish. However, the word can also mean a device fixed to the outside wall of a building that is designed to pick up television signals from digital transmitters. An attractive lady can also be termed a dish on the grounds that she is good enough to eat. As a verb, 'to dish' means to hand out, to distribute: 'I must dish out the entrance tickets.'

dismiss

If you **dismiss** someone from your employment, you sack them, you get rid of them. If you dismiss something as being of little importance, then you regard it as unworthy of serious consideration. Many people dismiss Jeffrey Archer as unworthy of serious consideration as a novelist.

dispatch

When you **dispatch** something, you send it off to a specific destination. Hence you dispatch a parcel to Scunthorpe or a letter to Swindon. If you receive a dispatch, then you receive a report from an overseas journalist or a report from a military commander. If you accomplish something with dispatch, you deal with it quickly. You may watch the English cricket team dispatch the Australians for a low total. If you dispatch someone with a bullet to his heart, then you are probably guilty of murder. As you can see, the verb 'to dispatch' always entails a movement from one sort of position to another. Even the noun 'dispatch' will contain data likely to entail some new assessment of the current situation.

dispense

When you **dispense** something, you give it out, you distribute it to others. The chemist will dispense a prescription to you. Yet, with an almost opposite meaning, you can dispense with someone's services (i.e. no longer require them) or you can dispense with your car (i.e. get rid of it) because you feel that you are now too old to drive.

displacement

This word always denotes the action of moving something from one place to another, but the contexts in which it can operate are so disparate that **displacement** needs to be counted as a homonym. There may, for instance, be the displacement of people from where they live to some other area because of the urgencies of war or physical disaster. If you have water in a bottle, and then place a weight in that bottle, there occurs a displacement of some of the water. In psychoanalysis, the unconscious transfer of an intense emotion from one object to another is known as displacement.

disposition

A person's **disposition** is his or her inherent qualities of mind and character. Some of your friends are of a placid disposition; others, no doubt, are much more volatile. But disposition can also mean the way in which something is arranged or positioned. Hence the disposition of the vases of flowers in your drawing room was most attractive.

dissent *see* **descent**

dissolve

Many things will **dissolve** in water; even more will dissolve in acid. In other words, they will lose their solid form and become incorporated into the liquid. However, you can also dissolve something by closing it down. It was decided to dissolve the Bedminster Brass Band because it was becoming increasingly difficult to find adequate players of the trombone. You personally can also dissolve into tears – possibly as a result of watching a party political broadcast. Films at the cinema often have one scene dissolving into another one. Hence the verb 'to dissolve' always entails a change of state, but, as the examples illustrate, those changes of state can be very diverse.

distaff

This used to be a cleft stick about three feet long on which flax or wool was wound ready for spinning. This stick was called the distaff. Because the spinning was normally done by women, the word **distaff** began to be used in reference to the female side of a family or organisation.

distemper

When someone wants to dilute their Scotch with water, they could say that they wanted to **distemper** their drink. I have never heard anyone use the word in this way. Nor have I heard anyone saying that they were suffering from a distemper, meaning that they were feeling ill-humoured. Both these meanings can still be found in the dictionary, but the only common uses for distemper today are to describe a method of painting in which the colours are mixed with some glutinous substance soluble in water, or to denote a catarrhal disease of dogs.

distinguish

The verb 'to **distinguish**' means to be able to recognise a difference between object A and object B. 'My daughter can distinguish between cows and bulls, but it is not easy for anyone to distinguish between appearance and reality.' However, it is also possible for people to distinguish themselves. 'Peter certainly distinguished himself when he unexpectedly won the 100 metres front crawl last Saturday, and I expect that Janet will distinguish herself in the cooking competition next month.'

ditch

A **ditch** is a long, narrow hollow that has been dug into the ground. You often find ditches along the sides of fields or roads. But you can also ditch someone by no longer associating with them. You often hear teenage girls saying that they are about to ditch their boyfriend. If you are an airline pilot, you may have to ditch your plane if, through some technical fault, it becomes impossible to keep it airborne.

dive

As a verb, to **dive** means to plunge headfirst into some water or, in an aircraft, to lose altitude rapidly. As a noun, the word has come to signify some less than respectable establishment like an unsavoury pub, casino or lap dancing venue.

divers

Since a diver is someone who plunges head first into water, **divers** clearly represents more than one person so doing, yet the word is also an adjective meaning 'several'.

divert

If you **divert** traffic, you force it to go from A to B by a different route. Equally you can divert attention away from one topic by deliberately raising another one. But you can also divert people by amusing them or catching their attention is some way or other. You may be diverted by a particular television programme or by a cartoonist in the newspaper.

divide

To **divide** something, you split it up into separate parts. Thus you may divide your land into sixteen small holdings, or divide your library into three parts, fiction, non-fiction and reference. You can also divide numbers. If you divide the number six by two, you get the answer three because two will go into six three times. However, 'divide' can also mean to disagree. Creationists and evolutionists divide deeply over the topic of Darwinism.

divine

Something is **divine** if it has a close connection with God or some religion. Thus Jerusalem is a divine city to both Christians and Muslims. By extension, art, music and literature can be called divine because they appeal to man's higher faculties. However, divine can also be a verb, in which case it means to discover something by supernatural means. You can find such miracle workers at any fair, normally equipped with tarot cards or crystal balls.

division

If you separate something into parts, you are indulging in an act of **division**. Hence you may organise the division of your land into a series of fields. But a division may also mark a difference or disagreement between you and someone else. Perhaps there was a division between you and your sister as to who should stay in next Saturday night. It is often said that there is a division between the north of England and the south in terms of living standards. Furthermore, a large organisation might be divided into separate divisions, one for sales, one for accounts, and so on. In botany and zoology, a division is a section in the classification system for those subjects. In a factory, there is likely to be a division of labour between administrative staff, shop floor staff, sales staff and so on. Nationwide sports are often organised into divisions. Hence, in football in Britain, if a team is in the Premier Division, it is likely to be a more skilled team than one in a lower division.

djinn, gin

A **djinn** (often spelt **jinn**) is an intelligent spirit of lower rank than the angels that is able to appear in human and animal forms. **Gin**, of course, is an alcoholic drink, often mixed with tonic or a fruit juice, but it is also a card game, a trap for catching birds and small animals, a machine for separating cotton from its seeds, a machine for raising and moving heavy weights, or an offensive Australian term for an Aboriginal woman.

dob

If you **dob** someone, you betray them. But you can also dob (give) some money to a good cause, or dob (persuade) someone to do a job for you. The word is basically Australian.

doc, dock

To be fair, **doc** is not really a word. However, as an abbreviation for 'doctor', it is so commonly used that it seemed unfair to omit it. A **dock** though is very much a real word with at least four meanings. First of all, a dock is a plant of the genus *Rumex* which, as a child, I used to diminish the pain of a nettle sting. Secondly, it is an artificial basin into which ships are received for repair. As a result, almost any object can be described as being in dock when it is in the process of being repaired. Thirdly, you appear in the dock when you are placed on trial in a criminal court. Finally, when an animal has part of its tail removed it is said that the tail has been docked.

dodder

If you **dodder** around, you move slowly and hesitantly, normally because of old age. As a noun, a dodder is a parasitic climbing plant of the convolvulus family.

doe, doh, dough

A **doe** is a female deer, hare or rabbit, **doh** is the first note of the diatonic scale, and **dough** is a paste of moistened flour waiting to be baked into bread. All are homophones with each other.

doer, dour

If you are a **doer,** you are a person who does something. If you are **dour**, you are severe, strict and unsmiling.

does, doze

A group of female deer is a gathering of **does**, and a fairly brief sleep on the train or in your easy chair is a **doze**. Note that 'does' as a group of deer is pronounced quite different from 'does', the third person singular present form of the verb 'to do'.

dog

Most of us are acquainted with the domestic quadruped often sentimentally referred to as 'man's best friend'. Indeed, given the devotion that many people feel towards their pet dogs, it is somewhat odd that if you call a person (normally a male) a dog, you are insulting that person and implying that he is a surly, worthless fellow. Equally when something goes to the dogs, you imply that it has been ruined in some way. However, **dog** can also be verb, one that means 'to follow'. If you closely follow someone, you are behaving in the same way that their dog would behave. The word is also an integral part of many idiomatic expressions: dog collar, dog days, dog in the manger, let sleeping dogs lie, etc.

dogger

Dogger is the sandy ironstone of the Lower Oolite or a two-masted fishing vessel.

dole

If you **dole** out some money, you distribute it among a number of people, though the word has a connotation that this act of sharing is being done in a niggardly fashion. That is because, when you became unemployed, you went on the dole, namely queued up each week at the Unemployment Office to receive your inadequate unemployment benefit. If you are unemployed (i.e. on the dole) you are likely also to be full of dole, because the word can also mean grief or sorrow. The word originates from the Old English *dal* which meant 'share'.

dolly

Perhaps the most common use of the word **dolly** today is as a pet name for a child's doll, but the word does have other meanings. A 'dolly bird', for instance, is a slang expression used to denote an attractive and sexually alluring young lady. As a child I remember my mother putting the clothes in a large metal bowl of soapy water and pounding the resulting mixture with a wooden implement known as a dolly. This, of course, was before the days of washing machines. Today the word is commonly used to mean a wheeled platform for cameras, etc. Apparently a dolly can also be an offering of fruit, flowers or sweetmeats presented normally on a tray. A dolly catch at cricket is a very easy catch. In 1996 the name Dolly was given to the world's first cloned sheep.

dolphin

This is best known as a toothed whale, but a **dolphin** can also be a buoy for mooring boats or a structure for protecting the pier of a bridge.

domain

We mostly like to have our own **domain**, an area or territory that we can call our own. For some it is the study in their house, for others their garden, for some it is even their office at work. But one can also have a personal domain in the sense of following some specialised activity or study. Your domain might be the poetry of Hopkins, someone else's might be Scottish dancing. 'Domain' is also a technical term in computing, biochemistry, physics and maths, meaning something different in each field.

domino

If you have ever played the game, you will know that a **domino** is a small oblong piece with pips from nought to six on each half of one side. There are 28 dominoes in each set. But a domino is also a loose cloak, normally black and tending to be worn by highwaymen or at masked balls. Indeed, the black ebony pieces used in the game of dominoes might have gained their name from the black cloak and the black mask that often accompanied it.

don, done, dun

A **don** can be a Spanish lord or a university lecturer (or, presumably, both at the same time). Furthermore, if you don your clothes, you put them on. **Done** is the past tense of the verb 'to do', and means completed, executed, finished or settled. **Dun** is a dingy brown colour quite often seen on horses, though the word can also mean the act of demanding payment for something, or a hill or hill fort.

donjon, dungeon

The great tower or innermost keep of a castle was called a **donjon**. A **dungeon** is a dark, underground prison cell.

donkey

A **donkey** is a quadruped somewhat similar to a horse. Most donkeys have a rather appealing facial expression of total vacuity, and this may be why, if you call someone a donkey, you imply that he or she is a half-wit.

dop

A **dop** can be a pupa case or a copper cup into which a diamond is placed for cutting or polishing.

dope

Many people take some form of **dope** because in the twentieth century it became a catch-all label for a variety of drugs like heroin and cocaine, and smoking or injecting such substances became, although illegal, almost fashionable. Yet the word is also used as a derisive label for someone. If you call someone a dope, you imply that they are foolish.

dorado

This is either an edible marine fish of warm seas, or a South American freshwater fish.

dork

Whether referring to a socially inept person or to the penis, the word **dork** is at the best an informal word.

dory

A **dory** can be a fish, *Zeus faber*, often called a John Dory, or a flat-bottomed boat often used in sea fisheries.

doss

This is a slang word for sleep or even a bed upon which to sleep. There is also a dialect verb **doss** which means to push with the horns as bulls are prone to do.

dost, dust

The word **dost** is an old-fashioned form of the second person singular present of the verb 'to do'. **Dust** is a grey powder that magically appears in your absence on desks, furniture, window sills, etc. Rumour has it that some people go around with dusters and try to remove this powder. This is fairly pointless because it always comes back.

dot

This word has a number of aliases, both as a noun and a verb. As a noun, a **dot** is a small round mark or spot just like the full stop that ends this sentence. If someone is a long way away and you can barely see them, you might say that they are a dot on the horizon. It is also one of the signals in the Morse Code. As a verb, you can dot something by putting a series of dots on it, but you can also dot someone by hitting him. DOT stands for directly observed therapy.

double

This is a somewhat complicated word. Perhaps its most common meaning is when it is used to indicate that something has been increased by the same amount as the original. Thus, if I had two bars of chocolate, and was then given another two bars, the amount of chocolate I possessed would have doubled. If you double two, you get four, if you double four, you get eight, and so on. At the same time, it is possible that you have a double, that is, someone who looks exactly like you. I once encountered a well-known television actor on an Underground platform. When I had congratulated him on his most recent role, he explained that this was always happening to him, but that he was not in fact the actor concerned. He was the actor's double. It is also possible that you have a double personality. At home you are sweetness and light, marked by your consideration and charm. When, however, you go to a race meeting, you immediately become bellicose, demanding, loud-mouthed and altogether tiresome. However, as you can see, 'double' almost invariably implies an increase, and you can see that in the many words of which 'double' is a part: double-barrelled, double-breasted, double-cross, double-faced, etc.

dour *see* **doer**

down

As the opposite of 'up', **down** indicates a position lower than something else. If you fall down the stairs, you end up at a lower altitude than you started. If you are down on your luck, you are feeling less prosperous than you were. If you are down in the dumps, you are much less contented than is your norm. If your marks in your history exam were down from last year's, then you did not score as high a mark. But a down can also be an area of elevated land, often an area on which people walk or have a picnic. In addition, regardless of altitude, one often goes down to a particular place: 'I'm going down to Southport this weekend', or, 'Rachel went down to her mother's yesterday.' Absurdly, one could just as well use the word 'up' in the above instances, though, in Britain's quaint conventions, one always goes up to London and up to Oxford. Do not expect anyone to explain this. 'Down' is also the fine fluffy feathers which form the first covering of a young bird.

drab

If something is **drab**, it is unappealing, colourless, depressing. 'Jocelyn always wears such drab dresses.' 'Stephen lives in such a drab area.' But 'drab' can also mean a wooden case into which salt is put when it is taken out of the boiling pan, or be a slang word for a slatternly woman.

draft, draught

You may be writing an article on Peruvian history, and are just completing your first **draft**. Here 'draft' means a preliminary attempt. On the other hand, you may working in the police force and be selected to be among the first draft of officers detailed to search Clapham Common for evidence. Here 'draft' means a portion from a larger body. The word **draught** has even more meanings. Its most common is a current of air, and few of us like sitting in a draught. It also means the depth of water needed to float a boat, a counter in a game of draughts, a type of beer favoured by CAMRA, and is an adjective to describe an animal used for pulling things. Thus a horse used for pulling a plough is a draught animal.

dragoon

A **dragoon** is the name given to a member of the cavalry, but it can also be a verb meaning to force someone to do something. Hence you may dragoon your son into the Boy Scouts or dragoon your husband into doing the washing up.

drain

As a noun, a **drain** is a channel or pipe carrying off surplus liquid. Hence, as a verb, you can drain a swimming pool, a field or a river. But 'drain' is not confined to physical activities. You may drain your mind through lack of sleep, or drain your body through excessive exercise. Equally certain things may be a drain on your purse, things like council tax or bus fares. If it matters, The Drain is also the nickname for the Waterloo and City Line on the London Underground.

drake

A **drake** is a male duck, a small cannon or a beaked galley.

draw

You may **draw** a picture with your pencil, in which case you are trying to create a pleasing representation of something in the world, a house, a hill, a vase of flowers, or whatever. In this usage of the word, you are putting something in, creating something new. In most of the other uses of the word, one is extracting something. Thus you can draw money from your bank, draw up water from the well, draw on someone's good nature to do you a favour, or draw on your inner reserves to complete a task. You can draw a cork out of a bottle, draw a chair up to the table, draw blood from out of a vein, draw a net through the sea, or draw a woman into your arms. As you can see, it is close to impossible to provide a comprehensive definition for the word 'draw'. To confuse things even more, when Arsenal and West Ham both score the same number of goals in a football match, the result is a draw. A lot of chess matches end in a draw, which always strikes me as a shame.

drawer

Clearly a **drawer** is someone who draws, but it is also a box-like storage compartment without a lid made to slide horizontally in and out of a desk, a person who writes a cheque, or, in the plural, another name for knickers.

drawn

This is the past participle of the verb 'to draw', but a person can look **drawn** if they appear strained or under pressure.

dray, drey

A **dray** is a cart or truck without sides. A **drey** is the nest of a squirrel.

dredge

A **dredge** is an implement or machine used for scouring a river bed, a lake or some form of channel in order to locate and bring to the surface objects that are lying at the bottom. It is also a word used to indicate that a field is sown with a mixture of grains, normally oats and barley, or a verb meaning to sprinkle food with a powdered substance like sugar or flour.

dress

For a woman, a **dress** is a one-piece garment that covers most of the body. As a verb, to dress is to clothe oneself, but one can also dress a salad or a wound, very different actions in both cases. If you are putting on a play, the final rehearsal is called the dress rehearsal.

drift

If something is moved along by a current of water, it is said to **drift**. Thus if your boat becomes unfastened during the night, it is likely to drift out to sea. Even on a voyage, a ship may drift off its course because of winds and/or currents. Similarly the wind might drive the snow so that it forms a snow drift. Equally a drift may be the direction in which your speech or thought are tending. When explaining how work on chaos in the realm of physics has influenced weather forecasting, you may say to your audience, because it is a complex subject, 'Do you get my drift?' There can also be a drift in the population as more and more people leave the countryside to live in towns.

drill

A **drill** is an instrument or machine for boring holes. You may have experienced a drill on your teeth when you have visited the dentist, and you are likely to have heard a drill in the road when council workmen are engaged in their function of delaying traffic. Yet drill can also be the execution of a series of pre-agreed actions. Thus you may at work have a fire alarm drill. Here no one is drilling holes into anything. Instead you are merely practising the operation of leaving the building in an orderly and efficient manner. The armed forces frequently have a physical drill in order to keep them fit and agile. Indeed you can develop a drill for almost anything, learning Latin declensions, ploughing a field, making coffee, etc. A drill is also a dark brown baboon and a coarse twilled cotton or linen fabric.

drive

As a noun, a **drive** might be a ride in the car ('They went for a drive to Oxford'), a short road leading from a public road to your house, a massive urge ('He had a drive to learn Chinese'), an organised effort to achieve something ('The drive to reduce car theft was very demanding'), or an organised meeting to play cards (a whist drive). As a verb, the word is mostly restricted to using a motor vehicle ('I drive a Ford') or to urging people to accomplish a task ('I drive my employees very hard').

driver

This may be someone who drives a vehicle or an animal, a part in a mechanism that imparts motion to another part, or a golf club.

drone

A **drone** is a male honey bee or a monotonous noise. The three lower pipes of a bagpipe are called the drones.

droop, drupe

The verb 'to **droop**' means to bend or hang down limply. You and I tend to droop when we are physically very tired or when we are feeling dejected. A **drupe**, however, can be a fleshy fruit with thin skin and a central stone (e.g. plum, cherry, olive) or a small marine mollusc with a thick knobbly shell.

drop

As a noun, a **drop** can be the smallest amount of liquid that falls in a spherical form. Thus you may see drops of rain sliding down the window. The word has been extended to apply to relatively small amounts of any liquid. Thus Ian will say, 'I'll just have a drop of Scotch,' as he helps himself to a large glassful. As a verb, 'to drop' means to fall from one higher position to one lower one. Thus your post drops on the mat each morning, the apples drop from the tree as you contemplate the nature of gravity, and your corn flakes drop from your spoon as you try to turn over the pages of your newspaper.

drove

Drove is the past tense of the verb 'to drive' and a road along which horses or cattle are driven.

drum

This is a percussive musical instrument, the tympanum of the ear, a cylinder round which a belt passes, an evening assembly of fashionable people at a private house, a ridge separating two valleys, or a verb meaning to make a noise like a drum.

drunk

Drunk is the past tense of the verb 'to drink' and a name for someone who has become overcome by alcoholic liquor.

drupe *see* droop

druse

A crust of small crystals lining the sides of a cavity in a rock is called a **druse**. The name is also applied to one of the political and religious sects of Muslim origin.

dry

Something is **dry** if it is not wet. But there can also be dry humour, which tends to be understated and matter-of-fact, and dry wine, which is not sweet and can be almost acidic.

dual, duel

The adjective **dual** means pertaining to two, while a **duel** is a fight or contest between two people.

dub

When the Queen makes you a knight by touching your shoulder with her sword, she has just dubbed you. However, you can also **dub** leather by smearing it with grease, or dub a film by providing it with a soundtrack in a different language from its original one.

duck

A **duck** is a swimming bird of the genus *Anas* and is traditionally found swimming on the village pond. It is also a strong untwilled line fabric, and a verb meaning either to lower the head suddenly (normally to avoid a flying ball or a low rafter), or to plunge one's head into water and to emerge from thence quickly.

ducked, duct

If you have been **ducked,** your head has been rapidly immersed in water. A **duct** is a tube or passageway in a building or machine for air, liquid, cables and whatever.

due *see* dew

dumb

Someone who does not or cannot speak is **dumb**. However, the word is often applied to foolish or stupid people as well.

dummy

In the game of whist, an imaginary player whose hand is exposed and played by its partner is called the **dummy**. There is a similar situation in bridge. A plastic outline of the human form and used to model clothes in shop windows is also called a dummy. So too is a bulbous-shaped object that the British are prone to stick into the mouths of their very young children in order to keep them quiet. If someone is associated with a group of others but takes no decisions with them and generally just accepts what the others decide, he or she is likely to be termed a dummy. You can also have a dummy in a game of soccer or rugby when a player pretends to go in one direction but suddenly darts off in a different one.

dump

This word can mean two or three things, none of them very alluring. As a noun, **dump** normally means a site for depositing rubbish, but it can also be unflatteringly applied to your house ('Why do you live in such a dump?'), or refer to the transfer of data from one computer memory location to another. As a verb, to dump something means to dispose of it.

dungeon *see* donjon

dust *see* dost

dwarf

A **dwarf** is a human being who is considerably below average height, but the word has been extended as a verb into a comparative word. Hence, if you passed a massive lorry on the road one day, you might say, 'Our car is dwarfed by that vehicle.' It can be applied to talents as well. Hence you could say, 'Mozart's genius dwarfs Salieri's genuine skill.'

dyeing, dying

If you are **dyeing** something, you are attempting to change its colour. If you are **dying**, you are approaching death, 'the undiscovered country from whose bourne no traveller returns'.

dyer *see* dire

dyke *see* dike

E

E, e

The single letter can be used as a class of academic mark, the fifth file from the left on a chessboard, or the lowest-earning socio-economic category for marketing purposes. It is also a symbol for energy, and the third note of the diatonic scale of C.

eagle

Most of us think of an **eagle** as a large bird of prey, but in golf it is a score of two strokes under par at a hole. An eagle also used to be an American gold coin worth ten dollars.

ear

We all know that the **ear** is the organ of hearing in men and animals, but it is also the part of a cereal plant like wheat that contains the seeds of the plant.

earn, erne, urn

The verb 'to **earn**' means 'to deserve' or 'to merit', and most of us go to work in order to earn money. An **erne** is an eagle, and an **urn** is an earthenware or metal vessel of a rounded or ovaloid form and with a circular base.

earnest

One is most likely to think of **earnest** as an adjective meaning solemn, serious and committed, but it can also signify money given in part-payment for something: 'He gave me £1,000 as an earnest of his intentions.'

earth, Earth

For most of us, **earth** is the surface covering of our planet, and mostly comprises soil and fragments of minerals and plants. With a capital letter, **Earth** is the name of our planet, one that we seem to be destroying. But an earth can also be an electrical connection, and there is also the idiomatic expression when you run something to earth meaning that you capture it or find it. Earth used to be regarded as one of the four elements making up the universe, and it is also the underground lair of a fox or badger.

ease

When one is at **ease**, one is feeling relaxed and comfortable, not plagued with any worries. One can also use the word as a verb. If you ease something, you diminish it. Hence you might take an aspirin to ease a headache. You can also ease something into something else, meaning that the operation is conducted slowly and with care. Thus you might ease yourself into your tightly fitting jeans, or ease some blade between two objects. Share prices which have been rising are also said to ease when their value decreases.

eave, eve

One is not accustomed to seeing the word **eave**, because one almost invariably talks about the eaves. The eaves are the projecting edges of a roof that overhang the side of the house or building. Clearly an 'eave' is just one side of the eaves, but, in my experience, no one ever mentions it. **Eve**, which sounds identical to 'eave', is either a synonym for 'evening' or refers to the time immediately preceding some event.

écarté

This noun can be either a card game for two players, or a position in ballet.

echo

In certain circumstances, if one speaks or shouts, a diminished repetition of one's words can be heard because of the reflection of the sound waves by some obstacle. This repetition is known as an **echo**, but the word has since been extended to apply more widely. Hence, if you write an article about South American snakes, some less than friendly critic might say, 'Your article was just an echo of what Professor Creepy has already said on the subject.' 'Echo' is also a code word in radio communication standing for the letter E, a particular tactic in the game of bridge, and part of the title of some newspapers like the *South Wales Echo*.

eclipse

We normally think of an **eclipse** as being the obscuring of the light of one heavenly body by another. Thus you can have an eclipse of the sun when the moon moves between it and Earth. Since the astronomical eclipse entails the hiding of one object by another, the word has naturally been used metaphorically in a similar manner. 'The work of Professor Maxim has eclipsed all others in this field,' for example. In ornithology, the word 'eclipse' relates to the period when the markings of a male duck are obscured by the moulting of the breeding plumage.

economy

The **economy** is that management of work, taxation, wages, supplies, employment and so on that is the special preserve of the Chancellor of the Exchequer. Since it is beyond the comprehension of most people (including the Chancellor of the Exchequer), it is a subject upon which the British people tend to have strongly held (but massively ill-informed) views. However, away from national concerns about tariffs or pensions, the word 'economy' can also be used to refer to habits of personal frugality: 'On an income of £9,000 per year, I need to exercise considerable care with my economy.' Because economy for many people is a matter of eking out sparse resources, the word 'economy' can often be used as a synonym for 'cutting down' or depriving oneself, and things that are inexpensive or long-lasting are often described as being 'economic'. The people who manage the economy (politicians, entrepreneurs, bankers, etc.) are also often accused of using considerable economy with the truth.

ecstasy, Ecstasy

The lower-case 'ecstasy' refers to a state of indescribable happiness or joy, but the upper-case 'Ecstasy' is the name of an illegal amphetamine-based drug.

ectoplasm

In the world of biological fact, **ectoplasm** is the viscous, clear outer layer of the cytoplasm in amoeboid cells. In the world of make-believe, ectoplasm is the supernatural viscous substance that supposedly exudes from the body of a medium during a trance.

edge

Here is another four-letter word that performs a multitude of tasks. The outside limit of an object is often called its **edge**: 'My hip caught the edge of the table', or, 'The ball glanced off the edge of his bat.' The word is also used to depict the sharpened side of a blade: 'The edge of the knife was placed against his throat.' If someone or something has the edge, they are displaying a superiority: 'In the derby match between United and City, it was United who had the edge.' You can also edge away from something, in which case you are moving unobtrusively away. As applied to the voice, the word can denote a certain bitterness: ' "Do you really attribute your success to talent?" she asked, with a real edge to her voice.'

effects

'The **effects** of the computer revolution have been vast.' That sentence shows the most common usage of 'effects' as the consequences and results of some preceding event. However, the word is also used to denominate the sound, lighting and scenery in a play, film or television show. Your personal belongings can also be referred to as your effects, often in a legal context: 'The insurance fortunately covered my effects.'

effusive

This adjective is used to describe someone expressing him- or herself in an unrestrained or heartfelt manner. Thus, if someone saves your life by rescuing you from a sinking ship, you are likely to be **effusive** in your thanks. The adjective is also used in geology to describe rock that was poured out when molten.

egg

An **egg** is that oval hard-shelled object that is produced by female birds. They subsequently hatch out into the young of the species, or are taken by other animals (including humans) and eaten. The word is also used for the female reproductive organ which, when fertilised by the male sperm, can develop into an embryo. 'Egg' can also be used as a verb. If you egg someone on, you encourage them or incite them to pursue a particular course of action.

Eh! *see* **A**

eight *see* **ate**

ejaculate

This is a verb often used to describe the spurting out of semen from a penis, but **ejaculate** can also mean saying something quickly and urgently: 'Get down!' he ejaculated.

elaborate

If something is very **elaborate**, it is complicated and complex. You might build something very elaborate with your Lego, or you might find the London Underground system too elaborate for you to master. Equally 'elaborate' can be a verb where it can mean to produce or develop by labour, or, more commonly, to expand verbally (or in writing) about something that you have mentioned before.

elastic

Most of us know **elastic** as a cord, tape or fabric that is woven with strips of rubber, with the result that, when pulled out of shape, it rapidly, when released, returns to its former form. The word is used as an adjective to describe the same process. In economics the word is used to describe a state where demand and supply are sensitive to changes in price or income.

elder

An **elder** is a low tree or shrub, but also the comparative degree of 'old': old, elder, eldest. In the early Christian church, officials were referred to as elders.

elect

In a general election, the population get the chance to **elect** their next government. Equally officials for the local bowling club can be elected by the members of the club. To elect someone is to choose them by voting, and consequently appointing the one who receives the most votes. In Calvinist theology, however, the elect are those lucky souls who have been predestined for salvation.

electrify

Unsurprisingly, the word **electrify** is a verb concerned with the transmission of electricity. You might, for instance, decide to electrify the railway between Bolas Magna and Lower Bugthorpe. Equally unsurprisingly, the instant power of electricity has been transferred metaphorically to human emotions and reactions. Hence you might electrify the audience with your wondrous performance of Beethoven's 'Moonlight Sonata'.

elegant

When a woman is described as **elegant**, we mean that she is stylish and graceful in manner and/or appearance. The same would be true for the arch of a cathedral or the curve of a drive. Yet the word is also not infrequently used within the scientific community to describe a theory when that theory has a compact and graceful mathematical underpinning.

element

Because of scientific development, the word **element** means different things depending upon which historical period you are referring to. Over 2,000 years ago there were four basic substances: earth, water, fire and air. Each one of these was called an element, and you still hear this old scientific view reflected in remarks like 'I must go out and brave the elements.' Nowadays, of course, an element is a substance which cannot be broken down into anything simpler. Thus nitrogen, copper and carbon are all elements, whereas sulphuric acid isn't an element because it can be broken down to sodium, hydrogen and oxygen. In a non-scientific context, the word 'element' is still used to express the essential core of something. 'A major element in Beethoven's music is his exploration of harmonic boundaries,' someone might say. 'Ironic control is the surpassing element of Jane Austen's genius,' someone else might say. Reference can also be made to the environment in which a creature is most at home: 'Richard is in his element at dinner parties.' The word 'element' is also used sometimes in reference to the heating appliance within an electric kettle, heater or cooker.

elephant

Most of us are acquainted with that large, vegetable-eating animal of Africa and southern Asia, but the word **elephant** is also applied to a size of paper, 28 x 23 inches.

elevator

An **elevator** is the American term for what in Britain is called a lift, but an elevator is also a machine for lifting grain to an upper storey of a barn, a hinged flap on the tailplane of an aircraft, and a muscle whose contraction raises the appropriate part of the body.

elicit, illicit

The verb **elicit** means 'to draw forth', 'to extract'. Hence you might elicit information from a witness to an accident, or you might elicit some knowledge about your ancestors from poring over the parish registers. If something is **illicit**, it is not allowed, it is against the rules or against the law. It is, for instance, illicit to sell opium in York Minster (and lots of other places too).

elite

Since the **elite** are people who are considered to be superior to others, most of us regard ourselves as belonging to some sort of elite. The word also signifies a typeface size providing twelve characters to the inch.

ember

An **ember** is a small piece of wood or coal in a smouldering fire, or the name given to the four periods of fasting that were established by the Council of Placentia in 1095. The word is also used to identify a type of goose.

embrace

If you **embrace** someone, you hold them closely in your arms. You can also embrace a point of view in that you become convinced of its validity. You can also embrace a variety of elements in your life: 'Although Wajn Sing was primarily a pianist, he also found time to embrace competitive cross country running and spasmodic work as a crossword setter.'

emerge, immerge

When you cleaned your teeth this morning, you doubtless pressed the toothpaste tube and watched the toothpaste **emerge** from the nozzle. The verb 'to emerge' means 'to come out of'. Hence the spy who has been following you over the last week might silently emerge from a tunnel and creep towards your back garden. The sun can emerge from behind a cloud, the problem of single mothers might emerge from a council discussion, or weeds might begin to emerge out of the soil as spring develops. The verb 'to **immerge**' has almost an opposite meaning to 'emerge'. If you immerge something, you dip it into a liquid. Indeed, its meaning is virtually identical to 'immerse'.

emu

The **emu** is a large, flightless bird rather like the ostrich and resident in Australia, but is also an abbreviation for 'electric multiple unit'.

en *see* N

enamel

This is an opaque or semi-transparent glossy substance that is a type of glass, the hard glossy substance that covers the crown of a tooth, and a type of paint that dries to give a smooth, hard coat.

enclosure

An **enclosure** is an area of land that is demarcated by a fence or barrier of some sort, and often used for enclosing deer or other animals. A section of a racecourse is also often called an enclosure, normally the area restricted to members. If you write a letter and also enclose some other object or document with your letter, the extra item is called an enclosure. In late eighteenth- and early nineteenth-century Britain, there was also the Enclosure Movement where open fields were hedged or fenced around so as to indicate that the land was private property.

end

There are two basic meanings for **end**. The first is to refer to an extremity or furthermost point of an object. Hence the end of a pencil is at the tip of its sharpened lead, the end of a fence is where it abuts at right-angles to a wall or other fence, and so on. Obviously most objects will have two ends, the two points most widely separated from each other. Thus one end of your washing line might be attached to the wall of your house, while the other end is attached to a pole in the garden.

The second meaning of 'end' refers to the conclusion of something, the moment when an activity ceases to occur. In August you are likely to say, 'It is nearly the end of summer now.' You may be nearing the end of the novel that you are currently reading. The end of all our lives is death.

endorse

If you **endorse** something, you declare your support for it. However, you endorse a cheque by writing your name on the back of it, and the police endorse your driving licence when they catch you speeding.

enforce

If you **enforce** something, you could be doing one of two things. You could be strengthening something, making it more stable or firm. Hence you might enforce the fence at the back of the garden. Alternatively, you could compel something to happen, insist on the observance of a rule. 'You were not popular when you decided to enforce the parking regulations in Bridge Street.'

engineer

As a noun, an **engineer** is someone who applies practical and technical skills in an attempt to create something useful or to repair something that is broken. You can be an electrical engineer, a road engineer, a chemical engineer, and so on. As a verb, however, the word has come to mean the effective accomplishment of something in almost any field. Thus you could engineer an invitation to the Lord Mayor's Banquet, a method of getting home after the last bus had gone, or an improved way of searching a database. There is a slight connotation of deviousness attached to the word.

enter

This word always carries the concept of coming into something. Thus you can enter a room, enter the army as a cadet, enter a horse for a race, or enter a record in your diary. On a computer keyboard, you can press the 'Enter' key in order to perform various functions.

entertain

You can **entertain** a group of people with your witty conversation, or you can entertain the idea of writing a series of cookery books. The first meaning implies amusement and enjoyment, the second denotes an intellectual concept or scheme.

entrance

What this word means depends on how you pronounce it. If you emphasise the -trance and lengthen the syllable, it is a verb meaning to captivate, to bewitch, to delight. If both syllables have a more or less equal emphasis, then the word is a noun meaning a door, a way in, a place of ingress.

entry

The most common meaning for **entry** is to signify the act of going. Thus refugees can seek entry to a new country, the oboe makes an entry at the beginning of Beethoven's eighth symphony, while *The Winter's Tale* begins with the entry of Camillo and Archidamus. You can also make an entry into your diary, your account book, or whatever. You can also be an entry in a race or a competition. So, although the concept of going in is always present, the contexts can be so diverse as to give 'entry' homonymic status.

equation

This is a mathematical expression where the values on the left-hand side of the equals sign are equal to the values on the right-hand side. More loosely, the word is also used whenever one is trying to determine the respective significance of a number of factors. Hence, when your parish council is trying to decide on which date to hold the swimming gala, one member of the council might say, 'Well don't forget that the state of the harvest comes into the equation.' In chemistry an equation denotes the changes that occur in a chemical reaction.

equity

While **equity** as a concept denotes the quality of being fair, impartial and just, the word is also given to a branch of law devoted to those qualities, to the value of shares that are issued by a company, and to the value of your property after all the mortgage costs have been deducted. Equity is also the name for the trade union of the acting profession.

e're, ere, err see air

erect

This is a verb meaning to build or to set up: 'We need to erect the garden shed next.' As an adjective, it denotes the state of being rigidly upright.

errant

If your husband goes out for the evening and comes home in a drunken state, you can describe him as **errant**. It denotes the straying from accepted standards. Once upon a time, however, you could be a knight errant, that is, one travelling in search of adventures and glory. In zoology, the word is also applied to worms that move about actively and are not confined to any specific area.

erupt, irrupt

These two words have similar meanings. The verb 'to **erupt**' means 'to break out suddenly, to be ejected from'. Hence you can see lava erupt from a volcano, fighting erupt between rival gangs, or even spots erupt upon one's skin. You can even erupt with laughter. If something irrupts, rather than being expelled in an outward direction, it is suddenly impelled inwards. Hence birds can irrupt into a new area or a crowd can irrupt into a room.

escape

Basically the verb 'to **escape**' means to break free from one's existing state, but the contexts in which the verb can be used and the differing connotations that it carries in those contexts qualify it as a homonym. At its simplest, one can physically escape from a situation. Thus one might break out of jail, or evade a pursuing gang. Something can also escape from one's mind. 'When talking to the Prime Minister the other day, his name escaped me, and I inadvertently called him Mr Wilson.' An escape can also be non-purposeful. Gas, for instance, can escape from a pipe, though the gas has no motive like a convicted convict. Similarly, after you have fallen down the stairs, you might thankfully comment, 'At least I escaped from breaking anything.' There is also an escape key on a computer keyboard. Sometimes it works.

escutcheon

Normally we think of an **escutcheon** as being the shield or shield-shaped surface on which a coat of arms is depicted, but it can also refer to the oval depression behind the beaks of certain bivalves, or the compartment in the middle of a ship's stern where her name is written.

even

This word has as many meanings as it has letters. It can be used to refer to the latter part of the day, though it is more commonly seen as a compound word in 'eventide' or 'evenfall'. **Even** can also indicate that something is uniform throughout, free from variations. Thus a flat area of land can be referred to as 'even', or two weights on the opposing sides of a scale will be described as even if they equal each other in weight. You may also wish to get even with someone, normally, regrettably, because you feel that they have done you a wrong and you wish to be equally unpleasant in return. Finally, 'even' can be a particle emphasising with surprise that something is the case: 'Even Peter agreed about this', or, 'We walked to the cave even though we were so tired.'

ever

This word has two meanings directly connected with time. It can signify eternity or always: 'I will love you for ever.' Or it can mean at any time: 'If ever I become rich, I'll buy you an apartment in Park Lane.' 'Ever' is also used in comparisons for emphasis as in 'I feel better than ever before', or even to express astonishment as in 'Who ever heard of such stupidity?'

ewe, Ewe, yew, you

A **ewe** is a female sheep, a **yew** is a type of tree, and **you** is the second person personal pronoun, both singular and plural, as in 'Are you going out?' A **Ewe** is a member of a West African people who live in Ghana, Togo and Benin.

ewes, use, yews

A group of **ewes** is a group of female sheep, **use** is a verb meaning 'to apply', 'to handle', 'to employ', and **yews** signifies more than one yew tree.

exact

If something is **exact**, it is precise, admitting of no deviation, and totally accurate. If, however, you need to exact some money from your brother, you are going to demand it, to insist that it is being paid. Hence it is possible for the school bully to exact an exact number of sweets from your son.

example

If something is an **example**, it can be one of two things. First of all, it can be a model to be admired and imitated. Harold is an example to all aspiring long-distance runners. Secondly, it can be a typical instance. A chimpanzee is an example of a primate.

exchange

The verb 'to **exchange**' often means the same as 'to swap'. You exchange your CD of Schubert's *Octet* for a CD of Brahm's *Alto Rhapsody*. So to exchange is to engage in a reciprocal act. Indeed, every time you buy something, you exchange some money for the item bought. But 'exchange' is also used to indicate the place where business is carried out. The Stock Exchange is the most obvious example.

excise

An **excise** is a toll or tax. It was wonderfully defined by Samuel Johnson in his Dictionary: '*Excise*: a hateful tax levied upon commodities, and adjudged not by the common judges of property, but wretches hired by those to whom excise is paid.' But if you excise something, you cut it out, you obliterate it.

excuse

If you **excuse** someone, you seek to diminish their culpability. 'It was easy to excuse Joe for being late because we all knew that his wife was not feeling well.' Thus the verb turns automatically into a noun: 'Joe's excuse for being late was that his wife was feeling ill.' But 'excuse' can have a slightly different meaning when it is used to signify that someone has received permission not to attend some function or other: 'I decided to excuse Barry from being present tonight because he's been under a lot of pressure recently.' The word, of course, is also frequently used as a social convention, so it is polite to say 'Excuse me' as you squeeze past someone in a crowd.

execute

If you **execute** a person, you bring their life to an end. If you execute a task, you complete it.

exercise

Many people **exercise** in order to keep fit. Hence they go for a run, do press-ups, lift weights, and so on. This is very different from doing an exercise in quadratic equations or Bulgarian irregular verbs. Here the object is to improve one's skill in some intellectual or commercial sphere.

exhaust

The **exhaust** is that part of a machine through which steam or combustion products exit from the system. It is also a verb which can mean to use up completely – 'If I send out the invitations, I will exhaust my supply of stamps' – or to be deprived of physical energy – 'I will exhaust myself if I run up that hill.'

expedition

If you go on an **expedition**, you will be undertaking a journey, normally a journey with a particular purpose like observing baboons in the wild, trying to find the yeti, or even just doing the week's shopping. If you do something with expedition, you perform the task promptly.

expire

If you **expire** you either die or breathe out from your lungs. Hence this verb can be applied to something that you only ever do once, or to something that you do countless times each day.

exponent

Imagine that you are a firm believer in the power of the astral signs. You are likely then to be an avid **exponent** of the virtues of astrology. More sensibly perhaps, you could be an exponent of the philosophy of Aquinas or the principles of Montessori education. Whatever the specific case, you would be someone who supports a theory and attempts to convince others of its validity. Equally you could be someone with a particular skill who displays that skill for the delight of others: 'There has been no finer exponent of the piano in my lifetime than Alfred Brendel.' In mathematics, an exponent is a quantity that represents the power to which a given number is raised.

exposure

This word always carries the sense of something being revealed. Thus, if your quaint habit of walking round the garden naked at three o'clock in the morning while playing the banjo is revealed in the local paper, you have been subject to **exposure**. Less embarrassingly, someone at work lets slip that your seminal work on cobalt is nearing completion, and this is exposed in a scientific journal. A film needs exposure before it can be seen. Even if you suffer from exposure on a mountain top, this suffering is the result of not wearing adequate clothing for the conditions, i.e. you reveal too much of yourself to the elements.

express

If you **express** yourself, you speak or write, you articulate your thoughts in words. If something travels express, it proceeds as quickly as it can.

extract

An **extract** is a portion taken from a book, play or film and cited for illustrative purposes, but 'extract' as a verb means to force something out of something else. Thus you might extract some glass from your car tyre, some enzyme from a plant, or some information from your daughter.

eye *see* aye

eyed, I'd, ide

If you **eyed** someone, you would be glancing at them, being visually aware that they were there. **I'd** is a common contraction for 'I would' or 'I had', and an **ide** is a freshwater cyprinoid fish of northern Europe.

eyelet, islet

An **eyelet** is a small hole through which you thread something. Thus you often have eyelets in shoes through which laces are threaded. An **islet** is a small island.

eyespot

An **eyespot** is a light-sensitive pigmented spot on the bodies of invertebrates such as flatworms, starfish and microscopic crustaceans, a rounded eye-like marking on an animal, or a fungal disease of cereals.

F

fabric

We mostly think of a **fabric** as being a cloth produced by weaving or knitting, but the word is also used to denote the walls, floor and roof of a building, and the body of a car or aircraft. The word derives from the Latin *fabrica* meaning something skilfully produced.

face

We recognise most people by looking at their **face**, that front part of the head extending from the chin to the forehead. The word is also used for the surface of almost anything. Hence you can have the face of a coin, a clock face, the front or face of a building, the coal face of a mine, the face of the moon, and so on. The word can also be a verb. You can face up to something when you decide to confront a problem. If you confront someone face to face, it implies that you are attempting to resolve an issue. The word is also a colloquialism for 'impudence' or 'effrontery', and has been so since the sixteenth century. Equally colloquially, it can be a shorthand term for make-up: 'She took off her face before going to bed.' The word comes from Old French based on the Latin *facies* meaning 'form, appearance, face'.

facies

There is a medical condition called **facies** that forces the face of the individual suffering from it to assume a particular expression. The same word is used by geologists to refer to the character of a rock as expressed by its formation, composition and fossil content.

facility

A **facility** can be a special talent that a person possesses – you may have a facility for remembering phone numbers or for discovering the lair of a snow leopard – or a facility may be a special feature of a machine or service: 'Our digital TV recorder has the facility of being able to record two programmes simultaneously.'

factor

As a noun, **factor** has a number of separate meanings. In broad terms, it means a circumstance, fact or influence that contributes to a result, but within that umbrella definition, there are a number of specialist applications. Thus a factor can be a gene that determines a hereditary characteristic, the Rhesus factor being a well-known example. In mathematics, a factor is a number that, when multiplied, produces another number with no remainder. Thus two and three are both factors of six. In physiology, a factor is any one of a number of substances in the blood that are involved in coagulation. In business, a factor is a person who buys and sells goods on commission. A factor is also an element to be considered in a situation. In deciding whether or not to go for a walk, the state of the weather, the time that you have available, and the condition of your shoes are all factors that need to be considered. A person who acts for someone else in a commercial operation is also called a factor. The word derives from the Latin verb *facere* meaning 'to do', as, of course, do words like 'factory' and 'factotum'.

facts, fax

Facts are things that are demonstrably true. Hence the battle of Hastings was in 1066, Jane Austen wrote *Emma*, and the chimpanzee is a primate are all facts. The word, however, can be used metaphorically. When a politician says, 'The facts of the matter are . . . ', he actually means 'The most self-flattering way of looking at this situation is . . . ' A **fax** is a widespread image transmission technology. A document is first scanned and the resulting signal is then transmitted by wire or radio. The word 'fax' did not become really well-known until the 1970s.

faculty

If you or an organisation has the **faculty** of doing something, then you or it will presumably go ahead and do it. For instance, you have the faculty of seeing with your eyes, and exercise that faculty every day. The company Scrooge & Fagin have the faculty of extorting payments from their clients and do so on a regular basis. A faculty, however, need not simply be the ability, aptitude or capacity of doing something. Normally with a capital F, a Faculty may also be a department within a college or university. Hence you may study within the Faculty of Law or the Faculty of Theology. Neither Faculty may be pleased when you point out to them that the word 'faculty' derives from the Latin *facilis* which means 'easy'. They might, however, respond by telling you that *facilis* itself comes from *facere*, a verb meaning 'to do' or 'to make'.

fag

This simple three-letter word has at least four different meanings. First of all, a **fag** can be an activity that causes weariness: 'It is a fag having to sweep the courtyard every morning.' Secondly, in some English public schools, a fag is a junior pupil in the school who performs certain duties for a senior pupil. A fag is also a slang word for a cigarette, a male homosexual, and a disease that afflicts sheep. There is also the colloquial expression 'at the fag end of a conversation', meaning towards the end of said conversation.

faggot

A **faggot** can be a ball or roll of seasoned chopped liver (the word is normally used in the plural in this context), a bundle of sticks bound together as fuel, a bundle of iron rods bound together for reheating, and an American slang term for a male homosexual.

fain, feign

The word **fain**, from an Old English word meaning 'to rejoice', now normally means 'to be necessitated' or 'obliged'. Hence you could say, 'I must fain go now and begin to prepare for dinner.' **Feign** on the other hand means 'to pretend', 'to invent' or 'to dissemble'.

faint, feint

If you are feeling **faint**, you are sluggish, lacking in energy and generally feeble. If in fact you do faint, you swoon into a brief unconsciousness. The word can also refer to a hope or opportunity, and if that hope is a faint one, it means that it has little chance of being fulfilled. Similarly, if you detect a faint smell, sight or sound, the impression you gain is a very slight one. A **feint** is an action intended to deceive. An army may look as if it is about to attack from the left, whereas in fact they are going to surprise from the right. This is a feint. In boxing you may feint with your left hand and then aim a real blow with your right.

fair, fare

As a noun, a **fair** is a periodic gathering of people for some commercial event. Thus you can have a sheep fair where sheep are bought and sold, a horse fair, a cattle fair, and so on. A fair can also be a combination of stalls and rides calculated to appeal to children, sometimes devised by a charitable organisation to raise funds, more often run by a travelling company who erect helter-skelters and ghost trains as a living. Ironically, this use of 'fair' derives from the Latin *feria* which means 'holy day', because fairs in the middle ages were often held on saints' days. As an adjective, 'fair' can signify something that is attractive to look at ('women are the fair sex'), something that is light in colour ('just look at her fair hair'), something that is just and equitable ('that was a fair trial'), something that is clear and distinct ('you get a fair view from the tower'), or even to indicate a noticeable length of time ('I had to wait a fair time'). As a noun, **fare** can signify the amount of money charged for a journey (bus fare, train fare, etc.), or an amount of food ('a cheese salad will be my fare tonight'). As a verb, 'fare' can indicate one's state of being ('I fare pretty well at the moment').

fairing, faring

Apparently **fairing** can be a complimentary gift, and the *Shorter Oxford* suggests that originally it was one bought or given at a fair. The action of fairing is also that of making an aircraft smooth and streamlined. **Faring** is a word used when you want to indicate a state of progress. You may ask a friend, 'How are you faring?' or you may reply in answer to a question, 'I'm faring pretty well at the moment.'

fairway, fareway

These are alternative spellings of the same word which means either a navigable channel in a river or between rocks, or the smooth part of a golf course that lies between the tee and the putting green.

fairy

Most people have a number of these at the bottom of the garden – or at least, such is a popular and jocular saying. A **fairy** is a supernatural being, small in size, traditionally equipped with wings, and capable of doing good or evil to the human beings it encounters. It is also a colloquial term for a homosexual and a Central and South American humming bird. The word is also an essential component of other nouns: fairy cake, fairy floss, fairy fly, fairy godmother, fairyland, fairy lights, fairy ring, fairy shrimp, fairy story, fairy tern, fairy wren.

faithful

This is word often used purely to indicate sexual fidelity: 'He's always been faithful to his wife.' But **faithful** has a much broader meaning too, since it means the state of being true to one's word, of being loyal to a cause, of being conscientious in one's duty.

faker, fakir

These two words are hardly homophones since the '-ir' of **fakir** ought to be clearly stressed, but, as always, it depends on who is pronouncing it. A **faker** is someone who fakes, who pretends that something false is in fact true, or tries to pass off as genuine something that he or she knocked up in the garden shed this morning. A fakir is a poor Hindu ascetic, unless, of course, it is a faker pretending to religious humility in order to cadge some money off you.

fall

A **fall** is always unfortunate, but it has a diversity of applications. The simplest is when one accidentally drops from a higher elevation to a lower one. Thus someone may have a fall in the street, and change from being upright to being prone on the ground. There may be a fall in the temperature, and so the air feels cooler. Someone may give you some bad news, and so your face falls, and you have a mournful expression. You may have a moral fall, in that yesterday you were training for the priesthood, but today have decided to become a dealer in drugs. (Some might argue that there is no moral difference between those two professions.) Music, as Orlando notes in the first scene of *Twelfth Night*, may have a dying fall. There is also, of course, the fall, the mythical event when Adam and Eve in the Garden of Eden disobeyed God and hence introduced human death and suffering into the world. In North America, fall is a synonym for autumn, and since the 1960s the expression 'fall about' has meant to 'to laugh'.

familiar

If something is **familiar** to you, then you are accustomed to it and well acquainted with it. You are doubtless familiar, for instance, with the drink of tea since, for the British, it is the universal panacea. Equally you are likely to be on familiar terms with at least some of your friends. However, the word can also be a noun, it which case it refers to an official who belongs to the household of the Pope or a bishop and who performs domestic duties. Once upon a time, a familiar was a spirit slave who took human, cat or raven shape, and who assisted a witch or wizard. Shakespeare's *Henry VI, Part 2* has the strange line, 'Away with him! he has a familiar under his tongue.'

family

We all know that a **family** is a group of individuals who are genetically related to each other, and who often live with each other: parents and children, for instance. In biology, however, a family is a taxonomic category ranking above genus and below order. In mathematics, a family is a group of curves or surfaces obtained by varying the value of a constant in the equation generating them. Languages that are related to each other are also often grouped into a family.

fan

A **fan** can be a triangular-shaped object that one waves in front of one's face in order to produce a slight current of cooling air, an electrical or wind-powered implement that produces a current of air for ventilation, the flukes of a whale's tail, or an enthusiast for something (normally pop stars or football teams). Originally the Old English word *fann* denoted a device for winnowing grain.

fancy

If something is **fancy**, then it is ornate or decorative, and exists largely for ornamental purposes: 'Your dress is very fancy.' Your fancy, however, can also be your imagination or your belief in something that cannot be proved: 'I fancy that Tranmere Rovers will win the FA Cup this year.' You may also fancy someone, in that you are sexually attracted to them. The word can also be an exclamation of surprise.

fare *see* **fair**

fareway *see* **fairway**

faring *see* **fairing**

farm

A **farm** is an establishment in which agricultural activities like breeding cattle, growing crops, etc. are carried out. But the word can also be a verb meaning, obviously, to engage in agricultural activities, but also to let out a property or an employment to someone else: 'I decided to farm out the database search to young Kevin.' You can also farm out a footballer to another team, or a child to a childminder.

fashion

For women in particular, **fashion** is of intense interest, since it is the changing modes of attire that are dreamt up by clothing establishments for sale at ludicrous prices. It is interesting that 'fashion' as a noun has developed this meaning, because 'fashion' as a verb simply means to create, to make: 'I must fashion some way of making all the relevant addresses available to the committee.' Consequently the phrase 'out of fashion' originally meant 'out of shape'. The word can also be used to denote current practice: 'It is the fashion here to have a jam tart during afternoon tea break.'

fast

If you run a race quickly, you are going to cover the ground in an extremely **fast** fashion, though clearly you will not be anything like as fast as a galloping horse or a racing car. Clearly, then, 'fast' indicates swift motion, though, at the same time, we often call a clock or watch fast if its hands go round that little bit more quickly than they ought. If, however, you tie something fast to the wall, you are thereby ensuring that whatever is tied doesn't move at all. Something that is fast in this sense is secure, fixed and stable. A colour too can be fast, indicating that it does not diminish in intensity if it is washed. You can be fast asleep, indicating that your sleep is deep and unbroken. In photography, a fast film is one that only requires a short exposure. Quite differently, you may decide to fast, which means that you abstain from food. Equally differently, if you are described as a fast woman, the implication is that you are loose and casual in your social connections, and probably undiscriminating in your sexual behaviour. Hence this word has at least six differing connotations, some of which are conceptually entirely disparate.

fat

All animal body tissues contain **fat**, a natural oily substance, and that is the root meaning of this word. However, animals (particularly humans) that have too much fat in their body tissues are simply, and disapprovingly, referred to as fat, so the body substance 'fat' is extended in meaning from its entirely neutral chemical definition, to include the connotation of an obese, corpulent creature, unattractive in appearance. 'Fat' is also metaphorically extended in a different way. If you say 'Michael is getting fat since he started working at Grogan's,' you don't necessarily mean that he is becoming obese. Instead you could be implying that his salary has considerably increased, that his perks are plentiful and that he is now living a life of considerable ease. The word is also used informally to indicate that there is very little chance of something happening: 'There's fat chance of that taking place.'

fate, fête

The word **fate** denotes some mystical force which determines our ends. Thus you were fated to forget Mrs Robinson's birthday, fated to become a historian, or fated to be late at the wedding. There were in Roman mythology three Fates, goddesses who presided over the birth and life of humans. A **fête** is an entertainment of some kind, often held out of doors, and frequently occasioned by some pressing need to raise funds for the church restoration. A fête is often marked by stalls offering second-hand goods for sale and, if you are very unlucky, by displays of morris dancing and chances to guess the weight of the pig.

fated, fêted

If something is **fated**, it was inevitably going to happen. If something is **fêted**, it is celebrated.

father

Each of us has or had a **father**, the male person whose seed combined with the mother's egg to create a new human being. Because one's father is one of the essential begetters of this new life, the word has been figuratively used to describe any person who originated a new process or movement. Abraham Darby, with his invention of a new smelting process, is sometimes called the father of the Industrial Revolution. In addition, a priest (particularly in the Roman Catholic Church) is often called Father, and Christian theologians of the first five centuries AD are sometimes called the Fathers. The word is also sometimes gratuitously given to any aged male person, as well as being bestowed upon an entirely mythical creature called Father Christmas.

fathom

A **fathom** used to be a measure of length, one originally determined by the stretching of one's arms in a straight line to a full length, and equal to six feet. It is now little used as a measurement except for measuring the depth of sea water, but the word is still used as a verb meaning 'to comprehend, to understand'. Hence you can hear someone say, 'I need to fathom this out before I can make any more progress.' There is an interesting conceptual link between the two meanings of the word. If you hold out your arms, it looks as if you are ready to embrace, and if you embrace something, you seek to understand it.

fatigue

As a noun, **fatigue** means extreme tiredness. Hence you are likely to suffer fatigue if you go for a six-mile run, climb Mount Snowdon, memorise the dates of all the English kings and queens or watch a party-political broadcast. The word is also used to denote a weakness in metal or other materials caused by repeated variations of stress.

fault

If something is your **fault**, then you have made a mistake, committed some error. A fault is a failing, a defect, an imperfection. In the game of tennis, a fault is a service or shot in which the ball fails to land within the prescribed limits. In hunting, a fault is when the hounds lose the scent. In geology, a fault is where there is a break in the continuity of the strata.

faun, fawn

A **faun** was a god or demigod worshipped by farmers and shepherds. Represented as men with horns and the tails of a goat, they were reputedly extremely lustful. A **fawn** is a young deer, or, as a verb, the act of showing servile delight and joy in someone else's presence.

faux, foe

If something is **faux**, it has been made in imitation of something else. Hence you could have a string of faux pearls. A **foe** is an opponent, an enemy.

favour

When you do a kindness to someone else, then you have done them a **favour**. It may be that at work, you favour one colleague above all the others, which may or may not breed resentment among those others. Yet 'favour' can also refer to outward appearance. In *Love's Labour's Lost*, Shakespeare has one character saying, 'This favour shalt thou wear.'

fawn *see* faun

fax *see* facts

fay, fey

A **fay** is a fairy, though the *Shorter Oxford* doesn't admit this, and instead thinks that 'fay' is a verb meaning 'to fit, adapt or join'. If you are **fey**, you give an impression of being other-worldly, too vague to be fully connected to reality.

fays, faze, phase

It is rare to have three words all sounding virtually identical. **Fays** is just the plural of 'fay' and hence means 'fairies'. **Faze** is a verb meaning to 'discompose', and always seems to be used with a preceding 'not': 'I was not fazed by his interruption.' A **phase** can be a number of things. The moon passes through sundry phases, depending upon the degree of illumination that it receives from the sun. Human beings, children in particular, are said to go through phases, each phase being a stage in their mental and emotional development. In physics, a phase is a particular change or point in a recurring sequence of movements. In systemic grammar, a phase is the relationship between a catenative verb and the verb that follows it.

feat, feet

A **feat** is an exceptional act, a remarkable accomplishment: 'It is still a major feat to swim the English Channel.' **Feet**, of course, are the flattened appendages at the end of the legs that are in contact with the ground when walking or running, though in the old Imperial measurement system, feet are also a measurement of distance, twelve inches making up one foot. In Britain, people's height is still normally registered in feet and inches.

feather

Apart from being an epidermal appendage of a bird, **feather** can also be a verb denoting a rowing action.

feature

This word used to be confined to an aspect of a greater whole. Thus you could have a **feature** of the landscape, a feature of someone's work, or a feature of someone's face. Today, however, a feature can be any television programme, magazine article or film for which they are unable to invent a more revealing label.

feel

Broadly speaking, the verb 'to **feel**' can relate to the physical sense of touching something or being touched by it, and hence experiencing it as a texture against one's skin or body, or the mental sense of experiencing an emotion or reaction. Hence you can physically feel the silk against your skin, and mentally feel disappointed that you were not elected head gardener of Hinstock Hall.

feet *see* feat

feign *see* fain

feint *see* faint

fell

This word is the past tense of the verb 'to fall'. It is also the skin or hide of an animal, a hill or mountain, lead ore in its rough state, or, as an adjective or adverb, **fell** can mean fierce, savage, unrelenting. As a verb, you can fell a man or a tree, in the first case by knocking the man down, and in the second by chopping the tree down.

felon

Most of us think of a **felon** as a criminal, legally someone who has committed a felony, but the word can also mean a small abscess or boil.

felt

This is the past tense of the verb 'to feel', as well as being a kind of cloth made of wool.

female

In the animal kingdom, the **female** is the sex that bears offspring, but among human beings, the word is entirely impossible to define, the sex to which it refers being so varied, disparate and contradictory.

fen

A **fen** is a low-lying area almost entirely covered by water, but it can also be a mould that attacks the hop plant, or a synonym for 'forbid' and so used apparently by boys playing marbles. It is also a monetary unit of China, equal to one hundredth of a yuan.

fence

A **fence** is a barrier, normally made of wood or metal, that separates one entity from another. Hence you have fences around fields, parks, houses or monuments. The word is also a colloquial term for a receiver of stolen goods, and, as a verb, relates to a type of sword combat. From that last usage, the meaning can be extended to verbal combat also.

feral

An adjective, **feral** relates either to death or to being wild and untamed. Hence you could refer to a feral disease or to the feral atmosphere at the undertakers. Alternatively, you could mention that your garden is in a feral state, or that your son has become feral since joining the Bash Street Kids' Gang.

ferment

If a liquid ferments, some of its contents turn into alcohol. But you can also **ferment** trouble by stirring up agitation.

ferrate, ferret

Something that is **ferrate** is a salt of ferric acid. A **ferret** is a half-tamed polecat, and since ferrets were used to eliminate unwanted other animals, the word has since transposed into a verb meaning 'to search out'. The respective pronunciations of these words are distinct enough to make their entry in this dictionary extremely dubious.

fess

In the quaint world of heraldry, a **fess** is an ordinary in the form of a broad horizontal stripe across the middle of the shield. The word is also sometimes used as an informal and casual adaptation of the verb 'confess': 'Come on, Jason. Fess up. What were you doing in the dormitory?'

festoon

If you **festoon** someone or something, you place a chain or garland of flowers, leaves or ribbons upon then as a decoration. A festoon is also a Eurasian butterfly or moth patterned with dark arcs on a lighter background.

fetch

All English speakers know the verb **fetch** as meaning 'to go in quest of and to bring back'. Hence you go into the house to fetch your car keys. The word though can also mean a considerable distance: 'It's a fair fetch to Wissendine from here.' An item in an auction can also fetch a particular price. The word can also mean the distance travelled by wind or waves across open water. More alarmingly, a fetch can also be an apparition of someone still alive, and is interpreted as a sign of their impending death.

fetish

A **fetish** is an inanimate object that is worshipped for its supposedly magical powers, but for most people today a fetish is some relatively bizarre sexual practice or desire, or even an irrational and excessive devotion to any kind of practice. Licking chocolate off your lover's toes would be seen as a sexual fetish; saluting every time you saw the Prime Minister on television would be seen as a political fetish (or possibly just as insanity).

few, phew

Few is an adjective that means 'not many': 'There were few people out in the rain to witness the ceremonial hanging of Tony Blair.' **Phew**, which has a slightly more breathy sound than 'few', is an exclamation meaning 'Good gracious', and is normally used when one has just escaped from some imminent danger.

fey *see* fay

fiat

Apart from the being the name of a well-known car, **fiat** is a synonym for 'command', 'order' or 'demand'. You might say, 'Nothing can be done without the mayor's fiat.' However, in the Vulgate, the command '*Fiat lux*' (Let there be light), means that 'fiat', in religious circles, tends to have the connotation of creation, not just command.

fibula

The **fibula** is a bone between the knee and the ankle, and, in archaeology, a brooch or clasp.

fiddle

In musical terms, a **fiddle** is a somewhat slang word for the violin, but if you fiddle with something, you are just inconsequently handling it in an abstracted fashion. A fiddle is also a barely legal dodge whereby you charge more for something than you should or gain some benefit to which you are not entitled. At sea, a fiddle is a rack or frame designed to prevent things rolling off the table. In agriculture, a fiddle is a long wooden bar attached to the traces of a horse and designed to drag loose hay or straw on the ground.

fiddler

Self-evidently, a **fiddler** is someone who fiddles, either because they play the violin, or because they are prone to cheat others. The word is also used to denote at least three different animals, a fly resembling a cockroach, the angel or shark-ray, and a small crab.

field

Physically a **field** is an enclosed stretch of land used for grazing animals or growing crops. However, equally physically, the word is also used for the land on which certain games are played. Hence you have a cricket field, a football field, a hockey field and so on. Non-physically, a field is an area of intellectual interest. Your field might be the novels of Bulwer Lytton, while someone else's field is the role of black holes in the universe. A field is also in computing the space taken up by an item of data. The word can also be a verb in that you can field a ball in certain sports like cricket, field a candidate in an election (i.e. put one up to be elected), field a number of tricky questions, or field an army on a battlefield.

fiend

A **fiend** can be an evil spirit or demon, or a fanatic for some activity like football.

fig

While a **fig** is a fruit from the fig tree, the word has also come to signify a contemptuous dismissal – 'I don't give a fig for what Alan says.' It can also be an informal term for smart clothes: 'Gerald was in fine fig at the regimental dinner.'

figure

Something's **figure** is its outward appearance, its shape and form. Hence you might say that the ocean liner cut a fine figure as it sailed across the Pacific, or you might admire the figure of Miss World. But the word is also used in a variety of other instances. A number like 2, 6 or 9 is a figure. If you are selling something, you might be asked to put a figure on it, that is, state an expected price. A diagram in a scientific textbook can be called a figure. An imagistic or metaphorical use of words can be called a figure. A musical phrase can be termed a figure. In certain types of dancing, you and the other dancers create a figure. In logic a figure is a syllogism. It can even be used as a verb, so that if you figure something out, you sort out its proper meaning. Equally, if you figure in something, you play a significant part in it.

filament

A **filament** is a slender, thread-like object or fibre, especially one found in animal or plant structures. In electronics, a filament is a conducting wire or thread with a high melting point.

file, phial

As noun or verb, **file** can signify a number of things. The most practical is that metal instrument that you use to grind away at the bars on your prison cell window before making your daring escape. Such instruments have at least one of their sides covered with small cutting edges or teeth so that they can gradually wear away the substance against which they are being rubbed. A file is also a collection of documents relating to some topic or case. You can have a file of people marching in unison. Every chessboard has eight files, stretching across the board from player to player. When queuing at the supermarket checkout, you tend to stand in file with other customers. You tend to file your important documents in a filing cabinet so that you can find them when needed. **Phial**, however, simply means a small container or bottle for liquids.

fill

The verb 'to **fill**' can mean three slightly different things. The most common of them is to cause a space or container to contain more things than it initially does. Hence you might fill a bottle with water, a suitcase with clothes, or a box with screws and washers. Equally you can fill up a hole with earth, or a cave with debris. However, if someone in your company resigns, you will need to fill his or her position. Clearly this is a different sort of filling from that of filling a cup with a drink of tea. Thirdly, you may have some spare time, and you decide to fill it by learning Serbo-Croat or dissecting a rabbit. As a noun, the word can be used to signify an amount of something which is as much as one can take at any one time: 'I have eaten my fill', or, 'I have had my fill of surprises for one day.'

fillet

Many of us only experience a **fillet** when we buy the undercut of a sirloin or the middle part of a leg of veal or a slice of fish. Such fleshy, easily detachable slices of meat are generally referred to as fillets. But a fillet can also be a band of material for binding one's hair, a thin, narrow strip of almost anything, a horizontal band on a shield, or a narrow flat band separating two mouldings on a building.

fills, fils

Fills is the form of the verb 'to fill' normally only used in the third person singular form of the present tense: he fills, she fills, it fills. According to a file on the Internet, a **fils** is one one-thousandth of an Iraqi dinar. I doubt if you knew that before.

film

Most of the time we think of a **film** as a story that we watch on television or at the cinema (*King Kong* or *Dr No*), or as a thin flexible strip of plastic which we load into a camera in order to take pictures of our loved ones. From time to time, though, our eyes may film over when they appear to become covered with a thin layer of something.

filter, philtre

A **filter** is a material through which liquids are passed in order to extract from the liquid any foreign bodies. Filter can also be used as a verb, so that when you are listening to Rosemary explaining about her holiday, you filter out any unnecessary material and only retain that she had a wonderful time. There may also be a filter lane on the road along which you are travelling. This is an arrangement whereby a vehicle may turn left (or right) while the rest of the traffic is halted by some traffic lights. A **philtre** is a love potion. Apart from the fact that philtres don't work, it is always difficult ensuring that the requisite dosage is imbibed by your loved one.

find, fined

If you **find** something, you discover something for which you were looking. If you are **fined**, you are charged a sum of money in recompense for your evil in breaking some law or regulation.

fine

This innocent-looking word can serve as a noun, a verb, an adverb and an adjective. As a noun, it can denote those very small particles found in milling or mining, a sum of money extracted from you as a punishment for some evil act you have committed, a high-quality French brandy, or a musical direction indicating that the musical piece has ended (in which case it is a two-syllable word). As an adjective, **fine** can indicate high quality ('This is a very fine suit'), something thin or narrow ('a fine nylon thread'), or a position on the cricket field like fine leg. As a verb, you can fine beer or wine by causing the precipitation of sediment during production, or you can fine someone for parking in the wrong place. As an adverb, the word indicates that things are pleasing or at least satisfactory: 'My new job is going along fine.'

finger

Eight of the digits protruding from our hands are called fingers, and they, together with the two thumbs, provide human beings with much of their manual dexterity. Consequently there has been a tendency to label anything that protrudes from anything else, a **finger**. The word 'finger' has also developed a few figurative uses as well. If you finger someone, you identify them as the source of whatever is currently concerning you. You habitually finger people if you are a pickpocket. Literal fingers are also used in a variety of gesticulations, most of which have extremely rude connotations.

finish, Finnish

If you **finish** something, you complete it. Hence you might finish reading a novel, finish running a race, finish knitting a sweater and so on. The word can also be used to denote the external appearance of something: 'That coat of paint gives a nice finish to the fence.' The homophone **Finnish** should not appear in this dictionary because it is a proper noun and simply refers to someone who was born in Finland.

fir, fur, furr

Fir is the name given to a number of coniferous trees. **Fur** is the hairy, external covering of many animals, and is consequently often used to make expensive coats for the morally insensitive rich. The word 'fur' is also often used to describe material which, through chemical reactions, deposits itself on other objects. Thus a kettle can fur up because of the carbonate of lime that is deposited on the element of the kettle as a deposit from the water it boils. According to an Internet source, **furr** is to separate with strips of wood, but I am unable to find this word in the full *OED*, the *Shorter Oxford* or anything else, so I think that we are safe in assuming that it is another example of Internet invention.

fire

As we all know, **fire** is that extremely hot entity that is produced when combustible objects are set alight. A fire is normally associated also with flames and smoke. As a verb, 'fire' means to discharge a gun or other weapon in order to propel something (a bullet or an arrow) at something else. It is also possible for a person to be on fire with something, namely very excited and enthusiastic. Indeed, his enthusiasm for it may be sufficient to fire up someone else with a similar passion. In addition, of course, the word 'fire' is an essential component of many other words: firearm, firebrand, fireguard, fireproof and firewall, for instance.

firm

If something is **firm**, it is stable, not easily moved, fixed. A firm is also a business establishment, a plumber, a grocer, an electrician and so on. Presumably the term came about because the establishment was itself stable and reliable and hence was a firm establishment.

fish

A **fish** is a limbless cold-blooded animal that lives in water. It is also a sign of the Zodiac, and a flat plate that is fixed on a beam or across a joint in order to give additional strength. As a verb, one can fish for fish (i.e. attempt to catch fish) or one can fish for a compliment (i.e. attempt to extort one), or fish in a pocket for something that you are trying to find.

fisher, fissure

These are not complete homophones, but once again slovenly pronunciation often makes them so. A **fisher** is someone who fishes, normally for fish, but sometimes for compliments, and in the case of the apostles and other evangelicals, for men. A **fissure** is a cleft in the earth, and as such of interest to geologists and of danger to walkers.

fit

This simple word has manifold uses. If you have a **fit** you are seized by a sudden paroxysm which may cause you to faint. If you buy a new garment, you obviously make sure that it fits you; clothes that don't fit look unkempt and absurd. If you care for your health, you may take steps to keep fit, to keep your body in good running order. You may wish to attend a class on pottery for beginners, but, alas, it does not fit in with your other commitments. It may be that you are so dismayed with the recent actions of the government that you have a fit of depression. So, three simple letters and we have a word that is a noun for a sudden seizure, a verb indicating that your clothes are of the right measurement, an adjective indicating physical ability, a verb indicating congruence with other concerns, and a noun meaning a period of time.

fix

As a verb, **fix** has a number of roughly related meanings. If you fix something, you fasten it securely to something else. Hence you might fix a door knob to the door itself. If you fix your eyes on something, you stare at it with concentration. 'Every time that I visit the National Gallery in London, I fix my eyes on Leonardo's *Virgin of the Rocks* because it is the most miraculous painting that I have ever seen.' If your digital camera ceases to work, you may be able to fix it by inserting new batteries. If your daughter is coming to visit you, it may be possible to fix a dinner engagement with Patrick whom you know she likes. In the forthcoming match between Manchester United and Chelsea, and which you desperately want Chelsea to win, you may be able to fix it by offering Alex Ferguson, the United manager, a free pack of chewing gum. (To put it mildly, this is unlikely.) In all these instances, the verb 'to fix', despite the widely differing contexts, denotes the concept of changing situation A into situation B. As a noun, 'fix' can signify four different things. If you are in a fix, you are in a difficult situation. If you have a fix, you take some drug to which you are addicted. If you engineer a fix, you dishonestly ensure some particular outcome. If you get a fix on something, you are likely to gain visual or radio bearings on the position of something.

fixture

A **fixture** can be an object that is fixed into a particular position in a building, site or a vehicle. Thus the Cenotaph is a fixture in Whitehall, and the gear lever is a fixture in your car. A fixture is also an event, often a sporting one, that has been arranged for a particular date.

flag

Perhaps the first object that the word **flag** suggests is a piece of bunting, normally rectangular in shape, that hangs from a pole and waves in the wind, and represents a country or organisation. The Union Jack is the flag of Great Britain. But a flag can also be a slab of paving stone, often a constituent of a pavement, or a plant with sword-shaped leaves that grow from a rhizome. The word can also be a verb. If you stand in the road and violently wave at an approaching car, you are trying to flag the car down so that it will stop. (Presumably you know the driver and are merely attempting to cadge a lift home.) Alternatively, during a cross-country race, you may begin to flag after about five miles. Here flag means a loss of energy and determination. Most of us begin to flag towards the end of the day.

flair, flare

If you have a **flair** for something, you have an inherent ability. Thus some have a flair for dressmaking, others for cooking or playing the piano. I was amazed to discover that my 1965 printing of the *Shorter Oxford* makes no mention of this common meaning, a meaning that dates at least from the nineteenth century. A **flare** is a bright but normally short-lived light, though the word can also be a verb meaning to break out suddenly. Thus you might flare up in temper, or your normally quiescent ulcer might flare up in pain.

flake

Probably most of us think of a **flake** of snow, yet this word has a number of much less common meanings. It is a frame or rack for storing provisions, a frame for drying fish, a portion of ignited material thrown off into the air during burning, a thin piece of wood or other material broken off accidentally, a lock of hair or even a kind of carnation. Interestingly, in 1906, the word 'flake' was adopted as a replacement for the term 'dogfish', it being felt that the name 'dogfish' discouraged sales. One assumes that 'flake' wasn't terribly successful either, since in 1931 it too was jettisoned and replaced by 'rock salmon'.

flame

A **flame** is a tongue of fire emitted from a match, lighter, fire or furnace. The word is also used to denote a member of the opposite sex with whom you are having a sexual relationship of some kind, though in this context the noun is often preceded by the adjective 'old', indicating that the romantic connection no longer exists.

flank

If one is a man, one's **flank** is the fleshy part between the ribs and the hip, but the word can be used to denote the side of almost anything. Thus it can be used to signify the side of a building, or the right or left side of a military formation.

flannel

A **flannel** is a small square of cloth used for wiping one's hands and face. It is also a cloth material often used for the making of trousers, and thus inspired Kipling's impious remark about 'the flannelled fools at the wicket'. Flannel is also often used to denote evasive or flattering talk.

flap

A flag will **flap** in the wind, that is, it will move from side to side as it responds to the breeze. As a noun, the word can be applied to loose skin attached to the body only at its base. A flap can also be a colloquial term to denote a short period of chaos and confusion.

flare *see* flair

flash

Like so many words, **flash** can be a noun, adjective or verb. As a noun, a flash is a sudden, bright burst of light, a camera attachment that produces such a light, a sudden burst of insight or inspiration, or the public exhibition of one's genitals. The verb usages are all directly derived from the four definitions just given. As an adjective, 'flash' indicates something rather ostentatious and expensive: 'He had a flash car.'

flat

If something is **flat**, it is horizontally level. Hence the surface of a table is flat. But the word is also used in a variety of other ways. An apartment in a building in which one or more people live is often called a flat. A speech or event that is devoid of real interest could be described as flat. If a note is a semi-tone lower than the pure note, it will be described as flat. A sparkling wine, if left open for too long, will go flat. An unvarying charge for some service can be termed a flat rate. An upright section of stage scenery is often referred to as a flat.

flathead

A **flathead** is an edible tropical marine fish or a member of certain North American Indian people.

flea, flee

A **flea** is a small wingless insect that feeds off the blood of man and other animals. Most of us are likely to **flee** (run away) if confronted by a swarm of

fleas

flecks, flex

A fleck is a tiny speck of something, and flecks is simply the plural of that word. It is a homophone with flex, a verb meaning to bend, or a noun signifying flexible, insulating wire.

fleece

The **fleece** of a sheep or goat is the woolly covering of their bodies. As a verb, to fleece someone is to fraudulently overcharge them.

fleet

As a noun, **fleet** signifies a sea force or naval company, though it can also be a dialect word for a marshland creek. As an adjective, 'fleet' means rapid or swift, and as an adverb the word can signify that something is at or to a small depth.

flesh

The **flesh** of a human being or other animal is that substance lying beneath the skin consisting of muscle and fat. As a verb, if you flesh out, you put weight on. You can also flesh something out when you give more details to add to the bare outline that your audience has so far received.

flew, flue

The word **flew** is the past tense of the verbs 'to flee' or 'to fly', while **flue** is a noun denoting a passageway for hot gases or liquids to escape. 'Flu' is also a common abbreviation for the illness of influenza.

flex *see* flecks

flic, flick

A **flic** is a computer file containing computer animation. If you **flick** something, you give it a light, passing blow with your hand or a whip. If you flick through a book, you rapidly scan its contents. The word is also a slang word for a film, used first in the 1920s, probably because films then tended to flicker.

flight

As a noun, the word **flight** can signify the process of something flying through the air. Hence you can watch the flight of some birds or the flight of a cricket ball. If you travel by aircraft, you might be on a flight to Rome. The word also denotes the action of fleeing from danger or persecution. An example would be the flight of the Israelites from Egypt under the leadership of Moses. You can also have a flight of capital when stocks and shares are sold in great numbers and drop massively in price. You can also climb a flight of stairs, a set that connects one floor with another. You might even have a flight of fancy when you imagined that you were Superman or Batwoman. The feathers at the end of an arrow are also called the flight.

fling

To **fling** something is to throw it away, to toss it aside. The word is also a colloquial noun meaning a carefree, joyous time.

flip

We are, perhaps, most used to **flip** as a verb, because when we flip over a card or flip over the pages of the newspaper, we are rapidly turning something over. You can also flip coins into the air, and the waves can flip your dingy over. If you flip your lid, you lose emotional control, and if you receive some good news, there is often a flip side, i.e. less desirable elements. As a noun, a flip is a sudden, quick movement, or, apparently, another term for egg-nog.

float

If something floats on the water, it rests on the surface of the water. Indeed, many things naturally **float**, being of a lower specific density than the water itself. Since floating in water is an inactive and gentle activity, the word is extended to any activity that seems effortless. Thus a slim and elegant woman can seem to float into the room. The American boxer Muhammad Ali claimed that he could 'float like a butterfly, sting like a bee'. Because you are naturally talented, you can float through your exams. A float can also be a noun. Anglers have a float among their equipment, a small object that floats on the water. A plasterer uses a float in order to give a smooth finish to the plaster. A polishing block used in marble-working is called a float. If you take a loan in order to begin a new business, this can be known as a float. The word is also a technical term in weaving and geology. Since 1965, the word has also been used in reference to the international exchange rate. A currency is said to 'float' if it is allowed to fluctuate with regard to that rate: 'The decision to let the mark float was forced on the German authorities by a sudden inflow of funds.'

flock

We normally think of a **flock** of sheep, but 'flock' as a collective noun can be used for any band or company of creatures. Hence you could have a flock of centipedes or a flock of bison, though the word is more usually confined to sheep, and birds, though you sometimes hear vicars talking piously about their flocks of parishioners. A flock is also a tuft of wool, a soft material for stuffing cushions, and a verb meaning to gather together in a company or to come and go *en masse*.

flocks, phlox

You may see **flocks** of sheep at the agricultural fair, since 'flocks' un-surprisingly is simply the plural of the word defined immediately above. It is also, though, a homophone with **phlox,** a North American herbaceous plant. The two words are also dangerously close to being a homophone with 'flux'.

floe, flow

A **floe** is a sheet of floating ice, while the verb 'to **flow**' indicates a movement, normally one of smoothness and inevitability. Thus a river is said to flow to the sea, a musician can make a piece of music flow, and rural populations often seem to flow into the towns.

flog

This is a verb meaning to beat or chastise with a rod or whip. In fishing, it denotes the action of casting the fly-line over a stream repeatedly. In cricket, if you punish the bowling severely you are said to **flog** it. It is also a slang word meaning 'to sell'.

flood

A **flood** is an event when water covers and submerges areas where it does not usually exist. The overflowing of the Nile floods the land of the delta on an annual basis. A broken pipe in your kitchen might flood your house. But the word is also widely used metaphorically for any unusual inundation. Hence the murder of a well-known television star will see the area flooded by reporters. People flood into the National Gallery if they have a major exhibition.

floor

We all walk on the **floor** of our house or any other building that we enter, and such floors are normally made of wood, stone or brick and covered with linoleum or carpets. You can also floor someone by knocking them down with a powerful fist, or intellectually floor someone by asking a question that they are unable to answer.

flop

If you **flop** on the bed, you lie on it in a loose and ungainly fashion. If your latest play was a flop, it failed to gain critical or audience support.

floss

Floss is the rough silk which envelops the cocoon of the silk-worm, but also the fluid glass floating upon the iron in a puddling furnace. You also floss your teeth by inserting a narrow thread in between them so as to dislodge any remnants of food.

flounder

The **flounder** is a small flat-fish, or a tool used by a boot maker to stretch the leather of a boot front. It is also a verb meaning to flop around, normally in water, in an uncoordinated and clumsy fashion, and consequently the word is often extended to denote any unproductive and undisciplined activity: 'I expect to flounder in my Latin exam', or, 'The men floundered in the wood in their search for the missing bracelet.'

flour, flower

Flour is a word that can be applied to any powered substance, but most of us know it as the white powder that we buy at the grocers. Derived from wheat, flour can be an ingredient in cakes, puddings and other meals. A **flower** is a plant that, with stem, leaves and petals, is often attractive and hence grown for its beauty. The word is then applied to people when the person in question shows themselves off to particular advantage: 'As a solo violinist, Scraper only began to flower after his successful recital at Carnegie Hall.'

flourish

If you **flourish**, you do very well in health and development. You may find that daffodils flourish in your garden, whereas moles flourish in mine. If you do something with a flourish, you do something extravagant in order to attract attention.

flow *see* floe

flower *see* flour

flue *see* flew

fluff

A piece of **fluff** is anything small, light and feathery, and fluff is normally picked up by the vacuum when you are cleaning the carpet. A woman can also be described as a bit of fluff, thereby indicating that she is not, for her current male companion, a serious romantic interest. A television programme or any form of entertainment that is described as 'fluff' is merely trivial and superficial.

fluke

Most of us think of a **fluke** as an extremely unexpected piece of good fortune. Thus it was a fluke that you found a priceless diamond on the common this morning, or that it stopped raining just long enough for you to get the shopping done. A fluke is also the plates of iron on the arms of an anchor, another name for the flat-fish often termed a flounder, a parasitic trematoid worm, a variety of kidney potato or part of the tail of a whale.

flush

This word has a number of quite unconnected meanings. You can talk about a **flush** of water, and, indeed, the word turns into a verb when you flush the toilet. But it does not have to be water; you can have a flush of almost anything. There can be a flush of people if it so happens that a number of people enter the same room at the same time. There can be a flush of light on the stage when the director has called for some of the spotlights to be turned on. The basic meaning of 'flush' in such instances is of a sudden flow, a rapid emergence. I suppose the same could be said about a flush of the cheeks. Some people, when embarrassed, have an automatic reaction of their cheeks reddening. Since this effect is caused by a sudden rush of blood to their faces, one might argue that the basic meaning of 'flush' is still preserved. However, if you are playing cards and happen to hold a hand in which every card is of the same suit, then you are holding a flush hand. If you have plenty of money on your person, then you can be described as being flush with money. If you instal a shelf that is precisely adjacent to another such shelf, then the two shelves are said to be flush with each other. The word 'flush' is also used as a technical term for an action in weaving, so one can hardly say that it is a redundant word.

flute

While the **flute** is a well-known wind instrument in the orchestra, it is also an ornamental vertical groove in a column, a trumpet-shaped frill on a dress, or a tall narrow wine glass.

flutter

This word describes a somewhat agitated or disorganised state. Thus a flag can **flutter** in the breeze as the wind tosses it to and fro. Equally your heart may flutter when you see the object of your dreams. Birds and butterflies tend to flutter. The word is also a colloquial term for indulging in a spate of betting: 'I had a flutter on the horses this afternoon.'

flux

As a noun, a **flux** is the action or process of flowing, often used in scientific contexts to describe the flux of ions across a membrane or an abnormal discharge of blood. The word can also signify a continual change: 'The political scene was in a state of flux.'

fly

In one of its common manifestations, **fly** is a verb meaning to travel through the air. Thus birds fly in the air, cricket balls fly through the air, and aircraft do the same. Consequently, a common winged insect is also called a fly, though it is not by any means the only insect that flies. Even in other contexts, the word 'fly' sometimes carries the connotation of motion. Thus in printing, the fly is the operation that removes the sheets from the press. In the early nineteenth century, a fly was a one-horsed light covered carriage. Money is sometimes said to fly from one's pocket. This connection with motion is absent when one refers to a strip of cloth on a garment that is designed to hide the button holes or zip of the garment in question. In a theatre, the space over the proscenium is also called the fly. Sometimes a person can be described as fly, and this means that he (it is normally a man) is astute and somewhat self-seeking in his approach.

fob

Originally a **fob** was a small pocket in the waistband of a man's trousers that was used for carrying a watch. However, the expression 'to fob off' means to put off or to get rid of, often in a somewhat dubious manner. The three letters have also been turned into an acronym, 'Friend of Bill', a reference to the lying, dishonest, immoral but highly intelligent and personally captivating Bill Clinton.

focal

This adjective is generally used to relate to the centre or most important aspect of the matter being considered. Hence you might claim that the **focal** matter for attention in the music of Wagner was harmonic advance, or that Dickens's use of imagery was focal to his art. More specifically, focal is used with reference to the focus of a lens, and, medically, to a disease occurring in one particular part of the body.

focus

If one decides to **focus** on something, one concentrates on that particular topic or issue. For instance, for many people their focus of attention is global warming. But if 'focus' is a mental attention, the word is also much more concrete. If something is 'in focus', it can be clearly seen, and one focuses one's telescope or microscope in an attempt to achieve this clarity.

foil

As a verb, 'to **foil**' means to prevent the action of someone else: 'I must foil Richard's scheme at once.' As a noun, foil tends to mean some metal (normally aluminium) that has been hammered into an extremely thin sheet and is then used for the protective wrapping of food. This usage of the word entered the language in 1946. A foil is also a thin weapon used in fencing.

fold, foaled

As a noun, a **fold** is an enclosure or pen for farming animals like sheep. As a verb, if you fold something, you reduce its surface area by bending it so that one part of the object now lies over another part. Thus you may fold a towel, a sheet of paper, or a shirt. Colloquially, it is also possible for you to fold. You may be having an argument with a friend, and the friend suddenly produces a fact or a factor that you had not previously considered. As a result, you folded up, i.e. ceased arguing. If a mare **foaled**, she gave birth to a baby horse.

follow

Although the five or so meanings of the verb **follow** are all at least vaguely related, they are certainly distinct enough for the word to be an internal homonym. The most common of those meanings is to come after something or someone else: 'The police tried to follow the stolen car', or, 'Julie's boyfriend was prone to follow her everywhere.' Naturally an event that takes place after an earlier event is said to follow the former: 'It was planned that Miss Prendergast's singing would follow Mr Hodge's poetry recitation.' Thirdly, if you obey some instructions that you have been given, then it can be said that you followed instructions. You can also follow (earn your living at) a profession or occupation. You can follow (support) a football club. It follows, therefore, that 'follow' is an adaptable word.

font

A **font** is a receptacle, usually made of stone, that holds the water necessary for the baptism of a baby in church, the so-called christening ceremony. A font is also a type-face. *I might decide to change to an italic font*, or possibly to Franklin Gothic Medium. There are scores to choose from.

fool

We are all accustomed to regarding a **fool** as an individual who acts unwisely or imprudently, but as a verb, the word means to trick or deceive. There is also a cold dessert of fruit and cream that is termed a 'fool'.

foot

The **foot**, as you know, is the lowest part of the leg and upon which you walk. From that fact, it is not surprising that the bottom of many things also tends to be called the foot: the foot of the page, the foot of a hill, and so on. Also the measurement of 12 inches (0.3048 of a metre) became known as a foot because it was thought to be the average length of most feet. A foot is also a division in the scansion of poetry. If a line of verse has a regular rhythm, each instance of that rhythm is called a foot.

for, four, fore

There are no problems with **four**. It is simply a number, one greater than three and one less than five. **For**, however, has manifold uses. It can be used as a word signifying replacement or exchange: 'I gave him £900 for his car.' It can indicate purpose: 'I'm going to the conference for the sole purpose of voting for a new chairman.' It might signify a duration of time: 'I stayed for three hours.' It might even be a synonym for 'because': 'I did not go for good reason.' 'For' is one of those indispensable words that must perplex people learning English considerably because so much of its usage is idiomatic: 'for good or bad', 'for all that', 'for goodness' sake', and so on. **Fore** is simpler. It is the cry that a golfer utters when he is about to drive a ball that might, if it hits you, give more than a slight headache. Basically the word means 'in front' and that sense is clear in the many ways in which the word is used as a prefix: forebode, forecourt, foreground, forelock, forerunner and so on.

foreward, forward

The first of these is the introduction to a book, usually by someone other than the author of the book. The second is the adverb meaning to advance or progress in movement or status: 'I moved forward in the queue', or, 'From being tea-boy, I moved forward rapidly, becoming chief inspector in just under six years.' If you look **forward**, you are looking towards the future. If you walk forward, you are moving to a point beyond your current one. If you forward a message to someone else, you are advancing the state of information in the world. Hence the word 'forward' always seems to carry the connotation of progress, of advancement. This may indeed be the case. After all, if you are a forward in a game of football, you are in front of at least six members of your own team. If your behaviour is criticised for being too forward, it is because you were clumsily and insensitively trying to press onward with your preferences. Even so, the contexts within which 'forward' can be used are so diverse that the word must be counted as an internal homonym.

fork

Most of us use a knife and **fork** when eating a meal. The fork is an instrument comprising a longish straight handle furnished at the end with two or more prongs. Depending upon its size, a fork can be used for placing food in one's mouth, digging the garden or hurling at an enemy. The word can also mean a division. When one reaches a fork in the road or path, there are two options open, to take the right-hand fork or the left-hand one. You can also have a fork or flash of lightning.

form

In one of its senses, the word **form** indicates shape, the outward appearance of something. Hence you might admire the form of a diamond, a woman, a poem or a report. But the word also means a long, backless seat, the home of a hare, a class in a school, the success rate of a competitor, and, as a verb, means to conceive, to fashion, to mould and to create.

formally, formerly

The adverb **formally** is a word that implies doing things in accordance with set routine, something that is laid down by convention or enmeshed with a network of other requirements. Wearing a dinner jacket would be labelled formal wear, the new railway station will be formally opened by the mayor, and the prose of Edward Gibbon is formally complex. **Formerly**, also an adverb, relates things back to the past, to some former situation or context. Sri Lanka was formally called Ceylon, and my accountant son was formerly a rock musician.

fort, fought

A **fort** was a place designed to withstand attack. Thus it might have a moat, thick stone walls, and vantage points from which to attack the approaching enemy. **Fought** is the past tense of the verb 'to fight': 'He fought Jackie Mills in 1948.'

forth, fourth

If you go **forth**, you go forwards. The word is somewhat archaic now. If you are **fourth** in a competition, you have scored less than the person who came third, but more than the person who came fifth. In other words, 'fourth' is the ordinal number belonging to the cardinal four.

foul, fowl

If, in a sport, you commit a **foul**, you do something that is against the rules. That is very different from living in a foul house, one that is dirty, untidy, smelly and ugly. That too is different from using foul language, language that is gross and obscene and calculated to offend any maiden aunts in the vicinity. Hence 'foul' is an internal homonym, as well as being a homophone with **fowl**, a winged creature, though the word is often confined to domestic birds like chickens, hens, geese and turkeys that are reared for their eggs and their flesh.

found

If you **found** a school, a hospital or any other institution, you provide the money for that establishment to be set up. If you found some metal, you melt it and pour it into a mould. If you found a coin in the garden, you would have discovered something of whose whereabouts you were previously ignorant. Hence 'found' has three distinct and separate meanings.

founder

If a ship should happen to **founder**, it unfortunately fills up with water and sinks. If a horse happens to founder, it stumbles or falls down from exhaustion. Of course, it is also possible for a human being to be a founder: Baden Powell was the founder of the Boy Scout movement.

four *see* **for**

fox

The **fox** is a four-legged animal of the genus *Vulpes*, but it is also possible to fox someone by misleading them in some fashion.

fracture

Many of us have had a **fracture**, since it is the cracking or breaking of one of our bones. The word is also used for similar mishaps with other materials. Thus you can have a fracture in a rock, a wall or a piece of wood. Entirely differently, a fracture is what takes place when a single vowel is replaced by a diphthong.

frame

A **frame** is a structure to which other elements will be added in order to make it a complete entity. The frame of a building normally merely consists of the uprights and girders that dictate its eventual size and shape. The frame of the human body is the skeleton of bones to which the flesh, blood vessels and nerves are attached. You can also create a mental frame as to how next to accomplish a task. All those meanings carry the connotation of underlying structure. If, however, you frame someone, you make him or her appear guilty of something of which they are innocent. The word is also used for a game of snooker.

franc, frank, Frank

The **franc** used to be a French coin until they moved over to the Euro. If you are **frank**, you are honest, open and plain-speaking, often to the discomfort of those with you. You can also frank a letter so that it can then be delivered with no further charge. If you were a **Frank**, you were a member of a Germanic tribe who attacked Gaul in the sixth century.

fray

A **fray** is a fight or brawl, an unproductive event often witnessed after closing time of the pubs in Britain. As a verb, it means to frighten, or, in the case of deer, to rub against a tree. Clothes often fray also in that the threads composing them become split and as a result hang out a little from the main fabric.

frays, phrase

A fray is a quarrel or fight, and so **frays** is more than one of them. A **phrase** is a group of words equivalent to a noun, adjective or adverb and possessing no verb of its own. Many phrases become so well known that they become clichés. A short sequence of notes in music can also be termed a phrase.

free

As an adjective, **free** can mean being able to act as one wishes, not subject to any other commitments, being no longer confined, not physically obstructed, or even not being constrained by the rules. As an adverb, free means with no cost or payment: 'Children were admitted free.' As a verb, 'to free' can mean to release from confinement (' "Free me from jail," he cried'), to remove something undesirable ('It is good to be free from the brambles'), or to be available ('I am free for the concert on Monday').

frees, freeze, frieze

If someone **frees** you from armed robbers, you are doubtless very grateful. The word 'frees' is the present tense third person singular of the verb 'to free' meaning to release, to relieve, or to set at liberty. **Freeze** is another verb, this time meaning to chill something so much that it changes state from being a liquid to being a solid. Water, as most of us know, freezes at o degrees centigrade, turning into ice at that temperature. The verb can also be used metaphorically. Hence you can freeze someone out of a discussion by ignoring anything that they try to say, or you can freeze a bank account, preventing withdrawals for a stated time. A **frieze** is a band of painted or sculptured decoration. Many living rooms in Britain have a frieze of wallpaper at the point where the wall meets the ceiling. But a frieze can also be a kind of coarse woollen cloth, the nap or down on a plant, the decoration on a silver plate, or a verb to signify the embroidering of something in gold.

frequent

When something happens at **frequent** intervals, it happens repeatedly with only short gaps between. If you frequent the library, you visit it quite often.

fresh

If something is **fresh**, it can either be new within that particular context ('Mary was a fresh arrival to the scene') or it can mean that something is unspotted, full of life and eager ('Wilfred felt very fresh after his shower'). Fresh water is water that is not salty, fresh food is food that has just been made or bought, and a fresh wind is fairly strong and rather cool. You can also be fresh by behaving in a bumptious and sexually overt way.

fret

To **fret** about something is to worry or to feel vexed about something. But a fret or example of fret work is an ornamental pattern.

friar, fryer

A **friar** is a brother or member of any religious order, but in particular the Dominicans, the Augustines, the Franciscans and the Carmelites. A friar is also an Australian bird. A **fryer** is someone who is frying something.

fritter

A portion of batter enclosing apple, oyster or some other food, is called a **fritter**, but the word is also a verb meaning to waste, to mis-spend. Hence you can fritter time away by watching some mindless drivel on television or by 'reading' the *Sun*.

frog

While most of us think of a **frog** as a tailless amphibious animal that is unlikely to win many prizes in an animal beauty contest, the word also relates to a disease of the throat or mouth ('I've a frog in my throat'), an elastic horny substance growing in the middle of a horse's hoof, an attachment to the waistbelt for carrying a sword, a piece of iron placed at the junction of the rails where one track crosses another or the fastening for a military coat. The word is also a nickname for the French, a name derived from their ancient heraldic device which depicted three frogs or toads.

front

The **front** is the foremost part of something. Hence the front of a book is its outside dustjacket, the front of a person is his or her face, chest, etc., the front of an army is its foremost line, and so on. However, one can also present a front to someone when one is attempting to give an impression that is not an entirely accurate one.

fry

If you **fry** something, you cook it in fat. Young fishes just produced from the spawn are also called fry. If sentenced to death by the electric chair, you are said to fry.

fudge

This substance is soft and chewy, and is made from sugar, butter and milk. However, when you are dealing with something of which you are uncertain, you may decide to **fudge** the issue by talking in vague generalities. The word can also be a slang term for 'nonsense'. In the 1980s, the word became a common one in political circles, and meant an unsatisfactory or makeshift solution.

full

As an adjective, **full** tends to mean having no empty space ('The jar was full of sweets'), having no spare time ('His life was so full that he was unable to take a holiday'), being complete ('There was a full range of equipment at the gym'), or being amply proportioned ('She had a full figure'). As an adverb, full can mean 'straight' ('She looked him full in the face') or 'very' ('He knew full well what the answer was'). The word can even be a verb so that if you full some cloth, you clean and shrink it by heat, pressure and moisture.

function

You can attend a **function**, because in such a context the word means a formal social event. In mathematics, though, a function is a relation or expression involving one or more variables. The most common usage of the word, however, is to express an activity or state that is the *raison d'être* of the object in question. Hence it is the function of a teacher to teach, of a bridge to provide access over water or some other obstacle, of the nose to smell things, and so on.

fungous, fungus

If something is **fungous**, it is related to or pertains to a **fungus** or to fungi. A fungus is a plant like a mushroom or toadstool that lacks any chlorophyll.

funk

If you **funk** something, you avoid it out of fear. Hence I have always funked sailing over Victoria Falls in a canoe. Funk is also a style of popular dance music of US black origin.

furry

Something that is made out of fur, can be called **furry**. The word is also the name of a festival held at Helston in Cornwall at which the furry dance is performed.

furs, furze

Furs is simply the plural of 'fur', the short, fine hair of sundry animals like the otter, leopard, bear, etc. **Furze** is a spiny evergreen shrub with yellow flowers.

further

This is a word that gives rise to argument about its homonymic validity. It can act as an adverb or as an adjective, but always gives the sense of movement. You can move further away from something. You can advance further in your studies. You can walk further than your neighbour. You can add a further point to the discussion. You can cook something for a further ten minutes. Always there is a sense of addition and comparison; more has been added compared to what there was before. Hence conceptually the word is not really homonymic, but its range of reference makes it so.

fuse

A **fuse** is a length of material along which a small flame moves until it connects with a bomb which then explodes. A fuse is also part of an electrical appliance, the absence of which renders the appliance inactive. As a verb, when two or more things fuse together, they blend into a single entity. Electrical appliances are said to fuse when their fuse ceases to operate.

fuzz

Apart from being a slang term for the police since the 1920s, a **fuzz** is also a fizzy mass of hair, a blurred image, or a buzzing sound.

G

G, g, gee

The key of **G** in music is one which has G, the fifth note of the diatonic scale of C major, as its tonic note. The letter is also used in physics to stand for gravity, and in chess is the seventh file from the left as viewed from White's side of the board. **Gee** was an American exclamation of surprise, a child's word for a horse, a slang word meaning 'to get on well together', 'to suit', and, in combination with 'up', a command to increase the speed, often a command given to a horse. In the USA, a 'gee' (or 'g') is often used to denote a thousand.

gab

The most common usage of **gab** is a verb meaning 'to talk too much', and there tends to be a connotation of the resulting verbiage as being slightly suspect, stemming perhaps from malice or from a desire to conceal. Furthermore, if you say that someone has 'the gift of the gab', you are not normally being very complimentary. The word also means 'to lie'. Apparently too the word can be a noun denoting a hook or open notch in a rod or lever.

gad

If you have ever used the word **gad** it is likely to have been as a synonym for 'going out', 'going for a random wander' or something along those lines. My next-door neighbour is always gadding about, while I stay at home working on this dictionary! Yet the word is also a noun signifying a number of objects. It can be a sharp spike of metal, a bar of metal, a pointed tool of iron or steel, a measuring rod for land, a division of an open pasture, or a band or rope made of twisted fibres of rough twigs. Milton even uses it to denote a struggling plant: 'Wild thyme and the gadding vine'. You also occasionally hear it as a euphemism for God: 'By gad! Arsenal lost on Saturday.'

gaff, gaffe

The far from common word **gaff** can denote an iron hook, a barbed fishing spear, stuff and nonsense, one's own home, or a public place of amusement like a fair. There is also the common expression 'to blow the gaff', where 'gaff' means 'a secret' or 'a plot'. **Gaffe**, on the other hand, has only one meaning, to make a mistake, to utter an indiscreet remark, to commit a *faux pas*.

gag

A **gag** can be something forced into the mouth to prevent your speaking, a joke or amusing story, or, more figuratively, a closure motion in Parliament so as to prevent further discussion of a particular matter. According to *Brewer's*, a gag, in theatrical parlance, is an interpolation of lines that are not actually in the received text.

gage, gauge

Sometimes, when you are having a disagreement with your friend Felix, you get so incensed that you throw down your glove and challenge him to a duel. This is known as throwing down your **gage**. Equally you may give £2,000 to your local drama group on condition that they do a performance of Dekker's *The Shoemaker's Holiday*. If they fail to carry out their promise, you are entitled to demand repayment of the money, and this too is known as a gage. The word is also occasionally used as an abbreviation for a greengage. A **gauge**, though it has a number of different meanings, is always concerned with measurement. It can be a standard measure for the capacity of a barrel, the diameter of a bullet, or the thickness of sheet iron. It can relate to the width of a railway track, or the depth to which a ship sinks when fully laden. You can have instruments to gauge the strength of the wind, to display the contents of a boiler, or even to regulate the penetration of a cutting tool.

gain

If you **gain** something, you obtain or secure it. Thus you may gain £1,000,000 on the lottery, half a stone in weight as a result of Christmas, or respect because of your unstinting work for the RSPCC. The factor by which power or voltage is increased in an electronic device is usually expressed as a logarithm and is known as a gain.

gait, gate

One can often be recognised by one's **gait**, namely the way in which one walks. You can also judge something about the condition of a horse from its gait. The homophone **gate** normally refers to the wooden or metal structure that has been placed in a gap of a hedge or wall so as to afford access. If you open the gate, you can then enter the field, courtyard or whatever the gate was enclosing. If you are a tiresome Oxbridge undergraduate, your tutor may announce that he is going to gate you, i.e. confine you to college so as to curtail your penchant for public disorder. Both words probably have the same origin, the Old Norse *gata*, and the spelling *gait* was rare until the seventeenth century.

gal

This is a North American term for a girl or young woman, but in physics a **gal** is a unit of gravitational acceleration equal to one centimetre per second per second.

galah

This is a small Australian cockatoo, but also Australian slang for a stupid person.

gale

While a **gale** is a very strong wind, you can also be overcome by a gale of laughter.

gall

If you act with **gall**, you are behaving in a bold and impudent fashion: 'I'm afraid, your Majesty, that I regard the Royal Family as an expensive and irrelevant anachronism.' But 'gall' is also the contents of the gall bladder, and an abnormal growth formed in response to insect larvae or fungi resting on trees. The first of these – contents of the gall bladder – is apparently extremely bitter, and so gall has become an emblem for bitterness.

gallery

A **gallery** is a building in which, normally, works of art are displayed. The word can also denote a balcony or upper floor in a church, theatre, cinema or concert hall. A horizontal underground passage in a mine is also called a gallery.

galley, gally

A **galley** is a low flat-built sea-going vessel with one deck, propelled by sails and oars that used to be common in the Mediterranean. The rowers were mostly slaves or condemned criminals. Earlier still, a galley was a Greek or Roman war ship. In printing, however, a galley is an oblong tray to which the type is transferred. To **gally** is to frighten or scare.

gallop, galop

Horses **gallop**, a word used when they are running as fast as they can, though the word can also be applied to other animals including humans. A **galop** is a lively dance in three/four time.

galvanic

This adjective is used to describe events or experiments that involve electric currents that have been produced by chemical action, but the word can also be applied to any sudden or dramatic event.

gamble, gambol

If you **gamble**, you take a chance. Thus you might gamble on it being a nice day tomorrow and therefore plan a picnic for the family, or you might place money on a horse to win the Grand National, or you might do the football pools every week. A **gambol** is a leap or spring in dancing, the bound of a horse, or the active play of children. The word is probably used more as a verb than as a noun.

game

A **game** is a competitive activity following set rules and usually indulged in for one's personal amusement, and comes from the Old English word *gamen* meaning 'amusement' or 'fun'. Animals and birds that are hunted for pleasure or for food are also known as game. One can also have a game leg, that is, an injured one. This usage was originally a north Midland dialect.

gammon

If you eat **gammon**, you will be eating ham which has been cured or smoked like bacon. If you say that someone is talking gammon, you mean that he or she is talking nonsense. If you achieve a gammon, you have managed to remove all your backgammon pieces before your opponent has removed any.

gander

A **gander** is a male goose, and a verb meaning to look at.

gang, gangue

In normal speech, a **gang** is a group of people who gather together for some specific purpose. Thus you might have a gang working to weed the allotment, a gang working on widening the A32, a gang robbing a bank, or a gang just hanging around on the street corner. The word is related to the Scottish *gang* which means 'go'. **Gangue** is the earth or stony matter in a mineral deposit.

gannet

A **gannet** is a large seabird and a colloquial term for a greedy person, a usage which first appeared in the 1920s.

gantry

A **gantry** can be a bridge-like overhead structure with a platform, a tall framework supporting a space rocket prior to launching, or a structure containing inverted bottles that have been fitted with optics for serving measures.

garage

A **garage** can be a building in which you house your car, an establishment that sells petrol and/or repairs cars, or a style of unpolished, energetic rock music.

garb

If you **garb** yourself, you clothe yourself, often in somewhat unusual garments: 'She was garbed in Indian shawls.' In heraldry, a garb is a sheaf of wheat.

garibaldi

In Britain a **garibaldi** is a biscuit containing a layer of compressed currents. In the USA, it is a small bright orange marine fish found off California. In Europe, a garibaldi can refer to a woman's or child's loose blouse of the type that was originally worn by the Italian liberator Giuseppe Garibaldi (1807–82).

garnish

If you **garnish** something, you decorate or embellish it, a usage dating from the late seventeenth century. The word is most frequently applied to food. Hence you can garnish your stew with sprigs of radish, or your trifle with a dollop of sour cream. In legal terms, to garnish is to serve notice on a third party for the purpose of seizing money belonging to a debtor or defendant.

gas

Substances can be divided into solids, liquids and gases, and by definition a **gas** is a substance that can normally be neither seen nor felt, but which will expand to fill any available space. The word was invented by the Belgian chemist J. B. van Helmont (1577–1644) to denote an occult principle which he believed to exist in all matter. The word is also an American term for petrol, and a colloquial term for an entertaining or amusing person or event.

gate *see* gait

gauge *see* gage

gavel

A **gavel** can be a quantity of corn cut and ready to be made into a sheaf, a partition of land among the whole tribe when a large landowner has died, or a kind of mallet occasionally hammered loudly on the desk in public meetings or law courts to restore order to the proceedings.

gawk

If you **gawk** at something, you stare at it, though the word is sometimes a noun signifying a simpleton or fool.

gay

Once upon a time the word **gay** simply meant 'cheerful', 'light-hearted' or 'full of mirth', but these days it is more frequently a reference to a homosexual man. Originally, in the USA, 'gay' meant 'sexually dissolute', and its narrowing down to homosexual did not take place until the 1930s, and the term was not established until the 1960s. As *The Oxford Dictionary of Phrase and Fable* comments, 'The centuries-old other senses of gay meaning either "carefree" or "bright and showy" have more or less dropped out of natural use.'

gays, gaze

A number of **gays** is a collection of male homosexuals, while the verb 'to **gaze**' means to look, often with rather a vacant air.

gazette

A **gazette** is a news-sheet or periodical publication, while to gazette means to publish in a gazette.

gear

There are at least two very different meanings for this word. The first is a mechanical device that you encounter in cars, bicycles and various pieces of equipment where the **gear** that you are in to some extent dictates the speed at which the vehicle or machine is able to work. Secondly, gear can be a general word for one's belongings. If you are about to go on holiday, you may say, 'We must get our gear together.' Indeed, the word can be applied to any activity that demands special dress or equipment. Thus you will get your riding gear ready if you are about to go hunting, you will get your sports gear ready if you are about to play football for Chelsea, and so on. It can also be an informal word for illegal drugs.

geek

A **geek** is an informal word for an unfashionable or socially inept person, or for someone who is obsessive about a particular activity – 'He's a computer geek.' In Australia and New Zealand the word is a synonym for a look: 'I wanted to have a geek at the Rosetta Stone.'

gel, jell

Gel is a jelly-like material formed by the coagulation of a colloidal liquid, a jelly-like substance used in cosmetic or medicinal products, a socially superior girl, the process of an idea or project beginning to take shape ('My half-formed notion was beginning to gel into something really practical') or the process of a human relationship beginning to become meaningful ('After about half an hour, he and I began to really gel'). The verb **jell** means 'to congeal or become jelly'.

geld

During the Middle Ages, a **geld** was a tax paid by landowners to the Crown. As a verb, to geld means to dispose of unnecessary elements of an organism. Thus you can geld trees of unnecessary branches. More commonly, though, to geld means to castrate, and few men would regard the removal of their genitals as the disposal of unnecessary elements.

gene, jean

Many of the characteristics of animals are inherited from their parents, and the blueprint for such inheritance is contained in genes. The word itself was invented in 1911 by W. Johannsen who wrote, 'The **gene** is nothing but a very applicable little word, easily combined with others, and hence it may be useful as an expression for the "unit-factors", "elements" or "allelomorphs" in the gametes . . . ' **Jean**, apart from being a female Christian name, is a twilled cotton cloth.

general

A **general** is a commander of the army, something which poses no difficulties of definition. As an adjective, however, 'general' is much less precise. By and large, the word indicates an overall embracingness. (My spell checker thinks that I've invented the word 'embracingness', but I'm sure that you know what I mean.) Thus when you talk about the general public, you mean the entire population. When someone says that 'The general feeling is . . . ' he or she means that the majority view would appear to be such and such. When you argue that the general thesis of a book is whatever, you are claiming that the basic tenet of the book is what you are just about to expound. To ask a general question is very different from asking a specific one.

gest, geste, guest

The first two words here are just alternative spellings of the same word. *Collins Dictionary* gives **gest** and **geste** as being archaic words, and the *Oxford Dictionary of English* (2nd edn 2003) doesn't list it at all, but the *Shorter Oxford* defines the word as meaning a notable deed or exploit, and makes no comment on its current currency. We are, of course, much safer with **guest**, which is very definitely a current word, and means a person who is staying somewhere as a visitor.

geyser

This is a hot spring in which water intermittently boils, sending a tall column of water and steam into the air. The word is also used for a gas-fired water heater through which water flows as it is rapidly heated (or, in the case of my own **geyser**, very slowly heated).

ghost

Most of us know about those shadowy figures that are supposed to be apparitions of the dead, though few of us can genuinely claim to have seen a **ghost**. The word, though, does have two less alarming meanings. If you are a ghost writer, you earn your living by putting into comprehensible prose the inarticulate witterings of a football star or pop singer, and you might have the ghost of a smile on your face as you do so. A ghost writer (first used in 1927) writes for someone else, and a ghost of a smile means a slight trace or vestige of a smile.

gib

Apparently a **gib** is the name for a male cat (in some dialects, a castrated cat), the hooked gristle which grows at the end of the lower jaw of a male salmon after spawning, or a piece of wood or metal used to keep some part of a machine in place.

gift

A **gift** can be a tangible object given to someone as a present, or an in-born ability: 'I gave a piano as a gift to Harold because he obviously has a gift for music.' There is also an acronym GIFT standing for gamete intrafallopian transfer.

gig

Today a **gig** is most likely to be taken as a performance by some pop group or other (first so used in 1926), but the word is still used to refer to a one-horsed, two-wheeled carriage, and also as a form of light boat. You can also encounter it as an abbreviation for gigabyte.

gild, gilled, guild

If you **gild** something, you cover or adorn it with gold or with something that makes it look valuable and impressive. As Shakespeare pointed out, this operation of showing off can be overdone:

> To gild refinèd gold, to paint the lily . . .
> Is wasteful and ridiculous excess.   (*King John*)

The Middle English word *gilt* is the old past participle of 'gild'. All fishes are **gilled** in that they have gills as an integral part of their obtaining oxygen. In the Middle Ages a **guild** was a gathering of people who were involved in the same trade or occupation. They are thus seen as a sort of precursor of the trade union, though the guild was much more a gathering of merchants and employers than it was of workers.

gill

A **gill** is the organ of respiration in fish and other aquatic animals, but it is also the name for a deep, rocky ravine, a female ferret, and a measurement for liquids (normally about a quarter of a pint).

gilt, guilt

Today **gilt**, if used at all, is a slang term for money, though the word can also be used to denote a young sow, or to describe an object that has been thinly covered with gold leaf. **Guilt**, of course, is the feeling that you have when you have just been rude to the mother-in-law. More seriously, guilt is the state one is in when one has committed a crime or some act of rudeness or lack of consideration.

gimp

Gimp is a silk, worsted or cotton twist with a cord or wire running through it, a fishing-line composed of silk, etc., a neckerchief worn by a man, a physically disabled person, or a verb meaning to give a scalloped or indented outline.

gin, jinn

Most of us doubtless think of **gin** as an alcoholic drink, a spirit distilled from grain or malt, and often diluted with tonic water or bitter lemon. However it is also an apparatus for hoisting heavy weights, a machine for separating cotton from its seeds, an offensive Australian term for an aboriginal woman, or a pulley frame used in unloading cargo from a ship. A **jinn** is a demon or spirit in Muslim demonology.

ginger

The rhizome of the tropical plant *Zingiber officinale* is called **ginger**, and its hot spicy taste is often used in cookery and medicine. The word is also used to denote a light, sandy colour, and, metaphorically, as a verb meaning to activate, to put spirit into something, to mettle something up.

gird

There is a common expression, '**gird** up your loins', which gives some hint that one meaning for the verb 'to gird' is 'to prepare oneself for future action', though that conceptual meaning clearly derives from a previous and still current definition, 'to secure a garment by means of a belt'. You also gird someone when you make a cutting remark to them.

girdle

A **girdle** is a belt or cord worn round the waist, a woman's elasticated corset, the part of a cut gem dividing the crown from the base, or a ring made around a tree by removing some of its bark.

glair, glare

The white of an egg can be called **glair**, as can anything made from the white of an egg. A **glare** is that dazzling brilliance of light that you get when the sun shines on some reflecting substance, or when a powerful spotlight is directed towards your eyes. But it can also be a powerful and disapproving look from the eyes of someone else, the sort of thing that you used to get from your teacher when you were chewing gum in class.

glance

You **glance** at something when you take a rapid look at it. When playing cricket, the ball may strike the edge of the bat and dart off at an angle. This is known as a glance. Indeed, when anything strikes something at an angle and bounces off obliquely, the term 'glance' can be applied. Light too can glance off something at an angle. A glance is also a shiny black or grey sulphide ore of lead, copper or other metal.

gland

One sometimes hears the complaint, 'It's my glands, you know,' and, like all other parts of the body, a **gland** can sometimes malfunction. A gland is an organ which separates from the blood certain constituents for use in the body. For a mechanic, however, a gland can be a sleeve employed to press a packing tight on a piston-rod, or, to a motor mechanic, a clutch which enables a car to move.

glare *see* **glair**

glassy

Something is **glassy** if it possesses the physical properties of glass, but eyes are sometimes described as being glassy when they show no interest or animation in what is going on around them.

glean

Originally the verb 'to **glean**' meant the activity of gathering up leftover grain after a harvest, but the word has been extended to denote the activity of gaining information, often with difficulty, from libraries, museums and other research sources.

glee

If you happen to be full of **glee**, you are excitedly happy, but a glee is also a musical composition for three or more unaccompanied voices.

glide

This word is always associated with movement, but the contexts in which it can be used are very different. It implies a smooth, quiet, continuous movement. Thus you can **glide** on your skates over the ice. If you are in an unpowered aircraft, you will glide on the wind. If you gently glance a cricket ball with your bat, the stroke may be termed a glide. In phonetics, a glide is the sound produced as the vocal organs move towards or away from the articulation of a vowel or consonant.

gloss

If you put a **gloss** on something, you are giving the object concerned a superficial lustre, a possibly misleading impression of it being more splendid and shining than it actually is. Thus you might disguise the tatty nature of your garden fence by painting it gold, or you might try to hide your own intellectual imperfections by memorising some impressive Latin phrases. Very differently, if you gloss something, you are normally inserting something into a text in order to explain something that is obscure. Hence, if you are editing *King Lear*, you might want to gloss the word *benison* and explain that it means *blessing*.

glutenous, glutinous

If something is **glutenous**, it contains the nitrogenous part of the flour of wheat or other grain. If something is **glutinous**, it partakes of the nature of glue.

gnaw, nor

If you **gnaw** something, you repeatedly bite at it in an attempt to wear it away or to consume it. Non-physically, some worry can gnaw away at your mind as well. **Nor** is a conjunction which is used in conjunction with the word 'neither': 'I neither like him nor trust him.'

gneiss, nice

Gneiss is a metamorphic rock similar to granite. **Nice** is an all-purpose adjective used to convey a general feeling of approval: 'It's a nice day.'

gnome

A **gnome** is a legendary dwarfish creature supposed to guard the earth's treasures underground. It is a British habit to have stone or clay represent-ations of one or more of these creatures decorating gardens, a trait which must surely interest those specialising in psychology. However, in the 1960s, the Prime Minister Harold Wilson referred to Swiss financiers as 'all the little gnomes in Zürich', and since then the word 'gnome' has been used as a synonym for sinister Alpine bankers.

gnomic, nomic

Something **gnomic** consists of general maxims of a proverbial nature, and can hence be taken as distilling received wisdom. Something **nomic** partakes of the character of Greek musical nomes.

gnu, knew, new

Sometimes known as the wildebeest, the **gnu** is a South African quadruped that resembles the ox. **Knew** is the past tense of the verb 'to know', and **new** is an adjective describing something that is a recent arrival or recent purchase: 'The kingfisher is new to this stretch of the river', or, 'Do you like my new hat?'

goal

In football and similar games, the **goal** is the posts at each end of the field through which a ball has to be driven. By hitting a ball into the goal, you score a goal! But a goal is also the object of an exercise, the purpose of a venture. Hence your goal may be to win the London Marathon, and therefore you run at least ten miles a day, and more at the weekends.

goat

A **goat** is a domesticated ruminant mammal that is kept for its milk and meat, but the word is also a slang term for a lecherous man. In common clichés like 'stop acting the goat', the word is being used as a synonym for 'half-witted fool'. In addition, since Matthew in his gospel talks about separating 'the sheep from the goats', the goat has been taken as a symbol of a damned sinner.

gob

Most of us, I imagine, think of **gob** as a slang word for the mouth – 'Shut your gob!' – but the word is also applied to a slimy lump, the space from which coal has been extracted, and, as a verb, the action of choking up a furnace.

gofer see gopher

golden

Clearly something is **golden** if it is made of gold, but the word is also used metaphorically so that a golden age is one marked by numerous virtues and achievements, a golden opportunity is a chance to be seized, a golden girl is a popular and successful young woman, and so on. The word is common in sundry mythologies: the golden apple of Hesperides, the Golden Ass of Apuleius, the golden fleece of Jason, and so on.

goose

A **goose** is a large web-footed bird, a tailor's smoothing iron, or, as a verb, the action of hissing or expressing disapproval at the theatre, or interfering with someone manually, usually in a playful manner. There also used to be a royal game of goose, a game played with counters on a board divided into sections, some of which had a goose depicted on them. Since the goose is traditionally regarded as a stupid bird, if you call someone a goose, you are implying that their mental abilities are less than outstanding.

gooseberry

This is a round, edible, yellowish-green berry of the genus *Ribes*, and the same name is given to the bush upon which it grows, but if you play **gooseberry**, you are acting as the often unwanted chaperon of someone else.

gopher, gofer

This word can be applied to a variety of animals: a burrowing rodent, a burrowing squirrel, a burrowing land-tortoise or a large burrowing snake of the southern USA. According to the book of Genesis, **gopher** was the wood out of which Noah's ark was made. With a capital G, the word is also used for the menu-based system which allows Internet users to search for and retrieve documents on topics of interest. A **gofer** is a menial hired to fetch things.

gored, gourd

These two words are not quite homophones, but once again in conversation they often sound identical. **Gored** is the past participle of the verb 'to gore', to pierce or stab with dagger or tusks. A **gourd** is the large, fleshy fruit of the climbing plant *Lagenaria vulgaris*.

gorilla, guerrilla

A **gorilla** is a large ape, while a **guerrilla** is an irregular soldier who normally acts by sabotage and surprise rather than engage in open combat.

goulash

A **goulash** is a highly seasoned Hungarian soup or stew of meat and vegetables, but the word is also used to denote a system of dealing out the cards in a variation of bridge.

grace

If one acts with **grace**, one displays a smoothness and elegance of movement that is attractive to behold. But Grace (normally capitalised) is the free and unmerited favour of God, and (uncapitalised) a short prayer of thanksgiving made at the beginning of each meal. A limited number of people, dukes, duchesses and archbishops, are also addressed as 'Your Grace', and in Greek mythology, the three Graces were said to bestow charm, grace and beauty. In music, a grace note is an extra note added as an embellishment and not essential to the harmony or melody.

grade, greyed

The word **grade** refers to the process of assessment or judgement. When you take an exam, you are graded and emerge with 73% or 29% or whatever. At work, you can be allocated to a grade – second-class bottle washer, for instance – and, as the years elapse, you are likely to rise in your grading to positions of real power like first-class carpet inspector. We all tend to grade things, and our lives are permeated by examples like *Top of the Pops*, the Booker Prize, and league football. If, however, something is **greyed**, it has simply turned grey.

graft, graphed

If you **graft** something, you insert some tissue from one place on to another. Hence skin from one part of your body might be removed and grafted on to another part, a leaf from one plant might be grafted on to another plant, fruit from one tree might be grafted on to another, and so on. One might also graft an idea or system on to another idea or system, and consequently produce a new hybrid. But 'graft' is also a colloquial synonym for 'work': ' "It's hard graft this job," he wearily muttered.' If something is **graphed**, the past tense of the verb 'to graph', data is transformed into a quasi-pictorial form as here. ➤

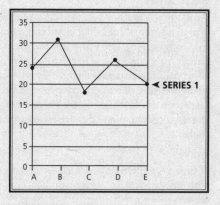

grain

Grain is a word used in reference to cereal crops like wheat, barley, etc. Strictly speaking, grain is the seed of such crops. Because the fruit of cereal crops is small and hard, small particles of other hard substances are often referred to as the grain of such items. Thus you can have grains of salt, grains of gold, and so on. Quite differently, the longitudinal arrangement of wood fibre in a plank, a table or whatever is also called the grain.

gram

A **gram** (sometimes spelt 'gramme') is a unit of weight in the metric system, but the name is also applied to any kind of pulse used for horses. With a capital G, Gram was the name given in Norse legend to Sigurd's sword.

grant

As a verb, 'to **grant**' means to bestow, to allow, to give. Hence you can grant your son permission to go to the cinema tonight, you can grant access to your house for the decorator who is painting your kitchen, and you are prepared to grant that the local bus service has improved. As a noun, 'grant' tends to refer to a sum of money provided for a specific purpose by an outside body. Local authorities used to provide grants for people to go to university, and may still award a grant for the dredging of the local canal or the erection of a statue of some local worthy. In law a grant is a conveyance by deed.

grass

Many of us think of **grass** as that green plant which, in summer, we have to keep on mowing in order to keep our lawns tidy, but 'grass' is also an informal term for cannabis, and, as a verb, means to inform the police of someone's criminal activities or plans. This final meaning probably derives from *grasshopper*, which was rhyming slang for *copper*.

grate, great

As a noun, a **grate** is a framework of metal bars, either serving to bar an entrance while still allowing verbal communication, or to act as a sort of cage in which burning fuel can warm the room. As a verb, 'to grate' means to irritate, to set on edge, or to rub roughly against something. Thus the sound of virtually any pop song might grate on your ears, the constant criticisms of your mother-in-law might grate your nerves, and the noise of the boiler as it warms up might grate you for no very comprehensible reason. The word **great**, of course, is an adjective meaning 'important', 'significant', or even 'bulky'.

grave

A **grave** is a place of burial, or, as an adjective, a word meaning 'serious', 'solemn' or 'weighty'. It can also be a verb with a meaning very similar to 'engrave'.

grayed *see* **grade**

grays, greys, graze

The first two words are merely alternative spellings for the same word signifying a number of tints of that undistinguished colour that rests dully between black and white. Sheep are normally content to **graze** in the field, i.e. chew away contentedly at the grass. So, of course, are a number of other animals. However, it is also possible for you to graze your arm or any other part of your body when something brushes against it in passing. Thus a bullet might graze your cheek, or you might graze your knee while climbing up a rocky hill.

great *see* **grate**

greave, grieve

A **greave** is armour for the leg below the shin. To **grieve** for someone is to mourn them, to feel grief, though the verb is colloquially used as a synonym for irritate, to harass. In the middle ages a grieve was a governor of a province or town.

green

This is a well-known colour, the colour of grass and the leaves of many trees, and hence associated with growth and nature, though Shakespeare has memorably linked it with jealousy:

> O beware, my lord, of jealousy;
> It is the green-eyed monster which doth mock
> The meat it feeds on. (*Othello*)

However, if a person is green, then he or she is inexperienced, immature or undeveloped. In physics, green is one of the three colours of a quark. The Green Party wishes to combat global warming by better use of the environment.

greet

In normal parlance, to **greet** means to give a word or so of acknowledgement to someone when you meet them, but in Scotland the word can mean to weep or cry.

grenade

This is a small explosive shell, often thrown at the enemy during war. It is also a dish of larded veal-collops, with six pigeons and a ragout in the middle.

grieve *see* **greave**

griff

This word, which you are unlikely to have ever used, none the less has five distinct meanings. It can be an Anglo-Indian verb meaning to take in or to fool, a rare term for a claw, news or reliable information, the offspring of a mulatto and a negro, or, in weaving, a frame composed of horizontal bars.

griffin

A **griffin** was a mythical beast having the head and wings of an eagle and the body and hindquarters of a lion. The word was also used to denominate a newcomer to India, someone unused to Indian ways. It could also be used as a synonym for 'griff' when that word meant a mulatto.

grill, grille

As a verb, **grill** can mean to cook something on bars under or over radiant heat, or to interrogate someone in the hope of extracting information from them. A **grille** is a grating, a frame for incubating fish eggs or a rectangular pattern of small dots impressed on postage stamps.

grip, grippe

If you **grip** something, you hold it firmly, you grasp it strongly. If you have the **grippe**, you have the flu.

gripe

The most common use of the verb to **gripe** is as a synonym for 'to grumble' or 'to complain': 'It's difficult not to gripe about the food here.' But the word is also a synonym for 'grip' meaning to grasp or hold on to. In surgery one can also gripe an artery by compressing it with one's fingers, and the word is sometimes used to indicate a pain or spasm in the bowels. In nautical parlance, a gripe refers to the lashings formed by an assemblage of ropes used to secure a boat on the deck of a ship. As a noun, the gripe is either a minor complaint ('My only gripe is that there were no chocolates'), or a gastric or intestinal pain sometimes known as colic.

grisette

A **grisette** is a common edible woodland mushroom, or a young working-class French woman.

grisly, gristly, grizzly

Something that is **grisly** tends to induce shock, horror and nausea, since grisly objects like men lying dead on a battlefield or someone undergoing an operation to remove his spleen or a public hanging are not normally appealing visions for most reasonably sensitive human beings. Things that are **gristly** are not normally wildly attractive to look at either, since they are cartilaginous objects full of gristle. Something that is **grizzly**, greyish like an old squirrel or a bear, can, however, be attractive to see, though one would want to be a safe enough distance from the bear. In the USA, 'grizzly' can be a mining term referring to a grating of parallel iron bars.

grist

There is a common expression '**grist** to the mill', and this reveals that one meaning for this word is simply corn that is waiting to be ground. The word also means the size or thickness of rope, and, in the USA, it can mean a quantity of, a number of. Grist can also be useful material, especially that which is useful in supporting an argument.

grit

Grit is a hard substance broken down into small particles. Hence you tend to get grit flying around when workers are mending the road, and local authorities shower roads with grit when there has been a deep freeze in the hope that the grit will enable cars not to skid. The word also describes a human quality, one of courage and determination: 'Only someone with a lot of grit could have restored that ruin of a house so well.' One is also said to grit one's teeth when facing something unpleasant.

grizzle

Young children are prone to **grizzle**, that is, utter fretful cries for no very apparent reason. If, however, you are grizzle-haired, you have a mixture of dark and white hairs.

groan, grown

One tends to **groan** when in pain, since it is a deep, anguished sound expressive of grief. **Grown** is the past participle of the verb 'to grow', and indicates that something or someone has increased in size and/or matured.

grocer, grosser

Many of us buy our fruit and vegetables from a **grocer**, who stocks such foodstuffs, though originally the word meant 'a person who sold things by the gross'. Grocer was also *Private Eye*'s nickname for the Conservative Prime Minister, Edward Heath. **Grosser** is the comparative term of 'gross' and hence means more stout, corpulent or burly than something else. Of course, since 'gross' is now also a less specific term of abuse, 'grosser' could also mean more seamy, more abhorrent than something else.

grommet

A **grommet** can be an eyelet placed in a hole to protect or insulate a cable or rope, a tube surgically implanted in the eardrum to drain fluid from the middle ear, or, informally, a young or inexperienced surfer.

groom

As a noun, a **groom** is either a man-servant who attends to horses, an officer in the Royal Household, or a shortening of the word 'bridegroom'. As a verb, 'groom' means to ensure that an animal or human is looking at its best. Thus a groom will lovingly brush the hair of a dog to make sure that the animal is looking resplendent, or will ensure that the Prince of Wales has a superbly pressed suit, and that his tie matches his shirt. It is also possible to groom someone for a new role in life. If you, previously a coal miner, have suddenly been appointed British Consul to Australia, you will be groomed for the job and taught what the words of 'Waltzing Matilda' really mean.

groove

A **groove** is normally thought of as being a channel, either literal or metaphorical. Hence, in the days before CDs, a needle ran along the groove of a gramophone record, and from that there developed the expression 'in the groove' to denote that someone was performing well. One would have a groove above and below a sliding door along which the door could run. You might be stuck in your groove as a clarinettist of the Wigan Symphony Orchestra, and be unable to break out and realise your ambition of being conductor at La Scala. In some dialects, however, a groove is a name for a mining shaft, and this was, indeed, its original meaning.

gross

As an adjective, **gross** can mean unattractively fat or bloated, very rude and coarse, very obvious and unacceptable, without deduction of tax when talking of one's earnings, or large-scale. As a noun, gross can signify an amount equal to twelve dozen (144).

grosser *see* grocer

ground

As we all know, the **ground** is what we walk on, the surface of the Earth, be it pavements, fields, moors or the floors of our house. But the word also has a purely conceptual meaning in that it can mean the basis or foundation of something. Hence you could say that the ground for your current skill as a pianist was the hours you spent as a six-year-old practising your scales. A large number of terrorists, suicide bombers, etc. claim that the ground for their activities is their strong religious beliefs. Ground is also the substance used to prepare a surface ready for painting upon. In music, a *ground* bass is a short melodic bass line that is repeated over and over again. The word is also the past tense and the past participle of the verb 'to grind'.

groundling

A **groundling** is best known from the reference in Shakespeare's *Hamlet*. They were the people who stood in the arena of theatres like the Globe, and were, on the whole, the unsophisticated and less critical members of the sixteenth-century playgoing public. But a groundling is also a person on the ground as opposed to one in a spacecraft or aircraft, a creeping or dwarf plant, and a fish that lives at the bottom of lakes and streams.

group

The insertion of **group** in a dictionary of homonyms is, like so many other words, an arguable inclusion because it always carries the basic meaning of a number of people or objects linked together by some common purpose or quality. None the less, its contexts can be so varied that I feel it demands an entry. First of all, a group is a collection of people who work together or share similar beliefs or interests. You may associate with a group of chess players, work with a group of accountants, or go to the theatre with a group of friends. In chemistry a group is a set of elements that share the same column in the period table and consequently have similar properties. In mathematics, a group is a set of elements which contains an inverse for each element. In linguistics, a group is a level of structure between clause and word. I have little doubt that other fields of activity have similar specialist usages. Today the most common usage of the word is to denote an ensemble of pop musicians, though even here, 'group' has tended to be replaced by 'band'.

grouse

A **grouse** is a game bird (i.e. one that people like to shoot), but also a verb meaning 'to grumble'.

grout

This word can mean the infusion of malt before and during fermentation, or the fluid mortar which is poured into the interstices of masonry and woodwork.

growler

You might quite reasonably feel that a **growler** is simply a human being or animal that growls, and so it is, but a growler can also be a small iceberg, a four-wheeled hansom cab, or, in the USA, a bucket used for carrying drink, especially beer.

guard

As a verb, to **guard** is to watch over and protect someone or something. As a noun, a guard is someone who does such watching and protecting, but it is also a defensive posture of the kind that you see in boxing, an official in charge of a railway train, and a player in American football.

guerrilla *see* gorilla

guessed, guest

Guessed is the past tense of the verb 'to guess', and a **guest** is someone who is entertained and/or fed at someone else's residence.

guide, guyed

A **guide** is someone who shows you the way or instructs you in some technique to which you are new. It is also someone who is a member of the Girl Guides' Association. Something is **guyed** when it is secured with a rope or wire.

guild *see* gild

guillotine

The **guillotine** is famous for its usage during the French Revolution when it was used to cut off the heads of aristocrats and other enemies of the regime. This it did by means of a large blade which was released from a height above and consequently sliced through the neck of the kneeling victim. A more pacific version can be found in most offices where it is used for slicing paper. In Parliament, in order to hasten proceedings, a guillotine may be placed upon a bill under discussion, which means that only a predetermined amount of time is allowed for each clause of the bill.

guise, guys

Your **guise** is your external appearance, and you can sometimes use that external appearance to deceive. Hence you might call at a house in the guise of the local vicar whereas you are really a thief wanting to steal their spare cash rather than their soul. A guy is a colloquial term for a man, and hence **guys** is simply the plural of that. But 'guy' can also be a verb. If you guy someone, you imitate him or her with the object of poking fun at them.

gull

A **gull** is a long-winged bird of the family *Laridae*, and is often to be observed at the seaside. A gull is also someone who has been fooled, and to gull someone is to dupe them in some way.

gulf

A **gulf** can be a deep inlet of the sea, a deep ravine, or a large difference or division between people.

gunnel, gunwale

Despite their very different spellings, these two words are homophones. A **gunnel** is a small, eel-shaped marine fish, and a **gunwale** is the upper edge of a ship's side.

gutter

A **gutter** is a shallow trough fixed beneath the edge of a roof for carrying off rainwater, a channel at the side of a street for carrying off rainwater, or the blank space between facing pages of a book or between adjacent columns of type or stamps in a sheet. Shoddy and sensational newspapers are often referred to as being the gutter press, though the term stems from the English writer and journalist Gerald Priestland (1927–1991) who wrote, 'Journalists belong in the gutter because that is where the ruling classes throw their guilty secrets.' As a verb, a small flame as in a candle can gutter in that it flickers and burns unsteadily.

guy

In the USA a **guy** can be a person of either sex, though in Britain the word has hitherto been confined to males. A guy is also an effigy of Guy Fawkes, traditionally burnt on a bonfire on 5 November each year. If you guy someone, you make fun of them, and if you put up a tent, you will need a guy (or guy rope) to secure that tent to the ground.

H

habit

As you doubtless know, a **habit** is an action that someone repeatedly performs. Hence it may be someone's habit to have a shower every morning when he or she awakes. It may be someone else's habit to have a cigar every evening just after dinner. But the word also denotes one's bodily attire, though these days it more frequently refers merely to the garb, a long loose robe, of a religious order. The word stems from the Latin *habitus*, 'condition, appearance', and it was not until the sixteenth century that 'habit' referred to a habitual practice. A biologist uses the word to refer to the characteristic mode and appearance of an animal or plant.

hack

If you attack something with an axe, you are said to **hack** at the object concerned. The word denotes a somewhat random and undisciplined chopping action, and probably derives from the Old English *haccian*, which meant 'cut to pieces'. The same word applies in a football game when a player lunges with his feet at another player. Used as an adjective or noun, 'hack' can be applied to horses or writers. A hack horse is one let out for hire, and therefore sometimes referred to simply as a hack. The word is an abbreviation of *hackney* which probably derives from the East London area of Hackney where horses were pastured. A hack writer is one who writes articles on virtually anything, depending upon the instructions given to him by his editor or publisher. Oliver Goldsmith wrote an epitaph for a hack writer:

> Here lies poor Ned Purdon, from misery freed,
> Who long was a bookseller's hack:
> He led such a damnable life in this world,
> I don't think he'll wish to come back.

The board on which a hawk's meat is placed is also called a hack, as is a frame for drying bricks, cheeses, etc. These days you can also hack into someone else's computer system, steal their data and possibly infect them with a virus. You can also hack someone off, i.e. annoy or infuriate them, or simply hack around, namely pass one's time with no definite purpose.

hackle

This word, which most of us have never used, can mean a covering of any kind like a bird's feathers or a snake's skin, the straw roofing of a bee hive, the long shining feathers on the neck of a cock, peacock or pigeon, a comb for splitting and combing out the fibres of flax or hemp, a local name for a stickleback, an artificial fly used in fishing, a bunch of feathers in a military headdress, or, as a verb, to cut roughly. Even with these eight definitions, it is still unlikely that **hackle** is a word that you will encounter frequently other than in the plural e.g. 'His hackles rose'. This derives from the use of the word to describe the long narrow feather on the neck of a cock.

hag

If you describe Mrs Evans who lives three doors away from you as a **hag**, you are not being complimentary. In mythology, a hag was an evil spirit or demon or witch. By extension, the word has since been applied to any ugly and repulsive woman (like Mrs Evans), and the word normally carries a connotation of the woman concerned being malicious and spiteful. Macbeth is not being flattering when he addresses the witches with the words, 'How now, you secret, black and midnight hags.' Yet a hag can also be a fish allied to the lamprey, a wooden enclosure, the stump of a tree left after the tree itself has been felled, a pit or break in moss land, the vertical marking of a peat-cutting, or, as a verb, 'to urge' or 'to egg on'.

ha-ha

This can simply be a representation of laughter or a boundary to a garden or park. Since the boundary comprises a ditch with a wall on its inner side below ground level, its name, ha-ha, is said by the *Oxford Dictionary of Phrase and Fable* to represent a cry of surprise on suddenly encountering such an obstacle.

hail, hale

If you **hail** someone, you are simply greeting them with a welcoming salutation, though it is also possible to hail a ship or something else when you merely wish to attract their attention. This is much more pleasant than being deluged with hail, frozen raindrops falling in pellets, or, even worse, being met by a hail (large number) of bullets. If you are **hale**, you are fit and healthy, though, as a verb, you can hale something along by pulling or tugging it.

hair, hare

Hair is a filament that grows on the skin of animals, especially mammals, though occasionally in plants there is an outgrowth of the epidermis that looks very like an animal hair. Its homophone **hare** is a rodent very similar to a rabbit. The verb 'to hare' means to run at great speed, something that the long-eared mammal is itself prone to do.

hake

This is a fish somewhat resembling the cod, but a **hake** can also be a wooden frame suspended from the roof for drying cheeses or a verb meaning to go about idly from place to place.

halcyon

This supposedly was a bird that bred about the time of the winter solstice in a nest floating on the sea. It was reputedly credited with charming the wind and waves so that the sea became especially calm. Consequently **halcyon** also became an adjective meaning peaceful and undisturbed. But a halcyon is also a tropical African or Asian kingfisher with brightly coloured plumage.

hale *see* hail

hall, haul

A **hall** is a large room used for receptions and banquets, an open area covered by a roof and normally part of a palace, court or temple, a university building containing rooms for students to live in, or the vestibule to a house. The word can also be applied to the house itself, as you see with Haddon Hall, Darlington Hall and so on. Whatever the actual building may be, the word 'hall' gives a connotation of space. Indeed, the word used to be an exclamation urging people to provide more space, and there is a good example of this usage in Shakespeare's *Romeo and Juliet*: 'A hall, a hall, give room, and foot it girls.' If you **haul** something, you pull or drag it. The word is a variant of the archaic verb *hale* which meant 'drag forcibly'.

hallow

If you emit a **hallow**, you are uttering a cry or shout, normally to assist dogs in their pursuit of some hapless fox. At the same time, if you hallow something, you consecrate it as sacred to God. Indeed, until the fifteenth century, a hallow meant a saint.

halt

If you come to a **halt**, you come to a stop. If you halt something, you force it to cease or stand still. If you are halt, one of your legs is injured with the result that you limp. If your sheep is halt, it has the disease of foot-rot.

ham

The **ham** is part of the leg at the back of the knee, the thigh of a slaughtered animal used for food, and, as a verb, the process of over-acting. Ham as a noun to describe an excessively theatrical actor was originally coined in the USA, and might derive from the first syllable of the word 'amateur'. In the early twentieth century, the word 'ham' also came to be applied to an amateur radio operator.

hammer

As a noun, a **hammer** is a tool with a solid head that is used for breaking things up or driving nails in. It has been metaphorically used to denote a fierce and warlike person: Edward I was the Hammer of the Scots. As a verb, it can obviously be used as the equivalent of the noun – 'I must hammer these rocks to gravel' – but it can also be used figuratively: 'I must hammer these German irregular verbs into my head.' If you defeat someone comprehensively in a sport or competition, you can say that you hammered them. In the Stock Exchange, the verb means to beat down the price of a stock or to declare a company or person to be a defaulter.

hamper

You can pack a **hamper**, a large basket-like container, with provisions for your planned family picnic in the Malvern Hills. Indeed, you can pack a hamper with virtually anything you like. As a verb, though, 'to hamper' means to handicap, to obstruct, to fetter or to impede.

hand

While we are all acquainted with the physical entity that is attached to our arms and which, with its fingers and thumbs, enables us to manipulate so many things, the word **hand** is so often used in a metaphorical fashion that it has to be counted as a homonym. We talk about the hand of God, we ask for someone's hand in marriage, we claim that some robbery shows the hand of Dirty Dennis, you may be a great hand at washing up or engraving or playing canasta, and so on. But apart from such emblematic usages, the word 'hand' is homonymic in a physical sense too. You hold a hand of cards, you look at the hands of a clock, and you measure a horse in hands. The word also occurs in scores of idiomatic expressions: you have to hand it to him, I've got my hands full, the right hand doesn't know what the left hand's doing, he never does a hand's turn, and so on.

hang

The word **hang** is most commonly used as a verb. You can hang a picture from the wall by means of a hook, and one can often see meat hanging from hooks in the butchers. You can hang a person by slipping a noose around his neck and then raising him from the ground or, more humanely, causing him to drop suddenly so that he is instantly throttled. One can hang around waiting for something. A computer operation can hang when it suddenly ceases to continue. As a noun the word is rare, but one can talk about the hang of his head when referring to a drooping posture, or the hang of one's clothes depending upon whether one's clothes fit one perfectly or hang so loosely as to resemble a marquee. One can also use 'Hang!' as a simple exclamation of annoyance.

hangar, hanger

A **hangar** is a sort of garage for aircraft, and, **hanger** an object from which something hangs. A hanger can also be a sword or a hillside wood.

harbour

We use the word **harbour** most frequently to describe a place where a boat can reside safe from the ravages of the sea, and as a verb, 'to harbour' does mean 'to provide a lodging for', 'to shelter' or 'to sojourn'. Apparently in glass making, a harbour is a trough-like box for holding the mixed ingredients and conveying them to the pot for fusion.

hard

If something is **hard**, it is either solid to the touch and not easily penetrated, or it is difficult to accomplish. Hence granite is hard, and so is calculus. But 'hard' is widely used in a variety of metaphorical senses. One can be a hard man, i.e. tough and unemotional. One can drink a hard drink, i.e. a spirit. One can work hard, i.e. with effort and duration. One can drink hard water, i.e. water that contains mineral salts.

harden

One can **harden** something by making it firmer, more solid, as one does with clay pots in the oven. One can also harden something to new conditions by gradually increasing its exposure to those conditions.

hare *see* hair

harmony

Harmony is either a number of sounds occurring simultaneously and creating a pleasing noise and is therefore most frequently used in the realm of music, or the word can be used to describe the pleasing combination of almost anything. Hence people can live together in harmony, the fields on yonder hillside combine in visual harmony, or Professor Bloodstock's views on genetic engineering can be in harmony with those of Dr Mutant.

harp

The **harp** is a musical instrument consisting of a frame supported a graduated series of parallel strings which are played by being plucked with the fingers. As a verb, 'harp' is almost invariably followed by the preposition 'on', and 'to harp on' means to talk or write persistently and tediously on a particular topic.

harrow

A **harrow** is an agricultural implement equipped with iron teeth, and which is dragged over the field in order to break up clods and make the soil more suitable for the planting of seeds. As verb, 'to harrow' someone is to frighten or appal them in some way. Some find that going on the ghost train at a fair is enough to harrow them.

hart, heart

A **hart** is the male of the deer, especially the red deer. In Christian art, it is the emblem of solitude and purity of life. Its homophone, **heart**, is the organ in all animals that keeps up the circulation of the blood. Regarded as the seat of life, the heart has naturally been used metaphorically for centuries, being regarded as the progenitor of love, loyalty, courage and morality.

hash

Commonly the word **hash** signifies a dish, normally comprising small pieces of meat and vegetables, and served in gravy. The word can also be used to denote a mixture of almost anything, a jumble of things, a medley of items. These days it is often used to refer to an illegal drug, hashish.

hatch

A **hatch** is a half-door or gate through which items can be passed, as in a cargo hatch or a service hatch. It is also a verb signifying the process in which a bird's egg is tended until the young bird is able to break out of its confines. You can also hatch a door (i.e. close it), or cut, engrave or draw a series of lines, normally parallel.

haul *see* hall

haunch

In architecture, a **haunch** is the side of an arch, but the word is more frequently used to refer to the buttock and thigh of an animal or human.

haut, ho, hoe

The word **haut** is a French one that has been incorporated into the English language. It means 'high', 'lofty' or 'haughty'. **Ho** is a simple exclamation designed to attract attention or to persuade an animal to stop its progress. A **hoe** is a tool used chiefly for breaking up or loosening the surface of the ground and thus making it easier to weed that ground or to plant on it.

haw

A **haw** can be a hedge or encompassing fence and, by extension, the ground so enclosed, the fruit of the hawthorn, the nictitating membrane of a horse, dog, etc., or a kind of exclamation generally representing hesitation.

hawk

This term can denote any bird of prey used in falconry, a small quadrangular tool with a handle used in plastering, or, as a verb, to wander around offering items for sale. More figuratively, the word is also used to denote a person who advocates an aggressive policy.

hay, hey

The *Shorter Oxford* lists eight obsolete meanings for **hay**, but the two current ones denote grass cut down and dried so as to provide fodder for animals, and a country dance having a serpentine movement. **Hey** is simply a call to attract attention.

hays, haze

If you have more than one type of hay, you will refer to them as **hays**. A **haze** is a thin misty appearance in the atmosphere normally caused by heat. At sea, though, you can haze someone by imposing hard and unnecessary work upon them. You can also haze cattle by driving them in a particular direction from horseback.

hazard

Most of us think of a **hazard** as being a potential source of danger. If you are playing golf, a bunker is a hazard. If you are crossing the road, careless drivers are a hazard. Hazard is also a gambling game using two dice, and in billiards, a stroke with which a ball is pocketed.

head

As we all know, the **head** is that part of an animal that contains the brain, the eyes, nose, ears and mouth. But you can also be the head of something, in which case you are the most important and directing person of that establishment or operation. The anterior parts of plants are also often referred to as their heads. The cutting, striking or operational end of a tool is often referred to as its head. Indeed, the word can be applied in a vast area of contexts. It can also be a verb. You can head a ball, head a procession, head for promotion, head off a potential danger, and so on.

header

Although I have never heard it used in this way, a **header** can be one who heads an organisation or operation. The word can also be used for a tool or machine which removes the heads of plants. In building, a header is a brick or stone which is laid with its head or end in the face of the wall. You are taking a header when you dive into the swimming pool. When playing football, a header is when a player directs the ball with his head rather than his feet. Most common of all, a header can mark a subdivision in a piece of writing. If you are writing an article about the music of Mozart, you could have headers which label specific comments on the piano concertos, the operas, the string quartets and so on. Even so, the word 'heading' is much more common in this context.

heal, heel, he'll

To **heal** someone is to enable them to recover from a disease, though most minor physical injuries like cuts and bruises heal themselves. The **heel** is the hinder part of the foot and, because of Achilles, is often used figuratively as being a weak spot in someone or something. A heel is also a dishonest and unscrupulous person, the part of the palm of the hand next to the wrist, the end of a violin bow at which it is held, and the part of the head of a golf club that is nearest to the shaft. As a verb, you can heel a shoe by fitting a new one, heel a ball by hitting it with the back of your foot, or heel during a dance by touching the ground with your heel. The word is also used as a command to a dog. The word **he'll** is simply a contraction of 'he will'.

hear, here

If you can **hear** something, you are able to perceive it with your auditory senses. Hence you can hear other people speak, play music or walk along the street, just as you can hear birds sing, traffic pass or thunder roar. **Here** is an adverb indicating that something is present or taking place at this very spot: 'It was here that I saw Mrs Griffiths.'

heard, herd

Heard is simply the past tense of the verb 'to hear' – 'I heard the cattle lowing in the field' – and a **herd** is a company of animals – a herd of cattle – or, as a verb, the process of bringing animals together into one place.

heart *see* hart

heat

The quality of **heat** signifies that something is warm or hot, or at least warmer or hotter than something else to which it is being compared. As a verb, if you heat something, you raise its temperature. But the word is often used figuratively. If you speak with heat, you speak with passion, possibly with anger. In addition, before a race, heats may be held to determine who is worthy enough to enter the race itself. If you come first in a heat, you are then able to enter the major race itself.

heave

Basically this verb means to lift something, and the word implies that great effort is needed. Hence you may **heave** a sack of coal on to your shoulders, or heave yourself out of bed. It is, however, also possible to heave a sigh of relief, or for your stomach to heave when you are being sick. A boat or ship heaves to when it comes to a stop.

heavy

Something that is **heavy** is of considerable weight, but the word has many metaphorical uses too. You can have a heavy heart when you are overtaken by sadness, you can indulge in heavy humour when your wit is particularly ponderous, you can see heavy clouds when the sky is threatening rain, or you can find a book somewhat heavy going. Clearly such instances have nothing to do with physical weight, but instead imply a slow, serious or even threatening mode. Thus you could have a heavy burden when you were carrying a bale of straw, or trying to cope with the unexpected death of your beloved daughter. The one is physically heavy, the other emotionally so.

heckle

If you **heckle** during a speech, you interrupt that speech with some derisive or aggressive comments, a usage that arose in the mid-seventeenth century. Much earlier usage was confined to the fact that you can heckle flax or hemp by splitting and straightening the fibres ready for spinning.

he'd, heed

The apostrophised word **he'd** is simply a contraction of 'he would' as in 'He'd never support Arsenal.' The word **heed** is a verb meaning 'to listen', 'to observe', 'to pay attention'.

hedge

As a noun, a **hedge** is a fence or boundary formed by closely growing bushes or shrubs. However you can also hedge against financial loss by spreading your investments. When asked a question, you can also hedge by failing to give a straightforward answer to that question.

heel, he'll *see* heal

heigh, hi, hie, high

Heigh is simply an exclamation of greeting or encouragement, as is **hi**. If you decide to **hie** off to the shops, you have opted for doing some fairly rushed buying. 'Hie' means to go, to depart, to speed away, and tends only to be used these days by literate people being consciously archaic. **High** means lofty, tall or possessing height, and is used mostly in a perfectly straight-forward fashion: 'That is a high wall', 'The snow drift was six feet high' and so on. However, the word is also used metaphorically to describe rank – 'He's someone high in the Foreign Office' – the amount of money that one uses in gambling – 'They played for high stakes' – or in reference to musical sounds – 'Top C is too high for most sopranos.' Somewhat oddly, the word is also used to describe meat or cheese that is very close to rotting. In addition, 'high' is often an integral adjective to nouns, and its meaning in such contexts often seems to denote consequence, importance or sig-nificance. High Church, High German, High Mass, high priest and high treason are good examples.

heir *see* air

help

As a verb, **help** means to assist, to aid, but if you help yourself to something, then you take something without anyone else's assistance, and it can be a synonym for stealing. As a noun, a help can be a piece of assistance in some task, or a domestic employee who cleans and tidies. Help is also a cry for assistance, or a computer program that purportedly guides you through sundry computer activities and operations, but in fact buries you in jargon.

herd *see* heard

here *see* hear

hermetic, Hermetic

If something is **hermetic**, it is complete and airtight. Hence you could have a hermetic seal or even a hermetic society. However the word is used also to refer to something that is difficult to understand because it is confined to a specialised minority. Thus database design is a hermetic activity for most of us, as is the mating of drosophila, or the sprung rhythm of G. M. Hopkins. With a capital letter, Hermetic relates to an ancient occult tradition.

heroin, heroine

Heroin is a drug derived from morphine, while a **heroine** is a female hero or the chief female character in a book, film or play.

heteronym

This word is a good illustration as to how confusing the world of homonyms and language usage in general actually is. The *Oxford Dictionary of English* gives three definitions of **heteronym** as follows:

1 each of two or more words which are spelled identically but have different sounds and meanings, such as *tear* meaning 'rip' and *tear* meaning 'liquid from the eye'.
2 each of two or more words which are used to refer to the identical thing in different geographical areas of a speech community, such as *nappy* and *diaper*.
3 each of two words having the same meaning but derived from unrelated sources, for example *preface* and *foreword*.

It is difficult to see how one word can have three different definitions within the same intellectual ambit. It is surely like having sulphuric acid mean a liquid with the chemical formula H_2SO_4 (which is true) and a gas with the formula HSO (which isn't). My edition of the *Shorter Oxford* then confuses things even more. It begins with the less than helpful definition: 'One or other of two heteronymous terms', but then continues:

2 A word spelt like another but having a different sound and meaning;
3 A name of a thing in one language which is a translation of the same in another language.

The full *Oxford* is virtually identical, and I will not insult your intelligence by spelling out how they differ from their more recent companion, the *Oxford Dictionary of English*. If you have read the Introduction to this dictionary, you will be aware that I do not even mention the word 'heteronym' in that preface. Yet, in so far as one can make any sense of the varied Oxford definitions of 'heteronym', it would seem to be an exact synonym for 'homonym'. As such, it is completely unnecessary, and you should forget about its existence immediately.

hew, hue

If you **hew** at something, you attack it with an axe. Hence you might hew a tree down. In North America, the verb can mean 'to conform to'. Hence an organisation could hew to high ethical standards. A **hue** is either a variety of any colour, an outcry normally raised by a crowd that see something to which they object, or a hunting cry.

hey *see* hay

hi, hie, high *see* heigh

hiccup

There are two meanings for **hiccup**, both of which most of us encounter very frequently. The first is an involuntary spasm of the diaphragm and respiratory organs which tends to produce a gulping sound that reminds one of a drowning frog. The second is a temporary or minor problem or setback, like discovering that you have forgotten your pen as you attempt to begin an exam.

hide, hied

When you **hide** something, you place it in a position where you hope that it will not be found. The hide of an animal is its skin. A hide was also a measurement of land in medieval times, and was defined as enough to support one family. **Hied** is an old-fashioned past tense of the verb 'to hie', and means 'hurried': 'He hied his way to the Sheriff.'

hie *see* heigh, hi, high

high *see* heigh, hi, hie

higher, hire

When something is **higher** than something else, it is taller or at a greater elevation. Thus a skyscraper is higher than your bungalow, and someone standing on the summit of Ben Nevis is higher than someone else standing on the sea shore. More figuratively, one can have a higher position in one's profession than someone else, or one can have one or more higher degrees. To **hire** something is to pay for its temporary use. Hence you might hire a car for a day trip, hire a lawn mower for obvious reasons, or hire a person to rewire your house.

hike

This verb most commonly means 'to travel', either on foot – 'I'm going for a hike in the Peak District' – or by cadging a lift from a passing motorist. It can also mean 'to raise up', either in something very tangible like 'He hiked up his trousers', or something more abstract like, 'The unrest in the Middle East is bound to produce a hike in the price of oil.'

him, hymn

In grammatical jargon, **him** is the accusative or dative third person singular of the personal pronoun 'he'. A **hymn** is a song of praise to God, and, like most nouns, can be used as a verb, though not necessarily with a religious connotation.

hind

A **hind** is the female of the red deer, one of the various fishes of the family *Serranidae*, a bailiff or steward on a farm, or an adjective to denote the back part of something.

hinny

This noun either refers to the offspring of a female donkey and a male horse, or is a Scottish term of endearment.

hip

A **hip** is the fruit of the wild rose, the projecting part of the body on each side formed by the pelvis, the first part of the cheering acclamation 'Hip, hip, hooray', a projecting inclined edge on a roof, and an adjective meaning trendy much used by teenagers.

hit

For most of the time, a **hit** is a blow given to something. Hence you can hit somebody on the nose with your fist, a cricket ball with your bat, a football with your foot, and so on. But a hit is also something that has become very successful. Pop songs that sell a lot are known as hits, plays that attract large audiences are known as hits, and so on. The word is also used when you have achieved a target. If you intended to become manager of your local Lloyds Bank and did so at the age of thirty-eight, you would say that you had hit your target.

hitch

Most of us use the word **hitch** when we want to refer to a temporary delay or stoppage: 'The only hitch on our trip was when we got caught up in some carnival in Lyon.' But a hitch can be the action of catching something on a hook, a noose or knot by which a rope is caught round some object, or a slight fault or dislocation of a stratum. As a verb, 'to hitch' can mean to tie together or even to marry. It is also a part of the compound word 'hitch-hike', and either part can be used singly.

ho, hoe *see* **haut**

hoar, whore

Something that is **hoar** is venerable or grey-haired with age. A **whore** is a woman who earns her living as a prostitute, though the word is often used just as a general insult.

hoard, horde, whored

If you **hoard** something, you amass it and store it away for preservation or for future use. With humans being such idiosyncratic creatures, one does hear of hoards being kept of love letters, shoes, Superman comics, etc., as well as jewels and other financially valuable items. A **horde** is a company of some size of animals or humans. Hence you can have a horde of wolves on the prowl or a horde of nomadic Arabs in the desert. **Whored** is the past tense of the verb 'to whore' which means to offer oneself as a sexual plaything, normally for payment.

hoarse, horse

Hoarse is an adjective normally applied to the human voice, and it signifies that the voice concerned is deep and somewhat rough. One is frequently hoarse when one has a cold. The word is also applied to animals that have a deep-sounding voice, a frog or raven for example. A **horse** is a solid-hoofed quadruped that can be used for riding upon (or betting upon). In colloquial speech, one can horse around, namely frolic energetically rather like a horse cavorting in a field.

hoary

If someone is **hoary**, they have grey or white hair. In a similar way, the word is used to describe animals and plants that are covered with whitish fur or short hairs. Quite differently, if you describe a story as being hoary, you mean that it is overused, unoriginal or trite.

hob

As a noun, a **hob** can be a cooking appliance or the flat top part of a cooker, a flat metal shelf at the side of a fireplace used for heating pans, a machine tool used for cutting gears, a male ferret, or a peg or pin used as a mark in throwing games. In *A Midsummer Night's Dream*, Shakespeare used the word to signify a sprite or hobgoblin, though, according to *Brewer's*, the word is also a short form of Robin.

hobby

A **hobby** is a small or middle-sized horse, a small species of falcon, or an activity or topic which one pursues for one's personal enjoyment; stamp collecting, dancing and archery are all hobbies. A hobby horse is a particular obsession that one may have. Thus you might have a hobby horse about making boxing illegal, combating global warming, or obesity.

hock

The joint in the hinder leg of a quadruped between the true knee and the fetlock is called the **hock**. It is also the name for some German white wine. If something is in hock, it is residing at the pawn shop, and interestingly this usage comes from the Dutch word *hok* which means 'hutch, prison, debt'.

hoe *see* haut

hog

As a noun, a **hog** can be a male pig, a young sheep that has not been shorn, a greedy and coarse person, a selfish and reckless driver on the road, a device in paper-making that agitates the pulp, or a sort of brush for cleaning a ship's bottom. As a verb, 'to hog' means to appropriate something for one's own exclusive use, or to bend or arch the back in an upwards direction. If you go the whole hog, you do something completely and thoroughly. This phrase may derive from one of William Cowper's poems which discusses Muslim uncertainty about which parts of the pig are acceptable as food. Clearly if you go the whole hog, you decide that it is permitted to consume the entire pig.

hold, holed

To **hold** something is to grasp it, to keep it in one's hand. That, obviously, is a physical action, but one can also hold something conceptually. Most people hold the multiplication tables in their heads. One can also hold an office or position, and the word is part of countless idiomatic expressions: hold good, hold a candle to, hold one's breath, hold the fort, etc. As a noun, a 'hold' is the interior cavity of a ship in which the cargo is stored. If something is **holed**, it is because it is full of holes (like some of my shirts) or because it is a golf ball that has just entered a hole on the green.

hole, whole

A **hole** is a hollow place or a cavity in the ground in which one can stumble. A hole can also be an aperture passing through an object like a hole in one's shirt, a button hole on one's coat, a hole in a wall for the water pipes to pass through, and so on. It is also possible to have an intellectual hole. If, for instance, you wrote a brilliant book about narrative techniques in the English novel, but totally omitted the epistolary novels of Richardson and others, this would be a hole in your thesis. Golf links have holes for the golf ball to be aimed at, and the word is also used metaphorically to describe a dingy lodging or an unappealing area. You can also be metaphorically in a hole if you are in a tricky situation. If something is **whole**, it is complete and/or in good condition. You may this afternoon read a whole book, knit a whole cardigan, ensure that the whole train set is packed away, or alternatively waste the whole time by watching snooker on the television.

holey, holy, wholly

If something is **holey**, it is full of holes. If someone or something is **holy**, it is regarded as sacred. If something is **wholly** satisfactory, it is completely so.

hollow

Something is **hollow** if it has a hole or empty space inside itself. But something is also hollow if it has no real substance or meaningful *raison d'être*. Both the Conservative Party and New Labour come to mind.

home

Although, tritely, we all know that there is no place like **home**, the word does carry a number of differing meanings. The most common, of course, is the place where you live, either on your own or with relatives. A home is also an institution in which people needing professional care live. A sports fixture may be held at home or away. A horse in a race might fall four fences away from home.

homonym

There is some confusion with respect to this word. Some regard it as being a word that sounds the same as another word that is spelt differently, words like *stare* and *stair*. Others regard it as a word that is spelt the same as another word but with a different pronunciation, as a violin *bow* and a *bow* to the Queen. There are also words that are spelt identically and sound identically, but none the less have two or more meanings, words like *fluke* or *boil*. The most sensible course is to accept all these examples as homonyms, a stance adopted by this dictionary. However, according to the *Shorter Oxford*, a homonym can also be a nickname for someone or something. See also the entry on 'heteronym'.

honesty

This is a human quality that is indispensable for civilised human contact, because, unless people tell the truth to each other, chaos is inevitable. Hence acting with **honesty** is morally good and practically convenient. However, there is also a European plant with purple or white flowers that is called honesty, with no reference at all to its moral standing, but so named because its diaphanous seed pods' translucency seemed to symbolise lack of deceit.

honey

Honey is a sweet substance created by bees from the nectar of flowers. The word is consequently used to refer to almost anything that is sweet, and also frequently used as a term of endearment to a woman.

honour

If someone is held in **honour**, then he or she is highly regarded because of their probity and industry. To a few of such people, an honour is sometimes awarded, an honour here being a medal or title bestowed upon them like the OBE or a knighthood. It is also possible for you to feel that it is an honour to meet someone, someone whom you particularly admire. In the game of bridge, the top cards of each suit (ace, king, queen, jack, ten) are called honours.

hoodoo

Most of us regard a **hoodoo** as being a run of bad luck, a run that is often associated with one particular person or activity. In North America, however, a hoodoo is a column or pinnacle of weathered rock.

hook

A **hook** is a piece of metal or other hard material curved or bent back at an angle, and used for hanging things like clothes or pictures. It can also be a curved cutting instrument used in reaping or shearing, a stroke in cricket and golf, a blow in boxing, and a curved promontory of land jutting out to sea.

hooker

A **hooker** can be a rugby player, a one-masted sailing boat, a glass of some spirit like scotch or brandy, or a prostitute.

hoot

A **hoot** is a somewhat strident sound that tends to echo in the air. Owls hoot, as do cars when jammed in traffic jams. Human beings can hoot in derision or merriment, yet at the same time one can describe something that is very amusing as being a hoot.

hop

If you **hop**, you proceed by moving forward on one foot only, a mode of locomotion that is tiring and ungainly and is employed only in games. Birds also hop because they move both their feet simultaneously. If, however, you are in a rush, you might describe yourself as hopping around to get things done. You might even be caught on the hop, i.e. in an unprepared state. If someone doesn't like your company, you might be told to hop off, i.e. go away. But the word 'hop' is also a noun relating to a climbing plant which is used in brewing beer.

horde *see* hoard

horn

Certain animals are equipped with horns, bony projections from the head, and most of us have seen them on cattle, goats and deer. The horn was a symbol of power and dominion, and as such it is found in classical writers and the Old Testament. The warning sound of a car is also called a **horn**, and a musical wind instrument can also be a horn. Other horns include a projection at each corner of the altar in a Jewish temple, the land projection semi-enclosing a bay, a reed-stop on an organ, and the extremity of a crescent moon. As a verb, you can horn in on something, i.e. intrude or interfere. In the West Indies, to horn is to be unfaithful to one's husband or wife.

horny

Something is **horny** if it possesses horns on its head, or if it is feeling sexually aroused.

horse *see* hoarse

hose

Hose is a general term to refer to socks, stockings and such clothing for the legs and feet. A hose is also a flexible tube for conveying a liquid to where it is needed.

host

A **host** is a collection of people, a great company, from the Latin *hostis*, 'enemy', or a man who entertains and feeds others in his own house, from the Latin *hospes*, 'a guest'. The same word refers to the bread consecrated in a Christian service as a symbol of Christ's body, from the Latin *hostia*, 'a sacrifice'. A person or animal that has received transplanted tissue is also a host, as is a computer that supervises multiple access to a database. In biology, a host is a living cell in which a parasite or virus lodges.

hot

Something is **hot** if it is at a high temperature. Food can be described as hot if it contains spices or peppers that produce a burning sensation. Your temper or imagination may be hot if you are filled with strong emotion about some issue. A film or book may be hot if it contains explicitly sexual material. News may be hot if it has only just been released. A topic may be hot if a lot of people are discussing it. Goods may be hot if they have just been stolen, and the thief or thieves now want to get rid of them.

hotel

A **hotel** is an establishment that provides accommodation and meals for visitors and travellers, but in radio communication it is used as an unambiguous, unconfusable sound signifying 'h', because over a wireless network 'h' can easily be misheard as 'a'.

hour, our

An **hour** is a length of time, sixty minutes, though the word is often used more loosely and generally to indicate that a particular time is appropriate for someone or something. Thus you might say, 'Today is the hour for Gladys to shine', and one's darkest hour might last for a week or month. **Our** is a personal pronoun meaning 'possessed by us'.

house

A **house** is a building for human habitation, a building set aside for a particular activity (a house of prayer, for example), a firm or institution (the House of Fraser), a residential building at boarding school, a religious community that occupies a particular building, part of a legislative body (the House of Commons), an old-fashioned term for Bingo, an imaginary entity in a debate ('This house would legalise cannabis'), or, in astrology, the twelfth division of the celestial sphere. There are also scores of phrases in which 'house' is an integral part: clearing house, country house, halfway house, open house, rough house, and so on.

how

This adverb is employed in asking questions as to in what way something works or what it means or in what manner something was done. It is also supposedly the greeting of the North American Indians, the equivalent of our 'Hello'.

hub

The central part of a wheel is called the **hub**, but the word can be conceptually extended to refer to the centre or crux of political, intellectual and emotional concerns. Thus one could say that the hub of Britain's drug problems lies in the decline of religious belief, the failure to control immigration, or whatever took your fancy as a viable explanation.

hue *see* hew

huff

A **huff** can be a puff of wind, the blowing out of air loudly on account of exertion, a spasm of injured pride or petty annoyance, or, in the game of draughts, the removal of an opponent's piece because he or she had failed to take a piece that was *en prise*.

hull

The **hull** of a ship is its body or frame. The pod of peas and beans is also called the hull.

hum

A **hum** can be a low, continuous sound of the sort that is made by bees or by an audience just before the play or concert starts. Slightly differently, one can also hum a tune. A hum can also be a disagreeable smell.

humbug

A **humbug** is a boiled sweet, especially one flavoured with peppermint, but the word also denotes the general concept of deception and falsity or can be applied to a specific hypocritical person.

humerus, humorous

The **humerus** is a bone of the upper arm. It is often called the funny bone because of its similarity to **humorous** which is an adjective meaning comic, funny or whimsical.

humour

Humour is the quality of being amusing or comic, and people searching for a partner in contact magazines always specify that the potential person must have a good sense of humour. However, the word can also signify one's general mood ('I'm in a bad humour today'), or, as a verb, denote a weary compliance with someone's idiosyncrasies so as to keep them in an equable mood. In the middle ages it was believed that each person was made up of a mixture of four fluids, each of which was known as a humour.

hump

A **hump** is a protuberance, particularly one on the back, which occurs naturally in animals like the camel but which can occur in humans as a deformity. If one takes the hump, then one is offended by the words or actions of someone else. If you hump a sack up the stairs, then you carry it. If you hump your next-door neighbour, you have sexual intercourse with them.

hundred

If you count to ninety-nine, then the next number is one **hundred**. A subdivision of a county, a subdivision that possesses its own law court, is also called a hundred, gaining its name from the fact that it originally comprised a hundred hides.

hung

If, after a General Election, no one party has an overall majority, then the resulting Parliament is said to be **hung**. The same word is used for a jury that is unable to agree. If a man is described as well hung, it denotes that he has quite large genitals. Of course, the most frequent use of this word is as the past tense of the verb 'to hang', and you can often hear such well-worn phrases as 'I've just hung out the washing.'

hunt

This verb normally describes the activity of pursuing and killing a wild animal as in fox hunting, though the word can be used to describe any seeking of almost any object. Hence you can hunt for your car keys, gold, a missing invoice, or, in my case, your diary. 'Hunt' is a homonym, however, because in bell ringing the word signifies the moving of a bell in a simple progression.

husband

Apart from being a noun signifying a married male, **husband** can also be a verb meaning to till the ground, to cultivate, or to administer something well, or to use resources economically. In nautical usage, a husband is an agent provided by a ship's owners to see that the ship in port is well provided in all respects.

hymn *see* **him**

I

I *see* **aye, eye**

ice

Ice is formed when water freezes, and so, in cold weather, you can see lakes covered with ice. You can also freeze water in lump form so that people can have ice with their drinks. But you can also ice a cake, and this has nothing to do with frozen water. Instead the cake is covered with a sugary substance that, for small children at least, increases the appeal (and taste) of the cake. The use of the word 'ice' in confectionery arose during the eighteenth century. Metaphorically it is also possible to add ice to a situation by acting in a disapproving and censorious fashion. In somewhat slangy senses, ice is also a synonym for diamonds or for the verb 'to kill'. The word is also used as an adjective for a variety of nouns: ice age, ice cube, ice pick, ice plant, and many more. The phrase 'break the ice' dates from the late sixteenth century, and then referred to breaking up sea ice so as to make a passage for a ship.

icon

An **icon** was originally the name for a devotional painting of Christ or some other holy figure, but it has since the 1950s been used to exalt any sort of celebrity ('Rock Hudson is an icon of the cinema', for example) and also to refer to a symbol or graphic representation on a computer monitor. Apparently the word is also used in linguistics when a word shares a quality with the very thing that the word represents, as, for example, in onomatopoeic words or words like 'snarl' when they are pronounced in a snarling manner.

I'd, ide

I'd is a contraction of 'I would' or 'I had' and an **ide** is a freshwater fish. The word *ides* is also 'ide' in its singular, but no one ever seems to use the singular form. It was a Latin word for a series of specific dates – March 15, May 15, July 15, October 15, and the 13 of all other months – but Shakespeare (and everybody else) talks about the ides of March, not the ide.

idle, idol, idyl

If you are **idle**, you are not doing anything that requires any effort. Sometimes people describe themselves as idle because they are unemployed, but most idle people are so because they prefer some non-strenuous activity in which they need make no mental or physical effort. The word comes from the Old English *idel*, which meant 'empty, useless'. The verb 'to idle' can also be used with reference to an engine that is just ticking over but not being called upon to perform any meaningful function. An **idol** is something or someone that is worshipped. Pop stars, footballers and film actors are often idols to some members of the population. Originally, of course, an idol was a graphic representation of some god, and people would kneel before the idol and beseech it. While 'idle' and 'idol' are homophones, the word **idyl**, when correctly pronounced, shouldn't appear in this dictionary at all, but its similarity in spelling, and the vagaries of human diction, just about merit its inclusion. An idyl is a personal version of paradise. For you, a week on the Norfolk Broads might be an idyl. For someone else, their idyl might be a tour of Florence, a session of fell walking, listening to the Mozart piano concertos, or surfing off the Australian coast.

I'll *see* **aisle**

I'll, ill
These are a long way from being homophones, but **I'll** is a contraction of 'I will', and **ill** is an adjective describing a state of physical or moral sickness. Hence you can be ill with flu or ill with envy. The adjective can also be used metaphorically in a wide variety of contexts: 'It was an ill day for politics when Tony Blair became Prime Minister'; 'You did an ill piece of homework last night, Smithers.'

illegitimate
A person is **illegitimate** if they were born of an unmarried mother, but in a much more general sense, something is illegitimate if it is intellectually invalid, socially frowned upon or emotionally injurious. Thus it is illegitimate to claim that the ontological argument proves the existence of God, it is illegitimate to throw noisy parties when your neighbours are trying to sleep, and it is illegitimate to punish a colour-blind child for drawing a tree trunk green instead of brown.

illicit *see* **elicit**

illumination
This word has a physical and mental meaning. Physically **illumination** signifies the lighting up of an area (a building, park, town, etc.) for some festive reason. Mentally, illumination comes when understanding is achieved.

imago
In entomology, an **imago** is the final and fully developed stage of an insect, but in psychoanalysis it is an unconscious idealised mental image of someone that influences your behaviour.

immanent, imminent

If something is **immanent**, it is inherent. Hence the ability to think is immanent in human beings. If something is **imminent**, it is shortly going to occur. As you watch the approaching clouds, you might say, 'I think rain is imminent.'

immersion

The noun **immersion** either means the total covering of something by water or some other liquid, or the complete mental involvement in something. Hence, if you become a convert to some Christian sect, this conversion may be marked by a ceremony in which you are totally immersed in water. Equally if you are writing a Ph.D. thesis on the poetry of William Cowper, you are likely to have total immersion in his writings. There is also a further technical usage in that astronomers describe the disappearance of a celestial body in the shadow of or behind another as being an immersion.

imp

By and large, the word **imp** is used playfully to refer to a mischievous child, but it can also refer to a piece added on to something else, and is specifically so used in falconry to denote feathers that are engrafted on to a damaged wing.

impact

Impact is what occurs when one body crashes into another one. Cars crashing into one another produce an impact. So does a rock falling into the valley, a fist on to a chin, or a snooker ball hitting another. But an impact can also be some less physical event that none the less leaves a marked impression. The poetry of Hardy had a deep impact on Philip Larkin, the music of Mahler had a deep impact on Hans Keller, and the work of Charles Darwin had a deep impact on Richard Dawkins. This figurative use of 'impact' where it means the effect of something on someone dates from the early nineteenth century.

imperfect

Self-evidently something that is **imperfect** is something that is lacking in perfection, something that is incomplete in some way, not fully formed. However, a number can also be imperfect when it is not equal to the sum of its aliquot parts, and in grammar an imperfect tense is one which applies to actions that are going on but have not yet been completed. The word is sometimes used in music to denote a diminished chord.

imperial

Imperial is an adjective referring to matters that pertain to the state or to the possessions and lands of that state, and comes from the Latin *imperialis* meaning 'pertaining to an emperor or empire'. It is also a term relating to a number of diverse entities. Before metrification it was a standard size of printing and writing paper of 30 x 22 inches. There was an eighteenth-century Russian gold coin called the imperial, a trunk for luggage adapted for the roof of a coach, a tuft of hair on the chin (a fashion set by Napoleon III), and a wine bottle containing about 6 litres.

impersonal

If something is **impersonal**, it is not influenced by personal feelings. If you are marking a set of examination scripts done by students whom you have never met, you can be completely impersonal because you have no attitudes or feelings towards the students concerned. In English grammar, an impersonal verb is one that is used only with a formal subject and which expresses an action that is not attributable to a definite subject. The sentence 'It is raining' would be an example.

implicit

If something is **implicit**, then it is assumed that it is too obvious to need any specific mention. If you go along to a clarinet teacher and ask for some lessons, he or she will assume that you possess a clarinet. That fact is implicit in your request. Equally implicit can mean that something is implied without being directly mentioned. When, at your AGM, concerns are expressed about recent vandalism, those concerns contain an implicit criticism of the caretaker. Finally, implicit can mean total or complete. When someone says that they have implicit faith in the Prime Minister, they mean that they trust him or her completely. I do not know if there is psychiatric help for this condition.

import

This word can mean the action of bringing goods into one's own country, goods (imports) that have been purchased somewhere else, just as exports are goods taken from one's own country and sold elsewhere. One can also import data from one computer to another, and one can import ideas from one civilisation into another one. But to **import** something also signifies that you have said something to which you attach some significance: 'I tried to import my ideas about the cosmological argument to the audience, but I do not really think that they understood their import.'

impotent

To be **impotent** implies that you are powerless to do anything effective about some particular matter, but the word is often used more specifically to denote a sexual failure, normally a man's failure to gain an erection.

impound

If you **impound** something, you seize it and take legal custody of it. Customs are prone to impound bags of heroin that they find in your luggage. You can also impound animals by placing them in an enclosure. Dams are also said to impound water when they hold it back.

impregnate

If you **impregnate** a cloth with window cleaning liquid (or anything else), you saturate it. If your financial report to your company is deeply pessimistic, you may impregnate your company with despair. If a woman or female animal has been impregnated, she has been made pregnant.

impress

If you **impress** someone, you affect or influence them strongly, but you can also impress people into the armed services (normally by force), or mark something by stamping a word, character or design upon it.

impure

The two meanings of **impure** are conceptually akin. Something can be physically impure by having some other element mixed in with it. Thus water will be impure if it contains unnecessary and possibly dangerous chemicals within it. Equally some person or concept can be impure if it contains morally unworthy elements within it. Thus Peter was being impure when he denied knowing who Jesus was, John Major (a British Prime Minister) was being impure when he had an affair with one of his ministers, and Descartes' *cogito ergo sum* (I think, therefore I am) is an impure philosophical concept because it rests upon an unproven assumption.

in, inn

In is an extremely common word, but its range of uses tends to surprise one. It has certainly been used as a verb, though this is no longer common practice. Most of the time 'in' is a preposition expressing the concept of inclusion: 'I am in church', 'I am in hot water', 'I am in my old age.' It can also be an adverb used in relation to motion or direction: 'Let us go in the pub', 'The batsman stayed in for over three hours', 'Always keep the fire in.' Many Latin phrases using 'in' are also still used: '*in extremis*', '*in situ*', '*in toto*' and so on. 'In' is also a prefix for many, many words where it can mean 'not' as in 'infertile', or 'within' as in 'inborn'. The *Oxford Dictionary of Word Histories* contains a useful list of such words. An **inn** is another name for a hotel or tavern. The word is Old English and originally meant a private dwelling house.

inc, ink

The word **inc**, often given with a capital I, should not appear in this dictionary because it is an abbreviation for 'incorporated', but the abbreviation has become so common that it would be pointless pedantry to exclude it. **Ink** is a writing fluid that, in the days of fountain pens (or quills), was used for handwriting on paper. These days it has been replaced by felt-tipped pens, ballpoint pens, etc.

incandescent

An **incandescent** light is one that has a filament that glows white-hot when heated by a current. If you yourself are incandescent, you are aflame with something, either incandescent with anger (i.e. very, very angry indeed) or incandescent with love (i.e. totally besotted).

incense

If you go round a cathedral, you are likely to find **incense**, an aromatic gum, burning in sundry receptacles. As a verb, 'incense' means to make very angry. You will, therefore, incense the priests (rouse them to anger) if you attempt to put out the incense. There is a tree called the incense cedar that grows in North America, and that has leaves that smell of turpentine.

incidence, incidents

The word **incidence** is strangely difficult to define. The *Shorter Oxford* offers, 'The act or fact of falling upon, or coming into contact with', and this is fair enough, but seems a little amorphous. A few examples might clarify things. You could talk about the incidence of malaria in Berkshire being very low, or the correlation between alcohol consumption and the incidence of fatal car crashes. The word 'incident' is easier. An incident is a happening, an event which occurred, a chance occurrence. 'There was a slight incident this morning when I saw two boys throwing stones at a dog and I tried to intervene.' 'Last night there was an incident at the Rose and Crown when some fellow accidentally spilt his beer down a woman's dress.' Clearly, of course, **incidents** is the plural of 'incident', and I have just told you about two incidents.

incite, insight

In order to **incite** something, you need to provoke it, to stimulate it in some way. Thus you might incite a riot in the High Street by demanding an end to vagrant beggars, you might incite a riot in church by arguing that the Trinity was a false doctrine, or you might incite joy in your son by allowing him to go hang gliding. If you have **insight**, you have a perception below the surface of things. Thus you see that Mr Skimpole in *Bleak House* is not just a comic character but also an evil one, that your daughter is depressed not just because she did badly in her maths exam but also because her boyfriend is putting pressure on her, and that Aunt Hilda wants to visit you partly because she would like to go to the annual flower show.

inclination

If something has an **inclination**, then it slopes away from or towards another body. Thus you might say that a road had an inclination of one foot in every 100 yards. In mathematics, the direction of a line, surface or body with respect to another line, surface or body which has a different direction is called its inclination, and one can measure the angle of inclination. As far as human tastes are concerned, an inclination is a tendency towards or a preference for one course of action over another. Thus this afternoon you may have an inclination to go for a walk, though your sister is more inclined to finish her novel.

incubus

An **incubus** is a parasitic genus of hymenopterous insects, but the word is more generally known as signifying an evil spirit who enters into you one night while you are asleep and proceeds to pervert your normal actions into actions that are much more sinister, or, even more commonly, ravishes a woman while she is asleep.

indeed

This adverb can be used with a variety of connotations. It can be a simple exclamation of surprise. It can be used to emphasise: 'It was a very good performance indeed.' It can be used to express scepticism: 'You think Mr Jones is a Chinese spy. Indeed!'

indent

As a noun, **indent** can mean an incision in the edge of a thing, a certificate of a money claim, or an official requisition for stores. These nouns can be transferred into verbs in the normal fashion, but the verb 'to indent' also has an additional meaning in printing where it means to set back from the margin the beginning of a line. Hence you might indent at the beginning of every paragraph. Apparently the word originally meant 'to give a zigzag outline to, to divide by a zigzag line'.

independence, independents

The state of **independence** means that one is free and able to control one's own affairs. Hence a country which gains independence ceases to be under the control of another power, and is henceforth able to conduct its own affairs. A son or daughter who leaves home and acquires their own living space and employment has acquired independence. They are therefore both **independents**, responsible for their own lives. The word 'independents' is, however, sometimes used to describe political candidates in an election who are not members of an established political party.

index

Many non-fiction books have an **index** so that it is relatively easy to look up specific topics. Normally printed at the end of the book, an index is an alphabetical list of subjects dealt with in that book. Thus the index to a book is a pointer to topics that you might wish to look up, and the Latin word index actually meant 'forefinger, informer, sign'. Hence you can refer to your index finger. The word can also be used as a sort of scale of measurement: 'The superb exam results are something of an index of Mr Huntley's skill as a teacher.' In mathematics, an index is an exponent appended to a quantity. In printing, an index is a symbol shaped like a pointing hand, used to draw attention to a note. The *Index Librorum Prohibitorum*, a list of books that Roman Catholics are not allowed to read, is also commonly known as the Index. Authors who have been thus prohibited include Addison, Bacon, Chaucer, Descartes, Gibbon, Goldsmith and Milton, which would suggest that the Roman Catholic Church has not been in the forefront of literary appreciation.

Indian

This earns its homonymic status because it is a word that can be used to describe a person who lives in India or who comes from India, a person from the West Indies, or a native North American. The word **Indian** is also used as an adjective for a variety of objects: Indian ink, for instance, comes from China, an Indian summer is a term of US origin, and an Indian club is a bottle-shaped club used by jugglers.

indict, indite

If you **indict** someone, you charge them with some offence. If you **indite**, you put it into writing.

indigence, indigents

The state of **indigence** is the state of wanting or needing something, normally the very means of existence like food, water and shelter. Consequently an indigent is a person who lacks those necessities, and regrettably some areas of the world have large numbers of **indigents**.

inflection, inflexion

These are just alternative spellings for the same word, but it is a word that has at least four different meanings. The first signifies a bending or curvature. Thus a river may experience an inflection when it encounters an obstacle. In geometry, an inflection is a change of curvature from convex to concave. In grammar an inflection is the change of a word to express a differing grammatical relation. Thus, in Latin, *puella* is used when the girl is the subject of the sentence, but is inflected to *puellam* when the girl is the object of the sentence. Finally, an inflection or tone in one's speech can indicate the attitude that you are objecting to the matter under discussion: 'I gathered from his inflection that he was not happy with the proposal.'

initial

As an adjective, **initial** normally signifies the beginning of something. A building contractor might say, 'We are in the initial stages of building a sports complex.' As a noun, an initial is the first letter of someone's name or some organisation's name. Thus JFK are the initials for John Fitzgerald Kennedy and UK are the initials for the United Kingdom.

ink see inc

inn see in

innocence, innocents

To be in a state that is without guilt is to be in a state of **innocence**. Consequently, when being interviewed by the police in connection with a bank robbery, you are likely to protest your innocence. Sometimes innocence can be used almost as a synonym for ignorance: 'Frieda had a total innocence of the art of flower arranging.' The word is also often used to indicate sexual purity: 'Sheila's innocence was completely unsullied by libidinous thoughts.' Obviously, if you are full of innocence, you are going to be an innocent person. A collection of innocent people will be a collection of innocents.

insight see incite

inspiration

In the most basic of senses, **inspiration** simply means the drawing in of breath, something that you and I do constantly until we die. However, most of us use the word to signify the operation of a great mind either having some brilliant insight into an intellectual problem or producing a work of art of everlasting value. Occasionally the word is also used to indicate that the recipient has been influenced by God.

institute

As a noun, an **institute** tends to be an organisation or establishment set up to teach, to tend the sick or to promote some activity. As a verb, if you institute something you start it off or establish it for the first time.

insula, insular

In Latin the word **insula** meant 'an island', and it has been incorporated into English to denote a block of buildings, a square or space mapped out or divided off, the central lobe of the cerebrum, or a clot of blood floating in serum. The conceptual link to an island can be seen in each case. Unsurprisingly, the adjective **insular** also has island connotations. If you are an insular person, you tend to cut yourself off from everyday life and live a cloistered and self-contained existence, as if you were a solitary island of humanity. You can also, of course, live an insular life, either by living literally on an island or by having little contact with society.

intelligence

There are two broad meanings for **intelligence**. The first refers to an inborn mental faculty that is very difficult to define, but which can sensibly be said to be the ability to see connections. The second can be defined as information received. Thus you have received intelligence that your local primary school will be closed next Thursday because of council elections.

intension, intention

If an argument strikes you with considerable **intension**, then it impresses itself upon you with force and depth. If you have the **intention** of doing something, then you propose to take that particular course of action. As we all know, the road to Hell is paved with good intentions.

inter

The verb **inter**, pronounced with the emphasis on '-ter', means to bury something in the ground. The Latin preposition 'inter', pronounced with the emphasis on 'in-', has been incorporated into English in such phrases as *inter alia*, 'among other things'. 'Inter' is also the prefix for a very large number of words: intercede, intercourse, interlude, and so on.

interest

If you have an **interest** in something, you find that your attention is captured by it, that you find the subject matter or issue an absorbing one. Most of us have an interest in something or other, be it the fortunes of Tottenham Hotspur, the geology of Chile, or the best way of cooking rabbit. Equally you can have an interest in something that doesn't actually interest you at all. Your company is trying to decide whether to buy some Dell computers or some IBM ones. You are consulted on the matter, and say, 'Actually I'd better declare an interest here because I have a Dell computer myself.' As it happens, you only use your personal computer as a word processor, and have neither interest nor knowledge about operating systems or database management, but you declare your 'interest' just in case someone argues that your opinion was biased in favour of Dell. It is also quite likely that you are paying interest on your computer. When you borrow money, you are charged interest on that money, which means that you pay back more than you borrowed. You paid a £20 deposit on your computer, and are paying off the rest by monthly payments of £15. If you had bought the computer outright it would have cost you £795; by using hire purchase, it will cost you £1,683.74. Hence you will end up paying £888 in interest. That fact is certain to interest you!

intimate

This word has two pronunciations. The first, with the emphasis on the 'in-', denotes a state of being close, intrinsic and familiar. Hence you are likely to be intimate with your wife or husband and your children. The word is also used somewhat euphemistically as a synonym for sexual relations: 'I was intimate the other night with Ted.' The second pronunciation, with the emphasis on the '-mate', means to make known: 'I did intimate that the fault might have serious repercussions.'

invalid

This word has two pronunciations. The first, with a slight emphasis on the 'in-', denotes someone who is infirm from sickness or disease. The second, with an emphasis on the '-val-', indicates that the argument being advanced or the solution being proposed is a weak and ineffective one. Thus it is **invalid** to argue that, since Timothy comes from Birmingham, and Timothy is a liar, it follows that all the inhabitants of Birmingham are liars. If you argue in Birmingham itself that everyone there is a liar, you might end up as an invalid.

iris

Apart from **Iris** being a female first name (and the name of a Greek goddess), the word also denotes a rainbow-like appearance, a membrane in the eye, and a genus of plants.

iron

Iron is a metallic element, an implement for removing creases in clothes, and a type of golf club. As an adjective, it is often used as a synonym for 'hard' or even 'cruel'. Hence Bismarck was called the Iron Chancellor and Margaret Thatcher the Iron Lady.

isle *see* aisle

islet *see* eyelet

issue

This is a common word, and one rarely thinks how many different uses it possesses, conceptually linked though most of them are. To start with, an **issue** can be something that comes out. Thus you might have an issue of blood from your nose, you might purchase an issue of the *Guardian* from your newsagent, or you might decide to disinherit your issue (i.e. your children). Equally an issue may be some matter of concern that is avidly discussed among the interested parties. Thus reducing unemployment may be an important government issue, gaining promotion at the office may be an issue for you, and whether or not to take cannabis may be an issue for your daughter.

it's, its

It's is a contraction of 'it is' or 'it has', while **its** is a possessive pronoun.

J

J, j, jay

J is the tenth letter of the alphabet, and although it is used as a symbol in mathematics and physics, the letter has no place in a dictionary of homonyms other than the fact that it is pronounced exactly like the word **jay**. The jay is a common European bird similar to the magpie, though the word can also be used to denote a impertinent chatterer, a showy, flashy or insubstantial woman, a simpleton, or a person who is flashily dressed.

jack

Although, with a capital letter, **Jack** is a proper noun (normally a friendly version of John) and often used as an emblem for the common man (every Jack and Jill), the word has a number of lower-case meanings as well. It can be a synonym for a sailor, a court card in a pack of playing cards (also known as the knave), a socket with two or more pairs of terminals designed to receive a jack plug, a marine fish, and the figure of a man who strikes the bell on the outside of a clock. A jack is also a tool used for lifting something heavy off the ground; one uses a jack to raise a side of a car so that one can slide under the car to correct some fault or change a tyre. It is also an implement for easing one's shoes or boots on and off, the smallest bowl in a game of bowls, and an item in sundry instruments or machines from a harpsichord to a telephone, from a carding machine to a spinning machine. The word is often used to denote maleness as in jack crow, jack-fish and jackass, and the general sense of the common man or labourer survives in words like 'lumberjack' and 'steeplejack'. The name also appears in certain common wild plants: Jack-at-the-hedge (cleavers), Jack-by-the-hedge (garlic mustard), Jack-go-to-bed-at-noon (goat's beard), and so on, though all these have the proper name in mind, and so their inclusion here is dubious.

jacket

In its most common usage, a **jacket** is an outer garment for the upper part of the body, but it can also be the paper cover for a hardback book, the skin of a potato when it is cooked with the skin on, or the word for the outer covering of almost anything.

Jacobin

The Jacobins were a radical group formed during the days of the French Revolution, but a **Jacobin** can also be a breed of pigeon or a Central and South American humming bird.

jade

Although **jade** is an attractive hard translucent green stone, the word is also used to denote an inferior horse and a disreputable woman.

jam, jamb

A **jam** can be a static or slow-moving collection of objects or people. You normally get a traffic jam at rush hour, a jam of people when the sales open, or a jam-packed spare room when you are paranoid about throwing anything away. Jam is also a sticky substance composed of fruit and sugar that is often smeared on bread to make a sandwich. This usage came into being in the mid-eighteenth century. A jam session is an improvised performance by a group of jazz musicians, a usage that dates from the 1920s. If you jam on the brakes of your car, you stop very abruptly. A **jamb** is the leg of an animal represented on a coat of arms, the leg piece from a suit of armour, each of the side posts of a door, a bed of clay or stone running across a mineral vein or seam, and a projecting columnar part of a wall.

jar

A **jar** is a cylindrical vessel of earthenware, stoneware or glass in which objects can be stored, especially food like jam and fruit. Something that is strident, inharmonious or embarrassing can be said to jar you.

jay *see* J

jean *see* gene

jerk

A sharp sudden pull is a **jerk**, though the word can also be applied to involuntary movements of the face or limbs. It is also a slang word for a useless and unproductive man. As a verb, the word can mean to cure meat by cutting it into strips and drying it. Alternatively you can jerk by preparing pork or chicken in a barbecue, having first marinated the meat in spices. In contemporary slang, 'to jerk off' is to masturbate.

jet

A **jet** is a hard compact black form of lignite, an aircraft powered by jet engines, a stream of water or other liquid streaming out of a small hole in a rock or from a hose, or a channel or tube for pouring melted metal into a mould. As an acronym, JET stands for Joint European Torus, a machine for conducting experiments in nuclear fusion.

jewel, joule

A **jewel** is a small decorative object like a ring or brooch worn for adornment. If someone is regarded as outstanding in some way they might be termed a jewel to their profession. A **joule** is the amount of work done or heat generated by a current of one ampere acting for one second against a resistance of one ohm.

jib

A **jib** is a triangular stay-sail, the projecting arm of a crane, or the action of stopping moving when confronted by an obstacle.

jig

A **jig** is a lively dance with leaping movements, a device that holds a piece of work and guides the tool operating upon it, or a type of artificial bait that is jerked up and down in the water.

joint

A **joint** is a junction where two entities meet, be they bones in the arm, rocks underground, pipes in a water system or rods in a machine. A joint committee is one chosen by two or more bodies. Thus a parliamentary joint committee is one selected by the House of Commons and the House of Lords. A joint is also a portion of meat and a somewhat disrespectful term for a building. It is also slang for a cannabis cigarette.

jumper

Most of us think of a **jumper** as being a knitted garment with long sleeves that is worn on the upper body, but a jumper can also be a person or animal that jumps, a heavy chisel-ended iron bar for drilling blast holes, a short wire used to shorten an electric circuit, a rope made fast to keep a yard or mast from jumping, or a mushroom-shaped brass part in a tap which supports the washer.

junk

For most of us, **junk** is the miscellaneous assortment of useless objects that we find stored away in the attic, but the word also denotes a Chinese sailing boat, part of the tissue of a sperm whale, and the salt meat used in the past as food on a long sea voyage. It is also a colloquial word for heroin.

just

Something is **just** if it is fair and equitable, and a number of rulers have been named 'the Just' as a tribute to their equitable reign. The word can also be an adverb signifying an approximation: 'He was just on time', or, 'That looks just enough.'

jute, Jute

The fibre from the bark of the Corchorus plants is known as **jute**, but a **Jute** was a member of a Low German tribe that invaded England in the fifth and sixth centuries.

K

K, k

This is the eleventh letter of the alphabet, and is only used as an abbreviation or symbol for, in upper case, the Köchel catalogue of Mozart's works, the king in chess games, and the element potassium, and in lower case, kilobytes (520k), knit (as opposed to purl), a thousand (£5k) and kilometres.

kaiser

This was the title given to the German emperor (Kaiser Wilhelm II), and is also a North American term for a crisp bread roll in the shape of a pin wheel.

kangaroo

This large plant-eating marsupial found only in Australia and New Guinea would find no entry in this dictionary if it had not given rise to two adjectives, one for a **kangaroo** court, an official and *ad hoc* court that often pays scant regard to evidence, and a kangaroo closure, an occasion in the British Parliament when a committee agrees to select some amendments and ignore others.

keel, Keele

A **keel** is the lowest longitudinal timber of a boat, though in architecture it is the ridge or edge on a rounded moulding. It is also a ridge along the breastbone of many birds, and a prow-shaped pair of petals present in members of the pea family. **Keele** is a small village in north Staffordshire and in no way merits an inclusion in this dictionary, but I took my first two degrees at Keele and have such fond memories of the place that this invalid entry is my tribute.

keen

Something with a very sharp edge – a knife, for instance – can be described as **keen**. Equally a sharp, stinging drink can be termed keen, as can a piercing wind. The expression 'as keen as mustard' arose because mustard gives an edge to the food. If your eyes are alert and sensitive, they too can be described as keen, yet the most common usage of the word is to describe a state of eager, ardent enthusiasm. Thus you can be keen on Aston Villa Football Club, collecting wild flowers, or reading Jane Austen. The word is also used as a verb when it means to wail bitterly, normally at a funeral.

keep

Many castles possess a **keep**, the central tower of the castle and the final refuge. More commonly we encounter 'keep' as a verb meaning 'to hold in possession': 'I will keep this necklace for ever.' But 'keep' has a number of slightly different connotations. Thus you can keep the books when you are an accountant and are maintaining a constant record of your company's financial dealings. You can earn your keep when the services you perform cover the cost of food and lodging. And 'keep' alters its meaning depending upon which adverb follows it: 'keep away', 'keep off', 'keep in', 'keep from', 'keep up', and so on. Even in a language as rich, diverse and confusing as English, 'keep' must be one of its most chameleon words. How does one explain 'keep one's word', 'keep up with the Joneses', and many others?

kelpie

Somewhat alarmingly, a **kelpie** is a water spirit of Scottish folklore, typically taking the form of a horse and reputed to delight in drowning travellers. Much less worryingly, a kelpie is also a sheepdog of an Australian breed.

ken

Most of us know that Ken is the shortened form of the first name Kenneth, but the word can also mean the range of one's vision (I cannot **ken** the Wrekin this morning because of the mist) and the degree of your understanding (I do not ken what you mean). The word is also an informal one for a thief's house.

kern

A **kern** is either a light-armed Irish foot soldier, a grain of wheat or sand, or, in printing, a part of a metal type projecting beyond the body or shank. The verb 'to kern' means to adjust the spacing between characters in a piece of text to be printed.

kernel *see* colonel

key, qui

As a physical object, a **key** can be (a) a shaped metal object with incisions cut into it so that it is capable of opening a lock, (b) a letter or symbol button on a keyboard that, when pressed, causes an action to be carried out, (c) the dry winged fruit of an ash, maple or sycamore tree, (d) the part of a first coat of wall plaster that passes between the laths and so secures the rest, (e) a low-lying island or reef (see 'cay') or (f) the keyhole-shaped area marked on a basketball court near each basket. As a non-physical thing, a key can be (a) the tonality of a piece of music, (b) the secret of one's success, or (c) the clue to solving a problem. Interestingly the word used to be used to rhyme with *day*, *play*, *say*, etc. and this pronunciation seems to have been standard until the end of the seventeenth century. **Qui** is a French word meaning 'Who?' but has been incorporated into English in a number of expressions like 'Qui vive'.

kick

Most of us think of a **kick** as a striking outwards with the foot with the intention of hitting some object with that foot. One sees lots of kicks in a football match. But a kick is also the recoil from a gun immediately after it has been fired, an indentation in the bottom of a glass bottle so that the bottle holds less than you would at first assume, the projection on the tang of a pocket-knife blade, a sudden forceful jolt, the thrill of some excitement, and the rough contact between two snooker or billiard balls.

kicker

Obviously someone who kicks a ball (or anything else) is a **kicker**, but the word also denotes an unexpected and unwelcome discovery or turn of events, an extra clause in a contract, a small outboard motor, or, in poker, a high third card retained in the hand with a pair at the draw.

kid

If you **kid** someone, you tell them something which is not true in order to watch their reaction. The word 'kid' implies that your hoax is not a serious or malicious one. A kid is also the young of a goat, the skin of such an animal often used for making gloves, and an informal term for a young human child.

kill

Clearly the meaning that all of us know for **kill** is the action of taking someone else's life, but the word is also used in many contexts where it signifies the end of something. Hence you might kill a computer program (stop it), or kill the ball in cricket or soccer by rendering it motionless.

kind

This word can signify the class of object to which something belongs, as when you say 'It is a **kind** of spy thriller', or, 'There were so many differences in detail that it almost belonged to a different kind.' As an adjective, 'kind' denotes a friendly, helpful and generous approach or action: 'It was kind to give £5 to that beggar', or, 'She is always kind to the children.' The word can also be used to denote both elements (bread and wine) of the Eucharist.

king

A **king** is the titular head of a country, one of the court cards in a pack of playing cards, or the most important piece in a game of chess. The sobriquet 'the King' has been given to a number of people considered peerless in their field.

kip

You might have used the word **kip** as a synonym for 'sleep', but its other meanings are less common. In Scotland it can mean a bed, in Ireland it can be an unpleasant, dirty place, in Australia it is a small piece of wood from which coins are spun in a game, and in Laos it is the basic monetary unit. The only other English usage is as the hide of a young or small animal. According to the *Oxford Dictionary of Words*, 'kip' was first used to mean a brothel.

kiss

All meanings of the verb 'to **kiss**' entail the action of touching. Between humans, a kiss is the pressing of the lips to a part of another person's body, lips to lips being the most intimate kind, and lips to cheek being not much more than a social convention. Equally if a snooker ball gently touches another ball, that touch is described as a kiss. The same is true for the game of bowls.

kit

A **kit** is a collection of articles necessary for the effective carrying out of some function. Hence, if you are off to play football for Dereham United, you will take with you your football kit (boots, shorts, singlet, etc.). If you are a soldier, you will carry your kit with you when on duty. According to *Twentieth Century Words* 'kit' came to mean clothes in the 1990s, used mainly in the phrase 'Get your kit off' where the speaker was a lecherous onlooker. But a kit is also a circular wooden vessel made of hooped staves, normally used for carrying milk. It is also a small violin used by dancing masters, and the young of certain animals like the beaver, ferret and mink.

kite

Many of us have flown a **kite**, a toy consisting of a light frame with paper stretched upon it, and so constructed as to be easily flown in a strong wind or breeze, with the operator controlling it by means of a long string attached to it. A kite is also a bird of prey, with long wings, and, in commercial slang, a bill of exchange. An aircraft is often referred to as a kite, as is a fraudulent cheque.

kitten

We think of a **kitten** as being a young cat, but it is also the young of other animals like the rabbit and beaver. It is also a stout furry grey and white moth.

kitty

This can be a child's name for a cat or kitten, a pool of money in some gambling game, or the jack in a game of bowls.

knag, nag

A **knag** is a short projection from the trunk or branch of a tree, or a knot in wood, or a pointed rock. The verb 'to **nag**' means the activity of continuous fault-finding or scolding. It is normally associated with women. As a noun, a nag can be a small horse or pony.

knap, nap

Knap is either the summit of a hill, or a verb meaning to break with a hammer. A **nap** can be a short sleep, the rough layer of projecting threads or fibres on the surface of a textile fabric, or a card game.

knave, nave

A **knave** is a rogue or dishonest man. It is also the lowest of the court cards in a pack of playing cards. A **nave** is either the central part of a wheel, or the central part of a church stretching from the west front to the chancel.

knead, need

The verb 'to **knead**' refers to the action of mixing dough so as to make an object ready for baking into a loaf of bread, though one can also knead clay to create a dish or ornament. If you **need** something, you feel that it is essential either to your existence or to your contentment.

knickers, nickers

Knickers are most commonly thought of as the female equivalent to male underpants, but the word can also refer to marbles of baked clay, or a large flat button of metal that is used as a pitcher in the game 'On the line'. **Nickers** are either the hard seeds of the bondue tree, or people who in their throwing manage to hit the target. There is also the slang verb 'to nick' meaning to steal, so I suppose 'nickers' could be a slang word for 'thieves'.

knight, night

During the middle ages the word **knight** could be employed to describe the champion of a lady – the knight of the Red Cross was Una's protector in Spenser's *Faerie Queene* – or the military servant of the king or a baron. The king could also bestow a knighthood upon some worthy person whom he wished to distinguish. Today knighthoods are bestowed technically by the monarch but in reality by the Prime Minister to reward those who have given massive donations to the relevant political party. A knight is also a piece in a game of chess. **Night** is that portion of the day when one receives no illumination from the sun. The word is also metaphorically used to denote something that is dark in one's life.

knit, nit

To **knit** is the process of combining together a substance or substances so that they combine to make a finished object. You can knit your hands together so they become one intertwined entity. You can negotiate with the Latvian government so that you knit together a viable policy on bee keeping. Of course, the most common usage of knit today is the operation where, with two needles and a ball of wool, one can knit together a pair of socks, a sweater or some other article of clothing. A **nit** is the egg of a louse or some other parasitic insect, or a young version of the insect itself.

knob, nob

You often find a **knob** on a door, because a knob is a small rounded object projecting from some other object. Clearly you use a door knob to open or close the door in question, but you can see knobs on many other objects as well, including one's own head shortly after you have walked into something. A **nob** is a slang term for an important person, and a slang term for the head. Apparently in the game of cribbage, a nob is a knave of the same suit as the turn-up card.

knock, nock

A **knock** is the action of rapping or striking something else, normally with your fist. Hence you knock at a door if you desire admittance. Of course, you can knock against someone else by accident, and an innings in cricket is often referred to as a knock. A **nock** is a notch in an arrow into which the bowstring can fit. It is also the foremost upper corner of boomsails and of staysails cut with a square tack.

knoll

A **knoll** is either the rounded top of a mountain or hill, or a verb meaning to ring or toll a bell. The latter meaning is probably an imitative alteration of 'knell'.

knot, not

A **knot** is what you get if you intertwine two pieces of rope or string in such a fashion that they will remain affixed to each other. Hence you tie the knot when you get married. It is also a unit of speed at sea, and a tightly grouped collection of people is often called a knot of people. There is also a small sandpiper called a knot. 'Knot' is also used as an adjective in 'a knot garden', a formal garden laid out in an intricate design. **Not** is normally an adverb negating the action of the verb: 'I will not' or 'I should not'.

know, no

If you **know** something or someone, you are in possession of information about them. Hence if you know anything about drosophila, you will know that it is the fruit fly. If you know anything about Queen Victoria, you are likely to know that she died in 1901. However, if you know a person, the word implies that you have developed some sort of relationship with them. **No** is a word of negation. You will use it when refusing to do something or admitting ignorance: 'Will you mow the lawn?' 'No'; 'Do you know where the paper is?' 'No.'

knows, noes, nose

If someone is in possession of some piece of information, you are likely to say, 'She **knows** the answer.' The word is the third person singular form of the present tense of the verb 'to know'. If a vote is held in Parliament, and those against the motion achieve a majority, the Speaker of the House is likely to say, 'The **noes** have it.' Most animals possess a **nose**, an organ that projects from the face and is used for breathing.

L

L, l

The letter **L** is not a word, but just scrapes into this dictionary because L is the symbol for fifty in Roman numerals, and because L or l can be part of a hyphenated word like L-shaped or L-plate. It can also be an abbreviation for a number of things. L on a car means learner driver, and the letter can also stand for litre, lire, lake, laevorotatory and left.

laager, lager

A **laager** is an encampment, especially one in the open marked out by a circle of wagons. **Lager** is a light beer.

labium

In entomology a **labium** is a fused mouthpart which forms the floor of the mouth of an insect. In botany the labium is the lower lip of the flower of a plant of the mint family.

labour

As most of us know, **labour** means work or effort. It is also, normally capitalised, the name of a British political party, and also, in lower case, the process of childbirth from the start of uterine contractions to delivery.

labyrinth

This is a maze or some complicated network in which it is difficult to plot a meaningful path. In anatomy, a **labyrinth** is a complex structure in the inner ear.

lac, lack

Until compiling this dictionary, I had never encountered **lac**, but it is, according to the *Shorter Oxford*, a dark-red resinous incrustation produced on certain trees by the puncture of an insect and used in the East as a scarlet dye. In Anglo-Indian (more usually spelt lakh) it also stands for one hundred thousand or, occasionally, an indefinite number. According to the *Oxford Dictionary of English*, it is also an adjective denoting the ability of normal strains of the bacterium *E. coli* to metabolise lactose or the genetic factors involved in this ability. The verb 'to **lack**' means to be without something, to stand in need of, or to be wanting or missing something: 'I would go for a run, but I lack any suitable footware.' 'Lack' as a noun denotes a defect, failing, want or need: 'The Kenyans lack food.'

lace

This word can be a verb, in which case it means 'to fasten or tighten'. The noun denotes a delicate open-work fabric of linen, cotton, silk, or even metal, so that the resulting clothing or decorative barrier has a trellis-like appearance. A **lace** can also be a string or cord used to fasten something or bring something together. Thus you might tie your shoe lace. As a verb, 'lace' has a couple of more specialist meanings. You can lace an innocuous drink with some alcoholic addition, or you can lace a chicken, i.e. make incisions in its breast. At a more colloquial level, you can lace into something, which implies that you are tackling some task or opportunity with gusto.

lackey

We normally think of a **lackey** as some obsequious servant, but there is also a brownish European moth of woods or hedgerows that is called the lackey moth.

lacks, lax

The word **lacks** is either the plural of 'lack' or the third person singular of the present tense of 'to lack' (see **lac, lack**). If you are **lax**, you are careless or negligent about something.

ladder

Associated with window cleaners but used by scores of other occupations, a **ladder** is a piece of equipment consisting of a series of bars or steps between two upright lengths of wood, metal or rope, and is used for climbing up and down. The word can also be used figuratively, so you can be climbing the ladder to success in your profession, or be at the bottom of the ladder in the race for promotion. Of course, a ladder can also be a vertical strip of unravelled fabric in tights or stockings.

lade

A **lade** can be a channel for leading water to a mill-wheel, or a verb meaning 'to load' or 'to remove water from a river, a vessel or whatever with a ladle'.

lag

As a noun, **lag** can mean the stave of a barrel, the retardation in a current or movement of any kind, a period of time between one event and another, or a convict. As a verb, 'to lag' means to progress too slowly, to fall behind, or to enclose or cover a boiler, pipes, etc. with material that provides heat insulation.

lain, lane

Lain is the past participle of the verb 'to lie': 'I have lain on this sofa all afternoon.' A **lane** is a narrow passageway between houses or hedges or even over an open moor. You will encounter lanes more commonly in the countryside than in towns.

lair

In Britain a **lair** is either a place where a wild animal lives, or a secret and confined place in which a person seeks concealment or seclusion. In Australia and New Zealand, it is a colloquial noun for a flashily dressed man who enjoys showing off.

lam, lamb

According to the *Shorter Oxford*, a **lam** can be either pieces of wood in a loom connected with the treadles and healds or a verb meaning 'to beat soundly, to thrash'. A lam is also a headlong flight, normally from the police. Almost all of us know that the **lamb** is the young of the sheep, though, since the lamb is taken as a symbol of meekness and innocence, parents can sometimes call their offspring 'lambs'. Jesus Christ, of course, was called the Lamb of God.

lama, llama

A **lama** is a Buddhist priest of Mongolia or Tibet. A **llama** is a South American ruminant quadruped used in the Andes as a beast of burden.

lame

A person who is **lame** is injured or crippled in one of his legs, but the word is also often used figuratively to denote something that is imperfect or defective: 'He made a lame excuse.' An ineffective person is often called a lame duck.

lance

A **lance** used to be a medieval weapon, a long pointed article used for unseating people from their horses. Today the word is used for almost any pointed instrument, and surgeons are prone to lance an ailment with a lance. The word is also used to denote a metal pipe supplying a jet of oxygen to a furnace, or a rigid tube at the end of a hose for pumping or spraying liquid. In lance corporal and lance sergeant, the word is also part of two army rankings.

land

As a verb, you **land** when you arrive at port in a ship, touch down at an airport, or hit the ground when jumping or falling from something that is higher. 'Land', of course, is the solid portion of the Earth (or any other planet), though people curtail the word quite often in order to refer to their own country: Scotland, Ireland, Swaziland, etc. Thus you get expressions like 'it is the most beautiful valley in the land'. The word is also used in a variety of colloquial expressions: 'I landed up with Myrtle', 'We will live off the land', 'He is in the land of Nod', and so on.

landmark

A **landmark** is an object in town or country that stands out in some way. Hence a hill can be a landmark, as can a tower, a castle, an abbey and so on.

The word is also used figuratively. Thus a significant event can be a landmark in a country's history, Kepler's laws of planetary motion were a landmark in astrophysics, and Beethoven's Eroica symphony was a landmark in his development as a composer.

lane *see* **lain**

lap, Lapp

If you have ever sat on someone's **lap**, you will know that the lap is that portion of a human between the waist and the knees when that person is sitting down. There are, however, a number of technical meanings as well. A lap is the distance traversed by a slide-valve beyond what is needed to close the passage of steam to or from the cylinder. It is also a layer or sheet into which cotton, wool or flax is formed in certain stages of its manufacture, or a hanging flap on a garment or saddle. A lap is one complete circuit of a running track, and if you are lapped, it means that someone has overtaken you, having completed one more lap than yourself. A cat and some other animals take up liquid with quick movements of the tongue, and they are said to lap at their drink. A **Lapp** is one of a Mongoloid race inhabiting the north of Scandinavia. It is also the Finno-Ugrian language of the Lapps.

laps, lapse

A lap is a circuit of a racing track, and so **laps** is the plural of that noun, and of all other substantive meanings that the word possesses. It is also the third person present tense singular of the verb 'to lap', meaning 'to take up liquid with the tongue'. A **lapse** is either an error ('My forgetting the nine times table was an unfortunate lapse'), a breaking away from some previously held belief ('I am a lapsed Catholic'), or an interval of time ('Obviously there was a lapse in the excitement at half time').

lard

Lard is fat from the abdomen of a pig that is rendered and clarified for use in cooking. As a verb, the word means to do to excess some pretentious or exculpatory action: 'He larded his speech with too many quotations.'

large

Most of the time, **large** means 'big, ample, spacious', but it can also mean 'free, unconfined' in expressions like 'he was at large for three days', or 'we can take a large view'.

lark

A **lark** is the general name for any bird of the family *Alaudidae*, and an episode of unfettered play, often directed at poking fun at someone else: 'We thought it would be a lark to ring the doorbell and then run away.'

laser, lazar

A **laser** is a gum-resin obtained from a plant called *laserpicium*, but we are more likely today to think of a laser as a narrow, concentrated beam of light. A **lazar** is a poor and diseased person, one suffering from a loathsome disease like leprosy.

lash

As a noun, **lash** is a sharp blow with a whip or rope, the flexible leather part of a whip used for delivering blows, or a frequent abbreviation of eyelash. As a verb, to lash is to strike repeatedly at something or somebody, or to fasten something down securely with cord or rope. One can also lash out, which normally means the excessive expenditure of money.

last

As a noun, a **last** is a model of the foot on which shoemakers shape boots and shoes. It is also a commercial weight, and that weight varies depending upon the industry concerned. Thus a last of cod is 12 barrels, but a last of grain is 80 bushels. As an adjective, 'last' indicates that there are no more to follow: 'Peter was the last to complete the race.' This meaning is enshrined in a number of common expressions: the last-chance saloon, the Last Day, one's last gasp, the Last Night of the Proms, etc. It can also be a verb indicating that something will continue for or can survive a predetermined length of time: 'The concert will last for about three hours. Can you last that long?'

late

If you are **late** for something, then you fail to present yourself on time. One year a plant may be late in flowering; all too often, a train is late in arriving. However, in an idiosyncratic speech form, if you speak of the late Mrs Pearson, you are referring to someone who is dead, not someone whose arrival is tardy. Ironically, given these meanings, 'late' can also mean 'current' or 'most recent': 'Have you heard the late news?'

law, lore

Despite their considerably different spellings and meanings, these two words are actually homophones. **Law** is the body of rules by which most states attempt to ensure order within themselves. Thus it is against the law for any of us to murder our next-door neighbour, great though the temptation may sometimes be. However, there are also laws in the observational sciences. Here the law is not an edict that we have to obey, but a principle that governs animate and inanimate objects. Thus the law of gravity governs us all, Kepler's laws of planetary motion describe how the planets have to move, Boyle's laws describe inevitable consequences concerning the volume and pressure of gases, and so on. The word **lore** tends these days to refer to accumulated knowledge within a particular field. Hence you may be an expert in the lore of forestry management, tuning a piano, or divorce settlements.

lawn

Most of us are acquainted with the typical British **lawn**, a small stretch of flat grass-covered ground in front of the house. Lawn is also a fine linen, resembling cambric.

lax *see* lacks

lay, lei

Lay has a number of meanings. It is most often a verb, but you can lay a surprising number of things: an egg, a bet, a tax, a lawn, a table, a proposition. You can also link the verb with a number of prepositions, each of them imparting a different connotation: lay on, lay out, lay to, lay together, lay over, etc. The *Shorter Oxford* disentangles the word into six basic verbal meanings: to prostrate, to deposit, to place, set or apply, to present or put forward, to impose as a burden, and to dispose or arrange properly over a surface. As an adjective, 'lay' can be used to demonstrate that someone is not a member of the clergy, even though he or she can be active in the church: 'Stephen is a lay preacher.' The word can also be a noun. A lay can be a short lyric song, a place of lodging, or a share in a whaling venture. **Lei** is not listed by the *Shorter Oxford*, but is defined by an Internet source as 'a flower necklace' and by the *Oxford Dictionary of English* as 'a Polynesian garland of flowers'. 'Lei' can also be seen as the plural of leu, which, as you all know, is the basic monetary unit of Romania.

layer

As a noun, a **layer** can be a sheet, quantity or thickness of material covering a surface or body, a level of seniority in an organisation, a person or thing that lays something, or a shoot fastened down to take root while still attached to the parent plant. As a verb or adjective, you can layer hair when you cut it into overlapping layers, propagate a plant as a layer, or arrange objects as layers.

lays, laze, leis

Lays and **leis** are simply the plurals of 'lay' and 'lei', and are only cited because they are homophones with **laze**, a word delightfully defined by an Internet source as meaning 'to recline with extreme prejudice', though the *Shorter Oxford*, one feels, evades the issue: 'To lie, move, act or enjoy oneself lazily.'

lazar *see* laser

lea, lee, li

A **lea** is pasture land or grass land on a farm, a measure of yarn, or a tract of open ground. As LEA, it is an acronym for Local Education Authority. A **lee** is a sheltered place, a refuge, or the sediment from wine. A **li** is a Chinese weight or the distance of about one-third of a mile.

leach, leech

The verb 'to **leach**' indicates the action of a mineral or chemical being slowly removed from a substance (soil, most commonly) by the force of percolating water. Thus pesticides can leach into rivers. A **leech** is a blood-sucking worm, and the word is often used figuratively to describe a money-lender.

lead, led

As a noun, **lead** is either a metallic element of a pale bluish-grey colour, a small stick of graphite for filling a pencil, or a thin strip of type-metal used in type-composition to separate the lines. The noun 'lead' is pronounced exactly the same way as **led**, but the verb 'to lead' is pronounced as if it was spelt 'leed'. As a verb, 'to lead' means to bring or take to a place, to guide, to mark the course for, to march at the head, to precede, or even to govern: 'I will lead you to salvation', 'I will lead the government to economic bliss', 'I will lead you along the Pennine Way', and so on. There are also a number of common figurative expressions like 'to lead a dog's life' or 'to lead someone up the garden path'. 'Led' is the past participle of 'lead': 'I led them to salvation / economic bliss / the Pennine Way / the pub.'

leader, lieder

A **leader** is self-evidently someone who leads, someone who gets others to follow him or her, be it on a route-march, a choir or a political movement. A leader can also be the chief violinist in an orchestra, an article of comment in a newspaper, a short strip of non-functioning material at each end of a film reel or recording tape, or a shoot of a plant at the apex of a stem or main branch. **Lieder** is the German word given for songs, normally with piano accompaniment, and the word is normally applied to the song cycles of Schubert, Schumann, etc.

leaf, lief

A **leaf** is the expanded organ of a plant, usually green, produced laterally from a stem or branch. It is also a sheet of paper, either loose or as part of a book. The hinged part of a door, table or drawbridge can also be called a leaf. As a verb, a plant or tree can leaf, i.e. begin to grow leaves. You can also leaf through a book or magazine by turning over the pages casually without much attention. **Lief**, obviously a German word, can be used as an adjective or adverb. It conveys the sense of willingness, preference, agreement or desire. Hence you could say 'I would lief go home' meaning 'I would rather go home'.

league

A **league** can be a combination of people, organisations or countries linked together because of some common interest. The League of Nations was such a body on an international scale; the Childs Ercall Cat League would (if it existed) be such a body on a village scale. But a league is also a distance, normally in Britain about three miles, though the word is used today as a synonym for any considerable distance. A league can also be a group of sports clubs which play each other over the length of a season.

leak, leek

A **leak** is a hole or fissure in a vessel that could contain liquid. The result is that the liquid slowly escapes from the vessel because it drips continually from the aperture. The word is also used when information is divulged to people and organisations who were not intended to have such data. A **leek**, the national emblem of the Welsh, is a herb related to the onion but having long flat leaves and a small cylindrical bulb.

lean, lien

If an animal or human is described as **lean**, then it means that the body tissue of the object concerned is largely muscle and very little fat. But the adjective can also be used to indicate scarcity: 'We had a lean time of it at Quebec.' The word is also a verb meaning to stand or lie at an oblique angle. If you lean against a lamppost, you are not standing upright but are supporting your upper body to some extent upon the lamppost. The word **lien** is invariably encountered in a legal context. The right to retain a property until the person holding it is paid a debt is known as holding a property in lien.

leas, lees

Leas is simply the plural of 'lea' (qv), whereas **lees** are the dregs, often of a wine bottle, though the word can be applied to virtually anything else.

leased, least

If something is **leased**, it is rented out to someone. The **least** you can do is the minimum, though the word can also be used superlatively: 'Of all the examinees, I did the least revision.'

leave

Most of the time, **leave** is a verb. You can leave a place or person (i.e. depart from it or them), you can leave some cake (i.e. retain it) to gobble in bed tonight, you can leave (bequeath) your DVDs to Meg, or you can leave a job (defer it) until tomorrow. As a noun, leave is time off from your normal job or occupation. People in the forces get leave, though most other occupations take a holiday, the two events being identical.

led *see* lead

ledge

A **ledge** is a narrow horizontal surface projecting from a wall, cliff or other surface, an underwater ridge, or a stratum of metal or ore-bearing rock.

ledger

A **ledger** is a book of financial accounts, a flat stone slab covering a grave, a horizontal scaffolding pole, parallel to the face of the building, or a weight used on a fishing line without a float, to anchor the bait in a particular place.

lee *see* lea

leech *see* leach

leek *see* leak

leet

A **leet** in Scotland is a list of candidates selected for a post. In England in the middle ages, a leet was a yearly or half-yearly court of record. According to *Brewer's*, in East Anglia a leet was a division of the hundred.

left

The word **left** indicates the relative position of something: 'You will find the Post Office to the left of the statue.' It is thus the complement of 'right': 'Turn left at the traffic lights and then take the second turning to the right.' The word also means something that has not been used, consumed or taken: 'I meant to take my cycle clips, but left them behind'; 'There was very little food left after the party.' The word also denotes a political and social position, normally one that is liberal, democratic and believes in equality: 'Tony Blair is marginally to the left of Attila the Hun.'

leg

As we all know, a **leg** is one of the limbs of an animal or human. It is also one of the supports of a chair, table, etc. It can be a section or stage of a journey or a multi-part sporting fixture, one half of a cricket field, or a deferential action.

lei *see* lay

lends, lens

Of course, the 'd' of **lends** should give it a different sound from **lens**, but it frequently doesn't, and the two words can end up as homophones. 'Lends' is the third person singular present tense of the verb 'to lend', and a lens is a piece of manufactured glass so curved as to magnify what is being looked out through it.

lent, Lent

With a lower-case 'l', **lent** is the past participle of the verb 'to lend', but with an upper-case 'l', **Lent** denotes the period in the Christian calendar extending from Ash Wednesday to Easter-eve. This is supposed to be a period of fasting and penitence.

lessen, lesson

Lessen means 'to become less, to decrease.' A **lesson** is a time of instruction, and although you have formal lessons at school, the mere act of living is a constant lesson.

let

If you **let** Barry go home, you give him permission so to do. If you let your house, you allow others to live in it in return for payment. If your service in tennis clips the top of the net, it is known as a let.

letter

There are 26 letters in the English alphabet, and the **letter** E is much more commonly used than the letter Z. Yet, although the word 'letter' signifies an individual one from those 26, the word also denotes a missive written to a friend or to a company or to an official. Such missives contain your address, and normally begin 'Dear Alice' or 'Dear Sir', and then continue with the matter that you wish to communicate to your correspondent.

levee, levy

The word **levee** has two entirely dissimilar meanings. It can be an embankment to prevent the overflow of a river, or the act of rising from one's bed, normally surrounded by a number of visitors. It would, for instance, be the first ceremonial act of Louis XIV's day.

level

As a noun, a **level** is a horizontal plane or line with respect to the distance above or below a given point. It can also be a position on a scale: 'there was a high level of unemployment', 'he played chess at an advanced level.' It can also denote that something was flat or flattish, as in a tract of land.

ley

A **ley** is a piece of land that is put down to grass or clover for a single season or a limited number of years instead of being a permanent pasture. The word is also used to signify a supposed straight line connecting three or more prehistoric sites. This line is sometimes regarded as marking the line of a former track, while others see it as some mystical line of energy.

li see lea

liaison

Most of us think of a **liaison** as being a relationship, either between two people, or between organisations. Thus Antony and Cleopatra had a liaison, but so did England and Prussia in the Napoleonic Wars. However, a liaison can also be the binding or thickening agent of a sauce, or the sounding of a consonant that is normally silent at the end of a word, because the next word begins with a vowel.

liar, lyre

A **liar** is an untruthful person. A **lyre** is a musical instrument rather like the harp.

liberty

The state of being free is known as **liberty**, yet a presumptuous remark or action is also known as a liberty. An instance of being too free!

licence, license

A noun, **licence** relates to a document which gives permission for some activity to take place. Thus you need a licence to run a public house, a bookmakers, a carnival, to get married, and so on. The verb **license** means 'to give permission' or 'to tolerate'. There is also a disapproving usage: 'Pubs open all day are giving too much licence.' There is also artistic licence, by which an artist in words or paint is allowed to break conventions of normality.

lichen

Lichen is a simple slow-growing plant which typically forms a low crust-like, leaf-like, or branching growth on rocks, walls and trees. It is also a skin disease in which small, hard, round lesions occur close together.

lick

As a verb, to **lick** is to pass the tongue over something in order to taste it, moisten it or clean it. It is also a colloquial term to signify a defeat: 'Arsenal licked Aston Villa on Saturday.' It can also be a short, sharp blow: 'If you don't stop whistling, I will give you a lick.' Hence, by extension, it can be a small amount or quick application of something: 'The fence needs a quick lick of paint.'

licker, liquor

A **licker** is one or something that licks. Most dogs are lickers. **Liquor** normally denotes an alcoholic spirit of some sort, but it can be used for any sort of liquid, or for the water or fat in which meat has been boiled.

lickerish, licorice, liquorice

Something that is **lickerish** is delightful to the taste. The word can also be used as an adjective for a skilled cook. **Licorice** is the North American spelling of **liquorice** and the words refer to a perennial Mediterranean leguminous shrub, the dried root of which can be used as a laxative or as a sweet.

lie, lye

If you **lie**, you tell an untruth or you are in a prostrate or recumbent position. Hence you could lie about where you were last night, or you could lie on your bed. An inanimate object can also lie upon the ground, a ship can lie in a berth, a stratum can lie upon a bed of clay, and a golf ball can lie in a bunker. A **lye** is a caustic solution that is strongly alkaline, and hence can be used as a detergent.

lien *see* lean

lieu, loo

The French word **lieu**, always used with the word 'in' preceding it, means 'place' or 'stead', so that you can say, 'I went to Paris in lieu of Gerald'. The word **loo** means a card game of which there are two varieties, three-card loo and five-card loo, a velvet mask partly covering the face used by women to protect the complexion, a cry to incite a dog in the chase, or a slang term for the toilet.

lift

As a verb, to **lift** means the action of raising something from one position to a higher one. Thus you might lift a bag from the floor on to the table, or a stack of bricks from the ground to the third storey. The word can also be used metaphorically, so that you might get an emotional lift from walking in the Peak District or playing a Beethoven string quartet. As a noun, a lift is an enclosed compartment in which people can be transported from one floor of a building to another, either upwards or downwards. It can also be a means of free transport in someone else's vehicle, the act of lifting a heavy weight, a rise in price, level or amount, or a feeling of confidence or cheerfulness. There are also one or two technical uses as well. Thus a lift is a layer of leather in the heel of a boot, a set of pumps in a mine, or, on a ship, ropes which reach from each mast-head to their respective yard-arms.

light, lite

As a noun, **light** is the illumination that proceeds from the sun, a star, a torch or a fire. As an adjective, light is the opposite of heavy. The word can also be used metaphorically in both senses. Hence reading a book can cast light upon your understanding of the decline and fall of the Roman Empire or whatever, while resolving a problem with your mother can make you feel light in spirit. Entertainment can also be light in that it requires little intelligence to enjoy, and stimulates neither the brain nor the soul. The word **lite** means little, not much, or few.

lightening, lightning

If something is **lightening**, then it removes or diminishes a weight to be handled or a puzzle to be pondered. The purchase of a lawn mower is lightening the hours that you have to spend in the garden, and your son's purchase of a flat is lightening your concerns over his welfare. **Lightning**, of course, is that visible discharge of electricity in the sky that can both thrill and frighten.

lighter

A **lighter** is either a device that produces a small flame used to light cigars or cigarettes, or a flat-bottomed barge used to transfer goods to and from ships in harbour.

like

If you **like** someone, you view them with affection. If you like a particular activity, you enjoy indulging in it. Thus you might like your aunt Peggy, ice cream and the poetry of Spenser. If you are like someone else, you resemble them in a number of ways.

limb, limn

A **limb** is an appendage to a body, like an arm or a leg, the branch of a tree, or the edge or boundary of a surface. To **limn** is to portray or delineate something or someone.

limbo

Limbo, in some Christian beliefs, is a sort of halfway house between Heaven and Hell. It is where the souls of unbaptised babies will go. In more general parlance, limbo is an uncertain period of awaiting a decision or resolution. It is also a West Indian dance.

lime

As a chemical entity, **lime** is calcium oxide, a white caustic alkaline substance obtained by heating limestone. As a biological entity, lime is a rounded citrus fruit similar to a lemon but greener, smaller, and with a distinctive acid flavour. It is also a deciduous tree with heart-shaped leaves. In West Indian English, lime can be a verb meaning to sit or stand around with others casually chatting.

linch, lynch

As a noun, **linch** is a piece of rising ground, but as a verb, 'to linch' means to fasten with a linch pin. To **lynch** someone is to illegally hunt them down and then hang them. It is a frequent activity in cowboy films.

line

As a noun, **line** has a variety of meanings that are all conceptually akin. A line can be a long, narrow mark or band, a length of cord, rope or wire, a horizontal row of printed words, a row of people or things, or a connected series of military fieldworks. Much less conceptually linked, a line can also be an area or branch of activity: 'George's line is ceramics, whereas my line is tapestries.' Many of these can be turned into verbs with no difficulty or alteration, but there is also the verb 'to line' that denotes the covering of the inside surface of something. Hence you can line a coat with fabric or line a dish with butter.

liner

A **liner** is a large passenger ship, a fine paintbrush used for painting thin lines, a cosmetic used for outlining a facial feature, a boat engaged in sea fishing with lines rather than nets, a ferret held on a leash while it is rabbiting, or the inside covering of something like the lining of a garment.

links, lynx

Links can be interlocking items in a chain or necklace, personal contacts with friends and acquaintances, torches of pitch and tow that used to be used for lighting the way in dark streets, and the driveways and greens of a golf course. A **lynx** is a wild, feral cat.

list

A **list** is a number of items normally written in a column form, a selvedge of a piece of fabric, or an instance of a ship leaning to one side.

lite *see* light

literal, littoral

To be **literal** is to accept words in their primary sense, and to be oblivious to metaphor or irony. This is appropriate when reading a railway timetable, but unilluminating when reading Jane Austen. If something is **littoral**, it pertains to the shoreline.

litter

This can be stray refuse (cigarette packets, sweet wrappings, paper bags, etc.) casually dropped to despoil the streets or countryside, granular, absorbent material lining a tray in which a cat can urinate and defecate, a vehicle containing a couch, shut in by curtains, and carried on men's shoulders or by animals, straw, rushes and the like serving as bedding, or the young brought forth at birth as in a **litter** of pigs, kittens, etc.

livid

If you are **livid** you can either be furiously angry or be displaying a bruise that is dark bluish grey in colour.

llama *see* lama

lo, low

The first, **lo**, is simply an exclamation of surprise, as in the Wesley hymn 'Lo, he comes with clouds descending.' The second, **low**, is an adjective being the opposite of 'high' and applied to relative spacial position, depth of voice, social status, or even cultural activity.

load, lode, lowed

A **load** can be materials being carried by a person or any vehicle. When you visit the market on Wednesdays, the goods that you have to carry home are your load. The cargo of a ship is its load. A **lode** is a water-course, an aqueduct or an open drain. **Lowed** is the past tense of the verb 'to low', a verb depicting the mooing sound of a cow.

loan, lone

If you **loan** something to someone, you allow them to borrow it. If you live a **lone** life, you have no companions, you live a solitary existence.

lob

A **lob** is a country bumpkin, a lump of something, a thick mixture in the brewing industry, a slow, under-hand ball, or a stroke in tennis.

loch, lock

A **loch** is the Scottish equivalent of 'lake'. A **lock** is a mechanism for securing an object safely. Thus one locks one's doors when one goes out, or locks one's car or bicycle when one is out. A lock can also be a tress of hair, a contrivance for raising or lowering a boat on a canal, a hospital for treating venereal diseases, the extreme turning of the front wheels of a car, or a receiver of stolen goods.

locks, lox

Locks is clearly the plural of 'lock' (see immediately above), and **lox** is a kind of smoked salmon.

locus

In mathematics, a **locus** is a curve or other figure formed by all the points satisfying a particular equation of the relation between coordinates. For a biologist, a locus is the position of a gene or mutation on a chromosome. For the rest of us, a locus is a particular place or situation where something significant happens: 'The locus of Ket's Rebellion was in Norfolk.' Indeed, 'locus' is the Latin for 'place', and it is used with that meaning in a number of classical expressions that have been incorporated into English.

lodge

As a noun, a **lodge** is a small dwelling, a house or cottage at the entrance of a park, the place of meeting for members of a Freemason branch, the den or lair of a beaver or otter, the residence of the head of a college at Cambridge University, or the tent of a North American Indian. As a verb, 'to lodge' means to inhabit a dwelling on a temporary basis.

lone *see* loan

long

With regards to spatial measurement, the adjective **long** indicates greater length than other objects to which it can validly be compared. Thus the Marathon is a long race in comparison with the one hundred metres. The word can also be applied to time. An hour can be a very long time when you are listening to Dr Tedium Circumlocution deliver a lecture on East Sussex weaving patterns. As a verb, you may long for the company of your spouse, you may long for the end of the working day, or you may long for a cup of tea. In other words, 'to long' means to yearn, to desire, to pine for.

loom

A **loom** is a machine in which yarn or thread is woven into fabric, or, as a verb, loom means to come into sight or to be ominously close.

loon, lune

A **loon** is the name for certain aquatic birds of the family *Gaviidae* (divers), or, in colloquial speech, a silly or foolish person. A **lune** is a leash for a hawk, a crescent shape or the figure formed on the surface of a sphere or plane by two arcs of circles that enclose a space.

loop, loupe

A **loop** is what is formed when the two ends of a rope, ribbon, metal pipe and so on meet each other while leaving an aperture between the bulk of their lengths. This often creates a shape that is close to a circle. Hence, when we have a series of circles that are intermeshed in such a way as to create a chain, we talk about the links of the chain. According to an Internet source, a **loupe** is a jeweller's monocular magnifier, and this is confirmed by the *Oxford Dictionary of English*, though the word is not cited by either the *OED* or the *Shorter Oxford*.

loot, lute

The proceeds of a burglary or robbery are often referred to as the **loot**. It is the ill-gotten gains of some illegal activity. A **lute** is a stringed musical instrument much in vogue in the sixteenth century, a tenacious clay or cement, or a straight-edged piece of wood for scraping off superfluous clay from a brick-mould.

lop

If we use the word **lop** at all, it usually as a verb meaning to cut off: 'I must lop off those branches of the tree.' However, the word does have one meaning as a noun and two as an adjective also. It can be the smaller branches and twigs of a tree, a state of the sea when the waves are short and lumpy, and a variety of rabbit with long drooping ears.

lore *see* **law**

lot

We not infrequently talk about our **lot** in life, in which sense 'lot' is being used as a synonym for 'destiny'. But we may also have a lot of CDs, in which case 'lot' is a synonym for 'great quantity'. We may have a lot in a sub-divided stretch of land, namely a portion of this land on which we grow vegetables. We may place something for sale in an auction, and it may be assigned Lot 62.

lounge

As a noun, **lounge** denotes the sitting room in a house. As a verb, 'to lounge' means to recline indolently, to laze around.

low

This word has a number of meanings, though they are mostly conceptually linked in that they suggest a comparative inferiority. Thus if you are low in cash, this means that you have little money, an inferior state to being awash with it. If an area of town is a low area, it is poorer, dirtier and more criminal than a higher area. If a bridge is a low bridge, it is less grandiose than a high bridge. If you have a low opinion of your vicar, you do not esteem him very highly. If you are low church, you prefer a less ornate and ceremonial approach to worship than someone who is high church. If you lie low, you attempt not to be observed. If you have a low voice, your speech or singing has a lower vibration rate than a soprano. Holland and Belgium are called the Low Countries because they are very flat and have no hills. The only instance where 'low' loses this comparative inferiority is as a verb. A cow is said to low, and this is neither better nor worse than a sheep bleating, or a horse neighing.

lug

It is unlikely that you use the word **lug** very often, yet it has at least three separate meanings. Now confined to dialect usage, a lug is a long stick or pole, or even a branch of a tree. Mostly confined to Scotland, a lug is one of the flaps of a cap or bonnet that can be pulled over the ears, or even the ear itself. In North America, a lug can be a loutish man. It can also be an abbreviation for a lugworm. As a verb, to lug is to pull or tug.

lull

As a noun, a **lull** is a cessation or diminution of some current activity. Hence, if the Hotwells Hooligans and the Ashton Anarchists, normally engaged in street warfare, have no pitched battles for a fortnight, we might say that there is a lull in their activities. When the workmen, drilling away adjacent to your office, troop off to lunch, there will be a lull in the noise. As a verb, however, to lull means to soothe, even to induce sleep. Sometimes someone may lull you into a feeling of security, only then to take you by surprise and pull some nefarious and damaging trick upon you.

lumbar, lumber

The validity of these is arguable because of the difference between the '-ar' and '-er' endings, but in 'normal' speech you barely notice the difference. **Lumbar** is an adjective relating to the loin area of the human body. Thus you can have lumbar arteries and veins. **Lumber** means timber, especially when cut up, or a collection of unwanted items, often furniture, that take up room, but have now no real purpose.

lump

Lump, like so many words, has various conceptually linked meanings. Its most common is to denote a compact mass of something, a lump of clay, a lump of earth, a lump of rock. It is also used figuratively to describe a dull, unstimulating sort of person. There are also specific, technical usages. Hence a lump may be a barge or lighter used in dockyards, a nipple-seat on a gun-barrel, or an uncouth-looking spiny-finned fish of a leaden-blue colour, *Cyclopterus lumpus*. It can also be a verb. You might say, 'I'll just have to lump it,' when you feel that you have been subject to some unfair conduct but can find no retribution.

lune *see* loon

lunette

A **lunette** is an arched aperture, a fortification with two faces forming a projecting angle, in church a holder for the consecrated host in a monstrance, a broad, shallow mound of wind-blown material along the leeward side of a lake, or a ring fixed to a vehicle by which it can be towed.

lunge

As a noun, a **lunge** can be a long rope used in training horses, a thrust with a sword or other weapon, a sudden forward movement, or the Great Lake trout.

lurch

We normally use this word as a verb meaning to move suddenly and unsteadily, the sort of movement that drunken people are prone to do. It can also be a noun to describe the state of a game where one person is far ahead of anyone else.

lyre *see* liar

M, m, em

The thirteenth letter of the alphabet does not form a word, but sneaks in here largely because it was the Roman symbol for 1,000. **M** is also a symbol on cricket score cards for a maiden over, the international vehicle registration for Malta, and an abbreviation for sundry items: metres, miles, married, masculine and minutes. M was also the code name for James Bond's boss, and hence is now part of that escapist fantasy. In printing, an em is a square space in any size of type.

macaroni

Many of us are familiar with the food **macaroni**, a kind of wheaten paste formed into long slender tubes and dried for use as food. Equally most of us, not being alive in the eighteenth century, will not know that young men who had travelled and consequently affected continental tastes and manners were known as macaroni. Indeed, it was this clique that popularised the eating of macaroni. The word is also the name for a species of crested penguin.

macaw

A **macaw** is a parrot from tropical and subtropical America remarkable for its gaudy plumage; also the West Indian name for palms of the genus *Aerocomia*.

mace

Originally a weapon of war, a **mace** is now a symbol of office, often carried by the mayor of a town and by the Speaker of the House of Commons. It is a heavy staff or club, with its rounded head often being spiked. It is also a spice made from the dried outer covering of the nutmeg, and a Malay currency.

made, maid

Made is the past participle of the verb 'to make', while a **maid** is either a woman who has never had sexual intercourse or a young lady who serves food and drinks to the table for the convenience of customers or guests and/or performs household duties.

magazine

A **magazine** can be a storehouse of munitions, a chamber in a repeating rifle, or a periodical publication containing articles, mostly of an ephemeral nature.

maid *see* made

maiden

A **maiden** was once an instrument, similar to a guillotine, formally used in Edinburgh for beheading criminals. Today the word is more likely to denote an unmarried woman, or, in cricket, an over in which no runs were scored.

mail, male

Mail can be armour composed of interlaced rings or chain-work, or, more commonly today, letters and parcels delivered to one's house or business by the postman. A **male** is the masculine of a species.

main, mane

If something is the **main** attraction, it is the principal one, the primary one. If an animal possesses a **mane**, as the horse and lion do, then it possesses long hair on the back of its neck and shoulders.

maize, maze

Maize is a grain crop similar to wheat or barley. A **maze** is a confusing network of winding and intercommunicating paths in which one can easily get lost. The word can also be used to indicate a state of bewilderment, and as a verb to denote a trick or deception.

major

A **major** is an officer in the army. As an adjective, something is major if it is of significant importance: 'Horse-riding is of major importance in my life.' The word is also used in music for intervals and keys. In America, you major at a college or university in a particular subject or subjects, namely those subjects that constitute the bulk of your course.

make

As a verb, 'to **make**' means to create, to construct. The word can also be a noun when it refers to the thing that has been made or constructed: 'What make is your car?'

man

A **man** is an adult male person, but the word also signifies one of the pieces in chess, backgammon or draughts. The word can also be a verb, so if you man something, you take an active part in running it.

mane *see* **main**

manifest

If something is **manifest**, it is almost self-evident. Yet 'manifest' can also be a noun, it which case it is a public declaration, not unlike the word 'manifesto'. In shipping, a manifest can be a list of the ship's cargo.

manna

In the book of Exodus, the Israelites are travelling through the wilderness, and are bereft of food. God accordingly provides a substance for them that is called **manna**, and the word has since been used for any last-minute and vital assistance. However, there is also a literal manna, the sweet pale yellow or whitish concrete juice obtained from incisions in the bark of the Manna ash.

manner, manor

Your customary mode of behaving or your normal way of working can be called your **manner**. You might say that someone has a supercilious manner or a humble manner. A **manor** in medieval times was a unit of fields, woodland, cottages and castle or stately house, all of which were under the control of the lord of the manor. Since 1924, 'manor' has been slang for the area in which a police officer works.

mantle

A **mantle** is always a covering for something, but its application is so diverse as to raise it to homonym status. The most familiar usage for most of us will be to denote a cloak-like garment, but it can be the covering, envelope or shade employed in various mechanical contrivances, the covering in birds when the plumage of the back and wings is distinct from the rest of the bird, the covering or scum that can form on the top of liquids, and even a blush that covers the human face. Originally the physical mantle was a symbol of authority, and when someone succeeded to the position of a predecessor, he was said to assume 'the mantle of Elisha'. The full story is told in 1 Kings 19.

manual

This can be a noun denoting a book, normally a book of instructions for the maintenance of a car or other technical equipment. It can also be an adjective indicating that something is performed by hand. Thus, if you are bricklayer, you have a manual occupation. If you are a spade (which is impossible), you are a manual tool.

marc, mark, marque

Marc is the refuse that remains after the pressing of grapes or other fruits. A **mark** can be a variety of things: a name in medieval Germany for the tract of land held in common by a village, the sign of a boundary or position, a device, sign, seal, label or emblem indicating the ownership of something, or a pre-decimal German currency. Originally a **marque** was a licence granted by a sovereign to a subject authorising said subject to take reprisals against a hostile state. Later it became a licence to fit out an armed vessel, and to use that vessel as a sort of pirate ship against the enemy.

march

Apart from being the third month of the year (with a capital M), a march can be an ordered progression on foot from A to B, or a tune originally designed to assist such a progression by setting out a tempo for the disciplined walking. A march is also a tract of land on the border of a country.

mare, mayor

A **mare** is the female of a horse or other equine animal. The word, with a very different pronunciation, is also the Latin word for 'sea', and as such has been used to denote the large, level basalt plain on the surface of the moon. A **mayor** is the head of a town, borough or county council.

mark *see* marc

marque *see* marc

marshal, martial

As a verb, **marshal** is relatively straightforward. It basically means to arrange in a proper order (the things needing arranging can be a crowd at a football match), to draw up soldiers for review, or to supervise an exhibition or dinner. As a noun, 'marshal' is more varied. In some armies, it can be an office of the highest rank. It can be a man or woman charged with supervising a ceremony. It is an officer of the corporation of the City of London. In the USA, a marshal is a civil officer answering to the sheriff of a county. **Martial**, however, is an adjective that means 'of or pertaining to war'.

marten, martin

A **marten** is a semi-arboreal weasel-like animal found in Eurasia and North America. A **martin** is a swiftly flying insectivorous bird of the swallow family.

maser, mazer

A **maser** is a device using the stimulated emission of radiation by excited atoms to amplify or generate coherent monochromatic electromagnetic radiation in the microwave range. A **mazer** is a hardwood drinking bowl.

mash

Most of the meanings of **mash** entail some sort of mixing or combining operation. Thus if you mash malt with hot water, you end up with wort, sometimes called mash. If you mix warm boiled grain, bran or meal together, the resulting mash is a food for horses and cattle. Indeed, if you mix almost anything together into a soft pulp, the result can be called mash. There is, though, a quite different slangy meaning. If you mash someone, you excite a sentimental and sexual admiration in them.

mask, masque

A **mask** is a covering for the face made of velvet or cloth so as to hide your features and make you unrecognisable. They were traditionally worn by highwaymen, and are more commonly worn today at parties. A **masque** is a masked ball, or a lavish entertainment.

Mass, mass

A **Mass**, normally capitalised, is either the Eucharist service in a Roman Catholic church, or a musical setting of those parts of the Mass which are usually sung. A **mass** normally signifies a body of matter of sufficient size to be an obstacle or to need attention. However, the word can also be extended to objects that have little or no physical significance: 'I have a mass of work to do', or, 'The speaker deluged us with a mass of thoughts.' The verb 'to mass' means to gather together into a crowd or group.

massed, mast

Massed is the past tense of the verb 'to mass' – 'We massed in the square.' A **mast** is a long pole normally used for flying a flag or supporting the sails of a ship.

mat, matt, matte

Most of us think of a **mat** as being a coarse material placed on the floor for people to wipe their feet on, though you can, of course, have beer mats for resting your tankard on, or table mats to protect the table from the heat of the serving dish that you are about to place upon that table. You can also have a mouse mat for your computer mouse to move along, a mat of hair (untidy and long), and be on the mat for some error that you have committed. **Matt** is an adjective to describe a surface that is dull and flat, without a shine. **Matte** can be the impure product of the smelting of sulphide ores, or a mask used to obscure part of the image in a film, thus allowing another image to be substituted, and thereby combining the two.

match

A **match** can be a contest between two people or two teams, as in a chess match or a rugby match. It can also be one of a pair. You may find a sock in a drawer, and then spend half an hour looking for a match. You may admit that someone is a good match when they are of equal ability to yourself. If you are thinking of marrying Elsa, you might ask yourself if she is a good match. Equally, of course, she could ask herself the same about you. And then, totally differently, a match is a short, thin piece of wood tipped by some combustible material that, when rubbed against some rough substance, will burst into a flame.

mate

When animals (including humans) **mate**, they have sexual intercourse. Yet your mate can also be a friend with whom you have no sexual congress. Mate is also what you say in a game of chess when you have placed your opponent's king is such a position that he cannot be moved out of check.

matter

Everything that has a physical existence is composed of **matter**, because the word is just a general term for the substance or substances of which an object is composed. Yet the word is probably even more commonly used in a non-physical sense. When we say, 'What's the matter?' we are not normally looking at some material in a test tube. Instead we are enquiring about what is concerning our friend, and may well get the answer, 'Oh, I'm worried about Simon's first day at school,' or something like that. The word can also be used to describe the contents of a book: 'The basic matter of this book is concerned with vegetable distribution in the English Fens.' Hence 'matter' denotes something entirely physical and something entirely mental. Only the context of the remark will reveal which.

maxim

'A man's house is his castle' is a well-known **maxim**, since a maxim is a proposition that is thought to express some general truth, even though many are highly questionable. A maxim is also a single-barrelled quick-firing machine gun.

maze *see* **maize**

me, mi

Me is a personal pronoun referring to oneself: 'He gave the flowers to me.' **Mi** is the cause of one of the *OED*'s most opaque definitions: 'The third note in Guido's hexachords, retained in solmization as the third note of the octave.' To make this comprehensible, all that we have to know is that the notes of an octave were each given names: doh, re, mi, fah, soh, la, ti, doh, and so, as we can see, 'mi' is the third note in the diatonic scale.

mean, mien

The word **mean** in most instances means 'to intend, to have in mind as a purpose, to design': 'What I mean is that John should not be allowed to drink any alcohol during his stay.' The word can also signify an ungiving spirit: 'Victor was remarkably mean with his allowance to his son.' Since the 1920s 'mean' has also been a colloquial word for 'adroit, formidable'. The word **mien** means the way in which a person appears to others, the way in which a person bears himself or herself: 'His mien was what you would expect from an army sergeant, upright and commanding.'

meat, meet, mete

Unless we are vegetarians, most of us eat **meat** at least once a week. It is the cooked flesh of an animal, normally beef from a cow, pork from a pig, or lamb from a sheep, though poultry like chicken, geese and turkey are also often cooked and eaten. In fact, of course, meat is quite frequently used as a synonym for food in general, which must be irritating for vegetarians. In parts of Devon, potatoes for the table are still called meat potatoes, as opposed to feed potatoes for livestock or seed potatoes for planting. The word can also be figuratively extended, so that that someone can say, 'The paintings of Cézanne are meat to my soul.' **Meet** is a verb meaning 'to encounter, to come face to face with, to find'. Hence you may meet a friend for coffee, meet a business colleague to discuss strategy, or meet a problem and try to solve it. The verb is also used in a variety of idiomatic expressions. 'To meet one's maker' is to die. To meet someone halfway is to make a compromise. A meeting of minds indicates an agreement or understanding. **Mete** is the least common of these homophones. In legal circles it means a boundary or limit. As a verb, it means 'to administer, to allot, to apportion', often with a connotation of reward or blame.

medal, meddle

One tends to be awarded a **medal** in return for some act of considerable bravery or self-sacrifice. Hence medals, normally fairly small discs of metal, tend to be more frequently awarded during a time of warfare. **Meddle** is a verb which means 'to concern oneself with, to interfere, to busy oneself'. It normally carries a somewhat disapproving tone.

meddler, medlar

A **meddler** is someone who meddles (see above), while a **medlar** is a small bushy tree of the rose family bearing a small brown apple-like fruit.

medium

If something is **medium**, it is fairly average, neither good nor bad. But if the word is used as a noun, then a medium can be a substance through which something else passes. Thus air is the medium through which sound travels. A person who claims to be able to receive messages from the dead is also called a medium.

meet see meat

mell

In Scotland and some northern dialects, **mell** is a noun meaning a heavy hammer. For most of us, though, it is a verb meaning 'to mix, to mingle, to meddle'.

Mercury, mercury

With a capital M, **Mercury** can either be the Roman god of eloquence, skill, trading and thieving who was the messenger of the gods, or the smallest of the planets in our solar system, the one nearest to the sun. In astrology, Mercury, according to *Brewer's*, 'signifieth subtill men, ingenious, inconstant rymers, poets, advocates, orators, philosophers, arithmeticians, and busie fellows'. In lower case, **mercury** is one of the elements, a heavy silver-white liquid metal.

mere

A **mere** is a lake, a fact that is marked by the Shropshire town of Ellesmere, which means 'the lake or pool of a man called Elli'. The word is also used in Derbyshire for a stretch of land that contains lead ore, and can also signify a boundary or a landmark. As an adjective or adverb, its most common meaning is 'nothing more than': 'The building was erected by a mere six men.'

mess

Normally taken to denote a muddle or a confusion, **mess** is also associated with food in that meals are served in a mess in the armed services, and the word can also be applied to the food itself. This is not to imply that the mess served in the mess is a mess. On the contrary, the meal served in an RAF dining room can often be immaculately presented and taste delicious. You will recall that Esau sold his birthright for a mess of pottage.

metal, metel, mettle

The natural metals are gold, silver, copper, iron, lead and tin, but alloys of them all are now common. By and large, a **metal** is ductile and is a good conductor of heat and electricity. In the middle ages, metals were divided into two classes, noble and base. The noble ones, gold, silver and platinum, were not affected by air. The others suffered from oxidation, and decayed. **Metel** is the specific name of the hairy thorn-apple, *Datura Metel*. **Mettle** is a word used to indicate that an animal or a human is keyed up to perform well or possesses spirit and courage.

mete *see* meat

meter, metre

A **meter** is an apparatus for automatically measuring the amount of gas or fluid flowing through. A **metre** is a unit of length in the metric system, namely 39.37 inches. The word is also used to denote any form of poetic rhythm.

mew

Most of us probably think of a **mew** as being the cry of a cat, but a common name for the common gull is sea-mew. A mew is also the cage of hawks while they are moulting, and the word can also be used as a verb to describe such a process.

mewle, mule

If you **mewle**, you whimper like a child. A **mule** is the offspring of a female horse and a male donkey.

mews, muse

A **mews** these days is a somewhat select cul-de-sac for the upper middle class. I wonder how many of them know that it used to be the name for the stables. The nine daughters of Zeus and Mnemosyne (Memory) became the nine muses, each one being the **muse** for a different artistic activity.

mho, moo, moue

The **mho** is the reciprocal of an ohm. As all country dwellers know, cows **moo**. It is a low, normally prolonged noise which sounds like a profound comment on government policy. A **moue** is a disdainful or pouting look. The word is taken directly from the French, and describes an action normally taken by attractive young ladies when they are offered half a bitter rather than a gin and tonic.

middy, midi, Midi, MIDI

A **middy** can be an informal term for a midshipman, a woman or child's loose blouse with a sailor collar, or, in Australia, a beer glass containing half a pint. A **midi** is a woman's calf-length skirt, dress or coat. The **Midi** is the south of France, and the **MIDI** is a widely used standard for interconnecting electronic musical instruments and computers.

mien *see* mean

might, mite

The word **might** indicates the ability of being able to do something – 'I might visit Dora's tonight' – or, more forcefully, it denotes power and strength – 'The Romans had sufficient might to overrun the English.' A **mite** is either a small insect or a generic word for a very small offering or contribution. Colloquially one can use 'mite' as if it was a synonym for 'little' in sentences like 'Sorry about my brief letter, but I'm a mite busy at the moment.'

mil, mill

A **mil** is one-thousandth of an inch and an abbreviation for millilitres, millimetres and millions. A **mill** is a building that threshes or grinds something like corn or coffee, though the term has been extended to include any machine that is powered by wind or water. The word is also used for other mechanical operations like the stamping of coins and bank-note printing. It is also used for buildings in which manufacturing processes are carried out. The cotton mills of Lancashire were once a common example. The word is also used figuratively in expressions like 'I was put through the mill today.'

millenary, millinery

Millenary denotes the passage of a thousand years. **Millinery** is the trade or business of a milliner, someone who makes or sells women's hats.

mince, mints

Not quite homophones, but difficult to tell apart. **Mince** is what is produced when meat is cut into small pieces. However, you can also mince your words when you are trying to avoid giving offence, and you mince in your gait when you choose to walk in an affected manner. **Mints** are sweets which we chew or suck and which have a very distinctive taste. However, the word could also be the third person singular of the verb 'to mint', or the plural of the noun 'mint'.

mind, mined

There is a great deal of scientific discussion about the nature of the **mind**. For dictionary makers it is simply the portion of the brain that is engaged in memory, purpose, thoughts and emotions. The word is also a verb meaning to look after, to care. **Mined** is simply the past tense of the verb 'to mine'.

miner, minor

A **miner** digs for something, be it coal or to undermine a castle, and a **minor** is either a young person not allowed to do a number of things, like have sex or drive a car. To describe an object as 'minor' is to indicate that it is of little importance.

minister

As a noun, **minister** can refer to anyone who helps another or others, to someone who is in charge of a government department like the Minister of Education, or to a priest. As a verb, the word means to serve, dispense, supply or execute.

minor *see* miner

mints *see* mince

minute

With the emphasis on the second syllable, **minute** is an adjective meaning extremely small. With the emphasis on the first syllable, the word means the duration of time of sixty seconds, or, more casually, a short time. It can also be a summary of what took place at a meeting, or an official memorandum authorising a particular course.

Miss, miss

With a capital letter, **Miss** is the title for an unmarried lady or girl. Since 1922 it has also been the appellation for a lady who has been voted the winner of a beauty contest. Thus you have Miss World, Miss America or Miss Scunthorpe. As a noun, **miss** is what you get when you fail to achieve a target. Thus if you are aiming for double twenty on a dartboard, but instead hit double five, you have achieved a miss. As a verb, it has exactly the same meaning: 'I would miss the train if I stayed for lunch.'

missed, mist

Missed is the past tense of the verb 'to miss' – 'I missed the plane because of a delay in Berlin' – and **mist** is a light fog or haze.

misses, Misses, Mrs

Misses is either a collection of unmarried ladies, though the word is rarely used like this, or the third person singular present tense of the verb 'to miss'. The title **Mrs** is applied to married, widowed or divorced ladies.

mite see **might**

mitre

Most of us think of a **mitre** as being the tall headdress worn by a bishop, but it can also refer to a headband worn by women in ancient Greece, or a joint in which the line of junction bisects the angle between the two pieces.

moan, mown

A **moan** is a low mournful murmur, either emitted at a time of grief or when one is suffering some relatively slight ache. **Mown** is the past participle of the verb 'to mow'. Thus most people are pleased when the lawn is mown.

moat, mote

A **moat** is a deep and wide ditch, normally filled with water, surrounding a town, castle or house. A **mote** can be something very small like a speck of dust, or a mound at the top of which a castle is normally erected.

mode, mowed

As keys are to the music of Mozart, so a **mode** was in ancient Greek music. Indeed modes lasted through most of the middle ages, and were much used in church plainsong. Today a mode is a fashion, an accepted way of doing things among the self-proclaimed elite. **Mowed** is the past tense of the verb 'to mow': 'I have mowed the lawn.'

moderate

This word indicates an avoidance of extremes. Thus if we say 'The weather was **moderate**', we mean that it was not too hot, nor too cold, was not too rainy, nor too dry, and so on. If we say that Phyllis is a moderate scholar, we mean that she is not intellectually outstanding, but not massively stupid either. The word only sneaks into this dictionary because it can occasionally be used to mean 'arbitrate'. Thus, if someone is called in to moderate a dispute between a trade union and an employer, he or she is called to moderate between the two sides and to achieve some sort of settlement.

moiré, moray

An Internet source defines **moiré** as being an optical illusion. In fact the adjective is generally used in connection with metals, and means the metals in question have a watered or clouded appearance. A **moray** is a tropical eel.

mole

A **mole** is a small mammal that lives mostly underground, but occasionally comes to the surface, thereby making an unwanted hole in your lawn. Because of the mole's hidden existence, the word 'mole' has been adopted to refer to a spy working unseen within the enemy's camp, though this usage did not emerge until the 1970s.

monitor

In our IT world, we now perhaps most often think of a **monitor** as being the screen attached to a computer system, a screen which enables us to keep track of the instructions that we give the computer. In general terms, however, a monitor is someone who supervises and possibly reprimands someone else. Thus a prefect at school is, to some extent, a monitor. Yet the word is also a type of lizard, an ironclad ship, a jointed nozzle used in hydraulic mining, or, in the USA, a raised part of the roof.

mood, mooed

We tend to think of a **mood** as being the frame of mind or state of feelings of a person, that state being reflected in their behaviour. Thus someone in an irritable mood is likely to be curt in their remarks and abrupt in their actions. Yet the word also has much more technical meanings. In logic the mood is any one of the classes into which a syllogism can be placed. In grammar the mood is any one of the groups of forms in the conjugation of a verb which serve to indicate the function in which the verb is used. **Mooed** is simply the past tense of the verb 'to moo'. An Internet source delightfully defines it as 'what the loquacious cow did'.

moor, more

A **moor** is a tract of unenclosed waste ground, a member of a North African Muslim people, or a verb meaning to secure a ship by means of anchors or cables of steel or rope attached to the shore. **More** is an adverb or adjective indicating that something is of greater quality, size or importance than something else: 'The daisy is more beautiful than the buttercup.' It can also indicate where improvement is needed: 'You need to do more work on your Latin.'

moose, mousse

A **moose** is an elk-like animal native to North America. A **mousse** is a dessert of whipped cream and eggs, though, from the 1980s, the word has also meant a substance for setting or colouring the hair.

moot

A **moot** is a meeting or the place where such a meeting takes place. Normally the meeting has a judicial purpose, and the word is still used at Gray's Inn when students of law meet to discuss a hypothetical case. As an adjective, 'moot' means debatable, something about which there can be disagreement.

moral, morel

Something that is **moral** has an ethical basis. Alas, moral judgements and conduct are so complex that an entire school of philosophy has developed round the topic. Fortunately a **morel** is more straightforward. It is a name for various kinds of nightshade, a morello cherry, or an edible fungus. Thus 'morel' only has three conceivable meanings, whereas 'moral' has hundreds, from torturing Afghan prisoners to denying abundant scientific evidence about evolution.

moray *see* moiré

mordant, mordent

Mordant as an adjective is often used to describe a dry and ironic sense of humour. As a noun, a mordant can be a substance, typically an inorganic oxide, that combines with a dye or stain and thereby fixes it in the material, or it can be a corrosive liquid used for etching the lines on a printing plate. In music, a **mordent** is an ornament consisting of a rapid alternation of the note written with the one immediately above or below it.

morn, mourn

Morn is an abbreviation for 'morning', and **mourn** is a verb meaning 'to grieve'.

morning, mourning

The **morning** is that portion of the day between sunrise and noon. **Mourning** is the process of grieving.

mort

A **mort** is the note sounded on the horn at the death of a deer, the salmon in its third year, a great quantity or number, or a harlot.

mould

Mould is the debris matter deposited by a decaying body, be it vegetable or animal. It is also a hollow form into which fluid or malleable matter may be placed so as to create the shape wanted. Consequently moulds are used by bricklayers, shipbuilders, masons, plasterers, painters, cooks and so on.

mount

For most of us, a **mount** is a hill or small mountain. For a soldier, a mount is a quantity of earth thrown up to resist an attack. For a palmist, a mount is one of the prominences on the palm of the hand. For a horse rider, his or her mount is the horse they happen to be riding. Indeed, as a verb, 'to mount' is often used in connection with a horse, though you can also mount a bicycle, or, presumably, almost any quadruped animal, though you are likely to raise some eyebrows if you mount your hippopotamus to do the weekend shopping.

movement

This is a noun derived from the verb 'to move', but **movement** has so many different applications that it has to count as an internal homonym. At its simplest, a movement is when someone or something moves. Thus athletes move efficiently, clocks and watches move accurately, and snails move slowly. Yet a painting, which is essentially static, can depict movement or be said to possess movement. A symphony or sonata is normally divided into several movements. When stocks and shares are being sold unusually rapidly, there is said to be movement in the Stock Exchange. An organisation that seeks to change the existing order, organisations like Cancer Research or the Wetherby Campaign against Yorkshire Pudding (which I've just invented), are all called movements.

mowed *see* mode

mucous, mucus

If something is **mucous**, it tends to produce **mucus**, which is a slimy material secreted by animals for the purpose of lubrication. Thus if your nose is mucous, it will tend to drip with mucus thereby causing you to search desperately for a handkerchief.

mud

For a geologist, **mud** is the product of water and small particles of rock, but when you say that Ethel's name is mud, you imply that she has no reputation left for honesty or probity.

muff

A **muff** is a covering of cylindrical shape into which both hands are thrust from opposite ends to keep them warm. A muff can also be a tuft of feathers on some domestic fowls, a cylinder of blown glass for fastening on to a plate, a short hollow cylinder surrounding an object, or used to connect two adjoining pipes, or, most disparately, a dialect word for the whitethroat bird. However, if you muff your lines in a play, you get them wrong or forget them. Indeed, if you muff anything, you are a failure. Hence you could muff a catch in the slips at cricket, muff a shot at billiards, or muff your opening speech in Parliament.

mug

A **mug** is a drinking vessel, an informal term for a face, or the labelling of someone as being an idiot. Since the late 1940s it has also been a verb meaning to attack and rob someone, though this usage did not enter Britain until the 1970s.

mule *see* mewle

mum

To keep **mum** is to remain silent. As a noun, it is a kind of beer originally brewed in Brunswick, or a pet name for 'mother'.

mummy

A **mummy** is an embalmed dead body or a child's name for 'mother'.

muscle, mussel

A **muscle** is a contractile fibrous band capable of producing movement in the animal body. A **mussel** is a bivalve mollusc.

muse *see* mews

mustard, mustered

This pair are not quite homophones, but once again hardly anyone will detect the difference between them. **Mustard** is a spicy yellow sauce. **Mustered** is the past tense of the verb 'to muster' which means to call together for a meeting, for roll call or for a battle.

N

N, n, en

N, the fourteenth letter of the alphabet, is used in mathematics to indicate an indefinite number. In chemistry it represents nitrogen, and, more generally, is used in numerous abbreviations for north, national and new. It is also sometimes used as an abbreviation for knight in chess games, and stands for Norway in international vehicle registration. **En** is encountered as a unit of measurement in printing (half an em) or as part of adopted French expressions like *en famille* and *en suite*.

nab

A **nab**, mostly in Scotland and northern English counties, is a protection from a hill or rock. The word is also a verb meaning to apprehend, to capture, to arrest.

naff

Naff is a slang word in two senses. As a verb, you can ask someone to naff off, that is, go away. In 1982 Princess Anne became extremely cross with a group of journalists and told them to naff off. As an adjective, if you describe something as naff you mean that it is lacking in taste or style. This seems to have no connection with the verbal form, but its origin is unknown even though this usage only became common in the 1950s.

nag *see* knag

nail

A **nail** is either a protective covering at the end of the fingers or toes, or a small metal spike that can be driven with a hammer into wood or plaster. The word can also be used as a verb where it means to fix, secure or even outwit.

name

Although the word **name** has only one central meaning – the word or words by which a person is addressed or known – there are at least two variations that are worth noting. First of all, if you are a 'name', you are to some degree or other, a celebrity of some kind. Secondly, in the UK a name is an insurance underwriter belonging to the Lloyd's syndicate. Obviously, of course, the word can also be used as a verb. Indeed, in the House of Commons, if the speaker names an MP, that MP is barred from the Commons for five days.

nap

The rough layer of projecting fibres on a textile fabric or a snooker table is known as the **nap**. It is also a card game and a short sleep. On the race course, a nap can be a tipster's prediction of a winner.

Napoleon, napoleon

The upper-case **Napoleon**, the name of three emperors of France, only gets a mention here because the name is shared (lower-case) by a gold twenty-franc coin minted during the time of Napoleon I, and by a napoleon boot that was worn by men in the nineteenth century. In North America there is also a flaky rectangular pastry called a napoleon.

narrow

If something is **narrow**, it is of small width – a narrow bridge, for example – but you can also be narrow in your views, meaning that you are insular and possibly bigoted, or have a narrow victory, meaning that your margin over the opposition was very slight.

naught, nought

These two words are very close to being synonyms. **Naught** means 'nothing', and so does **nought**, except that the latter is more usually confined to arithmetic and accounts, and therefore signifies o, while 'naught' more commonly denotes moral or legal nullity.

naval, navel

Something that is **naval** is connected with the sea or the navy. Thus you can have a naval victory, a naval officer, naval stores and so on. The **navel** is the rounded depression in the middle of the stomach that marks where the umbilical cord was originally attached.

navy

The **navy** is the nation's sea-borne armed force, but also a dark blue colour.

nay, neigh

The word **nay** is an archaic way of saying 'No', and I imagine that the word is used today only in a semi-jocular context. A **neigh** is the horse's equivalent of the dog's bark or the cow's moo.

neap, neep

The word **neap** is a noun denoting the pole or tongue of a cart, an adjective describing a tide that occurs after the first and third quarters of the moon in which the high-water level stands at its lowest point, or a verb meaning to become lower. A **neep** is a turnip.

neat

This word is an archaic way of referring to an ox-like animal. Much more commonly, **neat** is an adjective indicating that something is tidy, elegant, cleverly done, or well expressed.

neck

The **neck** we all know is that body part that supports the head and connects it to the shoulders. By extension, the word is also used to describe other narrow and connecting objects. Thus you can have a neck of land, a bottle neck, or the neck of a garment. As a verb, 'to neck' depicts the activity of two people standing or sitting together and kissing and caressing each other.

need *see* **knead**

neep *see* **neap**

neigh *see* **nay**

nerve

In strictly factual terms, a **nerve** is a fibre or bundle of fibres arising from the brain, spinal cord, or other ganglionic organ that serves to convey impulses between the brain and other parts of the body. But the word is also used much more loosely to indicate the bravery, courage and determination with which one approaches a particular task. At times the word can imply impudence or cheek.

net

A **net** is an open-meshed object made of cord or twine and designed to capture fish at sea. It is also the 'goal' in netball and basketball, a matrix of interconnected computers, and a radio network. Quite differently, 'net' also signifies the amount of money left after all deductions like tax have been taken from it, and, more generally, whatever is left in a situation when the necessary deductions have been made.

nettle

Nettle as a noun refers to a herbaceous plant, but as a verb means to irritate or annoy.

new *see* **knew**

nick

If you see a **nick** in one of your clothes, or on a garden post, or on a sheet of paper, then you are likely to assume that the slit or notch in the material has been caused accidentally. Sometimes though a nick can be a deliberate method of keeping tally of something. The word is also a slang verb for 'to thieve', and a disrespectful name for the Devil.

nickers *see* **knickers**

night *see* **knight**

nipper

In one obvious fashion, a **nipper** is something that nips. This might be an animal or a manufactured instrument similar to forceps or pincers. In nautical fields a nipper is a piece of braided cordage used to prevent a cable from slipping. The word is also used to describe a thick woollen mitten used by codfishers to protect their wrists and hands. In Britain it is also a slang word for a small child, normally a boy.

nit

A **nit** is the egg of a louse or other insect parasitic on man or animals. The word is applied to the insect itself in its young state. It is also a slang term of abuse to a person, as well as being an integral part of the word 'nitwit'.

nix

This little word is not common, but it has three quite different meanings. First of all, **nix** is a synonym for 'nothing', but can also refer to a water sprite or be a signal exclamation to warn that someone is approaching.

no *see* know

nob

This is a slang term for the head, and an equally slang term for someone wealthy and important. In the game of cribbage, however, a **nob** is the knave of the same suit as the turn-up card.

nock *see* knock

nod

When you **nod** to someone, you just make a slight inclination of your head towards them. However, if you are in the land of nod, you are asleep.

nog

A **nog** can be a peg, pin or small block of wood serving virtually any purpose. In East Anglia, a nog is a kind of strong beer.

non, none

Non does not exist as an English word, but is an essential part of many Latin expressions that are part of educated English usage, expressions like *non nobis*, *non sequitur* and *non plus ultra*. It is also an essential prefix in many English words like 'non-human', 'non-believer' and so on. As a pronoun, **none** indicates the absence of persons or things. As an adjective, 'none' is rarely used today, but it is common enough as an adverb, especially in the expression 'none the less'.

nor *see* gnaw

norm

If something is the **norm**, then it is likely to be the standard by which any deviations are judged. Hence, in Britain, it is the norm to shake hands with someone to whom you are introduced. In mathematics, however, 'norm' has a much more technical meaning. It is the product of a complex number and its conjugate, equal to the sum of the squares of its real and imaginary components, or the positive square root of this sum.

nose

We are all acquainted with the body part that juts out from our face and whose function is to smell things. The same word, though, is used for the front end of an aeroplane, car or other vehicle. As a verb, to **nose** around is to look around, to pry. If a vehicle attempts to nose through the traffic, it tries to manoeuvre its way forward.

not see knot

note

In its musical form, a **note** is a single tone of a definite pitch. In its written form, a note is a brief communication to someone else. In a financial sense, a note is an article of currency in paper form like a £10 note. In a conceptual sense, a note is a mental determination to remember something.

notice

As a noun, a **notice** is normally a written or spoken declaration of some event or proposed course of action. Hence, on your town hall, you may find a notice of the next meeting of the councillors. If you notice that notice, then you have become aware of it.

nought see naught

novel

If something is **novel**, it is new. As a noun, a novel is a lengthy piece of fictional prose writing.

number

This word is easy to miss as a homonym because its two pronunciations are so different. With the 'b' pronounced, a **number** is a word representing a quantity. You have 2 ears and 2,538 books, and both 2 and 2,538 are numbers. You might decide to number (i.e. find out the sum of) the libraries in your town. Some things, like the stars in the sky, seem to be beyond number. 'Number', without the 'b' being sounded, means that something has less feeling, less awareness than something else: 'After my walk through the snow and ice, my feet were feeling number than G. W. Bush's synapses.'

nut

A **nut** can be the fruit of a plant or tree, a fruit that is enclosed by a hard exterior. It can also be a small metal projection on a spindle, furnished with teeth and engaging in a cogwheel. It is also an informal word for a crazy or eccentric person.

nymph

Most of us think of a **nymph** as being a mythological spirit of nature always imagined as a beautiful maiden inhabiting rivers, woods or other locations, but the word also denotes an immature form of an insect, an artificial fishing fly, or a breed of butterfly.

O

O, o

The fifteenth letter of the alphabet, used to be an exclamation, but has been replaced by 'Oh'. Today it is used in addressing somebody or something, 'O Death, where is thy sting?', for a human blood type, as an abbreviation for oxygen, and sometimes used as a symbol for a circle. It can also be mistaken for the number nought, and is a prefix in Irish names like O'Neill. In lower case, o is often used as an abbreviation for 'of' in expressions like 'a cup o'coffee' or 'nine o'clock'.

oar, or, ore see awe

oath

An **oath** can be a solemn promise, often entailing some invocation of a divine witness. It can also be a profane expression exclaimed in moments of anger or surprise.

object

As a verb, **object** presents no problems. If you object to something, you are disapproving of it. Thus you might object to the Home Secretary, to the building of a housing estate on woodland, or to your neighbour playing Louis Armstrong loudly. As a noun, 'object' presents more problems. First of all it is simply something of which you are aware. You see an object on your chair, and that object could be a letter, a book, a sock, or anything else that can fit on to a chair. There is no moral disapproval attached to any of those possible objects, yet if you say someone made an object of themselves, you are being strongly disapproving, implying that they attracted un-welcome attention to themselves. In English grammar, the object is a substantive word, phrase or clause that is governed by a verb. Thus in the sentence 'Peter kicked the ball', the object is 'the ball' governed by the verb 'kicked'. In games like snooker or croquet, the object ball is the ball that is being aimed at. In philosophy, the object under consideration is the concept or problem that is being discussed.

objective

This word has two quite different meanings. In one sense, it is the opposite of subjective. Hence, if you are being **objective**, you are considering a matter with no preconceptions, no bias, but purely on the grounds of the evidence provided. The other sense is when you have an objective (i.e. a purpose) in mind. Hence it may be your objective this weekend to get the lawn mowed. These, then, are the two customary meanings of 'objective', but there are one or two more specialist ones as well. In medicine, objective observations are those carried out by qualified medical staff rather than the patient him- or herself. In grammar the objective is that which expresses or denotes the object of an action. You might focus a telescope upon an objective, namely an object that you wish to view.

oblique

In the realms of grammar, a case that is **oblique** is any case other than the nominative or vocative. In the realm of communication, something that is oblique is something done by implication rather than directly. In the realm of geometry, a line or plane that is attached to another line or plane at other than a right-angle is said to be oblique.

obscure

If something is **obscure**, it can either be very little known (Shakespeare's use of imagery in *Titus Andronicus*, for example) or be so unclearly expressed as to be incomprehensible to most people (Joyce's *Finnegans Wake*, for example).

observe

If you **observe** something, you notice it, you see it. However, if you observe that the government appears to be run by maniacs, then you are making a comment, you are speaking. Equally, if you observe a strict diet, then you follow a course of action, you adhere to a plan.

obsolete

If something is **obsolete**, it is no longer used, out of date. Thus the word 'eke' is now obsolete, and black-and-white televisions are almost obsolete. For a biologist, however, a part or characteristic of an organism that is rudimentary or vestigial is termed obsolete.

obtuse

In geometry, an obtuse angle is one that is greater than a right angle. In less specialised usage, something that is obtuse is something that is blunt, not sharp or pointed. In informal speech, if you are called obtuse, you are being termed stupid, imperceptive or insensible.

obverse

If something is **obverse**, it is narrower at its base or point of attachment than it is at the apex or top. The obverse side of a coin or medal is the side on which the head of the monarch appears. Most commonly of all, the obverse of something is the opposite of something else. Thus witchcraft is the obverse of medicine, anarchy the obverse of order, and so on.

occasion

An **occasion** is an event, a happening of some note: 'My daughter's wedding was an occasion of great joy.' Sometimes though the word can express a necessity, something that cannot be avoided: 'It was a pity that during one of the most moving episodes in Bach's B-minor Mass, I had occasion to sneeze.' The word can also be a verb when it means 'incurred' or 'caused': 'I occasioned much mirth with my after-dinner speech.'

occlusion

In medicine, an **occlusion** is the blockage or closing of a blood vessel or hollow organ. In meteorology, an occlusion is a process by which the cold front of a rotating low-pressure system catches up with a warm front. In dentistry, an occlusion is the position of the teeth when the jaws are closed.

occupy

This verb can mean to reside in, to live in: 'I had to **occupy** the spare bedroom when my wife had scarlet fever.' It also means to take control of a place, especially a country, by means of military conquest. It also means to work at, to employ: 'I occupy myself by trying to memorise the whole of *Paradise Lost*.'

octave

The most common usage of the word **octave** is a musical one. In this context it denotes the note that is eight diatonic degrees above or below another note. But an octave is also eight lines of verse, most commonly the first eight lines of a sonnet. In ecclesiastical circles, the eighth day after a festival is often called the octave. It can also be a small wine-cask holding thirteen and a half gallons, and there also is a fencing position called in full octave parade.

Od, 'od, odd

Both these first two were abbreviated versions of God in seventeenth-century Britain, and still survive (just) in colloquial expressions like Od's bodikins (God's body), Od-zounds (God's wounds) and Od rot 'em. **Od** was also the name given to the force that according to Baron von Reichenbach (1788–1869) pervaded all nature. The adjective **odd** can relate to a number that cannot be divided by two, to a person or object that is unusual in some way, or to an object that is surplus to requirements. The final definition is still seen in colloquial expressions like 'odd man out'.

ode, owed

An **ode** is a lyric poem, though it is difficult to give any more precise definition because the length and nature of odes can vary considerably. If you are **owed** something, then some person or organisation is in your debt.

of

This tiny preposition is a word that we use so often that we rarely consider the variety of functions that it performs. First of all, it can indicate possession: 'I am a man **of** Devon'; 'These are the books of Megan.' Secondly it can indicate the relationship between a part and the whole: 'the sleeve of his coat'. It can indicate authorship: 'the plays of Shakespeare'. It can indicate cause: 'he died of cancer'. It can express an age: 'a boy of fifteen'. It can indicate the substance of which something is composed: 'The wall was made of brick.' Indeed, 'of' is so frequent a word that its manifold uses have to be picked up idiomatically rather than by rule book.

off

If anything, **off** is even worse than 'of', since 'off' can be an adverb, preposition, adjective, noun or verb. Let us take them in terms of increasing complexity.

Noun: only used in sporting contexts. The horses, runners or cars in a race can be ready for the off.

Verb: the word can mean to leave – 'I offed it to the town' – or to kill: 'She might off a policeman.'

Adjective: in this role, 'off' can mean below par ('I had an off day'), not fresh ('The fish was off'), unfair ('To charge him full price was a bit off'), or unfriendly or rude ('That assistant was a bit off').

Preposition: 'off' can indicate movement ('We needed to get off the platform'), a direction away from the central action ('Stanford Place lies just off Inns Court Avenue'), to be removed or separated from ('It's a huge burden off my shoulders'), and to indicate a temporary dislike ('I'm off watching soaps at the moment').

Adverb: in this role 'off' can indicate departure ('She dashed off to the shops'), to be removed or separated from ('He whipped off his cap'), the beginning of a journey ('We set off for Pembroke'), to bring something to an end ('He broke off his speech'), to indicate that something was not working ('The electricity was off for the rest of the day'), or to indicate possession ('I am very well off for CDs').

office

This word indicates a room in which mostly clerical work is done – 'The filing cabinet is in my **office**' – or the position held by a person in his or her employment – 'I hold the office of chief cashier.' The word also denotes a religious service (e.g. the Office for the Dead), and in some cases the premises or title of a government department (e.g. the Home Office).

offset

As a verb, **offset** has a variety of meanings. It can indicate a sort of equivalence, the way in which one thing offsets or compensates for another: 'The death of her husband was very distressing, but at least it is offset to some extent by the fact that she'll never again have to watch a football match on television.' The noun can indicate that something is out of line: 'These wheels have an offset of four inches.' It is also a printing process and a technical noun in at least four other disciplines. In biology, an offset is a side shoot from a plant, in mountaineering, an offset is a spur in a mountain range, in architecture, an offset is a sloping ledge in a wall, and in plumbing, an offset is a bend in a pipe to carry it past an obstacle.

ogive

In architecture, an **ogive** is a pointed or Gothic arch. In statistics, it is a cumulative frequency graph.

oh, owe

Oh is a simple exclamation that can express surprise, regret or pain. If you **owe** something, you are indebted in some way. You may owe money, thanks or loyalty.

oil

In a world apparently dominated by **oil**, it is difficult not to know that it is a viscous liquid derived from petroleum for use as a fuel or lubricant. A chemist, however, would count any natural esters of glycerol and various fatty acids as oils. In Australia 'oil' is a slang word for information or facts.

old

Although **old** has one normal and unambiguous meaning – something that is advanced in years – it is also used colloquially in a variety of contexts that have nothing to do with age. When you meet Gerald at the pub, you might greet him with the words, 'Hallo, my dear old fellow', even though Gerald is only thirty-seven. Equally you can be an old boy of Eton (or anywhere else) from the age of eighteen. Nor is the old-boy network limited to septua-genarians. You can also be an old hand at weaving, recorder playing or whatever long before you are chronologically old. As always, idiomatic usage defies logic.

olive

The **olive** is an evergreen tree, and the same name is given to the fruit of the tree, and to the colour of that fruit. There is also a gastropod mollusc called the olive, and a button in the shape of the plant olive. Anatomically, an olive is one of a pair of smooth, oval swellings in the medulla oblongata.

omer

An **omer** was an ancient Hebrew dry measure equivalent to the tenth part of an ephah. It was also a sheaf of corn or an omer of grain presented as an offering on the second day of the Passover.

omnibus

Usually, indeed almost invariably, shortened to 'bus', an **omnibus** is an internal combustion vehicle designed to carry passengers. The word was first used in France in 1828, and was adopted in England the following year. An omnibus is also a book that carries stories of the same type (e.g. *A Ghost*

Omnibus) or binds together a number of the writings of the same author (e.g. *A Sherlock Holmes Omnibus*). A bill going through Parliament that contains clauses dealing with a wide variety of topics can be called an Omnibus Bill.

on

Most of the work of **on** is done as a preposition. It can be used to indicate that object A was resting on the surface of object B: 'on the table was a jug', 'the smile on her face', 'it is the house on the corner', and so on. It can point to the topic under consideration: 'This is a book on African wild life.' It can indicate membership of or involvement in something: 'He sat on the finance committee', 'We marched on the CND march', and so on. It affirms that something is being broadcast: '*University Challenge* is on tonight.' It can indicate the timing of an event: 'She was cheered on arriving at the stadium.' This does not exhaust the prepositional usages, but it gives some indication of their range. As a adverb, 'on' can indicate physical contact ('She sat with her boots on'), the fact that some action or event is in progress ('He drove on'), or that some electrical appliance is working ('They left the iron on'). 'On' can even be a noun, since in cricket there is the on side and the off side.

once

As an adverb, **once** either refers to a single occasion – 'He only once hit the target' – or to some time in the past – 'In his youth Graham had once been a very talented cricketer.' The word can also be a conjunction when it more or less means 'as soon as': 'Once the party had started, Fiona began to relax.'

one, won

This pair are not precise homophones, but once again the difference in pronunciation is so slight as to be undetectable on most occasions. **One** is a simple number, and its singularity is reflected in scores of idiomatic expressions: 'one-armed bandit', 'one foot in the grave', 'one-night stand', 'one swallow does not make a summer', 'one-track mind', and so on. Ironically, 'one' can often refer to a great number: 'One cannot go down that road', does, after all, indirectly refer to everyone in the world. If you have **won** something, you have been victorious in some event, be it the Olympic 100 metres, the company's raffle or the Lottery.

only

As an adverb, **only** can signify that something is confined in quantity: 'There were only three biscuits left' or 'Gareth was sustained only by his faith.' Equally 'only' can be a modifier of time: 'Sharon's letter only reached him yesterday' or 'The new drug was discovered only last year.' The word can also be used to depict an inevitability: 'More training will only produce exhaustion.' As an adjective, 'only' signifies something being single or solitary: 'He was an only child.' As a conjunction, 'only' can almost substitute for 'but': 'Clarissa was very like her sister, only even prettier.'

oohs, ooze

When confronted with something that is very surprising or very skilful, many of us respond with **oohs** and ahs. They are virtually involuntary sounds of amazement. **Ooze** is mud, slime or some thick, slow-moving semi-liquid substance that oozes along.

open

Something is **open** when it permits entrance. Thus a stop is open when you can enter it to buy things, a door is open when it is not latched, and a box is open when its lid is removed. Equally something is open when it is clear and apparent: 'Emily's mind is an open book.' Open countryside is country-side that is not over-cluttered with roads, houses and trees. An open mind is one that is not too hampered by prejudice and previous assumptions. As you can see, the word 'open' always carries a conceptual similarity in its numerous applications, but there seems such a difference between the open sea, an open violin string and an open invitation that it is impossible to deny the word homonymic status.

opener

An **opener** can either be an implement that helps to open something – a tin opener, for example – or can be the initial event in an action. The batsman who opens the innings in a game of cricket is called the opener, the player who makes the first bid in bridge is the opener, and so on.

operation

If you go into hospital for surgery, you will be having an **operation**. If a hotel or any organisation opened yesterday for the first time, you can say that it is now in operation. If you devise a business scheme, it might be called the Clarke Operation (or whatever your particular surname happens to be). A calculation in mathematics which requires the manipulation of numbers, quantities or expression is also called an operation. In all these instances, there is an overriding sense of a function being performed, though the disparity of those functions merits 'operation' being according homonymic status.

optic

As an adjective, **optic** refers to the eye or vision, and is sometimes used as a synonym for 'optical'. As a noun, an optic is a lens or other optical component in an optical instrument. You can also encounter a very different kind of optic in a pub. When you order a gin, scotch or vodka, the landlord takes a glass and places it beneath an inverted bottle of the relevant spirit. He then pushes upward and a minuscule amount of the spirit is then released into the glass. This mechanism is called an optic.

or *see* **awe**

oracle *see* **auricle**

oral *see* **aural**

orange

Apart from being a plant from which grows the fruit that we call an **orange**, there is also the colour and an ultra-Protestant party in Northern Ireland. In addition there is a butterfly with orange wings.

orbit

The planets all follow a regular elliptical course round a star, and this is called an **orbit**. Yet the word is extended to mean the area of interest or influence a person or movement can embrace. Thus child cruelty falls within the orbit of Save the Children, while Egyptian irrigation schemes do not.

order

Although the word **order** always carries a sense of arrangement, it has a number of applications within that broad category. First of all, order can signify your rank within an organisation. Angels, for instance, though you may not encounter them very frequently, are actually grouped into nine ranks: seraphim, cherubim, thrones, dominations, principalities, powers, virtues, archangels and angels. No information is available to indicate whether cherubim, for instance, who wish to rise to the order of thrones have to take a written examination. More practically, if you are a member of the church, you are said to be in holy orders, and your specific order can be priest, deacon, bishop and so on. In natural history, an order is a subdivision of a class. In mathematics, equations are divided into orders depending upon their complexity. In classical architecture, there are five Orders. In each of these very different cases, the order to which an object belongs tells you something about its rank. Secondly, though, order might indicate simply a sequence. You are arranging a school photograph, and you arrange the pupils into a specific order, first year on the front row and sixth formers at the back. Thirdly, a group of people might be rioting, and so you call in the police or army to restore order. Alternatively, there might be a very large group of people protesting against some aspect of governmental policy – in Great Britain this is unlikely to be much more than sixty million – yet this massive group behaved with total order. When the Speaker wishes to subdue the riotous behaviour of members of the House of Commons, he shouts, 'Order'. There are also a number of distinctions that can be bestowed upon people that carry this word in their title: Order of Merit, Order of the British Empire, Most Noble Order of the Garter, etc.

ordinary

This extremely common word is not one that many of us ever think about. If something is **ordinary**, then it has nothing terribly unusual or distinctive about it. When you go to work, you are likely to have a perfectly ordinary day, a day very much like yesterday and the day before. Yet the word 'ordinary' has a number of specialist meanings of which most of us are unaware. In civil law, an ordinary is a judge who has the authority to take cognisance of cases in his own right and not by delegation. There is a similar status for a judge in ecclesiastical and common law. In heraldry the ordinary is a simple charge, such as the chief, pale, fesse, bend, bar, chevron, cross or saltire.

organ

An **organ** is a musical instrument which has keyboards exactly like a piano, but which also has a number of pipes supplied with air by means of bellows. An organ is also a part of a living being. Thus a petal, heart, root, liver, leaf and spleen are all organs. The word can also be used metaphorically. Thus *The Bell-Ringer's Gazette* could be described as the organ for all campanologists throughout Britain.

origin

If we talk about the **origin** of something, we talk about the point or place where something begins or arises. Thus the origin of human beings seems to have been in Africa, the origin of computers can certainly be traced back to Babbage's calculating machines in the first half of the nineteenth century, and so on. In anatomy, however, the origin is the more fixed end or attachment of a muscle. In mathematics, an origin is a fixed point from which coordinates are measured.

original

As an adjective, an **original** is something that was present or existing from the beginning: 'This font is the original one, placed there when the church was built in 1157.' The word can also be used to signify that some object is not a copy: 'This is an original Rembrandt.' Perhaps most commonly we describe some work as original when we wish to indicate that it is dependent on no one else's ideas. Each of those adjectival meanings can be transferred into acting as a noun, but there is also the occasional use of the word to denote an eccentric or unusual person: 'Stephen was a real original.'

oriole *see* aureole

Orphism

Orphism was a mystic religion of ancient Greece, and a short-lived art movement within cubism.

ostrich

An **ostrich** is a large, flightless African bird, but the word has also been adopted to refer to a person who refuses to accept the facts or to face reality or to keep up to date. This metaphorical usage stems from the belief that when an ostrich buries its head in the sand, the fact that it then cannot see anything leads it to assume that it also cannot be seen.

ought *see* aught

ounce

The **ounce** is a unit of weight, though it is slowly disappearing in our metrical world. Ounce also used to be the name for the common lynx, though the *Oxford Dictionary of English* tells me that it is another name for the snow leopard.

our *see* hour

out, owt

The word **out** in one sense means exclusion or to be disbarred. Thus if you are a batsman in a game of cricket and are caught, bowled, stumped or run out, then you are out and have to return to the pavilion. If you are a town councillor and fail to gain sufficient votes in a council election, then you are voted out. The word can also mean to be in the open air rather than indoors. 'I'm going out,' shouts your son as he slams the kitchen door. Equally your whole family might decide to go out for a picnic. The word can also signify a failure. 'My calculations were out by about six per cent,' the aspirant accountant might complain. You might also decide to reveal something that had not previously been known: 'The secretary of the NUT came out when he told us that he was gay.' You might extinguish something that was a potential threat. Thus you might knock out a troublemaker, put out a fire, or set out things for sale. There are also, of course, many idiomatic expressions in which the word 'out' plays an integral part: 'out like a light', 'out of sorts', 'out of the blue', 'out of this world', and so on. The word **owt** is a northern dialect word meaning 'something': 'Did you get owt at the sale?'

outfit

This word can refer to the assembly of clothes that someone was wearing – 'Joan's outfit was very becoming' – or to a complete set of equipment – 'Did you bring the first-aid outfit?' – or to a group of people who undertake a particular activity together, like a rock group or a business concern.

over

If something is **over** it is completed. Thus you might arrive at the concert so late that it was over before you arrived. Equally the word can signify that some object is higher than another. Hence you place an umbrella over your head. In cricket, an over is when one bowler has completed his allotted number of balls, normally six. The word also indicates a greater quantity than something else: 'Throughout the season I scored over 60 per game.' The word is also used for indicating movement: 'I rolled over in bed'; 'We travelled all over the Lake District this summer.' There are also, of course, the inevitable idiomatic expressions like 'over the hill' to describe people past their prime, 'over the moon' to describe extreme delight, and 'over the top' to denote excessive or gross behaviour.

overdo, overdue

If you **overdo** something, you carry it to excess. Thus you might overdo your sunbathing sessions on the lawn, and as a result, suffer sun burns. You might overdo the amount of work you do, and as a result become tetchy, tired and impatient. If something is **overdue**, the time for doing it has passed. You might be overdue with a library book and have to pay a fine. You might be overdue to see the dentist, and as a result now need an extraction rather than a filling.

overlook

If you stand on your veranda, you can **overlook** the Wye valley. Thus the word means to survey from a higher position. But it can also mean to miss, to forget, to fail to notice. Thus you might overlook your wallet on the table when you were going out, and discover when you got to the pub that you had no money.

oversea, oversee

The word **oversea** is much more commonly found in its plural form, but it means 'of or pertaining to movement or transport over the sea'. If you **oversee** something, you keep watch over it.

overture

An **overture** is a purely orchestral opening to an opera, intended to set the mood for the drama that is about to follow. Occasionally, however, composers have composed overtures with no opera to follow. This, of course, saves two or three hours' time. An overture is also an approach or proposal made to someone else with a view to establishing some sort of relationship, business or social.

owe *see* oh

owed *see* ode

owt *see* out

Oz

This word is a colloquialism for Australia, the name of the magical country inhabited by the wizard of Oz, and a magazine of the 1960s.

P

P, p, pea, pee

This sixteenth letter of the English alphabet only stands as a single letter when one is told to mind one's p's and q's, though it does stand for an abbreviation on a number of occasions: P (potassium), p (pawn), p (piano) and so on. A **pea**, on the other hand, is a very common vegetable, while to **pee** is to urinate, though it can also be a coat of coarse cloth, the portion common to two veins where they intersect, or, in mining, a small piece of ore.

pace

If you take a single **pace**, you have taken one step, yet as a verb, 'pace' can imply either measurement or speed. If you pace out the distance for your run up, you are trying to ensure that as you lope towards the high jump, you will land on exactly the right foot as you hurl yourself upward. Equally, if you walk at a brisk pace, you are walking quickly. Of course, a word with the same spelling but with a hard c and with an elongated e is a Latin adoption, and is used when you disagree with someone but none the less want to be polite in your disagreement: 'Pace Professor Holmes, but Namier's work is now somewhat discredited.'

paced, paste

If something is **paced**, it is measured out by footsteps. **Paste**, though, can mean a number of things. In cookery, paste is what is produced when one mixes flour, butter and water together. A similar substance is used to apply wallpaper to the relevant wall. Artificially made gem stones are also referred to as paste, and in mining, a mineral substance in which other minerals are embedded is known as paste. One can also have shrimp paste or similar substances composed of minced meat or fish. As a verb, apart from the obvious one of pasting the sitting room wall, you can also paste someone in a game when you overwhelmingly defeat them, or even paste them by physically overcoming them in combat.

pacific, Pacific

If you are a **pacific** soul, you are peaceful in character or intent. The **Pacific** is one of the great oceans of the Earth, but it is also a steam locomotive of a 4–6–2 wheel arrangement and a time zone of the world.

pack

As a noun, a **pack** normally denotes a bundle of things put together in a bag, box or rucksack. Yet a number of animals gathered together or working together can be referred to as a pack of hounds, a pack of deer, a pack of flies, and so on. One can even refer to a pack of human beings, though words like 'gang' or 'lot' are more common here, though you do get instances like a brat pack or the rat pack. One can also have a pack of cards, a pack of ice, or a body pack when a body is swathed in a wet sheet. As a verb, 'to pack' can signify the activity of assembling a bundle of things into a parcel or suitcase, to get rid of ('I packed him off'), or to assemble in close proximity ('We were packed into the bus'). We also have a pack of rugby players forming a scrum, and you might try to pack your nostrils with cotton wool. Inevitably there are idiomatic uses too like pack a punch, a pack of lies, or, from a First World War song, 'Pack up your troubles in your old kit bag'.

packed, pact

This pair are not exact homophones, but close enough to make little difference. **Packed** can be deduced from the entry immediately above, and a **pact** is an agreement of some kind, sometimes between individuals, sometimes organisations, and sometimes countries.

pad

In most cases, a **pad** is something relatively soft that is designed either to increase comfort like a cushion, or designed to clean something without abrading the object being cleaned. The word is also used to denote the sole of the foot, a protection for the leg in cricket, the socket of a brace, the relatively soft sound of footsteps, or, as a verb, to elongate a story.

paddle

A **paddle** is a short pole with a broad blade at one or both ends used for propelling a canoe. In North America it can also be a table tennis bat, or a paddle-shaped instrument used for inflicting corporal punishment. In medicine it can be a plastic-covered electrode used in cardiac stimulation, and in space travel it is a flat array of solar cells projecting from a space craft. As a verb, 'to paddle' can, unsurprisingly, mean to propel a boat with a paddle, to beat someone with a paddle, or, more surprisingly, to walk with bare feet in shallow water. As an idiom, *to paddle one's own canoe* has come to mean the virtue of being self-reliant, the image first being used in a poem in *Harper's Magazine* for May 1854.

paddy, Paddy

A **paddy** is a fit of temper or a field where rice is grown. The name **Paddy** has come to be used as a generalised label for an Irishman.

paean, peon

A **paean** is a hymn of thanksgiving for deliverance or victory. A **peon** is a day-labourer or a foot-soldier, or even, in Mexico, a debtor held in servitude by his creditor until the debt is paid off.

page

You may feel that you know exactly what a **page** is because you are looking at one now, but, apart from being one side of a leaf of a book, a page can also be a boy or lad employed as a servant or attendant, or, occasionally, be a little boy fancifully dressed at a wedding ceremony to bear the bride's train. In the middle ages a page could be a boy in training for knighthood. As a verb, apart from assigning numbers to the pages of a book or magazine, or looking through the pages of a book or magazine, the word can also mean summoning someone over a public address system so as to pass on a message.

pail, pale

The word **pail** is simply a synonym for 'bucket', a vessel with a hooped handle used for carrying liquids like milk or water. As a noun, a **pale** can be a vertical strut in a fence, an area of land, a conceptual boundary – hence you can be 'beyond the pale' – or, in heraldry, a vertical stripe in the middle of the shield. As an adjective, 'pale' means wan or pallid – 'She was pale and drawn' – or unimpressive – 'He was but a pale imitation of Matisse.'

pain, pane

Pain, as most of us know, is the opposite of pleasure, the feeling of discomfort or agony. A **pane** is normally taken to be a section of a window. Thus a window may have one pane, four panes, or whatever, each pane being an individual piece of glass, normally rectangular in shape.

paint

Most of us know that **paint** is a coloured substance which you spread over something like your wall, drawing paper or fence, and that 'to paint' depicts the activity of so doing. However, in North America, 'paint' can be an adjective for a piebald horse (a paint mare), and the name of an area on a basketball court. It is also possible to paint conceptually: 'The Prime Minister painted a grim picture of a Britain deprived of his genius.' A number of clichés have also developed which use 'paint' somewhat figuratively: 'to paint oneself into a corner', to be 'as smart as paint', 'to paint the town red', and women's make-up is often referred to as 'war paint'.

painter

Obviously a **painter** is someone who applies paint, whether it be to create a masterpiece like Leonardo da Vinci's *Mona Lisa* or to change the colour of the bathroom wall. A painter is also a rope attached to the bow of a boat for tying it to a quay.

pair, pare, pear

A set of two is known as a **pair**. Thus you can have a pair of shoes, a pair of trousers (only one item but it has two legs), a pair of tigers, and so on. If an

MP has to miss a vote on some House of Commons issue, he or she will normally seek to pair themselves with another MP of the opposing party so that their absences cancel each other out. If you **pare** something, you trim it, reduce it in size, or prune it. The **pear** is a well-known fruit and the tree upon which the fruit grows. There is also the quaint expression to go pear-shaped, which means 'to go wrong'. Although it only became common in Britain in the 1980s, its actual origin stems from the RAF. When an aircraft crashes nose down, it almost literally does resemble a pear.

palate, palette, pallet

The **palate** is the roof of the mouth, popularly considered to be the seat of taste. It can be metaphorically extended so that it is possible to say 'I find the long vowel sounds in so much of Tennyson's poetry wearisome to my palate.' There is also a technical sense in the field of botany. Here the word means a convex projection of the lower lip closing the throat of the corolla of personate flowers. A **palette** is a thin board or slab on which an artist lays and mixes colours, or, more conceptually, the range or selection of available items. As for **pallet**, this word has a number of meanings, but you are unlikely to have encountered them since they all apply in moderately specialised fields. For the brick maker, a pallet is a flat board for carrying away a newly moulded brick. For the bookbinder, it is a tool for impressing letters on the back of a book. A pallet is also one of the valves in the upper part of the wind-chest of an organ, and a projection on a machine part, serving to change the mode of motion of a wheel.

pale *see* pail

pall, pawl

A **pall** can be a rich covering like an altar cloth and is usually associated with religious contexts. In the same context, a pall can be a garment or vestment. Quite differently, you can have a pall of smoke settling over an area, or even a pall of depression afflicting you. Yet, as a verb, if something palls, it becomes stale and uninteresting. The word **pawl** only seems to exist in nautical contexts. It is each of the short stout bars made to engage with the whelps, and prevent a capstan or windlass from recoiling.

pallet *see* palate

palm

For the botanist, the **palm** comprises a large family of monocotyledons, chiefly tropical. Yet the palm can also refer to the obverse of the hand, the part of a glove that covers the palm of the hand, the flat widened part at the end of an arm of any tool like an oar, or, as a verb, to conceal in the palm of the hand as in cheating at cards or dice.

pan, Pan

A **pan** is a vessel, normally made of metal, in which you place water and the relevant vegetable, and then boil for lunch or dinner. The word is also used to denote a hard substratum of soil which is impervious to moisture. As a verb, to pan means to wash gravel or some similar substance in order to extract any precious metal like gold that may be lurking within the material. You can also in film-making swing or pan a camera so as to move it vertically or horizontally. If you pan a film, novel or play, you criticise it extremely severely. There is also the idiomatic expression *to pan out*, which means to turn out or to happen, and stems, of course, from the activity of panning for gold. Pan is also a common prefix in words like pan-African, pancake, pancreas, pantheism, and so on. **Pan** was the Greek god of flocks and herds.

panda

A **panda** is a bear-like mammal with black and white markings. A panda is also a Brahmin expert in genealogy, who provides religious guidance and acts as a family priest. The police these days have panda cars, so called from their black and white colouring.

pane *see* pain

panel

A typically rectangular piece of wood or glass forming or set into the surface of a door, window or ceiling is called a **panel**. It can also be a piece of material forming part of a garment, a flat board in which instruments or controls are fixed, or a small group of people brought together to interview someone, investigate something, or take part in a quiz show. Apparently in Scottish law, a panel can be a person or people charged with an offence.

panic

A **panic** is a person or group of people being seized by uncontrollable fear. They tend to occur during earthquakes, avalanches and suchlike natural disasters, or during sudden slumps on the Stock Exchange. Panic is also a cereal and fodder grass of a group including millet.

pannier

A **pannier** is normally one of a pair of baskets carried by a beast of burden or on a motorcycle or bicycle. They hang each side of the animal or cycle so as to achieve balance. A skirt looped up round the hips used to be called a pannier, though nowadays only a historian is likely to use the word.

pansy

This is the common name for the flower *Viola tricolour*, and a slang word for someone who is cowardly or effete. In South Africa, a **pansy** is a sand dollar with a flower-like purple marking on the shell.

pap

Pap is a bland, soft or semi-liquid food suitable for babies. The word is also applied to trivial and insubstantial reading matter, and to a woman's breast or nipple. In Africa and the Caribbean, pap can denote porridge. There is also the Pap test, carried out on a cervical smear to detect cancer, and named after George Papanicolaou.

paper

Most of us think of the **paper** as the article that we purchase each day and in which we read about news across the world. But, of course, paper is also the material on which the paper is printed, and one can also draw or write on paper. The word also has a number of quasi-technical usages. Thus you might sit an examination paper, read a government paper, present a paper to a learned society, or hand in your exam paper (i.e. your answers). The word itself comes from the Egyptian papyrus, a plant of the sedge family from which the ancient Egyptians manufactured a writing material.

par, parr

The word **par** normally signifies an equality of value or standing. Thus your position at work as chief desk tidier may be on par with Beryl's position as tea-bag provider. When you visit the USA, $1.50 may be the par rate of exchange for £1.00. In golf, par is the number of strokes that a first-class player should normally require for a particular hole. If you are not feeling very well, you might describe yourself as being a bit under par. A **parr** is a young salmon before it becomes a smolt.

parasitic

If something is **parasitic**, it lives off some other organism. Thus the mistletoe draws its sustenance from trees, and someone who does little work but draws his or her salary can be parasitic on your company. Equally you can have a parasitic disease when some bacterium or virus eats away at one or more of your organs. In phonetics, the word 'parasitic' applies to a speech sound that is inserted with no etymological justification. The 'b' in 'thimble' would be an example.

pare see pair

parity

If two or more things or people have **parity**, then they are roughly equal to each other in size, merit, position, or what have you. In mathematics, two numbers have parity if they are both odd or even. In physics, parity is where the property of a spatial wave equation remains the same – even parity – or changes sign – odd parity – under a given transformation. In medicine, parity is the fact or condition of having borne children. In computing, a parity bit checks on a set of binary values.

park

A **park** is an enclosed stretch of land which may be used as an area upon which people may walk and sit upon the grass to have a picnic, or an area in which animals are kept. As a verb, 'to park' normally indicates the prolonged and technically difficult operation whereby the British find some legal space in which to leave their car while they go shopping. You can, however, park almost anything: 'I parked my folders on your desk, Doris', or, 'I will park the kids next door.'

parley

In North America, 'to **parley**' is to turn an initial stake or winnings from a previous bet into a greater one by betting again. In Britain, though, to parley is to discuss issues with the opposing side in the hope of reaching a negotiated settlement.

parr see par

parrot

While a **parrot** is a bird of the order *Psittaci* and much loved by young children, the word is also used contemptuously to describe someone who is prone to repeat or imitate someone else.

part

As a verb, 'to **part**' means to separate, to leave. Thus you meet a friend in London, but have to part when it is time for you to catch your train home. 'To part' can also mean 'to divide'. You might part the twins because they are squabbling, or you might part your coin collection into two separate display cases. As a noun, a part can be a section of something bigger – 'Harold took part of his cigarette card collection to school' – a role in a play – 'Mary was playing the part of Ophelia' – the melody assigned to a particular voice or instrument, or an area of land: 'Which part of France do you come from?' If you take someone's part, you demonstrate that you support them.

partial

This word can denote something that only exists in an incomplete state – 'We only have a partial answer here' – something that is biased towards one side – 'The French newspapers gave a very partial view of the situation' – or to indicate a liking for something or someone – 'I am very partial to the music of Franck.'

particle

A **particle** can be any one of a number of subatomic objects (electrons, protons, etc.), in mathematics, a hypothetical object having mass but no physical size, in general speech, something that is very, very small, and in English grammar, any of the class of words like 'in, up, off, over, etc.' that are used with verbs to make phrasal verbs.

parting

When two friends separate, there is a **parting**. Indeed, there is a parting when any object or objects leave the purview of another object. Thus there was a political parting when Serbia and Montenegro became separate countries, an emotional parting when X and Y decide to have a divorce, and an intellectual parting when an atheist decides to become a deist. Many people also have a parting in their hair, a thin line which separates the hair brushed one way from the hair brushed in the opposite direction.

party

A **party** can be a celebratory event where a number of people gather together to eat and drink in order to mark something like a birthday, an anniversary, or a festival like Christmas. A party is also a collection of people who have joined together in order to pursue some social or political cause. The Conservative Party would be an example, though, like all political parties, it is not always easy to discern what cause they are pursuing. A party can also be a single person or a group who are on one side of a legal contract or action.

pas, pass

The first of these, **pas**, is a French word meaning 'step, pace', and has been incorporated into English as part of a number of expressions like *pas de deux*. The 's' is not sounded, and so it is not a homophone with **pass**, and since the spelling is not identical either, 'pas' should not really be included here were it not for the British almost total incompetence with languages (including, most of the time, their own). Anyway 'pass' is a manifold homonym on its own. As a noun, a pass can be narrow passageway through mountains or some other obstacle, a successful mark in an examination, a token or voucher that entitles one to admittance to some event or other, a token or voucher that allows one travel on a train, bus, boat or aircraft, the transference of the ball from one player to another in a game of football, or a slightly improper amorous approach to a member of the opposite sex. As a verb, pass means to overtake someone on foot or by vehicle, to achieve success in an exam, to travel through an area, to be changed from one form or state into another or to execute a successful thrust in fencing. Clichés involving 'pass' include to pass the buck, to pass the day, to pass the hat round, and to bring to pass.

passage

When you read a **passage** in a book or listen to a passage of music, you are attending to an extract from the work in question. That, so far as I can see, is the only meaning of 'passage' that does not relate to travel of some sort. Thus you can book a sea passage, watch the passage of birds overhead, observe the slow passage of a bill into law, or encounter someone in the passage or alleyway between the houses.

passed, past

If you **passed** someone on the way to work this morning, you were close enough to them as you overtook them or met them coming in the opposite direction to be aware of their proximity. Nor does it have to be another human being that you encountered. It is perfectly acceptable to use the word in connection with natural objects or man-made ones: 'It was not long after I passed the Wrekin that I also passed St Oswald's Church.' The word can also be used to signify examination success – 'I passed English, history and maths, but failed geology, Arabic and seismology.' Something that is in the **past** is something that occurred some time ago, and, unless it is the very recent past, is the preserve of historians. 'Past' is also a grammatical term denoting tenses of verbs that refer to actions that have been completed: 'I walked to the Post Office this morning.'

passing

As an adjective, **passing** can be used in three different ways. It can denote the movement of time: 'To revise my Estonian verbs, I needed every passing moment.' It can signify something ephemeral or insubstantial: 'He gave him a passing glance.' Finally, it can signify a slight resemblance: 'She had a passing resemblance to Felicity.' As a noun, the word can mean the ending of something ('The passing of the Cold War'), the duration of time ('With the passing of the years, his hair got greyer and greyer'), the death of someone ('The passing away of Derek saddened us all') and the handing over of something to someone else ('Charlton's passing of the ball was superb').

Passion, passion

The suffering of Christ on the cross is often referred to as the **Passion**, but the word in lower case is more generally used to denote either a major enthusiasm – 'I have a passion for the music of Nielsen' – or a romantic or sexual yearning or attachment of considerable intensity.

passive

A verb is **passive** when the subject of the sentence experiences the action that the verb denotes: 'They were beaten.' You are passive when you make no effort. A metal can be passive when it is unreactive because of a thin covering of oxide.

past *see* passed

paste *see* paced

pastoral

If something is **pastoral**, it is associated with country life. Pastoral land is land devoted to grazing animals, normally sheep or cattle. However, an officer of the church has a pastoral responsibility to his flock in that he must attempt to give them spiritual guidance. A teacher too has a pastoral responsibility to his or her pupils, being concerned not only with their academic progress but also with their general well-being.

pasty

A **pasty**, pronounced with a short 'a', is a pastry case filled with meat and vegetables. Something or someone that is 'pasty', pronounced with a long 'a', is very pale.

pat

If you **pat** something, you strike it an extremely light blow so that no hurt is occasioned, and the action can be taken as affectionate rather than hostile. Of course, if you are patting an inanimate object, the action is inspired less by affection than by a desire to level or flatten the object concerned. The word can also be applied to the sound that such an action produces: 'I heard a tap at the window.' Very differently, however, if you do something that was exactly appropriate for the occasion, you can be said to have been extremely pat for the event. In poker a pat hand is one that is so good that drawing other cards is unlikely to improve it. As an adjective, if something is pat it is made to appear simple, glib and somewhat unconvincing. Hence you get a lot of pat answers at Prime Minister's Question Time in the House of Commons.

patch

On first encountering this word, most of us are likely to think of a piece of cloth or other material which is used to mend or strengthen a torn or weak point. Yet a **patch** can also be a pad worn over a sightless or injured eye, an area that is different from its surrounding areas (a bald patch, for example), a small area of land, a particular period of time ('I'm going through a bad patch at the moment'), a segment of computer code inserted into a program to correct a fault, or, in the seventeenth and eighteenth centuries, a black disc of silk worn on the face for adornment. Naturally there are the corresponding verbal equivalents to these nouns.

paten *see* pattern

patience, patients

You will doubtless recall that **patience** is a virtue, a truism that often strikes me as being patently false. However, patience is that calm forbearance in waiting without getting angry or irritated. It is also a variety of card games where one attempts to use all one's cards in some predefined sequence. **Patients**, on the other hand, are sufferers of some medical complaint who are being treated by the doctor, vet or faith healer.

patrol

A **patrol** is an expedition to keep watch over an area. It is also a unit of six to eight Guides or Scouts that form part of a troop.

patronise

If you **patronise** someone, you treat them very much as an inferior. If you patronise a particular store, restaurant or whatever, you go to it with at least moderate regularity. If you patronise a cause, you give it financial or other support.

patten *see* pattern

patter

'To **patter**' is to trot in small steps at a slightly faster rate than a walk. Young children tend to patter; so do horses. Couples wanting to conceive are often said to yearn for the patter of tiny feet. Yet the word can also be used for speech, either somewhat rapid and disorganised speech or the speech of a particular clique like a salesman's patter or a comedian's patter. You could also patter if you were repeating the Paternoster.

pattern, paten, patten

A repeated decorative design on wallpaper, clothes or any other surface is called a **pattern**. A repeated sequence of actions can also be called a pattern. Thus if you rise at 6.00 each morning, make breakfast, go to work, come home at 17.30, eat dinner and then watch television until going to bed at 22.00, your life has an unvarying pattern. However, should your work for Amnesty International be active and unceasing, you could be said to be a pattern to others, i.e. a model that others would be well advised to imitate. Indeed, 'pattern' comes from the same root as 'patron', and a patron is supposed to set an example to others. A **paten** is a Cummunion plate, and a **patten** is a wooden shoe.

paunch

We normally use the word **paunch** when we are commenting on the obtrusive beer-belly of some friend or acquaintance, but technically the word means the first and largest stomach of a ruminant. It also means a thick strong mat made of interlaced spun yarn or strands of rope used on a ship to prevent chafing.

pause, paws

A **pause** is a brief break in some activity. Thus, if you were digging the garden to create a new flower bed, you might have a pause to have a cup of tea and regain your energy. In music, a pause is indicated by the top half of a circle with a dot placed between the two lines at the diameter point. A paw is the foot of a cat-like animal, and so **paws** is more than one such foot. To paw something is to handle it in a somewhat inconsequential and casual fashion, and so you could say, 'He paws the neck of the horse in an abstracted manner.'

pawl *see* pall

pawn

A **pawn** is the least valuable piece in the game of chess, or a thing (or person) left in another's keeping as security for a debt.

pay

When you buy something in a shop, you have to **pay** for the article with money. But you may also, from time to time, have to pay attention to something, and if you forget your wife's birthday, you may have to pay for that omission with your life. There are conceptual similarities between those three usages, but paying money, paying attention, and paying for a mistake are surely different enough to be accounted as homonymic. In addition, of course, you can pay a visit, pay a compliment, or pay your respects. Apparently, if you are told to pay the deck of a wooden ship, you will be expected to seal it with tar or pitch in order to prevent leakage.

pea *see* P

peace, piece

Peace is the opposite of war, a condition of freedom from disturbance, conflict or dissension. Slightly differently, peace can also be the opposite of noise, a state of quietude and calm. A **piece** is normally a portion, bit, part or fragment of a larger entity. Thus you may have mislaid a chess piece, bought a piece of land, fastened a piece of jewellery to your dress, or have rehearsed a piece of music.

peach

A **peach** is a round stoned fruit with juicy yellow flesh, but the word can be used metaphorically to signify an exceptionally good or attractive person or thing. The word can also be used colloquially as a verb meaning 'to inform on'.

peak, peek, pique

If you reach the top of a mountain, you have reached its **peak**. The word can also mean a projecting point, like the peak of a man's hat, the narrowed frontal part of a ship, or the two peaks of a bay at sea. The word is also used more metaphorically. Thus your performance last night of Beethoven's Opus 111 piano sonata was so sublime that it was described by the journalist from the *Market Drayton and Newport Advertiser* as being the peak of your career. The verb 'to **peek**' means to look at somewhat hastily and secretly. Thus you might peek through a crevice in the rock at the sunbathers on the beach, peek round a curtain at Mrs Harris rehearsing the part of Lady Macbeth, or take a quick peek at Boris's collection of Etruscan coins. If you feel **pique**, you are feeling somewhat irritated or offended. Hence you might feel pique when your so-called friend Felix described your voice as sounding like gravel being shaken in a tin can. Equally, having dressed in your finest for the opening of the new aquarium, you might be piqued when you discovered that everyone was looking at that blatantly exhibitionist girl Wendy from the finance department. Perhaps I ought also to mention the Pekinese, a small dog much favoured by old ladies in Kensington, and often abbreviated to a **Peke**. However, they are absurd animals, so perhaps I won't mention them.

peal, peel

Every Sunday you are delighted to hear the **peal** of bells from your local church. You are, though, less delighted to be walking in your nice summer frock down by the canal when you hear the peal of thunder. Hence a peal is an outburst of sound, and the verb is normally applied to bells, guns, laughter or thunder. As a verb, 'to **peel**' means to remove the outer layer of something. Thus you can peel an orange by removing its skin, peel off your clothes for a shower, or peel the potatoes for lunch. 'To peel' also means to send another player's ball through a hoop in the game of croquet. As a noun, a peel is a shovel-like instrument used for thrusting bread and pies into the oven or the outer covering or rind of a fruit or vegetable. It can also be a small square defensive tower built in the sixteenth century in the border counties of England and Scotland.

pear *see* pair

pearl, pirl, purl

A **pearl** is a nacreous concretion formed within the shell of various bivalve molluscs, and extracted from the shells to be used as a jewel for the adornment of women. Metaphorically you might describe your secretary as a pearl, particularly when she has just saved you from some foolish blunder. Perhaps **pirl**, a verb meaning to twist, wind or spin threads into a cord, is too archaic to be included, but I believe that it is still used in some dialects and/ or scientific contexts. In knitting, a **purl** stitch is one where the wool is inverted, producing a ribbed appearance of the surface. As a verb, a stream or river can be said to purl when it flows with a whirling motion.

peck

Once upon a time, a **peck** used to be a measure of capacity for dry goods, equivalent to the fourth part of a bushel. For most of us, though, a peck is an action taken by birds as they attempt to extract food from a nut, a fruit or a milk bottle. A brief and entirely meaningless kiss on someone's cheek is also called a peck. So too is a horse's stumble.

pectoral

As an adjective, **pectoral** relates to the breast or chest. As a noun, it is either the pectoral muscle or an ornamental breastplate.

peculiar

As an adjective, **peculiar** denotes something different or unfamiliar, as in: 'He wore very peculiar clothes.' Sometimes though it can mean specific, as in 'Learning Basque presents difficulties peculiar to that language.' As a noun, a peculiar is a church that is exempt from the jurisdiction of the diocese in which it lies.

pedal, peddle

A **pedal** is a lever worked by the foot. 'To pedal' is to operate such a lever, as on a bicycle. As an adjective 'pedal' means pertaining to the foot. However, 'to **peddle**' means 'to trade, to deal, to sell', and the verb is traditionally associated with a pedlar.

pediment

In architecture, a **pediment** is the triangular upper part of the front of a classical building, typically surmounting a portico. In geology, a pediment is a gently sloping expanse of rock debris extending outwards from the foot of a mountain slope, especially in a desert.

pee *see* P

peek *see* peak

peel *see* peal

peep

As a noun, a **peep** can be a feeble, high-pitched sound made by a young bird or mammal, a quick or furtive look, or, in North America, a small sandpiper or similar wading bird. To peep also means to take a peek or to peek at something.

peer, pier

As a noun, a **peer** is someone who is your equal in status. With one of those numerous absurdities that makes the English language so endearing, the word 'peer' also refers to a member of the nobility, someone who, by definition, is not equalled in status by many. As a verb, 'to peer' means to look earnestly at. Hence you peer at the horizon to see if you can see your vagrant son, or you peer at the *Mona Lisa* to see if you can interpret her smile. For most of us, a **pier** is a structure extending from the shore into the sea and along which you can normally find lots of slot machines and possibly a theatre or ballroom. However the word can also mean a support for a bridge.

peewee

A **peewee** can be one of any number of birds that emit a sound that sounds very much like 'peewee', but in North America the word is used to denote a level of amateur sport that involves children, and, in the days when children played marbles, a peewee was a small marble.

peg

Normally a **peg** is a short object of wood or metal which protrudes from a wall and on which coats and other articles can be hung. However, a pin or bolt that is driven into the ground and used to hold one of the ropes of a tent is called a tent peg, and a small, pincer-like object used for securing clothes to a line is called a clothes peg. You can also ask for a peg of whisky, and might refer to someone's legs as his pegs. The word also has a number of idiomatic uses: off the peg, bring someone down a peg or two, peg away, peg out, etc. PEG is also an abbreviation for polyethylene glycol.

pelt

A **pelt** is the skin of a sheep or goat or, indeed, any fur-bearing animal. The verb 'to pelt' means to strike repeatedly. Thus it can pelt with rain, air missiles can pelt a city, or you can pelt with your fists some enemy of yours. On occasions, pelt can also mean 'to run rapidly': 'I will just pelt to the Post Office.'

pen

A **pen** is a writing instrument. Once upon a time it used to be the quill pen, which is appropriate since the word 'pen' comes from the Latin *penna*, meaning 'a feather'. Then it was followed by one with a metal nib that you had periodically to fill with ink. These days it tends to be the fibre-tipped variety. A pen is also an enclosure for animals, and the tapering cartilaginous internal shell of a squid.

pence, pents

These are not quite homophones, but near enough, one feels, to make no difference. **Pence** is the quaint plural for penny, and there are a hundred pence in a pound. A pent is a sloping roof or covering, and so **pents** will be more than one of them.

pend, penned

The verb 'to pend' means that awful feeling when you know that something is going to happen, but you don't know when: 'The fear of redundancy was allowed to pend over the men for a fortnight.' If something is **penned**, it is enclosed in a fenced-off area much smaller than its usual habitat. Thus sheep might be penned into an enclosure when the farmer needs to give them all an injection.

pendant, pendent

Apart from the fact that **pendant** is a noun and **pendent** is an adjective, the meanings of these two words are virtually identical. A pendant is an ornament that can be seen hanging from a roof, tree, neck or arm, while you could describe a pendent necklace or a pendent rope, meaning 'hanging' in both cases. Both words are derived from the Latin *pendere*, to hang.

penetrate

This verb means 'to go into', and although this meaning is present in all the uses of **penetrate**, those uses are so diverse that we have to count the word as a homonym. Thus you might want a tunnel to penetrate 600 yards into the rock face, as a spy you might want to penetrate ICI so as to learn secrets of their proposed development, as a publisher of computer books, you might want to penetrate the university market, and as a student you might wish that the oddities of the German gender system could penetrate your mind.

penitence, penitents

These two words are closely related. **Penitence** is the state of regret and shame that overcomes you when you have done something wrong. **Penitents** are the people who are so afflicted with this feeling of remorse.

peon *see* paean

pep, PEP

If you put **pep** into something, you liven it up, make it more interesting and lively. If you have pep, you have energy, high spirits and enthusiasm. A PEP is a personal equity plan, though the abbreviation has, by now, almost made the full phrase redundant. The three letters can also stand for political and economic planning, though this is much less common, presumably because political and economic planning is so rarely undertaken.

per, purr

Per is a Latin preposition meaning 'through, by, by means of' which has been incorporated into English, sometimes in an original Latin expression like per capita, but often as a native English word in expressions like 'per person'. A **purr** is the low vibratory sound made by a contented cat.

perch

A **perch** is a common, spiny-finned European freshwater fish, a pole set up in a river or the sea to serve as a mark for navigation, anything serving for a bird to rest upon, a measure of length equal to a quarter of a chain, a measure of area equal to 160th of an acre, or a wooden bar, or frame of two parallel bars, used in examining cloth, blankets, etc.

perfect

If someone or something is **perfect**, it is without flaw. In mathematics, a number is perfect if it is equal to the sum of its divisors. Thus six is perfect because it can be divided by one, two and three, which, added up, come to six. In grammar there is also the perfect tense, which denotes a completed action or a state that began in the past: 'They *have eaten* their ice creams.' In botany a flower is perfect if it has both carpels and stamens present and functional. As a verb, the emphasis is on '-fect' rather than the 'per-'. If you per*fect* something, you improve it so that it is without faults.

period

Most frequently a **period** is an extent of time: 'I spent a period of time in the garden.' In astronomy the word is made more precise, since a period is the length of time taken by a planet or satellite to complete a revolution around its sun. In physics too the word tends to be used to describe any portion of time taken by the single duration of a recurring process. In chemistry a period is a set of elements occupying one horizontal row in the period table. In English grammar a period is a synonym for a full stop. For women, the period is the monthly occurrence of blood being released from the uterus to escape down the vagina.

perk

As a noun, a **perk** is a benefit to which you are entitled because of your rank or position. As a verb, 'to perk' is a casual way of saying 'to percolate'. The word is also often used in connection with 'up' when it means 'to enliven': 'She seemed to perk up last week.'

perm

A **perm** is a method of setting the hair in waves, but it is also a permutation, especially when selecting matches in a football pool.

permit

As a verb, 'to **permit**' means 'to allow, to grant permission to'. As a noun, a permit is normally a slip of paper that allows entrance to a building or allows a specific activity to be performed. A permit is also a deep-bodied fish of the jack family.

perpendicular, Perpendicular

Something is **perpendicular** if it is at 90 degrees to a given line, surface or plane. In England, churches from the late fourteenth to the mid-sixteenth centuries were built in the **Perpendicular** style.

person

We all know what a **person** is. It is a human being. But it is also a category used in the classification of pronouns and verbs.

persuasion

Brian is frightened about twisting his ankle, and so he needs a lot of **persuasion** to accompany you in an ascent of Cader Idris. Persuasion, thus, is the act of persuading someone to do something that they are initially reluctant to attempt. The word can also be used to signify a set of beliefs: 'Cynthia was of the Roman Catholic persuasion.'

pestle

A **pestle** is usually associated with a mortar, because a pestle is a club-like instrument used for pounding a substance in a bowl known as a mortar. Most of us encounter a pestle and mortar only in science labs at school. Apparently though, a pestle can also be the leg of certain animals used for food.

pet, PET

A **pet** is a domesticated animal much favoured by its owner or owners. Cats, dogs and canaries are common pets in Britain; bison, sharks and vultures much less so. The word is also often used in reference to human beings, particularly by aunts and uncles referring to their smiling and compliant nephews and nieces. People can also be given pet names. Thus the staid and ultra-respectable financier Sir Horace Probity is called Tiger by his wife. However, the word 'pet' can also signify a fit of ill humour. If your sister steals your boyfriend, you might get into a real pet with her. The acronym PET stands for polyethylene terephthalate.

peter

Apart from being a common male first name, the verb 'to **peter**' means 'to decrease, to fade away'. As a noun, 'peter' is one of the innumerable slang words for a penis, a safe or trunk, a term in the game of bridge, or, in the Antipodes, a prison cell.

petit, petty

Basically these two words are the same as each other. **Petit** is an adjective used in legal contexts, and it means 'trivial' or 'insignificant'. Hence you can be fined for petit larceny. **Petty** is a word more generally used, but it too means 'trivial' or 'insignificant'. 'Jean is petty in insisting that none of the women ever wears trousers.'

petrify

This verb can mean to change organic matter into a stony substance, or to terrify someone so much that they are unable to move. The conceptual link between these two meanings is obvious.

phase *see* **faze**

phew *see* **few**

phial *see* **file**

phlox *see* **flocks**

phone

Apart from being the universally used abbreviation for telephone, a **phone** is also the smallest discrete segment of sound in a stream of speech.

phosphorous, phosphorus

Phosphorus is one of the chemical elements, a yellowish translucent substance, and consequently **phosphorous** is an adjective indicating that something is abounding in phosphorus.

pi, pie

Many of us will remember **pi** from our school days. It is, of course, a Greek letter of the alphabet (the sixteenth), but is used in maths to express the ratio of the circumference of a circle to its diameter. The word can also be used as a slightly contemptuous abbreviation of 'pious'. A **pie** is a dish of meat, vegetables or fruit that is covered by a layer of pastry and baked in the oven. It can also be an abbreviation for the magpie, and there are types of woodpecker that are called French pie, rain-pie or wood-pie. A pie also used to be the smallest Anglo-Indian coin equal to one-twelfth of an anna.

piano

Strictly speaking, **piano** is an abbreviation for 'pianoforte', but you very rarely hear the full name. Consequently the piano is a percussive musical instrument where keys are hit by one's fingers and those keys act as levers so that metal strings are hit by hammers. Piano is also an Italian word meaning 'softly' or 'quietly' and is used as a dynamic instruction on pieces of music.

pica, pika

Pica is a type size, though also a perverted craving for substances unfit for food. A **pika** is a small rodent allied to the guinea pig.

pick

A **pick** is a tool consisting of a curved iron bar tapering to a point at one end and used for breaking up roads, rocks and other hard substances. It is also the cast or throw of the shuttle in weaving, the best of the items available from a selection, or a speck of hardened ink or dirt that gets into the hollows of the type during printing and causes a blot on the printed page. As a verb, if you pick something, you select an item from the ones available, and normally, of course, you pick the best.

picker

Obviously a **picker** is someone who picks, whether it be an engagement ring or peas in a field. The word does, however, have a number of more technical meanings. In agriculture, a picker is a sort of mattock or pickaxe. In the textile industries, it is a machine for separating and cleansing the fibres of cotton, wool and so on. In mining, at least in Cornwall, a picker is a miner's hand chisel. In founding, a picker is a light pointed steel rod used for lifting small patterns from the sand into which they have been rammed. More colloquially, you could be a picker of quarrels.

picket

Perhaps in modern days we think of a **picket** as being a member of a trade union who, when the union is on strike, tries to persuade other workers from going to work. The word, however, has much older meanings. It can be a pointed stake, post or peg driven into the ground, a small detached body of troops sent out to detect the approach of the enemy, or an elongated rifle bullet.

pickle

A **pickle** can be a vegetable or fruit preserved in vinegar or brine, a difficult situation, or an acid solution for cleaning metal objects.

picks, pix, pyx

Picks is obviously the plural of the nouns listed immediately above, and the third person singular present tense of the verb. **Pix** and **pyx** are alternative spellings of the same word which means a box or coffer. The box in which the consecrated bread is kept for Mass is called a pyx, as is the box at the Royal Mint where gold and silver coins are kept prior to being tested.

picnic, pyknic

A **picnic** is a simple meal outdoors. The entire family decide that they would like an afternoon on Snowdon or by Chew Lake or wherever, and you make some sandwiches, cut a few slices of cake, and take a couple of bottles of orange squash. As you eat these delicacies in the car as you shelter from the unexpected rain, this is a typical British picnic. The word **pyknic** does not appear in the *OED*, or my edition of the *Shorter*, but it does exist, and means a human being who has a stocky physique with a rounded body and head, thickset trunk and a tendency to fat.

pidgin, pigeon

Pidgin is an adjective normally placed before the word English to signify that the English being spoken is an uneasy mixture of English and the native tongue of the speaker. The term 'Pidgin English' was originally applied to a form of Anglo-Chinese jargon which developed on the China coast from the seventeenth century. 'Pidgin' itself is a alteration of 'business', and you might say, 'That's not my pidgin' when disavowing any knowledge of or connection with something that your boss or your friend wants to lever in your direction. A **pigeon** is a bird similar to the dove, though someone inexperienced in some art or craft can also be called a pigeon. Pigeons are apparently very easily caught by snares. Hence in the criminal word, rogues and their dupes are called 'rooks and pigeons'. In military slang the word 'pigeon' denotes an aircraft from one's own side.

pie *see* pi

piece *see* peace

pier *see* peer

pig

Although we all think of a **pig** as that grunting animal that provides us with pork, a pig can also be an oblong mass of metal or, in northern dialects, an earthenware pot. The word is also used as a label for a disgusting and unclean person. As a verb, the word means to crowd together, to give birth to piglets, or to operate a pig within an oil or gas pipeline.

pigeonhole

As the word would suggest, a **pigeonhole** can be a small recess for a domestic pigeon to rest in, but it can also be an open-fronted compartment in a workplace where one's letters are left, or a category into which people are placed: 'I was a teacher for ten years, and even now people pigeonhole me as being pernickety, bloody-minded and humourless.'

pike

This is a versatile word. A **pike** can be a pickaxe, a sharp point at the end of a staff, a mountain or hill (especially in the Lake District), a large, voracious freshwater fish, and a toll-bar or toll-gate.

pile

Many humans, being less than perfectly tidy, tend to accumulate a **pile** of newspapers in the lounge, a pile of books beside the bed, a pile of clothes in the laundry basket, or a pile of CDs beside the hi-fi system. In other words, a pile is a heaped collection of objects, evidence, according to my tidy friends, of a disordered mind and a lack of self-respect. Yet the word can also be applied to hair, or to man-made objects with a hairy surface. Thus one can talk about brushing the pile of a carpet or the whiteness of a sheep's pile. Pile is also a disease characterised by tumours of the veins of the lower rectum, though this is almost universally referred to as 'piles'. One can refer to an imposing building as a pile, and a series of plates of dissimilar metals laid one on another alternately to produce an electric current is also known as a pile.

pill

Most of us assume that a **pill** is a small, hard tablet or sphere prescribed to us by the doctor in order to cure some ailment or, for a woman, to prevent herself becoming pregnant, and that we obediently swallow three times a day or whatever. However, the word has other manifestations too. Since the pill is associated with illness, it can also be metaphorically transferred to any task that is disagreeable: 'Having to apologise to Mr Smith was a hard pill to swallow.' The word can also be used as a shortened version of pillage, to denote a small cannonball, and, on both sides of the Bristol Channel, to describe a tidal creek on the coast. In the USA from the 1870s onwards, a pill was a tiresome or annoying person, and this usage was common in Britain in the first half of the twentieth century.

pillar

Since a **pillar** is a vertical structure of metal, wood, stone or brick often used to support some superstructure like a ceiling, the word is often extended to refer to people who help to support organisations or events: 'Mrs Brand is a pillar of the Women's Institute.' The word can also be used to indicate a central idea or concept: 'Sonata form was the pillar of Haydn's symphonic writing.'

pilot

A **pilot** can be a person in charge of flying an aircraft, or a trial run for a television or radio programme, or a scheme or project that is tried out before introducing it more widely.

pin

Most of the time, a **pin** is a thin piece of metal with a sharp point at one end. It can, though, also be a small broach, a metal peg that holds down the activating lever of a hand grenade, a peg round which one string of a musical instrument is wound, a metal projection from an electric plug, a move in chess that prevents an opponent's piece from moving, or a skittle in bowling.

pincer, pincher, pinscher

A **pincer**, or, more commonly, a pair of pincers, is a tool made up of two pieces of metal with blunt concave jaws that are arranged like the blades of scissors, and used for gripping and pulling things. It can also be the front claw of a lobster, crab or similar crustacean. A **pincher** is someone who pinches, though that can mean a painful nipping of flesh between finger and thumb or the act of stealing. An Internet source tells me that a **pinscher** is a terrier dog, but I was unable to find the word in any of my dictionaries. However, a tipoff from a friend enabled me to find **Doberman pinscher** in *Collins English Dictionary* where I learnt that this was a fairly large, slender but muscular breed of dog with a glossy black-and-tan coat.

pinch

If you **pinch** someone, you take a small portion of their flesh between a finger and your thumb and squeeze sharply and briefly. Traditionally men are supposed to wander around pinching ladies' bottoms, though I have never seen anything to support this myth. Unsurprisingly, the word can also be used for other instances when skin is painfully compressed. Thus one's shoes might pinch one's feet. You may also be so poor that you have to live very frugally i.e. pinch your way through life. You may also pinch a plant by removing its buds or leaves so as to encourage a bushy growth. You might hold a pinch of salt (a very small amount) between your thumb and finger. Finally, and most common usage of all, the verb 'to pinch' means to steal.

pincher *see* pincer

pine

The **pine** is a tree of the genus *Pinus*, and, as a verb, means to languish or waste away through grief of some nature.

pineapple

Apart from being a large, juicy tropical fruit, a **pineapple** is also an informal term for a hand grenade.

pinion

A **pinion** is the distal or terminal segment of a bird's wing, a small cog-wheel, or, as a verb, means to shackle in some fashion.

pink

Most of us think of **pink** as a pale red colour, but the word is also used to denote a small sailing vessel, a young salmon, a garden flower, or the most perfect condition (I am in the pink). As a verb, pink can be used to describe the activity of making small holes in a substance or, in some dialects, to wink or look slyly at someone or something. More informally, 'pink' can denote left-wing tendencies, or an association with homosexuals.

pinole

This is a game of cards rather like bezique or, in the USA, a meal made from parched cornflour mixed with sweet flour of mesquite-beans or with sugar and spice.

pinscher *see* pincer

pip

Pip is a disease of poultry, each of the spots on a playing card or die, or a star on an army officer's uniform. You can also pip someone to the post, meaning that you just beat them in some race or contest.

pipe

Most of the time a **pipe** is a cylindrical tube, usually made of metal, that carries gas, water or vapour from A to B, but it can be a generalised name for some musical instruments, a command in computing that causes the output from one routine to be the input for another one, an instrument for placing in the mouth and drawing up the smoke of burning tobacco into the mouth, or a large cask for beer, cider, beef, fish, and so on.

pipeline

We normally think of a **pipeline** as being a long pipe, typically underground, for conveying gas, oil, etc. over long distances, but it can also be a channel or system for conveying goods or information from one place to another, in computing, a linear sequence of specialised modules, or, in surfing, the hollow formed by the breaking of a very large wave.

pique *see* **peak**

piracy
Traditionally we think of **piracy** as the activity of attacking and robbing ships at sea, but the word is also used for the unauthorised use of another's work.

piscina
Today a **piscina** is a stone basin near the altar in Roman Catholic and pre-Reformation churches for draining water used in the Mass, but in ancient Rome it was a pool or pond for bathing or swimming.

pistil, pistol
A **pistil** is the seed-bearing organ of a flower, while a **pistol** is a hand gun which it is to be hoped you do not use. The word 'pistol' probably derives from the Italian city Pistoia, which was famous for making weapons.

pit
A **pit** is a large hole in the ground, or an area reserved for some specific purpose like the orchestra pit at the opera or the refuelling area for racing cars. It is also used for the vertical shaft that marks the entry point to some mining operation; hence coal pit, copper pit, etc. The word is also used to denote a small indentation in one's skin, and is slang for a bed.

pitch
If you wish to ensure that your ship does not allow water to enter between its planks, you are likely to coat those planks with **pitch**. This is a tenacious, resinous substance obtained by boiling tar or distilling turpentine. If you pitch a ball, you throw it in some fashion, and consequently the word is often applied in the sports of cricket and baseball. If you are a singer, you will want to get the pitch of your voice exactly right so that it is in harmony with the piano or orchestra that is accompanying. You can also apply the word to the speaking voice: 'His voice had a low pitch.' The word can also be used to indicate the degree of slope that something possesses: 'That hill is at too great a pitch for granny to manage.' As you doubtless know, a number of sports are played on a grass pitch (football, cricket, hockey, etc.), a salesman when trying to persuade you to buy something will deliver his impassioned pitch, in a storm a ship may pitch or sway from side to side, and the word is often used to indicate the intensity of something: 'On his first day, Stephen worked at a very high pitch.' There are further nuances to the word, but at least this listing gives you some idea of the homonymic range that 'pitch' can cover.

pitta
Pitta is a flat, hollow, slightly leavened bread which can be split open to hold a filling. A pitta is also a small, ground-dwelling thrush-like bird found in the Tropics.

place, plaice

A **place** is a spot, a location, an area where someone or something is situated. Hence the word can refer to something extremely precise like just in front of the door of No. 12 Union Street, or to quite a wide area like the Lake District. The word can also refer to one's position in society, and, after over a century of the Labour Party and its supposedly egalitarian creed, it is still important to know one's place. As a verb, 'to place' means to position, to arrange, to set out. Hence you might decide to place the vase of wall flowers on the mantelpiece. As the governor of an orphanage, you may also need to place your entrants into suitable homes. In a race, the entrants are labelled as coming in first place, second place or what have you. A **plaice** is a European flat fish, much eaten in Britain with chips.

plague

A **plague** is a contagious bacterial disease, but the word is also used to describe an excess of some undesirable element. Thus you may be plagued with a plague of flies, regard all estate agents as a plague upon humanity, or be assailed by your children with a plague of questions.

plain, plane

A **plain** is an open, and flat area of countryside very useful for growing wheat. The word can also be an adjective. If you describe something as plain, you are likely to mean that it is uncluttered by irrelevancies, that it is relatively easy to understand, or that it is uncluttered with a pattern. If you describe a person as being plain, you might mean that they are no beauty, that their face is unremarkable to the point of tedium. Plain is also a type of knitting stitch. A **plane** is a tree of the genus *Platinus*, a tool resembling a plasterer's trowel, a tool used by carpenters for levelling a piece of wood, or a widely used abbreviation of the word 'aeroplane'. As an adjective, 'plane' has almost the same meaning as 'plain' in that it means perfectly flat and level.

plait, plat

If you **plait** something, you interweave its strands into a firmer entity. It used to be the fashion for girls with long hair to have their hair plaited into two plaits secured at the end further away from the head by a fabric bow. While one might think that 'plait' ought to be a homophone with 'plate', it fact it sounds exactly like **plat**, a word that can mean a flat surface or, more usually, a small patch of ground.

plant

We are all accustomed to the living organism that grows in one's garden, in fields and in woods. This is a **plant**. But the word is also used to denote a place where industrial or manufacturing procedures take place (a car plant, for example), and a person placed in a group as a spy or informer is known as a plant. When someone places in your locker the new designs for an vertical take-off helicopter, hoping thereby to get you dismissed as a spy, that too is a plant. In snooker a plant is when the cue ball hits another ball thereby causing a third ball to be moved.

plasma

This is the colourless part of blood, lymph or milk in which fat globules are suspended. **Plasma** is also an ionised gas, a translucent variety of quartz, or a shortened term for cytoplasm or protoplasm.

plaster

When we cut our finger or graze our knee, we are likely to put a **plaster** on it, an adhesive strip of material for covering cuts and wounds. But plaster can also be a soft mixture of sand and cement and sometimes lime with water for spreading on walls and ceilings to form a smooth hard surface when dried. There is also plaster of Paris, a hard white substance used for holding broken bones in place or for making sculptures and casts.

plastron

This is a large pad worn by a fencer to protect the chest. It can also be the ornamental front of a woman's bodice, a man's starched shirt front, or, in zoology, the underside part of a turtle or tortoise's shell.

plate

A **plate** can be a flat sheet of metal, a thin plate organic structure, the portion of a denture which fits to the mouth and holds the teeth, a thin sheet of metal, porcelain or glass coated with a film sensitive to light on which photographs are taken, or a thin, flattish circular piece of china, earthenware or whatever on which food is placed to be eaten. There are specialist meanings in biology and geology also. If you plate something, you cover it with a thin layer of another substance. If you are overburdened with things to do, you are said to have a lot on your plate.

platform

As a physical entity, a **platform** is a raised level surface on which people or things can stand, but a platform can also be the declared policy of a political party or other organisation.

plating

The **plating** of an object is the thin coating of metal that has been applied to it. It is also the process of knitting two yarns together so that each yarn appears mainly on one side of the finished piece, and the racing of horses in which the prize for the winner is a plate.

play

A **play** is a fictional drama staged normally in a theatre for the pleasure of the attending audience. As a verb, though, 'to play' means to take part in any activity from crosswords to rugby, from hang gliding to chess undertaken almost solely for the participant's pleasure. There is also the slightly different instance of playing a musical instrument. Your eight-year-old son may not enjoy practising his scales on the piano, but he is still playing. You can also play a fish stuck on the end of your hook until the poor creature is too exhausted to struggle any more. The word occurs in countless idiomatic expressions: play ball, play footsie, play fast and loose, play gooseberry, play hookey, and many more.

pleas, please

A plea is either a suit or action at law, or an earnest request or cry for help. Hence **pleas** are two or more of such actions. **Please** is either a verb meaning 'to give pleasure', or a word that polite people add to any request they may make.

plenary

If you make a **plenary** promise, that means that it applies to all who are involved in the matter under discussion. Thus, for example, the Pope offered a plenary indulgence to all who went on the Crusade. If you attend a plenary meeting, that means that it was attended by everyone.

pleural, plural

A pleuron is the lateral part of the body wall, and hence the adjective **pleural** relates to anything connected with or pertaining to the pleuron. The adjective **plural** denotes anything that is more than one in number. It is also a grammatical term. Hence 'I' is singular, but 'we' is plural.

plonk

If you **plonk** something down on the table, you shove it on to the table heavily and carelessly. If you drink plonk, you drink cheap and inferior wine. If you plonk away on the piano, you play the instrument unskilfully and with little dynamic range.

plot

A **plot** is the story line of a novel, short story or play. Thus the plot of *Macbeth* concerns the ambitions of a great warrior who is urged by his wife to kill the existing king and take over the throne himself. However, you can also have a plot of land, an area devoted to some activity or other. Hence you can have a building plot, a garden plot, or a recreation plot. A plot can also be a plan, usually devious, to secure some desired end. You might, for instance, have a plot to make the Green Party into the governing party of the British Isles. A plot can also be a graph showing the relationship between two variables.

plough, Plough

A **plough** is a farm instrument used for turning over the soil. As a verb, though, while it is obviously applied to the activity of land tilling, it is also used for clearing snow, to describe the progress of a heedless and inconsiderate driver ('He ploughed his way through the traffic'), and to indicate a slow and painstaking attention to detail ('She ploughed her way through the textbook on economic history'). More informally still, it can indicate that you have failed an exam ('Michael ploughed in his chemistry paper'). The **Plough**, of course, is part of the constellation of Ursa Major and is sometimes referred to as the big dipper.

pluck

If you **pluck** a chicken, you pull off its feathers. If you pluck the strings of a guitar, you twang those strings with your fingers. If you pluck off your jacket, you hastily remove it. So 'to pluck' means to pull off or twitch with your fingers or hand. If you have pluck, you have courage. As the American sage Emerson commented, 'The one thing the English value is pluck.'

plug

If you **plug** something, you insert something into an object so as to stop the entrance or exit of any other material. You might plug a hole in a wooden chair so as to prevent the entry into that hole of a carpenter wasp. You will put a plug into your bath when you want to have a bath. A dentist plugs one of your teeth when a hole has been created in it. But a plug is also the object that is placed into an electric socket so that you can operate the cooker or vacuum the floor. More recently, the word has been used as a synonym for advertise. Thus an author visits book shops throughout the country to plug his or her most recent book.

plum, plumb

A **plum** is the fruit of sundry trees of the genus *Prunus*. If you have a plum job, you have an easy, undemanding and well-paid one. Figuratively, if you describe Lianne as the plum of the cast, you imply that she is the most outstanding performer. A **plumb** is a small weight attached to a string which is used to ensure that something is completely vertical. In cricket the word is also used to describe a pitch that is completely level. If you plumb a lake, you establish its depth. If you plumb someone's mind, you understand them completely. Much more practically, if you plumb you carry out the sort of activity for which plumbers are employed.

plume

A **plume** is a long, soft feather or group of feathers displayed by some birds or worn in some ladies' hats. It can also denote a long cloud of smoke or vapour, or, in geology, be a localised column of hotter magma rising by convection.

plump

If you are a **plump** person, you are chubby, of a full and rounded form. But you can also plump for something, which means that you select it. Hence you plumped to read history at university because it was the subject that most interested you.

plunk

As a verb, you can **plunk** a keyboard or stringed instrument in a mechanical and inexpressive way, or you can place something heavily or abruptly upon something else ('She plunked her case upon the table'), or, in the USA, you can hit someone abruptly. The noun instances of the word are simply parallels to the verbal usages.

ply

As a noun, **ply** can signify the thickness or layer of a material. Thus a piece of yarn can be two-ply to eight-ply. The word is also often used as an abbreviation for plywood, and, in a game like chess, ply denotes the number of levels at which branching occurs in a tree of possible outcomes. As a verb, 'to ply' can mean the activity of working steadily at some task ('She plied at her knitting all afternoon'), or denote a regular transport system ('The ship plies between Dover and Calais every day'). You can also ply someone with food and drink. Car and lorry tyres also have a ply rating indicating the strength of a tyre casing.

poach

If you **poach** on someone's land, you are walking or whatever on land that is not open to the public. You may be on this land because you want to poach some game illegally, namely, steal it. If you are a doubles tennis player, you may poach a ball, namely, return a ball that would more properly have been left for your partner. To stamp down something with your feet is also to poach, though I have never heard this usage. You can also poach an egg, which is a process of cooking the egg by enveloping it with steam.

pocket

A **pocket** is a cavity in your jacket or dress in which it is possible to put loose change, your keys or any other small items. If you pocket something, you put the item concerned in your pocket, though the verbal form often implies that you have done so illegally. Billiard and snooker tables also have pockets into which the balls fall. The word can also be used to indicate small isolated groups ('There were pockets of resistance in Cheshire'). Because pockets on jackets or snooker tables are fairly small, the word 'pocket' has consequently become an adjective for lots of fairly small objects: pocket watch, pocket money, even a pocket battleship.

pocks, pox

If you pock someone, you mark them with disfiguring spots. Hence having the pock or the pocks indicates that you have a disease characterised by pustules, a disease like small**pox**. The words 'pock' and 'pocks' have, however, been largely displaced by pox.

pod

A **pod** is the elongated seed vessel of peas and beans, the egg case of a locust, a narrow-necked purse for catching eels, a body of rock or sediment whose length greatly exceeds its other dimensions, a small herd of marine animals like whales, or a detachable or self-contained unit of an aircraft, vehicle or vessel that has a particular function.

poi

This is a Hawaiian dish made from the fermented root of the taro, or a small, light ball of woven flax swung rhythmically on the end of a string in Maori songs and dances.

point

This word takes four columns in the *Shorter Oxford*, and it certainly does have a variety of uses. A point can be a small dot indicating a precise position. It can also be the nub of an thesis that you are trying to expound: 'The point of the government's human rights legislation is that, instead of protecting human rights, it removes them.' This point that you have made can be described as your point of view. If something tapers to a sharp end as a sword or pair of compasses do, then the sharp end is called the point. A point on the railways is where a line splits into two alternatives and, according to how the point is set, the train is forced to take one of the alternatives. A fielder on a cricket field who is positioned more or less in line with the war memorial is said to be standing at point. If a passerby asks you where the war memorial is, you may with your arm point him or her in the right direction. So, as we can see, 'point' is an invaluable word, and there are innumerable idiomatic expressions: point of order, case in point, point of view, point of honour, point of no return, cardinal point, and so on.

pointer

A **pointer** is normally a thin piece of metal which points to some measurement on a dial, or a dog that stands still pointing in the direction of the game being sought.

pointing

The action of **pointing** is to indicate with a raised arm the direction in which someone needs to go or to direct their attention to something at which you want them to look. Pointing is also the insertion of punctuation into a piece of writing, as well as the insertion of strong mortar into the joints of brickwork. For a yacht, pointing is the action of sailing with the prow close to the wind. It is also the insertion of points on a railway track.

poise

We all want to have **poise**, the graceful and elegant bearing that indicates composure and dignity. Few of us, however, are likely to know that poise is also a unit of dynamic viscosity, such that a tangential force of one dyne per square centimetre causes a velocity change of one centimetre per second between two parallel planes separated by one centimetre in a liquid.

poke

Most of us think of **poke** as a verb meaning to thrust with a finger or some object like a poker or a stick, and this, of course, is quite accurate. Figuratively too the same concept is preserved when someone is accused of poking their nose into someone else's affairs. But the word can also be a noun and mean a small sack, a morbid bag-like swelling on the neck, a bag growing under the jaws in a sheep, a contrivance fastened upon cattle, pigs, etc. to prevent them from breaking through fences, or a name for the American species of *Phylolacca*. One must also beware of buying a pig in a poke. Someone would try to sell a pig in a sack (a poke), whereas, in fact, the sack was filled with a cat, and the buyer did not realise this until he got home and released the 'pig'. Hence too, of course, the origin of the expression of letting the cat out of the bag.

polar, poler

If something is described as being **polar**, it indicates that it is connected in some way with the North or South Poles of the Earth. Thus snow bears are polar, and a magnet is polar because it is orientated towards the poles. If two objects or ideas are polar opposites, it means that they could not be more widely different from each other, just as the north and south poles are as widely separated from each other as they can be. The word is consequently often used in physics to indicate forces opposed to each other. A **poler** is anyone who uses a pole, but the word has specific currency for those who propel a barge or punt by means of a pole.

pole, Pole, poll

A **pole** is a long, slender and cylindrical object, normally made of wood, which is used as a support for tents, telegraph wire or climbing plants. It is also the trade sign for a barber, a ship's mast, each of the two points of the celestial sphere, each of the two terminal points of an electric cell, or a species of deep-water flounder. These days we are also treated to pole dancers, erotic ladies who drape themselves suggestively around a vertical pole. A **Pole** is someone who lives in or comes from Poland. A **poll** is a method of gauging human sentiments on any controversial issue by asking a sample of those humans what their feelings are. Hence you could have a poll on bringing back the death penalty, growing organic food, or the efficiency of the National Health Service. The word itself is of Germanic origin and means 'the head'. Hence, by conducting a poll, you are counting heads. A poll is also a semi-humorous name for a parrot, a rare label for the head, a label for animals with horns, or a name for an act of plunder.

poler *see* **polar**

polish, Polish

If you **polish** the furniture (or anything else), you rub it, possibly with a prepared substance called polish, in order to make it brighter, cleaner and/or more supple. If someone or something is Polish, it comes from Poland.

politic, politick

To be **politic** is to be sensible and judicious in the circumstances that confront you. **Politick** is not listed by the *Shorter Oxford* and the *Oxford Dictionary of English* merely cites it as an alternative and archaic spelling of 'politic'. I am not so sure. I think that 'politick' is still sometimes used, and always with the connotation of somewhat devious and underhand politics.

polo

This is, perhaps, a dubious entry. **Polo** is normally thought of as being a game where people on horseback armed with long-handled clubs try to score goals into the opposing side's goal. However, there is also a ball game with goals played by swimmers and called water polo, and a similar game played on skates and called rink polo. Finally, of course, there is a circular mint sweet with a hole in it that is called Polo.

polyp

This is a solitary or sedentary form of a coelenterate such as a sea anemone, or, in medicine, a small growth, usually benign, protruding from a mucous membrane.

pommel

A **pommel** is a rounded knob on the end of the handle of a sword, dagger or old-fashioned gun, or the upward curving or projecting part of a saddle in front of the rider.

pone, pony

The leader, or the leader's partner, is called the **pone** in some card games. A **pony** is a small horse and slang for £25.

pontoon

A **pontoon** is a flat-bottomed boat, and the name of a card game.

poof

Apart from being a derogatory term for a homosexual, **poof** is also used as an exclamation to indicate contemptuous dismissal ('Poof, Robert, you can't expect me to believe that') or sudden disappearance ('Miranda was talking to Claude, then, poof, she was gone').

pool

A small body of standing water is called a **pool**, but the same name is applied to the collective amount of the stakes laid down in a game, a snooker-type game in which each player has a ball of a distinctive colour, a contest in which each rifle-shooter pays a certain sum for every shot he fires, and the process in coal mining where the coal is undermined so as to cause it to fall.

poor, pore, pour

If you are **poor**, you have little money or few material possessions. Compilers of homonym dictionaries fall into this category. But you can also be poor in less materialistic ways. Hence your vocabulary may be poor, your spiritual insight may be poor, your physical coordination may be poor, and so on. A **pore** is a minute opening or orifice through which liquids may be able to pass. Thus humans have pores on their skin, and plants have them on their leaves. The word is also a verb meaning 'to look intently'. The verb **pour** means to emit in a stream. Thus it can pour with rain, a river may pour strongly along its course, or you may pour yourself a cup of tea. That last example is itself interesting because you don't actually pour the cup at all.

pop

A **pop** is a sharp, short sound, the sort that you get from the crack of a rifle, or the removal of the cork from a bottle of champagne. The word is also a casual synonym for 'father', a fizzy drink of the lemonade variety, a brand of popular music almost entirely lacking in merit, and a social and debating club at Eton College. As a verb, you can pop a question when you rapidly and without warning fire a question at someone.

popery, pot-pourri

Popery is the slightly insulting label given to the practices and beliefs of the Roman Catholic Church. A **pot-pourri**, which does sound astonishingly like 'popery' despite the wide difference in spelling, is a mixture, normally of the petals of different flowers mixed with spices, though the word is often used to signify a mixture of almost anything.

popper

This is a colloquial name for a press stud, an equally informal name for a small vial of amyl nitrite, or, in fishing, an artificial lure which makes a popping sound when moved over the surface of the water.

populace, populous

Populace means the mass of the population, though the word is frequently used in a pejorative sense, signifying the unlettered and uncultured mob, i.e. those who don't consult dictionaries of homonyms. If an area is **populous**, it is densely populated.

pore *see* poor

porridge

This is an oatmeal dish boiled in water or milk, or a time spent in prison.

port

A **port** is a place on the coastline where ships are able to shelter from storms or load and unload goods. The same word is sometimes used for a gateway, usually one within a town or city wall, the opening in the side of a ship for exit and entrance, the manner in which one carries oneself (he had a stately port), a strong, dark-red wine from Portugal, or a naval term for 'the left side'.

portal

This is an opening or gateway, or an Internet site providing a link to other sites. In anatomy, a **portal** is an opening in an organ through which major blood vessels pass, and the portal system relates to the system of blood vessels.

porter

A **porter** is a person employed to carry luggage or other loads, or a dark brown bitter beer.

pose

If you **pose** for an artist, you assume a specified position and maintain it while he or she draws or paints you in that pose. Less formally, we all of us adopt different poses for differing contexts. If you are being interviewed by the chief constable of North Yorkshire, your pose is going to be very different from the one that you adopt when lounging by the swimming pool. So a pose is an attitude or posture of the body. However, you might also decide to pose a question. Here you are querying a situation or seeking fuller understanding, so here 'to pose' means 'to question, to query, to put forward an alternative situation' and so on.

position

This is an interesting word because, although we rarely think about it, it has a number of varying meanings. For most of us most of the time, a **position** denotes the place occupied by a thing: 'I always position my husband's photograph on the bookcase because he is always buried in a book.' 'The pub is positioned appropriately between the church and the school.' But the word has a number of more technical meanings. In logic, the position is an affirmation. In arithmetic, a position is a method of finding the value of an unknown quantity by positing one or more values for it, finding the error as indicated by the results, and then adjusting it. In military jargon, a position is the site chosen for occupation. You can also have a position in society, and if you are the Countess of Suffolk and president of the Landed Gentry Guild, your position is regarded as higher than that of a bus driver or academic.

positive

If you are **positive** about something, you are either very enthusiastic about it or feel that the matter concerned admits of no doubt. If you are positive about your child's progress in Icelandic, you feel that he or she is making progress. An electric current is positive if it has a higher electrical potential than another point. A positive number is one greater than zero.

post

A **post** is a stout length of square or cylindrical timber used in a vertical position as a support or barrier. The post is also the collection of useless free offers that the postman delivers most mornings (together, perhaps, with more relevant items). The post you hold at work is the position that you occupy within a company. The post is the place where a soldier is stationed. In book-keeping, to post is to carry or transfer an entry from an auxiliary book to a more formal one. You post a boat by attaching or mooring it to a post, though you can also post a boat by publishing its name as overdue or missing. The word is also an integral part of many Latin expressions like post mortem, and the prefix for many words like postcard or postscript.

pot

A **pot** is a vessel of rounded form, deeper than it is broad, made of earthenware or metal, and used to hold liquids or solids. 'To pot' is to make such objects on a potter's wheel. The word is also used as a slang word to denote a large sum of money, cannabis or a large stomach. As a verb, 'to pot' can also mean the planting of a flower or vegetable in a pot, to transfer crude sugar from the coolers to perforated pots, or to knock a ball into a pocket in billiards or snooker.

potent

If a person or substance is **potent**, it possesses great power. More informally, a man is potent if he can easily achieve an erection.

pot-pourri see popery

potted

Obviously something that is placed in a pot is **potted**, but the word also means the presentation of some relatively complex matter in a short and simplified fashion: 'I have just written a potted history of Uganda.'

pounce

We are most likely to think of **pounce** as a verb meaning 'to swoop down on' or 'to spring suddenly', the sort of action associated with birds of prey, cats upon mice, and journalists upon so-called celebrities. However, the word can also denote a fine powder, an action in embossing metal work by raising the surface, or the action of cutting a garment into points and scallops.

pound

In Britain the **pound** used to be a weight. Hence you could go to the shops and ask for three pounds of apples or eight pounds of potatoes. Indeed, you can still do this, but increasingly the pound is being replaced by the kilo, and one will soon not have to know that there are 16 ounces to the pound in avoirdupois, but only 14 ounces to the pound in troy weight. The pound also used to be a value of money equal in value to 20 shillings or 240 pence. In our decimal world, the pound still survives, but is now equal to 100 pence, and shillings have vanished completely. Apart from being an almost obsolete weight, and a decimalised currency, a pound can also be an enclosure for animals, an apparatus for crushing apples, or, as a verb, the action of beating heavily upon something: 'He pounded on the door.'

pour *see* poor

practice, practise

I suspect that quite a lot of English natives don't know the difference between these two words. **Practice** is a noun, and **practise** is a verb. A practice is the action of doing something, a method of working: 'It is my practice to learn ten Russian verbs before breakfast.' A practice is also the method of procedure in the law courts, and in some cases like lawyers and doctors, the exercise of a profession. Of course, you are likely to practise your Russian verbs by reciting them on the bus as you travel to work, and no doubt most doctors have to practise their patience every time they have a surgery.

praise, prays, preys

If you **praise** someone, you commend them, you applaud their efforts or abilities. The verb 'to pray' means to beseech or to ask for. No doubt the Archbishop of Canterbury **prays** to God every day. Although a verb like 'to pray' is normally used within a religious context, it is perfectly valid to use it more widely. The verb 'to prey' can mean to plunder and pillage, to kill, or to exercise an unhealthy and damaging influence upon. Thus the lion **preys** upon the deer, the blackmailer preys upon his victim, and the tax man preys upon us all.

pray, prey

As is obvious from the entry immediately above, 'to **pray**' means 'to beseech', but **prey**, apart from being a verb meaning 'to plunder' or 'to kill', is also a noun meaning that which is taken in war or by violence.

precedence, precedents, presidents

If someone is regarded as being more significant or important than others, then that person is likely to be granted **precedence**. Thus at the Lord Mayor's dinner, the lord mayor him- or herself will be given the best position at the table, will be served first, and no one will leave the table until the lord mayor has done so. A precedent is a previous example of some action or ruling, and so **precedents** is simply the plural of that word. Thus, for instance, there are ample precedents for believing that blasphemy is an illegal act that is no longer regarded in Britain with any great seriousness. A president is the governor or leader of an organisation, a province or a country. Thus there have been many **presidents** of Balliol College, Oxford, of the Privy Council, and of the USA.

precious

Something that is **precious** is something that means a lot to its owner. Hence you may have your grandfather's Bible, which is probably worth now about 25p but is none the less precious to you because you know how much it meant to him. Of course, some things are precious without any sentimental value at all, and some jewels are automatically termed precious because they are made up of minerals like diamond, ruby and so on that are valued in our quaint society. The word 'precious' also has a third meaning which is very different. If you call someone 'precious', you are implying that he is affected, absurd in some rather pretentious way. You can also term an activity precious when it strikes you as being ludicrous in some quasi-snobbish way. Some television 'celebrities' are precious because their self-importance contrasts violently with their almost total lack of talent.

preen

A bird is often known to **preen** itself when it trims its feathers with its beak. A human also preens him- or herself when the person concerned ensures that they are immaculately clean and tidy. Yet in Scotland and some northern areas of England, to preen means to fasten with a pin.

premium

One's **premium** is the amount that has to be paid for a contract of insurance, a sum added to an ordinary price, a bonus, the amount by which a share or other security exceeds its issue price, or something given as a reward, prize or incentive.

presence, presents

If something happens in your **presence**, then you are there to witness it. Equally, of course, your presence may be demanded at the AGM of your company. But 'presence' can also mean something striking or impressive in a person's carriage, demeanour or bearing. **Presents** are what you get at Christmas, gifts received from others. The word can also be a verb. When Julia Green presents Nancy Hedge to Mark Stoddard, she is introducing him to her. When you present *West Side Story* to the population of Nantwich, you are introducing your particular production of that work to the lucky inhabitants of the Cheshire town.

presentation

A **presentation** is giving of something to someone, especially in a formal ceremony. A presentation is also a speech in which a new product, idea or piece of work is shown and explained to an audience, or the position of the fetus in relation to the cervix at the time of delivery. The Presentation of Christ is another term for Candlemas.

presidents *see* precedence

press

This word can be a verb meaning 'to exert pressure' as in 'He pressed my hand'. It can also mean 'to burden, to weigh down' as in 'Worries about my debts continually **press** me down.' Verbally, the word can also mean 'to urge on, to encourage', as in 'I wish my uncle wouldn't continually press me to have trombone lessons.' As a noun, a press can be a machine for printing things, a collective noun for publishers, particularly newspaper publishers, a tightly packed crowd, or a now extinct method of forcing people to join the armed services.

prevail

This verb can mean to win a victory because you or your arguments or forces were too strong for your opponent. The word can also mean to persuade: 'Can I prevail upon you to go round with the cakes?'

prey *see* pray

prick

As a noun, a prick can be the act of piercing someone or something with a sharp point, the sensation of feeling a sharp point prick you, the penis, or a stupid man.

prickly

Something is **prickly** if it is capable of pricking you, but the word can also be used metaphorically so that you might raise a prickly subject, namely one that is likely to rouse some heat and resentment in the assembled company.

pride, pried

Depending upon your moral stance, **pride** is either a major sin or a major virtue. If you have an overweening opinion of your own talents, achievements or possessions, then you have the sort of pride against which most religions fulminate. If you take pride in doing a good and fair job, then most people will praise you. For no very clear reason that I can detect, a pride is also the collective noun for a company of lions. Presumably it would be unwise if you **pried** into a company of lions, because 'pried' is the past tense of the verb 'to pry' which means 'to spy, to look at closely'.

pries, prize

You are normally annoyed if someone **pries** into your affairs. As you can see, 'pries' is the third person singular present tense of the verb 'to pry', and the British traditionally dislike anyone prying into their affairs. A **prize**, on the other hand, is to be welcomed, because it is an award gained, either as a result of chance (lottery, raffle, etc.) or as a reward for merit (Nobel Prize, victor ludorum prize at school, etc.).

prime

Something that is **prime** is of the first importance: 'Dr Hargreaves is the prime scholar in Britain of tropical butterflies.' Something that is prime is of the highest quality: 'These chicken breasts are prime.' Something that is prime has all the typical characteristics of its type: '*Clarissa* is a prime example of the epistolary novel.' A prime number is one divisible only by itself and 1. The prime position in fencing is the first of the eight parrying positions. As a verb, if you prime something, you get it ready for use or action.

prince, prints

A **prince** is normally the son of the reigning monarch, or possibly a title awarded by a grateful (or corrupt) government for outstanding services to the state. The word can also be used metaphorically to denote supreme excellence. Hence John Smith could be the prince of gymnastics, Tom Brown could be the prince of horse jumping, and so on. **Prints** is not quite a homophone because of the 't' sound, but once again, the difference is scarcely detectable in everyday life. 'Prints' can be products of a printing press: 'I received prints of my article today.' Alternatively it can be the third person present tense of the verb 'to print'.

principal, principle

A **principal** is the head of an organisation, often, in Britain, a college. The principal can also be a sum of money that is lent to some organisation, and consequently gains interest while it remains borrowed. In law, a principal is the person responsible for a crime. The word is also used for each of the combatants in a duel, a main rafter supporting purlins, and an organ stop sounding a main register of open flue pipes. A **principle** can be a fundamental element, a general law, an ultimate edict. Hence you might regard it as a principle to treat people as you would wish to be treated yourself. The reason that alchemy died out is because it offended against the principles of chemistry.

prior, pryer

A **prior** is the superior officer in a religious house. As an adverb, prior indicates that event A occurred before or prior to event B. A **pryer** is someone who pries into things, and is therefore a blot on the landscape and a social pariah.

private

A **private** is the lowest rank in the army, but when the word is used as an adjective, it has no martial connotations. If something is private, it is secret to one person or a small group of people. There are also private schools where parents choose to pay for their children's education rather than receiving it free from the state. The same system applies in the medical profession.

profit, prophet

All businessmen want to make a **profit** from their business. Profit is the excess money that is left when all expenses have been covered. Hence profit is the gain that one makes from a transaction. But profit may not be materialistic. You may gain great profit from listening to Bach's organ music, or reading the poetry of Pope, or watching your son learn to walk. Here the gain is not tangible, but still very real. A **prophet** is someone who is able to foretell the future. A number of the books of the Bible were supposedly written by prophets (Isaiah, Daniel, Hosea, etc.). According to the Koran, the holy book of Islam, there have been 200,000 prophets, but only five of them (Adam, Abraham, Moses, Jesus and Mohammed) brought in new laws.

promise

A **promise** is an assurance that person A will do something, like fetch you a loaf of bread from the market, or make Britain a wonderful place in which to live, like the Prime Minister promises. A promise can also be rather vaguer and more uncertain: 'The clouds look as if they promise rain.' Promise can also be the potential that someone displays: 'Hilda has considerable promise on the clarinet.'

promotion

If you are offered a higher position in your workplace, then you are offered **promotion**. But promotion can also mean the advertising of an event or the giving of money and support to a cause.

prompt

If you are **prompt,** you arrive somewhere on time. If you prompt someone, you help them speak their lines in a play or master the intricacies of some task.

proof

If **proof** is provided for something, its validity is demonstrated beyond reasonable doubt. In printing, a proof is a trial impression of a page used for making final corrections. Proof is also the strength of distilled alcoholic spirits.

pros, prose

The word **pros** is a commonly used abbreviation for 'professionals', and is the opposite of amateurs. Pros are also arguments or factors in favour of something, and are normally contrasted with the antis, that is, arguments against the proposed matter. An issue like abortion gathers large numbers of pros and antis. **Prose** is the sort of English that we all read every day in the newspaper, in our library books, and so on. It is the sort of English that you read in this dictionary

> Whereas were I to write like this,
> You'd think it verse that you'd like to miss.

So, prose and poetry are the two basic ways of writing, and prose is much the more common because it is much easier to write than poetry.

prune

A **prune** is a plum preserved by drying, but the word is sometimes used as a derogatory label for a disagreeable person. As a verb, 'to prune' means to trim a tree, bush or shrub. One might also prune the typescript of a book to remove errors and lapses in taste before it is published.

psalter, salter

A **psalter** is quite simply a book of psalms. A **salter** is someone who manufactures or deals in salt.

psi, sigh, xi

psi is the 23rd letter of the Greek alphabet, though knowing this is unlikely to be useful even in the most abstruse of pub quizzes. However, if you are regarded as being psi, it is supposed that you possess parapsychological or psychic powers. A **sigh** is a slow, low-sounding exhalation of breath, normally indicative of grief, puzzlement or pure irritation. **xi** is the 14th letter of the Greek alphabet.

puff

As a noun, a **puff** can be a short, explosive burst of breath or wind, a light pastry case, a very favourable review of a book, film or play, an advertisement, also of a wildly praising nature, a gathered mass of material in a dress, or a rolled protuberant mass of hair.

pull

As a verb, to **pull** something is to exert force on someone or something so that the object or person is forced to move towards you. But the movement does not have to be physical. You can attract a member of the opposite sex (or the same one, for that matter), so that they feel pulled towards you. Your advertising can pull people into your theatre. A pull is also a stroke in cricket.

pun

For most of us, a **pun** is a disease of those who enjoy playing with words. It uses words that have different meanings but sound the same to create a joke or ambiguity. Shakespeare is very prone to puns. Mercutio in *Romeo and Juliet* says this as he is dying: 'Ask for me tomorrow, and you will find me a *grave* man.' But the verb 'to pun' does not only mean playing with words. It can also mean consolidating earth or rubbish by pounding it.

punt

As a noun, a **punt** is a long, narrow, flat-bottomed boat that undergraduates at Cambridge are fond of easing along the River Cam. As a noun and verb, punt can mean to kick a ball some considerable distance.

pupal, pupil

Pupal is an adjective used to indicate that an insect is in the state between larva and adult. A **pupil** is one who is taught by another, or the dark circular opening in the centre of the eye.

purl *see* pearl

purr *see* per

puttee, putty

Puttee is a Hindi word for a garment, that comprises a long strip of cloth wound spirally round the leg from the ankle to the knee. **Putty** is a fine mortar or cement made of lime and water without sand.

pyknic *see* picnic

pyx *see* picks

Q

Q, q
The seventeenth letter of the English alphabet, and is a homonym with **cue** and **queue**.

quack
A **quack** is the sound made by a duck, or someone pretending to be a doctor, though quite often the term is extended to include any fraudster pretending to knowledge in any occupation. Hence you could be a quack solicitor, a quack architect or whatever.

quad
A **quad** is one of four children born of the same mother on the same day. It is also the universal abbreviation for 'quadrangle', a square or rectangular space surrounded on all sides by the walls or buildings of a palace, university college or cathedral. A quad can also be a group of four insulated conductors twisted together, usually forming two circuits. A radio aerial in the form of a square or rectangle is also called a quad, as is large spaces used in letterpress printing. A four-wheeled roller skate is colloquially referred to as a quad.

quadrature
In mathematics, **quadrature** is the action or process of squaring, as in the expression of an area bounded by an arc or circle by means of the equivalent square. In astronomy, a quadrature is one of the two points in space or time in which the moon is 90° distant from the sun. It can also be the position of one heavenly body from another when they are 90° apart.

quadrilateral
This can be an adjective describing any figure that is bounded by four sides. It can also be a noun denoting the space lying between and defended by four castles.

quadrille
A **quadrille** can be a card game played by four persons with forty playing cards, the eights, nines and tens of the ordinary pack being discarded, a square dance of French origin, a piece of music for such a dance, a ruled grid of small squares, or one of four groups of horsemen taking part in a tournament.

quadruplex
In electrical telegraphy, a **quadruplex** system is one in which four messages can be sent along the same wire simultaneously. In engineering the word is used for an engine in which the expansion of steam is used four times in cylinders of increasing diameter.

quail

A **quail** is a bird allied to the partridge family, or a verb meaning to cower away, to be frightened.

qualify

If you **qualify** for something, then you have the necessary qualifications and/or experience for the position under consideration. If you qualify something, then you modify it or express certain doubts about the current state of it.

quark

A **quark** is any of a number of subatomic particles carrying a fractional electronic charge. It is also a type of low-fat cured cheese.

quarrel

We are all acquainted with the situation when we have a violent disagreement with someone else. This is a **quarrel**, and can be used as a noun or a verb in the normal way. You may not, however, have known that a quarrel can be a short, heavy, square-headed arrow or bolt formerly used with the cross-bow, or a square or diamond-shaped window used in making lattice windows.

quarry

Typically, a **quarry** is a large deep pit from which stone of some nature has been extracted. A quarry is also an animal being pursued, or a diamond-shaped pane of glass as used in lattice windows.

quart

A **quart** is an English measure of capacity, namely, a quarter of a gallon. It can also be a position in fencing.

quarter

A **quarter** is a fourth part of something. Hence 4 is a quarter of 16, spring is a quarter of the year, and so on. But the word can be used much more loosely to indicate a rough locality: 'He lives in the Latin quarter.' You can also be quartered in Edinburgh when you are posted there as a soldier, policeman or what have you. Entirely differently, to give quarter means to give mercy.

quarts, quartz

Clearly **quarts** is the plural of **quart**, while **quartz** is a crystalline rock.

quay *see* key

quean, queen

Although **quean** is not, I think, in the current vocabulary, it used to mean a bold or ill-behaved woman, and Shakespeare uses the word in this sense in at least three of his plays. A **queen** is the wife or consort of a king, a ruler in her own right, the leading female among bees, wasps and ants, the most powerful chess piece, a court playing card or an effeminate male homosexual.

queer

This word used to be an adjective meaning 'strange, odd, peculiar', and is, indeed, still used in this fashion, but increasingly these days **queer** is used as a noun meaning 'a homosexual'. As a verb, queer can also be used in the sense of spoiling something, cheating or imposing upon. There is also the strange expression 'Queer Street', which is an imaginary street where people in difficulties are reputed to live.

queue see cue

qui see key

quick

If something is **quick**, it is alive, a usage most frequently encountered in the expression 'the quick and the dead'. If something is quick, it can also denote that the object or person concerned is rapid or brisk in motion, though someone can be called quick who is also mentally alert. The soft tender flesh below the growing part of a toenail or fingernail is also called the quick.

quid, Quid

A **quid** is either a lump of tobacco for chewing, or a casual term for one pound sterling. **Quid** was the name given to a section of the American Republican Party in 1805–11.

quiet

Something that is **quiet**, can either be making no noise, or can be restrained and soothing in appearance. Hence an audience will be quiet during a recital, and the wallpaper, curtains and carpeting in the drawing room are quiet in their effect.

quince, quints

The hard, acid, yellowish, pear-shaped fruit of *Pyrus Cydonia* is known as **quince**, and is used in preserving other fruits. A quint is a tax of one-fifth, the musical interval of a fifth, an organ stop, or a sequence of five cards of the same suit in piquet. Hence the word **quints** is the plural of any of those.

quire see choir

quoin see coin

quoit

A **quoit** is a ring of iron, rope or rubber thrown in a game to encircle or land as near as possible to an upright peg, the flat covering stone of a dolmen, or, in Australia, a colloquial term for a person's buttocks.

quotation

If I say or write, 'Nay but this dotage of our general's o'er flows the measure', I am proffering a **quotation** from Shakespeare's *Antony and Cleopatra*. Hence a quotation is a group of words taken from someone else's work, though it is, of course, possible to quote from an earlier work of one's own as well. There can be quotations in music too. Thus Shostakovich quotes in one of his symphonies from Beethoven, Rossini and Wagner. A quotation can also be a formal statement setting out the estimated cost for a particular job or service, or registration granted to a company enabling their shares to be officially listed and traded.

quotidian

As an adjective, **quotidian** mostly is used as a synonym for 'daily': 'Trevor nosed his way through the quotidian traffic.' In medicine, however, quotidian refers to a the malignant form of malaria.

R

R, r, are

The eighteenth letter of the alphabet, **R**, sounds exactly like the word **are** (qv), but otherwise, apart from its role in abbreviations like RSPCC, RIP, RC, and so on, has no homonymic interests, unless you count the three Rs (reading, writing and arithmetic) which are regarded as the fundamentals of learning, but only one of which begins with an R.

rabbet, rabbit

A **rabbet** is a channel, groove or slot cut along the edge or face of a piece or surface of wood or stone, and intended to receive the edge or end of another piece or pieces. Hence, if you rabbet, you join on or lap over by means of a rabbet. The word 'rabbet' is also an archaic or North American term for 'rebate'. A **rabbit** is a burrowing rodent of the hare family, though the word can also be used as an insult when you wish to imply that someone is cowardly. It is also used to indicate that someone is inexperienced or a novice at something. You can also rabbit on about something, which means that you talk at length about it.

rabid

If you are **rabid** about something, you are fanatical about it. You may be a rabid feminist, a rabid supporter of Chelsea Football Club or a rabid advocate of wind farms. An animal can be rabid if it has contracted the disease of rabies.

race

A **race** is a running contest between humans, boats, horses, vehicles, greyhounds, or, for all I know, tortoises. Apart from being a showcase for the humans, machines or animals involved, they are also an excellent excuse for humans to indulge in betting on the projected result, thus enabling bookmakers to live lives of affluence. A race is also a collection of humans who are linked genetically, and for some people marriage between differing races is deeply disapproved of. Indeed, many people dislike living close to people of a different race, and consequently many of our cities are marred by conflicts occasioned by racial tension.

rack, wrack

The **rack** used to be an instrument of torture whereby the victim's arms and legs were slowly stretched out of their sockets, thereby causing intense agony. This barbaric practice is still figuratively referred to when people undergoing suspense or tension of some kind say, 'I was on the rack', or when they intimate that something is going 'to rack and ruin'. Today a rack is more commonly going to mean a method of storing something. Thus wine can be placed in a wine rack, food for cattle or horses can be placed in a farm rack or stable rack, and so on. An overhead shelf on a coach, train or plane for stowing luggage is also called a rack, as is the triangular structure for positioning the balls in a game of pool or snooker. Rack is also a particular gait in horses, a joint of meat, typically lamb, that includes the front ribs, and, as a verb, the action of drawing off the sediment from a barrel of beer or wine. **Wrack** is an old-fashioned word for 'wreck', and is rarely used today, though the word can also denote any of a number of coarse, brown seaweeds which grow on the shoreline, or a mass of high, thick, fast-moving cloud.

racket, racquet

A **racket** can be a bat used in rackets, tennis, badminton, etc., a ball game for four persons played in a plain, four-walled room, an illegal moneymaking scheme, or a clamour or noise-producing event. A **racquet** is a woven bat for tennis.

rad

Apart from being an abbreviation for 'radians' and an informal term for a political radical, a **rad** is a unit of absorbed dose of ionising radiation, corresponding to the absorption of 0.01 joule per kilogramme of absorbing material. In North Amerca, 'rad' can also be an adjective meaning 'excellent' or 'impressive'.

radius

In mathematics, the **radius** is a straight line from the centre of a circle to the circumference. In biology, the radius is the thicker and shorter of the two bones in the human forearm.

radix

In mathematics, the **radix** is the base of a system of numeration. In more literary circles, a radix is the source of something.

raft

Most of us think of a **raft** as being a number of logs tied together and thence used as a primitive boat. A raft, however, can also be a layer of reinforced concrete forming the foundation of a building, or a large amount of something, e.g. a raft of Government legislation.

rag

We normally take a **rag** to be a small, worthless fragment of some woven material, though it is also, of course, a fund-raising event in aid of charity put on annually by most universities and comprising a variety of lunatic activities by undergraduates. As a verb, if you rag someone, you tease them to the point of causing tears or psychological harm. It can also denote the action of wasting time in a game of ice hockey by keeping possession of the puck, or, as a noun again, a rag can be a large coarse roofing slate. The word is also short for ragtime, a type of music.

rage

You are in a **rage** when you are seized by uncontrollable anger, an event that tends to occur when watching a Conservative Party political broadcast. Yet very differently, something can be all the rage when it becomes subject to a widespread enthusiasm. Hoola hoops were once all the rage among the children of Britain, particularly the girls.

ragged

If you are wearing old and torn clothes, you might be described as looking **ragged**. Something with a rough and irregular surface or edge can also be described as ragged, a coastline, for instance. If your breathing is uncontrolled and uneven, it too can be ragged. You are also likely to look ragged after running the marathon, in that you will look exhausted and worn out.

rail

A **rail** is a horizontal bar-like object that can be adapted for many purposes. A number of rails can be affixed together to form a fence, rails can be used to guide modes of transport like trains and trams, an altar rail separates the altar from the nave, and so on. In electronics, a conductor which is maintained at a fixed potential and to which other parts of a circuit are attached is also called a rail. As a verb, 'to rail' means to lose one's temper, to berate violently. Hence the expression 'to go off the rails'.

rain, reign, rein

For those living in Britain, **rain** is a frequent occurrence. It is the condensed vapour of the atmosphere falling in liquid drops, and normally occurs when you are having a picnic at some local beauty spot or are waiting for a bus to arrive. The word is often used metaphorically too: 'He rained compliments on his new secretary'; 'Sharon's presence was like a gentle shower of rain on a lovely bed of flowers.' Kings and queens are said to **reign** over their respective countries, though anyone who exercises power or influence over some organisation, region or event is often said to reign over their particular domain. Thus Mrs Snodgrass reigns over the Tibberton Women's Institute, Carlos Spinetti reigns over the Lambeth drug trade, and Maurice Spellcheck reigns over the National Union of Teachers. A **rein** is a long narrow strap of leather attached to the bridle of a horse, which is then used to guide the direction of the horse.

raise, rase, rays, raze

The verb 'to **raise**' is frequently used for the physical activities of lifting, erecting or constructing. Thus a lift can raise you from the ground floor to the first floor, it is unusual these days to see someone raise their hat to a lady, many buildings were raised from the ashes in the years following the Blitz on London, and so on. The verb can also be used in a more conceptual manner. Hence you might gain a raise in your salary, the office boy might gain a raise in status when he is appointed to the post of Stamper of Office Post, and so on. Equally, of course, your spirits might raise when you listen to some music, you may be impressed by the way that Alice and Gareth raise their children, and you might want to raise a question at the next AGM. These contexts are very different, but 'raise' always maintains a conceptual identity. **Rase** is very rarely used today, but it used to mean to scrape away with a knife, and so has a similarity with 'raze'. **Rays** are beams of light or any other luminous or electro-magnetic source like X-rays, laser rays or uranium rays. A ray is also a selachian fish, and so rays will be a number of them. If you **raze** something, you obliterate it, sweep it away. Raze is the antonym of 'raise'.

rake

You might use a **rake** for breaking up, levelling or tidying your garden. It is an implement consisting of a bar fixed across a long handle and fitted with teeth pointing downward. A rake is also a man of loose habits and immoral character against whom you warn your daughters, or a number of railway carriages coupled together. As a verb, you may rake in the money at a casino, rake the leaves off your drive, or rake over past memories when you look at your graduation photographs.

rally

If you **rally** people together, you assemble them and try to encourage them in a joint effort. In tennis, a rally is a number of strokes that take place before the point is won. To rally someone can mean that you attempt by humour or friendly ridicule to raise their spirits.

ram

A **ram** is an uncastrated male sheep, the constellation Aries, a cylindrical piece of timber that you use for battering down a door, the falling weight of a piledriving machine, a hydraulic water-raising or lifting machine, or the piston of a hydrostatic press.

ramble

A **ramble** is a gentle, untaxing walk, normally in the countryside. If, however, you ramble, this might be because you talk with little sense of direction or coherence. A plant can ramble when it puts out long shoots and grows over walls and other plants.

ramp

A **ramp** can be a slope leading up to something, or a swindle of some kind. It can also be an electrical waveform in which the voltage increases or decreases linearly with time.

rancour, ranker

If something fills you with **rancour**, then it arouses ill-feeling, bitterness and animosity. A **ranker** is either someone who arranges things in ranks, as, for instance, in the army, or it is an adverb indicating that object A smells even more vilely than object B.

rand

The **rand** is the basic monetary unit of South Africa, a strip of leather placed under the back part of a shoe, or, in South Africa, a long rocky ridge.

range

In mathematics, a **range** is a set of points on a straight line, and so we talk about a range of houses that are set in a straight line, a range of cliffs, and so on. But range need not be so precise, since the word can apply to a collection of almost anything, whether or not they are in a straight line. Hence your tailor might have a range of suits, your wife may have a range of sauces, and your son might have a range of computer games. A fire, oven, grill, sink and so on can be called a kitchen range. Yet the word can also apply to geographical areas. Thus the snow leopard has a limited range of land over which it roams. Your cat and dog doubtless also have their own ranges, out of which they do not venture. You studied at school a range of subjects. A firing weapon will also have a range i.e. a distance over which it is effective. More academically useful, a range is the area of variation between upper and lower limits. You can also range yourself against someone else when you challenge him or her to an arm wrestling contest.

rank

Your **rank** can be your position within an organisation, particularly the armed services. Hence your rank could be vice admiral, corporal, field marshal, private, etc. or, outside the armed forces, chief administrator, personnel officer or junior typist. Articles or humans can be organised into ranks. Hence you might see a rank of the Coldstream Guards marching or a rank of computers ranged on the desks. Should you be woefully obese, your personage might be described as rank. If you have been lying dead in the sun for the last few days, your odour will certainly be described as rank. Your unsubtle attempts to lure Wendy to bed with you could also be described as rank, particularly when you know that she's just got engaged to Tom. The weeds in your garden could be described as rank when they jostle close to each other. The ordinary members of an organisation are known as the rank and file.

rap, wrap

The word **rap** is normally associated with the action of striking something, like a sharp rap on the door, though in the eighteenth century a rap was a counterfeit coin worth about half a farthing. A rap can also be an impromptu conversation, a criminal charge, the smallest amount ('He doesn't give a rap what happens to Mary'), or a type of popular music. **Wrap** is normally a verb meaning to cover something. When you were a child, your mother would wrap you up warmly in winter. You doubtless wrap up Christmas presents for your friends.

rape

The barbarous action of having sexual intercourse with a woman (or man) against her (or his) will is known as **rape**. Every civilised person strongly disapproves of rape, yet millions buy salacious newspapers in order to read about alleged acts of rape. There seems to be some psychological double-mindedness going on. Rape is also a plant commonly grown in Britain for the rape oil that it provides or as a food for sheep. It was also the name for each of the six ancient divisions of Sussex.

rapped, rapt, wrapped

You might have **rapped** Tommy on the knuckles during his maths class in order to direct his attention to quadratic equations. Clearly the word 'rapped' is the past tense of the verb 'to rap'. If you are **rapt**, you are in a state of unearthly wonderment. It is a state induced by listening to great music, having a religious revelation, or being absorbed by your charismatic lecturer discoursing on the philosophy of Plato. There are also stories of being rapt and in that state being transported from one place to another without any tangible means. Something that is **wrapped** is something that is securely covered and possibly tied up in a convenient shape for transport or handing over to someone else.

rare

If something is **rare** it is uncommonly found. Thus the snow leopard is a rare animal, the Penny Blue is a rare stamp, and to be able to play the piano like Alfred Brendel is a rare gift. The word is also used to indicate that something has not yet been cooked, or, in the case of meat, has been undercooked.

rase *see* raise

rash

As a noun, a **rash** denotes a marking of the skin by red spots or patches, as in measles or scarlet fever. A rash can also be a smooth textile fabric made of silk or worsted. As an adjective or adverb, rash signifies an impetuous action, an ill-considered deed or reckless speech.

rasp

A **rasp** can be a coarse file designed to scrape or grate in a rough manner. It is also the radula of a mollusc.

rat

A **rat** is a rodent prone to inhabit sewers and other unhygienic areas, and consequently a frequent carrier of disease. The word can also be a verb meaning to desert or betray the side or party to which one once belonged, or just a random insult. In the USA a rat can be a pad used to give shape and fullness to a woman's hair.

rate

Rate can signify the level of income or the expected level of outcome for a job, activity or event. Thus the rate of pay for a steward might be £6.50 an hour, the rate of expected immigration for 2011 might be 300,000 a month, and the rate of water loss through leaks might be 3 million gallons a year. The word is also used in relation to speed: 'Aunt Aggie walks at a slow rate', or, 'The car sped round the track at an almost incredible rate.' In addition, 'rate' can be a verb of evaluation: 'I don't rate Gauguin as a painter anything like as much as Cézanne.'

rather

This adverb can be used in four different ways. First of all, it can indicate a preference: 'I would **rather** go swimming this afternoon.' Secondly, it can suggest a degree: 'David was rather odd yesterday' which is less extreme than very odd and possibly more emphatic than slightly odd. Thirdly, it can emphasise an opposite: 'Alison did not fail through lack of ability. Rather she failed through a total lack of work.' Finally, the word can sometimes be used as an exclamation of enthusiastic agreement: 'You ask if I'd like to go to Florence. Rather!'

rational

Used as an adjective or an adverb, **rational** indicates the faculty of reasoning, the ability to assess, the operation of logic. In mathematics, a rational number is one which contains quantities which are expressible as a ratio of whole numbers. Yet as a noun, a rational used to be an ornament worn on the breast by bishops.

rationalise (or rationalize)

You have just inherited the company of Lunatic Logic Ltd. You decide to subject the company to an analysis so that you can detect where, if anywhere, there is duplication of effort and superfluity of workers. You will then act on your findings. This process is your attempt to **rationalise** the company, that is, make the company more efficient, logical and consistent. Very differently, you are detected taking your new secretary out to dinner one evening.

When a fellow director enquires about this next day, you attempt to rationalise the matter. 'Well, Hazel is new to the company, and I thought that she'd more easily divulge any difficulties that she was encountering in the relaxed atmosphere of a restaurant than in the arid context of the office.' This, of course, is codswallop, and your fellow director knows it, but your rationalisation is not one that he can easily attack. Finally, in mathematics, a rationalisation is the action of converting a function or expression to a rational form.

rattle

As a verb, there are four differing uses of **rattle**. You are in the street one Saturday morning collecting money for the St Basil Church Restoration Fund. You have a metal tin with a slot at its top into which people drop their money. If you shake this tin, it will rattle. Infants have a toy which rattles when it is shaken, and sometimes money will rattle in your pocket. Secondly, the word can denote a state of alarm or apprehension: 'Sir Felix always manages to rattle me when he asks me about our current profit and loss account.' Your next-door neighbour, Mrs Oswald, tends to rattle on end-lessly about the progress of her granddaughter. In other words, she talks at length and inanely. Finally, 'to rattle' can signify the operation of saying or producing something rapidly: 'She rattled off the Health and Safety Regulations with the greatest of ease.' 'Rattle' as a noun produces no surprises: 'The baby played with his rattle'; 'Mrs Oswald is a rattle.'

rave

As a verb, **rave** can mean two things. If you rave about the new procedures for claiming back expenses, you are likely to be virtually incoherent with anger because you regard them as humiliating and time-consuming. If you rave about the music of Mozart, you are likely to be enthusiastic and praise-worthy. It is easy to transfer both those verbs into an appropriate noun, but a rave can also be a lively party, often accompanied by music of extreme loudness and no merit.

raven

When pronounced with a long 'a', a **raven** is a large black bird of Europe and Asia (a member of the crow family) which feeds on carrion, though the word can also be used to signify a deep and dark black colour. When pronounced with a short 'a', raven becomes a verb meaning to seize or plunder, often for food.

ravish

If you **ravish** someone, you are likely to seize them and carry them off by force, which is not going to please them at all, or you are going to fill them with intense delight, which presumably is going to please them a great deal.

raw

Most of the time we probably think of **raw** as denoting something that is uncooked, but your skin can be raw when it has been abraded by contact with something, your emotions can be raw when they depict some basic emotion like sorrow, rage or love, the weather can be raw when it is painfully inclement, and you can be raw when you are beginning a new job and you are not yet familiar with its codes.

ray, re

A **ray** is a narrow beam of light, a straight line extending from a point, any of the bony or cartilaginous spines of the fin of a fish, a thin beam of electromagnetic radiation, any strand of tissue that runs radially through the vascular tissue of some higher plants, or a selachian fish of the family *Raiidae*. The *Shorter Oxford*'s definition of **re** reads as follows: 'The second note of Guido's hexachords and of the octave in modern solmization.' The *Shorter Oxford* (and its full-scale parent) are fond of these user-friendly definitions. In fact, as far as its musical definition is concerned, 're' is an alternative spelling for 'ray'. In tonic-sol-fa, 're' or 'ray' is the second degree of any major scale, and most of us have, from time to time, sung doh-re-mi in the operation of learning our musical intervals. But *re* is also often used as a short-hand way of saying 'in reference to', and is the chemical symbol for rhenium.

rays *see* **raise**

raze *see* **raise**

re *see* **ray**

reach

I was doubtful about including **reach** because its meanings do seem to be conceptually linked. At a physical level, you reach for something when you stretch out to touch or grasp it. The word can also signify the act of arriving at a particular place: 'I will be glad when we reach the café.' It can also mean attaining a particular level: 'I want to reach Grade 8 in my piano lessons.' I can also indicate the act of communication: 'At least I can reach Sybil by phone.' It can signify contact of some kind: 'This television programme will reach at least eighty million people.' There are, of course, corresponding noun versions, but there is one noun version of 'reach' which is somewhat different. One can talk about travelling along the upper reaches of the Amazon, or even, I suppose, about walking along the reaches of the Shropshire Union Canal. Here a reach is a stretch of unbroken river or canal.

read, red

When pronounced like the word **red**, the word **read** is the past tense of the verb 'to read' (pronounced like 'reed'). *Red* itself, of course, is a colour, and one that has been used as a symbol for left-wing politics, or for getting extremely angry. If you are in the red, you are overdrawn at the bank. In heraldry, red is said to signify magnanimity and fortitude. In folklore, red is the colour of magic.

read, rede, reed

To be able to **read** is one of the essentials of life in advanced society. It indicates that you are able to understand markings like these, and translate those markings into some meaningful message. The word is used in innumerable contexts, both literally and metaphorically. Not only can one read words, but one can read music, faces, the sky, the gas meter and doubtless scores of other things. One can even read between the lines, read someone like a book, read lips, and read something into something else. Those thousands who leave school every year still unable to read can never lead more than half a life. If you are given **rede**, you are given counsel or advice, and *to rede* is to take counsel together, though the word is rare today. A **reed** is one of the tall, straight stalks formed by plants of the genera *Phragmites* and *Arunde*. It can also be a piece of thin cane or metal which vibrates in a current of air to produce the sound of various musical instruments, an electrical contact used in a magnetically operated switch or relay, or a weaver's comb-like instrument for separating weft from warp.

reader

A **reader** is someone who reads or, quite frequently, reads aloud. A reader is also a title given to a university don who is primarily concerned with research rather than teaching, or, in the Inns of Court, to a lecturer who lectures on law. Sometimes the word is applied to a primary school book designed to aid children in the early stages of reading. In a publisher's office, a reader is someone who reads and reports on manuscripts submitted for publication.

reading, reeding

The activity of **reading** is the process of perusing written or printed matter, something that you are doing this very moment. The reading stage is also a stage through which a bill in Parliament must pass before it becomes an Act. The action of **reeding** could denote the activity of collecting reeds or of decorating something with reeds. The word, though, is also applied to a small semicylindrical moulding, or to the milling on the edge of a coin.

ready

If something or someone is **ready**, then they are in a suitable state for immediate action: 'I am ready to go out now.' The word can also signify a preparedness to do something, even if the person concerned doesn't really want to: 'I am ready to apologise if you think that is the only way of smoothing over the situation.' Finally, 'ready' can indicate that things are easily available: 'There was a ready supply of drink.'

real, reel

Something that is **real** purports to possess an objective existence. Thus tigers are real, but hobbits are not. The word is also used to distinguish between a genuine article and a fake: 'This is a real Picasso; that is a clumsy imitation.' In slovenly English, 'real' can also be a synonym of 'very': 'My head hurts real bad.' (Even my word processor objects to that last sentence.) There is also the doctrine of the real presence, the doctrine that Christ himself is present in the bread and wine of the Eucharist. Since 1994, the real has been the basic monetary unit of Brazil. A **reel** is a rotatory instrument on which thread or wire is wound, a small cylinder round which thread is wound, a lively dance, the music for such a dance, or the action of walking in an extremely unsteady fashion.

ream

A **ream** is 480–500 sheets of paper, a verb meaning to enlarge a hole or the bore of a gun, or, in Scotland, a verb meaning 'to foam or froth'.

reap

As a noun, a **reap** is a bundle or sheaf of corn. As a verb, it denotes the cutting of corn or, indeed, other plants. The word is also used figuratively in expressions like 'you only reap what you sow', a somewhat gloating homily delivered to those who bemoan their hangover after a night on the town.

rear

Clearly it is possible to **rear** children, chickens, dogs or cobras, where 'rear' means 'to bring up, to sustain, to bring to maturity'. But 'rear' also means the hindmost part of any congregation of objects. Thus you can have the rear of the army, the rear of a procession, or the rear of the competitors in the London Marathon. *Rear* can also mean 'to lift up': 'He reared himself to his feet.'

rebound

This word can denote an entirely physical event when, for instance, a ball thrown at a wall can be seen to **rebound** off the wall and return, perhaps, into the hands of the thrower. It can also signify a recovery after a slump: 'We saw the shares of Micro Magic Ltd rebound to their previous value after a mid-summer slump.'

recall

This verb can denote the activity of your dimly remembering something from the past: 'Yes, I dimly **recall** visiting Stokesay Castle when I was a schoolboy.' It can also be a firm order to someone to return to a previous position: 'I have received a recall to the camp in Tiverton.'

recede, reseed

If you **recede** from something, you move away from it, you become more distant: 'We watched the water recede from the fields.' It can also denote a hope or expectation becoming less firm: 'The approaching clouds made the hope of a rainless day recede.' Many men also see their hair recede, though I always claim that this only happens to men of extremely high intelligence and strong sexual stamina. If you **reseed** a flower border, you put fresh plant seeds into the border, presumably because the old ones have died or been uprooted by next door's dog.

receipt, reseat

When you pay for something, you often get a **receipt** that provides written evidence that you have paid for the object concerned. But, less formally, when you receive something from anyone, then you are in receipt of the article concerned. If someone at the theatre complains that a pillar prevents them from seeing all the action on the stage, then you may be able to **reseat** them in a more suitable seat.

receiver

A **receiver** is the part of a telephone apparatus contained in the earpiece, in which the electrical signals are converted to sound. It is also a person who receives something from someone else, a person who buys or accepts goods which he or she knows to be stolen, the person to whom the ball is served in tennis, a person or company who tidies up the affairs of a company or person that has gone bankrupt, and a chemical container for collecting the products of distillation or any other process.

receptacle

Most of us use this word as a general-purpose word to indicate a container of some sort into which we can put things. Thus we could have a **receptacle** for screws, used tins, dirty washing, five-pence pieces or virtually anything else. The word does, however, have more specialised meanings in botany. It can be an enlarged area at the apex of a stem on which the parts of a flower or the florets of a flower head are inserted, or it can be a structure supporting the sexual organs in some algae, mosses and liverworts.

recess

We normally think of a **recess** as being a period of time when proceedings are suspended for a while. In a court of law, there may be a recess while the judge consults with one of the counsel, in a cricket match there may a recess while a shower passes over the ground, and so on. But a recess is also a small space created by building part of a wall further back than the rest. A recess thus becomes an ideal place for storing lumber.

recessional

As an adjective, **recessional** can relate to an economic recession, denote astronomical motion away from the observer, or depict a moraine or other deposit left during a pause in the retreat of a glacier. As a noun, a recessional is a hymn sung while the clergy and choir process out of church at the end of a service.

recessive

In genetics, a **recessive** gene is one that only manifests itself when passed on by both parents. Economic markets can also be recessive since they will be reflecting an overall depression. In phonetics, the stress on a word or phrase is recessive when it falls on the first syllable.

reciprocal

Last week you helped Ada clear away the furniture after a Women's Institute meeting. This week she helped you do the washing up. This was a **reciprocal** action, a favour done in return for one previously done by you. In mathematics the word describes a quantity or function related to another so that their product is unity. In grammar a pronoun or verb can be reciprocal if it expresses a mutual action or relationship.

reck, wreck

Though hardly a common word today, the verb 'to **reck**' means 'to take care of, to care about, to take heed'. It perhaps survives most commonly in the expression 'reck one's own rede' (be governed by one's better judgement). A **wreck** is the remains of something that has been destroyed. Hence you might see the wreck of a ship in the bay, the wreck of a car on the pavement, or the wreck of a person in a hospital bed.

reckon

If you **reckon** up the amount of money in the pockets of all your jackets, you are engaged in an arithmetical calculation. If you reckon that Basil will be at the dance tonight, you are making an informed guess. As you can see, 'reckon' depends a great deal on the adverb that follows it: reckon up, reckon that, reckon on, reckon by, and so on.

reconcile

Reconcile has two meanings that are conceptually similar, but certainly distinct enough to be included in this dictionary. If you reconcile Jerome with Patricia, you have done a worthy thing in bringing to an end an animosity that existed between them. If you reconcile the cost accounts with the financial ones, then you have succeeded in presenting a coherent set of figures that will pass the auditor's eye.

record

There are two obvious pronunciations of this word, one with the emphasis on the 're-' and the other with the stress on the '-cord'. With the stress on the 're-', the word **record** is a noun signifying a written account of something, a legal report, or a circular disc that can be revolved on a gramophone so as to emit sound. It can also be a list of the criminal convictions that someone has undergone. With the emphasis on '-cord', the word becomes a verbal equivalent to the nouns just mentioned above.

recorder

Clearly a **recorder** is one who records, whether it be someone who sets down train usage in Kings Lynn, or someone else who places on disc or tape a piece of music. A recorder can also be an apparatus which records sound, pictures or data. It is also a simple woodwind instrument through which many children gain their first experience of making music. With a capital 'r', a Recorder is a barrister appointed to serve as a part-time judge.

recovery

If you are ill, all your friends hope for a speedy **recovery**, that is, a return to health. If you are burgled, all your friends hope for a speedy recovery of the eighteenth-century egg cups that were stolen. In science and industry, recovery is the process of removing or extracting an energy source or industrial chemical for use, reuse or waste treatment.

rectify

For 60-odd years, I have assumed (quite rightly) that **rectify** is a verb meaning to put right or to correct, but apparently it also means to convert from alternating current to direct current, and to find a straight line equal in length to a curve.

rector

In the Church of England, a **rector** is virtually the same as a vicar. Some schools, colleges and universities are headed by a Rector, and in Scotland a rector is the elected student representative on a university's governing body.

red *see* **read**

rede *see* **read**

red-eye

Red-eye is an undesirable effect of flash photography whereby the people being photographed all appear to have red eyes. The red-eye is also a freshwater fish with red eyes, a tiring overnight flight, and a slang term in the USA for cheap whisky.

red-hot

If something is **red-hot**, it is so hot that it glows in a reddish fashion. Equally, though, red-hot can be a casual term denoting excellence: 'Mr Parsons is a red-hot physics teacher.'

redress

If you **redress** something, you put something right that was previously wrong. Equally, of course, you might decide to redress (i.e. clothe yourself again) when you realised that your red gown was a little strident for President Martin's funeral.

redstart

The **redstart** is two types of bird, the Eurasian and N. African songbird related to the chats, and the American warbler.

reduce

On its own with no adverb following it, **reduce** means to make smaller or to diminish: 'I must reduce the size of this class.' If the verb is followed by *to*, as it so often is, the verb can take a variety of meanings:

a)   to bring someone or something to a less desirable state: 'The block of flats was reduced to rubble';

b)   to be forced by circumstances to do something different: 'If I lose this case, I will be reduced to begging';

c)   to change a substance to a more basic form: 'Left to itself, the lava will reduce to dust.'

In addition, in chemistry you can reduce something by causing it to combine with hydrogen.

reed *see* read

reef

In nautical contexts a **reef** is one of the horizontal portions of a sail which may be successively rolled or folded up in order to reduce the extent of canvas exposed to the wind. But a reef can also be a narrow ridge of rocks.

reek, wreak

Something can be said to **reek** when it emits vapour, steam or fumes. The word is most often used when the emission is foul-smelling. The verb 'to **wreak**' tends to be used in a vengeful context. You might wreak your anger against Mrs Talbot by taking the heads off her tulips, or you might wreak your fury at the latest increase in council tax by calling for a public demonstration outside the Council House.

reel *see* real

reeve

The **reeve** was a local government official in medieval England, and Chaucer has one in his *Canterbury Tales*. It can also be a female version of the bird called the ruff, or a verb meaning to pass a rope through a hole.

reference

When you mention or allude to something in passing, you are making **reference** to it. Equally you might refer to a work of reference when you need to look up some item of information. This dictionary is a work of reference. Finally you might cite Jason Block as a reference to your potential new employers because Jason knows you well and can comment knowledgeably about your expertise in Latvian (or whatever).

reflect

When light hits certain materials, the light itself can be thrown back and in doing so can **reflect** the object that it has encountered. Hence you see your reflection in a mirror, the adjacent rocks reflect in the lake, and the light of the moon can reflect on the ice. Just as surfaces reflect light that shines upon them, so our actions are often said to reflect our character. Ian's habit of forcing his son to sleep in the dog kennel reflects badly on Ian's sense of humanity, while Constance's sterling work for Save the Children does the very reverse. Very differently, you and I can reflect when we give ourselves time to think about the issues that make up our lives. We may reflect upon our decision to join the Great Urkington Drama Group, upon our daughter's decision to go and live with Melvyn, upon the strength, if any, of the cosmological argument for proving the existence of God, and so on.

refuse

If you **refuse** to do something (with the emphasis on '-fuse'), then you positively decline to do the thing concerned. If you put the refuse (with the emphasis on 'ref-') in the bin, then you are dealing with rubbish that needs disposing of.

register

A **register** is an official book listing names or items. Most of us answered the register at school each morning. One's voice also possesses a register and each musical instrument has a register, that is, a range of notes that it can play. The word also has specific meanings in linguistics, art, electronics, printing and doubtless other fields.

registrar

As one might expect, a **registrar** is an official responsible for keeping a register, for example the registrar for birth and deaths in Smethick. A middle-ranking hospital doctor undergoing training as a specialist is also called a registrar. The Registrar General in Britain is the official responsible for holding a population census.

registration

This is the state of being registered. Thus you have to have **registration** in the birth register, you have to have your car registered, you have to have registration for your marriage, and so on. Very differently, the combination of stops used when playing the organ is known as the instrument's registration.

regressive

Something is **regressive** if it moves someone or something from one state to a lower, less desirable one. A tax is also regressive if it takes a proportionally greater amount from the poor than it does from the rich. In philosophy an argument is regressive if it proceeds from effect to cause or from particular to universal.

regular

Visually something is **regular** if it forms a uniform pattern. Thus the daisies on your wallpaper occur at regular intervals, the paving stones on your drive form a regular pattern, and your check shirt has a regular pattern. 'Regular' can also relate to time. Mr Hopkins is regular in his habits, always going for the newspaper at 8.05 in the morning, visiting his daughter at 11.00 every Saturday, and going to Frinton on holiday in the first week of August every year. In grammar a regular verb is one that follows the normal pattern of I build, you build, he builds, we build, you build, and they build, instead of something wildly eccentric like I am, you are, he is, we are, you are, they are. In geometry a regular figure is one that has all its sides and angles equal.

reign see rain

rein see rain

relate

If you **relate** one thing to another, you show a connection between them. Thus you might want to relate global warming to the widespread use of the internal combustion engine in cars and lorries. If you relate to Aunt Nancy in her grief at the death of her son Arnold, then you feel a fellow sympathy with her and you identify with her. Finally, if you relate to Mavis exactly how the accident occurred at the junction of Hallows Road, then you give her an account of the incident, you relate the sequence of events to her.

relation

A **relation** is someone who is genetically akin to you, a relative. Hence your son, uncle, niece, grandmother and so on are all your relations. A relation can also be a narration of a story or of an account. Thus you might listen to Aunt Doris's relation of the night that the Post Office was raided. More conceptually, a relation is a kinship between ideas, schemes, objectives, entities and so on. Thus Spanish and Italian have a close relation to Latin, the Labour Party has a close relation to the trade union movement, the paintings of Cézanne have a relation to the paintings of Picasso, and so on.

relative

Relative can be a synonym for 'relation' with respect to members of your extended family. Hence Uncle Harry can be described as your relation or your relative. But the word 'relative' has many other functions too. It can be used when you want to assess the impact of item A on item B. For instance, the success of the Shrewsbury Flower Show is going to be relative to the amount of rain that we received in the months preceding the show. In English grammar, a clause can be a relative clause if it refers to something that is antecedent to the matter being discussed. Thus, in the sentence 'Tom, who had been a very good swimmer at school, wondered whether or not to join his company's swimming club', the clause 'who had been . . . at school' is a relative clause. The key of C minor is relative to the key of C major because they have the same key signature. A rank in the RAF can be relative to a rank in the navy if they carry much the same responsibility.

relay

As a noun, a **relay** can be a group of people detailed to accomplish a task. Thus a relay force of 43 men may be sent out to demolish the Town Hall. Equally you can have a relay of horses pulling the wagons to the next site. You may, at school, have taken part in a relay race. This is when one runner carrying a baton runs a certain distance and then passes the baton on to the next runner. Four runners in a relay is the normal situation.

relief

Emotionally you feel considerable **relief** when your son returns from his mountaineering trip to the Pyrenees. *Relief* here is a release brought about by the removal of the cause for worry. On a less emotional level, you also experience relief when you have been on guard duty for several hours, and someone else comes to take your place. You could also make a *relief* model of the Lake District. Here *relief* indicates that the model will be a three-dimensional one that, in miniature, depicts the physical layout of the countryside. On a two-dimensional map, relief lines try to give some indication of the area's physical make-up. Relief can also be financial or practical assistance given to you when you are in need or difficulty.

remedy

As most of us know, a **remedy** is a cure for some disease or problem. Aspirin can be a remedy for a headache, and improved working practices can be a remedy for underproduction at the factory. Much less well known is the fact that 'remedy' can be the amount of deviance from the ideal manifested by a newly minted coin. In some public schools, a remedy is another name for a school holiday.

remote

If something is **remote** it is far-off, distant, or removed, but these days the word is also used to designate the portable hand control with which you change channels on a television or skip tracks on a CD or DVD. It is also possible to be remote in one's behaviour by being aloof and unfriendly.

remove

If you **remove** something, you take the object concerned from where it is and place it somewhere else. Even more extreme, 'remove' can signify the abolition or destruction of something: 'We must remove that fence in order to give us more space.' The word can also indicate an intellectual or conceptual distance: 'Maths in schools today is at a far remove from the maths I did forty years ago.' In some schools, the Remove is also the name of a particular class.

render

Most commonly, the verb 'to **render**' means to give or provide: 'I must render assistance to the new Astronomer Royal.' Quite often, though, 'to render' means that something has happened to affect something else: 'I fear that the rain will render my walk to Ollerton impossible.' The word can even mean 'done' or 'achieved', normally in some artistic context: 'The cornfields in Ambrose's paintings are extremely well rendered', or, 'I render the deep sadness of the C-minor concerto extraordinarily well.'

renew

The three meanings of **renew** are all similar, but sufficiently distinct to count as homonymic. First of all, you can renew an activity after it has been interrupted: 'After Gladys had enquired about the seating arrangements for dinner, I was able to renew my attempt at the crossword.' Secondly, the word can imply a fresh vigour and enthusiasm: 'My week in France enabled me to renew my attack on irregular verbs with fresh vigour.' Finally, the word can signify the replacement of something old with something new: 'I was able to tear down the old curtains and renew them with much more pleasing ones.'

rennet

Rennet can be the mass of curdled milk found in the stomach of an unweaned calf, or one of a large class of dessert apples of French origin.

rent

If you live in a house that is not your own, it is likely that you pay **rent**, a payment proffered for the use of an object owned by someone else. It is also possible to rent cars, lawnmowers, offices, allotments and a host of other objects. A rent is also a tear or split in a garment, a schism within a party or organisation, or a plane of cleavage running across a seam of coal or other geological layering.

repair

If you **repair** something, you remedy a fault so as to return the object concerned to full working order. It is also possible to repair home. Here the word means to go to, to betake oneself, to resort to.

repent

Most of us have had to **repent** something or other most days. To repent something is to regret an action or speech that one made. Hence you may repent this evening that you were rude to Mrs Tomlinson this morning, or you may repent that you failed to help your son with his homework last night. Only if you are infallible – i.e. a politician – can you get through life without regretting many of your own actions. However, in biology, *repent* is an adjective meaning 'creeping', especially growing along the ground or just under the surface and sending out roots at intervals.

report

Under normal circumstances, a **report** is a calm, considered assessment of some state or issue. There can, of course, be scrappy and rushed reports; there can even be oral reports, but most of the time a report is a formal document prepared with care. A report can also be a loud noise like the shot of a gun or a car backfiring. You also report yourself as being present at some function or other, and bills passing through Parliament go through a report stage.

repose

If you are in a state of **repose**, you are in a relaxed state. Indeed, you may even be asleep or watching a game of cricket – the two states are similar. Alternatively, you may repose your confidence in someone or something. In other words, you give someone your trust.

represent

If you **represent** someone or some organisation, you are at that moment entitled to speak on their behalf. Hence your solicitor represents you in your dispute with your neighbour. The verb can also mean 'constitute' or 'amount to'. Your bank statement may represent your current state of affluence (or poverty). An item can also represent something outside itself in the real world. A halo in a painting represents that the character portrayed was a saintly being, just as your four-year-old son's drawing of an evil witch represents you at your most becoming. You also should represent the facts of the case when you make a formal 'Nothing to declare' statement at customs.

representative

Mr and Mrs Brown who live next door to you are entirely **representative** of middle-class England. In other words, they are entirely typical in tastes, habits and expenditure of a particular class. In a similar fashion, the pea plant is a representative legume, the zebra is a representative ruminant, and *The Sun* is a representative tabloid newspaper. More formally, perhaps, the House of Commons can be said to be representative of the British population because each of its members was chosen to act and speak on behalf of the population that elected them. Sometimes too the word can be used when something is a symbol of something else. The maple leaf is representative of Canada.

reproof

Most of the time a **reproof** is a telling-off, an expression of blame. Hence a wife may give her husband a reproof for leaving his dirty socks on the bathroom floor yet again. But 'reproof' can be a verb. If your mackintosh no longer keeps out the rain, you will have to reproof it in order to restore it to its waterproof state. In addition, if the proof of your latest novel gets lost at your publishers, they will have to order a reproof.

reservation

A **reservation** is when something is excluded from general use but is instead commandeered for the exclusive use of a particular person or organisation. Hence when you reserve a seat at Covent Garden, that seat is confined to your personal usage. A deer reservation is set aside for the grazing of deer only, and so on. On the other hand, a reservation can be when you harbour some doubts as to the veracity of something presented as fact. When your daughter tells you that she has no homework because the French mistress forgot to give any, you might have a slight reservation about this story. When the Prime Minister announces that identification cards will greatly protect human rights, you might have very considerable reservations about his or her veracity.

reserved

When a seat at the theatre has been **reserved**, then you know that it is for the use of someone who booked in advance. When someone is reserved in their manner or approach, you might find them somewhat cold or reticent, because a reserved person is restrained and uncommunicative in their social behaviour.

residence, residents

A **residence** is an establishment where people live, whether it be a normal home for a family or an institution like an orphanage or old people's home. The people who live in a residence or a hotel or a caravan or whatever are the **residents**. However, in North America, residents can also be medical graduates engaged in specialised practice under supervision in a hospital.

resign

If you **resign** from your post as janitor of Middlepark Primary School, you announce that you wish to terminate your current employment at that establishment. If you resign yourself to the fact that your son is never going to be any good at playing chess, you regretfully accept something that cannot be altered.

resinate, resonate

A **resinate** is a salt formed by the action of a resinous acid on a base. The verb 'to **resonate**' depicts the sound produced when the original sound reflects itself and the sound vibrations are prolonged. Clearly the two words are not exact homophones, but British vowel oral laxness virtually makes them so.

resistance

As a noun, **resistance** can mean the refusal to accept some proposal or argument – 'Our vicar displayed a complete resistance to the idea of lady priests' – an ability to withstand some outside influence – 'Martin seems to have a complete resistance to the flu virus' – or the ability to stop or impede an electric current, in which the degree of resistance is measured in ohms.

resister, resistor

A **resister** is someone who resists. A man may be a resister when the police attempt to arrest him, and children are normally resisters when you explain that it is time for bed. A **resistor** is an electrical component designed to introduce a known value of resistance into a circuit.

resolution

If you make a **resolution**, you make a firm decision to do something or to refrain from doing something else. Hence you may make a resolution to help Annie in her decorating, or a resolution never to smoke another cigar.

The word can also mean the quality of being determined: 'Confronted by the angry parent, Gareth acted with great resolution.' A resolution can also be a solving of a problem or, in music, the passing of a discord into a concord. In chemistry, a resolution is the breaking down of a compound into its constituent parts. There are also technical meanings in physics and astronomy. Understandably, you find a similar spread of meanings with the verb 'to resolve'.

resonance

If you hear **resonance** in a voice or any sort of sound, you hear a rich deepness, a noise that has a full and reverberating quality. Bass voices and tubas and trombones tend to have resonance. This, then, is the meaning that one will normally encounter, but the word is used in a number of specialist contexts also. In physics it refers to the prolongation of sound from a surface. In chemistry it denotes the state of having a molecular structure which cannot adequately be represented by a single structural formula but is a composite of two or more structures of higher energy. In astronomy resonance is the occurrence of a simple ratio between the periods of revolution of two bodies about a single primary. Apart from such scientific applications, 'resonance' can also be used metaphorically. You might, for instance, say that the poetry of Hopkins has resonance in your mind when you mean that the dark sonnets or 'The Wreck of the Deutschland' reverberate in your mind long after you have read the poem or poems concerned.

resort

It may be that every summer you and your family venture off to a seaside **resort** for a fortnight. A resort is a place that is frequented for holidays or recreation. As a verb though, 'to resort' means to adopt a course of action. You had forgotten your umbrella and so, on the way home, you had to resort to holding a newspaper over your head.

responsible

If someone is **responsible**, they have an obligation to do something or to superintend something. 'Mrs Pratt is responsible for putting fresh flowers in church each Saturday.' 'Donald Prescott is responsible for increasing the export markets of Fluran & Co.' But the word has a more general use as well. If you describe someone as being a responsible person, you mean that they are law-abiding, courteous, helpful and generally an asset to the community. From time to time, 'responsible' can also have a causative meaning. 'Cook's score of 174 was primarily responsible for England's first innings' lead in the match against India.'

rest, wrest

If you are at **rest**, then you are relaxed, at repose. But the word has several other meanings too. A rest in music, indicated in a score by a variety of symbols depending upon the length of the rest needed, simply means that the instrument concerned does not play. A support for a firearm is called a rest. When you have been using some consumables, those that remain unused are simply called the rest. To be dead is often referred as being at rest. If, however, you **wrest** something from someone else, you turn and twist the article in dispute in order to gain it yourself. Even if it entails no physical contact, to wrest something always implies a degree of force. Indeed the instrument used for tuning a harp or spinet is called a wrest because it involves twisting the strings of the musical instrument.

restraint

If something or someone is kept under **restraint**, it is being kept under control in some fashion. Thus a prison cell will keep Desperate Dan under restraint, a dog lead will keep Fido under restraint, and liberal use of weedkiller will keep your weeds under control. But 'restraint' can also mean dispassionate or moderate behaviour. Thus when someone pushes into a queue, your saying 'Excuse me, but the end of the queue is back there' would be acting with more restraint than shooting the interloper with your stun gun.

retail

The word **retail** most commonly refers to the practice of selling goods in relatively small quantities to the general public. However, you can also retail a story or incident to others, in which case 'retail' is a synonym of 'relate'.

retard

The **retard** is the gap between the transit of the moon and the high tide that follows it. As a verb, 'to retard' is to delay, slow down, hinder. In informal speech, 'retard' is sometimes used as a label for someone with learning difficulties.

retch, wretch

The verb 'to **retch**' means to vomit or to make earnest efforts so to do. For reasons entirely beyond my understanding, an Internet source defines 'retch' as 'call Ralph on the porcelain telephone'. A **wretch** is a person or animal who is in some sort of distress, physical, financial or emotional. Unfortunately perhaps, the word is normally used in unsympathetic tones, though this is not invariably the case.

reticulum

A **reticulum** is either a fine network or net-like structure, or the second stomach of a ruminant.

retire

There are two basic meanings for the verb 'to **retire**'. The first is 'to withdraw, to remove oneself'. The third battalion on the battlefield may find themselves being worsted by the enemy forces, and consequently retire from combat in order to reassess the situation. You might be having an argument with Shirley Hampden about whether *Measure for Measure* is a comedy or a tragedy, but, since you are losing this particular scrap, you decide to retire. You can even do something as simple as decide to retire to bed. The second meaning is when a person gives up their working life and, through age, enters the period of retirement. In Britain women used to retire at the age of sixty and men at the age of sixty-five, but the retiring age is certainly going to rise during the first decade or so of the twenty-first century.

retired

Fairly obviously, **retired** is the past tense of the verb 'to retire', and a person can be a retired gardener, a retired policeman, or whatever. The word can also describe a place that is secluded and peaceful.

retort

You arrive at work a fraction late one morning. Your office manager says to you, 'Well done, Alex. I hope getting out of bed was not too great a strain.' You instantly reply, 'It was a strain, Brian, but at least I got out of bed conscious.' Your reply could be described as a **retort**, a sharp or incisive reply that turns the preceding remark against the person who made it. A retort is also a vessel, usually made of glass and provided with a long neck, bent downwards, in which liquids, subject to distillation, are heated. A furnace in which iron is heated with carbon to produce steel can also be termed a retort.

retreat

As a verb, to **retreat** means to give up ground to a superior force. Hence you are likely to retreat if you are threatened by a gang of unfriendly youths one evening. The army will retreat if the opposing forces are overwhelmingly larger, and there is a specific bugle call that is called the retreat. Somewhat differently, you may have a room in your house that is known as your retreat. Into it you retire when you want to work on your forthcoming analysis of the poetry of John Donne. Your wife and children observe the unspoken rule that you are not to be disturbed.

retrieve

If you **retrieve** an object, you go and fetch it back from the place it currently occupies. Hence Tony might need to retrieve his ball from the garden of his next-door neighbour. You might also need to extract data from a computer, and the verb 'to retrieve' is often used for this process. Sometimes too it is desirable to try and restore a previously amicable situation from its current tension. You have objected to your neighbour constantly having bonfires in his back garden. Relations between the pair of you are considerably strained. One night his wife, René, pops round and explains that the bonfires will end very shortly, but that they needed to destroy a lot of wooden things in the process of having their kitchen refitted. Her explanation and apology do a great deal to retrieve the situation.

return

You go to visit your aunt in Harrogate and **return** home to Wetherby that evening. This is the most common usage of 'return', to come back to a place or person that you had previously left. Equally, of course, having borrowed a book off Ben, you will naturally return it to him. Yet 'return' can also have financial implications. You invested £15,000 in ICI, and got a return of £831 (i.e. a profit in interest) after only six months. Furthermore, in an election, you return a candidate to the House of Commons even if he or she has never been an MP before. Naturally, of course, there are noun equivalents to these verbal examples.

reverse

As most of us know, if you **reverse** your car, you begin moving in the opposite direction to your normal forward movement. You might, for instance, want to go backwards into your garage, and so you reverse into it. But reverse can also mean a set-back, an instance of bad fortune: 'My building company was doing very nicely, but since September there has been a reverse, and work has been very difficult to pick up.' Indeed, 'reverse' can indicate 'the opposite' in a number of contexts: 'His remarks were the reverse of complimentary'; 'Her work was the reverse of tidy' and so on. Again, on a coin or a banknote, the side that is the opposite to the face side is often termed the reverse side.

reversion

Reversion is the return to a previous state, practice or belief. Griff was brought up in a Roman Catholic household. When an undergraduate, he became an atheist, but in his 40s he experienced a reversion to Catholicism. In law a reversion is the right, especially of the original owner or their heirs, to possess or succeed to property on the death of the present possessor or at the end of a lease. In insurance a reversion is the sum payable on a person's death, especially by way of life insurance. There is also a reversion disease which can afflict the blackcurrant.

review, revue

A **review** can be an evaluation of some work. Thus a book review judges the book in question, a film review does the same, and the so-called quality newspapers all carry book, film, play and art reviews on a weekly basis. Slightly differently but with the same evaluative object in mind, your factory might be the subject of a review to see if it fulfils health and safely regulations and so on. A judge might review some sentences that were imposed last year, and might conclude that the sentences imposed were too lenient, too harsh or entirely invalid. A **revue** is much less weighty. It is a theatrical entertainment normally comprising a series of different acts from a series of different performers.

revolution

A **revolution** occurs when something moving in an orbit of some kind completes such an orbit and arrives back at exactly the same position from which it started. The Earth performs a revolution around the sun, a wheel completes a revolution round its axis, and runners in a mile race along a 440-yard track will complete four revolutions to complete the distance. But, as we all know, a revolution can also signify a great change. The French Revolution saw France change from a monarchy into a republic. The Newtonian Revolution saw terrestrial and planetary motion being unified under a number of laws. In relatively trivial worlds like those of fashion or pop music, revolutions are frequent.

revue *see* review

Rhea, rhea

Rhea, in Greek mythology, was one of the Titans, and it is also the name given to a satellite of Saturn. In lower case, a **rhea** is a flightless bird of South American grasslands.

rheum, room

Rheum is the watery matter secreted by the mucous glands. **Room**, alas, is much more varied. As a noun, a room indicates a space, normally an enclosed space bounded by four walls, a floor and a ceiling. But the word can also be much more indefinite than that. If you say, 'I need room', there is no indication as to the size of the area that you need. Here 'room' is an undefined concept. Of course, there is a large difference between your spare bedroom and the ballroom of Blenheim Palace, but they are both defined rooms with very finite measurements. When someone says, 'I need room to think' or 'I need room to build an intergalactic missile' or 'I need room to be myself', in at least two of the statements it is impossible to set down any temporal dimensions. Indeed, the word 'room' is being used more meta-phorically than literally in such statements. This technique is amazingly common in English. For a nation who, by and large, despise poetry, pride themselves on calling a spade a spade, and appear to have the imaginative capacity of an armadillo, the British manage with amazing frequency to turn a perfectly utilitarian word into one packed with innuendo, symbolism and poetic overtones.

rheumy, roomie, roomy

If you are unfortunate enough to be **rheumy**, you have a watery discharge of mucus emerging from your eyes, nose or mouth. Apparently **roomie** is a colloquial term for a roommate, and if something is **roomy**, it has lots of space.

rho, roe, row

Rho is the seventeenth letter of the Greek alphabet, **roe** is a small species of deer or the mass of eggs contained in the ovarian membrane of a fish, and a **row** is a number of objects (seats, people, bottles, etc.) arranged in a straight line. It can also be a verb meaning to propel a water vehicle manually by means of oars. Pronounced with a short 'o', it becomes a noun or verb signifying a sharp disagreement.

rhubarb

A member of the dock family, the stalks of the **rhubarb** are often cooked for food. The word though is traditionally the word that is supposed to be uttered by actors when they are trying to provide an indistinct background conversation. The word is also used as a synonym for 'nonsense': 'The story of Margaret and me getting married is all rhubarb.'

rhumb, rum

A **rhumb** is any one of the set of lines drawn through a point on a map or chart and indicating the course of an object moving always in the same direction. **Rum** is a spirit distilled from various products of the sugar-cane and traditionally drunk by sailors. However, if you describe something as 'rum', you mean that it is strange and perplexing.

rhyme, rime

When one word shares the same basic sound as another word – fill, spill, for example – they are said to **rhyme**. For centuries English poetry and verse have used rhyme as one of their techniques:

> I look into my glass,
> And view my wasting skin,
> And say, 'Would God it came to pass
> My heart had shrunk as thin!'

The word 'rhyme' used, until the seventeenth century, to be spelt 'rime', but today the word **rime** denotes a hoar-frost or frozen mist.

rib

A **rib** is one of the curved bones articulated in pairs to the spine in men and animals, and enclosing the thoracic cavity. Because of its biological function and shape, the word has also been used to describe a curved frame-timber in a ship extending from the keel to the top of the hull, a piece of timber forming part of the roof of a house, an arch supporting a vault, a hard or rocky portion of a mountain, a bar or ridge of metal made on each barrel of a double-barrelled gun and numerous other specialised usages which it would be redundant to list. Quite differently, however, 'rib' can be a verb meaning 'to tease'.

riband, ribband

A **riband** is a narrow strip of something, a ribbon, while a **ribband** is one of a number of long narrow flexible pieces of timber which are nailed or bolted externally to the ribs of a ship from stem to stern. A ribband can also be a wood scantling used in the construction of a gun or mortar platform.

rich

If you have a great deal of money, you are **rich**. Equally, of course, you can be rich in other things rather than money. You might have a rich collection of CDs, be rich in wisdom, have a rich head of hair, or be rich in the number and steadfastness of your friends. Land can also be rich if it invariably produces an abundant crop. A sound or colour can be rich, normally indicating that either is deep and strong. Occasionally too the word is used as an exclamation of derision. When Frieda, who has the energy levels of the average sloth, tells you that she is entering for the 100 metres in the county sports, you might exclaim, 'Oh Frieda, that's rich.'

rick

One can **rick** one's ankle or one's wrist by spraining it or wrenching it in some way. As a noun, a rick can be a stack of corn, hay, peas, etc. built up into a heap or pile.

riddle

A **riddle** can be a statement, situation or question asked or posed in such a way as to be deliberately puzzling. It can also be a coarse-meshed sieve. According to *Brewer's*, there is also a riddle of claret, a phrase that apparently denotes thirteen bottles of claret, an amount that was presented in a riddle by magistrates invited to a celebratory dinner at the local golf club. (Yes, I know it sounds bizarre, but the English are.)

ride

As a verb, 'to **ride**' denotes that you are sitting on an animal like a horse or sitting in a vehicle like a car and are in control of this mode of transport and are using it to travel from A to B. Sometimes the word is used when you are carried or supported by something over which you do not have complete control. Hence you can ride the waves at sea, ride the markets at the Stock Exchange, or ride the air currents in your glider. In a boxing match, you can also ride a punch in that your body is moving away from it as it lands, and hence its force is greatly diminished. The word is also sometimes used colloquially for sexual intercourse. There are noun counterparts for most of these, though a path in the woods is also called a ride when it allows someone on horseback to trot along it. There are sundry idiomatic expressions using the word 'ride': ride a cockhorse, ride for a fall, ride shotgun, etc.

rider

Clearly a **rider** is someone who rides, be it a horse, bicycle or any other mode of transport. Once upon a time, a rider was also a gold coin of Flanders and Holland that had a horseman on its obverse side. In the game of curling, a rider is a stone driven so as to dislodge other stones blocking the tee. A rider is also an additional set of timbers or iron plates used to strengthen the frame of a ship. It can also be an amending clause attached to a parliamentary Bill, or any additional factor that might impinge on the central matter under discussion.

Riding, riding

The county of Yorkshire was for many years divided into three administrative districts that were called Ridings. With a lower-case 'r', the word is simply the present participle of the verb 'to ride', or a noun in a sentence like 'We went for a riding this afternoon.'

riffle

A **riffle** can be a rocky obstruction in the bed of a river, a device for catching gold in a river, or, as a verb, the action of bending up the cards when shuffling them or the action of handling something in a hesitant manner so as to produce a slight rattle.

rifle

A **rifle** is a gun, or a verb meaning to search rapidly though something in an attempt to find the object or objects that you want.

rift

When you get a crack or split in something like clouds or a rock, it is called a **rift**. The same word is used for a break in friendly communications with someone.

rig

As a verb, 'to **rig**' means to equip a boat with sails and associated tackle, to set up equipment in a hasty fashion, or to provide someone with clothes of a particular type. Sometimes you may even rig the results or the mode of procedure of an election in such a way as to arrive at an unfair result.

rigger, rigour

A **rigger** is someone who makes a ship ready for sailing or an aircraft ready for flight, whereas if you do something with **rigour**, you do it with exactitude, allowing no latitude in any direction.

right, rite, wright, write

Four homophones in a row are rare. The first, **right**, is an internal homophone of its own. As you know, right can be the opposite of wrong, and the opposite of left. It can also denote a legal status: 'I have the right to see my solicitor.' The word can also carry a considerable aura of moral feeling and correctness: 'It is only right that her feelings should be considered.' 'Right' can also depict a political position, normally one concerned with conserving the status quo rather than radical innovation. A **rite** is much more straightforward. It is a formal ceremony, often associated with a religious ceremony like the rite of the Mass, or a civic ceremony of some sort like the inauguration of a new mayor. Quasi-secret societies often indulge in rites in order to give some spurious validity to their quaint practices. A **wright** is a handicraftsman or artificer of some kind. Some crafts have been merged into one word like cartwright, shipwright and wheelwright. To **write** is to form letters and other symbols in such a way as to make coherent sense. Only in the loosest of ways could producing a phrase like wohg owh bwpdsioe zoehh be described as writing, since such a phrase makes no sense.

righting, writing

The activity of **righting** a wrong is an admirable activity in which the legal profession, the police and many charities are constantly engaged. The activity of **writing** is what engages you when you pen a letter to a friend, leave a note for the milkman, or compile a dictionary of homonyms.

rim

The upper or outer edge of an object like a cup, wheel or planetary system is called the **rim**. The word is also used to denote the sucking or licking of someone's anus as a method of sexual stimulation.

rime *see* rhyme

ring, wring

Most of us think of a **ring** as a small circlet of real or simulated precious metal, often set with stones, for wearing on the finger. None the less, almost anything circular in form can be termed a ring. Throw a stone into a pond, and rings of water spread out from the point of impact. Have an accident in the street, and a ring of people will almost instantly surround you. Perversely, though, a boxing ring is square. However, a ring can be conceptual rather than physical. A group of people dedicated to some cause or other might be called the Save the Children ring, or the ring of drug pushers. Equally a ring can be a sound. Most door bells ring. Church bells ring. The sound of metal on metal produces a ring. Some musical instruments can ring out. Even a voice can ring out on occasions. Finally there is a quartet of operas by Wagner that is customarily known as the Ring, and regarded by some as being the greatest operatic achievement of all time. The verb 'to **wring**' is less varied. It means to press, twist, squeeze or afflict. Thus you might wring a flannel to rid it of excess water, wring someone's heart with a touching story, or wring someone's neck when they annoy you beyond endurance.

riot

In most circumstances one thinks of a **riot** as being a violent disturbance of some sort, but you could also talk about a garden being a riot of colour, or of someone being so amusing at some event or other that everyone agreed that he or she had been a riot.

rip

If one makes a tear in something, one has made a **rip**. Thus you might rip your trousers on the barbed wire, or rip some junk mail into pieces. The verb can also denote rapid movement. Hence a fire might rip through a building. You might also rip someone off, which indicates that you have cheated him. All these are common enough usages, but as a noun, 'rip' can denote a stretch of fast-flowing and rough water, or an immoral or unpleasant person. In addition there are two abbreviations, RIP standing for Rest in Peace, and RIP standing for raster image processor.

ripe

Fruit becomes **ripe** and is then suitable for eating. Beer or other alcoholic liquids become ripe, and are then fit for drinking. You might be described as ripe in years when you are in your 70s or 80s. The word can also signify that something is ready: 'The time was ripe for the development of Jocelyn's tactics.' If you describe someone's language as 'ripe', you generally mean that it was coarse. A female fish or insect is ripe when it is ready to lay eggs or spawn.

ripple

A **ripple** is an implement toothed like a comb, and used for cleaning flax or hemp. The wind might cause a ripple across the lake, a ripple being a slight ruffling of the surface. It is also a type of ice cream which has wavy lines of coloured flavoured syrup running through it.

rise, ryes

Although the word **rise** does carry a general connotation of lifting up, of elevating in some way, its range of reference is so great and diverse as to make it a manifold internal homonym. You can see the sun rise each morning. You doubtless rise from bed most mornings. Voices and instruments rise in pitch as they travel from middle C to top C. Your Post Office is situated on the rise of a hill, which does make walking to it more taxing than you ideally wish. Doubtless you are hoping for a rise in salary this year. You often see the fish rise to the surface in your village pond. I expect the winds will rise this evening. As you can see from such examples, 'rise' is a valuable and versatile word. Rye is a food-grain obtained from the plant *Secale cereale*, and so **ryes** is the plural of that plant.

rite *see* **right**

road, rode, rowed

A **road** is a hard-surfaced line of physical communication between places used by pedestrians, cyclists and motorists. The word is also used metaphorically: 'The road to success in learning Latin is to memorise the conjugations and declensions as early as possible.' The word **rode** is the past tense of the verb 'to ride', just as **rowed** is the past tense of the verb 'to row'.

rock

As a verb, 'to rock' means to move gently to and fro, as in a cradle or a rocking chair. As a noun, a rock is a large rugged mass of stone. Metaphorically it can be claimed that Jason is the rock of the Hinstock Chess Club, since without him, it would probably collapse. There are also claims that 'rock' is a type of music, often linked together with 'roll' to create 'rock and roll'. From the inadequate evidence that it has been possible to glean, this 'music' would appear to be loud, rhythmically monotonous, harmonically unadventurous and lyrically asinine.

rocket

The cruciferous annual *Eruca sativa* that possesses purple-veined white flowers is called a **rocket**, though it is obviously very different from a cylindrical object that can be powered to shoot upwards into the sky, which is also called a rocket. If someone gives you a rocket, you have been rebuked most soundly.

rocky

If the terrain is **rocky** it is littered with rocks, but if a marriage is rocky it seems doomed to collapse.

rod

Most of the time a **rod** is a thin, straight bar of wood or metal, but it can also be a shortened way of referring to a fishing rod, a light-sensitive cell present in the retina of the eye, or a slang term for the penis.

rode *see* road

roe, row

The **roe** is a small Eurasian deer, or the mass of eggs contained in the ovaries of a female fish or shellfish. A **row** is a number of people or things standing more or less in a straight line.

rogue

A **rogue** is a dishonest or unprincipled man, or an elephant or other large animal that is living away from the pack and having destructive tendencies. The word can also be a verb, in which case it means to remove inferior plants or seedlings from a crop.

roil, royal

The verb 'to **roil**' tends now to be used only in the USA. It means to render water or any liquid turbid or muddy by stirring up its sediment, or to rouse someone's temper or to irritate someone. Something that is **royal** is either related in blood to the royal family or belongs to or is used by that royal family. The word can be used metaphorically. If you call the lion a royal animal, you mean that it possesses majesty and is king of the large cats.

roll, role

A **roll** can be a number of things. It can be a sheet or sheets of paper wound up without creasing into a cylindrical form. It can be a cylindrical piece of wood or metal used to facilitate the moving of something. The peal of thunder is often called a roll of thunder. Children like lying down at the top of a grassy hill and allowing gravity to roll them down the hill. One can roll one's eyes in despair, irritation or humour. One can take the roll at some organisation like a school when one checks off that all the people who are supposed to be there actually are. One can even be on a roll, which means that you are full of energy, ideas and commitment. A **role**, however, is simply the part that one plays on a particular occasion. You might have the role of Shylock in Shakespeare's play *The Merchant of Venice*, you might one night have to take the role of babysitter, you might have to take the role of cook one evening when the normal cook in your household is ill, and so on.

rood, rude, rued

A **rood** is a crucifix, and the word is often used when referring to the cross upon which Christ died. The word also once signified a linear measure of six to eight yards or a measure of land equal to about forty square poles. If someone is **rude,** they are impolite, uncivilised or barbaric. If you tell someone that their face resembles that of a half-witted bison, you are being rude, but that is not the same meaning as describing the Twitototal tribe as living in rude conditions. If something is **rued,** it is regretted. It is the past tense of the verb 'to rue'.

roof

A **roof** is the structure that covers a building or vehicle, and hence prevents the rain from drowning the bedroom or the car. There is also the idiom of hitting the roof which means suddenly becoming very angry.

rook

A **rook** is a black raucous-voiced bird that belongs to the crow family. A rook is also a chess piece, often called a castle. 'To rook' someone is to cheat or defraud them.

room *see* rheum

roost

Domestic fowl perch on a **roost.** The tumultuous tidal race formed by the meeting of conflicting currents off various parts of the Orkney and Shetland Islands is also called a roost.

root, route

That part of a plant or tree that is below the surface of the ground is divided into tendrils that absorb water and nutrients, each of which is called a **root.** If you are trying to find the source of almost anything, you might say that you are looking for the root of the matter. The word also has technical usages in mathematics, philology and music. As a verb, if you root around for something, you are trying to find it. I am always rooting around for a pen. If you root for someone, you give them support and encouragement. A **route** is a way from A to B. Hence, if you wanted to go from Bristol to London, it would be a sensible route to travel via Bath, Swindon and Reading, but an idiotic route to travel via Birmingham, Norwich and Ipswich.

rose, rows

The **rose,** of which there are many varieties, is one of the most loved flowers in Britain. Equally if you describe your friend Yvonne as the rose of Basingstoke, you are paying her a compliment (assuming, that is, that she does live in Basingstoke). The word is also the past tense of the verb 'to rise': 'The sun rose at 5.47 this morning.' **Rows** is the plural of 'row'. Consequently it could signify objects or people arranged in lines, or a series of sharp disagreements.

rostrum

Normally seen on a stage or dais, a **rostrum** is a raised platform on which a person stands to make a public speech, receive an award, play music or conduct an orchestra. The same word is used to depict a beak-like projection, especially a stiff snout or anterior prolongation of the head in an insect, crustacean or cetacean.

rot

If today you killed your cat and left its corpse on the back lawn, it would quite rapidly begin to **rot**. In other words, it would putrefy, decay and smell. If a friend tries to convince you that astrology is a serious subject and you cried, 'This is rot,' then you would be indicating that you regarded the matter as nonsense.

rotate

The verb **rotate** indicates motion, the motion of moving in a circle around some axis. Thus the planets rotate round the sun, just as a fan rotates round its axis. The word is also used conceptually. The English department at Swineshire University rotates round its dynamic professor, Dr Imagist Structure. (Please excuse my crass naming inventions.) More practically, the word is also used for the rotation of jobs: 'We rotate the position of chairman, and this month it is my turn.' And, as Turnip Townshend inaugurated in the eighteenth century, many farmers rotate their crops, wheat in Field A this year, carrots next, and so on.

rote, wrote

If you do something by **rote**, you tend to be doing so because continued practice has made it second-nature. Few of us, for instance, devote much thought to laying the table; we do it by rote. In the USA, however, 'rote' can denote the roaring of the sea, and in Britain in the middle ages a 'rote' was a musical instrument, probably of the stringed variety.

rough, ruff

Ground that is uneven, untended and clogged with stones and weeds can be described as **rough** ground. When the wind is blowing, the rain streaming down, the lightning flashing, then it will be agreed that the weather is rough. When a man in the pub, clad in rags and unshaven, threatens to punch your lights out (eyes) if you don't stop looking at his bird (woman), then that man could be described as being of a rough character. As you can see, 'rough' always means untamed, untended, or with violent tendencies, but its wide range of possible application makes it into an internal homonym of its own. A **ruff** can be more disparate, since a ruff is a sea-bream or other sparoid fish, an article of neckwear common in Elizabethan and Jacobean England, the act of trumping at cards, or the male of a bird of the sandpiper family.

round

Something that is spherical, globular or circular can be described as **round**. A dance in which the participants move round in a circle is also called a round. If you go for a walk, you might say, 'I just went round the castle grounds,' indicating that your walk was very roughly a circular one. If four of you play one hand of bridge, you might later say that you'd had a round of bridge. When going to the pub with your friends, you might buy the first round of drinks (i.e. you buy a drink for yourself and everyone else). If you sing in a round, you take part in some canonical piece of music. If you fire a single shot from your rifle, you have shot a round. If you are not sure quite how many attended your Christmas party, you might say that it was round forty. As you can see, 'round' is another versatile word.

row *see* rho

rowed *see* road

rub

In the game of bowls, an impediment by which a bowl is hindered in, or diverted from, its proper course is called a **rub**. Indeed, the word can be applied to an obstacle of almost any kind, and the clichéd clause, 'Ay, there's the rub,' is a common one whenever one meets some sort of difficulty. Even more common is the use of 'rub' as a verb, when it means that one applies pressure to some object, often with a cloth, in an attempt to clean the object or to rid it of unnecessary objects that have become stuck to it. Equally, of course, one can rub one's arm or leg if one has scratched or bruised it.

rubber

Rubber is a tough, elastic polymeric substance made from the latex of a tropical plant or synthetically. A rubber is also obviously something with which one rubs. You might rub your body with a towel after a shower or bath. You might rub your cup that you gained for winning the town's hockey competition with a cloth. In both instances, the towel and cloth are acting as rubbers. A piece of India-rubber is often used for erasing marks made by a pencil. But a rubber is also the name for a set of games (often three or five) that establish an overall winner. Thus you can have a rubber of bridge, bowls, cribbage, whist and so on. Even a test-match series at cricket is often called the rubber.

rule

As a noun, a **rule** is a regulation that has to be obeyed. Thus it is a rule at the Adderley Working Men's Club that no woman can be served a drink. The word can also mean control or dominance. Thus one might say that the British rule over India was marked by an almost total ignorance of local practices, customs and sensibilities.

ruler

A **ruler** can be someone who rules over a country, province or organisation, or a straight strip of wood, plastic or metal used for measuring short distances or for drawing straight lines.

rum *see* rhumb

run

This verb has a surprising number of applications. The most obvious and common is to move at a speed faster than a walk. You perhaps needed to **run** for the bus this morning. Secondly, the word can be applied to the spread of news: 'The news that Helen was pregnant ran through the offices at the speed of light.' Thirdly, water or any other liquid can be run: 'I must go and run some water for my bath.' Streets, though they stay exactly where they are, are also said to run: 'The High Street runs south of the parish church.' More reasonably, trains, buses and other forms of transport also run, even when they are stuck in a traffic jam. If you manage some organisation or part of an organisation, you run it: 'Carolyn runs the stationery department.' A film, play or event will run for some days, weeks, months or years: '*The Mousetrap* seems fated to run for ever.' A habit, trait or genetic disease can run in a family: 'Dishonesty seems to run in the Patterson family.' If a newspaper reveals what is really happening in Lebanon, it is said to run the story. If you are a drug smuggler, you will run drugs into the country. There are, of course, noun equivalents to these verbal uses, and also one or two individual noun instances. Thus you can have a ski run, take a run at cricket, keep the hens in a run, have a run on berets in your clothes shop, or have the run of the office. There can be few words in English whose application is so varied.

rung, wrung

In its most common usage, **rung** is the past tense of the verb 'to ring'. It can also be the round or stave of a ladder. If something is **wrung**, it is squeezed, pressed or twisted, normally in order to expel water from it. It is the past tense of the verb 'to wring', and can also be used metaphorically. Hence your heart may be wrung by sadness.

runner

Clearly a **runner** is someone who runs, but it could also be someone who smuggles goods into the country, a rod or groove along which something slides, a plant that can spread out horizontally, or a long, narrow strip of carpet.

rye, wry

Rye is a type of grain, and **wry** indicates that something is twisted or contorted in some way. Hence a wry smile normally signifies regret or distaste.

ryes *see* rise

S

sable

The small carnivorous marten, *Mustela zibellina*, is commonly called the **sable**. It is native to arctic and sub-arctic regions. The word is also used to refer to several species of pyralid moths, and to an antelope. Sable is also the equivalent to 'black' in heraldic terminology, and the word is often used as an adjective to describe mourning garments, though the fur of the marten is actually dark brown.

sabot

A **sabot** is a kind of simple shoe, the box from which cards are dealt out at a casino, or a device which ensures the correct positioning of a bullet or shell in the barrel of a gun.

sac, sack

In current usage, **sac** is a biological term. It is any natural bag-like cavity with a membranous covering in an animal or vegetable organism. However, 'sac and soc' used to be the expression used in charters to denote certain rights of jurisdiction, which by custom belonged to the lord of the manor. Most of us think of a **sack** as being a large, oblong bag, open at one end, normally made of flax or hemp, and used for carrying and transporting corn, coal, flour, fruit and so on. It is also a common noun and verb for dismissing someone from their employment. It is also a general name for a class of white wine, and can be a verb signifying the plunder and destruction of a town or settlement captured by an opposing army.

sachet, sashay

A **sachet** is a small sealed packet containing something such as dry perfume to be placed among clothing. The *Shorter Oxford* doesn't list **sashay**, which is surprising because it is a not uncommon word meaning 'to strut, to flounce'. Attractive and confident women tend to sashay in the ballroom.

sack *see* sac

sacks, sax, saxe

Fairly obviously, **sacks** is the plural of 'sack' ('Please put the sacks of flour in the warehouse') or the third person singular of the verb 'to sack' ('Adrian always sacks anyone who is caught smoking'). **Sax** is a shortened form of 'saxophone', but, rather like 'bus', has become a standard form so that it barely counts as an abbreviation. A sax can also be a small axe used for cutting roof slates. **Saxe** is a light blue colour with a greyish tinge.

433

sad

Someone is **sad** if they are feeling and exhibiting sorrow, but the word is also used to describe dough that has failed to rise in the oven. Shakespeare calls it 'distressful bread'. In the USA, unleavened cakes are known as sad cakes.

saddle

Most of us have encountered the **saddle** of a bicycle or the saddle of a horse, in both cases a kind of seat designed for riding on. However, a saddle can also be a shaped support on which a cable, wire or pipe rests, the region of a curve between two high points, or a joint of meat consisting of the two loins.

saddleback

A **saddleback** is a tower roof which has two opposite gables connected by a pitched section, a hill with a ridge along the top that dips in the middle, a breed of pig, or a New Zealand wattlebird.

safe

A **safe** is a receptacle with a strong and complex locking mechanism into which one can place valuable objects (money, jewels, etc.) to protect them from thieves. In the USA it is also another name for a condom. The word is also an adjective or adverb indicating that something is free from danger: 'It is safe to walk along here', or, 'It is a safe procedure if you don't let the fat get too hot.'

sage

If someone is described as **sage**, you can assume that he or she is wise, prudent and judicious. But sage is also a plant, an aromatic culinary herb.

sail, sale

Before the invention of artificially powered ships in the nineteenth century, all ships sailed by having a **sail** or sails attached to them. This large piece of canvas was attached to a mast so that it could catch the wind and be powered by the force of that wind. Unsurprisingly, the word sail is also applied to objects that resemble a ship's sail. A **sale** is an event when person A exchanges an article in exchange for money from person B. Hence sales are constantly occurring in shops, and communities and charities often arrange special sales of their own in order to raise funds.

saint

Strictly speaking, a **saint** is only someone who has been canonised by the church, but the word is often used in connection with any very virtuous and kind person. People who compile dictionaries of homonyms should automatically be termed saints, but this usage has not yet caught on.

sake

This common noun is quite difficult to pin down to an unambiguous definition, because it can express purpose – 'I walk every day for the **sake** of my health' – or it can express consideration – 'I did that for the sake of Petula' – or it can even express impatience or annoyance – 'Why did you do that, for heaven's sake?' There is also the Japanese drink made from fermented rice, and pronounced with the e sounding like an i.

salad

A **salad** is a cold conglomeration of herbs or vegetables like lettuce, tomatoes, cress, etc., often flavoured with a dressing of salt, pepper, oil and vinegar. However, there is also the common expression 'in my salad days' which tends to mean when one was young and enthusiastic and naïve. The expression comes from Shakespeare's *Antony and Cleopatra*.

salamander

In mythology a **salamander** was a lizard-like creature that was said to live in fire. In real life, a salamander is a newt-like amphibian, which, because of its flame-like markings, was once thought, quite wrongly, to be able to endure fire. A salamander is also a metal plate heated and placed over food to brown it.

sale *see* sail

salient

As an adjective, **salient** means relevant, significant or important: 'The most salient point is . . . ' The word is also used to describe an animal standing on its hind legs. As a noun, a salient is a piece of land or fortification that juts out to form an angle.

sallow

If a person is **sallow**, their complexion has a sickly yellow colour, but the word also applies to a type of willow tree and to a European moth with dull yellow, orange and brown patterned wings.

sally

Apart from being a female first name, **sally** can also be a noun denoting a sudden rush out from a besieged place in order to attack the enemy, a sudden start into activity, a witticism, the woolly grip for the hands near the lower end of a bell rope, any of a number of acacias and eucalyptuses that resemble willows, or the first movement of a bell when 'set' for ringing.

salon

A **salon** can be a reception room in a large house, or an establishment where a beautician, hairdresser or couturier conducts trade.

saloon

Strictly speaking a **saloon** is a public room used for a specified purpose, but anyone who has seen a western film will assume that it is a public bar for the selling of alcoholic drinks. There are also saloon cars, each of which is often just called a saloon.

salsa

Salsa is a type of Latin American dance music, though it is also a spicy tomato sauce.

salt

Apart from **salt** being sodium chloride, a salt is also any chemical compound formed from the reaction of an acid with a base. The word is also often used metaphorically. You can call someone 'the salt of the earth' (a great compliment), you can 'rub salt into the wound' (increase the pain someone is enduring), or 'salt the books' (make fictitious entries so that the business looks more prosperous than it really is).

saltation

In biology a **saltation** is an abrupt evolutionary change, but in geology it denotes the transport of hard particles over an uneven surface.

salute

Today we tend to use the word **salute** in two different ways. The first refers to a conventional action, normally by a member of the armed forces, in which he or she raises an arm and touches the side of his or her head with the angled parts of the arm forming a lateral triangle. The other usage is a simple greeting. You meet Matthew in the street and salute him by calling out, 'Hi, Matthew, how are things?' or some other trite remark. However, there are other meanings too. The firing of guns at some ceremony is called a salute. The formal greeting in fencing just before the bout begins is called a salute. A kiss on the cheek between two friends can be called a salute. When the birds begin to sing in the dawn chorus, it can be said that they salute the morning. All of these instances have one thing in common. They are all an acknowledgement of one kind or another, but the instances are so diverse that it would be foolish not to call them homonymic.

salve

This word can be pronounced in two different ways, one so that it rhymes with 'valve', and the other with the final 'e' pronounced as it was in its Latin original. With the first pronunciation, **salve** can be a verb or noun meaning an ointment that is applied to a wound. It can also be the action of saving a ship or its cargo from loss at sea. With 'e' pronounced, the word retains its original Latin meaning, and is a simple greeting like 'Hail'.

salvo

We normally think of a **salvo** as being the simultaneous discharge of artillery, but the word can also denote a reservation in one's mind, often a somewhat dishonest reservation along the lines of 'If I say this, I'll still be able to do x, because my actual words don't actually exclude it, even though my disputant thinks they do.'

sandwich

A **sandwich** is two slices of buttered bread with some other food like cheese, salmon, beef or salad placed between them. One can also do a sandwich course in which one does a period of vocational training in between one's academic teaching.

sane, seine

If a person is **sane**, they are relatively normal and balanced in their mental and emotional make-up. Someone who is not sane might suffer from delusions, paranoia, ludicrous conspiracy theories, massive self-importance, and so on. One thinks of the House of Commons. Anyone referring to a dictionary of homonyms is, by definition, sane. A **seine**, apart from being the name of the French river that flows through Paris, is a fishing net designed to hang vertically in the water.

saner, seiner

Many of us regard ourselves as being **saner** than our friends (or, indeed, anyone else). That means that we regard ourselves as more mentally normal or balanced than most others. A **seiner** is someone who fishes with a net.

sanguine

Anyone who is a **sanguine** person is naturally cheerful and optimistic. Yet the word can also mean blood-red.

santero

The **santero** is the Mexican and Spanish-speaking areas of the south-western parts of the USA. It is also a priest of the santeria religious cult.

sap

Sap is the vital juice which circulates in plants, and the process of under-mining some building or wall by burrowing beneath it and thus weakening the entire structure. You can also sap someone else's work by insidious comments in the appropriate ears or by placing obstacles in their way. The word is also used to denote that someone is a half-wit.

sapling

A **sapling** is a young tree, especially one with a slender trunk. It is also a greyhound in its first year.

sardine

In the Biblical book of Revelation, it is stated that the person whom John saw in his vision 'was to look upon like a jasper and a **sardine** stone'. Consequently one must assume that sardine was a precious stone. Most of us, however, think of a sardine as being a small fish of the herring family.

sash

A **sash** can be a scarf-like object worn round the waist, or a sliding frame constituting part of a window.

sashay *see* sachet

satellite

In days of **satellite** television, we tend to think of a satellite as an artificial body that orbits the Earth (or, indeed, any other planet), but the word was first applied to celestial bodies that did orbit their own planet. Thus the moon is a satellite of the Earth. The word, however, is also applied to a person or establishment that is loosely connected to some central person or establishment. The freelance reporter who none the less mostly works for the *Daily Mail* might be regarded as a satellite of that paper. An insurance company based in New York might have satellite offices in London and Paris. A small independent country that is none the less tied by heritage, economy and language to a larger, more powerful country can be regarded as a satellite country. The word is also applied to portions of DNA that have repeating base sequences.

satisfaction

Your idea for a better system of classification at work has been accepted, your boss has just raised your salary by £5,000 a year, and your wife has just become pregnant. Consequently you are full of **satisfaction**, a general feeling of contentment. Unfortunately your colleague Gerard was recently accused wrongly by his Departmental Head of being a paedophile, and so Gerard quite understandably has demanded satisfaction. The two will be fighting a duel in the courtyard at 11.00 tomorrow morning. In addition, Penelope recently spent £6.30 of her own money in travelling to one of our branch offices. Fortunately she has received satisfaction from the Accounting Department and will be getting the money back at the end of the week.

satyr

In Greek mythology, a **satyr** was a lustful, drunken woodland god. Hence the impulse to have sexual intercourse with as many women as possible is known as satyriasis. The name also applies to a butterfly with dark brown wings.

sauce, source

A **sauce** is a material, usually liquid or soft, that can be added to a meal to provide extra taste. It is also a colloquial word denoting that someone is impertinent or cheeky. A **source** is the origin of something. The source of Shakespeare's history plays is often Holinshed's *Chronicles of England, Scotland and Ireland*. The source of the River Severn is to be found in mid-Wales.

save

Broadly speaking, the verb 'to **save**' means to keep safe or to rescue, but its applications are quite varied. You can save money, you can save time, you can save someone from danger, you can save appearances, and in computing you can save data. All these have a basic similarity to each other, but there are at least a couple of instances where 'save' is used somewhat differently. In the game of football, the goalkeeper can make a great save, yet he is not saving the ball or the goal in either the sense of keeping safe or of rescuing. Then there is the strange idiom that you find in sentences like 'The dining room was empty save for Priscilla.' Here 'save' is a synonym for 'except'.

saver, savour

These words are not quite homophones, but we are unlikely to notice that very often in most usages of the words. A **saver** is someone who saves. You may be a saver because you put money into the bank, because you rescue someone from drowning, or because you save your files on the hard disk of your computer. You can also buy a saver ticket on the trains, and apparently a hedging bet in horse racing is also called a saver. If you **savour** something, you taste it with relish. If a dish possesses savour, it has a distinctive taste.

saw

A **saw** is a cutting tool designed largely to cut through wood. It can also be a proverb or maxim of some kind, and the past tense of the verb 'to see'.

sawyer

Understandably a **sawyer** is someone who saws timber for a living, but it is also a large long-horned beetle. In the USA it can be an uprooted tree floating in the river, but fast at one end, and in New Zealand a sawyer is a large wingless cricket.

sax, saxe *see* sacks

say

If you **say** something, you utter words, you speak, and this is the way in which we all think of that verb. None the less there is another interestingly speculative meaning also. We often use 'say' when we are suggesting a hypothesis or proposing an alternative: 'Say we took Tim with us; would that be difficult?'

scab

The dry protective crust that forms over a cut or wound during healing is known as a **scab**, but the same word is applied to a number of fungal diseases of plants and to someone who refuses to come out on strike when his colleagues do so.

scald

One tends to **scald** oneself if one comes into contact with boiling liquid on one's skin, but the same word is used for a number of plant diseases which produce an effect similar to scalding.

scale

A weighing instrument consisting of a pair of dishes hanging from each side of a balance is called a **scale** or a pair of scales. The same name is applied to one of the thin membranes of the skin found in fishes and some reptiles and insects. In music a scale is the notes of a complete octave of any particular key. A scale can also be a series of gradations in a graph, a map, a list of prices or any arithmetical progression. One can also scale a mountain, the activity of climbing up the mountain.

scallop

The **scallop** is an edible bivalve mollusc with a ribbed fan-shaped shell. A small dish or pan that is shaped like that shell is called a scallop shell, and embroidery decorations of the same shape are called scallops. However, you can also scallop some vegetables by baking them with milk or a sauce.

scalp

The **scalp** is the skin covering the skull. American Indians had the unpleasant habit of removing the scalp (with hair attached) of defeated enemies. As a result, the word 'scalp' has become used to signify a convincing victory in a number of fields from the Stock Exchange to the football field.

scamp

This can be a rascally good-for-nothing, or a verb meaning to do a task negligently.

scan

If you **scan** something, you look at it fairly carefully, normally because you are looking for some specific item. However there is also an electronic scan when a machine scans your brain in search of tumours or scans your luggage at Heathrow in search of a bomb.

scape

In architecture a **scape** is the shaft of a column. In botany it is the long flower-stalk rising directly from the root. 'Scape' is occasionally used as a shortened version of landscape, and I gather that it is also the conventional imitation of the cry of the snipe.

scapular

This word always relates to the shoulder or shoulder blade (scapula), but the instances of its use are still very different. A short monastic cloak covering the shoulders is called a **scapular**, as is a bandage passing over and around the shoulders and a bird's feather taken from the shoulder region.

scarf

A **scarf** is a band of material worn round the neck in cold weather, though soldiers, churchmen and some officials have more ceremonial scarves. In carpentry a scarf is a joint by which two timbers are connected longitudinally. It is also the name given to an incision made in the blubber of a whale, and in North America it can be a verb meaning to eat or drink enthusiastically.

scavenger

A **scavenger** is an animal that feeds on carrion, a person who searches for and collects discarded items, and in chemistry a substance that reacts with and removes particular molecules and radicals.

scene, seen

In the theatre, a **scene** is a sub-division of a play or film, but it can also be something at which one is looking, or a disruption of normal social conventions by two or more people having some altercation. **Seen** is the past participle of the verb 'to see'.

scent see cent

schedule

A **schedule** is a plan for carrying out a process or procedure, giving lists of intended events and times. In law it can be an appendix to a formal document, and for the Inland Revenue it is their categorisation of the British population into wealth divisions so that they can more accurately carry out their time-honoured procedure of taxing the poor more than the rich.

school

As most of us know, a **school** is an establishment that we attend from the ages of five to sixteen or eighteen in order to gain knowledge and skills that will make us economically productive members of society. More loosely the word can also be applied to members of an academic trend: 'Nigel belongs to the school of linguistic philosophers.' A collection of fish, porpoises or whales swimming together while feeding or migrating is also called a school.

schooner

A **schooner** is a small, sea-going vessel, or a tall beer-glass holding about twice the normal quantity.

sclerosis

Sclerosis is an abnormal hardening of body tissue, but the word is also used to signify the tendency in humans to be resistant to change: 'The English department is subject to sclerosis because Mr Huntley refuses to teach any writer more modern than Shakespeare.'

scoff

As a verb, 'to **scoff**' is either to deride, or to gobble food in a voracious manner.

sconce

A **sconce** is a flat candlestick with a handle for carrying it, a small fort or earthwork, a fine levied by undergraduates upon one of their own community, or a seat at one side of the fireplace in an open chimney.

scoop

A **scoop** can be a ladle-like kitchen implement used for extracting substances from a container, a piece of news gathered by a newspaper or television channel before anyone else has discovered it, or an unpleasant glide from one note to another by a musical instrument or, more frequently, a voice. As a verb, one can also scoop out dirt or soil from a hole that one is digging, or one might scoop up all the clothes that your son has left lying on the bedroom floor and toss them out of the window into the garden.

score

It is possible to **score** a notch in a tree or piece of wood, to score runs in cricket, goals in football, and so on, or, colloquially, to score by persuading a lady to go to bed with you. A score is also a group or set of twenty, the result of a test that one has taken, or a written representation of a musical composition.

scour

One might **scour** a place in a desperate attempt to find something, one might scour the kitchen sink in an attempt to make it clean, and one would doubtless regret that one's cattle and pigs had scours, namely, diarrhoea.

scout

As a verb, 'to **scout**' means to wander over an area in an attempt to gain information of some kind. As a noun, a scout is a member of the movement founded by Baden Powell designed to foster skills and independence in young lads, a male college servant at Oxford University, or the local name for various sea birds. Interestingly, the word comes from the Old French *escoute* which means 'to spy'.

scrag

As a noun, a **scrag** can be an unattractively thin person or animal. As a verb, one can scrag in rugby by grasping an opponent by the neck, whereas if you did that in the street, you would end up in court.

scramble

If you are climbing Ben Nevis, there may be times when you are forced to **scramble**, that is, clamber up using your hands as well as your feet. Yet, when aircraft are told to scramble, they have to take off immediately because there is some sort of crisis. If you scramble something up, you turn a tidy situation into an untidy one, or an ordered situation into a disordered one. You can also scramble eggs, and eat the result on toast. Finally, when sending a radio message to your troops in Natal, you may scramble that message by putting it into code.

scrambler

Unsurprisingly a **scrambler** is someone who scrambles over the terrain, or a machine for scrambling a telephone conversation or a broadcast transmission, but it might also be a motor cycle engaged in racing over rough and hilly ground, or a plant with a long slender stem that is supported by other plants.

scrap

A **scrap** is a tiny fragment left of a meal or almost anything else, or an angry dispute frequently leading to physical violence.

scrape

As a verb, to **scrape** means to rub something against something else, either by accident or in a deliberate attempt to clean the item. One can also scrape through an exam by only just passing it. One might also scrape an acquaintance with someone, normally activated by motives of social prestige or greed. As a noun, a scrape can be a somewhat awkward and embarrassing situation in which one finds oneself.

scratch

If you **scratch** something, you mark it with a sharp or pointed object. You may also scratch out something that you have written (i.e. cross it out) because you want to substitute another word or phrase. You will also doubtless be sorry if you have to scratch (i.e. withdraw) Annabelle from the greyhound racing on Saturday. As a noun, scratch can signify the starting point of a race for a competitor who is given neither a handicap nor an advantage, or a slight wound, normally on one's arms or legs.

screw

A **screw** is a grooved tool that can be twisted into wood, metal or some other material so as to hang something from that material or to secure that material to another object. Thus you can hang a picture from a screw, replace a missing screw from your car, or screw your name-plate on to your study door. A billiard or snooker player can impart a twist to the cue-ball, and a bowler in cricket can impart a twist to the ball that he is bowling. Both can be called a screw. A screw is also slang for a prison warder. You might also screw some information out of someone by threatening them with some embarrassing revelation. If you screw Margaret, you will have sexual intercourse with her.

scrub

If you **scrub** the floor, you clean it by rubbing it with a hard brush and water. Yet scrub as a noun can be low stunted vegetation.

scull, skull

A **scull** is a kind of oar with which you scull along in a relatively light boat. A **skull** is the bony casement for the brain.

scum

Scum is dirt which rises to the surface of the water when you have a bath or when a pond is stagnant or when some liquid is fermenting. It is also a word used to refer to the lowest specimens of humanity.

scuttle

As a verb, 'to **scuttle**' can mean to run with quick hurried steps, or to cut a hole or holes in a ship with the object of sinking it. As a noun, a skuttle is a container for sifting corn or holding coal. It can also be a hole in a ship's deck used as a means of communication between deck and deck.

sea, see

A **sea** is a large expanse of saline water, though the word is often used metaphorically. If you are lost and confused about something, you might say that you were all at sea. You might describe a large crowd as a sea of faces. A **see**, however, is the area of land under the control of a bishop, though, more commonly, it is a verb meaning to perceive things with the eyes.

seal, seel

A **seal** is a member of the aquatic family *Phocidae*, and is an excellent swimmer. A seal can also be a device impressed upon a piece of wax as evidence of authenticity. 'To **seel**' is to close the eyes of a hawk or other bird by stitching up the eyelids.

seam, seem

A **seam** is what you get when you sew two pieces of fabric together. The seam is the junction that they create. In geology, when you have two large strata separated by a much thinner one, the thin is called the seam. The verb 'to **seem**' suggests that something looks fine, but that there is still room for doubt: 'Gordon Green seems a certainty to become Prime Minister, but politics is a wayward creature.'

seamen, semen

As you would expect, **seamen** are people who work by the sea or on it, tending the harbour, repairing boats, sailing the seas, and so on. **Semen** is the discharge from a man's penis when he reaches orgasm.

sear, seer

A **sear** is the catch in a gun-lock which keeps the hammer at full or half-cock. As a verb, 'to sear' means to wither away, to be impaired by too much heat. A **seer** is a prophet or one who see divine revelations. It is also a denomination of weight in various parts of India.

seas, sees, seize

Seas is the plural of 'sea', **sees** is the third person singular, present tense of the verb 'to see', and **seize** is a verb meaning to capture, to take possession of, or to grab.

season

We are all acquainted with the seasons of the year, and many of us have our personal favourite, be it the flowering of spring or the dying tinge of autumn. Not that, even in its temporal meaning, the word **season** need be confined to the four quarters of the year. The word can be used much more loosely: 'I fear that it is not the season for getting any leeway from the Chinese over this matter.' As a verb, 'to season' means to add spices and herbs to a dish in order to make it even more delicious. In addition, you can season wine or wood by keeping them in storage, and a person is said to be seasoned when he or she has had experience of some activity or other.

seat

A **seat** is something that has been designed to sit upon, like a chair or sofa. But the word also has a more rarefied meaning. One can talk about Chatsworth House being the seat of the Duke of Devonshire without meaning that he sits on the roof. One can talk about the liver being the seat of a disease, about the House of Commons being the seat of government, and about good primary school education being the seat of all education, when one is using 'seat' as a synonym for basis or source.

second

A **second** is a division of time, one sixtieth of a minute, a word used loosely to indicate a short duration of time ('I won't be a second'), a word indicating a placing or positioning between first and third, and a verb denoting support for an appointment or proposal ('I second that motion').

secrete

Almost all living things **secrete** matter from their bodies, either to perform some function within the body as would be the case with an enzyme, or to expel waste matter from the body as is the case with sweat. However, the word also has another meaning where something is removed from point A and placed at point B for the purpose of deceit, fraud or a simple game of hunt the slipper.

sects, sex

Not quite homophones, but close enough to cause confusion. **Sects** are relatively small religious bodies like the Plymouth Brethren, the Christadelphians or Jehovah's Witnesses who normally take a fundamentalist view towards the Scriptures, and have the comforting certainty that they are right. The word can be more loosely used to refer to splinters within almost any organisation or mode of thought like a trade union, a political party or an academic subject. **Sex** scarcely needs any definition, it being the division in living animals between male and female, and the act of coition that occurs between males and females. An Internet source defines 'sex' as follows: 'If you have to ask you are too young.'

see *see* sea

seed *see* cede

seeder *see* cedar

seek, Sikh

If you **seek** something, you look for it, you try to find it. A **Sikh** was originally a member of a military community belonging to the Punjab, where it was originally established as a religious sect by Nanak Shah in the early part of the sixteenth century.

seel *see* seal

seem *see* seam

seen *see* scene

seer *see* sear

sees *see* seas

seine *see* sane

seize *see* seas

sell *see* cell

seller *see* cellar

semen *see* seamen

sense

In a fairly concrete way, a **sense** is one of five faculties, touch, taste, sight, hearing and smell, but the word is also used in a variety of less tangible ways. If you say that Ernest has got some sense, you mean that the man is not unintelligent. If you sense that someone has been in your room, you have an almost indefinable intuition. If you fail to gather the sense of a passage in a book, you have failed to understand what the writer was meaning, something that may be your fault or the writer's. So, apart from the five senses, the word can mean an extra-sensory feeling, intelligence or apprehension.

sensible

If you describe someone as being **sensible**, you mean that he or she is a reasonable being, capable of logical thought. The word, though, can be used in a wider sense than this. You can be sensible to the gorgeous touch of Gwendoline's fingers, and equally you can be sensible to any of the other five senses. You can also be sensible in an emotional fashion: 'I was sensible that Emma's mood had changed.' Objects can be sensible too in that they may be regarded as more suitable than something else: 'Miranda insisted that Gloria should buy some sensible shoes.'

sensitive

This word has a very humdrum and scientific meaning in that it simply means that something is conscious of perceiving something. Thus plants are **sensitive** to water, and absorb it in order to grow. Indeed all things are sensitive to water, to light and to heat because, quite unconsciously, they respond to them in differing ways. But the word is also used as a compliment. 'He is so sensitive to music,' you might hear someone saying about someone else, and the word 'sensitive' here carries a touch of applause that someone's apprehensions should be so finely attuned. Information can be sensitive too when it is important that it should remain known only to a very confined circle: 'Scotland Yard felt that the information that they had gained about Angela Ford's membership of the Newcastle croquet club was very sensitive.' For reasons beyond my understanding, someone who claims to have contact with paranormal influences is also called sensitive.

sensor *see* **censer**

sent *see* cent

sentence

A **sentence** is a word or group of words that begins with a capital letter, ends with a full stop, and makes coherent sense. You just read a sentence. It is also the handing down of a punishment: 'I hereby sentence you to five years in Horfield Jail.'

sequence, sequents

When two or more things happen one after the other, they are said to be in **sequence**. Hence you might say, 'This afternoon I experienced a very odd sequence of events.' A sequent, as one might expect, is a follower or something that happens after something else. Hence **sequents** refers to a number of such things.

sere *see* cere

serf, surf

A **serf** is a slave or bondman. Wives have been known to say to their husbands, 'You treat me like a serf.' **Surf** is the swell of the sea as it breaks upon the shore.

serial

As a noun, a **serial** is a novel or play that appears in print, on radio or on television in a series of episodes. As an adjective, serial can mean repeating the same offence, refer to music that atonally manipulates a fixed series of notes, or in computing refer to data that is processing item after item rather than being multi-tasked.

series

All the applications of the word **series** tend to share the concept of succession, but that similarity does not debar it from homonymic status. If you range a number of objects in a line, you can point to them and say, 'Look at my series of bottles', or whatever. If there is an office or public appointment that has existed for a long time, the holders of that office create a series. Hence you might want to say that Robert Walpole was the first in Britain's series of Prime Ministers (though perhaps a better case can be made for Robert Harley in that role). Equally a long-running show on television can be called a series, and no doubt there are people who pride themselves on having seen every episode of *Coronation Street*. However, the word does have more technical applications. A set of successive deposits in geology is called a series. So is a number of cells or conductors so placed that the electric current passes through each in succession. There are technical uses in mathematics, music and phonetics also.

serious

If a person is **serious**, they are acting or speaking in a thoughtful and considered manner, with no hint of flippancy. If a subject is serious, it demands careful attention. Yet, somewhat oddly, the word can also mean 'substantial': 'He now had serious money to spend.'

serous *see* cirrus

serpent

As animals, serpents do not normally rank high in human affection. A **serpent** is a limbless reptile which, apart from having tempted Eve in the Garden of Eden, also arouses distaste because of its silent, underhand approach and the fact that a large number of serpents have a poisonous bite. Much more agreeable is the serpent, an obsolete bass wind instrument that tended to be about eight feet long.

serpentine

Most of us doubtless think of the Serpentine as a lake in Hyde Park, but the uncapitalised word can be an adjective meaning resembling a serpent. More unusually **serpentine** can also be a noun meaning a dark green mineral made up of hydrated magnesium silicate, a horse-riding exercise, or a kind of fifteenth- and sixteenth-century cannon.

serve

As a verb, **serve** means to assist, to help, to perform services for. Thus a waitress will serve your meal to you in a restaurant, someone might serve the church by providing and arranging flowers for it every week, and the Royal Infirmary serves the population of Bristol. Equally 'to serve' can be used in the sense of achieving something: 'This book will serve to provide me with all the information I need about Peruvian reptiles.' Less pleasantly, one can be served a summons or a writ demanding one's attendance in court. Very differently, a serve in a racket sport like tennis begins play in every game.

service

Fairly obviously, **service** is what you get when someone serves you, and you may be delighted with the service provided by your local grocery store. But the word also has a more generalised meaning. Hence we talk about a whole system as a service like the gas service, the water service, and so on. We also use the word for a system of periodic inspections. Thus every year the gas engineer comes round to service our central heating system. A ceremony of a religious nature is also called a service. A matching set of crockery or cutlery can also be called a service. Finally, the word can be used as a disrespectful and vulgar way of referring to sexual intercourse: 'I service my wife every night.'

session *see* cession

set

In most circumstances, a **set** is a collection of objects. Thus you may have a set of Dickens's novels, a set of tableware, or a set of car tools. In the bizarre scoring system employed in the game of tennis, a set is the number of games needed to produce a winner, three or five sets normally producing an entire match. You need to construct a set for the annual school play, listen to a jazz set at your local pub, possess a television set, or dance a set in the village hall. But 'set' can also be a verb. You can set things out on the table, that is, place things on the table normally in an organised manner as you do when you arrange knives, forks and spoons ready for a meal. You can also set someone to do a job, and you may have often heard your offspring say, 'Miss Howard's set us some spellings to learn.' You may also set up an argument for others to discuss, set off on a journey, or set your dog on a burglar. When you make a jelly, you wait for it to set (i.e. get hard) before eating it. The sun sets below the horizon, and you set your alarm every night. You can set something up, set something aside, set someone apart, set something off, set someone up, and so on. Women are prone, I believe, to have their hair set. Few words in English have so many applications.

settle

A **settle** is more or less a synonym for 'sofa' or possibly 'bench', though the word is not much used now. Much more common is 'settle' used as a verb. Here it means to be established in a particular place or position – 'My wife and I will settle in Devon' – or to subside or calm down – 'After the excitement of sports day, it took ages for Alex to settle down' – or to fix – 'I need to settle the arrangements for prize day.' It can also mean much the same as the verb 'to pay': 'Charles settled the bill.'

settlement

A **settlement** can be a location of people within a relatively confined space. Thus a leader and his tribe might establish a settlement at the estuary of the River Avon. A settlement may also be an agreement. Hence two nations may draw up a settlement agreeing that the boundary of their respective countries should be marked by the River Medea. The word can also mean subsidence of the ground or a structure built upon it.

severe

This word is not normally a very welcoming word. As an adjective, it is always used of something undesirable: 'We face a severe famine', 'The downpour was very severe.' It is often used in terms of punishment: 'The sentence handed down by the court was a very severe one', 'Wilkins was given a severe whipping.' You can even describe someone's dress as severe even to give an impression of starkness.

sew, so, sol, sow

The activity of fastening or attaching one piece of fabric to another by means of a thread is know as sewing, and once upon a time, girls learnt to **sew** as a matter of course. However, attaching fabric by needle and thread is not the only form of sewing. A surgeon can sew human flesh together, and a bookbinder can sew the sheets of a book together. The word is also used metaphorically. You can sew almost anything together: friendships, communities, countries, and so on. You can also complete something successfully: 'We should have this sewn up by lunchtime.' **So**, which can be both an adverb and a conjunction, has a variety of uses. As an adverb, it can indicate the degree or extent that pertains to an event or action: 'He served the tennis ball so fast that I could barely see it.' It can refer back to a previous remark: 'Did Glynis pass her exams?' 'I believe so.' As a conjunction, it can introduce an explanation: 'My hand still hurt, so I chopped it off.' It can preface a question: 'So, why did you go?' Indeed, the problem with 'so' is that it has so many usages that it is difficult to pin it down to any convenient rules. I can only direct you to a full dictionary for those. **Sol** is a note in the tonic sol-fa system and, in the key of C, would be G, in other words, a fifth up from its tonic note. It is pronounced without the 'l' being sounded at all. **Sow**, as a noun, is a female pig, or a large block of metal made by smelting. As a verb, 'to sow' means to scatter seeds on a ploughed field so as to ensure crops for the next harvest. Like its homophone 'sew', it can be used metaphorically also: 'We sow the seed of the Gospel among the wicked'; 'Mr Prior tried to sow a love of mathematics among his pupils.'

sewer, suer

Clearly a **sewer** is someone or something that sews things, but the word is also used, with a different pronunciation, to describe an artificial channel, normally underground, that helps to remove waste products from houses, factories and offices. A **suer** is someone who brings someone else to court charged with a civil or criminal offence. Thus someone can be a suer of a newspaper which they claim has libelled them.

sewn, sown

Something that is attached to something else by means of a thread and needle has been **sewn**. **Sown** is the past participle of the verb 'to sow'.

sex *see* sects

shabby

A person can be **shabby** because they are dressed in poor condition, or because their behaviour has been mean and unfair.

shadow

When the sun shines and we go out walking, a **shadow** of our figure is cast upon the ground. Children often have fun trying to run away from their shadow, an activity that is impossible while the sun still shines. Since shadows themselves are dark, it is perfectly possible to stand in the shadow of a building to gain shelter from the sun. This fact has given rise to a metaphorical usage of the word. If something ominous is approaching, you might say that we stand in the shadow of the approaching threat. Somewhat differently, if you are a spy and are about to secretly meet the Latvian head of anti-Estonian activities, someone might try to shadow you, that is follow you without being observed.

shady

A location is **shady** if it is protected from the direct rays of the sun by the branches of a tree or some other covering. An action or a person can be shady if they do something which they try to keep secret, and which is of dubious legality.

shaft

A **shaft** can be a long, narrow handle to a tool like the shaft of a spade, the shaft of an arrow, or the shaft of a golf club. It can also be the vertical drop to a mine, a ray of light, a bolt of lightning, or another of the numerous colloquial words for a man's penis.

shag

As well as being a colloquial verb meaning to have sexual intercourse, **shag** can also be a noun meaning rough, matted hair, a dance characterised by vigorous hopping from one foot to the other, a carpet or rug with a long, rough pile, or a bird related to the cormorant.

shake, sheik

If you see something **shake**, you see it vibrate, move irregularly from side to side or up and down. You can, of course, shake something yourself quite deliberately. Hence you might shake the branch of a tree in order to dislodge a ball that has become lodged in it, you might shake someone's hand in greeting, or you might shake your son or daughter when their behaviour is even more tiresome than usual. A **sheik**, sometimes spelt sheikh, is the head of an Arab family or tribe.

shame

If something is a **shame**, it is a matter of regret. Hence it is a shame that you lost your French dictionary yesterday, and it is a shame that Shawn can't come on holiday with us next month. But the word can also be used in a much stronger context. Something can be a shame, not because it is regrettable, but because it is a disgrace. Terry's drunken behaviour at the Royal Ball brought shame on himself and his family. For many people, the curtailment of civil rights in Great Britain has brought shame upon the country.

shank

The **shank** is that part of the leg which extends from the knee to the ankle, but the word is also applied to a joint of meat, the straight part of a pin or nail, the stem of a glass or goblet, the plane spaces between the grooves of a Doric triglyph, or a ladle which carries molten metal from the furnace to the mould.

shape

The **shape** of something is its external form, but the word quite reasonably is also used to describe geometrical figures like square and triangle. It can also be virtually a synonym for 'condition' when you say, 'Harold is looking in good shape these days.' There is also the slightly strange usage when one wants to indicate that someone is preparing to do something, normally in sports or athletics: 'I must shape up to take my next jump.'

share

When you **share** something with someone else, you divide the object in question into two as in a piece of cake, or allow someone else to use your possession as in sharing the use of a car. When you buy a share of IBM or Microsoft, you gain a portion of the company in question, thereby entitling you to receive a proportional share of the company's profits.

shark

A **shark** is a large voracious fish, but the word is also applied to humans who prey on others. There is also a shark moth.

sharp

Something that is **sharp** possesses an edge or point that is capable of cutting or piercing something else: 'The knife was sharp.' Something can be sharp because it produces a sudden and surprising effect: 'There was a sharp crack of thunder.' Something that is clear and distinct in outline can be called sharp, as can a sudden bend in the road, new and well tailored clothes, speed of comprehension, or a musical sound that is fractionally above normal pitch. You might be called sharp if you are comfortably above average intelligence, but you might also be called sharp if you are prone to capitalise on others' mistakes, particularly in a dishonest way. All these instances show 'sharp' as an adjective, but it has corresponding noun and verb usages. Interestingly, though, the word's uses as an adverb are different. It can either be a synonym for 'precisely' as in a sentence like 'The meeting starts sharp at two o'clock', or it can be a synonym for 'abruptly' as in 'Turn sharp right at the corner.'

shave

If you **shave** something, you remove a small amount from it. When men shave, they remove a small amount of facial hair. However, if you shave the corner with your car, you don't remove anything, you just get very close to doing so.

shear, sheer

To **shear** something is to cut it with a sharp instrument. Hence you can shear someone's hair, shear grass or shear off a couple of inches from your skirt. The word **sheer** is more adaptable. It can mean an abrupt deviation from one's course. You are in the market and, in the distance, see Mrs Montgomery approaching. Abruptly you sheer off to the right in order to avoid bumping into her. You can describe a material as being sheer if it is thin and diaphanous. A lady's nightgown might be sheer. A cliff might be sheer if it presents a completely perpendicular face. Pleasure may be unalloyed, 'She giggled with sheer delight.'

shed

A **shed** is a simple roofed structure, often made of wood, that one uses for garden implements or to temporarily house animals. The verb 'to shed' means to take off, just as one sheds one's clothes before going to bed, or a snake sometimes sheds its skin. The word can also mean to give out, just as the moon sheds its light at night time, or a lorry can shed its load into the road.

sheep

As most of us know, a **sheep** is a woolly animal accustomed to grazing in a grassy field, but the word is also used to describe people who are content to follow the social norm or some leader. The word is often used in this context to describe a devout Christian.

sheepskin

It will come as no great surprise to learn that a **sheepskin** is a sheep's skin with the wool left on. They are often made into a garment or a rug. In South Africa, though, a sheepskin is also a party with country dancing.

sheer *see* shear

sheet

For most of us, a **sheet** is a large oblong fabric which one uses on the bed, but the word can also apply to a piece of paper, the sail of a ship, the page of a newspaper, a broad expanse of almost anything like a sheet of water, and, somewhat differently, a rope or chain attached to either of the lower corners of a square sail.

sheik *see* **shake**

shell

A **shell** is the hard protective covering of a mollusc or crustacean, an explosive artillery projectile, the walls of an unfinished or gutted building, the metal framework of a vehicle body, the outer covering of an egg, or one of a set of orbitals around the nucleus of an atom.

shield

A **shield** can be a portable protection against blows and weapons, or a large rigid area of the Earth's crust.

shift

If you **shift** something, you move it from its current position, but it can also be a simple garment of a smock-like nature, or a period of work when the working day is divided into two or three different periods and each period is called a shift, with normally different workers operating on each shift.

shine

As a verb, 'to **shine**' means to emit a strong light, to be brilliant or excellent at something, or to make an object bright by rubbing or polishing it. As a noun, you can obviously say, 'Those knives have got a real shine,' but a colloquial usage also refers to a strong attraction as in, 'Sarah took a real shine to Hugo.'

shirr

This verb means to gather a portion of fabric by means of drawn or elasticised threads in parallel rows, but in the USA 'to **shirr**' is to bake an egg without its shell.

shive

Until compiling this dictionary, I had never encountered this word, but apparently it has at least three different meanings. It can be a slice of bread, a thin flat cork for stopping a wide-mouthed bottle, or a piece of thread or fluff on the surface of another fabric.

shock

Most of us have experienced a **shock**, that is, an unexpected, surprising event, but an extreme shock can also produce a medical condition also called shock in which one experiences a fall in blood pressure. A shock is also a group of twelve sheaves of grain placed upright and supporting each other to allow the grain to dry and ripen, or a thick bushy mass of hair.

shoe, shoo

A **shoe** is an article of clothing worn on the feet. The word **shoo** is an exclamation used to frighten away intruding animals or children.

shoot *see* chute

shooting star

A **shooting star** is really a meteor, but it is also a North American plant.

shop

A **shop** is a building in which you may buy things, shoes in a shoe shop, trousers in a clothes shop, and so on. It is also, of course, a verb indicating the activity of buying things. However, if you **shop** someone you reveal their involvement in some nefarious scheme and consequently get them imprisoned or killed.

shore

The **shore** is the area of sand and stones stretching from the sea edge to firm land. Clearly the area of shore that is visible will vary depending upon the state of the tide. It is also possible to shore something up. In this case, you wedge something against an unstable object in order to make it more stable. It is also possible emotionally to shore someone up when they are feeling depressed.

short

If something is **short**, it possesses relatively little length or height. Equally the word can be used for the duration of time. In both cases, the meaning of the word depends entirely on context. An adult human who is four feet tall is very short, but a domestic cat that was four feet tall would be a biological miracle. It is noticeable too that women have a different judgement of time from men. 'I'm just going shopping, dear; I'll only be a short time,' the wife announces, and you can confidently expect not to see her for the rest of the day. It is also possible to have an electrical short, a short syllable in phonetics, to be short in your speech to someone you dislike and distrust, make short pastry, which is very crumbly, and to be short of money (or anything else).

shot

Most of the time a **shot** signifies the firing of a weapon like a gun, bow or cannon, but it can also be a small drink of spirits, a photograph, or a heavy ball thrown by a shot putter.

should

This is such a common word that we rarely think of the different ways in which we use it. Most commonly perhaps, **should** indicates some form of obligation: 'I should go home.' Sometimes it is used to indicate what is probable: 'The cheque should arrive tomorrow.' It can express a polite request: 'I should like another slice, please.' It can be used for emphasis: 'You should have seen Basil's face.' Less usefully, 'should' often comes up in grammatical arguments about the usage of 'should' and 'would'.

shoulder

The **shoulder** is the part of the human body lying between the upper arm and the neck, and the word is often used figuratively in phrases like 'the shoulder of the hill'. As a verb, however, it can be used as a straight complement to the noun – 'He shouldered the stack of bricks' – but can also be metaphorically used in phrases like: 'I will shoulder all of Marie's debts', or, 'I wish I could shoulder Brenda's worries about her job.'

show

If you **show** something to someone else, you display it. Hence you might show a new dress to your friend. But it is also possible to show non-tangible things. Hence you might show marked ability in German at school, or show your placid nature when confronted by the work of a burglar in your house. You can also show someone the way to the nearest bread shop, or show someone how to do a mathematical equation. 'Show' can also be a noun. There can be a flower show in your town where scores and scores of flowers are on display.

shrew

A **shrew** is a small insectivorous mammal similar to a mouse, but the word is also applied to carping and complaining women.

shroud

The white cloth or sheet in which a corpse is laid out for burial is known as a **shroud**, and sometimes the word is used for any covering fabric. The word can also denote a set of ropes leading from the head of a mast and forming part of the rigging of a ship. As a verb, the word can signify a hiding from view: 'He shrouded his activities in darkness.'

shrub

A **shrub** is a woody plant smaller than a tree, or a drink made from orange or lemon juice.

shuffle

If you **shuffle** cards, you rapidly mix them up by flicking them from one hand into the other. If you **shuffle** along, you walk without really lifting your feet from the ground.

shutter

A **shutter** is each of a pair of hinged panels fixed inside or outside a window, a device that opens and closes to expose the film in a camera, or the blind enclosing the swell box in an organ.

shuttle

A **shuttle** is an instrument used in weaving, a floodgate which opens to allow the flow and replacement of the water in a mill-stream, or a frequent means of transport, normally by bus or train, between two places. The word has been applied since the 1970s in the expression shuttle diplomacy, whereby an intermediary dashes between two places to convey the views of power A to power B and vice versa. Since 1969 there have also been space shuttles in which a manned space vehicle can visit a space satellite.

shy

Someone who is timid and easily frightened is described as being **shy**, but a horse can shy by quickly jerking when it is suddenly startled, and one can take a shy at a coconut, or anything else, by quickly throwing something at it.

sic, sic bo, sick

The word **sic** is inserted into documents or books when something is being quoted, and the author of the quotation has made some factual error. The *sic* simply confirms that the compiler of the document is aware of the error and is only reproducing it for the sake of textual accuracy. There is also **sic bo**, a Chinese game in which bets are made on the throwing of three dice. To be **sick** is to be unwell, though it is possible to be sick from a disease, from mental disorder, from loathing at someone else's views or tastes, or from being disgusted at someone's behaviour.

side, sighed

Every physical object has one or more sides, yet the word **side** is very difficult to define accurately. In some instances, the side is the position to the left or right of an object, place or central point. If you look at your house, the roof represents its top, the floor its bottom, and the structures separating the two are the four sides of your house, though the side facing the road is normally called the front, and the side facing the garden is normally called the back. A car has two sides, the two equal areas that separate the boot from the bonnet. A die or cube has six sides, a page in a book two sides, and so on. The word also has meanings far removed from these positional quasi-geometrical ones. When teams play a game, each team can be called a side. If someone treats you in an offhand and haughty manner, he or she is displaying side. If you don't like the television programme that you are watching, you might decide to change sides and watch another channel. You may have two aunts, one from your father's side and one from your mother's. You might have a side dish with your dinner. If your two children are having a quarrel, you might take the side of your son against that of your daughter. You have a wonderful boss at work, but even he has a petulant side. After such variety, it is a relief to learn that **sighed** is just the past tense of the verb 'to sigh'.

sideline

A **sideline** is a leisure activity that you do as a contrast to your activities at work. Thus if you work as an accountant, you might have campanology as your sideline. A sideline is also either of the two long lines marked out for a football pitch.

sigh *see* psi

sigher, sire

Fairly obviously, a **sigher** is someone who sighs, while **sire** is an archaic word for someone of noble birth, now usually used in a semi-jocular fashion. 'Sire' can also be a verb meaning to procreate.

sighs, size

A sigh is an audible respiration, be it through exhaustion, relief or sadness, and so **sighs** is simply a number of such breaths. Most of the time, the **size** of something is simply its magnitude. A table is larger in size than a teacup. But size can also be a glutinous substance applied to paper so as to make the paper or similar substance suitable for gilding or painting.

sight *see* cite

sign, sine

A **sign** can be a number of things. It can be a gesture of the hand indicating permission to come on or an injunction to stop. It can be a symbol printed in a book or inscribed on a wall which, to the initiated, carries a specific meaning. Thus the + sign means add or plus. Some data can be interpreted as a sign of some development; the melting of Icelandic ice sheets is a sign of global warming. It can, as a verb, be the action of appending one's signature to some document. It can be a mode of communication to a deaf person. A **sine**, on the other hand, has a complex mathematical meaning concerned with trigonometry, but at least that is the only meaning.

signature

When one signs a letter or a cheque, on is appending one's **signature**. Each line of printed music begins with a key signature. In North America a signature can be the part of a medical prescription that gives instructions about the use of the medicine or drug prescribed.

signet *see* cygnet

sile

This little word, which most of us never use, has two different meanings. In Scotland and the North of England it means a strainer or sieve, especially for milk. Oddly enough, in the same British area, it can also stand for a small herring.

sill

A **sill** is a strong horizontal timber serving as the foundation of a wall or other structure. It can also be the piece of wood or stone that forms the lower horizontal part of a window, and there are similar usages in a ship or a castle. In the USA, a sill is one of the lower framing-timbers of a cart or railway-car.

silly

If a person is being **silly**, they are displaying a lack of common sense, a lack of normal rational control, and most of us are silly from time to time. The word is also part of the occasionally employed positions on a cricket field, positions like silly mid-off or silly point.

simple

If a problem is described as **simple**, it is regarded as easy to solve, but if a person is described as simple, it is intimated that he or she is not in full possession of their faculties. Equally the word can signify an uncluttered life, one marked by a lack of elaboration or ostentation.

sine *see* sign

sing

To **sing** is to use the voice so that, in succession, it emits noises of a particular pitch and in a predetermined rhythm. In other words, to sing is to use the voice as a musical instrument. However, someone in police custody might well sing in the hope of gaining a reduced sentence. Here to sing means to give information to the police that will help them capture other criminals.

single

If a person or object is on their own, then they are a **single** item. If a person is unmarried, they are single. If a person playing cricket hits the ball and is able to run only one run, then they have scored a single. If you want to travel from A to B but not return to A, they you buy a single ticket on the bus or train. If you do very badly in some test, then the supervisor may single you out for extra training.

singular

In grammar **singular** denotes that only one person is involved. Thus 'I run, you run, he, she or it runs' are all singular parts of the verb 'to run'. Equally in mathematics, something that is singular has properties that are not shared by other members of the same class. However, if you describe a person as being singular, you could mean that he or she is exceptional in some way.

sinister

If an organ of your body is described as lying on the **sinister** side, it means that it is lying on the left, and this was the meaning of the Latin word which has survived unchanged into our vocabulary. However, as you doubtless know, since then 'sinister' has come to mean something that is full of foreboding, something that is secretive and underhand. Thus we might find it sinister to be under the railway bridge at night time, or we might find the actions of our next-door neighbour sinister when he buries shroud-covered bodies in his garden at dusk.

sink, synch

As a noun, a **sink** can be a pool or pit in the ground for the reception of waste water and sewage. For most of us, a sink is a receptacle in the kitchen in which we do the washing up. As a verb, 'to sink' means to fall into some pool, lake or the sea and be submerged in water. Thus a ship can sink at sea, you and I can sink in the swimming pool, or have our keys sink in the garden pool. But the idea of being submerged can be conceptual as well. Thus one might sink under the amount of work that one has got to do, sink from exhaustion after a cross-country run, sink into a chair after a day's work, or sink into despair after looking at one's bank statement. Stocks and shares can also sink in value, and, to console yourself, you might sink a few pints after work. The noun **synch** means 'in time with'. Thus your feet tap in synch with the music, or you need to get your flash gun to work in synch with your camera.

sinker

A **sinker** can be one who engraves figures or designs on dies, one who sinks a mine shaft, or a weight used for sinking a fishing line or fishing net.

sinus

This can be an abscess, a curved recess in a shell, a rounded depression on the margin of a leaf, or a cavity in a bone.

Sioux, sou, sough, sue

The **Sioux** are a native American tribe, the **sou** is a French coin, a **sough** is a boggy or swampy place, or a rushing sound like that of the wind, and the verb 'to **sue**' is to prosecute an action at law.

siren

For the ancient Greeks, a **siren** was a creature, half woman, half bird, who lured men to destruction by making her enchanting singing impossible to resist. Much less melodious, a siren is a hooting or screeching noise made by emergency vehicles or a mechanism at work to signal the end of the working day, give a fire warning or something similar. A siren is also an eel-like American amphibian with tiny forelimbs.

sit

The verb to **sit** means to be in a position where one's weight is supported by one's buttocks, but objects without buttocks are said to sit in a particular position if they are semi-permanently lodged there: 'That flower pot always sits on the porch.' Furthermore, if you are a member of some body, you are likely to say, 'I sit on the borough council.' If you take an exam, you sit it.

site *see* cite

sitter

Obviously a **sitter** is someone who sits, but the word can also denote someone or something that is an easy target.

size *see* sighs

skank

A **skank** is a steady-paced dance to reggae music, or, in American slang, an unpleasant person.

skate

A **skate** is a large flat fish, or a steel-bladed attachment that one fits to one's feet so as to enable one to proceed with speed over ice. As a verb, to skate, apart from its obvious connection with ice, can also mean quick and easy progress.

skeleton

The **skeleton** of a human being or an animal is the framework of bone from which the rest of body tissue is supported. Unsurprisingly, therefore, a skeleton plan is an outline plan, a skeleton speech is the basic framework of a speech, and so on.

skelp

A **skelp** is a blow delivered with the flat of the hand or some other flat surface, or, in the north of England and Scotland, a thin narrow plate or strip of iron or steel which is then converted into the barrel of a gun.

sketch

A **sketch** can be a rough drawing which often serves as the genesis of a more polished and finished piece of work, or it can be a written piece of work which lacks detail but provides the basic outline of a topic. The same can be done in musical composition. Confusingly the word sketch is also applied to a perfectly completed short play or episode.

skew

A **skew** can be a stone specially adapted for being placed with other similar stones so as to form the sloping head of a gable. A skew can also be almost anything that is placed on a slant or obliquely. Cars, horses and other forms of transport can also go into a skew when they encounter ice or some other handicap in their travels.

skid

Most of us think of a **skid** as being an uncontrolled movement that occurs when we or a mode of transport encounters ice, grease or some other slippery material and consequently slides forward or sideways unintentionally. However, a skid can also be a beam, plank or piece of timber that supports something else, a beam or stone on which a ship is placed while undergoing repair, or a wooden fender on the outside of a ship to protect when hoisting cargo on board.

skim

As a noun, a **skim** is an addition to a plough which enables the surface of the ground to be pared off. As a verb, 'to skim' means to clear a liquid of any extraneous matter floating on its surface. One can also skim a book or newspaper by reading it in an extremely rapid and cursory fashion.

skin

The **skin** is the thin layer of tissue which forms the outer covering of humans and some other animals. The word is also used for the peel of an orange, the head of a drum, or the outermost layer of a structure. There is also the skin trade, which denotes involvement in pornography.

skink

A **skink** is a small lizard common in north Africa and Arabia, or a verb meaning to pour out or draw a drink or liquid.

skip

Many of us used to **skip** as children, either by waltzing in a carefree manner over the meadows or by using a skipping rope. We may also have been tempted to skip a number of disagreeable tasks like homework. Here 'skip' means to omit or leave out. One can also sometimes see a skip in someone's drive or in the street. Here a skip is an open container for the receiving of rubbish.

skirt

Either as part of a dress or as an article of clothing on its own, a **skirt** is a garment that covers a woman from the waist to her legs. It is also one of the flaps or lower portions of a saddle. As a verb, 'to skirt' means to touch only briefly a particular topic – 'I am going to skirt briefly the subject of Charles I's cultural pursuits' – or merely to go round the edge of an area or topic – 'We only skirted Manchester on our way to Hyde.'

skive

The verb 'to **skive**' means to avoid work, to idle one's time away. It can also mean to pare the edge of a piece of leather or other material so as to reduce its thickness.

skull *see* scull

slab

Something that is flat, broad and relatively thick is often called a **slab**. A paving stone can be described as a slab of stone. In some dialects, a slab is a muddy place.

slack

As a noun, a **slack** can be a small shallow valley, but the word is more often encountered as a noun, verb, adjective or adverb where it carries the meaning of failing to pay attention, of being careless, or of decreasing in effort or force. Walter was slack in his inspection of tyres, with the result that some got passed that should properly have been failed. Miriam was slack in her revision of French verbs, and consequently did badly in the test. But the word can also mean lacking in tension or loose. The rope was slack, which meant that the load on the back of the lorry was not ideally secure.

slam

A **slam** can be a severe blow, the violent closing of a door, a severely adverse criticism of a book, play, etc., or the fact of winning all the tricks in a game of cards.

slate

As a noun, a **slate** can be an argillaceous rock of sedimentary origin, a tablet of stone, usually framed in wood, that is used for writing on, or a rectangular object made of slate and used for roofing. As a verb, 'to slate' means to rebuke severely or to defeat heavily.

slay, sleigh, sley

If you **slay** someone, you kill them. A **sleigh** is a sledge constructed so as to carry humans or goods over ice and snow, and normally pulled by dogs. A **sley** is a tool used in weaving.

sleep

This is a condition where one's body goes into repose, rather like a car idling, and one loses consciousness and remains more or less motionless. Death is sometimes referred to as the eternal **sleep**. When you wake up from sleep, you sometimes need to rub the sleep from your eyes, a gummy secretion found in the corner of one's eyes. If you run a hotel, you might also say, 'This hotel can sleep one hundred and five people.' The word, used before 'with', is also a euphemism for sexual intercourse.

sleeve

A **sleeve** is the part of a garment that wholly or partially covers a person's arm. The same word is used for a protective or connecting tube fitting over a rod or smaller tube, the paper or cardboard cover for a record, and for a windsock.

sleigh *see* slay

sleight, slight

Sleight is the use of cunning to deceive. A card sharper uses sleight of hand; a financier uses verbal obscurity and technicality. If something is **slight** it is either small and thin, or too insignificant to be bothered with.

slender

A person or animal that is described as **slender** is thin. But one can also be of slender means, meaning that one has little income.

slew, slue

Slew is the past tense of the verb 'to slay'. **Slue** is merely a variant spelling.

slice

Most of us are accustomed to a **slice** of bread or a slice of cake, a relatively small and thin portion of the substance concerned, but you also slice the ball in golf when you hit it in such a manner that it curves away to the right or left.

slick

If something is done in a **slick** fashion, it is done smoothly and efficiently. Something looks slick if it is smooth and glossy.

slide

A **slide** is a structure with a smooth sloping surface for children to slide down, but it can also be a microscopic object mounted on a small rectangular piece of glass, or a shortened way of referring to a hair slide. As a verb, 'to slide' obviously refers to the action of sliding down a slide, but one can also slide on ice or sometimes on a wet road. Stocks and shares can also slide downwards and possibly produce a crash (as, indeed, can cars sliding on the ice, but it is a different sort of crash).

slight *see* sleight

slim

If an object or person is **slim**, they are thin or slender, but you can also slim something down by doing less of it, or have only a slim chance (slight chance) of achieving something that you would like.

sling

A **sling** can be an implement for throwing stones by hand, a device for holding large and heavy objects for the purpose of the raising or lowering of such objects, and a loop for supporting an injured arm.

slip

Most of the time we think of **slip** as a verb. Either one can slip on the ice or a polished floor, that is, lose one's footing inelegantly and struggle to remain upright, or one can slip away from some event or scene that is not holding our attention and go and do something more absorbing. Time too can slip by without our fully realising it, one can slip a stitch in knitting, or one can detach a carriage from a non-stop train so that that particular carriage does slowly come to rest. As a noun, though, 'slip' has at least an equal number of definitions, though they are not as well known. A slip can be a twig or small shoot from a plant or tree for the purpose of grafting, a semi-liquid material made of finely ground clay or flint mixed with water, a thin or slender person, an artificial slope of stone built or made beside navigable water to serve as a landing place, a leash for a dog, a woman's garment worn under her dress, an error in conduct, procedure or argument, a cord used in fastening the back of a book, or a pillow case. One can also have a small piece of paper, a slip of paper, which one uses as an interim bookmark or to write a brief reminder on, and so on.

slipper

A **slipper** can be a loose, light, casual form of footwear, a form of skid used to retard the speed of a vehicle going downhill, or a device used for conveying electricity from a conductor rail to a tram or train.

sloe, slow

A **sloe** is the small bluish-black fruit of the blackthorn. Something is **slow** if it moves or operates at a low speed.

slop

A **slop** can be a sort of loose jacket, a liquid overflow from a container or sink, a choppy sea, or a liquid or semi-liquid food unappealing in both appearance and taste. Slop without a definite or indefinite article is some crass and sentimental musical or literary material. In prison, to slop out means to empty your chamber pot.

slope

A **slope** is a piece of rising or falling ground, but as a verb, coupled with the word 'off', it can mean to disappear unobtrusively from a particular scene. Also, if you slope around, you wander in an aimless and undirected fashion.

slosh

If you **slosh** someone, you hit them, but if you slosh around in the bath or in the sea, you are engaged in the activity of splashing.

slot

This is certainly a common enough word, but it has a surprising number of applications. A **slot** can be a bar used to secure a door or window when it is closed. It can be an indentation in a piece of wood, normally long and narrow, into which something else fits. It can be a narrow slit in a machine for receiving money. According to the *Shorter Oxford*, it can also be the track or trail of an animal, though I have never encountered this usage. Perhaps most common of all, a slot is an opening of employment for someone: 'Do you think that you can fit into this slot?'

sloth

Sloth, one of the seven deadly sins, is a reluctance to engage in any work or make any sort of effort. The sloth is also a slow-moving American mammal.

slough

Well known from Bunyan's *Pilgrim's Progress* where we have the Slough of Despond, a slough is a piece of soft, miry or marshy ground, and the word in this sense is often used metaphorically so that one is in a slough when one is feeling depressed or one's business is not making any significant progress. The slough is also the outer skin of a snake which it periodically casts off. Hence in pathology, a slough is a layer of dead flesh.

slow *see* sloe

slub

A **slub** can be a lump or thick place in yarn or thread, or a piece of fabric that has an uneven appearance caused by uneven thickness of the warp. Slub is also wool that has been slightly twisted in preparation for spinning.

slug

A **slug** is a slow-moving slimy land-snail, and consequently the word is sometimes used to describe an inert human being or a slow-moving vehicle. However, it can also be a piece of metal for firing from a gun, an amount of liquor that is gulped down or poured out, or a line of type in Linotype printing. As a verb, 'to slug' can mean to hit someone.

sluice

A **sluice** is a sliding gate or other device for controlling the flow of water, but one can also sluice something (including oneself) with water by rinsing or showering.

slump

A **slump** can be an economic downturn, but you can also slump into a chair (i.e. sprawl heavily down into it).

slur

If you **slur** someone, you make a disparaging remark about them, but if you slur your words, you speak indistinctly. In music a slur is a curved line connecting two or more notes and indicating that these notes have to be played smoothly.

slush

All those who pine for a white Christmas tend to forget the **slush** that snow tends to turn into. As the snow melts, it turns into a messy, dirty hindrance that oozes into one's shoes, wets one's socks, and makes a mess of the kitchen floor. This is slush. But slush is also the nauseating sentiment with which romantic films tend to be clogged, backed by 'music' of cloying, minor-key inanity. In addition, you might have a slush fund, a sum of money kept on one side to cover unforeseen eventualities like needing to bribe someone or replace some bugging devices.

smack

A **smack** is a single-masted sailing boat, a blow delivered with the flat of the hand, the crack of a whip, or a colloquial term for a kiss. The word can also be used to indicate a trace of some taste as in 'This chocolate has a smack of coffee about it' or a trace of someone else's influence, as in 'This essay has a smack of A. J. P. Taylor about its argument.'

smart

'Jason is **smart**, but he will smart when he reads my review.' This sentence demonstrates that 'smart' can mean clever or intelligent, but can also mean a pain, whether physical or mental. Given the British long-standing distrust of anything approaching intelligence, it is wise not to be a smart aleck or a smart-arse.

smear

You **smear** something if you mark it with a greasy or sticky substance, but you also smear something or someone if you falsely accuse them of some dishonourable action.

smelt

A **smelt** can be a small fish allied to the salmon, the process of heating an ore in order to extract its metal, or the past tense of the verb 'to smell'.

smooth

If something is **smooth**, it is even and regular to the touch, and so, in a metaphorical usage, if you smooth over a dispute between friends, you overcome their irritation with each other, and restore the normal calm and cordial relations.

smut

Smut is a fungous affecting cereals, a black mark or stain, bad, soft earthy coal, a particle of soot, a very minute insect, or obscene or indecent language.

snag

For most of us, a **snag** is a sudden and often unexpected difficulty that we encounter, but it can also be a short stump jutting out from the trunk of a tree, or a broken piece of a tooth.

snap

A **snap** is the sudden and quick closing of the teeth, a method of fishing for pike, a card game, a sharp and sudden frost, a sudden break of something, or a terse and abrupt vocal remark.

snapper

A **snapper** is a marine fish, a slightly disrespectful term for a photographer, or the part of a Christmas cracker that makes a noise when the cracker is pulled.

snarl

You **snarl** something up when you entwine it with ropes or netting so that it cannot move. You also snarl when you make an angry sound, normally grimacing with your teeth at the same time. 'To snarl' is also a method of producing a raised pattern in metal by means of indirect percussion.

snatch

You can hear a **snatch** of conversation as you pass two people in the street, that is, a brief extract. You snatch something from someone else when you suddenly and unexpectedly seize something from their grasp. The same word is used to describe a rapid lifting of a weight in weight lifting, and is a coarse term for a woman's genitals.

snell

As a noun, a **snell** is a short line of gut or horsehair, but as an adjective or adverb the word can mean quick in movement or action, clever, smart or acute.

snipe

A **snipe** is a marshland bird with a long bill, but if you snipe at a group of people, you are firing a gun at them. It is also possible to snipe verbally by making unpleasant and damaging remarks.

snood

A **snood** is an ornamental hairnet, a wide ring of knitted material worn as a hood or scarf, or a short line attaching a hook to a main line in sea fishing.

snot

Mucus from the nose is often referred to as **snot**, but the word also denotes the burnt part of a candle wick.

snout

A mammal's **snout** is its nose, but the word is prison speak for tobacco, or a police informer.

snuff

In the eighteenth century it was common for men to inhale **snuff**, a preparation of powdered tobacco, through the nose. One can also snuff out a candle by putting it out, normally by placing something over the wick or by just squeezing the lower part of the wick.

so *see* sew

soak

As a verb, if you **soak** something, you immerse it in liquid, normally for a prolonged period, but the Chancellor of the Exchequer also soaks people by imposing heavy levels of taxation. A person can also be a soak by being a heavy drinker.

soap

A mixture of oils, fats and alkaline bases formed into convenient tablets and used for washing oneself is known as **soap**. Sometimes the word can be used as a verb to indicate the process of flattering someone. Today the word 'soap' is often used to denote a long-running television series like *Coronation Street*, though the term first came into use in 1939 in reference to similar radio instances.

soar, sore

The verb 'to **soar**' means to fly or mount upwards. Hence birds soar into the sky. Less than literately, one's hopes can also soar upwards. A **sore** on the other hand can be a bodily injury or an emotional hurt. Hence you might have a sore on your knee from bumping into a tree, or you might feel sore that you were not considered for the post of Mayor of London. It could also be argued that both these words should be linked with **saw**, since the difference in sound is so slight.

soared, sword

Something that has **soared** has mounted high into the air. A **sword** is a bladed weapon used in the middle ages for killing one's enemies, but only used today on ceremonial occasions.

sober

If you are **sober**, it could mean that you were not under the influence of alcohol, or that you were of a serious and restrained nature.

soc, sock

In North America, **soc** is used within an academic context for 'sociology'. A **sock** is a garment for the foot and lower leg, or a hard blow like a sock on the jaw. It can also be used metaphorically to indicate force or emphasis: 'I'll sock it to them at our next meeting.'

society

I seem to recall that Margaret Thatcher, a British Prime Minister from 1979 to 1990, once declared that there was no such thing as **society**. As in so much else, she was wrong. Society is the aggregate of people living together in a more or less ordered community. Thus you can have the society of Canadian people, and that very broad definition can be broken down loosely into numerous sections, like the high society of Canada, the trapping society of Canada, the academic society of Canada, and so on. There are also organisations specifically to gather together certain sections of society, and they call themselves by appropriate labels like the Society of Cacti Growers in Little Puddleton or the Royal Society of Taxidermists or whatever. The word can also be used just to signify the company of others: 'I enjoy the society of my fellow workers.'

sod

A **sod** is a piece of earth, square or rectangular in shape, that still has grass growing on it. It is also a generalised term of abuse, though sometimes used more specifically to denote a homosexual man.

soft

An article that is **soft** is yielding and malleable. Most pillows are soft. A person can be soft if they are easily persuaded, or if they are gentle and mild by nature. Soft music is music that is played gently and quietly. A soft drink is a non-alcoholic one.

sol *see* sew

sol

A **sol** is a Peruvian silver coin or a liquid solution or suspension of a colloid.

sola, solar

The **sola** is an Indian swamp plant of the pea family, or the feminine form of 'solus' which means 'unaccompanied', and tends to be used on stage directions. **Solar** is an adjective relating to the sun or a noun referring to the upper chamber in a medieval house.

soldier

A **soldier** is someone who serves in the army, a wingless caste of ant or termite which helps defend the community of insects concerned, a strip of bread or toast used for dipping into a soft-boiled egg, or an upright brick, timber or other building material. To 'soldier on' means to press on even in adversity

sole, soul

A **sole** is the under surface of a shoe, sandal or slipper. It can also be the floor of an oven or furnace, the horizontal piece of timber that in a coal mine is placed underneath a prop as a support, a common flat-fish, or the lowest part of a valley. As an adjective, sole tends to refer to people or objects that are alone. The **soul** is thought of by some as being the spiritual part of a human being, and most Christians regard the soul as being immortal. The word is often used metaphorically in remarks like 'Mozart speaks to my soul', or, 'I feel in my soul that Brenda is a hypocrite.'

soleplate

The **soleplate** is a metal plate forming the base of an electric iron, machine saw or other machine. The same name is given to the horizontal timber at the base of a wall frame.

solitaire

If we think of **solitaire** at all, we are likely to think of a game for one player that entails moving pegs in a board. However, it can also be a gem set by itself in a piece of jewellery, a large American thrush, or an extinct flightless bird.

solution

When one or more substances are dissolved in a liquid or gas, you then have a **solution**. When you are able to solve a problem, you have then arrived at a solution.

some, sum

Some can be an indefinite pronoun referring to an unspecific entity ('Some person hit my brother') or an unspecified quantity ('Here are some nuts'). It can also be an adjective, though again with the same sense of vagueness ('I shall be some time'). A **sum** can be an arithmetical problem of the sort most of us did at primary school, or the total amount of something, be it of money or a collection of objects.

son, sun

A **son** is a male offspring of his parents. The **sun** is a star that provides heat and light for the planet Earth. The word is often used metaphorically when one wishes to exalt someone or something: 'Jocelyn is the sun of my life.'

soon

As an adverb, **soon** can denote that something will happen in only a short space of time – 'Harold will soon be here' – or indicate a preference – 'I'd just as soon Jeremy did it.'

soot, suit

Soot is a black deposit left as the result of burning coal or almost any other fuel. A **suit** is a matching jacket and trousers, articles of clothing that tend to be worn on relatively formal occasions. It can also be a process in a court of law where A is suing B. As a verb, 'suit' tends to mean much the same as being suitable or agreeable. Hence someone might say, 'That dress suits you', or, 'I'd like some chocolate, but it doesn't suit my digestive system.' A suit is also a category of playing card. Any one card will be in a suit of clubs, diamonds, hearts or spades.

sop

Your husband (or wife) has indicated that they would prefer it if you could cease waking up at five in the working, going to the bathroom and loudly singing the Agnes Dei from the Verdi *Requiem*. However, you find it greatly refreshing to sing in the morning, but as a **sop** to your partner, you have decided to transfer your singing from the bathroom to the bedroom. A sop is a relatively trivial concession to someone else's wishes. It can also be a piece of bread dipped in gravy, soup or sauce.

sore

I very nearly placed this word with **saw** because, to my ears, they sound virtually identical, but a neighbour, the divine Janet, persuaded me differently. If you have a **sore** on your arm, you have a portion that is painful or aching. But the word can also mean annoyed or angry: 'He was sore at Mr Hawkins's lack of manners.' There are even instances when 'sore' can mean urgent: 'I am in sore need of some aspirin because my head feels sore and I'm pretty sore at Kiri failing to bring some from the chemists.'

sort

As a noun, **sort** refers to the kind of thing that one is talking about: 'Adrian is a sort of handyman, though his actual training was in electronics.' As a verb, to sort something means that you organise something in a greater degree of order. Hence, when you sort your books out, you put novels on one shelf, biographies on another, and so on.

sou, sough *see* Sioux

soul *see* **sole**

sound

Every day we are surrounded by **sound**, the sound of our children, the sound of the radio, the sound of traffic, and so on. Yet if you pronounce something as being sound, you are stating that it is fit for purpose, that it will carry out its function. Equally, as a verb, to sound tends to mean trying to measure the depth of something. You might lower a line and lead into your local lake to see if Toby's car has been submerged in it. You might sound Priscilla out as to how viable merging the Finance and Accounts departments actually is. You can also use the word to convey an impression: 'You sound very cheerful this morning.' Your cheerfulness, of course, could be the product of having experienced a sound night's sleep. Entirely removed from hearing, a sound can also be a narrow stretch of water forming an inlet or connecting two wider areas of water.

soup

Soup is a liquid dish, typically savoury and made by boiling meat, fish or vegetables in an appropriate stock. The same word is applied to virtually anything that looks like soup, even if it is a mixture of blood, water and washing up liquid. The word is also a colloquial term for nitroglycerine or gelignite, or a synonym for 'trouble' in an expression like 'You'll get me in the soup.'

sour

Something is **sour** if it has an acid taste like lemon, is deficient in lime, or is petroleum or a natural gas that contains a relatively high proportion of sulphur. However a person can be sour if he or she is feeling resentment, disappointment or anger.

source *see* **sauce**

souse

I would imagine that **souse** is a word that most of us never use, yet it has a number of different meanings. If you plunge something into water, you souse it. If you preserve fish or meat by storing it in some sort of pickle, you souse it. If you beat someone severely, you souse him. Parts of a pig, particularly the ears and feet, which have been preserved in pickle are known as the souse. It is also a slang term for a drunkard.

sovereign

The king or queen of a country is often referred to as the **sovereign**, and this idea of pre-eminence is preserved when the word is used to indicate that someone or something is pre-eminent: 'Stephen is sovereign at the bowls club, but a serf in his own home'; 'In terms of melodic invention, Verdi must be sovereign.' The sovereign also used to be a gold British coin.

sow *see* sew

space

I am extremely dubious about including this word because, although **space** has a number of different applications, they all carry the connotation of 'area'. Thus space can be a continuous area or expanse which is free or unoccupied, the totality of the universe, an interval of time, the amount of paper needed to write about a topic, or the freedom to live in the way that best suits oneself. The only application that does not carry this underlying sense comes from telecommunications where space can be one of two possible states of a signal.

spade, spayed

A **spade** is a digging implement for the garden, or a suit of cards. A female animal that has been sterilised has been **spayed**.

span

Strictly speaking, a **span** is the distance from the thumb to the little finger when the hand is fully spread out. Clearly though, in real life, the actual distance of a span would depend entirely on the size of the hand that was doing the measuring, and so the word has lapsed into a more general term. The area covered by the arch of a bridge is the bridge's span. Hence you span a river if you build a bridge over it. People talk about the span of an aircraft's wings, or of the span of a swimming pool. Consequently the word today is virtually a synonym for 'width'. However, it would appear that sometimes 'span' is used as a verb to indicate that someone is using a spanner.

spar

Either a **spar** is a beam of wood usually employed for holding up a roof, or it is a crystalline mineral. As a verb, however, it can apply to a relatively relaxed boxing bout in the ring, normally undertaken as part of training.

spare

We all use terms like **spare** room, spare money, spare tyre, and so on. From such usages, we can infer that 'spare' means 'something kept in reserve', but there is also a slightly different meaning in phrases like 'I will spare you the details.' Here 'spare' means 'forbear' or 'not burden you with'. There is also the colloquial use in sentences like 'He went spare', where 'spare' means 'livid with anger' or possibly 'frantic with worry'.

spark

A **spark** is a small particle of fire, but the word is frequently used metaphorically. If you say, 'He's a bright spark', you mean that the person in question is lively and stimulating. If you say, 'I couldn't get a spark out of her', you mean that she was unresponsive and inert.

spat

As a noun, a **spat** can be a short cloth gaiter covering the instep and ankle, a quarrel about an unimportant matter, or the spawn or larvae of shellfish. It is also the past tense of the verb 'to spit'.

spatula

A **spatula** is an implement with a broad, flat, blunt blade, used for mixing and spreading things, especially in cooking and painting. In Britain, however, it is also a flat thin wooden or metal instrument used in medical examinations.

spawn

The eggs of a fish, frog or mollusc are known as **spawn**, and one's own children can somewhat disrespectfully also be called spawn, as can the plentiful production of almost anything: 'The discovery of Atlantis spawned a remarkable number of books.' The same word is used for the mycelium of a fungus.

spayed *see* spade

spear

We normally think of a **spear** as being a thin pointed weapon which used to be thrown in the hope of piercing one's enemy, but the word is also used to denote the plumule or rudimentary shoot of a seed, a young tree, the thorn of a plant, a spike of a hedgehog, or the fin of a fish.

spec, speck

Spec is an abbreviation of 'specification', but it is frequently used by builders, decorators and so on who say, 'I'll let you have a spec by the weekend.' The word can also be used as a hope or aspiration: 'He bought the shares on spec, just hoping that they would soar in value.' A **speck** is a small spot of a different colour or substance from that upon which it can be seen. Hence you might get a speck of gravy on your shirt, a speck of paint on the wallpaper, and so on. The word is also used for fat meat like pork or bacon, the blubber of a whale, or the fat of a hippopotamus.

special

Something is **special** if it is different from the norm. Dustin Hoffman is a special film star because he can actually act, Richard Dawkins is a special scientist because he writes so well, and so on. In education, someone has special education or goes to a special school if they need specific attention in learning difficulties. In mathematics, a special group is one that consists of matrices of the unit determinant.

species

A **species** is a group of living organisms that are capable of interbreeding, but in non-scientific contexts the word is used, often semi-humorously, to denote a kind or sort of object: 'Sheila had a species of humour that was desert-like in its dryness', or, 'Derek belonged to that strange species of being known as librarians.' The *Oxford Dictionary of English* tells me that species also means the visible form of each of the elements of consecrated bread and wine in the Eucharist, but I fear that this definition leaves me no wiser. Perhaps you are much holier than me, and it makes perfect sense to you.

speck *see* spec

spectacle

A **spectacle** is something that can be seen. Thus when the circus comes to town, the advertising hoardings might say, 'The biggest spectacle in town'. Slightly differently, when your Aunt Lily goes to town dressed in her large yellow hat, her purple blouse, her jodhpurs, and a pair of clogs, someone might disapprovingly say, 'Lily made a spectacle of herself again.' Very differently, a spectacle can be a means of seeing, a lensed glass worn to correct a sight deficiency, though normally, of course, people wear a pair of spectacles, not just one.

spectral

As you wander through Thetford Wood at night, you suddenly see a faint figure in front of you. The figure, that of a young woman, lifts up her arms, utters a heart-breaking sigh and then magically vanishes. You have had a **spectral** experience, one concerned with a spectre or ghost. Equally if you shine light through a spectrum and watch the white light being split up into all the colours of the rainbow, you have just had a very different and more scientifically demonstrable spectral experience.

speed

Speed is a word that denotes one's rate of motion. A snail has a low speed, while your brother Trevor in a sports car has a hair-raising speed. The word is also used to denote the light-gathering power or f-number of a camera lens. Today, however, the word is also often used colloquially as a synonym for an illegal drug, particularly methamphetamine.

spell

The ability to **spell**, that is, the ability to write out words with the letters in the right order, is a skill by some considered over-valued in today's educational context. Affter all, dus it reely matter if I get sum words rong in there spelling if, none the less, I am saying sumthing significant? Much more interesting is the spell that a great actor, musician or artist can cast upon one. Here a spell is an almost other-worldly feeling of rapture that great skill in a great art form can induce. Scientists experience the same when absorbed in an experiment or working out a complex equation. Finally, there is the sort of spell that is cast by a wizard or witch. This, of course, tends to break all known biological or physical laws, and is best left in the world of fairy tales or Harry Potter.

spent

When you return from shopping, you might say, 'I have **spent** all my money.' You mean, of course, that you have used up all your money. Alternatively, being a frugal person, you might say, 'I have only spent £5.67,' in which case the household might be on starvation rations for the next week. Slightly differently, you are likely to be completely spent when you complete the cross-country run. In this case, you are exhausted.

sphere

As a physical entity, a **sphere** is a globular object. Thus the Earth is a sphere, as is a tennis ball. Sometimes, though, the word is used to describe a circle, or to relate to the elliptical passage of the planets round the sun. The word is also used conceptually. As Professor of English at the University of Mercia, you are asked by a student what is the best book on the poetry of W. B. Yeats. You reply, 'Sorry, that's not my sphere; I'm a seventeenth-century man.'

spicule

A **spicule** is a minute sharp-pointed object or structure that is typically present in large numbers like a cactus needle. In astronomy, a spicule is a short-lived relatively small radial jet of gas in the chromosphere or lower corona of the sun.

spike

For most of us most of the time, a **spike** is a sharp, pointed object, but it can also signify a great increase ('Last month there was an oil price spike'), a hostel ward offering temporary accommodation, the action of increasing the alcoholic strength of a drink, or a forceful downward fling in volleyball.

spikenard

Mentioned, I believe, in the Bible, **spikenard** was a costly perfumed ointment much valued in ancient times. Understandably, though, spikenard is also the name given to the Himalayan plant of the valerian family that produces the rhizome from which the ointment was produced.

spin

In the twenty-first century, the **spin** that almost everyone is familiar with is the practice of presenting things in the best possible light, even though all the available facts point to the fact that it was an unmitigated disaster. This is a practice particularly associated with politicians, but there seems no reason to doubt that everyone indulges in it. The old practice of drawing out and twisting the fibres of wool or other fabric so as to cause a continuous thread, a practice that once was so common that many, many girls learnt to spin in their childhood, is no longer part of the British scene. Nor is the practice of spin in a cricket game quite as common as it used to be. This is where a bowler twists the ball as he is bowling it, with the result that when the ball lands on the pitch, it spins to the left or the right, thus confusing the batsman. You also spin a coin if it is a simple one or the other choice, and, of course, the word spin can be applied to anything that turns or whirls around quickly. You can also spin (tell) a yarn, which brings us back to the deceits of politicians.

spindle

Before the cotton and woollen industries were mechanised in the Industrial Revolution, a **spindle** was a slender rounded rod used in hand spinning. It also became a measure of length for yarn, but today the word is used to describe a rod or pin that serves as an axis that revolves or on which something else revolves. There is also a spindle tree or bush, so called because its hard wood was formerly used for making spindles.

spine

As most of us know, our **spine** is our backbone, and consequently provides the basis of our posture and physical activities. Consequently the word is often used for anything else that is crucial for effective operation in the sense that Hutton and Washbrook used to provide the spine for the England cricket team and Einstein's theory of relativity has been the spine for most of world physics since 1905. The part of a book jacket that normally displays its title and authorship and connects the two larger covers is known as the spine, and so is a tall mass of viscous lava extruded from a volcano. Each spike of a hedgehog, a plant, a fish's fin, or a sea urchin can also be called a spine.

spinner

Clearly, given the entry above, a **spinner** can be a worker in textiles, a slow bowler, the tosser of a coin, or a storyteller, but the word is also applied to a type of fly in fishing or to a spider spinning a web.

spinule

A **spinule** is a small thorn or spine that is found in some lower forms of animal life. It is also a particular kind of larva.

spirit

It is often assumed that one's **spirit** is one's essential self, not one's physical being, but one's emotions and character. With a similar vagueness, an event or meeting can be said to have the spirit of amity or hostility or whatever. Equally one's words may be felt to be aminated by a spirit of repentance, forgiveness, cordiality or whatever. Much more concrete is a spirit that you order at the bar, a strong, distilled liquor like whisky, gin or vodka. As a verb, one might spirit up demons in the night, or, using the word as an adjective, enter the spirit world, namely, the world of ghosts and departed souls.

spit

Apart from being the fluid that is secreted by the glands of the mouth, a **spit** can also be a slender sharp-pointed rod often used for roasting meat over a fire, a skewer on which fish are hung to dry, a small low tongue of land projecting outwards into water, or the depth of earth that is penetrated by the full length of a spade-blade.

spitfire

The **Spitfire** was one of the most effective fighter aircraft in the Second World War, but a **spitfire** is anyone or anything that emits fire, though the term is usually a figurative one referring to anyone with a fiery temper.

splash

A **splash** is what occurs when something is thrown into a body of water. Thus you make a splash when you jump into the swimming pool. But the term is also used to indicate a moment of lavish show or lavish expenditure. 'The Royal Variety Performance ended with a real splash', or, 'Now that I've won the lottery I'm going to splash out on some gorgeous clothes.' The word is also applied to a garish scoop in a newspaper.

spleen

The **spleen** is a physical object in the abdomen responsible for the production and removal of blood cells, but the word is also used to denote a bad temper.

splenetic

If someone is **splenetic** they can be suffering from a disease of the spleen, but the word is more commonly used to denote a peevish or irritable disposition which may or may not have any connection with the condition of their spleen.

spline

A **spline** is a rectangular key fitting into grooves in the hub and shaft of a wheel, a slat of wood or metal, or the modifier for the word 'curve' because, in mathematics, a spline curve is a continuous curve constructed so as to pass through a given set of points.

splint

A **splint** can be one of the plates or strips of overlapping metal of which certain portions of medieval armour were sometimes composed, a usage that I imagine rarely crops up over dinner. It can also be a slender, moderately long and flexible rod of wood prepared for use in some manufacture, or a splinter of wood or stone. A splint can also be a callous tumour developing into a bony excrescence on the metacarpal bones of a horse's or mule's leg. Its most common usage, however, is as a thin piece of wood used to hold a fractured bone in position.

spoil

As a verb, to **spoil** means to damage something ('Jessica's tears at the party tended to spoil the atmosphere'), or, more seriously, one can spoil a dwelling or an area of land by totally wrecking it ('The Visigoths spoilt the village of Ebor by setting fire to all the huts'). As a noun, spoil refers to the goods and possessions that one seizes in the activity of spoiling an area or a town. Thus the Visigoths could carry off food, carpets, jewels and women as their spoil. The word as a noun can also be used as meaning payment for services rendered: 'Michael, for his excellent work in canvassing support, was awarded the post of Minister of Trivia and given a splendid new office in Whitehall as his spoils.'

spoke

As a noun, a **spoke** is one of the set of rods radiating from the hub of a wheel and extending to the rim. As a verb, spoke is the past tense of the verb 'to speak'.

sponge

In its natural state, a **sponge** is an aquatic animal belonging to the group *Porifera*, but most of us encounter a sponge as a cleansing aid in the bath or kitchen, characterised, like the animal, by interlaced fibres. The fermenting dough of which bread is made is also called a sponge, as is an immoderate drinker, someone who downs pint after pint. The word is also used figuratively to describe someone who absorbs facts as easily as a sponge absorbs water.

spoor, spore

The traces of its passage that an animal leaves behind it (footprints, faeces, hair, etc.) as it travels through the countryside are known as its **spoor**. A **spore**, however, is a minute reproductive body that is characteristic of flowerless plants.

sport

Most of us have played some kind of **sport** in our lives, be it football, cricket, hockey or rounders. A sport is a physical activity in which one person or one team battles to overcome another person or team in a manner vaguely congruent with the rules of that particular sport. More interestingly, a sport can also be a species of animal or plant that shows a marked difference from its parentage as the result of a spontaneous mutation. A human being can also be termed a good sport when he or she has accepted graciously some defeat or has been prepared to smile tolerantly when made the subject of some inane practical joke.

spot

If you get a **spot** of grease, ink, dirt or whatever on your shirt, you are normally a little irritated, and so, since a spot is a small physical mark, so the word can also be used to signify a small moral imperfection: 'Jill is a lovely girl, but she is marred by little spots of envy that appear from time to time.' There are also small circular marks on a snooker table known as spots indicating where certain balls need to be placed. Quite differently, if you spot someone in the street, you see them, you notice them, you observe them.

spout

A fairly narrow pipe-like object through which liquid is permitted to pass is often called a **spout**. Thus your tea-pot has a spout, as does your watering can, and, quite often, your guttering. Sometimes the word 'spout' is also applied to a gush of water being ejected in a vertical direction, and from that we get the figurative usage of the word to denote a ceaseless talker: 'Kevin Brown is prone to spout on endlessly about his pet lizards.'

sprag

A **sprag** is either a simple brake on a vehicle or a prop in a coal mine.

sprat

A **sprat** is a small fish common on the Atlantic coasts of Europe, but the word is also used as a term of contempt for someone regarded as insignificant.

spray

A small collection of twigs, often in flower, can be termed a **spray,** as can a scattering of water or other liquid so that the liquid comes from a small opening and then disperses in the air to cover a wider area.

spring

Apart from being one of the four seasons of the year, a **spring** is the point where water issues from the ground or a rock before careering along the ground as a small stream. It is also a quick jumping action, often witnessed when a child, hiding behind a bush, springs out upon his searching friend.

Indeed this bounding action is often seen in manufactured goods as well. The springs in your mattress adjust to the position of your body in bed.

springer

A **springer** is a small spaniel, a cow near to calving, the lowest stone in an arch, where the curve begins, or any of a number of fish known for leaping out of the water.

spruce

The **spruce**, more properly called the spruce fir, is a conifer that boasts several varieties. There is also a spruce beer made from its leaves. As an adjective and adverb, however, 'spruce' indicates a smart and neat appearance.

spud

Most of us know the word **spud** as an informal name for a potato, but it also means a small, narrow spade for cutting the roots of plants, a short length of pipe that is used for connecting two components, or an ice chisel. As a verb, 'to spud', apart from meaning to dig up plants, can also signify making the initial drilling for an oil well.

spur, spurr

Mostly we think of a **spur** as being something that urges us to do well. Thus a jockey sticks a pointed piece of metal into a horse's side in order to urge it to gallop faster, and the hope of getting to Balliol College, Oxford acts as a spur in our A-level work. While the spur used on a horse is a manufactured object and the spur urging us to work hard is a mental stimulus, some birds have a literal and natural spur in that cocks and others grow a sharp projection on their tarsus. A **spurr** is herbaceous plant of the genus *Spergula*.

spurt

Suddenly water might gush rapidly upwards out of some pipe or hole. You see a bus coming and so you suddenly dash towards the bus stop. In both cases, one witnesses a **spurt**, a sudden and short spell of activity. Perhaps, therefore, this word does not count as an internal homonym, but the difference between a sudden spurt of milk from the breast when you begin to feed your infant, and the spurt of revision you indulge in as the exams approach do seem so different.

spy

Through the novels of countless writers, we all know about the activities of a **spy** as he or she pursues the secretive business of finding out about A for the benefit of B despite the earnest efforts of C to keep A secret. It is understandable that a spy should be so named, because the verb 'to spy' means to watch, to keep observation.

squab

A **squab** is a newly hatched bird (usually a pigeon), or a verb meaning to stuff or stuff up or an adverb meaning with a heavy fall. It can also be the padded back or side of a vehicle seat.

squall

A **squall** can be a sudden gust of wind or short storm, or a scream or a loud harsh cry.

square

A **square** is a shape where there are four equal sides that meet each other at right angles. It can also be a tool for setting out right angles, or a market square where an area is almost completely enclosed by buildings arranged in a square shape. The word can also be a verb denoting the intention to redress an unfairness: 'I will square the matter with Gerald.' It is also a colloquial word indicating that something is not in fashion or, more commonly, that someone is out-of-date, lacks taste or is socially un-acceptable. The word can even mean directly, as in sentences like 'The ball hit me square on the forehead.' (Strictly speaking, since 'square' is there acting as an adverb, it ought to be 'squarely', but in common speech it often isn't.) Also, of course, if you square a number, you multiply it by itself. There are also sundry square positions on a cricket field, but these can be ignored because cricket fielding positions are an occult science.

squash

Squash is a racket game played inside a closed court, the unripe pod of a pea, a crush or crowd of people, a gourd produced by the plants of the genus *Cururbita*, or a verb meaning to squeeze or crush.

squat, squatt

If you **squat** you crouch down with your knees bent, or you unlawfully occupy a vacant building. Using the word as an adjective, a squat person is short and thick-set. A **squatt** is the larva of the common house fly, used by anglers as bait.

squeak

A **squeak** is a short, high-pitched cry, but you can also squeak through an exam, which means that you just managed to obtain a pass mark.

squeal

If you hear a **squeal**, you hear a sharp cry. Clearly then the verb 'to squeal' means to utter a sharp cry, but the verb can also mean to divulge a secret to others, often under the threat or actuality of torture.

squeeze

If you **squeeze** someone or something, you fairly gently hug them or it. Hence you can squeeze your aunt when you meet her at the station, or you can squeeze the trigger of a gun when you have decided that the next-door neighbour can no longer be tolerated. You can also squeeze through an opening when the opening is barely big enough to let you through. You may also be able to squeeze a diminution of Council Tax from your local authority after months of negotiation. As a noun, a squeeze can be a moulding or cast of an object, or, in America, a slang term for your boyfriend or girlfriend.

squelch

One tends to **squelch** when one is walking through mud or marshy ground and thereby making a soft sucking sound. But there is also a squelch circuit in electronics, a circuit that suppresses the output of a radio receiver if the signal strength falls below a certain level.

squib

A **squib** can be a small firework, a short piece of satirical writing, or a small weakly person.

SQUID, squid

In physics, **SQUID** is a device used in particular in sensitive magnetometers, which consists of a super-conducting ring containing one or more Josephson junctions. The word began as an acronym for superconducting quantum interference device, but, like so many acronyms, has become a valid word. A **squid** is an elongated, fast-swimming cephalopod mollusc.

squinch

As a noun, a **squinch** is a straight or arched structure across an interior angle of a square tower to carry a superstructure such as a dome. As a verb, to squinch is to tense up the muscles of one's eyes or face, or to crouch down so as to make oneself seem smaller or to occupy less space.

squire

In the later middle ages, a **squire** was a young man from the upper classes who was an attendant on a knight. Today, as a verb, you can squire a lady to an event, that is, escort the lady to the event in question and devote yourself to looking after her.

squirrel

A **squirrel** is an agile tree-dwelling rodent with a bushy tail. As a verb, to squirrel something away is to hide something of value in a place where you hope no one will find it. There is also a squirrel cage which rotates and a squirrel monkey which I assume doesn't, though it does leap through the trees of South America.

stable

A **stable** is a building in which horses are kept, but one can be described as stable if one is a well-balanced and unexcitable person. People in hospital are sometimes described as stable when they are showing no signs of improvement or deterioration.

stack

As a noun, a **stack** is a pile of objects, a chimney, or a measure for a pile of wood equal to 208 cubic feet. As a verb, if you stack a pack of cards, you shuffle them dishonestly so as to gain an advantage.

staff, staph

A **staff** is a rod or stick made of wood or metal that can be used as an aid in walking, a weapon for beating people with, an aid in measuring distances, or as a ceremonial adjunct. The word can also be used to refer to the total number of employees in an establishment: the staff of a school, the staff of a bakery, etc. **Staph** is a common abbreviation for 'stachylococcus', a particular bacterium.

stag

A **stag** is a male deer, a person who buys shares with a view to selling them immediately at a profit, or an adjective describing an all-male event.

stage

A **stage** can be a period in the development of a person or process. Hence Kiri may be at the stage of attempting to walk or the Nimbus Theatre may be at the stage of having its green rooms expanded. A stage is also a raised floor or platform from which people speak or actors act. In geology a stage is a range of strata corresponding to an age in time.

stagger

If a person is drunk or has been hit on the head by a flying missile, he or she may **stagger**, walk or move unsteadily. You are also likely to be staggered if you see flying elephants, that is be astonished or deeply shocked. You may also need to stagger entrance to your priceless collection of Renoir paintings otherwise the gallery will get far too full. Consequently you just let ten in at fifteen-minute intervals.

staid, stayed

The word **staid** is an adjective denoting a somewhat conventional and unexciting personality. **Stayed** is the past tense of the verb 'to stay'.

stair, stare

A **stair** is a simple structure that enables one to ascend in height. A number of them in succession constitutes a flight of stairs. The word is also used metaphorically. You may see being appointed cashier at a supermarket as the first stair in your ascent to directorial status. If you **stare**, you look fixedly at someone or something.

stake, steak

A **stake** is a stout stick or post, usually of wood, which is commonly used in making fences, tethering animals or burning someone alive. The word can also mean a sum of money which you wager on some event, or it could mean a metalworker's small anvil, or a territorial division of the Mormon Church. A **steak** is a thick slice of meat cut for grilling, roasting, frying or stewing.

stalk, stork

The petals of a flower grow at the end of the flower's **stalk**. Alternatively, if one follows someone in a quiet and stealthy manner, trying to remain undetected, then one is said to stalk that person. A **stork** is a large wading bird.

stall

A **stall** is a standing place for cattle or horses, an enclosed or semi-enclosed section of a church or cathedral, a seat on the ground floor of a theatre, a delay, or a pickpocket's assistant. As a verb, you can stall for time while you think of some escape from your present position, you can listen despairingly as your car stalls, or you can realise that your career has stalled and that you are doomed for ever to remain in your current lowly post.

stamp

A **stamp** occurs when something is brought down heavily upon something else. The same word is used for an instrument used in stamping or for the result of stamping. A small paper object that is placed on letters or parcels showing that you have paid for the delivery of that letter or parcel is also called a stamp, and when something is used to frank the stamp, you have an instance of a stamp on the stamp.

stand

If an animal or human supports itself in a stationary position by its legs, it is said to **stand**, as opposed to kneeling, crouching or lying. If you take a stand on some issue, you oppose those with a different view and indicate your willingness to fight, verbally or physically, for your position. If two batsmen in a game of cricket score a significant number of runs between them, it might be said that they have participated in a stand of 63 or 117 or whatever. Should you be accused wrongly of some shameful action, you might state that you cannot stand (endure) the unmerited disgrace. The word can also be followed by a number of prepositions which, on each occasion, change its meaning. Thus you can stand up to a bully, stand for a cause, stand against the Roman Catholic Church, stand apart from the crowd, stand down as a candidate, stand in for Felix, or stand out for your beauty.

standard

Standard can be level of achievement. Hence you want to attain an A standard in your embroidery. Standard can be a norm: 'Ties are standard for executives here.' A standard can be a flag of some sort, normally of a military or ceremonial nature.

standing

Self-evidently someone who is **standing** is in an erect position, using their feet to maintain that position. Someone may have considerable standing in the locality, namely, esteem and respect. Equally you may have had a grudge of long standing against your MP, ever since she refused to consider your financial grievances.

staple

As a noun, **staple** refers to a short piece of thin wire which is driven into paper and so bent as to secure several sheets of paper together, or to a short piece of iron which is similarly bent into a three-sided rectangle and driven into a wooden post so as to serve as a hook or hold for a lock, a door, fence or something similar. It can also be a town appointed by royal authority for merchants to have a monopoly on the purchase of certain goods which are then exported. A staple is also a fibre of wool that is graded according to its length and degree of fineness. Yet the most common usage of 'staple' is as an adjective where it denotes the major or prime factor in a particular context. Thus you could say 'The staple diet of the Patagonians is red meat', or, 'Anthea's staple skill was in pulling funny faces.'

star

We all know that a **star** is a luminous body seen in the sky, but stars have so bewitched men through the ages that the word has been borrowed in a number of ways. Someone who achieves fame in virtually any realm is a star. If you gain an outstanding first-class degree at university, it may be cited as a starred first. Many ornaments are created in the form of a star. Stars are also seen as determiners of one's destiny, a convenient excuse when you have just made a total mess of some task or other.

starch

An important constituent of the human diet, **starch** is an odourless, tasteless white substance occurring widely in plant tissue. But starch can also be a stiffness of manner, a humourless approach, typical of people who lack imagination or who are full of self-importance.

stare *see* stair

start

If you **start** something, you begin it. Hence you might start a course in Sanskrit, start the engine of a car, or start to develop ulcers. However, if someone jumps out at you from behind a corner, you are likely to start with surprise. Here 'start' means an involuntary jump.

starter

Self-evidently a **starter** is someone or something that starts. The person who starts a horse-race is the starter, some machines have an automatic starter, at the beginning of a discussion someone might say, 'Let me just ask this as a starter,' and so on. The first course of a meal might also be a starter, and a starter in bacterial culture might initiate the souring necessary to make yoghurt, cheese or butter.

state

As a noun, a **state** can refer to a condition of being: 'He was in a state of shock', or, 'The building was in a state of disrepair.' It can also refer to status: 'She rode in a golden carriage as befitted her state.' It can also refer to an independent entity: 'The state of Tibet was represented by a group of Buddhist priests', or, 'The Associated Society of Welders had grown so powerful that they were virtually a state within a state.'

static

Something that is **static** is lacking movement, activity or change, but an electric charge can also be static, and computer memory can be static if it does not need periodically refreshing by an applied voltage.

station

A **station** can be a stopping place, which is why places where you disembark from or enter buses and trains are called bus stations or railway stations. A station can also be one's rank: 'His station entitled him to seats in the front row.'

stationary, stationery

These two words are much beloved by English teachers because of the widespread inability of the nation's youth to remember that **stationary** means the state of being at rest, not moving or having a fixed position, and that **stationery** refers to the things that are needed for writing, like paper, pen, envelopes, etc.

stave

A **stave** is a narrow, thin plank of wood which, when placed together with other staves, forms the side of a cask or tub. It is also another name for a verse or stanza of a poem or song, and a set of lines along which musical notation is placed.

stay

As a noun, a **stay** is a large rope used to support the mast of a ship, a thing or person that provides support, or a stoppage of some nature. In law, a stay is a suspension or postponement of judicial proceedings. As a verb, 'to stay' can mean to cease motion, to remain in the same place, to support and sustain, or to stop, arrest or check.

steady

If something or someone is **steady**, it is firm, reliable and responsible. If you need to steady something, you need to ensure that it stops rocking, either physically or emotionally, and is returned to a state of calm.

steak *see* stake

steal, steel

To **steal** something is to take it without permission so to do. So, to steal something is to engage in an act of theft. You can, however, also steal away from an event or place, in which case you unobtrusively take your leave. **Steel**, of which there can be various kinds, is an artificially produced form of iron.

steep

Something is **steep** if it presents an arduous angle upwards to climb: 'I found the hill too steep to walk up with comfort.' The word can also be used to indicate difficulty ('I thought the maths questions were a bit steep'), or rudeness ('It was steep of Colin to leave without saying goodbye'), or instead of soak ('We need to steep the potatoes in water'). You may also find the price of an article too steep to pay.

steer

When one guides a vehicle of any kind, one is steering it. Thus you might **steer** a boat along the Thames, steer a car round the bollards, or steer a bicycle down the road. As a noun, a steer is a young ox, especially one which has been castrated.

stem

Just as a stalk is the main body of a flower, so a **stem** is the main body of a tree, bush or shrub. It can equally easily be used to denote anything that is supportive of anything else, like the stem of a wine glass. Linguistically the stem of a word is that part of it to which inflections are added. The word can also be a verb meaning to stop, to act as a barrier against, as in 'He did his best to stem the water pouring from the pipe.'

step, steppe

A **step** can be a single walking pace, an action taken in pursuit of some aim or objective, or something on which to place the foot when ascending or descending. A **steppe** is one of the vast treeless plains of south-eastern Europe or Siberia.

stereotype

A **stereotype** is a widely held picture of someone or something. Thus, when you hear that Travis Routh is a historian you immediately assume that he has no interest or knowledge of current affairs because he is buried in the past. Such is the widely misleading stereotype of historians. Very differently, a stereotype may also be a relief printing plate cast in a mould made from composed type or an original plate.

sterling

Sterling is the collective noun for the British currency, or an adjective indicating that something or someone is of the highest quality and totally to be relied upon.

stew

As a dish to eat, **stew** is a mixture of meat, vegetables, onions and spices cooked slowly together in gravy or wine in an oven. This combination of heat and length explains usages like having a stew in the bath when one just wants to relax and recover, stewing on the beach in the midday sun, or having a stew in a sauna. One might also be in a stew when one is worried about something, especially something that might cast discredit upon oneself.

stick

A **stick** is a rod or staff of wood, and the word can be applied to something of a similar shape like a stick of celery or a hockey stick. As a verb, you can stick something into something else, like sticking your finger in your mouth, or having to stick a nail into the fence. The verb can also mean to remain, to endure, or to persevere: 'I'm going to stick this out for as long as I can.' At times the verb is also used in connection with an adhesive quality. Thus you stick stamps on an envelope or labels on to a parcel. You can also stick with a person when they are in trouble. There is also a somewhat quaint usage where someone can be called a stick. This tends to mean that they are reliable, like a stick to lean on, though it can also mean that they are unchanging like a stick-in-the-mud.

stiff

As an adjective, the word **stiff** can mean hard and rigid like a knitting needle, strong like a stiff wind, or hard and difficult like a stiff exam. A dead body is also sometimes unappealingly referred to as a stiff.

stigma

In botany a **stigma** is the part of a pistil that receives the pollen during pollination. It can also be a visible mark on the skin that provides evidence of some disease. Much less concretely, a stigma can be a disgrace that you carry around with you all your days. If, for instance, you were once unfaithful to your wife (or husband), this could be a stigma that haunts you for evermore.

stile, style

A **stile** is an arrangement of steps so as to allow one passage through a fence, or, in carpentry, an upright in a framing or structure carrying a cross-piece. **Style** is the mode in which one operates. Thus Dickens's style of writing is very different from that of Jane Austen, Stanley Matthews's style of playing football was different from that of Thiery Henry, and so on.

still

In a laboratory, a **still** is an apparatus for distillation. It can also be a chamber or vessel for the preparation of bleaching powder. As an adverb, when something is still it is motionless – 'He lay as still as a log' – or it may indicate a determination to continue with some course – 'I am still going to go to Uganda.' As a verb, if you attempt to still something, you try to make it quiet or motionless.

stilt

Stilts come in pairs, so a **stilt** is one of a pair of upright poles with supports for the feet thus enabling users to walk about at a distance above the ground. The stilt is also a long-billed wading bird.

sting

A **sting** is a painful jab that you can receive from bees, wasps, ants and scorpions. It is also a carefully planned operation that is aimed at defrauding someone.

stir

If you need to **stir** something, you agitate it by moving an implement within it. Thus you stir the soup with a spoon, or stir the molten iron with a mechanical ladle. The verb can also be used more metaphorically. Hence you can stir up interest in global warming by giving a series of lectures on the subject, you can stir your wife/husband from lying in bed by pulling the duvet off, and so on. The word 'stir' is also a slang word for prison.

stitch

If one is running, one sometimes encounters a pain in one's side. This is known as the **stitch**. When one is sewing, each of the movements of the threaded needle is known as a stitch. In a similar fashion, when a surgeon is sewing up some wound, he does so with a series of stitches. A similar process can be seen in bookbinding.

stock

As a noun, a **stock** can be a tree-trunk deprived of its branches, the block of wood from which a bell is hung, a fund or store of objects, the subscribed capital of a trading company, the animals on a farm, a liquid used as the foundation of a soup or stew, a kind of close-fitting neckcloth, or a plant in the genus *Matthiola*. There are even more specialised meanings, and verbal equivalents for most of them, but at least these provide a reasonable range. The word is also a component part of other words or phrases: stockbroker, stock exchange, stock-in-trade, etc.

stole

This word is either the past tense of the verb 'to steal', or a noun denoting a long robe.

stone

A **stone** is a relatively small object made of rock or a hard mineral substance, though if the mineral substance happens to be a so-called precious stone like diamond or sapphire, you would be best advised not to throw that stone into the pond. Once upon a time, people convicted of certain crimes like adultery used to be stoned to death. A stone is a measure of weight equal to 14 pounds, though with decimalisation its usage is slowly disappearing. A stone is also the hard case of the kernel in the centre of some fruits, and a hard deposit formed in the kidney or bladder. To be stoned is to be under the influence of drugs or alcohol.

stony

Something that is **stony** is covered with stones, but the word is also used to indicate that a person displays no feelings or emotion.

stool

A **stool** is a wooden seat without arms or a back designed for one person. The word has also been used to denote a discharge of faecal matter, a bricklayer's shed, or the stump of a felled tree.

stoop, stoup

If you **stoop** to pick up something from off the ground, you bend your back and lower your body so to do. Consequently the word is often used figuratively to signify that you lower yourself socially and intellectually by speaking or dealing with someone whom you regard as your inferior, or, instead, that you have allowed your moral standards to drop by stooping so low as to steal from a blind man. A **stoup** is a drinking vessel, though the word is rarely used today.

stop

If you **stop** doing something, you cease doing it. Hence you stop driving your car when the traffic lights are red, you stop snoring when you wake up, and you stop talking when your favourite television programme starts. Unsurprisingly, the word is often used for objects that have the effect of stopping something. A stop in a clock prevents you over-winding the instrument, a stop on an organ opens or closes a particular set of pipes, a stop in boxing prevents a blow from getting home, and there are similar uses in architecture, card-playing, phonetics, wrestling, and doubtless other activities of which I know not. The word is sometimes used also as a shortened version of 'full-stop'.

store

As a noun, a **store** can be a collection of articles put away for use later, or a shop. It is also a synonym for computer memory. As a verb, 'to store' simply means to keep or accumulate something in a reasonably safe place.

storey, story

A **storey** is a layer of a building. A bungalow has only one storey, the ground floor, while a large department store may have five or six storeys. Most of the time, a **story** is a fictional account of an incident, episode, narrative or life. Traditionally all stories begin 'Once upon a time' and end 'And they all lived happily ever after', mythical though this tradition is. However, if you tell what happened in the office today, you will also be telling a story, factual though the content is.

stork *see* stalk

storm

A **storm** can be a strong atmospheric disturbance marked by high winds and usually rain, thunder and lightning. One can, though, also have an emotional storm, often marked by shouting, tears, and the throwing of random missiles. More weakly, the word is also used to indicate something unusual and controversial: 'There was a storm when Plunco appointed Lisa Burroughs as their managing director.'

stoup *see* stoop

stout

If a person is **stout**, they are fat. This obesity might conceivably be the result of drinking stout, a type of beer. However, one can also be stout with no reference to one's waistline at all. Thus one can be a stout supporter, i.e. a committed one, of some cause like Cancer Research or Amnesty International. The word is also sometimes used to indicate strength and endurance: 'The *Golden Hind* was a stout ship.'

stove

A **stove** is an apparatus for cooking or heating, or a hothouse for plants. As a verb, it can also be the past tense of the verb 'to stave'.

straight, strait

Something that is **straight** is not curved or curly, but is erect, without deviations. The Romans built straight roads, most tables have straight sides, and the walls of a building need to be straight. Because 'straight' denotes a physically undeviating line, so the word has been adopted to describe a person who is honest and fair in his or her dealings. A heterosexual person also describes themselves as 'straight', though the implication that homosexuals are crooked seems grossly unfair. A **strait** is a narrow passageway at sea or between the mountains, a tight-fitting garment, an indication that someone is strict, rigorous and puritanical in their approach to life, or a problem or difficulty.

strain

Something is a **strain** when it requires real effort or taxes one's mind or muscles. A strain can also be a particular breed, stock or variety of an animal or plant, as well as a utensil for draining water or any liquid from a solid object.

strand

The land bordering a lake or the sea is called the **strand**. So is a yarn which, when twisted together, forms a rope. Each of the threads or strips of a woven material is also called a strand. You can also, of course, have a strand of thought. As a verb, you can strand someone or something by leaving it in a place or position from which it is difficult to escape. One can also strand oneself; you come out of the cinema and discover that the last bus home has already departed. Consequently you are stranded in town for the night.

stratum

A **stratum** is a layer or series of layers of rock in the ground, or the status level to which people belong in society.

streak

If there is a long, thin line of a different substance or different colour evident on a surface, then one is seeing a **streak**. One can make a blue streak on a piece of paper with one's crayon; one can see a streak of iron ore in a rock. But the word can also signify a tinge of something different in a person's character: 'I think there was a streak of self-deception in what Gideon said last night.' A streak is also the act of running naked in a public place, an action taken presumably to amuse or shock.

stream

A **stream** is a small, narrow river, a continuous flow of liquid, air or gas, or a group of schoolchildren placed in that group because of their age, ability or both.

strength

If a person or animal has **strength**, they are strong in comparison with their peers. If someone or something is able to withstand great pressure, we are likely to say that they showed strength. A drug or drink can also have strength if it has a greater concentration of its active substance than usual. The word can also be used to indicate quantity: 'The army had a strength of 30,000 men.'

stretch

Something that is soft and elastic can be made to **stretch** by being pulled at opposite ends. Rubber, for instance, can stretch quite a long way before it snaps. One can also stretch one's own body to its full height, or you can stretch out a meeting by constantly interrupting. Your finances may be stretched when you redecorate, or you may be doing a stretch of five years in jail for your part in robbing Lady Constance Flamish.

stretcher

A **stretcher** is a framework of two poles with a canvas slung between them. They are used for carrying injured or dead people. A similar structure can also be used as a basis for a painting. The word stretcher is also used for the rod or bar that joins and supports chair legs, and for a brick or stone laid with its long side along the face of a wall.

stricture

A **stricture** can be a restriction on a person or an activity. Thus my local cinema cannot show the enlightening Korean film *Genocide as a Political Tactic* because of the strictures of the British Board of Film Censors. (I have, as I trust you realise, invented the film.) A stricture can also be an adversely critical remark, or an abnormal narrowing of a canal or duct in the body.

strike

If you **strike** someone, you hit them, either with your fists or with some other material. If you go on strike, you cease work, hoping thereby to persuade your employers to agree to higher wages or some other demand. If you strike sails on a ship, you lower the sails. If you strike ground after a swim or an aircraft flight, you arrive safely back on terra firma. You might hear a clock strike the hours, you might strike a match in order to produce a flame, you might strike out a passage of writing with your pen, you might strike camp by taking down all the tents, or you might strike off on your own by leaving the accepted path and plunging into the literal or metaphorical jungle. The word is also associated with scores of idioms like 'strike me pink', 'strike a chord' and 'strike it rich'.

string

Made normally of cotton or hemp, a **string** is a thread of material twisted together to make a firm, thin length that can be used for tying things together. The same word is used to describe a set of things tied together in a row like a string of beads or a string of onions. It can also be a tough thin fibre in some vegetables or meats. String theory is an exciting development in twenty-first-century physics concerning a hypothetical sub-atomic particle.

strip

As a verb, to strip means to remove everything. Thus you can strip the bed when you are changing the sheets, strip the wallpaper when you are decorating, or strip off your clothes when you are going to bed. You can, however, also strip someone of his or her rank, sell off the assets of a company, or tear the thread or teeth from a screw or gearwheel. As a noun, a strip can be the outfit worn by a team playing some sport, the act of undressing, a long, narrow piece of cloth, a comic strip, or a programme broadcast regularly at the same time.

stripe

In textile fabrics, a **stripe** is a long band which is a different colour or pattern than the surrounding material. Equally a wall could be painted in stripes of different colours. If, however, you stripe someone, you beat them, normally with a rod or whip.

stroke

Some animals like cats enjoy being stroked, and if you **stroke** a cat it is likely to purr contentedly in your ear. Here the action of stroking is a gentle rubbing of the animal's fur in the same direction that the fur itself is lying. At the other extreme, a stroke can be a blow. Hence you could be sentenced to six strokes of the cane. In addition, when there is a sudden lightning flash, we often say that we have seen a lightning stroke. A chiming clock chimes strokes of the hour, a conductor beats time with strokes of his baton, your butterfly stroke is improving in your swimming, an oarsman can increase the rapidity of his strokes, and a stroke is a cerebral affliction that can, in fact, kill.

strong

If a person is **strong**, they have the power to move heavy weights. But you can also be strong in maths and weak in English, strong at enduring force or pressure, and strong in the sense of very intense like a strong smell. In German there are strong verbs, and in physics the word strong can be used for describing the power of attraction between particles.

strut

A **strut** is a rod or bar forming part of a framework and designed to resist compression. If, however, you strut around, you walk with an arrogant, stiff, erect pose that can be guaranteed to antagonise.

stub

If you **stub** your toe against the stair (or anything else), you accidentally hit it against the stair and consequently cause at least a little pain. If you are using an article like a pencil or a cigarette, and there is only a little of it left, the small remainder is called a stub. When you tear a cheque out of your cheque book, the small amount of paper that remains is called the stub, and upon that you will write the date and recipient of the cheque. You can stub out a cigarette or cigar by pressing the lighted end against some hard object.

stud

A **stud** is something that is fixed to a surface and projects from that surface, as a football stud does from a football boot. It is also an establishment in which stallions and mares are kept for breeding, or a name for a sexually active man.

study

A **study** can be a room in which the owner retires in order to get on with some work, or at least that is the theory. The word is also a verb meaning to apply one's mind to the understanding of intellectual matters. However, the work can also mean a piece of work, normally one that is done in preparation for a more polished later piece. Thus an artist may do a pencil sketch of the landscape which he or she then expands into a finished oil painting. Some composers have also written studies as a guide to less experienced piano players.

stuff

Stuff is a vague word. When someone says, 'Shove that stuff in the cupboard,' the stuff concerned can be a conglomeration of almost anything. As a verb, however, 'to stuff' is much more specific. It means to place inside the body of a bird or beast some material that will improve its taste when cooked, or to fill the interior of the animal with material so that it then looks very much as it did when it was alive, and can consequently be displayed in a museum.

stump

A **stump** is the part remaining of an amputated limb, the portion of a felled tree that remains fixed in the ground, the part of a broken tooth that remains in the gum, one of the six upright pieces of wood that make up the two wickets in a game of cricket, the short remaining piece of an almost fully used pencil, or the heavy gait of a person, one who is perhaps lame or wooden-legged. Apart from the verbs that can be formed from the preceding nouns, it is also possible to stump someone by asking them a question that they cannot answer, to stump a batsman in cricket by removing the bails when he is out of his crease, or to stump the countryside seeking support in an election.

stunt

It is possible to **stunt** a person's development in a variety of ways. Keeping them in a darkened cellar for the first six years of their life is an effective method of stunting their social, emotional and intellectual development for ever. Most of us have stories about how our development in maths or whatever was stunted by the crass tedium of a teacher. But a stunt is also an action which seems to defy physical possibilities. For example, a trapeze artist may swing into the air from one trapeze, perform three somersaults, and then seize another trapeze with his toes. At a lower level, a stunt can be a publicity campaign that seeks to attract attention through its noise, colour and splendour rather than through its physical daring.

style *see* stile

subject

Almost everything in life can be placed under a **subject** heading. When you look at a flower, you are studying the subject of botany, albeit in a very casual and undisciplined way. When you look at a church, you are studying architecture, when you look something up in this dictionary, you are studying English, and so on. When you talk with a friend, there is always a subject, whether it be Spurs' loss to Manchester City last Saturday, or the pressing problem of whether or not Ralph and Fiona will ever get married. A subject, then, is a topic. Equally, almost every sentence ever written has a subject, not just a topic with which the sentence is concerned, but also a grammatical entity. Take the simple sentence, 'Alonso kicked the ball.' Here we have something (Alonso) doing something (kicked) to something else (the ball). The entity that is doing something is called the subject, the entity that is having something done to it is called the object, and the word that describes what is being done is called the verb. Hence if you wanted to turn 'the ball' from being the object of the sentence into being the subject, you could write, 'The ball smashed the glass', or thousands of other examples. Differently again, you are subject to the law. In other words, although you have a great deal of freedom, you are none the less bound to observe the laws of Great Britain. You are a subject of the United Kingdom. It could be, of course, that you get kidnapped by a gang of violent thugs. In that case, you will be subject to the gang in that you have no alternative but to obey their commands.

sublime

Most of the time, the word **sublime** relates to a feeling of awe, of being overcome by the beauty or majesty of something. Thus you might state that the G minor string quintet by Mozart is sublime, that lying in the arms of your lover is sublime, that the *Virgin of the Rocks* by Leonardo da Vinci is sublime, and so on. But the word also denotes some much less exalted scientific processes. For a substance to pass from the solid state to the gaseous state without going through a liquid state is for the subject to sublime. To cause a substance to pass into vapour by the action of the sun is to watch the substance sublime. The word can also be used as an honorific title, as is the case with some Turkish Sultans.

submission

When a person is confronted by a man holding a gun and bearing a very threatening expression, the person concerned is likely to adopt an attitude of submission, a state of accepting or yielding to a superior force. Very differently, you may be wanting to be appointed as the architect to design Tavistock's new town hall. Consequently you put in a submission for this role, namely a closely argued statement accompanied by sketches and plans for the new building. People prepare submissions designed to show that they are the best candidate or company to carry out a proposed schedule of work. Fairly obviously there is the same disparity in the usage of the verb 'to submit'.

subscribe

A person may decide to **subscribe** to the journal *Numismatics Research*, and so he or she will arrange for this journal to be delivered regularly to their house. Equally a person may subscribe to the views of the BNP, that is, they are in broad agreement with the insular and racist views of that organisation. Finally, your friend Eric may ask you to sign his will as a witness; in other words, you will be asked to subscribe his will.

substance

Any tangible object can be describe as having **substance**; the substance of which this suitcase is made is mostly leather, the fence was coated with a sticky substance, and so on. But 'substance' can also be used in a purely conceptual sense: 'I don't think that the ontological argument has any real substance'; 'The substance of Roberta's argument rested on the dubious claims first put forward by Descartes'; 'He is a man of substance.'

subtend

Subtend has two entirely different technical meanings. In geometry it concerns lines, arcs or figures forming an angle at a particular point when straight lines from their extremities are joined at that point. In botany it depicts the action of a bract extending under a flower so as to support or enfold it.

succeed

The verb **succeed** can mean to come next and take the place of its pre-decessor, just as Prince Charles will succeed his mother Elizabeth II, and become monarch in her place, or it can mean to do well, to accomplish a task, to attain a desired standard. Hence you may succeed in passing your German exam, succeed in capturing Josephine Elliot as your girlfriend, or succeed in becoming finance director of Cushing & Co.

succession

When a number of people or things of a similar type are seen following one another, they are said to be in **succession**. Thus you may see a line of schoolchildren in succession on their way to the swimming baths, or, in your company, you may have seen in your twenty years there a whole succession of chief executives come and go. Sometimes a succession comes about automatically. Thus, when the Duke of Mercia dies, his eldest son will inherit the title in succession to his father.

succour, sucker

Succour is a noun and associated verb meaning to provide help, to come to the assistance of. Thus you provide succour to an old lady who faints in the street, succour to a child who has got separated from its mother, or succour to an armed force that has got ambushed by the enemy. A **sucker** can be a young animal before it is weaned, one who lives at the expense of another, or any animal or machine that operates by sucking, yet I imagine the most common usage of the word is to describe some person who is so gullible as to be taken in by the most patent of deceits.

suck

This verb may indicate the action of drawing something into one's mouth as one does when sucking a lollipop, or it may denote the action of flattering your MD because if you suck up to him, he might appoint you as management director.

sucker

Apart from being someone or something that sucks, a **sucker** can also be a rubber cap that adheres to a surface, a gullible person, a shoot springing from the base of a tree or plant, or a freshwater fish with thick lips.

sue *see* Sioux

suede, swayed

Suede gloves, suede shoes or a suede coat are objects made out of tanned kid-skin or material that resembles it. **Swayed** is the past tense of the verb 'to sway'.

suffer

While the verb 'to **suffer**' is most commonly thought of as meaning having to endure some pain or ailment – 'I suffer from a gastric ulcer' – the word can also mean to tolerate or to allow. Hence you might say, 'I suffer Agnes to chatter on about her brother for the sake of eating her delicious damson pie.'

suffrage

We normally think of **suffrage** as being the ability to vote in local and general elections, but the word also embraces prayers uttered for the souls of the dead.

sugar

Naturally we think of **sugar** as that crystalline substance, consisting mostly of sucrose, that we use for cooking and for putting in our tea and coffee, but it is also a chemically wider term embracing glucose and others, a slang word for heroin or LSD, and a possible affectionate word used to your secretary/ wife/daughter or whomever.

suit *see* soot

suite, sweet

If you happen to be the Lord High Executioner of Cleethorpes (or wherever), you will normally wander around with an entire **suite** of followers, acolytes and flatterers. When you stay in a hotel, you are so important that you will be given a suite, that is, a number of rooms merged together as a unit. A suite can also be a musical work comprising a number of movements, or a group of minerals, rocks or fossils occurring together and characteristic of a location or period. Food can be **sweet** when it contains sugar, and most people enjoy sweet-tasting food like chocolate, cakes and trifle. A person can be sweet when they are charming, helpful, cheerful and other socially welcoming things.

sulphur

Sulphur is a yellow element (atomic number 6) that is very combustible, and an American butterfly.

sum *see* some

summary, summery

A **summary** is a brief statement or document that sums up the major points that are relevant to the topic being considered. If something is **summery**, it possesses the qualities of summer.

summer

Summer is a season of the year, lying between spring and autumn. It is also the main beam in a building.

sun *see* son

surf *see* serf

surprise

Most of us know that a **surprise** is something unexpected. Thus it is a surprise when Rosetta turns up one day because you haven't seen her for months. For the campanologist, however, a surprise is a complex method of change ringing.

survey

To **survey** something entails looking closely at it. Thus you might survey an area of land to see if it was suitable for building an estate of semi-detached houses upon it. A somewhat different kind of survey is when you survey a random section of the population to discover their views about capital punishment, abortion or whatever.

suspend

One can **suspend** something by hanging it from a nail. One can also suspend someone from work until investigations have been made into an alleged breach of company discipline. One can also suspend particles of a solid in a liquid or, in a piece of music, suspend or prolong a particular note.

sustain

If you **sustain** an injury at work, then you are likely to have been the subject of an accident. If you sustain carrying a heavy weight on your shoulders, you are demonstrating your strength. If you sustain a lengthy conversation with Professor Erudite Scholar, you demonstrate that you are both knowledge-able and intelligent. If you sustain your view that Pete Grundy is innocent, you do at least demonstrate your loyalty to a friend. In all these instances, 'sustain' carries the implication of duration, but the contexts are so varied that I do not think that one can deny homonymic status to the word.

swad

A **swad** is a country bumpkin, the pod or husk of peas, beans, etc., or, in the USA, a thick mass, clump or bunch.

swag

Swag can be a wreath or festoon of flowers, a thief's plunder, or a personal bundle of belongings.

swallow

You **swallow** something when you take it inside the mouth and then pass it down the gullet into the stomach. Thus, every time that a person eats, they swallow the food that they consume. A swallow is also a well-known migratory bird with long pointed wings and a forked tail. It can also be a deep hole or opening in the earth, or an abyss of water.

swamp

A **swamp** is a tract of low-lying marshy ground, or, as a verb, the action of being submerged, either literally as with water, or figuratively as with the amount of work that you have to do.

sway

If you see something **sway**, you watch it move gently to and fro. Thus a tree can sway in the wind. It is also possible to have sway or influence over something else. Thus as leader of the Harrogate Palm Court Orchestra, you have some sway over the concert programme for the forthcoming season.

swayed *see* suede

sweep

If you are a **sweep**, you have the job of seeing that people's chimneys are kept relatively clean. If you need to sweep the kitchen floor, you will use a brush or broom to gather together all the dirt and articles of refuse together so that it can then be put in the bin. You can also perform a conceptual sweep, when you survey a topic relatively briefly before moving in to a more detailed analysis of some aspect of that topic. Thus you might sweep in general over the nature of Romantic poetry before looking in detail at Keats's odes.

sweet *see* suite

swell

As a verb, to swell means to increase in bulk. When you blow into a balloon, it swells. When you eat too much over a long period, you swell. Swell is also an adjective indicating approval and praise. 'Carl is a swell fellow', 'We had a swell dinner', or, 'That is a swell view,' would all be typical instances.

swipe

If you take a **swipe** at someone, you aim a blow at them. If you swipe something, you steal it, though the *Shorter Oxford* seems to be unaware of this.

switch

A **switch** can be a lever as in a light switch, or a mechanism for altering the direction of something, as in a railway switch. As a verb, you can switch (change) from studying biology to bio-chemistry.

sword *see* soared

synch *see* sink

syzygy

This is such a splendid word that I'd have probably invented meanings for it if it hadn't already been an internal homonym. In astronomy it relates to both the conjunction and opposition of two heavenly bodies. In biology it is a suture or immovable union to two joints of a crinoid, or, equally, a conjunction of two organisms without loss of identity. In mathematics a **syzygy** is a group of rational integral functions so related that on their being severally multiplied by other rational integer functions, the sum of the products vanishes identically. So not only is syzygy a splendid word, its sundry definitions are incomprehensible also. **S** has been a letter packed with homonyms, but it could not have ended on a more rewarding one.

T

T, t, tea, tee, ti

T is the twentieth letter of the English alphabet, and is only seen on its own as a sort of adjectival prefix in words like T-junction and T-square. **Tea**, on the other hand, though grown in India, China and other eastern countries, is a British institution, with every person in the British Isles having an average of three cups a day. The leaves of the plant are stripped, prepared, and then have boiling water poured upon them. For many, milk and sugar are then added, and the resulting drink is mythically regarded as being responsible for the British imperturbability. However, the word tea can also mean an afternoon snack of sandwiches and cakes accompanied by a cup of tea. A **tee** is the point from which a ball is driven off at the beginning of a round of golf. It is also the mark made on the ice in a game of curling, a mark at which the stones are aimed. In addition, a metallic decoration in the form of an umbrella is called a tee in Burma and adjacent countries. **Ti** is a note in the tonic sol-fa system.

tab

This little word performs a variety of functions. A **tab** is a small flap or strip of material attached to or projecting from something else. It is the tally of items ordered in a bar or restaurant. In aeronautics, it is part of a control surface, typically hinged, that modifies the action or response of the surface. You can keep a tab on someone when you monitor their activities. It is a shortened form of tabulator. It can be a tablet, especially one containing illicit drugs. It can even be an abbreviation for typhoid-paratyphoid A and B vaccine, and in the antipodes, an abbreviation for Totalizator Agency Board.

tabby

A **tabby** is a general term for a silk taffeta, an abbreviation for tabby cat, a collector's name for two types of moth, an elderly maiden, or a concrete formed out of a mixture of lime, shells, gravel or stones.

tabernacle

Renowned for its use in the Bible, a **tabernacle** is a fixed or movable altar-like structure, but the word has been appropriated by the Mormons and some other nonconformist Christian groups to designate their place of worship. In Catholic churches, the tabernacle can be an ornamental receptacle for the sacrament. It is also a partly open socket or double post on a sailing boat's deck into which a mast is fixed.

table

A **table** is a flat surface, though the one with which we are most acquainted is a flat surface raised on legs around which one sits to eat. A table can also be an arrangement of items so as to exhibit some set of facts like this:

Author	Title	Date
Austen, Jane	*Persuasion*	1818
Gaskell, Elizabeth	*Mary Barton*	1848
Dickens, Charles	*Hard Times*	1854
Eliot, George	*Middlemarch*	1871–72

One can also table a motion at some meeting or other. Here one is either giving notice of some future topic for discussion or introducing a delaying tactic for a proposal already under discussion.

taboo, tabu

These are just alternative spellings of the same word, a word that signifies that something is forbidden: 'Smoking in the swimming baths is taboo.'

tabor, tabour

Again alternative spellings for the same object, a small drum.

tabula, tabular

The Latin word for 'table' is **tabula**, and the word has survived into English to signify an ancient writing tablet, a wooden or metal frontal for an altar, or the horizontal dissepiments in certain corals. As tabula is a noun, so **tabular** is an adjective meaning having the form of a table.

tacet, tacit

The musical term **tacet** is an adjective or adverb indicating that an instrument or voice has to be silent. The adjective **tacit** indicates that something is understood or implied without being stated.

tach, tack

Strictly speaking, **tach** should not be in this dictionary because it is a shortened form of 'tachometer', but the shortened usage is so common that it cannot be ignored. A **tack** is a small nail, an object that fastens two or more other objects together, a fastening for shoots in the garden, a long slight stitch used prior to the permanent sewing, a rope, wire or chain used in securing a sail, the tenure or tenancy of land, a smack, taste or flavour of something, the process of turning a ship's head to the wind, or the operation of changing direction. Something cheap and shoddy can also be referred to as tack.

tackle

Many occupations require specialist tools for their carrying out, and those tools, especially when they are portable ones, are often referred to as the workman's **tackle**. A fisherman uses fishing tackle. Attempts to seize the ball from an opponent in games like hockey, football and rugby are also referred to as a tackle, and, less physically, you might also tackle someone in an argument, or tackle a job of work that you have to do.

tacks, tax

Of the many nouns that the word 'tack' signifies, **tacks** is simply the plural, and the present tense third person singular in its verbal manifestations. **Tax** is one of the few certainties in life, a process by which the government takes money off each member of the state in order to use that money to pursue its own, normally misguided policies.

taenia

In anatomy, a **taenia** is a flat ribbon-like structure in the body, in architecture it is a fillet between a Doric architrave and frieze, and in ancient Greece it was a band or ribbon worn around a person's head.

tag

This three-lettered word has a surprising variety of meanings, most of which, I imagine, are used extremely rarely. If you slash the skirt of a garment so that the garment becomes a series of pendent pieces, each piece is called a **tag**, and, more loosely, the same word can be applied to any hanging material. Equally when a lace, string or strap ends in a metal attachment, that attachment is called a tag. So is the tip of the tail of an animal, the strip of parchment that bears the pendent seal of a deed, a tie-label attached at one end to a parcel or piece of luggage, something appended to a writing or speech to provide a slick conclusion, a brief and usually familiar quotation added for special effect, or the refrain of a song or poem. It is also a children's game in which one child chases the rest, and the one caught then becomes the pursuer. As a verb, one can also tag along, which means that one follows something or someone as a tolerated presence.

t'ai chi ch'uan

This is a Chinese martial art, but in Chinese philosophy it is the ultimate source and limit of reality, from which spring yin and yang and all of creation.

tail, tale

Lots of animals, like cats, dogs, horses and so on, have a **tail** hanging from their posterior region. As a result, lots of things that come at the end of something else can be called a tail: the tails of his coat, the tail of his speech, the tail of the procession, and so on. It is also the reverse side of a coin. As a verb, 'to tail' means to follow, often secretly. A **tale**, on the other hand, is a story, true or fictional.

tailer, tailor

According to an Internet source, a **tailer** is one who hauls in on a ship's line, but I can find the word in no other of my dictionaries with that definition. The *OED* does have 'tailer', but its definition is the less than illuminating 'A fish that tails'. Apparently this refers to a fish that displays its tail above the surface of the sea or lake. A **tailor** is one who makes clothes.

tales

If a tale is a story, then obviously **tales** means a number of stories, but the word also signifies persons taken from those available to serve on a jury in a case where one or more of the original jury has been forced to drop out.

talon

A **talon** is a claw of a bird or beast, but it can also be the curved back of a ship's rudder, the projection on the bolt of a lock against which the key presses, or the remainder of a pack of cards after the hands have been dealt out.

tambour

This word, which is unlikely to be in most people's active vocabulary, none the less has a variety of definitions. A **tambour** can be an instrument for recording pulsations, a small drum, a fish that makes a drumming sound, a species of embroidery, a circular frame for holding fabric taut, a sloping buttress or projection in a real tennis or fives court, the core of a Corinthian or Composite capital, or a small defensive work formed of palisades or earth.

tame

The verb 'to **tame**' refers to the domestication of a wild animal or even an anti-social human being. As an adjective, a tame television programme, film or talk is one that lacks excitement.

tang

Most of us tend to use this word to mean a trace, as in 'The cake had a **tang** of lemon', or, 'His writing has a tang of Hemingway about it.' Yet 'tang' can also mean a projecting pointed part, the tongue of a serpent, one of various fishes possessing spines, or the strong singing tone produced when a large sonorous bell is struck heavily.

tangent

A **tangent** is a straight line or plane that touches a curve or curved surface at a point, but if extended does not cross that point. In mathematics, a tangent is a trigonometric function that is equal to the ratio of the sides (other than the hypotenuse) opposite and adjacent to an angle in a right-angled triangle. Much less precisely, one's mind can go off at a tangent when one thinks of something totally unconnected with the matter under discussion. Thus one can be discussing with a friend the circumstances in which telling a lie is morally preferable to telling the truth, and quite suddenly be visited by the thought that one needs to buy some washing up liquid.

tango

A **tango** is a dance of South American origin, music written in the style of a tango, a word representing the letter T in wireless communications, or an orange-yellow colour.

tank

If we think of a **tank**, we are likely to think of an armoured vehicle with caterpillar wheels used for attacking an enemy in difficult country, or an artificial receptacle, usually rectangular or cylindrical, used for storing liquids or gases. However, in India a tank is a pool or lake used for irrigation. Apparently the word can also be used to signify a heavy defeat: 'Manchester United tanked Spurs 5–0.'

tanner

A **tanner** is someone who tans hides, though presumably today the same word would be applied to a machine that tans the skin of humans who are anxious to look macho. In addition, a tanner was a slang word for a sixpenny bit in pre-decimal Britain.

tap

Found in most kitchens, a **tap** is a metal device that, upon turning it, releases water. It can also be a gentle blow, often delivered with the knuckle upon the head, and administered by mathematics teachers who wish to hasten your attempted solution to a quadratic equation. In mechanics a tap is a tool used for cutting the thread of an internal screw, and in surgery it is a procedure of piercing the body wall of a person so as to draw off accumulated liquid. One can also tap a phone line so as to overhear any calls made to or from that line.

tape

A **tape** is a narrow strip, normally of some sort of cloth like linen or silk, that is used for binding together other articles. It is also suspended across the course of a rail track to mark the beginning of a race, suitably marked out it can act as a tape measure, and the same word is now used for a tape-like object on which recorded music or words can be stored.

taper, tapir

Perhaps the difference between the '-er' and the '-ir' sound ought to exclude **taper** and **tapir** from being classed as homonyms, but 'taper' is certainly an internal homonym anyway. It can denote a wax candle, or be a verb meaning gradually to diminish in breadth, thickness or sound. A tapir is an ungulate mammal of tropical America.

tar

Apart from being an informal word for a sailor, **tar** is also a dark, thick flammable liquid distilled from wood or coal.

tare, tear

The **tare** is the allowance made for the weight of packing materials. Hence, if you want to find out how heavy something is when its packing is removed, you just weigh the packing, the tare, and subtract that sum from the weight of the whole parcel. It is also a name for the common vetch. The verb **tear**, pronounced differently from the noun 'tear', means to rip asunder, to split, to pull.

tart

A **tart** is a flat, usually small, piece of pastry, with no crust on the top, and filled with jam or some other sweet substance. The word can also be an adjective meaning sharp, bitter or keen, and a colloquial noun for a woman who is somewhat free with her sexual favours.

tartar

A **Tartar** is a native inhabitant of a region of central Asia, but the word has come to be used to describe anyone who is impatient, irritable and bad-tempered. It is also a hard calcified deposit that forms on the teeth and contributes to their decay, and a crusty deposit that forms during the fermentation of wine.

taste

If you **taste** something, you eat it and are conscious of the flavour of the food that you have put into your mouth. Personally I hate the taste of vinegar, but some people can barely eat a meal in which that taste is absent. But taste also operates at a much more rarefied level. You have good taste in novel reading if you enjoy Jane Austen; you have bad taste if you enjoy Jeffrey Archer. You have good taste if you idolise Mozart; you have bad taste if you enjoy the Rolling Stones. There is never any attempt to justify these value judgements, and they can therefore be regarded as essentially meaningless.

taught, taut, tort

Taught is the past tense of the verb 'to teach', and something that is **taut** is tense, tightly drawn or stiff. A **tort** is the breach of a duty imposed by law.

taw

A **taw** is a large marble, or, as a verb, the process of turning hide into leather without the use of tannin.

tax *see* tacks

taxi

A **taxi** is a car with a driver that one hires to transport oneself from A to B. One might, for instance, hire a taxi from the railway station to take you home. As a verb, though, the word describes the motion of an aircraft when it is on the ground, either preparing to take off, or when, having just landed, it is manoeuvring to halt at a point sufficiently inconvenient for the passengers' exit door.

team, teem

A **team** is a group of humans or animals dedicated to achieving a desired end. Hence a team of footballers will be dedicated to defeating their opponents, and a team of horses will be dedicated to pulling the plough over a field. The verb **teem** means to be prolific. You can guarantee that the town will teem with drunkards on a Saturday night.

tear, teer, tier

A **tear** is a single example of the moisture that wells from the eyes when a human being is in pain or in grief. The verb 'to **teer**' means to daub with earth, clay or plaster. A **tier** is a row in a banked arrangement of seats, a rank of pipes in an organ controlled by one stop, or a row of ships moored at a particular place.

teas, tease, tees

Teas and **tees** are merely the plurals of words already dealt with in their singular form (*see* T), but **tease** is a verb meaning 'to irritate by pseudo-jocular comments', though one can also tease a fabric by combing it in an attempt to extract extraneous matter from its surface.

teddy

This word can signify a soft toy bear for children or a one-piece woman's undergarment.

teem *see* team

teer *see* tear

tees *see* teas

telegraph

Most of the time, we think of the **telegraph** as an electronic instrument used for transmitting messages, but one can also telegraph messages by waving and gesticulating from a distance, performing certain actions that will indicate that you'd like a cup of tea or whatever.

telescope

A **telescope** is an optical instrument that makes distant objects appear to be much closer, but when one slides or pushes one object into another one, one is said to have telescoped them.

tell

The most common usage of **tell** is as a verb meaning to impart information to someone else by means of verbal communication. Hence you can tell someone where the cheese is, tell them that the train departs at 14.37, or tell them that their lecture was very good. The word is also used for entirely interior awareness. Thus you can tell when your daughter is upset, tell that Mrs Soames is about to be tactless again, or tell that it is going to rain shortly. As a noun, a tell is a Middle Eastern word for an artificial mound formed by the accumulated remains of ancient settlements.

teller

A **teller** can be someone appointed to count votes, someone engaged to tell a story, or a cashpoint machine.

temper

Perhaps we think of this word most often when we lose our **temper**, but let us see what it is that we lose. Temper, in one meaning, refers to the make-up of something, the proper mixture of its elements. Hence, if you are making concrete, you need to get the temper right, the combination of its ingredients, so that it turns out to be satisfactory cement. Equally you and I need to have the mixture of qualities that we both possess well tempered, otherwise we will be depressed, or obsessed, or angry. It is when we are angry that we lose our temper. And this is basically all that 'temper' really means, and so it cannot be called a homonym. But its applications are so varied that I feel that it squeezes into the homonymic class. Bach, for instance, wrote *The Well-Tempered Klavier*, celebrating the fact that it was now possible to tune a keyboard instrument so that it sounded tonal all the time. You temper something when you restrain it so that it fits into normality. You temper paints by mixing them with oil. The basic concept of a proportional mixture is always there, but the applications are very different.

tender

While you are likely to think that **tender** means caring and sympathetic, so that you look for tender care when you are ill, the word can also refer to a boat employed to attend a larger one, a carriage specially employed to carry fuel and water for a locomotive, a formal offer made by one party to another, or the condition of being soft and delicate.

tenner, tenor

The word **tenner** is most frequently used to refer to a ten-pound note, while a **tenor** is a male voice pitched between a baritone and an alto, though there is also a tenor bell. The word tenor can also mean the general import of a document or what someone is saying. Thus you might say, 'The general tenor of the Prime Minister's remarks was to the effect that the poor must be made poorer and the rich made richer.'

tense, tents

Many of us will remember learning tenses at school. A **tense** is any one of the different forms in the conjugation of a verb. Thus *amo, amas, amat* is the beginning of the present tense of the verb 'to love' in Latin. As an adjective, however, 'tense' means tightly stretched, and can be applied to a guy rope or, more figuratively, to a nervous and anxious person. **Tents** is the plural of the noun 'tent', a portable shelter of canvas much used by Boy Scouts, Girl Guides or impoverished travellers.

term

A **term** is a duration of time. Thus the school year is divided into three terms, your railway pass lasts for the term of a year, and each British government is allowed a term of five years before it has to seek re-election. A term can also be a word or a phrase: 'The term *allegro ma non troppo* means "quickly but not too much so", and the term "relational database" refers to a database where it is possible to relate data in one table to identical data in other tables.'

tern, terne, turn

A **tern** is the common name of a group of sea birds of the genus *Sterna*, though the word can also be used to refer to a group of three. A **terne** or terneplate is a thin sheet-iron coated with an alloy of lead and tin. A **turn** can be a variety of things. It can refer to rotation, as in 'The car wheels turn.' It can refer to a change of direction, as in 'We need to turn off the High Street here and go down this alleyway.' It can simply refer to change in general, as in 'I hope the weather turns sunnier for our holiday.' It can refer to an action performed by an individual or group, as 'It's your turn now.'

test

I suppose that the most frequent usage of the word **test** is in the sense of examining something to see if it comes up to the required standard. Hence you may have a test done on your central heating system, on your golden brooch to see if it really is gold, or on the brakes of your car. The other common usage relates to those tiresome tests of knowledge that you experienced at school: 'Today we are going to have a test on the first three declensions of Latin nouns.' There is also the quaint usage associated with cricket. When there is a series of international matches between A and B, they are called test matches.

Thai, tie

Something with the adjective **Thai** comes from Thailand, and a **tie** can either be a draw in a contest between two people or teams, or a narrow strip of cloth that is knotted around a person's neck, the wearing of which is quaintly regarded as essential for formal occasions. As a verb, 'to tie' means the attaching together of two ends of a cord, thread or rope in a knot, or the attaching together of two different cords, threads or ropes with a knot. The word is also used metaphorically, so the act of marriage ties a man and woman together, or a workaholic is tied to his job.

the, thee

Depending upon where you come from, these two words are homophones. For many of us, however, this is not the case, because we pronounce **the** with a short 'e'. Anyway, 'the' is one of the most used words in the language. It is called the definite article, and is used before a noun when one wishes to refer to a specific object: 'The cat lying on the lawn belongs to the Browns next door.' The word is also used generically, when one wishes to refer to a specific class of things: 'The elephant can be a friendly animal.' **Thee** is an old-fashioned word for the singular 'you': 'Get thee hence!' It tends to be used today with an undertone of parody.

their, there, they're

The possessive pronoun **their** is used to denote an object or objects that are associated with a number of other objects. Thus if you were referring to the vulture in general, you would say, 'Their talons are long.' If you were referring to a group of schoolchildren being shepherded round the British Museum, you could say, 'Their expressions ranged from real interest to total boredom.' The demonstrative adverb **there** is used to indicate position – 'He is standing over there' – or to indicate the state of the situation – 'There are no trains to Barmouth tonight.' **They're** is merely a shortened version of 'they are'.

theme

The **theme** of something can be called its topic or argument. Hence you might say, 'The major theme at the Trades Union Congress this year was to resist any further privatisation.' Your local philosophical society might ask you to deliver a paper on the theme of justice. Equally a theme can be a melody in a piece of music: 'The theme of thanksgiving that begins the final movement of Beethoven's *Pastoral Symphony* is one of the most beautiful themes ever written.' Apparently astrologers also talk about themes in connection with the disposition of the heavenly bodies, but we have no need to concern ourselves with such nonsense.

there *see* their

they're *see* their

thick

If you talk about a **thick** book or a thick plank, you mean that there is an unusual distance between its sides. You can also talk about a thick forest or someone having thick hair. Here it means that the items concerned (trees or hairs) are closely packed together. You can also call a person thick. Here it means that the person concerned is stupid, or (which is much the same thing) happens to disagree with you.

thin

Something that is **thin** is slender or lean. Thus the stem of a daisy is thin, as is a Parisian model, a cotton thread, a cane or, comparatively, a telegraph pole. But the word is often used figuratively. Thus the audience at the History Society's talk on 'Peasant diet in thirteenth-century Macedonia' was very thin, as was the evidence upon which the speaker based his talk.

threw, through

Threw is the past tense of the verb 'to throw', and **through** normally suggests a passage from A to B. Thus a needle may go through the cloth, you may push your way through the crowd, you may read through a whole book before going to bed, or you may look through a telescope in order to see the moon more clearly.

throe, throw

A **throe** is a violent spasm or pang that might convulse the body. To **throw** is to project something through the air like a cricket ball or die, or to perform a wrestling hold that propels your opponent to the ground. You can also, more figuratively, throw a glance at your friend, or throw a remark into the discussion.

throne, thrown

If you are the king or queen of somewhere, you are likely from time to time to sit upon a **throne,** and such seating is also used by the Pope, bishops or beauty queens. **Thrown** is the past participle of the verb 'to throw'.

thyme, time

The herb **thyme** has fragrant, aromatic leaves, and is used in cooking. **Time** consumes a lot of space in the *Shorter Oxford* but basically refers to a specific moment – 'It is time to go to bed' – or to a duration – 'The seventeenth century was a time of unrest and rebellion in Britain.'

tic, tick

Tic is a disease or affliction characterised by spasmodic twitching of certain muscles, especially of the face. A **tick** is the common name for sundry mites, a mark like this (✓) signifying that something is correct, half the tick-tock sound of a clock, a light pat, a beat of the pulse, or credit at a shop ('Can I have it on tick?').

tide, tied

The **tide** is that regular coming in and retreating performed by the sea on the shores of Britain (and most other places). Since boats are dependent on the state of the tide, the word has been used to denote the ebb and flow of human fortunes too. You may be experiencing a high tide in your fortunes, or, conversely, a low one. **Tied** is the past participle of the verb 'to tie'.

tie *see* Thai

tied *see* tide

tighten, titan

Not perhaps complete homophones – the 't' sound in **titan** prevents that – but once again few people would notice any real difference between the two words. **Tighten** is a verb meaning to draw tight, to make taut. A **titan** tends to be a large and powerful machine, because in Greek mythology the titans were a family of giants.

till

As a noun, a **till** can be a simple machine for dealing with the receipt of money and the handing out of change in a shop, a board or shelf in an early printing hand-press, or a stiff clay, normally the boulder clay of a glacial period. As a verb, to till is to labour, particularly in the sense of preparing ground ready for the sowing of crops. As a preposition, till indicates a passage of time: 'I won't be ready till sundown.'

tip

After you have finished your meal at Claridges, you may decide to leave a **tip** for the waiter, that is, a small sum of money in appreciation of the good service received. Equally, at the race course, you may bet on Great Mogul, because you have received a tip (a supposedly informed guess) that he's likely to win the Pooh Bear steeplechase. More usefully, you may spend the afternoon clearing out the attic, and taking all the rubbish to the tip, a communal site for the jettisoning of all refuse. A tip is also the end of an object like the tip of a pen, the tip of a snooker cue, or the tip of your toes. As a verb, the word is often used to denote the accidental knocking over of something: 'I'm sorry, did I tip your glass?' Equally it can be perfectly deliberate as you tip your loose change into a box, or tip your beer over the head of irritating Mavis.

tire, tyer, tyre

The most common use of the word **tire** is as a verb indicating that one is becoming physically or mentally weaker through exertion. The word can also be used in falconry to depict the tearing of a morsel by the beak of the bird, or, outside falconry, to dress the head or hair, or to plaster or decorate a building. A **tyer** is simply someone who ties. An Internet source defines the noun **tyre** as one of those 'round, rubber things on your car'.

to, too, two

The preposition **to** is one of those irritating little words that has such a manifold range of uses that it is difficult to pin down. First of all, it can express motion: 'The bus is going to Stockport.' Secondly, it can express the duration of time: 'I just live from day to day.' It can express purpose: 'He hopes to finish this today.' It can express a limit: 'My pension was cut to half its previous amount.' It can indicate addition: 'Add some sugar to my tea, please.' It is part of the infinitive of every verb: to carry, to run, to walk. If you really need to know more, I can only suggest that you turn to the *Shorter Oxford*. **Too**, however, is much more limited. Basically it means 'also' or 'in addition' or 'excessively', as in sentences like 'Is Felix coming too?' or, 'It is too likely that Boris got drunk last night', or, 'The bed was too hard'. **Two** is even simpler, it being the cardinal number that follows one and precedes three.

toad, toed, towed

A **toad** is an amphibian animal similar to a frog, though the word is some-times used as a term of abuse. Something that is **toed** possesses a number of toes, though apparently the word can also be a technical term in carpentry where it refers to something that is secured by means of nails driven in obliquely. **Towed** is just the past participle of the verb 'to tow'.

tocsin, toxin

A **tocsin** is a signal, in particular, an alarm signal of bells pealing or hooters blowing. A **toxin** is a poison, especially one produced by a microbe.

tod

Normally a **tod** is a weight used in the wool trade, usually 28 pounds, but it is also a dialect word meaning a fox or a crafty person.

toe, tow

Apart from being one of the digits of the foot, a **toe** can be the front part of a shoe, sandal or boot, the lower extremity of almost anything, or the thin end of a hammer-head. If you **tow** something, you pull it along behind you. Hence you might drive your car with a caravan being towed behind you, or you might watch a boat towing another boat.

toed *see* toad

toffee, toffy

Two alternative spellings for the same word signifying a sweetmeat made from sugar or treacle, butter and sometimes a little flour.

toil

'Double, double, **toil** and trouble,' the witches begin *Macbeth*, and here 'toil' means trouble, contention, strife, turmoil or severe labour. The word can also denote a net or nets set in such a fashion as to enclose a space into which the quarry is driven.

told, tolled

These are both the past tenses of verbs, **told** being the past tense of 'to tell', and **tolled** being the past tense of 'to toll'.

tole, toll

Tole, not found in the *Shorter Oxford*, is painted, lacquered or enamelled tin plate used to make decorative domestic objects. A **toll** can be a payment, these days for using a bridge, a special section of the motorway, or some quasi-medieval path, but in the middle ages it was a payment exacted as a kind of tax in return for protection. There have also been tolls exacted as a religious penalty. The word, of course, is also a verb, where it refers to the ringing of a bell.

ton, tonne, tun

There is some confusion in the use of **ton**. We normally use the word as a weight, 2,240 lbs in the UK and 2,000 lbs in the USA, but it is also a unit used in measuring the carrying capacity of ships, normally 40 cubic feet, but there are variations. A **tonne** is a metric unit of weight equal to 1000 kg. A **tun** is a large cask or barrel used for liquids, especially wine, beer, etc.

tone

In musical terms, the word **tone** refers to the nature of the sound being emitted. It is loud or soft, gentle or harsh, clear or dull. But the word can also refer to the physical state of one's body, to the way one speaks, the moral state of a community, the quality of the colouring in a painting, or the social ambience of a situation.

tong, tongue

Perhaps this should be 'tongs, tongues' because we always talk about a pair of tongs, meaning an instrument comprising two limbs which is used for picking something up in a medical operation or placing coal from the scuttle on to the fire. Once might talk about one **tong** of a pair, but this is rare, and the singular form is not listed in the *Shorter Oxford* (but neither are lots of other things). The **tongue**, however, is much simpler. It is an organ possessed by most vertebrates which assists in the production of sound and speech. It is the tongue that enables you to say 'The Lethe police dismisseth us.' The word has been extended from the physical organ to refer to language in general: 'French is a Romance tongue.' The word is also used to refer to anything jutting out: 'A tongue of land jutted out into the bay.'

too *see* to

tool

Apart from being one of the numerous slang terms for the penis, a **tool** can be a generic name for any implement employed in helping in some physical task. Thus a chisel, paintbrush, drill, pencil, lathe and so on are all tools. A person can also be a tool when he or she allows themselves to be used for the benefit of someone else.

top

A **top** is a small, spinning object that many of us played with when school children. It also denotes the highest or uppermost part of something. More figuratively, it can signify someone or something that has reached the pinnacle of their field.

tope

As a noun, a **tope** is a small species of shark, a local name for a wren, a clump, grove or plantation of trees, or an ancient structure in the form of a dome or tumulus. As a verb, to tope means to drink.

topless

Fairly obviously, **topless** signifies something that is devoid of its top, but these days the word often denotes a woman who has no clothing above the waist and consequently is displaying her breasts.

tort *see* taught

tot

A small child is often referred to as a **tot**, and so is a small drink of spirits. As a verb, the word means to add up, to calculate.

tough, tuff

Someone or something that is **tough** is hard, capable of endurance or difficult to do. Thus a man can be tough if he is strong, a problem can be tough if you can't do it, and a rock can be tough if it is not easily worn away by the rain and wind. A **tuff** is a stratified, porous rock or something produced by the consolidation of volcanic ashes.

tow

As a noun, a **tow** is a fibre of flax, hemp or jute prepared for spinning. As a verb, to tow means to pull something along. Hence a boat may tow another boat, a tractor may tow a plough, or you may tow your unhappy son to the dentist.

towed *see* toad

toxin *see* tocsin

toy

As a noun, a **toy** is a plaything customarily used by children. As a verb, if you toy with something, you trifle with it, treating it casually.

tracked, tract

The past tense of the verb 'to track' is **tracked**. A **tract**, however, is a written work, normally of pamphlet size, discussing a matter of importance. It can also be a stretch of land or a stretch of time.

tray, trey

A **tray** is a flat object upon which other objects can be placed and then carried to where they are needed. **Trey** is the name for the number three in dice or card games.

trend

We tend to use the word **trend** when we want to identify a prevailing movement or tendency. Hence we might say, 'There is a trend nowadays to learning the cor anglais.' (I have invented this; most people don't know what a cor anglais is.) But a trend can also be that part of the shank of an anchor where it thickens towards the crown.

trifle

A **trifle** is a dessert of sponge cake, jelly, blancmange and suchlike, a matter of little importance, a kind of pewter of medium hardness, or a verb indicating that one is not treating a matter with any seriousness, that one is jesting.

trip

One can go on a **trip** when one travels to somewhere else, or one can trip someone up, either physically by causing them to stumble, or intellectually by causing them to make a factual or logical mistake.

troop, troup

Both these words mean a collection of humans, but a **troop** refers to a collection of soldiers, while a **troup** refers to a collection of actors or dancers.

trooper, trouper

A **trooper** is a single soldier, while a **trouper** is a staunch colleague.

truss

A **truss** is a framework supporting a roof, a surgical appliance worn to support a hernia, a bundle of old hay, a compact cluster of flowers or fruit growing on one stalk, or, in sailing, a heavy metal ring securing the lower yards to a mast.

trussed, trust

If something is **trussed**, it is tied up. If you **trust** someone or something, you place reliance upon them or it, and have confidence in it.

tube

A long, hollow cylinder of metal, glass or plastic is known as a **tube**, and they are normally used for holding or transporting something. The underground railway of London is also called the tube.

tuff *see* **tough**

tun *see* **ton**

tune

A **tune** is a melody, a sequence of musical notes that make up, as it were, a musical sentence or paragraph. However, you can also tune an engine, that is, adjust it so that it is running smoothly. You can also tune a radio or television so that you receive the programme you want clearly and without interference.

turtle

A **turtle** can be a marine reptile or a freshwater one. Also, if you turn turtle, you turn on your back instead of proceeding normally on your front.

twig

If you **twig** something, you understand it or suddenly realise it. As a noun, a twig is a small off-shoot from the branch of a tree, or the small branch of a blood vessel or nerve.

twist

As a verb, 'to **twist**' can mean to form something into a distorted shape, to rotate something round a stationary point, to dance the twist, to be dealt a playing card upwards, or to cheat. As a noun, it can also denote something with a spiral shape, an unusual aspect of someone's personality, a carpet with a tightly curled pile, or a drink consisting of two ingredients mixed together.

two *see* **to**

tyke

A **tyke** is a small child, often of a mischievous disposition. The word is also used to denote a coarse man, or a dog.

type

We are all accustomed to saying that so-and-so is a perfect **type** of the smart executive, or that Friesians are a type of cow. Here the word 'type' is being used to link together objects that have important things in common or that share characteristics. There is also an emblematic use of the word. Abraham is a type of God because he was prepared to kill his own son at God's command. Joseph is a type of Christ because he was rejected by his own people, yet saved them from famine all the same. As a verb, the word represents exactly what I am doing at the moment, striking keys in order to produce letters on paper or a screen.

tyre *see* **tire**

U, u, you

U, the twenty-first letter of the English alphabet, is used as a word only in mobile-phone text-messages as an abbreviation of its homonym, **you**. The personal pronoun itself can be second person singular or plural, and so the sentence 'You must eat your parsnips' could be addressed to just one person or to a whole multitude. 'U', however, is often used as a proper abbreviation: u for uranium, UK for United Kingdom, and so on, and can also be used as a prefix in expressions like U-turn or U-shaped.

ullage

The amount by which a cask or bottle falls short of being full is known as its **ullage**, though the word is also used for the waste metal that is cut away by a graving tool.

ultimate

This word can be pronounced in two different ways. Where the '-ate' sound is fully expressed, the word means a bringing to completion, but where '-ate' is swallowed up in a sort of guttural growl, **ultimate** indicates that nothing further can be known: 'The Hubble telescope reaches into the ultimate regions of the universe.'

umbra

Since few of us ever use the word **umbra**, it is a little surprising to discover that it has five different meanings. It is the fish more commonly called the grayling, it is the shade or spirit of someone dead, it is an uninvited guest, it is the earth's or moon's shadow in an eclipse, it is the penumbra of a sunspot, and, in algebra, it is a symbol that must be paired with another in order to denote a quantity.

umbrella

As an object designed to shelter us from the rain, the **umbrella** is well known to most of us, but the word is borrowed by botanists to denote parts of a plant that resemble the umbrella, and by zoologists to denote the shape of a jelly fish.

unbridled

A horse can be **unbridled** when it is not equipped with its bridle, but your rage can also be unbridled (i.e. insanely intense) when you discover that someone has stolen your favourite place for parking.

unbroken

Something that is **unbroken** is something that is intact – 'The bottle was unbroken despite falling off the shelf' – but the word can also mean uninterrupted or continuous – 'The music from Karl's room was unbroken throughout the afternoon.'

uncharged

This word can signify that something is free, that no money has been charged for it, or that something has not been assaulted by an opposing force, or that a gun has not been loaded ('It is uncharged'), or, finally, that some electrical implement or machine has not been charged with electricity.

uncle

If you have an **uncle**, he will be the brother of your mother or your father, but the word is also used loosely as an affectionate term for an elderly man or as slang for a pawnbroker.

unconscious

If you are **unconscious**, you are either insensible because you are asleep, under anaesthetic, or have been knocked out, or, equally commonly, because you are unaware. Hence you can be unconscious that your wife is dropping hints about your approaching anniversary even though you are fully awake.

unctuous

Something that is **unctuous** is marked by the presence of oil or fat, but the word is also used to depict a human being who is self-satisfied and who glows with self-esteem and condescension.

underhand

If you are **underhand**, you are devious and prone to doing disreputable things secretly, but it is also possible to bowl a ball underhand when you release the ball with your hand under the ball and lower than the shoulder.

undermine

You can **undermine** a structure by burrowing beneath it and thus weakening its foundations. The same thing can be done by underground water. But it is also possible to undermine someone's efforts by spreading false rumours about them or placing obstacles in their way.

undone

Something is **undone** if it is not completed. Hence your shoelace may be undone or your French homework or your changing of the wheel of your car. More finally, something can be said to be undone if it is brought to ruin or destroyed, and a person brought to bankruptcy might describe himself as undone.

unsavoury

If a meal turns out to be **unsavoury**, it means that it is tasteless or insipid or possesses a taste that you find disagreeable. If a person is unsavoury, he or she is morally offensive, i.e. a politician, an estate agent, etc.

up

Like so many small words in English, **up** can perform a variety of functions and act as a noun, verb, adjective, adverb and preposition. You can talk about Melvin being on an up when he has just won a power battle in the board room. The ground can be up, the train can be up, and the price can be up. You can up and leave or be up and doing. You can point out that the booking office is on the up platform. You may decide to pull up your stockings. You may comment that a pleasant breeze is getting up. In addition, of course, 'up' is a prefix for countless words: upwards, upgrade, upbringing and so on.

upset

If you **upset** a physical object like a teapot, a car or the wastepaper bin, you overturn it. If you upset a person, you disturb them, distress them, perturb them.

urn *see* **earn**

use *see* **ewes**

utter

As a verb, **utter** is a synonym for 'speak'; hence you utter words of warning to the children bathing in the river. As an adjective, however, 'utter' can signify the extreme limit: 'She is an utter idiot', or, 'Conditions in the Arctic test your powers of endurance to the utter limit.'

V

V, v

The twenty-second letter of the alphabet, **v** has no place in this dictionary since it is only used as a prefix in things like a V-necked sweater, or, as the Roman symbol for 5.

vacancy

There may be a **vacancy** in that there is a job for which no one has yet been appointed. Alternatively, Timothy may be gazing into vacancy, namely empty space, or possibly quite full space, but he is seeing nothing because his mind is absorbed by something else. Equally there may be a vacancy in Doris's mind because she is suffering from some mental complaint.

vain, vane, vein

Someone who is **vain** thinks extremely well of themselves, and should be avoided as a tedious bore. A **vane** is normally an object of wood or metal erected in a high position so as to show the direction in which the wind is blowing. A **vein** is a tubular vessel through which blood is carried back to the heart.

vale, veil

A **vale** is a stretch of land lying between hills on either side, though, with the 'e' pronounced at the end, it can also mean 'farewell'. A **veil** is a piece of fabric used for covering the face or some object, often of a religious nature.

valley

Normally used as a synonym for 'vale', the word **valley** is also often used figuratively as in the valley of despond or the valley between a woman's breasts. In anatomy the word is used to describe the depression between the hemispheres of the cerebellum.

value

As a verb the word means that you esteem a friend – 'I value Renata's friendship' – or that you are going to estimate the worth of some painting or other object. As a noun value is the inherent worth of some object or other or, in the plural, a set of moral priciples.

valve

A **valve** is a device for controlling the input and output of fluid through a pipe or duct, but the word also has specialist meanings in zoology and botany, being each of the halves of the hinged shell of a bivalve mollusc or each of the halves into which a dry fruit divides.

vamp

The upper part of a boot or shoe is called the **vamp**, as is the introductory passage to a jazz or popular music piece. It is also an informal term for a woman who uses sexual attraction to exploit men.

van

For most of us, a **van** is a motorised vehicle which tradesmen or repairers use for carrying their goods or tools. However, you can be in the van of a army or a procession, which means that you are among the foremost.

vane *see* vain

vanish

If something were to **vanish**, it would disappear, but in mathematics it would simply become zero.

variable

If someone or something is apt to change, then they are **variable**. Thus Gertrude is happy one minute, depressed the next, the weather is sunny now but it will rain in ten minutes, and so on. In mathematics and physics, a variable is a quantity that is capable of changing (just like Gertrude) but the change is due to mathematical calculations, and hence qualitatively different. **Variance**, **variant** and **variation** show similar disparities.

vault

A **vault** can be seen in an arched window or an arched roof, the inner portion of a steel furnace, and is also a wholly or partially underground burial chamber. A vault can also be an athletic action, normally one of leaping over something with the aid of the hands or a pole.

vector

In mathematics and physics, a **vector** is a quantity having direction as well as magnitude. In biology it is an organism that transmits a disease or parasite from one animal or plant to another. A vector is also the course to be taken by an aircraft.

veil *see* vale

vein *see* vain

vellum, velum

Vellum is a kind of parchment, and a **velum** is the soft membranous septum extending backwards from the hard palate of the mouth.

verge

If you are on the **verge** of something, you are on the edge of it. Thus you can be on the verge of a cliff, and thus in danger of toppling off it, or on the verge of writing to the City Council to complain about their refuse collection system. In watch making, a verge is the spindle of the balance in the old vertical escarpment.

verses, versus

Properly pronounced, these two words are not homophones, but few of us pronounce words with clarity. **Verses** are segments of a poem on occasions when the poem is deliberately divided into a sequence of identical stanzas. The Bible too is divided into small segments, each of which is called a verse. **Versus** is a preposition that means 'against' in expressions like England versus France at Wembley Park.

vert

Vert refers to green vegetation growing in a wood and capable of serving as a cover for deer. It also denotes a convert from one religion to another, and, in pathology or anatomy, can be a verb meaning to turn or twist out of the normal position.

vessel

A **vessel** almost invariably refers to something that is capable of holding something else, but since that can refer to a ship or aircraft capable of carrying hundreds of humans, and a small bowl capable of holding only a bunch of grapes, one feels that almost makes it a homonym alone. Various organs of the body are also referred to as vessels, and a human being might be termed a vessel for the teachings of someone else. Thus Mimesis Acolyte, a student at Trinity College, Cambridge, might be a vessel for the doctrines of Dr Cais Hardfast.

vial, vile, viol

A **vial** is a narrow glass container, someone who is **vile** is despicable, and the **viol** is a stringed instrument slightly larger than a violin.

vice

A **vice** is an implement composed of two jaws which can be screwed so as to hold fast something else that needs to be held firmly. Understandably, the word can be extended in expressions like, 'He held him in a vice-like grip.' Entirely differently, vice is also a quality of depravity, evil, immorality or even evidence of a bad habit like smoking. Clearly there is a marked difference between raping under-age girls and eating too many chocolates, yet both can be stigmatised with the use of the word 'vice'. 'Vice' can also mean 'next in rank' or 'a substitute for', as in 'Melvin Green, the vice president, chaired the meeting admirably.'

view

If you are looking out of the window, you have a **view** of your back garden or whatever, a view being a visual image of something. But you can also have an intellectual view. Thus you might hold the view that Keats's poetry is effete, that horse racing is the greatest sport, or that Van Gogh is the world's greatest painter. Your view would be mistaken in each case, but you are entitled to hold it.

vile, viol *see* **vial**

violet

The **violet** is an attractive garden flower, but it is also a bluish colour.

vixen

A **vixen** is a female fox, but the word is also used to denote an ill-tempered, embittered and spiteful woman.

vole

A **vole** is a mouse-like creature, or the winning of all the tricks in certain card games.

volume

A book can sometimes be referred to as a **volume**, though the term is usually reserved for weighty tomes of reference or scholarship. The word also has a scientific meaning when it denotes the cubic contents of an enclosed space.

vulgar

In normal parlance, something that is **vulgar** is coarse, rude or lacking in refinement, but the word can also be used in the sense of normal or prevalent in phrases like 'the vulgar tongue'. In mathematics there are also vulgar fractions.

vulture

The **vulture** is a large bird of prey, but the word is often applied to a rapacious person.

W, w

W, the twenty-third letter of the alphabet, is used only as an abbreviation. In upper case, it can stand for West or Western or the element tungsten, and in lower case it can be a wide or a wicket in the game of cricket, or a watt in electrical appliances.

wad

A **wad** can be a bundle of hay or straw or banknotes, a plug or disc that retains the powder and shot in a gun, or plumbago or black lead.

wade, weighed

When one has a paddle in the sea, one is said to be having a **wade**. Equally one can wade through swampy ground, or wade through all the documents connected with the Jack-the-Ripper case. If something is **weighed**, it is placed on a scales or measuring device in order to ascertain its weight. It is also possible to weigh something mentally, and you can argue that you have weighed all the evidence and come to the conclusion that global warming is a proximate threat to man's existence.

wader

Anything that wades through water or mud can be termed a **wader**, though the term is particularly used for some birds. The word is also used denominate boots or even a garment that is designed to protect against mud or water.

waffle

While a **waffle** is a small, crisp batter cake, the word is more often used to denote vague, ill-directed and vacuous talk.

wag

As a verb, 'to **wag**' means to shake, to sway in opposite directions. Hence a dog's tail wags, as does a flag in the wind. As a noun, a wag is one of those irritating people who entertains you with his or her (normally his) droll comments, comments indicated to show his wit and his laid-back attitude.

wail, wale, whale

Should an animal or human being **wail**, they are making a sound of lamentation. A **wale** is a ridge in a textile fabric, the gunwale of a boat, each of the horizontal bands round the body of a basket, or, as a verb, the action of picking out the best, normally from a collection of refuse or coal. The largest oceanic mammal is known as the **whale**, and although its 'h' stops it being a complete homophone, once again that 'h' is often missing in people's speech.

wain, wane

A **wain** is a large, open wagon, and Constable's painting 'The Hay Wain' depicts one. The verb 'to **wane**' means 'to decrease'. Thus the moon in the sky waxes and wanes, and your interest in horse racing tends to wane as you become poorer and poorer.

waist, waste

The portion of the human body between the ribs and the hip-bones is called the **waist**, and women in particular like to have narrow waists. The verb 'to **waste**' means 'to squander, to fritter away'. It can also mean to kill or severely injure, for the body to become progressively weaker and emaciated, to devastate or ruin a place, or be an adjective describing a desolated or barren place.

wait, weight

If you **wait** for something, you remain in readiness for its appearance or occurrence. If you wait on someone, you attempt to provide them with what they want, as a waiter does in a restaurant. The **weight** of something tells you how heavy the object concerned is, but the word is also used more figuratively so that one can say that Professor Rolo's arguments carried great weight, or that Mrs Leech was of great weight on the Women's Institute committee. The word is also used for the surface density of cloth.

waiter

A **waiter** is anyone who is waiting for something, a small tray, or a man whose job it is to serve customers at a restaurant.

waive, wave

If you **waive** the entrance fee to the flower show for the Lord Mayor, you fail to charge him for entrance. If you waive the rule against smoking for the visit of the American Congress, you fail to enforce that rule. Thus, 'to waive' means 'to abandon, to relinquish, to forbear'. When a portion of the sea rises up and then subsides, it has created a **wave**, and similar turbulence in the air is also sometimes called a wave of air. When one's hair curls in a similar up and down movement, one has wavy hair. When the temperature fluctuates, it is normally due to waves of atmospheric pressure. When you flap your hand in an up and down motion, you are probably giving a wave to a friend. Seismic movements along the crust of the earth are called waves. The basic concept of a wave being an up and down motion is common to all these examples, but their disparity ensures that the word 'wave' is an internal homonym.

wake

Most of us **wake** every morning from a condition of sleep, but when a friend dies we may attend the wake, a meeting together of sundry friends to mourn the passing of someone we valued. It is also possible to follow in the wake of someone or something else when we travel over the same route as they have done, only a little later.

wale *see* wail

wall

Normally a **wall** is a continuous vertical brick or stone structure that encloses a garden or divides an area of land, but it can be metaphorically used to represent a barrier: 'The Press met with a wall of silence.' It is also used in biology to denote the continuous outer layer of an organ (not the sort that you play Bach on).

wallop

If you **wallop** someone, you give them a heavy blow, but if you go into a pub and order a pint of wallop, you are asking for a pint of beer.

wand

Many of us grew up knowing that a **wand** was a small rod used by fairies (or possibly magicians) to perform magic, but as we grew older we realised that a wand was a hand-held electronic device which can be passed over a bar code to read the encoded data.

want, wont

If you **want** something, you desire it. **Wont**, however, is much rarer word. It often occurs in the construction, 'It is my wont to . . . ', and I suppose that its nearest equivalent is the word 'habit': 'It is my wont to always play Schubert before going to sleep at night.' There are also variations in its pronunciation, and so it is quite likely that, for you, it cannot be paired with 'want' at all.

wanton

If you indulge in a **wanton** action, you normally do something excessive and often cruel. If you are wanton, you are a sexually promiscuous woman, but if a plant is wanton, it is growing profusely over a particular area.

war, wore

Properly speaking, a **war** is an armed conflict between different nations, though the word is often extended to unarmed conflict between individuals or organisations. **Wore** is the past tense of the verb 'to wear': 'I wore my blue dress last Tuesday.'

ward, warred

If we need to stay in hospital, we are likely to be placed in a **ward**, a room in which patients lie in bed waiting for their operation or recovering from it. If we are canvassing for the local elections, we are likely to do so one ward at a time, a ward being a subdivision of a parish. If we are attacked by some flies, we might flap at them with the paper so as to ward them off. If we are fencing, we might adopt a ward, a defensive posture. We might have the guardianship of a child, who is consequently our ward. A department of a prison is called a ward. So we can see that ward is a versatile word. **Warred**, of course, is just the past tense of the verb 'to war'.

ware, wear, where

Articles of merchandise are often called **ware** – 'I've stored all the ware in the basement' – and more specifically the word often relates to the cargo of a ship. The verb 'to **wear**' relates to the clothes with which we cover our bodies – 'Shall I wear the green dress tonight?' – but also relates to the slow process of deterioration that articles undergo when they are being used – 'That engine will wear out rapidly if you run it at such a rate.' **Where** shouldn't really be here because its 'h' means that it sounds significantly different in sound from the other two words. Alas, though, that 'h' is often missing from people's speech, and so it sounds just like 'ware'. It is, of course, an interrogative word enquiring about the position of someone or something: 'Where is my pen?'

warm

If something is **warm**, it is at a comfortably high temperature, but you can also be warm in your enthusiasm for something, you can get warm in discovering something that was intended to remain unknown, and you can decorate your room in warm colours (normally yellow, red or orange).

warn, worn

You **warn** someone about some possible or approaching danger. Something is **worn** if it is being used as a garment by someone, though the word can also mean that something is not in tip-top condition because it has been used a lot. Thus your twenty-year-old car may be worn out by now, and after four years' arduous gardening, your overalls are looking very worn.

warp

If you twist something out of shape, you **warp** it. The warp of a cloth interweaves laterally with the weft. You can moor a ship with a length of rope called the warp.

warrantee, warranty

The first is one who is protected by a guarantee, and the second is the guarantee itself.

wart, wort

A **wart** is a small, round, dry, tough excrescence on the skin, while a **wort** is a plant, herb or vegetable used medically. Wort can also be the infusion of malt or other grain in the process of making beer.

wash

If you and I have a **wash**, we try to make ourselves clean by using soap and water, but you can also have a deep feeling of affection wash over you, apply a thin coat of paint (the wash) over the walls, feed kitchen slops (the wash) to the pigs, or be aware that your reason for being absent from work yesterday has not washed with your boss.

waste *see* waist

watch

As a verb, 'to **watch**' means 'to observe'. As a noun, it can be a timepiece carried on the wrist, or the period of time for which a sailor is on duty.

wave *see* waive

wax, whacks

A substance produced by bees, certain trees and a few vegetables, a substance that is marked by softness and adhesiveness, is called **wax**, but the word can also be a verb that indicates growth. Thus the moon waxes as it apparently grows larger in the sky, and your anger waxes as you gaze on the mess that young Philip has created in your study. A whack is a blow, and so **whacks** is a plurality of blows.

way, weigh, whey

The word **way** is always connected with traffic or progress. Thus you can be on your way to see Kevin, you can be following the way of the path through the forest, you can be trying to play the trumpet in the way that your teacher advised, and you have accepted the teachings of Christ as the way for you to follow. **Weigh** is more straightforward. If you weigh yourself, you do so to discover how heavy you are, and in the course of a day you may have to weigh a letter, a parcel, your luggage, or your son. It is, though, possible to use the word metaphorically. You might want to weigh the arguments of the Prime Minister in order to assess how powerful they are. **Whey** is best known through the nursery rhyme 'Little Bo Peep', yet most of us go through childhood without knowing that whey is the serum or watery part of milk which remains after the separation of the curd by coagulation, especially in the manufacture of cheese.

we, wee

We is the pronoun of the first person plural nominative, and denotes an action or intention by more than one person. **Wee** is a word largely used in

Scotland to signify something or someone that is extremely small, though, of course, it is a word used by children to denote urine or the act of urinating.

weak, week

If you are feeling **weak**, you lack strength, physically or emotionally. The word also signifies a class of verbs in Germanic languages, and some almost insignificant forces in physics. A **week** is the duration of seven days.

weal, we'll, wheel

A **weal** is a skin welt, or one's general condition and well-being. Another contraction, **we'll** is a shortened form of 'we will'. A **wheel** is a circular frame of wood or metal which, because it is propelled easily, is universally used in forms of transport or in machines where one or more elements needs to revolve. An Internet source amusingly defines 'wheel' as 'something that is always being reinvented'.

weald, wheeled, wield

A **weald** is a tract of countryside, **wheeled** is the past tense of the verb 'to wheel', and **wield** is a verb meaning to direct the movement of something, to use or handle with skill.

wean, ween

When a woman slowly accustoms her child to no longer having breast milk, she is said to **wean** the child. If you postulate something or make an informed guess, you might say, 'I **ween** that flying saucers come to us via a black hole.'

wear *see* ware

weather, wether, whether

A British obsession is the **weather**. We talk about it all the time. The condition of the atmosphere at any given time – is it hot or cold? is it wet or dry? – is the conversational fail-safe gambit. But the word can also be a verb. One talks of weathering the changes being introduced at work, or of a ship being able to weather the storms. Here the word means 'to withstand' or 'to cope with'. A **wether** is a castrated ram, or the fleece obtained from the second or any subsequent shearing of a sheep. **Whether**, which can be a pronoun, adjective or conjunction, is normally used for proposing alternatives: 'Whether we go to Cheddar or to Wells hardly matters to me.'

weave, we've

If one interlaces fibres one with another, so as to create a cloth or a garment, then one has been weaving, but one can also **weave** from side to side when one is trying to walk or ride through a crowd. It is also possible to weave ideas into some sort of thesis. **We've**, on the other hand, is a simple contraction of 'we have'.

we'd, weed

When we want to say 'we had' or 'we would', we often contract it to **'we'd'**. A **weed** is a plant that is neither valued for use nor beauty, and which consequently consumes time in being eradicated. A thin and physically weak person can also be called a weed.

wedge

A **wedge** is a piece of wood or metal having one thick end and tapering to a thin edge, that is driven between two objects or parts of an object to secure or separate them. It is also a golf club, or a shoe with a fairly high heel. You can also wedge pottery clay for use by cutting, kneading and throwing down to homogenise and remove air pockets.

week *see* weak

ween *see* wean

weigh *see* way

weighed *see* wade

weight *see* wait

weir, we're

A **weir** is a barrier or dam to restrain water, though often the word is applied to a waterfall, particularly one formed by such a barrier. **We're** is a contraction for 'we are'.

weld, welled

If you **weld** two things together, you conjoin them, you forge them together. Normally this is done by heating two pieces of metal, and merging them in a molten state, but the word can also be used conceptually in ways like 'I think that I helped to weld Janet and Damien more closely together today.' **Welled** is the past tense of the verb 'to well'.

well

If you are **well**, you are in good condition. If you do something well, you do it in a thorough manner. If you draw water from the well, you lower a bucket down a cavity to a source of subterranean water, fill the bucket, and then haul it up again. As an adverb, 'well' normally indicates ampleness as in phrases like 'well known', 'well adjusted' and so on. Of liquid, 'to well' means to rise to the surface and flow out.

we'll *see* weal

wen, when

These two words are not homophones because the 'h' of **when** should be noticeable. Most of the time, however, it is not. Hence its pairing with **wen**.

A wen is a cystic tumour under the skin. **When** is an interrogative word concerned with the placing of something in time: 'When did Hogarth live?'; 'When did you last play bingo?'

we're see **weir**

wet, whet

Once again the 'h' in **whet** should be audible, but it often isn't, and so it becomes a homophone with **wet**. As you know, 'wet' is the opposite of dry, and indicates that something exists in a liquid state or that something has been dampened by a liquid. The verb 'to whet' can mean 'to sharpen' as in a knife, but more commonly means 'to render more keen' as in sentences like 'I whetted his appetite for the Hitchcock film tonight.'

wether see **weather**

we've see **weave**

whacks see **wax**

whale see **wail**

what

Most of the time, **what** is an interrogative pronoun – 'What is your name?' – but sometimes it is an interrogative adverb – 'What did you do?' – and sometimes a determiner – 'Do you know what excuse he gave?'

wheel see **we'll**

wheeled see **weald**

when see **wen**

where see **ware**

whether see **weather**

whey see **way**

which, witch

Which is a pronoun for a person or thing referred to: 'The house, which is empty, has been sold', or an interrogative word wanting you to choose between alternatives: 'Which is your favourite opera?' A **witch** is a woman possessed of supernatural powers and supposedly capable of riding through the air on a broomstick. They tend to be of a malignant nature, and so you might call Mrs Robinson a witch if you found her extremely disagreeable.

whiff

A **whiff** can be a smell that is caught briefly or faintly, a puff of air or smoke, or an unsuccessful attempt to hit the ball in baseball.

Whig, wig

As far as the English are concerned, a **Whig** was a person who belonged to a very loose confederation of politicians in the eighteenth century who opposed the Tories. The word has also been used to denominate historians who see the past as the continuing victory of progress over reaction. In America, a Whig was someone who supported the American War of Independence. A **wig** is an artificial covering of hair for the head.

while, wile

The word **while** expresses duration: 'I will wait here while you collect the paper.' A **wile** is a cunning, deceitful stratagem.

whiled, wild

Whiled is the past tense of the verb 'to while', meaning to pass one's time in a moderately pointless manner: 'I whiled away my time in the dentist's waiting room by reading a two-year-old copy of *Autocar*.' **Wild** is the opposite of tame, and refers to something that is not domesticated, like a tiger, a vulture or the mother-in-law.

whin, win

Whin is another word for the furze or gorse, though the term is sometimes applied to almost any prickly shrub. The word **win** indicates a victory of some kind. Thus you can win a game by defeating your opponents, you can win over cancer by defeating the disease, you can win the lottery by choosing the correct numbers, or you can win a lady's hand by getting her to marry you.

whine, wine

If you **whine**, you make a noise or utter words that indicate a general dissatisfaction with the current state of affairs. Children tend to whine on the first day of term. **Wine** is an alcoholic drink made from grapes.

whined, wind, wined

Fairly obviously, **whined** is just the past tense of the verb 'to whine' (*see* immediately above). If you **wind** up some wool, you tend to form it into a ball. Alternatively you might wind some cotton back round its reel. However, if you wind up a meeting, you bring it to a close. (Note too that this 'wind' has a long 'i', while the wind that blows through the trees has a short 'i', and is not therefore part of this entry at all.) If you **wined** well tonight, you consumed a comforting amount of good wine.

whip

A **whip** is a strip of leather or cord, fastened to a handle, and used for flogging an animal or person. It is also an official of a political party in Britain appointed to enforce discipline within the party, a light fluffy dessert, a slender, unbranched shoot or plant, or a rope-and-pulley hoisting apparatus.

whirled, world

The verb 'to whirl' means to move in a circle, normally rapidly, and so **whirled** is simply the past tense of that verb. The word **world** is normally used in reference to the planet upon which we live, the Earth, but it can also be used when one is referring to the totality of something else. Thus one can talk about the world of ballroom dancing, the world of cacti growing, and so on.

whirred, word

'To whirr' is to move and in so doing make a vibratory noise. Thus a bird's wings can whirr, grasshoppers can whirr, and so on. **Whirred** is the past tense of that verb. A **word** is an individual unit of language, signifying an object, an action, a relation or a process.

whit, wit

Not quite homophones because of the 'h' sound in **whit**, but once again, too close for there to be any real difference in normal speech. A 'whit' is a tiny portion of something. You may not care a whit about something, you may only have a whit of cake at the wedding, and so on. **Wit** often denotes cleverness – 'Norman has a good wit' – but it is more commonly used to signify the comic ability to yoke together disparate objects into a surprising unity, or to play on words in a surprising and amusing fashion.

white, wight, wite

As we all know, **white** is a colour, the opposite of black, and often taken as being emblematic of purity, chastity, honesty and general virtue: 'He is compiling a dictionary of homonyms, so his soul must be as white as snow.' Once upon a time, the word **wight** was a synonym for a human being – 'He was a noble wight' – but the word is now only used in this sense in a semi-jocular way. In Anglo-Saxon England, **wite** meant punishment, but today, like 'wight', the word is used only in a self-consciously quasi-comic sense.

whither, wither

For much of the time, **whither** is a simple interrogative word: 'Whither are you going?' meaning 'Where are you going?' Often though, 'whither' can be a word that reveals a relationship: 'Whither Colin went, Susie was sure to follow.' For much of the time, **wither** can be a verb meaning to fade, to lose vigour, to dry up: 'The flowers will wither in the sun.' It can also be an adjective meaning hostile, adverse or fierce, but this usage is very rare now.

whoa, woe

Whoa is a command to halt, to stop, normally used as a direction to a horse. If, however, you are experiencing **woe**, you are afflicted with sadness or grief.

whole *see* hole

who's, whose

As the apostrophe indicates, **who's** is a contraction meaning 'who is'. **Whose** is an interrogative pronoun enquiring about the ownership of something: 'Whose is that bag?'

wicket

The three stumps and two bails placed at each end of a cricket pitch are called the **wicket**. It can also be a small door or gate, or, in America, a croquet hoop.

widow

A woman whose husband has died and who has not remarried again is called a **widow**. So too is a page of print that only has one word or the short end of a paragraph carried over from the preceding page.

wield *see* weald

wig *see* whig

wild *see* whiled

wile *see* while

will

A **will** is a legal document indicating what one wishes to be done with one's money and property after one's death. It is also a modal verb expressing the future tense.

wind

This word has two very different pronunciations. With a short 'i', it refers to the perceptible movement of air in a breeze or hurricane, the physical expelling of breath as occurs when playing the trombone or running a race, gas generated in the stomach by digestion, or empty and pompous talk. With a long 'i', it refers to wrapping something round something else – 'I must wind the cotton round this reel' – following a circuitous path – 'Does the path wind its way through the wood?' – or activating the clockwork mechanism of a clock or watch – 'I mustn't forget to wind the clock.'

wing

Most of us know that birds have wings, as do aircraft, and we may know that a large building may have a west **wing** and an east wing, and that football and rugby teams tend to have laterally placed players on the right and left wings, but it may not occur to you that it is possible for a bullet to wing you in the shoulder (i.e. graze you) or that it is possible to talk about groups within an organisation as wings within that organisation. The sides of a theatre stage are called the wings.

wit

If you possess **wit**, you have the capacity for rapid and inventive thought, but the word can also be used, somewhat archaically, as a verb meaning 'to know'.

witch *see* which

with

This preposition can mean 'accompanying' as in 'I'll have sprouts with the steak, please', or it can indicate the instrument used in some action as in 'He cut the grass with the shears', or it can indicate a mood as in 'She served lunch with pleasure', or it can denote a relation as in 'My father will be angry with me', or it can indicate responsibility as in 'Leave it with me.' As so often in English, these small insignificant words perform a multitude of tasks.

wither *see* whither

woe *see* whoa

won *see* one

wonder

There are two basic meanings to **wonder**. The first is a noun denoting amazement and awe: 'Charlie is a wonder in the 100 metres.' The second is as a verb expressing ignorance: 'I wonder why Stuart is so late.'

wont *see* want

wood, would

A **wood** is a relatively small collection of trees growing in close proximity to each other. Each individual tree has a trunk made of wood, and from that material a large number of objects are made: tables, bookcases, chests, etc. The word **would** expresses a desire or intention: 'I would help Mrs Pritchard if she wasn't so snappy'; 'I would go to Geneva if I could afford the air fare'; 'I would never hit my children.'

word *see* whirred

wore *see* war

world *see* whirled

worm

The **worm** is an invertebrate animal with a long slender body and no limbs, but also a computer program, normally unwelcome, that is able to propagate itself across an entire network. The word can also be used as a term of abuse. As a verb it can mean to insinuate oneself, to extract information (out of someone), to crawl or creep along a narrow place, or to rid an animal of parasitic worms.

worn *see* **warn**

worst, wurst

If you need to express a superlative degree of badness, you use the word **worst**. You may feel that Tommy Saunders is the worst boy in Elmsgrove Drive, that Beethoven's second symphony is the worst of the nine, or that Delia Cordot is the worst cook in the world. A **wurst** is a German sausage.

would *see* **wood**

wrack *see* **rack**

wrap *see* **rap**

wreak *see* **reek**

wreck *see* **reck**

wrest *see* **rest**

wretch *see* **retch**

wright *see* **right**

wring *see* **ring**

write *see* **right**

wrote *see* **rote**

wry *see* **rye**

X, x

The twenty-fourth letter of the alphabet is used singly to express the unknown or hidden, as a Roman number for 10, or as a cross denoting an error, but other than that, no X-word provides material for a dictionary of homonyms.

Y, y

The penultimate letter of the alphabet is a homophone with **why**, but since neither y nor why is a homonym with anything other than each other, and since y doesn't exist as an independent word of its own, there is no entry under W for this pairing.

yack, yak

If you should happen to **yack** with your neighbour, you will be having a chat of a relaxed and often gossipy kind. Indeed, you might be commenting on the **yak**, the long-haired Tibetan ox, that the Browns have just installed in their back garden.

yard

Before the British were forced to go metric, a **yard** was a unit of length equivalent to three feet. However, the word is still current to describe an area of enclosed ground normally used for storing materials. Many British houses have a back yard where there might be a shed for storing the bicycles and a washing line for drying the clothes in the open air.

yarn

If you tell a **yarn**, you tell a story or tale, but if use yarn in your weaving or knitting, you are employing a spun fibre like wool or cotton for that purpose.

yellow

While **yellow** is a colour, it can also be used as an adjective to describe someone who is cowardly.

yew *see* ewe

yoke, yolk

If you need to bind two oxen together so that they can jointly pull the heavy plough, then you are likely to use a **yoke** for this purpose. However, the word is more commonly used as a synonym for a burden: 'It is something of a yoke having my mother-in-law staying with us.' A **yolk** is the yellow centre of an egg.

yore, you're, your

We sometimes talk about the days of **yore**, by which we mean the days of the past. **You're** is a contraction of 'you are', and is often confused by the semi-literate with **your**, a possessive pronoun and adjective signifying that something belongs to you: your hat, your manners, your house.

you *see* ewe

you'll, yule

'You will' is often contracted to **you'll**, while **Yule** is an alternative term for Christmas.

Z

zip

When an opening is closed by pulling a slide along two interlocking strips of metal, the whole device is called a zip. The word can also be used to describe the light, sharp sound of a something like a bullet passing near by.

BIBLIOGRAPHY

A number of files from the Internet were useful, but it is barely possible to list these in any very meaningful manner because the majority were anonymous, and none made any pretensions either to scholarship or to completeness. Consequently I simply list the books that I consulted in the compilation of this dictionary.

Ball, Philip, *Critical Mass: How One Thing Leads to Another*, 2005

Brewer's *Dictionary of Phrase and Fable*, 17th edn, 2005

Brewer's *Dictionary of Phrase and Fable*, 1981 edn

Bryson, Bill, *Troublesome Words*, 3rd edn, 2001

Bullock, Alan *et al.*, *The Fontana Dictionary of Modern Thought*, 2nd edn, 1988

Collins English Dictionary, 1st edn, 1979

Crystal, David and Ben, *Shakespeare's Words*, 2002

Green, Jonathon, *The Cassell Dictionary of Slang*, 1999

Oxford Dictionary of English, 2nd edn, 2005

Parrish, Thomas, *The Grouchy Grammarian*, 2003

Partridge, Eric, *Usage and Abusage*, 1972 edn

Scholastic Dictionary of Synonyms, Antonyms and Homonyms, New York, 2001

The Compact Edition of the Oxford English Dictionary, 1979

The Oxford Dictionary of Phrase and Fable, ed. Elizabeth Knowles, 2000

The Shorter Oxford English Dictionary, 3rd edn, Oxford, 1965